D0358525

SPECIAL MESSAGE TO READERS

This book is published under the auspices of

THE ULVERSCROFT FOUNDATION

(registered charity No. 264873 UK)

Established in 1972 to provide funds for research, diagnosis and treatment of eye diseases. Examples of contributions made are: —

A Children's Assessment Unit at Moorfield's Hospital, London.

•

Twin operating theatres at the Western Ophthalmic Hospital, London.

•

A Chair of Ophthalmology at the Royal Australian College of Ophthalmologists.

•

The Ulverscroft Children's Eye Unit at the Great Ormond Street Hospital For Sick Children, London.

You can help further the work of the Foundation by making a donation or leaving a legacy. Every contribution, no matter how small, is received with gratitude. Please write for details to:

THE ULVERSCROFT FOUNDATION,
The Green, Bradgate Road, Anstey,
Leicester LE7 7FU, England.
Telephone: (0116) 236 4325

In Australia write to:
THE ULVERSCROFT FOUNDATION,
c/o The Royal Australian and New Zealand College of Ophthalmologists,
94-98 Chalmers Street, Surry Hills,
N.S.W. 2010, Australia

Lisa Jackson's books are number one bestsellers in America. She lives with her family, two cats and an eighty-pound dog in the Pacific Northwest.

You can find out more about Lisa and her books at:
www.lisajackson.com.

TWICE KISSED

Marquise Walker has vanished without a trace and Maggie McCrae knows her glamorous twin is in terrible trouble — possibly even dead. Stepping into Marquise's wild, uninhibited life, Maggie makes startling discoveries — and some of them are about Thane Walker, the only man she ever loved. Although he left her for Marquise and could even be a cold-blooded killer, Maggie knows he's the one man who can help her find out what has happened. The deeper she digs, the more she learns about a twisted family legacy of desperate deceit, betrayal and revenge. Each secret brings her closer to the truth — and to the identity of a killer who is closer than she thinks.

LISA JACKSON

TWICE KISSED

Complete and Unabridged

CHARNWOOD
Leicester

First published in Great Britain in 2008 by
Hodder & Stoughton
An Hachette Livre UK Company, London

First Charnwood Edition
published 2010
by arrangement with
Hodder & Stoughton
An Hachette Livre UK Company, London

All characters in this publication are fictitious and any resemblance to real persons, living or dead, is purely coincidental.

British Library CIP Data

Jackson, Lisa.
Twice kissed.
1. Twins- -Fiction. 2. Sisters- -Fiction. 3.Romantic suspense novels. 4. Large type books.
I. Title
813.5′4–dc22

ISBN 978–1–84782–955–9

Published by
F. A. Thorpe (Publishing)
Anstey, Leicestershire

Set by Words & Graphics Ltd.
Anstey, Leicestershire
Printed and bound in Great Britain by
T. J. International Ltd., Padstow, Cornwall

This book is printed on acid-free paper

Heartfelt thanks to all the people who helped with the research and structuring of this book, especially Ann Baumann, Nancy Bush, Matthew Crose, Michael Crose, Alexis Harrington, Sally Peters, Tess O'Shaughnessy, Dave Painter, John Ray, Robin Rue, John Scognamiglio, Joan Sean, Carl Simpson, Celia Stinson and Larry Sparks. Your help, patience and laughter were invaluable.

PART I

Settler's Ridge
Northern Idaho

November 1998

1

Help me!

Maggie froze.

The old Maxwell House coffee can she used as a grain scoop slipped from her fingers. It hit the floor. Bam! Oats sprayed. Horses tossed their heads and neighed. Her legs buckled, and she grabbed hold of a rough-hewn post supporting the hayloft.

Maggie, please! Only you can help me.

'Mary Theresa?' Maggie mouthed, though no sound passed her lips. Was it possible? After all these years would her sister's voice reach her? The barn seemed suddenly airless. Close. Cold sweat collected on her scalp though the mercury level in the old thermometer tacked onto the wall near the door dipped below fifty degrees.

It was Thane. He did this to me. The voice pulsed through her brain.

Thane Walker. Mary Theresa's ex-husband and the one man Maggie never wanted to lay eyes upon again.

'Did what?' This time she spoke out loud, though her throat was as tight as dried leather, any saliva that had been in her mouth long gone.

Maggie, please, don't let him get away with it . . .

'Where are you?' she cried, spinning, looking up to the ancient rafters where an owl had taken up residence. Feathers and dust motes swirled in the faint shaft of light from a lone, circular window mounted near the ceiling. She knew that spoken words were useless. Mary Theresa was hundreds of miles away. So far. So damned far. Squeezing her eyes shut, she tried to throw her thoughts to wherever her twin might be. But it wouldn't work. It never had. Nonetheless, she tried screaming in her mind: *Mary Theresa, can you hear me? Can you? What did that bastard do to you?*

She waited.

Nothing.

A restless mare snorted.

'If this is some kind of sick joke . . . ' she said, though her heart was pounding a million beats a second. 'Mary Theresa, I swear . . . '

Anxious, as if picking up the tension in the air, the horses shifted in their stalls, hooves rustling the straw, muscles quivering under coats that were becoming shaggy as winter approached.

Maggie shuddered, the inside of her skin quivering as it always had when Mary Theresa had contacted her through their own special means. Mental telepathy. Instinct. Magic. Witchcraft. ESP. Clairvoyance. Maggie had heard all the terms and slurs, knew that most people considered her eccentric at best and just plain crazy at worst. Slowly, her fingers sliding down the post and gathering slivers, she sank to her knees and rested her head against the solid wood.

She concentrated, willing her breathing to return to normal. *Come on, Mary Theresa, come on. One more time*. Eyes closed so tightly they ached, she strained to hear, but the only sounds that reached her ears were the constant rustle of hooves in straw, hot breath blowing out of nervous nostrils, the scratch of tiny claws as mice scurried along the concrete floor, hiding in the cracks and crevices of the old barn. 'Don't stop now,' she whispered, her teeth sinking into her lower lip until she tasted blood.

Nothing.

'Damn you, Mary Theresa . . . or Marquise or whoever you think you are. Talk to me!'

The inside of the barn felt as if it were freezing, and yet cold perspiration broke out all over her skin. 'Mary Theresa — '

'Mom?' Becca's voice sounded far away. The door to the barn creaked open, and a shaft of fading daylight sliced into the musty interior. 'Hey, are you okay?'

'Fine,' she forced out, climbing to her feet and dusting her hands on her jeans. She managed a weak smile, hoping it would mask her lie a little.

Becca with her freckled face, eyes a little too large and a lot too serious for the age of thirteen, was instantly suspicious. 'What were you doing in here?' She motioned to the post. 'Praying?'

'No — '

'You were on your knees, Mom. Did you, like, have a heart attack or a stroke or what?'

'I was just feeding the horses and I, um, needed . . . a rest.' Maggie cringed inside because the lie was so ridiculous, but what could she say? That her sister, whom she hadn't heard from in months, was finally contacting her through telepathy? She'd learned from past experience that no one would believe her, especially not her nearly estranged daughter.

Becca eyed the empty coffee can that had rolled against a burlap sack of feed. 'Right.'

'I was. I just . . . well, if you want to know the truth — '

'That would be a change.'

'Becca,' she reproached, then held her tongue. The strain between them was palpable. Mother and daughter. How had they grown so far apart when they had once been inseparable?

'I . . . ' Oh, God, how would she explain this — this connection she had with her twin? This weird way of communicating when it hadn't happened in years. 'It . . . It was . . . just a little spell.'

'A little spell?' Becca repeated, nodding her head as if she had expected just such an answer from a mother she could no longer trust, a woman who had single-handedly ruined her life. Turning away, she didn't bother hiding the fact that she rolled her eyes.

Frustration caused a headache to pound behind Maggie's eyes, and her fingers curled into fists. She'd love to tell Becca the truth, but then her daughter would just think she was crazy. Anyone who had heard her try and explain about the odd connection she had with Mary Theresa did. 'Yes. A spell. When you get older — '

'You're only thirty-seven, Mom. You keep telling me it's not exactly ancient.'

Thirty-seven and sometimes it feels like seventy.

'Maybe you should see a doctor. Another one.'

Was there just the hint of concern beneath the sarcasm?

'Maybe I will.' Maggie bent down, picked up the can and found a push broom hanging from a nail. 'Nothing to worry about.' She swept with long, sure strokes, though she was still shaken. There was a chance she hadn't heard anything after all. Maybe she was just overworked — exhausted from the move and the emotional turmoil that she'd been through.

Becca lifted a thin adolescent shoulder. Beneath her baggy polar fleece sweater and faded jeans, she showed off the beginnings of a womanly figure. 'I, um, thought I'd go for a ride.'

'The sun's gonna set soon.'

'I won't be gone long. What do you care anyway?'

'I care, okay?'

'But I'll take Jasper. You said yourself he's more surefooted than any other horse you've ever seen.'

It was useless to argue. No reason to. Becca was right. 'Just be back soon, okay? For dinner. Before it gets dark.' She hung up the broom and scooped another ration of oats.

'No one's gonna get me out here in the middle of nowhere,' Becca said as she pulled down a bridle. 'It's not like when we lived in California, you know, in the middle of civilization.'

'Just be careful.'

'Always am.'

'Take Barkley with you.'

'He'll come whether I want him to or not, but he's not much of a watchdog.'

'Just take him.'

'Fine.'

'And let Jasper finish his dinner first, okay?'

Becca rolled her eyes again, then let out a theatrical long-suffering sigh, but she did as she was told, leaving the bridle draped over the top rail of the stalls and even going so far as to grab the pitchfork and toss hay into the mangers. They worked in tense silence, the argument simmering between them. It took all of Maggie's willpower not to make small talk or criticize her daughter. *Patience*, she told herself. *The resentment will fade. Give it time. Lots of time*.

When Becca was in one of her the-world-is-against-me-and-it's-all-your-fault moods, anything Maggie said would only exacerbate the situation. She had learned it was better to hold her tongue. Besides, Becca wanted answers, and what could Maggie say? *I heard your flamboyant aunt's voice while I was feeding the stock. It came to me right here in this barn, hundreds, maybe thousands of miles away from her?* Yeah, right.

When Jasper had eaten his fill, Becca brushed and saddled him, then slid a bridle over his head and walked the gray gelding to the pasture. The rest of the small herd snorted, nipped at each other, and tossed their heads as if they, too, were restless within the confines of the barn. Maggie leaned a shoulder against the doorjamb and watched as Becca climbed into the saddle. Whistling to Barkley, their adopted German shepherd, Becca rode through a series of gates to the Forest Service land, where scrub brush was interrupted by stands of jack and lodgepole pine trees. The dog, with his mangled right ear and bad hind leg, followed right behind, loping easily on three legs across the dry acres that were guarded to the east by the Bitterroot Mountains.

Maggie rubbed her arms. Today, her jacket didn't seem to keep out the cold of coming winter; or maybe it was because she realized how very much she and Becca were alone. Just the way Maggie had wanted it. As far from the city and all the painful memories of L.A. as she could get.

Becca leaned low over Jasper's shoulders and eased him into a gallop. The scruffy dog, despite the injuries he'd sustained in a losing battle with a raccoon, loped easily behind as they approached the hills. Becca and Barkley. *Both broken souls*, Maggie thought anxiously as she ignored the first mournful cry of a coyote hidden somewhere in the distance.

The moon, a smiling crescent that shimmered in opalescent tones, had already risen, though the sun was still undecided about settling into the western horizon where a jet's wake sliced across the sky before disappearing into a thin veil of slowly gathering clouds. In the fields, cattle stirred, chewing their cuds, switching their tails, lumbering without much grace near a stream that sliced sharply through the fields.

Yes, it was peaceful here, she thought. And safe. The nearest neighbor was half a mile down the road, the closest town not much more than a stoplight, grocery store, post office, and gas station. Maggie considered Settler's Ridge, Idaho, to be as close to heaven-on-earth as a person could find. Becca was sure the tiny town was the embodiment of hell.

Once Becca had disappeared from sight, Maggie checked the water in the troughs, then walked to the back porch to yank sheets she'd been drying off the line. She'd collected two pins in her mouth and was gathering the yards of percale when the phone jangled. 'Great,' she mumbled around the pins.

A second, demanding ring.

'Yeah, yeah, I'm coming . . . I'm coming,' she grumbled, spitting out the pins and tossing the bedding into a wicker basket.

Brring!

She hauled the load into the old cabin, dumped it on the table, snagged the receiver, and heard the flat sound of a dial tone in her ear.

'Hello?' she said automatically, then started to hang up only to stare down at the instrument as she shrugged out of her jacket. Who had called? If only she lived in the city as before so that she could check caller ID. *Or you could buy a new battery for the answering machine and plug it in. You don't have to be a hermit*.

That much was true. She eyed the mouthpiece of the receiver, then placed the handset into its cradle. So someone had called. Big deal. It could have been one of Becca's friends. Though they didn't get many calls here, there were a few, and just because she'd thought she'd heard Mary Theresa's mental voice a little while ago was no reason to panic. *Just calm down*.

The truth was that Maggie had been hiding for nine months, turning her back on a world that had hurt her and her daughter one too many times.

Coward. Other people cope. Why can't you?

Drumming her fingers on the checkered cloth that covered the table, she frowned at the telephone. Could the caller have been Mary Theresa? It had been so long since they'd spoken, too long . . .

She picked up the receiver again and dialed rapidly before she let her pride get the better of her. The long-distance connection was made and she waited. One ring. Two. Three. Click.

'Hi.' Mary Theresa's breathy, upbeat voice brought a smile to Maggie's lips as she nervously twisted the ring on her right hand. 'This is Marquise. I can't come to the phone right now, but leave a message after the tone and I'll get back to you as soon as I can. I promise.'

The recorder beeped and Maggie steeled herself. 'Mary Theresa, this is Maggie. If you're there please pick up . . . Mary Theresa? . . . Oh, okay, Marquise, are you there?' she asked impatiently, using her sister's stage name, hoping that if Mary Theresa was within earshot she'd put aside her petulance and answer. A heartbeat. Two. Nothing. 'Look, I, um, I got a message from you — you know, the kind you used to send.' She glanced around the room and felt foolish. What if she'd dreamed up the whole thing? 'Well, at least I think I did, and I need to talk to you, so please call me back. I'm still at the ranch in Idaho.' She rattled off the number, waited a second or two in the fleeting hope that her sister was listening, then, sighing, hung up. 'Damn.'

The sun had finally set and the cabin felt cold and bereft, empty. Maggie checked the thermostat, then walked to a window and looked toward the mountains as if she could will her daughter's image to appear from the shadows. All the while her sister's cryptic message haunted her. What had Mary Theresa said? *Only you can help me. It was Thane. He did this to me.*

Did what?

Who knew? It was nothing. Had to be. She couldn't let her wild imagination get the better of her. Just because Maggie wrote mysteries for a living and had delved into true-crime stories, didn't mean she had to believe something horrible had happened to her sister.

With one eye on the clock, Maggie pulled out a serving bowl of stew she'd made earlier in the week, dumped the contents into a saucepan, and switched on the stove. She sliced bread, topped it with cheese, intending to broil the open-faced sandwiches as soon as Becca had put Jasper away for the night.

As the seconds ticked by, Maggie told herself not to worry, turned on a couple of lights, unloaded the dishwasher, and ignored her computer, which had been waiting for her all day, the monitor glowing with a screen saver of cartoon characters. The idea of working on any kind of story at the moment was about as appealing as day-old oatmeal.

She'd tackle chapter six after dinner.

No sign of Becca.

Don't be a worrywart. She'll be back. Sighing, she shut the door, snapped her hair into a ponytail and, as the cabin grew darker, flipped on a lamp near the front door.

Her thoughts crept down a forbidden path, a crooked trail that still led to Thane Walker. She hadn't seen him in years but imagined he was just as sexy and irreverent as ever, a lone-cowboy type complete with a Wyoming swagger and enough lines in his face to add an edge of severity to already-harsh features. The kind of man to avoid. The kind of man who attracted trouble. The only man who had ever been able to make Maggie's blood run hot with only one cynical glance.

'Forget it,' she told herself. She must've imagined the whole scene in the barn. She'd only thought she'd heard Mary Theresa's 'voice' because it had been so long, so many silent months without a word from her twin. She walked to the fireplace and plucked an old framed photo from the mantel. It had been taken nearly ten years earlier, when Mary Theresa, who had reinvented herself as simply Marquise, à la Cher or Madonna, was about to launch her own Denver-based talk show. The two sisters stood back to back, identical twins except that they were mirror images. Mary Theresa was left-handed, Maggie used her right; one side of Mary's mouth lifted more than the other, the opposite was true of her sister. One of Mary Theresa's pinkies turned inward — the right. On Maggie, it was the left.

Maggie felt a smile tease her lips as she ran a

finger over the faded snapshot. She and Mary Theresa both had auburn hair that curled wildly, but Mary Theresa's had been highlighted with gold and framed her face in soft layers while Maggie's had been scraped back into her ever-functional ponytail. Mary Theresa had worn a short, shimmering black dress, a designer original, complemented with a strand of pearls, black hose and three-inch heels. She'd been on her way to a party with some once-upon-a-time celebrities.

At that same frozen moment in time Maggie had worn sneakers, jeans, and a flannel shirt with a tail that flapped in the wind and had balanced three-year-old Becca on one outthrust hip. With the snow-shrouded Rocky Mountains as a backdrop, the two sisters braced themselves on each other, then swiveled their heads to grin into the camera. Bright I-can-take-on-the-world smiles, rosy cheeks, a smattering of freckles and green eyes that snapped with fire had stared into the lens.

It seemed like ages ago.

A lifetime.

She set the photo on the mantel, where it had been, between pictures of all stages of Becca's life as well as her own, then glanced outside. The evening was gathering fast, stars visible through the thin layer of clouds.

'Come on, Becca,' she worried aloud as she snapped on the exterior light and stepped onto the front porch. Silently she hoped for some sign of Jasper galloping toward the barn. But there was no sound of hoofbeats, no glimpse of a gray horse appearing over the slight rise of the field. Instead she heard a breath of wind sighing through the dry leaves that still clung to the trees and the clatter of a train rolling on far-off tracks. Again the howl of a coyote on some nearby hill.

Her gaze scoured the distance.

An answering soulful cry, lonely and echoing, reverberated across the land and put Maggie's teeth on edge. Leaning one hip against the porch rail, she tried to find the sense of calm, of well-being that she'd been looking for when she'd leased this place at the first of the year.

Everything's fine; you're just letting your overactive imagination get the better of you. If you were smart, Maggie-girl, you'd use this to your advantage, go inside, pour yourself a cup of coffee and start writing. You've got a deadline in your not-too-distant future.

Nervously she fidgeted with the wedding ring that she still wore on her hand. It was a joke really, something she'd have to give up, but couldn't quite. Not yet.

She'd reached for the door when she heard it — the muted rumble of an engine that got louder, then the crunch of gravel being flattened by heavy tires. Turning, she spied twin beams flashing through the night, the beacons broken by the trunks of trees as they passed, headlights from a truck that rolled to a stop not far from the barn. Black, slightly battered, sporting a canopy, the truck was unfamiliar.

A solitary man was behind the wheel — a man she thought she recognized.

'Oh, God,' she whispered.

It couldn't be. Or could it? Was her mind playing tricks on her? All the saliva in her throat disappeared.

The driver cut the engine and opened the door. 'Maggie?'

She'd know that voice anywhere, even after more than a dozen years.

Thane Walker, big as life, stepped out of the cab.

Her throat turned to sand, and her stupid heart jolted.

'Well, well, well,' she said, forcing the words past lips that were numb. As he slammed the door of his truck, she told herself that the accelerated beat of her heart was way out of line.

He started toward the porch.

Looking every bit like the devil he was.

The memory of Mary Theresa's 'voice' haunted her again. *It was Thane. He did this to me*. Maggie swallowed hard. She gripped the porch rail with nervous fingers and told herself she wasn't going to be taken in by him. Never again.

His slow Western saunter had disappeared, replaced by purposeful strides that ate up the gravel-strewn lot that separated the house from the barn. With a countenance as harsh as the windswept Wyoming plains he'd once called home, his features were grim and set, his jaw clenched, his eyes, even in the darkness, drilling into hers.

'Thane,' she said, not bothering with a smile as he stepped into the small circle of light cast by the porch light. 'Will wonders never cease?'

Somehow she hoped to cover up the fact that she was shell-shocked, that her heart was racing, and a dozen questions blitzed through her mind. 'You know, Walker, you're about the last person I expected to ever darken my door.'

He didn't crack a smile. 'Guess you're still sharpening your tongue, eh, Maggie?'

'Always,' she lied.

His lips flattened over his teeth for just a second. 'So that's how it's gonna be? We're gonna trade insults?' After all these years, he still had the ability to make her feel like a fool. 'Right now I don't have the time, the energy, or the desire.'

'Neither do I.'

'Well, that's a start.'

'What're you doing here?'

The intensity of the man didn't let up one iota. He hesitated just a second. 'I need your help.'

'My help?' she repeated, not trusting him as far as she could throw him. He was trouble. She'd learned that painful fact a long time ago; the last person she wanted in her life in any way, shape, or form. 'I can't imagine why.' Already shaking her head, she forced herself to stay calm. Just because she thought she'd heard Mary Theresa's 'voice' was no reason to panic. But the fact that he was here had to be more than simple coincidence. Didn't it? Besides, she wasn't one to believe in coincidence. Folding her arms over her chest, she met his narrowed gaze with her own. 'You know, Thane, you've got a helluva lot of nerve. After everything that happened between you and Mary Theresa, I can't imagine why I would ever consider helping you.'

'Because, if I remember right, that's the kind of person you are. Even after what happened.'

She stiffened, felt a jab of undeserved guilt, and refused to rise to the bait. Some things were better left dead and buried. She forced a cold smile. 'Maybe you'd better explain.'

'It's Mary Theresa.'

Her heart nearly stopped, though she'd expected as much.

'I don't know how to say this but to do it straight out,' he admitted, rubbing his hand over a jaw that was in dire need of a shave. 'Brace yourself.'

'Oh, God — '

'She's missing, Maggie. Been gone at least three days. No one knows where she is, but . . . ' He glanced away toward the shadowy hills, then took a deep breath. 'It looks bad.'

'How bad?' She held on to the rail of the porch for support, felt the slivers in the tips of her fingers that she hadn't bothered working out yet.

'Real bad. I thought she might be here.'

'No.' Her stomach twisted.

'I'm surprised the police haven't called you yet.'

She felt the breath of something cold and sinister against the back of her neck. 'You know Mary Theresa,' Maggie heard herself saying, denial running circles in her mind. 'This could just be one of her stunts. It's not like she hasn't run away before.'

A shadow flickered in his gaze. 'This time she doesn't have a husband to run from.'

'For the love of God, Thane, listen to you. Mary Theresa is fine. She's just . . . hiding.'

'But not here? Not with you?'

'No — '

He looked tired. Weary. As if he hadn't slept in days. As if he really believed that this time Mary Theresa had gotten herself into thick, dire trouble.

'There's more,' he said and his tone of voice — so flat and guarded — told her to beware.

'More?'

'The police and that television station she works for don't think that she just ran off. At least, they're considering other possibilities.'

Dread sliced into her soul.

'They suspect that she's been kidnapped or worse.'

A soft cry erupted from her throat. 'No — '

He held her gaze with eyes that were, in the gathering darkness, a dangerous shade of midnight blue. 'I'm sorry, Maggie.'

'Look, Thane, I don't want to hear this. It's nonsense. It . . . it just can't be. Mary Theresa is fine. She's in Denver and — '

'I was there. At her place. She wasn't there. Hadn't been for days. Thursday she stormed off the set, then Friday she didn't show up for work and missed a meeting with her new agent.'

'New agent?' Maggie repeated. 'She's not with Merle?'

'Oh, you haven't heard the news. Merle Lafayette's out. Ambrose King is in.'

'But she was with Merle for years . . . '

'Until she fired her about six months ago. King made her promises. Anyway, she stood him up.'

'She could just be out of town. You know how she is.'

His teeth clenched and a muscle worked in the corner of his jaw. 'The police will be calling.'

'Oh, God.' She shook her head. 'No,' she said with new determination. 'You're wrong. Something's going on, sure, but — '

'Why would I lie?'

The question stopped her cold. She opened her mouth, then snapped it closed.

'Why would I drive all this way just to tell you a lie?'

Her head thundered as night descended. She felt detached and alone, as if she were watching a drama that she was a part of. 'I — I don't know. You've lied before.'

'Not about this.'

'No, but — '

He grabbed her hand, held it in a strong grip that squeezed hard. 'I didn't come here to freak you out, Maggie. But I thought you'd want to know, to hear it from me face-to-face. So just hear me out.'

He looked so beleaguered she half-believed him, and then the pain began in earnest, the agony of what he was saying plunged deep into her soul. Tears burned in her eyes. 'I don't want to hear this.'

'And, believe me, I don't want to say it, but Maggie, you've got to listen. There's a detective with the Denver police who thinks that she . . . ' His voice trailed off to be replaced by the sounds of a calf bawling for his mother.

'What?'

His lips turned down at the corners. 'That she might be dead.'

'Oh, sweet Jesus, no — 'This was all happening too fast; Maggie was getting too much information, too much horrible information, too quickly. Her guts turned sour, and she thought she might be sick. 'Why? What would lead him to believe . . . ' She swallowed back the bile that rose in her throat.

'I don't know. They haven't found her body, at least not that I know of, but they keep searching.'

Tears rolled down her cheeks. 'I don't believe you, Thane. This is all too crazy. Mary Theresa is alive, dammit! If something had happened to her, I would know.' She hooked a thumb at her chest and jerked it in the direction of her heart. 'I would feel it.'

'How?'

'I don't know, but I would.'

'Because you're twins?' He didn't bother to hide his sarcasm.

'Because . . . well, yes. Yes! She and I are close.'

'You haven't spoken in months.'

But I heard from her. Just a little while ago. She called to me. Maggie started to utter the words, then held her tongue. She'd learned her lesson long ago. No one would believe her. Not the psychiatrists she'd visited, not her parents, who were now gone, and especially not Thane

Walker, her first love, her sister's ex-husband. Stiffening her spine, she refused to break down. 'I just think I would know. Don't ask me to explain it, okay?'

He hesitated, then shoved his hair out of his eyes with both hands.

'Is there something else?' she asked, determined not to let this man with his wild allegations get to her.

'Oh, yeah.'

Her insides churned. 'More speculation?'

'Maybe.' He mounted the steps. 'As I said, it looks like I might need your help.'

'You?'

'The detective in charge — his name is Henderson — he thinks I had something to do with Mary Theresa aka Marquise's disappearance.'

'You? But why — ?'

A sharp woof heralded Barkley's arrival. Three legs moving swiftly, the shepherd tore into the yard and raced up the steps. The hairs on the back of his neck bristled, his fangs flashed an evil white, and his mangled ear lay flat and menacing against his head as he smelled the intruder. He growled low in his throat, his black lips curling back, eyes centered on Thane.

'Where's Becca?' Maggie asked as if the dog could answer. Thoughts of her sister were thrust aside. Maggie's heart pounded. She scanned the darkness, searching for her daughter.

Barkley snarled and barked.

'What?' Thane asked, then commanded, 'Hush,' to the dog, who backed off but still growled from beneath the rusting porch swing.

Maggie, fear turning her heart to ice, walked down the steps and headed for the corral that opened to the trail Becca had taken. Her gaze pierced the night-darkened fields. 'Becca. She went riding about an hour ago. Barkley was with her . . . ' Maggie strained, hoping to see the horse and rider but spying nothing except a few head of cattle, dark shapes shifting against the grass. Why would the dog return alone? Goose bumps rose on her flesh. 'I hope something didn't happen . . . '

Brrring!

From the open door of the cabin the phone jangled.

Unnamed fear congealed deep in her soul. She turned on her heel, raced across the yard and up the steps to the house. Past Thane and through the screen door, she flew through the living room and snagged the receiver. 'Hello?'

The screen door banged shut, and Thane, with the growling dog guarding him, stared through the mesh.

'Ms. McCrae? Margaret Elizabeth Reilly McCrae?'

Her heart hammered wildly. 'Speaking,' she said, her eyes fixed on Thane's as dread took a stranglehold of her heart.

'This is Detective Henderson with the Denver police.'

Her knees buckled, and she sank against the wall. 'Yes?'

'Is Mary Theresa Gillette, also known by the single name of Marquise, your sister?'

Maggie began to shake. Her blood turned to ice. Biting her lip, she stared at Thane's face visible through the screen and nodded slowly, as if the detective could see her. 'Yes,' she whispered.

A beat.

She wanted to die.

Tears filled her throat.

'I'm afraid I have some bad news for you, Ms. McCrae,' Henderson said solemnly. Maggie's head pounded, her fingers tightened over the receiver. 'It's about your sister . . . '

2

Maggie replaced the receiver slowly and licked her dry lips. She couldn't breathe, could barely think. A thousand thoughts screamed through her head, a million denials. 'That was Detective Henderson,' she said dully, her head pounding, her world suddenly out of kilter.

Thane had entered the house during Maggie's short conversation and stood at the door, his expression intense, his eyes narrowed.

'I figured as much.'

'This detective. Henderson. Do . . . do you know him?'

'We've met.' Thane rubbed the back of his neck and sighed. 'He comes off like a damned bloodhound. Has a good reputation.'

'That's what we want, don't we?' she asked, and met eyes that were shuttered, an intense expression that didn't give an inch.

'Yep.'

Still reeling in disbelief, Maggie sagged into a chair and propped her forehead with one hand. She felt as if a ton of bricks was weighing her down, dragging her into an emotional abyss she'd seen before — one she'd tried desperately to avoid.

'You're right,' she admitted, as the shock gave way to pain. 'Henderson thinks Mary Theresa might be dead.' The words were horrible, echoing painfully in her heart and bringing tears she refused to shed to her eyes. 'I can't believe it,' she admitted, shaking her head in silent denial. 'I just can't believe it.'

'No one knows for sure what happened to her.' Thane took a cursory glance around the small, cozy room and walked to the river-rock fireplace where he studied the pictures gathering dust upon the old notched mantel. 'There's a chance she may still be alive.'

'She has to be.' Maggie wouldn't believe Mary Theresa was gone.

'What exactly did Henderson say?'

'Not much.' Not nearly enough. The sketchy details Henderson had given Maggie only begged more questions rather than answering any. 'Just that her secretary, Eve . . . Oh, I'm really losing it, I can't remember Eve's last name.'

'Lawrence.'

'That's it,' Maggie said, slightly disturbed that Thane knew so much about her sister's life when they'd been divorced for years. 'Anyway, Eve tried to get ahold of Mary Theresa and couldn't — and I think someone from the station called as well. Anyway, the police and the news crew, I think, drove to her house and found a way in. Mary Theresa wasn't home, and one of her cars was missing.'

'Didn't anyone call you?'

'No.' Maggie shook her head.

'Don't you think that's odd?'

'Yeah,' she said, then leaned back in her chair. 'But last weekend Becca and I drove up to Coeur d'Alene, and if anyone phoned, I wouldn't have known it because I don't have my answering machine hooked up.'

He looked at her hard. 'Why not?'

'It's a long story,' she said, evading the issue. It was bad enough that Thane put her on edge, but the entire situation had her doubting what was real, what was imagined. 'I moved here to get away from all the rat race and chaos of the city,' she admitted, hedging just a little. Never in a million years would she have thought that she would confide in Thane Walker, the one man who had, years before, stolen her heart and callously shredded it into a million painful pieces. The less this man knew about her personal life, the better.

He cocked one eyebrow. 'Seems like an answering machine would make life easier.'

'Sometimes, I guess.'

'Most of the time.' He picked up a recent picture of Becca, his eyes scanning the school photograph that showed off teeth still too big for her head, dark hair that refused to be tamed, and eyes that sparkled with the same green fire as Maggie's. 'Your daughter?'

'Yes.' No reason to lie. 'She's thirteen.'

'Pretty,' he said, slicing Maggie a glance. 'Looks like her mother.'

She wasn't about to fall for that line. At least not again. She was pushing forty, for God's sake, not a naive girl of seventeen any longer. 'People say she has my temper.'

The edges of his lips lifted a bit. 'I pity anyone who crosses her.'

'Unfortunately, it's usually me.'

'I imagine you can handle yourself.'

'Most of the time.' Maggie glanced at her watch, then gnawed nervously on the corner of her mouth and climbed to her feet. 'She should be home by now.' Walking to the large window by the front door, she flipped on the security lamp that was suspended on a pole near the barn. Instantly the gravel lot was washed with garish blue light.

'Where is she?'

'Riding. The ridge, I think.' Maggie folded her arms under her breasts and stared through the glass. 'She left when it was still light and I thought she'd be back by now.' Already worried sick about Mary Theresa, Maggie felt a gnawing anxiety about her daughter. Opening the door, she walked onto the porch and told herself to calm down, to ignore the rapid beating of her heart. Too much was going on. It wasn't enough that she had to deal with Thane again, or that he was still as earthy and irreverent as ever, or that Mary Theresa was missing. No, she had to be worried about Becca as well.

She heard Thane follow her outside, felt him standing close behind her, sensed the raw heat and intensity that seemed to radiate from him. *Come on, Becca,* she thought, wishing her daughter to appear.

The temperature had dropped with the nightfall. Winter was steadily on its way, chasing away any hint of Indian summer. 'I should never have let her go,' Maggie said, as much to herself as Thane.

Barkley let out a low, threatening growl, his

dark eyes fixed on the stranger who had dared enter his domain.

'She'll be okay.'

'How do you know?' Maggie whirled, her thin temper snapping. She nearly bumped into him as he stood so closely behind her, and she took one step back so that she could glare up at him. 'You don't know a thing about Becca, or this terrain, or her horse, or anything! You come riding up here with bad news, then . . . then . . . hang around and offer me platitudes about my daughter's safety.' She knew she was ranting, that her tongue was running away with her, but her emotions were strung tight as piano wires, her frayed nerves barely allowing any room for sanity.

He arched one cynical eyebrow, and she bit her tongue. She was on edge. Anxious. And being this close to him didn't help. All too vividly she remembered his embrace, the strength of ranch-tough muscles surrounding her, the feel of his lips against hers and then the aching, bleak days of living through the Stygian darkness of his betrayal.

For half a second he stared at her, and her breath got lost somewhere deep in her lungs. 'You're right,' he allowed, eyes thinning in the gloom. 'I don't know anything about you or your kid.'

The drum of hoofbeats reached Maggie's ears.

'Thank God.' She was down the two steps as Jasper, his coat shining silver in the moonglow, galloped through the open gate on the far side of the corral.

Maggie's heart nose-dived.

All her fears congealed.

No rider appeared on the gelding's back. His empty saddle was still in place, the loose stirrups flopping at his sides, the reins of his bridle dangling and dancing as he drew up short and reared. Maggie was already running, speeding across the lot and opening the gate to the corral where the gelding, eyes wild and white-rimmed, sweaty coat flecked with lather, pranced nervously.

'I take it this was her horse.' Thane was right behind her.

'You take it right,' she agreed, snatching the reins and wondering what she would do. Fear coiled deep in the middle of her, and she had to tell herself silently not to panic. She wanted to latch on to Thane's earlier bromides, to believe that her daughter was fine. 'Something happened. I've got to go find her.' She glanced toward the darkened hills, her mind racing a hundred miles a second.

'I'll help.'

'You don't have to — '

'Maggie, stop!' Thane's hands were on her shoulders, hard and firm.

'But — '

'I said 'I'll help,'' he repeated, and he gave her a tiny shake, as if to get her brain in gear. 'You might need me.'

That much was true, and Becca's safety was at stake. Nothing else mattered. 'You're right. I . . . I've got flashlights in the house.'

'Get them.' Squinting, he searched the

darkness. 'And a cell phone if you have it.'

'A cell phone?' she asked.

'In case we need to call for help.'

'Oh.' She couldn't think like that, wouldn't believe that Becca was seriously hurt. Not yet. 'I don't have one, and they don't work well here anyway.'

'I've got one in the truck. I'll get it.'

She didn't wait. As he strode to his pickup, she tore back to the house, grabbed two flashlights, extra batteries, a couple of blankets, her jacket, and a first-aid kit. She smelled something burning and remembered the stew. Passing the stove, she cranked off all burners and scrounged in a cupboard until she found an old canteen that had come with the place, rinsed it out, and filled it with cold water from the tap. She didn't want to think that Becca might be injured, but she had to be practical. There was a reason her daughter wasn't on her horse.

And it probably wasn't Becca's choice.

Heart in her throat, she tore out of the house with her supplies.

Jasper, minus his saddle, was tied to the top rail of the fence and seemed docile enough.

Maggie jogged across the yard.

Pale light streamed from the windows of the barn. Through the cracked panes, Maggie saw Thane saddling two fresh horses, a pinto named Diablo and a buckskin who had been dubbed Sandman. Shouldering open the barn door, she snagged a leather saddlebag from a peg, then stuffed it with things she hoped she wouldn't need.

'Here.' She handed Thane one of the flashlights.

'Thanks.' He took it from her, their fingers overlapping for a second. 'She's gonna be all right.'

'I know.' But she didn't. She bit her lip and turned back to the gelding. With deft fingers she adjusted the cinch on the buckskin's saddle. Her mind ran in circles, and images of Becca alone and hurt, bleeding and pale, frightened as night closed around her, played through Maggie's mind. She worked by rote, fastening buckles, shortening stirrups, attaching the saddlebag. 'We'll ride up to the ridge,' she said, smoothing a corner of Sandman's saddle blanket. 'It's . . . It's Becca's favorite spot. If she's not there, we'll double back on an old deer trail that winds along the creek. She could have stopped for a drink or to rest or . . . or, well, who knows? If there isn't any sign of her, we'll check the north basin, and if she isn't there, oh, my God, she has to be, she just has to — '

'Maggie!' Thane turned quickly and grabbed both her shoulders in his big, calloused hands. His fingers squeezed over the tops of her arms and his breath was hot against the back of her neck. 'Just slow down a minute, okay. You're working yourself into a lather.'

Words froze in her throat. She squeezed her eyes shut for a second, forcing the horrid pictures in her mind to retreat to the shadows. Taking deep breaths, she managed to grab the remnants of her composure. For once he was right. She nodded and felt his hands shift as he slowly rotated her to face him.

When she finally lifted her eyelids, she was staring into a craggy face that was hard and drawn, a face so close to hers she could see his pores, read the concern in his gaze as he stared at her with eyes that pierced deeply, searching for the bottom of her soul. 'We'll find her,' he promised.

Tears filled her eyes.

'Don't do this to yourself.'

Sandman snorted.

'Of course we'll . . . ' She swallowed hard, her throat tight, her lungs constricted.

He gave her another little shake. 'I said, 'We'll find her.'' His lips were flat over his teeth, his gaze unflinching as he stared down at her. 'Do you believe me?'

She didn't answer.

His fingers tightened, digging into the muscles of her forearms. 'Do you believe me?'

'Yes.'

'Good.' His grip relaxed a bit, though he didn't seem convinced of her answer. 'Now, let's get out of here. You'll have to lead the way.'

'I know.'

'Don't lose me.' He released her, and she nearly fell backward. The words, said so innocently, catapulted her to another time and place when she would have cut out her heart to hear him utter them.

'I . . . I won't,' she said, catching herself and reining in her runaway emotions. Clearing her throat, she grabbed the buckskin's reins and, determined not to break down again, led him smartly out of the barn. Outside, even with the security lamp, the night was dark, the breeze thick with the promise of winter. Clouds scudded across the slice of moon.

With a whistle to Barkley, Maggie swung into the saddle, turned the horse's nose into the wind, and pressed her knees into his sides. 'Let's go,' she urged, and the gelding sprang forward, kicking up dirt as his strides lengthened. They sped through the open gate and across a dry field before heading into the vast acres owned by the government.

'Becca!' she cried as the cold wind tore at her face and tugged at the strands of hair escaping from her ponytail.

'Becca!' The flashlight's beam bobbed as she swept it over the landscape with her right hand while holding the reins with her left. Barkley, swift on his three legs, tongue hanging out, raced earnestly beside the fleet horse.

Thane was right behind her, his pinto galloping stride for stride with Sandman, the beam from Thane's flashlight wobbling over the clumps of weeds, grass, and dead wildflowers covering the ground.

Straining to listen, hearing nothing other than the horses' labored breathing and the thunder of their hooves, Maggie wondered how they would ever find her daughter. The hills in this part of Idaho were steep craggy bluffs and precipices that dropped off to chasms as opaque as midnight.

Don't give up, she told herself. *Becca's a smart girl. Even if she's hurt, she'll use her head.*

Unless she's unconscious.

Or worse.

No! No! No! Fright was the ghost in the saddle with her, but she denied her worst fears, pushed aside the horrible, bloody scenarios that played at the edges of her brain, threatening to paralyze her. *Please, God, keep Becca safe. Protect her. She's just a baby. My baby.*

'Becca!' she screamed again, her fingers clutching the reins. 'Becca! Can you hear me?' *Answer, baby, please just answer me.* The ravine for the creek, a dark winding chasm, split the moon-silvered fields and loomed ahead. Pressing her knees against the buckskin's sides, Maggie leaned lower, urging Sandman ever forward. Anxious to run, he grabbed the bit in his teeth and flew over the land. She sensed his strides quickening, lengthening.

Ducking her head close to his neck, she felt him launch. They sailed over the dry gravel and shallow stream that sliced through these dusty acres.

With a jolt that jarred her bones, the horse landed. He missed a stride, grunted as he scrambled up the bank, then recovered and took off, speeding Maggie toward the dark foothills, where stands of pine and larch clustered like lonely, cold sentinels defending the hillside.

The shepherd, his coat slick with water, lagged behind.

'Careful!' Thane yelled, his voice close as she shined her light on the deer trail that switched back and forth through the thickets.

'Always,' she muttered under her breath. The

last thing she was concerned about was her own well-being, but the buckskin slowed of his own accord, picking his way along the path as Maggie swung the flashlight over his head, sending a solitary beacon up the hill, the thin stream of light weakly illuminating the underbrush and tree trunks.

'Becca!' she yelled, then whispered, 'Please, please, please, be okay.'

'Becca!' Thane's voice boomed through the hills, and for a second Maggie was grateful for his strength, for the fact that she wasn't alone, that there was someone upon whom she could lean.

Never, Maggie! You can never rely on this man, never trust him! Remember what he did to you — to Mary Theresa and, for God's sake, remember why he's here! Because he's in trouble. Somehow he's involved in Mary Theresa's disappearance. Her heart ached again, her head reverberated with trepidation. Right now she couldn't worry about Thane, could only use him for the help he gave. After they found Becca . . . *if* they found her . . . *No! When* they found her daughter, then Maggie would deal with Thane.

Her horse was sweating now, fighting gamely up the path as the flashlight's beam began to dim. Maggie yelled until she was hoarse, hollering at the top of her lungs, refusing to give in to the mind-numbing fear that she would never see her daughter again. Dark mountains spired around her, deep canyons gaped on either side of the ridgeline trail.

In her mind's eye Maggie saw her daughter again for the first time, red-faced and screaming as she was being brought into the world, then another mental image of Becca's second birthday party, where the guest of honor had delightedly placed both chubby hands in the middle of her cake while Mary Theresa had laughed and flirted outrageously with Dean . . .

'Mom! Over here!' The voice was faint.

'Becca!' Maggie pulled up short, her heart pounding, tears of relief filling her eyes as she stood in the stirrups and swung her flashlight as high as possible, creating the largest arc over the greatest area. 'Where are you?' Damn, but she couldn't see a thing!

'Mom! Help me.'

Thane drew up beside her, his eyes narrowed against the darkness. He aimed his beam into the underbrush.

'Becca. I can't see you — ' Maggie yelled.

'Here, by the stump — '

Pinpointing the sound, Thane shined his light on the jagged remains of what had once been a pine tree twenty yards off the trail. Lightning had shorn the tree, leaving only a ragged, blackened stump. Propped against the scorched bark was Becca, her face white and drawn, her dark hair falling over her eyes, one hand raised and waving to get Maggie's attention.

Heart in her throat, relief and adrenaline flowing through her blood, Maggie scrambled off her horse and ran the short distance over the uneven ground on legs that threatened to give way. 'Oh, my God, Becca, what happened? Are you hurt?' At Becca's side, she fell to her knees, thankful that her baby was alive.

'Damned Jasper threw me.' Becca's eyes were dark. Angry. Her eyebrows pulled into a single furious line. But beneath the fury there was a hint of terror, and the tracks of tears that ran down her cheeks belied her true emotions. Her teeth chattered and she shivered. 'He spooked for no reason. No damned reason at all.'

'Are you all right?' Maggie asked, seeing the scrapes and smudges on Becca's cheeks and elbows. Thane, still holding the flashlight so that its beam illuminated the area surrounding Becca, edged his horse closer.

'Yeah . . . Nah . . . it's . . . it's my ankle.'

'Let me see.' Gently Maggie removed Becca's boot and her daughter, after giving out one squeal of pain, bit her lip. A knot swelled above Becca's right foot.

'I don't know what happened to Jasper,' Becca grumbled ungraciously. 'I hope he's lost for good, and the coyotes eat him.'

'Too bad,' Maggie said with a half smile. 'He already made it back.'

'Figures,' Becca sniffed, angry at the horse, her mother, and the world in general. 'If I were you, I'd sell him for dog food.'

'I'll consider it,' Maggie agreed, though she had no intention of doing anything of the kind. She just wasn't in the mood for another argument, and Becca seemed more angry than hurt. Thank God.

'Who's he?' Becca asked, holding her arm over her eyes, shading her brow as she wrinkled her nose and stared up at Thane, who was dismounting and reaching into the saddlebag.

'He's — ' How could she explain? And why? 'He's a friend,' she said, her tongue tripping on the lie. She glanced over her shoulder at the source of her daughter's confusion, and for a split second her throat caught at the sight of him. A tall man holding the reins of his horse, he cut an imposing figure. Wide shoulders pulled at the seams of his jacket, and yet his hips and waist were lean enough that his worn jeans hung low on his hips. He wore his sensuality as if he didn't know it existed.

Not that she cared. Not anymore. 'Becca, this is Thane Walker.'

'Oh.' Her gaze thinned on him. 'Thane? Weren't you — ?'

'Your aunt's husband,' he cut in. 'A long time ago. Nice meeting you.' He handed Maggie a blanket.

'Yeah, right. Me too,' she said, but there wasn't a ring of sincerity in her words.

'Let's take a look at you,' Maggie said. Ignoring Thane, she placed the blanket over Becca's shoulders, then gently touched her ankle.

'Ouch. Watch it.' Becca drew in a swift, whistling breath as an owl hooted softly from one of the lodgepole pines that towered high above them. 'Jesus, Mom.'

'Just trying to help.'

'By killing me?' Becca accused.

Maggie rocked back on her heels and told herself that Becca's bad mood was good news. If she was angry, she wasn't injured all that badly. 'I'm not trying to hurt you, honey.'

'Yeah, yeah. I know.' Becca offered a faltering smile that fell away as quickly as it appeared.

Thane leaned down and squatted next to mother and daughter. Pinning Becca with his steady gaze, he asked, 'Think you can ride?'

Becca, expression wary, nodded slowly as she sized him up. 'Probably.'

'Good.' Balancing on one knee, he instructed her to sling an arm around his neck. As she did, he reached under her legs with one arm and clasped the other around her back. 'Hang on.' As if she weighed nothing, he lifted Becca off the ground and carried her, wrapped in the blanket, to the pinto. There was a part of Maggie that didn't want anything to do with Thane Walker, that objected to his touching her daughter, a part of him that made her nervous as hell, but she bit her tongue and reminded herself that, even if he was here for some ulterior motive, he had helped her locate Becca. And that, as they said, was worth something.

More gently than Maggie thought him capable of, he helped Becca onto the pinto's back. She let out a yelp as she settled into the saddle, sucked in her breath. Barkley, hidden in the shadows, snarled, and the horses shifted nervously.

'Okay?' Thane asked, once she was astride.

'I . . . I think so.' But she was pale as death.

'Good. Hold on to the saddle horn.' He placed her hands over the leather knob. 'And let me know if you get woozy. I don't want you falling off.'

'I won't.' Bravely she tossed her hair from her eyes.

'Becca, are you sure you can handle this?' Maggie asked.

'Have to.' She stiffened her thin shoulders.

Thane patted the pinto's thick neck, but looked up at Maggie's daughter. 'Let me know when you need to rest.'

'I will,' Becca promised.

'I'll hold you to it.' Using the pale beam of his flashlight as his guide, Thane started leading the pinto down the hill. Astride the buckskin, Maggie followed slowly behind and sent up a thankful prayer that her daughter was safe.

It didn't matter that Thane Walker was involved.

Or so she tried to convince herself.

* * *

'She'll live.' The doctor, a petite woman in a lab coat three sizes too large and a name tag that read 'Penny Cranston, M.D.,' gazed at Maggie over the tops of half glasses that threatened to slide off her short, straight nose. 'The ankle's sprained, but not too badly and I looked at the X-rays. Nothing broken that I can see. However, just to be on the side of caution, I'll send them to a specialist in case I missed something.'

'Thanks.' Maggie was relieved. She'd driven over an hour to an all-night clinic in Lewiston only to discover that Becca, though bruised and scraped, her pride wounded as badly as anything else, would be fine. In the glare of the overhead fluorescent lights, Becca looked small and pale, her eyes wide, the scratches on her skin red but not deep. The dirt had been washed from her face and hands, and, all in all, aside from the knot turning blue around her ankle, she seemed fine.

'Now.' Dr. Cranston trained her eyes on her patient again. 'You need to use crutches for a few days, maybe a week or two, until you're out of pain. I'll give you a prescription for the first couple of days, and I want you to rest, elevate the foot, and ice it for twenty-four to forty-eight hours.'

'So, no school, right?' Becca asked eagerly.

'Wellll . . . I think you can make it back to class. Maybe not for a couple of days, but then I think you'll be able to go back.' She winked at Becca, who rolled her eyes theatrically and, with Maggie's help, hobbled back to the old Jeep, another source of irritation to Becca, who didn't understand why they had to trade in a perfectly good BMW for a dilapidated, rugged vehicle with four-wheel drive and a dented right fender. But then Becca didn't understand about an expensive lease as opposed to a vehicle that, though battered, was paid for.

Once they were in the Jeep, Becca leaned her bucket seat back as far as possible and closed her eyes. 'Why is that Thane guy at our house?' she asked, as Maggie wheeled out of the parking lot and headed east. It was nearly midnight, and clouds had crept in, covering the stars and moon. As the lights of Lewiston faded behind them, the darkness of the night seemed to close in.

Maggie fiddled with the radio, found a country-and-western station, and recognized a Garth Brooks tune. 'He's here because there's a problem with Aunt Mary,' Maggie said, hedging a bit until she knew for certain what had happened to Mary Theresa.

'You mean Marquise,' Becca clarified, her voice taking on a snotty edge.

'I still think of her as Mary Theresa. Always will.'

'She changed her name years ago.' Without lifting her head, Becca turned and faced her mother. 'The least you could do is respect it.'

Becca wasn't going to bait her into this argument. 'Old habits are hard to break.'

'Not if you try, Mom.'

'Forget it.'

'So what's wrong with Marquise?'

'I don't know,' Maggie admitted truthfully. She shifted down for a sharp corner and spied a set of taillights winking on the ribbon of road far ahead. 'She's missing.'

'So? Sometimes she just takes off.'

'I know.' Maggie should have taken solace in the fact that her sister was flighty and had, in the past, disappeared for a few days. But this time was different. This time the police were involved. And Thane Walker, Mary Theresa's first husband, was waiting for Maggie at her house. 'No one seems to know where she is. No one.'

'Don't blame her. Lots of famous people need to get away.'

'That's true.'

Maggie had felt her twin growing further and further away, more distant as the months had passed, but she had been dealing with her own problems and had expected that Mary Theresa would eventually land on her feet again. It had always happened in the past.

But this time it's different.

She couldn't tell Becca the truth — well, not all of it; not until she was certain of what had happened herself.

'It's freezing in here,' Becca complained, and Maggie adjusted the thermostat. True, winter was just around the corner, and as the Jeep climbed higher into the mountains, the temperature dropped. Not surprising since the heater, which needed fixing, was down to two settings — hot as Hades, or cold as death. Take your pick. She opted for Hades as Becca seemed to think she was in danger of contracting frostbite.

'So you were telling me why the Thane guy's hanging out?' she asked, opening one eye and staring at Maggie, whose hands clenched over the steering wheel. 'He and Marquise were divorced a long time ago.'

'I guess he's just concerned about her.' Maggie nodded, preferring not to dwell on Thane or his reasons for being in Idaho.

'I didn't think you liked him.'

'I don't.' At least that wasn't a lie. At a fork in the road, she angled south. The terrain was rugged, high bluffs that were sheer and dark in the night. 'He just thought I might be able to tell him where Mary — Marquise is.'

'Why?' she asked thoughtfully. 'Is he still in love with her?'

Undoubtedly. Aren't they all? 'I don't know,' she said instead, and refused to acknowledge the ache in her heart when she remembered his betrayal, denied the hot sting of Mary Theresa's deceit.

'But he's waitin' for us at the house?'

'I think so. He was going to cool down the horses and lock them away.'

Becca yawned and sighed. 'Is he gonna spend the night?'

Maggie took in a sharp, quick breath. 'No.' She was emphatic.

'Where, then?'

Good question, Maggie thought sarcastically and one she wasn't going to dwell upon. Come hell or high water, Thane Walker wasn't going to spend the night under her roof.

* * *

Thane patted Diablo on his spotted rump, then switched off the lights of the barn and walked into the night. Clouds had gathered over the moon, and the wind had picked up, bringing with it the first swirling flakes of snow. Hiking his collar around his neck, Thane stared at the little cabin Maggie called home and wished he were anywhere else on earth. Seeing her again had been a mistake — a big one. But it was too late to second-guess himself. Too late for a lot of things.

He paused at his truck, reached into the breast pocket of his jacket, and found a crumpled pack of cigarettes. There was one Marlboro left, his last smoke if he chose to give in and light up. He'd been cutting down over a couple of months, determined that the carton of filter tips he'd purchased at the end of September would be his last. This lone cigarette was all that was left.

Seeing Maggie again, touching her, smelling that special scent that lingered on his skin, had brought back memories he'd tried like hell to repress.

He'd failed. Miserably. Once the dam on his recollections had started to crack, there had been no stopping the torrent of emotions and images that crashed through his brain. He remembered the first time he'd set eyes on her, a smart aleck of a high-school girl in cutoff jeans, cotton blouse, and freckles. Her eyes had been wide and green, her cheekbones high, her smile as bright as any he'd ever seen.

And she hadn't given him the time of day.

He'd sensed there was more to her than met the eye, a restless sadness that she'd tried like hell to keep hidden. She'd been a challenge, the first woman he'd had to pursue in years.

He'd been in lust from the first time she'd turned her back on him and, with a careless toss of mahogany-colored curls in a sassy ponytail, walked away. Things hadn't changed all that much since then.

After being with her today, he'd half convinced

himself that tonight was the night he needed that final smoky shot of nicotine, but he tucked his last little crutch back into its dilapidated home and shoved the pack back into his pocket. No doubt he'd need a smoke later.

He checked his watch and figured he had at least an hour before Maggie arrived. Maybe two. Feeling cold snow hit the back of his neck, he headed for the porch and kicked off his boots. He opened the door and ignored a warning growl from the crippled old shepherd lying on a rag rug near an antique rocker. 'I'm not gonna hurt anything,' he told the dog.

Eyeing the cozy cabin with its five small rooms and yellowed pine walls, he pulled a pair of gloves from his back pocket, stretched them over his fingers, and steeled his jaw. Without second-guessing himself, he stole down the short hallway to Maggie's bedroom.

At the doorway he paused, felt a tiny jab of guilt, then tossed it aside as he entered. The room was cramped with its double bed, dresser and a desk shoved under the corner windows.

The scent of Maggie's perfume lingered in the air and he had to remind himself that he was on a mission; he couldn't be distracted. According to the old alarm clock sitting on a bedside table, he had just long enough to do what he had to.

Before all hell broke loose.

3

Thane was waiting on the porch swing. Huddled in a sheepskin jacket, one booted heel propped on the opposite jeans-clad knee, he glowered into the night, rocking, the swing gently swaying as the wind cut across the valley. Barkley, turncoat that he was, lay docilely near the door.

Maggie braced herself as she cut the engine. She switched off headlights and radio and told herself that her nerves were shot because of Becca's accident and Mary Theresa's disappearance. It had nothing to do with Thane and his innate, earthy sexuality. Nothing. She was just tired. There wasn't a thing about the man that got to her. She was being a fool. Thane Walker was only a man, and a lying one at that.

Slowly he climbed to his feet, and his silhouette was cast in stark relief against the porch light. All male. And dangerous. Long legs covered by low-slung battered jeans, and a chest that was wide enough to be interesting without a lot of extra weight.

Just muscle.

Great.

His physique was the last thing she should notice.

'It's been too long,' she muttered. Too many months without a man.

'What?' Becca roused.

'Nothing, honey. We're home.' Pocketing her

keys, she touched Becca on the shoulder and looked away from the dark sensuality of a man she didn't trust, a man who'd stolen her heart only to break it.

Becca blinked and rubbed the sleep from her eyes as snowflakes hit the windshield, collecting on the wipers. She looked at the cabin, lights glowing warmly in the cold night, then rolled her eyes expressively. 'Terrific.'

'I'll get the crutches.'

'Don't need 'em.'

'Of course you do.' Shouldering open the door, Maggie ducked her head against the flurries of snow and dashed to the back of the Jeep. Over the noise of the wind, she heard Thane's boot steps steadily approaching, gravel crunching. Stupidly, her heart began to pound. 'Get a grip,' she admonished.

Don't even think about him.

'How is she?' he asked, pulling the crutches from the cargo space.

'She'll be okay. The doctor thinks it's just a sprain. Not a bad one at that.'

'Good.' He actually seemed relieved. As if he cared. What a joke. Maggie wasn't going to fall into that particular trap. Not when Thane Walker was involved. But as she slammed the Jeep's cargo door closed, she caught a glimpse of him helping Becca out of the Jeep. Rather than force her to use the crutches, he lifted her off her feet and, sheltering her body against the cold, carried her swiftly across the snow-dusted lot to the house. A twinge of unwelcome forgiveness tugged at her heart.

'Don't be fooled,' she warned herself, as she grabbed the crutches he'd left propped against a fender, then jogged to the porch where Thane, hugging Becca tight, waited until she opened the door. He carried Becca inside.

Barkley's back end was wiggling crazily, and he, on his three good legs, trotted through the closing door a minute before Maggie snagged the handle and walked inside too. 'Traitor,' she said to the dog, and old Barkley didn't even have the decency to look abashed. 'Fine watchdog you turned out to be.'

Once inside, she motioned toward the hallway. 'She should go right to bed . . . ' Maggie began to instruct, but Thane was already hauling Becca in the right direction.

Still toting the damned crutches, Maggie marched into the bedroom and watched Thane place her daughter on the single bed tucked into the corner of the chaos Becca unhappily called home. She thawed a little as she saw how tenderly he laid Becca on the old quilt, but she reminded herself that whatever Thane was doing, it was all an act. He was here with a purpose, and it had something to do with Mary Theresa.

Mary Theresa.

Dread assailed Maggie once again.

Where was she? What was that horrible, painful plea she'd heard earlier? Had Mary Theresa tried to contact her, or had it all been in her head, a great blip in the universe, a coincidence that she'd heard from her sister after months of silence?

Goose bumps rose on her arms as she stacked the crutches in a corner near the bookcase, then opened a wicker chest and pulled out a couple of extra pillows which she used to prop up Becca's foot. As if sensing mother and daughter should be alone, Thane winked at Becca, whistled to the dog, and slipped out of the room.

'Can I get you anything?' Maggie asked, pulling on the edges of the antique quilt that she'd bought at an estate sale years before. On the table, Becca's lava lamp was glowing an undulating blue.

'Nah.' Becca's eyes were beginning to close. Posters of teen idols adorned the walls, and the scatter rugs on the floor were covered with makeup, CDs, magazines and stuffed animals left over from her younger years.

'Not even some hot cocoa?' Maggie hovered over the bed. She was caught between wanting to push the wet strands of hair from her daughter's eyes and knowing it was best to leave her alone. She had a tendency to overmother. Becca hated it. 'Or I've got some of that stew — it's a little burned, but . . . '

Rolling her eyes, Becca sighed loudly. 'I said I didn't want *anything*.'

Maggie got the message. 'Look, I was just trying to help, okay? I'll get the ice pack and bring it back. If you need anything else, just let me know.'

Becca didn't respond, and Maggie held her tongue rather than lash out. Lately she and her daughter had been involved in some kind of struggle she didn't understand. Of course Becca blamed her for uprooting her in the middle of her last year of junior high and bringing her to some 'gawd-awful middle-of-nowhere place where only losers lived.' Well, too bad. Moving here was just what the doctor ordered. At least in Maggie's opinion.

Mentally counting to ten, and then on to twenty when she hadn't cooled off, she walked briskly out of Becca's room, down the short hallway to the kitchen where she found a Ziploc bag and some hand towels. Ancient pipes creaked as she turned on the hot water, waited and waited until it was steaming. Grabbing a hammer from the odds-and-ends drawer, she placed ice cubes in a plastic bag and beat them into tiny shards.

Thane, with the old shepherd on his heels, had walked outside again and returned with an armload of firewood. The shoulders of his jacket were dark with melting snow, his hair wet as well. She tried not to notice and continued whacking at the bag of ice.

'Jesus Christ, Maggie, it's dead already.' He dropped the firewood into a basket near the hearth.

'Very funny.' She wasn't amused and slammed the plastic bag with the hammer one more time for good measure. As he opened the damper and stacked kindling over a hefty backlog, she dumped the crushed ice into the pack and carried it, along with the warm washcloths, down the hallway. Becca's face was turned toward the wall and she was feigning sleep, even going so far as pretending to snore.

'This might be a little cold,' Maggie said, undeterred by her daughter's act. Gently, she placed the ice bag on Becca's leg.

'Ouch.' Becca jumped. Her eyes shot open. 'Can't you just leave me alone?'

'The doctor said that — '

'I don't care. I *don't* want that, okay?'

'No. It's not okay, Rebecca,' Maggie said, reverting to her daughter's given name as she always did when she was angry. 'Leave it on. And here are some cloths to clean up with.' She left the warm, wet rags on a paper bag on the nightstand.

'God, Mom, give me a break, will ya?'

'Just do what the doctor said, okay?'

'Yeah. Yeah.' Becca closed her eyes again, and Maggie, rather than be drawn into an argument that neither one of them would win, straightened and turned out the light. Her head was beginning to pound in earnest. Drawing a deep breath, she headed to the living room to face Thane.

The old saying that if it wasn't one thing, it was another certainly seemed to be raging tonight.

In the living room, the fire was crackling. Golden light played on the old pine walls, making them seem even more yellow than before, and the scent of burning wood filled the small rooms.

In the few months she'd been here, Maggie had come to love this little cottage nestled at the foot of these craggy northern Idaho hills. A part of her realized that she'd run away from her problems, that eventually they would catch up with her, but for now, she felt safe and secure thousands of miles from L.A. Safe from the accusations. Safe from the pain and guilt that sometimes stole into this private place and hid, deep in the shadows, ready to attack her when she least expected it.

Thane, hands in his back pockets, hitched his chin toward the hallway. 'How'd it go?'

'The same as always. I'm an ogre of a mother, can't possibly understand her, and she's just a poor victim.' The minute the words were out, she cringed. Just because her nerves were frayed, she didn't need to be bad-mouthing her only child, the reason she found a way to get up each and every morning. 'Sorry. That's not what I meant. She's in a lot of pain, and she's trying to sleep.'

'And giving you a bad time?'

She bristled inwardly. It was one thing for her to complain about Becca, another thing entirely for an outsider to make a deprecating comment. 'It goes with the territory. I can handle it.'

'Can you?' He didn't seem convinced, but she ignored the silent questions in his eyes and walked to the telephone. By rote, she dialed Mary Theresa's number and again was connected with the answering machine. Her stomach clenched when she heard her sister's recording. She drummed her fingers on the receiver. At the tone, she said, 'Hi, M.T., it's Maggie again.' Leaning a hip against the small table where the phone rested, she bit the corner of her lip and glanced up at Thane, who was watching her every movement. As she turned her back for a bit of privacy, she said, 'Look, Mary Theresa, I know I called earlier, but I'm worried. Call me back as soon as you get in, okay?' She rattled off her telephone number again, then slowly hung up, her fingers lingering on the receiver as if she expected the phone to jangle at any second.

'She's not gonna call back.'

Facing him again, Maggie said, 'She will.' *She has to*. Maggie couldn't comprehend, wouldn't give a second's thought to the horrid idea that something had happened to her sister. 'It might be a while, but she'll call.' She wasn't going to think of the other alternative and opened a cupboard to pull down a can of coffee. Shaking the grounds into the basket of the coffeemaker she felt the same dark fear that had attacked her in the barn earlier today start to stalk her all over again.

'I hope you're right.' He adjusted the screen in front of the fireplace, then dusted his hands together and unbuttoned his jacket.

'You planning on staying?' she asked, suddenly nervous as she filled the coffee carafe with water.

'For a while.' As if he'd lived here all his life, he tossed his jacket over the screen.

Maggie was instantly wary, her muscles tense. She glanced at him over her shoulder and sloshed some of the water onto the counter. *Damn*. The man made her so jittery, it was ludicrous. 'How long is 'a while?''

His eyes glinted, and a corner of his mouth lifted. 'Don't worry, Maggie, your virtue is safe with me.'

She gasped, nearly sputtered out some kind of lame reply, and bit her tongue until she had control of it. 'Still the same charmer you always were, aren't you, Thane?' she mocked, snapping on the coffeemaker, then swiping up the spill with a sponge.

'I try.' His smile widened into a familiar sexy grin that she wanted to slap off his face. The same cocky, self-assured expression that had won as many hearts as it had broken.

'Well, it won't work on me.'

'No?' he asked, one eyebrow lifting as if he sensed a dare.

'No.' She was firm.

'Good. That'll make things easier.' His gaze swept the mantel, lingered for a while on the photos of Becca growing up, of the framed picture of the two sisters back to back, then stopped short on the only wedding picture that Maggie displayed, one of her and Dean, smiling happily at each other, she in her ivory-colored dress, her veil falling off, her fingers around the nosegay of baby's breath and pink roses, Dean's tuxedo tie loosened, his eyes full of life — a spark that had extinguished early on.

Without comment, Thane took a seat in a worn wing-backed chair and propped one heel on the ottoman as the coffee began to perk.

'Easier? How?'

His smile slowly disappeared and he stared at her with an intensity that made her want to squirm. She wrung the sponge over the sink as he said, 'I have a favor to ask of you.'

'Shoot.' She was ready to say 'no,' to deny him

anything he might want from her, because she knew deep in her soul he wasn't a man to be trusted, wasn't a person she wanted anything to do with. 'What is it?'

'I want you to drive back to Denver with me.' Eyes never leaving hers, he nodded slowly. 'I think I might need you as a character witness.'

If he hadn't been so deadly earnest, she would have laughed. 'You're kidding, right?' she said. '*Me?* A character witness for *you?*'

'I've never been more serious in my life.'

In an instant she believed him. The expression on his face was determined: his jaw set, his eyes steady, his lips blade-thin and unforgiving. Not a hint of the man who had joked just a few seconds before.

'I don't think I owe you anything,' she said slowly, folding the cloth, eyeing the pan of cold, burned stew, and ignoring it. She wasn't hungry, hadn't been since Thane had walked back into her life.

'This isn't a matter of payback.'

'Then why?' She walked into the living room and took a seat on the arm of the sofa.

'You know I would never lift a finger to hurt Mary Theresa.'

Her heart squeezed painfully. Oh, how she knew it was true. From the minute Thane had set eyes on her more seductive twin, he'd been smitten. She suspected that Thane had never stopped loving Mary Theresa. He'd only stopped loving Maggie. 'Of course.'

'The police don't know it.'

In an instant, she understood. 'You mean, not

only do the police suspect foul play in Mary Theresa's disappearance, but they think you're involved.'

'That's about the size of it.'

It was Thane. He did this to me. Mary Theresa's cryptic message crept through her brain again, chilling her blood, causing her stomach to cramp.

'I wouldn't have come here if I didn't have to,' he said, and she knew he meant it.

'I just can't up and leave,' she began, then heard herself. This was her sister they were talking about. Her twin sister. The person most like her on this earth. And she was in trouble. 'There's Becca to consider and . . . ' She let her thoughts trail off. What if Mary Theresa needed her? The coffeemaker dinged, and she returned to the open kitchen to pour two cups with hands that weren't quite steady. 'I . . . I don't know,' she admitted, carrying the mugs of steaming coffee into the living room and handing one out to him. 'There's sugar or milk in the kitchen . . . '

'I take it black. Thanks.'

She remembered. Not that she wanted to. Not ever. She settled into a corner of the couch, tucked her feet onto the cushions, and blew across her cup. 'Tell me exactly what you want me to do,' she suggested. Maybe if she heard what he had on his mind, she would better understand the situation.

'I don't know what happened to Mary Theresa or Marquise or whoever you want to call her,' he admitted. 'No one seems to. Some people think she was kidnapped; there's even talk of murder, you know that.'

Maggie nodded mutely.

'Then there are those who think this is some kind of publicity stunt, or that she just left because the pressure was so great, and she needed some peace of mind.' He took a swallow from his cup, studied the dark liquid inside, and frowned. 'I'm not sure I believe that one, though.'

'Why not?'

'Because whenever the rat race got too much for her, the ratings were down on her show, her latest lover had taken a hike, or she needed to get away from the high-profile life she was living, she'd show up at my ranch.'

'Your ranch?' Maggie repeated, dumbstruck. She'd thought that Mary Theresa hadn't seen Thane since their divorce. Never had her sister confided that she'd spent time with her ex-husband.

'Sometimes the ranch in California, other times the one outside of Cheyenne.' Setting his cup on the window ledge, he leaned forward, his forearms resting on his knees. 'Sometimes I was there, but a lot of times I wasn't.'

'I . . . I never knew that she even saw you,' Maggie said, realizing for the first time how little she understood about the woman who was her twin. It was almost as if when Mary Theresa had changed her name to Marquise, she'd severed ties with her family.

His eyes were steady. As cold as the Arctic Ocean. 'There are lots of things you don't know about your sister, Maggie. Lots of things you'd rather not know.' He stood and looked out the window to stare into the night. His reflection, distorted in the cold panes, was pale and shimmering with a steady determination. She knew from experience that Thane Walker was as stubborn as he was sexy.

The phone jangled and Maggie jumped, nearly spilling coffee all over her lap. By the second ring she grabbed the receiver and felt her heart thudding a million miles a minute. Maybe Mary Theresa had finally gotten her messages. 'Hello?'

'Maggie? It's Connie.'

Maggie's soaring spirits crashed. She recognized her sister-in-law's voice and steeled herself for more bad news.

'Hi.'

'I know you're wondering why I'm calling so late, so I'll get right to the point. I heard that Marquise is missing. I have a friend who lives in Denver who knows we're related. Well, sort of. Anyway, I . . . I know this is awkward, but I wanted to call and see if you and Becca are all right.'

As if you cared. 'We're fine,' Maggie lied.

'Well, good. Good. I, um, wanted to offer to help out. Oh, I know we've had our differences in the past, and still do. But Becca is still my niece, damn it, and I care what happens to her.'

Or what happens to her share of her inheritance.

'Thank you,' Maggie said without much warmth.

'Have you heard from Marquise?'

'No. She hasn't called.'

'Oh. I . . . I don't know what to say. But, believe me, if I can be of any help, just let me know.'

'I will,' Maggie lied as she hung up.

Becca, in her room, waited until she heard the click, then replaced her receiver. Through the thin walls of the cabin, she'd heard most of the conversation between her mother and Thane Walker, Marquise's first husband. When the phone had rung, she'd picked up, but before she'd been able to answer, her mother had started talking.

From what she could gather, Marquise was missing, no one knew why, but Thane wanted her mother to go to Denver with him. Her mom was worried about her sister. Becca smiled to herself in the darkness. She wasn't worried about Marquise. Marquise was too smart and pretty, too much of a celebrity to be in any kind of real trouble.

Becca watched the blue bubbles gently rising in the base of her lava lamp. She liked the fact that Thane was trying to talk her mother into going to Denver. In fact, that was perfect. If Becca worked things right, she'd be able to con her mom into letting her visit her cousin in L.A. Hadn't Aunt Connie offered any kind of help?

For the first time in a long while, Becca felt a ray of hope. Maybe there was a chance that she could get out of this loser, hole-in-the-wall town that her mother thought was heaven. In Becca's opinion, Settler's Ridge, Idaho, was the pits.

* * *

'Just think on it,' Thane suggested as he shoved his arms through the sleeves of his jacket. He watched as a gamut of emotions crossed Maggie's face, and, along with a sense of satisfaction in knowing she was going to agree, he felt a second's hesitation, a tiny grain of guilt that pricked at his conscience.

'I'm not sure.' She glanced at the phone again, as if willing Marquise to call. It wasn't going to happen.

'I'll be back in the morning.' He reached for the door and saw the hesitation in her eyes. She didn't know whether to invite him to stay or not. Didn't matter. He wasn't about to spend the night here. 'You can let me know then.' As he walked through the door a blast of wind cut through him like a razor. He eyed the sky as snow continued to fall and hoped that they weren't in for a blizzard.

Inside the truck, he flicked on the engine, lights, and wipers, then switched the radio to a local news station. Above the static came a brief report that started with a local shooting. As he threw his rig into reverse, the beams from its headlights flashed against the house and he saw Maggie at the window, arms folded under her breasts, eyebrows drawn together pensively, mouth compressed. A beautiful woman. More beautiful than her more high-profile sister, though she didn't know it. Probably the reason she held so much more appeal.

Fool, his mind taunted, and he saw the

reflection of his eyes in the rearview mirror. Blue-gray, hard, and glinting with a twinge of lust. He'd always been an idiot where the Reilly girls were concerned, probably always would be. Calling himself a dozen kinds of moron, he cranked the wheel and drove down the lane until he found a wide spot in the road, where he pulled off and cut the engine.

Reaching behind him to the compartment that held his essentials, he dragged out a down sleeping bag, draped it around himself, then opened the glove box and retrieved a pocket flask. Unscrewing the cap, he smiled grimly to himself. 'Here's to you, Walker, you miserable son of a bitch.' He took a long tug, felt the rye whiskey splash against the back of his throat, then burn a welcome path to his gut. Not satisfied, he lifted the flask again to his lips, swallowed long and hard, then screwed on the cap and settled in for what promised to be a long, cold, and probably fruitless vigil. But he had to wait; he couldn't take a chance that he'd been played for a fool again.

* * *

Maggie, help me, please! Remember how Thane used you, how he used me. Whatever you do, don't trust Thane Walker!

Maggie's eyes flew open. Her heart pounded and sweat poured off her. Mary Theresa's voice was as clear as if she'd been in the room. But she wasn't. Maggie was alone in her bed, in the cabin near Settler's Ridge. She swallowed back the fear that dried her mouth and pounded through her brain as the digital clock blinked a bright red three-seventeen. The dream had been so real, she wasn't convinced it hadn't happened. The three of them, Mary Theresa, Thane, and Maggie, had been standing at the edge of a ravine, the precipice high over a black abyss that seemed to have no bottom. Mary Theresa, laughing and flirting, had stepped backward.

'Don't!' Maggie had cried.

'Here, grab my hand!' Thane had ordered, as Mary Theresa's bright expression had fallen away and sheer terror had contorted her face. The earth beneath her feet had crumbled. She'd scrambled, her skin blanching, her eyes wide with panic.

'Thane!' she'd cried, and he lunged forward as if to catch her.

Maggie had screamed as his expression had turned to hatred and the hand he'd offered her sister had been used to push her farther over the edge.

'No!' Maggie had yelled, but it had been far too late.

Marquise began falling, her arms and legs frantically flailing as she became ever fainter, and the yawning black hole swallowed her completely. Thane, his features once again calm, had turned and faced her as if she was his next victim. That's when she'd heard Mary Theresa's voice again.

Now, the nightmare still palpable, Maggie sat up and swung her legs over the edge of the bed.

Her insides were shaking, her pulse thudding deep in her brain.

'Mom?'

She gasped, only to see Becca, a pale figure in the doorway. 'Good Lord, you scared me,' she admitted, clicking on the bedside lamp.

'*You* scared me.' Becca, still wearing the jeans and sweatshirt she'd had on when she'd been thrown by Jasper, was leaning on the doorframe, her injured foot cocked, her other leg bearing all her weight. She blinked against the sudden wash of light, and her hair was a tangled mess, evidence that she'd been sleeping.

'Sorry. I had a bad dream. A nightmare.'

'About Marquise,' Becca guessed.

'Yes.' Giving herself a quick mental shake, she stood and walked to the doorway. 'I'm sorry, honey. I guess I'm just worried.'

'Me too.'

'Let's get you back to bed, and I'll get some more ice and — '

'I'm okay, Mom, really.' Becca yawned. 'You just weirded me out. You've been acting so strange lately. Today in the barn when you were on your knees, and now with the screaming.' Becca's teeth sunk into her lower lip. 'It's kinda creepy.'

'Oh, honey.' Without thinking, Maggie wrapped her arms around her daughter, and for once Becca didn't squirm away. 'The last thing I want is to be creepy.'

Becca managed a nervous giggle as she slid out of her mother's embrace. 'I know you're worried about Marquise, and I heard you and

Thane talking about you helping him.' Maggie's eyes narrowed on her daughter. 'I wasn't really eavesdropping, but I couldn't help but overhear,' Becca added hastily, her gaze sliding away from her mother's. 'So why don't you go find out what happened to her?'

'It's not that easy.'

'Sure it is. The neighbors will take care of the horses, your book isn't due for another couple of months, I could miss a few days of school and stay with my friends or Aunt Connie and Uncle Jim in L.A . . . '

'So that's what this is all about,' Maggie said, wondering how conniving her daughter was becoming. As the years rolled by it seemed that Becca was developing her own sense of how to manipulate people. *Just like Mary Theresa*.

'But you could help find Marquise.'

'I could?'

'You write mystery novels, Mom. True crime. You talk to policemen all the time, and you worked for a private investigator, didn't you?'

'That was a long time ago.'

Becca lifted a shoulder. 'Isn't it kind of like riding a bicycle?'

'Not quite,' Maggie said, chuckling a little as the effects of her nightmare faded away. 'Come on, let's get you back to bed.'

Becca offered a shy smile. 'How about that hot cocoa now?'

Maggie wasn't so groggy that she didn't realize she was being conned, but she couldn't help herself. If this was Becca's self-centered and manipulating way of bonding, so be it. 'Okay,

okay, but then back to bed, and don't try and talk me into this trip to Denver, okay? I'll decide on my own.'

She helped her daughter into the living area of the house, where Becca curled on the sofa with an afghan tossed over her shoulders. The fire had burned low until only red embers glowed behind the screen and the house was taking on the chill of night. Maggie, barefoot and shivering, took the time to throw on a fleece robe and slippers, then quickly heated water for the instant cocoa. As the cups circulated in the microwave, she rummaged in the pantry for marshmallows whose shelf life had expired eons before. 'Perfect,' she thought aloud. Culinary creativity had never been one of her attributes. She considered herself the Sergeant Friday of the kitchen: 'Just the facts, ma'am.'

Plopping the hard mini-marshmallows into the cups, she asked, 'What makes you think if I do go to Denver that I'll send you to — L.A.? Why wouldn't you stay with a friend here?'

'Who?'

Maggie stirred the cocoa. Becca had a point. They didn't know anyone well enough to leave her with for more than a night. 'I don't know.'

'This way I could see my friends.'

'And miss school?'

'I'd make it up.'

'Promise?' Maggie carried a cup to Becca, who, for the first time in weeks, grinned up at her. An eager spark lit her eyes as Maggie sat on the far corner of the couch, tucked her knees up inside the voluminous folds of her dressing gown, and pulled the edge of the afghan over her feet.

'Promise.' Becca blew over her cocoa.

'I'll think about it,' Maggie said, though her mind was half-made up. Something had to give. She and Becca were always at each other's throats, the cryptic messages from Mary Theresa, real or imagined, had to be dealt with, and finding out what had happened to her twin was a priority, whether she wanted it to be or not.

Maggie had never been one to sit back and let everyone else handle her problems and now, it seemed, Mary Theresa needed her.

'Mom?' Becca's face was serious again, worry evident in the way she chewed on the corner of her lip.

'Yeah?'

'Is something wrong with you?'

'You mean other than the fact that I can't seem to get along with my daughter?' she teased, as the marshmallows melted into a gooey white mass. She took a swallow of the sickeningly sweet brew.

'No. I mean like are you sick?' Becca swallowed hard and her gaze shifted away. 'You know . . . '

'No, honey, I'm not sick. Not physically. Not mentally.' She sighed and wished she could confide in her daughter, tell her the truth about hearing Mary Theresa's voice, but that would only add fuel to the fire, scare Becca and bring back all the old, painful memories and concerns that her mother might not be sane, just because Maggie had seen a psychiatrist after her husband's death. It hadn't been a big deal, but

Connie and Jim had insinuated time and time again that Maggie's mental health was an issue. Clearing her throat, she said, 'Drink up, then we'll go back to bed.'

'So what're you gonna do?' Becca asked. She took a final swallow, then handed her half-drunk cup to her mother.

'I wish I knew,' Maggie admitted. There wasn't an easy answer. None. Life was getting much more complicated than she'd ever imagined. She carried both cups to the sink, where she noticed the mug Thane had used earlier. Touching the rim with one finger, she wondered why he'd chosen to show up at her doorstep. He could have called and told her about Mary Theresa, yet he'd decided to drive hundreds and hundreds of miles to see her in person.

Drumming her fingers on the edge of the counter, she stared through the kitchen window. Snow covered the ground and bowed the branches of the trees. Without any light from the moon, the night was eerie, the solitude that she usually found so comforting oddly disturbing.

'Mom?' Becca's voice caught her up short. 'What's really going on?'

Maggie shook her head and sighed. Instead of acting as if she didn't know what Becca was talking about, she said, 'That seems to be the sixty-four-thousand-dollar question right now.' Running her fingers through her hair, she walked back to the living room and silently offered to help her daughter down the hallway. 'I wish I knew the answer, Becca. Damn, but I wish I knew.'

4

Detective Reed Henderson didn't like being played for a fool, and in this case, the one involving Marquise or whatever the hell she wanted to be called, he was certain that someone was out to dupe him.

He picked at his teeth with his thumbnail, reached into his top desk drawer for his cigarettes, and found, instead, a pack of nicotine gum. He hated the stuff but wadded a piece into his mouth and thought it a damn poor substitute for a Camel straight.

A picture of Mary Theresa Reilly Walker Gillette aka Marquise was pinned over his desk. She was a looker, no doubt about it. Model slim with thick red-brown hair, eyes as green as jade, straight nose and perfect teeth surrounded by lips that were stretched into a smile that would light up any man's day, she carried herself with the confidence of a truly beautiful woman who knew and calculated her effect on every man who happened to cross her path. Looking into the camera as if intent on seducing the man behind the lens, she exuded a sexual radiance that even he, after nearly twenty years on the force and the cynicism that came with the duty, recognized.

Marquise had star quality. Few men would be able to resist her.

Married twice, with a string of lovers, she

didn't seem particularly stable in her love life, but then, who could blame her? Men would've been salivating, their tongues dragging out of their mouths, if she so much as gave them a wink or a smile. Her first husband was a cowboy — a loner who had a temper that had put one man in the hospital. That was years ago, of course, when Thane Walker was barely sixteen, but Henderson believed that a man didn't change. Once a hothead, always one. In years past, it seemed, Walker was forever just one step in front of the law.

Then there was the second man to make the mistake of marrying Marquise — an older guy who liked his women young and flashy, but had trouble keeping this one under his thumb. Mary Theresa had become the third Mrs. Syd Gillette for a period of less than a year. He'd moved on, been married and divorced since. It was a wonder the guy still had any money.

Her last boyfriend was ten years younger than she, a model with long, curly hair and a brooding, dark look that women seemed to find sexy. As far as Henderson was concerned, Wade Pomeranian was a spoiled pain in the butt.

So what had happened to her? The question rattled around in his head like rocks in a hubcap — irritating and damned hard to dislodge. Was she dead? Murdered? Had she committed suicide? Had she just taken off on a lark? Or was this all just a publicity stunt, the actions of a desperate woman whose star, albeit not in the caliber of a Hollywood celebrity, had once flared bright but now had begun to fade?

'Hell if I know,' he admitted, leaning back in his desk chair until it groaned in protest. He fingered his old baseball, the one that had been signed by Sandy Koufax when Henderson was just a kid, then gave it a toss. It arced perfectly one inch below the fluorescent lights before dropping into his open, waiting fingers.

What the hell had happened to Marquise? The press was all over the case. As she was the cohost of *Denver AM* and hadn't shown up on the set, the producer of the show had gotten nervous, checked around, and eventually called someone she knew on the force.

In the intervening days Henderson had talked to most of the people associated with Ms. Gillette. He didn't much like any one of them. Including her surly first husband. That guy was hiding something. Henderson could feel it in his bones. He intended to find out what it was; he just needed a little more time.

He'd put out a nationwide APB on Marquise, with her description as well as that of her Jeep Wrangler and the license plate of the vehicle. He'd also filed a missing-person report through the National Crime Information Center via the FBI. Sooner or later, she'd show up — dead or alive, he couldn't begin to guess. An enigma, that one. But people didn't usually fall off the face of the earth.

Then again, years ago, when he was still at the academy, he'd made a bet that Jimmy Hoffa would eventually turn up. That five bucks was history; he'd be damned if the same thing happened anywhere near his jurisdiction.

The door to his office swung open and Hannah Wilkins poked her head inside. Though it was the weekend, she, too, was working. 'No news on the whereabouts of Thane Walker?' she asked, eyeing him with disapproval as he flipped the baseball toward the ceiling again. He knew she objected to his lack of reverence when it came to things of value. Hell, everyone did. But he didn't believe in gilded cages, and, because of it, he supposed, he'd lost Karen and the kids.

'Nope. Walker seems to have taken a hike. Along with his ex-wife.' He caught the ball, careful to avoid his fingers touching Sandy's signature, which was still intact, then gave it another toss toward the ceiling. 'You talk to anyone at his ranch in Wyoming?'

'Nope. No one answered.' She slid into the room and leaned against the doorframe. Folding her arms over her chest, stretching the blue wool of her jacket, she added, 'But I called his other place — the spread in California. Talked to a manager there. No one knows what happened to him.'

'Convenient.'

'Very.'

'Keep looking.'

'I will.' She nodded, her short blond hair moving a bit, brushing her collar. 'They both can't be lost.'

'You wouldn't think so.'

'And he claimed he didn't leave with her. Remember you questioned him yourself the day that she was reported missing.'

'I remember. He'd had a fight with her.'

'He wasn't the only one.'

'But he was the last. Good ol' Marquise was on a tear last week, wasn't she?' he muttered, recalling that she'd had it out with the cohost of her morning program and her latest boyfriend as well as her first husband. And those were only the ones he knew about.

'Walker's not on the up and up.' Henderson frowned and replaced the baseball in its stand, a small metal replica of a catcher's glove that once had been painted shiny gold, but now showed dull black where the paint had chipped away. Narrowing his eyes on the skyline of the city, visible through a thick, plate-glass window, he scratched with one finger at the itchy stubble beginning to shadow his jaw. 'I don't like the guy.'

'This isn't exactly a news flash,' Hannah remarked with that irritating half-smile of hers. 'You don't like anyone.'

With good reason, he thought. Most people weren't to be trusted. Especially ex-husbands with personal axes to grind.

* * *

'Looks like your lucky day,' Maggie said as she walked into Becca's room and lifted the shades of her windows. Sunlight danced over the patches of snow that clung to the ground, and the room was suddenly awash with bright morning light. But as Maggie looked out the window, she saw the storm clouds gathering in the distance, gray and threatening, promising more snow than had been left in the middle of the night.

Becca, groaning, rolled over in bed, and the ice bag, a Ziploc plastic container now filled with water, tumbled to the floor. Fortunately, it didn't burst open. 'What's so lucky about it?'

'You're flying to California.' Maggie picked up the bag.

Becca's eyes sprang open. She pushed herself into a sitting position. 'What happened?' she asked suspiciously as she rubbed her eyes and yawned.

'I decided you were right. I have to go to Denver.' Maggie sighed and sat on the window ledge as the bright morning began to fade and the storm clouds encroached. 'I don't know what happened to Mary Theresa,' she admitted, staring at the clear sagging bag of water that had once been ice. 'And I'm the only family she has left, so I'm going to Denver.'

'Cool.' Becca didn't seem too worried about her missing aunt.

'Now, let's look at that ankle of yours.' She walked to the bed and Becca willingly showed off her bruised and swollen foot. Gingerly, Maggie ran a finger over her daughter's skin. Becca didn't wince.

'It's better.'

'It is?'

'Much,' Becca assured her. It seemed as if the swelling had, indeed, gone down, though the area around Becca's ankle had turned an even uglier shade of green-blue this morning and the discoloration had spread, running down to the back of her heel.

'If you say so.' She forced a smile as she straightened, then walked to the bathroom, where she dumped the contents of the bag into the sink and tossed the used plastic into a wastebasket. 'This isn't the greatest time for you to visit Connie and Jim,' she said, returning to Becca's room. It looked as if the proverbial cyclone had hit with the clothes, towels, books, and magazines scattered helter-skelter on the floor and every other available surface.

'Sure it is.' Becca wasn't going to relinquish her mother's promise. 'You can't change your mind.'

'I won't.' Maggie hated leaving Becca while the kid was still struggling with crutches. Not that she had much choice in the matter, considering the circumstances. 'So, I've already called Connie, and the airlines, and your teacher at home,' Maggie said, updating her daughter and ignoring her unease at leaving Becca with Dean's relatives, who sometimes seemed more interested in the family money than they were in their own daughter. 'We'll pick up your assignments from school on the way to Boise, and you'll fly from there to L.A. Connie will meet you at the airport. She told me Jenny is beside herself. She can't wait for you to get there.' Forcing a smile she didn't feel, Maggie opened the closet and, standing on her tiptoes, dragged down an athletic bag that was precariously balanced on the top shelf. 'I guess we'd better both get packed.'

Becca threw back the covers and, using one crutch, hobbled to her dresser. 'This is so great,' she said, her eyes bright, any groggy little hint of sleep long vanished from her eyes. 'I mean, I'm worried about Marquise and all, but nothing's really wrong with her. She's just missing. Like before. She'll turn up, don't ya think?'

'Sure.' No reason to dampen Becca's suddenly bright spirits, though Maggie wasn't certain of anything. True, Mary Theresa was flighty and had, over an argument with her agent, a fight with a lover, or a battle with the production company of the few movies she'd acted in, been known to walk off the set, take off for a few days, only to return refreshed and ready to do battle. Since working in Denver, Mary Theresa hadn't been much happier, though Maggie hadn't heard of her temper tantrums and never before had Maggie received an anguished, silent call from her sister. More to the point, never before had Thane Walker shown up on her doorstep.

This time was different.

'If you need any help in the shower, just let me know,' Maggie said. 'Breakfast'll be on the table in fifteen.'

' 'Kay,' Becca mumbled, but Maggie doubted if the information registered in her daughter's brain as she was into sorting through T-shirts, shorts, and jeans — warm weather wear for Southern California.

Maggie paused at the door. 'Pack enough for a week.'

Becca's head snapped around in her mother's direction. 'A week?' She couldn't hide the delight in her eyes. 'Really?'

'I don't know. But you know my motto — 'better safe than — '

''Sorry,' yeah, yeah, I've heard it before.' Rolling her eyes expressively, Becca once again dug through her underwear drawer.

Maggie had already showered, dressed, and packed. Her suitcase, laptop computer, briefcase and oversize purse were piled near the front door. She'd listened to the weather service and, upon hearing that the area was in for an early snowstorm, thrown her ski jacket, gloves, and hat onto the growing pile.

The coffee had perked, and she popped two waffles into the toaster. Nothing fancy this morning. Just the basics. She heard the creak of the water pipes as Becca turned on the faucet and a few seconds later Becca's off-key singing floated down the hallway over the rush of water as she showered.

How long had it been since Becca had sung spontaneously? How long had it been since she'd been truly lighthearted and happy? It seemed like ages. *Stop it,* Maggie warned herself. *No good comes of second-guessing yourself.*

The waffles popped up, and Barkley, ever vigilant under the table, lifted his head and cocked an ear. He let out a low, warning 'woof' about the same time as Maggie heard the sound of a truck's engine rumble up the drive.

Thane.

Her heart knocked in a stupid cadence as she spied his old Ford nose through the trees. *Get a grip, McCrae,* she told herself as she watched him stretch out of the cab, his legs seeming even longer than she remembered. He was wearing reflective aviator sunglasses and a stern expression that Maggie was certain would sour milk. *He's just a man. Nothing more. So what if he lied and betrayed you? So what if he got involved with your prettier sister, so what if he married her and now is wanted for questioning in her disappearance?*

She swallowed hard.

This was all so damned bizarre. And scary.

Barkley began making a racket in earnest.

'Shh! Barkley, hush!'

Careful not to burn herself, she plucked the waffles from the toaster and dropped them onto a plate about the time she heard the pipes groan again as Becca turned off the water.

Thane rapped loudly on the front door.

'It's open,' she called over Barkley's disgruntled growls.

'Hey, don't you remember me?' Thane stepped into the cabin, and the stupid dog's rear end went into immediate motion. His apprehensive growls turned into an embarrassed snort. 'I thought so.' Thane paused to rub Barkley behind his good ear.

'Looks like you won someone over,' she said.

'It's a start.' He squatted, patting Barkley's graying head, then spied the suitcases.

Maggie's stomach tightened as he scrutinized her. 'You decided to come back to Denver with me?'

'Yep.' She called down the hallway, 'Becca — breakfast.'

'Coming.'

With a curious lift of his eyebrows Thane straightened and sauntered into the kitchen area. 'What changed your mind?'

'Not you. Excuse me.' She moved around him and opened the refrigerator door.

'Talk to the police again?'

'What? No.' Retrieving a carton of orange juice she avoided touching him, found a glass in the cupboard, and poured. 'You want some?'

'Nah. Just coffee.'

'Help yourself.' The phone rang loudly, and she picked up the receiver as she managed to set the glass of juice on the old table. Becca, wearing cutoff overalls and a T-shirt, limped with one crutch into the room, slanted a wary glance at Thane, then slid into her seat. 'Hello?' Maggie said into the mouthpiece as Thane poured coffee and she reached around him to find a sticky bottle of syrup on the second shelf of the pantry.

'Maggie? Charlie here. Emma said you called, asked us to take care of the stock while you're gone.' Charlie and Emma Sandquist lived on the next ranch over. Maggie had spoken to Emma this morning while her husband was out feeding his cattle.

'Where's the butter?' Becca asked, and Maggie pointed to the counter. Thane handed the dish with a half-used cube to Becca, and she regarded him with a suspicious, puzzled expression.

'That's right. I shouldn't be gone more than four or five days,' Maggie said, propping the phone next to her ear with her shoulder as she stretched the phone cord and handed Becca the bottle of maple syrup. 'A week at the most.'

'It don't make no never mind,' her neighbor replied. 'A few days either way won't make much difference.'

'I really appreciate it. And if I can ever return the favor, just let me know.' While she gave instructions about the horses and dog, she finished putting a few dishes into the dishwasher and swiped crumbs, syrup, and coffee spills from the counters. Thane had moved out of the way and stood, drinking from a chipped mug she'd gotten as a wedding-shower gift years before. When she finally hung up, Becca was done with her breakfast and had, with the use of one crutch, returned to her bedroom.

'You packed?' Maggie called down the hallway as she checked her watch.

'Just about.'

'I'll help her carry it out.' Thane left his cup in the sink.

'Wait a minute.' She grabbed hold of the crook of his elbow, then dropped her hand quickly. 'Let's talk about what's going on here. Yes, I'm going to Denver to find out about Mary Theresa, but I think I should just buy a plane ticket and fly there.'

'Rather than go with me?' One cynical eyebrow cocked, and she felt her blood pressure elevate a bit.

'Right.'

'Why?'

She thought about hedging again, but decided at a time like this the truth was the best, if the last resort. 'Because I don't trust you,' she admitted.

His lips compressed and he rubbed a jaw that was darkened with better than a day's growth of beard. He didn't have to say anything; the clouds that crossed his eyes convinced her that he got the message. 'As long as we understand each other.'

'Exactly.'

'I'll be on my best behavior.'

'I'm not sure that's good enough, Thane,' she admitted.

'It's the best I can offer.' His jaw was rock-hard, his blue-gray eyes steady and focused on her so intently she saw his pupils dilate.

The back of her throat went dry, and a small, very feminine part of her wanted to believe in him, to put the deception of the past behind her, to give him the benefit of the doubt. 'You're . . . you're asking a lot.'

'I know.' He was serious, pain evidenced in the lines fanning from his eyes. 'But I have to ask. I could be in trouble, Maggie. The police act like they think I was somehow responsible for Mary Theresa's disappearance.'

Maggie thought of the desperate voice she'd heard while feeding the horses. Her sister's voice.

'What do you say?' he asked.

Maggie didn't answer. She didn't know what to say.

He snorted and shook his head. 'You don't believe me, either.' His voice was flat, without judgment. 'Well, hell, I suppose I deserve this, but I'm tellin' you right here and now, I didn't do anything to harm her.'

If only she could believe him, trust in those cold blue eyes, see beyond the cynical man in rawhide and denim and peer into the depths of his inky soul. What would she find, she wondered, then decided she was better off not knowing. 'All right,' she heard herself saying, 'I'll ride with you, Thane. You've got over a thousand miles to convince me that you're on a mission of mercy, that you're just interested in the safety and whereabouts of your ex-wife, that Mary Theresa's welfare is your primary objective.'

He didn't so much as flinch at the barbs of sarcasm in her words. 'Let's get a move on.' His gaze swept the interior of the cabin, to the fireplace, where only dead ash was testament of last night's fire. 'You've taken care of everything here?'

'Yep.' She nodded. 'As soon as Becca's packed, I'm ready. Barkley's going to camp out in the barn with the other animals until Charlie can pick him up and take him to his place. So' — she looked around her home one last time to see that everything was as it should be — 'I guess we're all set.'

He nodded and walked down the short hallway to Becca's room, when the phone rang again. Maggie snatched it up, crossing her fingers in the hope that it was her sister.

'Ms. McCrae?' A male voice. Her heart nose-dived. 'This is Craig Beaumont. I work with your sister, and I was just checking to see if you had any idea where she might be.'

Maggie sagged against the cupboards. 'No,'

she said, her throat closing. This was all starting to be too real. She'd never met Beaumont, only knew he was a 'pretty boy who would sell his mother to the devil for higher ratings,' according to Mary Theresa. Craig was worried, he claimed, and explained how Marquise hadn't come in to work last Friday, how everyone at the station was worried, and how they'd been checking around. ' . . . we tried to call earlier, but couldn't get hold of you.'

'I'm sorry.' She hung up a few seconds later and felt dead inside, her hopes dashed.

'Trouble?' Thane asked as he walked into the kitchen, carrying her athletic bag and a smaller case that housed Becca's portable CD player.

'That was the man Mary Theresa works with.'

'Ron Bishop, the station manager.'

'No, her cohost.'

'Beaumont.'

'Yes. They were just checking.'

'So she hasn't shown up anywhere yet.'

'No.' She shook her head and decided that the sooner she got to Denver, the better. 'We'd better get going.'

'I'll load up.' Maggie helped Becca out to the truck, apologized profusely to Barkley as she locked him in a stall with the horses, then closed her ears to the sound of his whining as she slammed the door of the barn shut behind her.

With one eye to the clouds that gathered in the morning sky, Thane stowed the bags beneath a canopy covering the bed of his truck, then climbed behind the wheel. They were squeezed together more tightly than Maggie liked, but she held her tongue.

As soon as they put Becca on the plane, there would be more distance between Thane and her. She found little comfort in the thought, however, because from that point on she and the one man she'd sworn never to trust would be alone, driving through a desolate part of the country where sometimes the radio reception was so bad that they would be forced to keep each other company.

Becca, seemingly oblivious to the tension between her mother and her aunt's ex-husband, scrounged in her CD case, found a disc she wanted, shoved it into the player, and placed the headphones over her ears. Her head swaying in rhythm to the music, she cranked up the volume to a decibel loud enough that Maggie could make out some of the lyrics.

Thane shoved the truck into gear, and, as the first snowflakes of the morning began to drift from a graying sky, they left the cabin behind.

* * *

Something was going on. Something big. But Becca couldn't figure out what it was. Listening to an old Nirvana CD, she couldn't get into the music that usually swept her away. Neither Kurt Cobain nor his hard guitar chords dispelled her sense of the immediate tension that was thick between her mother and Thane Walker, Marquise's ex-husband. Weird. Maybe Marquise was in worse trouble than they were saying.

Becca stole a look at her mother from the corner of her eye. Beneath the fringe of her lashes she caught a glimpse of Maggie, white-faced and biting on the edge of a thumbnail. Sitting stiffly, almost as if she had a case of rigor mortis, her mother stared out the windshield. Her lips were turned down at the corners and she looked worried, the way she had when she'd told Becca about the divorce just over a year ago.

Inside, Becca's stomach churned and she closed her mind to thoughts of her parents. Sure they'd fought. Big deal. Everyone's parents had fights. But somehow theirs had escalated to the point of divorce.

And then her dad had died.

The back of her eyes burned for a second, and she gritted her teeth as Kurt Cobain sang on and on. The empty part of her, the part that still hurt, burned again and she refused to think of her father or the fact that he wouldn't have died if it hadn't been for that last ugly fight.

'Shit,' she mumbled.

'What?' Her mother's head swung in her direction.

'Nothin'.' She didn't want to go into it and closed her eyes as the song ended. For a few seconds the silence in the pickup was deafening, then a crash of guitar chords started the next tune. Thank God. She'd listen. And instead of thinking about her parents and the crummy past, she'd concentrate on her future. And L.A. She smiled and decided she wasn't going back to Idaho ever again. It was like nowhere. Real hicksville. Aunt Connie would take her in; Jennifer had said so. And Jennifer had also promised on her next visit to take her to a party to meet some guys. She also said that they'd get their navels pierced and maybe even go to a tattoo parlor for some body art.

It would be so cool.

And her mom would flip.

Excellent. Becca slunk lower in the seat and bobbed her head in time with the drumbeats. She wasn't sure what kind of tattoo she'd get, but she wanted to put it on her ankle so people could see it when she wasn't wearing socks. A butterfly would be cool, but was kinda common. Not in Idaho, of course, but in L.A. A spider was a little too creepy, but a hummingbird might be just right. She smiled to herself, envisioning the colorful creature hovering just above her heel, its long beak dipping into a small flower. Yeah, that would do it.

And Mom will freak out.

Perfect.

A little twinge of guilt pricked her conscience, but she refused to think about it. For now she'd concentrate on having the time of her life in Los Angeles.

Later, as they passed over White Bird Hill, she sneaked a peek at Thane. Grim-faced, wearing sunglasses and concentrating on the snow that had started falling from the sky in small, icy pellets, he stared straight ahead. As if there wasn't another soul in the pickup. For an old guy, he was okay-looking, if you liked the rangy cowboy type. He looked like he'd rather be riding a bucking bronco or at least a huge motorcycle. There was an edge to him that even Becca, at age thirteen, could feel. So what was the deal with him and her mother? Why did they act as if they couldn't stand each other?

Becca had never heard much talk about Marquise's first husband, only that Maggie had never approved of the marriage and had always changed the subject whenever it had been brought up. She seemed to hate this guy.

Not that it mattered one way or the other. The only thing that Becca cared about was that she was about to be free, and she never intended to return to Backwoods USA again. In a few hours, she'd be outta there. For good.

It was about time.

* * *

Chewing on a toothpick he'd picked up at the airport restaurant, Thane watched the jet scream down the runway. Snow was building on either side of the tarmac, and the silver bird's wings had been de-iced before takeoff, yet he felt Maggie's case of nerves as if they were his own. Beside him, her face pressed to the glass, she seemed to hold her breath as the jet lifted its nose to the air, then took flight.

'This is the first time I've let her fly on her own,' she admitted, as her daughter's plane disappeared into the clouds.

'She'll be fine.'

The look she shot him told him she didn't believe it for a minute, but then she'd been prickly from the moment he'd set eyes on her last night. Her body language as well as her words convinced him that she didn't trust him. But then, she'd always been the smarter of the two sisters.

'She's going to be with relatives, right?'

'Not mine.'

'Your husband's.'

She nodded, her eyes darkening a bit. 'Dean's brother and sister-in-law. They have a girl, Jennifer, a few years older. Becca idolizes her.'

'And you don't?'

'I think she's on a faster track than she should be.'

'All kids are these days,' he observed.

'You don't understand.' Maggie seemed as if she were going to say something more, then thought better of it and held her tongue.

'Enlighten me.'

The look she leveled at him would cut through stone. 'I don't have enough years in my life left.'

His mouth twitched despite his bad mood, but she wasn't kidding. 'Look, I'll call Connie and Jim tonight. Make sure that Becca got there.' Her eyes were as clouded as the Boise sky, her skin pale. She glanced his way. 'Okay, so let's get this show on the road.' As if she'd given herself a swift mental kick, she turned away from the viewing window and headed down the concourse. Thane tried not to notice the jut of her chin or the lines of agitation that creased her usually smooth brow. Nor did he let his eyes wander to the sway of her hips as she strode so purposefully along the hallway. Sometimes she looked so much like Mary Theresa that his emotions got the better of him — rage and distrust charged into his soul.

And now good ole Mary Theresa, no, make that Marquise, was exacting her final revenge. On him. It was fitting somehow, a fine case of irony if there ever was one.

Outside the terminal, snow was blowing across the parking lot, scattering in the bitter wind that tore mercilessly down from northern Canada. He glanced at the sky, muttered an oath under his breath, and prayed they would find some way to outrun the storm that was predicted to chase them all the way to Colorado.

He unlocked the passenger side of the truck and waited until Maggie was tucked inside, then he slammed the door shut and knew in his gut that he was about to make the biggest mistake of his life — well, second biggest. The first had been marrying Mary Theresa Riley.

He had no choice. He had a job to do. Nothing more. He couldn't forget his objective for a second. He slid a surreptitious look at the woman seated so close to him. Beautiful. Smart. Treacherous. Just like her sister. Or the rest of womankind for that matter. In Thane's opinion, they were all alike. Every damned one of them.

* * *

'Okay, so you be good for Aunt Connie and Uncle Jim, okay?' Maggie said into the mouthpiece of the pay telephone.

'I will, Mom.' Becca sounded distracted, ready

to bolt; she was in California and didn't need or want to deal with her mother.

'I'll call when I get to Denver.' It was dark, and outside the phone booth snow swirled in a fine powder that piled on the roof of the roadside cafe and covered the parking lot.

'Fine. Whatever.'

'Becca — ' she reproached and caught sight of filthy words and telephone numbers scratched into the metal where a missing phone book had once been tethered. *For a good time call Pamela. Randy loves Jill*. Hearts. Arrows. And the usual four letters.

'I said 'fine.' '

There was no reason to try and reprimand her from hundreds of miles away. 'Okay. Love ya. Bye.'

'Bye.' Click. Becca had hung up, and Maggie stared at the receiver for a few heart-wrenching seconds. Her baby was growing away from her, taking off with all the restless energy of a pent-up colt at the gate. *Give her time*, she told herself as she hung up. *Remember how you were at thirteen*.

Inside the diner the smells of grilled onions, smoke, and day-old grease lingered in an invisible cloud near the rafters. The heating system was wheezing as it worked overtime against the dropping outdoor temperature. Colored lights, strung over the windows as if it was nearly Christmas rather than early November, winked merrily. Someone had plugged a jukebox full of quarters, and country music played on and on, accompanied by the tinkle of silverware, the murmur of conversation, and the ripple of discordant riffs of laughter.

Thane sat on one side of a wooden booth, his jacket hung on a peg. A few glints of gray appeared in the stubble darkening his chin, and the lines radiating from the corners of his eyes aged him a bit, but he still possessed that raw animal magnetism that she'd found fascinating at nineteen, an innate sexuality that some men were cursed with all of their lives.

'Get her?' he asked, looking up from a plastic-encased menu that sported more than its share of burn marks from cigarettes smoked long ago.

'Yep.'

'Everything okay?'

'Other than rampant teenage attitude?' She picked up her menu, scanned the dinner selections, and avoided the questions in his eyes. Her relationship with her daughter was none of his business. 'Have you ordered?'

'Just coffee.'

A slim waitress in a checked blouse, tight jeans, and scarf tied loosely around her long neck appeared with two cups and a thermal pot. 'Regular?' she asked, and poured as they nodded. 'Made up yer minds on dinner?'

'Burger and fries.' Maggie wasn't in the mood to count calories or fat grams or anything else for that matter. 'With the works.'

'Same — but cheese on the burger,' Thane ordered.

'You got it.' She whisked away, slapping the

order on the counter separating the kitchen from the dining area.

'How far to Denver?'

'Too far.' Thane looked into the night. 'We can't outrun the storm, so we just have to drive as far as we can. Probably Salt Lake. I've got studs on the tires, chains in the back if we need 'em. We won't be stranded.'

'How do you know?'

He swung his gaze back to her. 'I won't let that happen.'

'So now you're God?'

His lips pursed. 'Just don't worry.'

'You take more risks than I do.'

'I'll get us through this.'

'Look, Thane, I said I'd go to Denver with you. I said I'd talk to the police. I even said that I'd vouch for you, though God knows I don't trust you for a second, but I've learned over the years that I shouldn't rely on anyone, that I can stand on my own two feet, and that they're steadier than anyone's shoulder I've ever made the mistake of leaning on, including yours.'

A muscle worked near his temple. 'So now we're down to it, aren't we?'

'Just forget it.'

'You know, Maggie,' he said, resting his head against the wooden back of the booth, 'you're starting to sound like a bitter woman.'

'I wonder why?' she threw back at him. She was edgy and nervous, saw no reason to hide it. 'And really, who cares?'

'You do.'

'Do I?' She nearly laughed but he'd hit too close to the mark.

'It's not like the girl I remember.'

She stopped short, her breath caught in her lungs. *Don't fall for this, Maggie. You're way too smart, and you've been burned before*. 'I think we'd better not go into what you or I remember.'

'Why not?'

Was that her heart drumming? 'Water under the bridge, cowboy. That's all it is.' She took a sip of her coffee and was grateful that her hand was steady. This conversation was getting way too personal.

'I don't think so.' Suddenly he leaned forward, his elbows landing on the Formica tabletop. 'I think you're scared.'

Damned straight. 'Of what?'

'Me, for starters.'

'In your dreams.'

'Not my dreams, kid. My nightmares.'

'Let's not get into this, okay? It's not the time, or the place. All we have to concentrate on is Mary Theresa.'

His steady gaze called her a liar.

'And whatever you do, Walker, don't try and second-guess me or psychoanalyze my motives, or read more into my words.' She hooked her thumb at her chest. 'I tell it just like it is, okay?'

The waitress returned on hushed shoes. A plastic smile curved her glossy apricot-hued lips as she slid two platters onto the table. 'Can I get you anything else?'

Yeah, a one-way ticket back home.

'This'll do,' Thane said, then quirked an eyebrow at Maggie, inviting her opinion without saying a word.

'Just catsup.'

'Comin' right up.' She turned, snagged a plastic squirt bottle from the counter, and plopped it in front of Maggie.

'Thanks.'

'If ya need anything, just give a holler.' She motioned to the counter, where a refrigerated case spun slowly, showing off an array of confections. 'You just might want dessert, and our lemon meringue pie is to die for. No kiddin'. Baked fresh.' She pivoted on a soft-soled pump and focused her attention on a table of men with round bellies, flushed faces, baseball caps of various colors, and toothpicks wedged into the sides of their mouths.

Maggie ate in silence, and Thane didn't bother trying to break into her thoughts or making meaningless chitchat. In a small diner where everyone talked, laughed, smoked, and flirted, they ate in stony silence, the past edging into Maggie's thoughts, eroding her equilibrium while the future towered in a dark mysterious cloud ahead. When they were finished with burgers, fries, and a wedge of pecan pie with ice cream at Thane's insistence, he reached for his wallet.

Maggie delved into her purse.

'This is mine,' he said, eyeing her as she extracted her wallet.

'No way.'

'I practically shanghaied you to get you to come with me.'

She pulled out a ten and rested her elbows on either side of her half-eaten hamburger and the goo that had been most of her dessert. 'Look, Walker, let's get one thing straight, okay? I pay my own way. Yes, you talked me into coming, but I would have flown to Denver anyway to find out what happened to my sister. So we'll split everything down the middle.' With that she reached for her ski jacket.

'Is that so I don't get the wrong idea?'

The tops of her ears started to burn as she stood and shoved her arms down the jacket's thick sleeves. Quickly, she forced her hands through the gloves that she'd stashed in one pocket. 'I guess.'

She wanted to wipe the amused smile from his beard-shadowed chin. 'You want to make sure I don't think this is some kind of convoluted date, right?'

'You're so damned conceited, it's unbelievable.'

'It beats paranoia.'

'Barely.'

His smile faded as he tossed a matching bill onto the table. Anger flashed in his eyes. Without another word, he grabbed his jacket with one hand and Maggie's elbow with the other.

'What're you doing . . . wait.'

Silently he pulled, forcing her past the front desk, through double glass doors to the vestibule and into the dark night, where snow continued to fall. A quiet seething rage emanated from him as they strode to his truck. He unlocked the door for her, then climbed into the driver's side. After tossing his jacket into the space behind the seat where her laptop was stowed, he jabbed his key into the ignition. The engine turned over as she buckled her seat belt. He crammed the gearshift into reverse and backed out of his parking space.

'Let's get one thing straight,' he said as he threw the truck into first, maneuvered around a semi rolling into the truck stop, and eyed the desolate stretch of highway heading southeast. 'I need your help. Period. I don't expect anything more than your help in finding that damned sister of yours and helping me clear my name.' He clicked his headlights onto high beam, and snow swirled and danced in the glow. 'You don't owe me a thing, so I thought I'd take care of the expenses. This isn't part of some grand seduction, Maggie, it's a simple case of paying you back for your inconvenience.'

Her face was hot, her cheeks burning, but hopefully he didn't notice in the dark cab as he scowled and squinted through the windshield.

He flipped on the wipers, then adjusted the control for the defroster. 'Got it?'

'Got it,' she replied tightly, and felt like a fool. Of course he wasn't interested in her, that wasn't the point. She thought about holding her tongue, then decided it was best to clear the air. 'I just wanted to lay down the ground rules,' she said, slowly forcing her hands to relax from their clenched fists. 'It wasn't that big of a deal.'

'Amen.' A car appeared around the corner, flashing the interior of his truck with white, artificial light. She noticed his profile: Hard. Set. Determined. One hundred percent male. A strong, sometimes fierce man. Someone who didn't always tell the truth; she knew that from the past. So what secrets was he keeping? What was he hiding? She looked away, through the passenger window to the trees, tall heavy-boughed guardians of the night. Snow clung to their branches, and in other circumstances she would have found them and the steep hillsides they were climbing breathtaking. Tonight they seemed foreboding, casting a spell of fear and desolation.

Where was Mary Theresa? Was she alive? Oh, God, she had to be. Maggie's throat thickened. Staring into the stormy night, she crossed her fingers and sent up silent prayer after silent prayer for her sister.

Surely Mary Theresa was safe. Surely when they got to Denver they'd find out that the ever-flighty Marquise had just left town for a few days and forgotten to tell anyone. But as much as she tried to convince herself, she felt a chill in her blood that had nothing to do with the weather, and as the snow turned to icy pellets that battered the hood of the truck and slickened the road Maggie couldn't shake the feeling that something was wrong. Terribly and irreversibly wrong.

Be safe, Mary, she thought, closing her eyes and remembering her sister as she always had been — a free spirit who, though selfcentered, was a person everyone fell in love with. Everyone including Thane Walker. Even he hadn't been immune to Mary Theresa's charms. But then why would he have been? He had been a man, and all men, it seemed, were susceptible to Mary Theresa Reilly.

Maggie had first noticed it years ago, when Mitchell, their cousin who had been raised as their brother, had been alive. They'd been young then, barely seventeen, only a few years older than Becca was now, but already Mary Theresa was developing her charms, honing them on all the boys they knew, including the one whom Maggie had considered her brother . . .

PART II

Rio Verde
Northern California

1979

5

From beneath the water's shimmering surface, Maggie saw Mary Theresa, sunglasses propped on the bridge of her nose, string bikini showing off every inch of her tan, stroll along the edge of the swimming pool. She kicked out a lounge chair, away from the overhang and shade of the eucalyptus tree, then plopped down just as Maggie's lungs, burning from her length of time under the water, forced her to swim frantically upward. Shooting through the surface, Maggie gasped, gulped in air, and tossed her wet hair out of her eyes.

'What are you doing?' her twin asked, the corners of her mouth turned down in flat-out disapproval.

'What does it look like? Underwater laps.'

'Why?'

'I'm gonna try out for the swim team.'

'Again?' Mary Theresa sighed dramatically and dabbed at the corner of her mouth where a canker sore dared show on her lips. 'You know you're not going to make it. Just like the last time you tried out when we were in high school. Junior college will be lots tougher.'

'But I talked to the coach. So did Mitch.'

Mary Theresa's pouty little mouth acted as if it had been drawn together by purse strings, and she swatted at a bee that buzzed near her head. ‘You asked Mitchell to put in a good word for you?’

‘Yeah.’

‘With the women’s coach at the college?’ Mary Theresa asked, as if Maggie was dense as tar.

Maggie flipped onto her back and started swimming backward. She didn’t need any of Mary Theresa’s crap. Not today. ‘Uh-huh.’

‘Will wonders never cease?’

‘What’s it to you?’ Maggie knew she shouldn’t let Mary Theresa get to her, but she couldn’t help it. Mary Theresa had become more and more distant and it seemed to have started three or four years ago, about the time her sister’s breasts had developed into ‘round, ripe melons,’ as Billy Norton had been so proud of saying when they’d all been in the eighth grade. Billy was a pimply-faced geek whose talent for math made him think he was God’s gift to teachers and all females on this earth.

‘Your sister has the biggest tits in the whole damned school, and that includes Mrs. Nelson, so what happened to you?’ He’d looked to his circle of friends for some support as they’d stood in the hallway near the library. It was just after lunch about two days before they’d graduated from George Washington Junior High. The other boys had sniggered loudly, but had been blessed with enough decency to look embarrassed. ‘I thought you were supposed to be identical twins.’ Billy was always persistent.

‘And I thought you were supposed to be smart. You figure it out,’ she’d retorted angrily, though she’d been dying inside and had wanted to drop through the stain-covered carpeted floor. What was it about boys that found a girl's breasts so fascinating? It was as if they'd been weaned too early and were, ever since, dying for a peek, or a touch, or even grosser yet, a taste of some girl's tits. The bigger, the better.

'You're just jealous 'cause you got sold short,' he'd hooted.

'Tell me about it,' she'd said, then narrowed her gaze on his oversize shorts in the area where his alleged male anatomy had been hidden. She'd breezed off, wounded on the inside, her cheeks burning, her eyes filled with unshed tears. Around the corner she made a mad dash to the bathroom, where it took almost ten minutes to regain her composure. By the time she'd returned to the library, class had started. All the kids, sitting in their seats, had stared at her as she'd taken the only desk left, in the front of the room.

Mrs. Brady didn't ask any questions, just scribbled on a yellow pad, and handed Maggie a copy without so much as faltering over one single syllable as she ranted on and on about the new computer system the school was supposed to get — if there was enough funding, of course. Money was tight in all the public schools, but Mrs. Brady was ever-hopeful. Maggie had clutched the tardy slip in her sweaty fingers, slunk to the desk, and prayed for the humiliating day to be over.

'Hey, what's the difference between Maggie Reilly and a singer who's off-key?' Billy had whispered loud enough for her to hear. She felt hot tears glistening in her eyes.

No one answered, and Maggie hardly dared breathe.

'Nothin',' Billy said under his breath. 'They're both flat.'

More nervous chuckles. Maggie snapped her pencil in two. Mrs. Brady's eyes, behind the shield of thick glasses, narrowed on Billy. A tear drizzled from Maggie's eye, and she brushed it angrily aside before enduring the longest forty minutes of her life.

In the end, because of the tardy slip, she'd had to suffer through work detail, cleaning the hallways of litter before she'd been allowed to graduate.

Billy Norton hadn't been one to let sleeping dogs lie. He'd found out what day her work detail was scheduled and, knowing she would have to clean it up, had spread the remains of his lunch — an uneaten sloppy joe and french fries drizzled in catsup — on the floor. To add insult to injury, he'd also filled a condom that was probably way too big for him with meat from his sloppy joe, then left the ugly mess in the hallway by the seventh-grade stairs. He and his gang had gotten away scot-free while Maggie had to pick up the icky thin sheath and discard it, along with the rest of the garbage, into a big plastic bag.

All because she had been blessed with smaller boobs than Mary Theresa.

What a joke.

Now, as she stroked easily backward through the sun-warmed water, she told herself not to let Mary Theresa bug her. Lately Mary had been edgy, restless, and secretive. Several times Maggie had come upon her sister and cousin Mitch, whom her parents had adopted before the twins had been born and after his mother had died. They just hung out watching TV or listening to tapes of the Rolling Stones or Pink Floyd. They'd been laughing and talking, pushing each other. Upon spying Maggie, they'd both shut up, smiled falsely, and acted like stone statues. They pretended that nothing was out of the ordinary when there were all sorts of weird vibes sizzling through the air.

It was as if Maggie was suddenly the outsider, when, for most of her time on this earth, she and Mary Theresa had considered Mitch a pain in the butt — the one member of their family who hadn't fit in.

Mitch had worked hard to foster that separateness, not wanting his younger, dweeby cousins-cum-sisters anywhere near him from the time he'd entered kindergarten. He'd acted as if Maggie and Mary Theresa were strychnine, and his attitude had only gotten worse as the years rolled on.

When the girls had been in second grade, their mother insisted that he walk them to school. He'd grudgingly agreed, as he'd had no choice in the matter, but the minute they turned the corner and were out of view from the kitchen window, he'd ditched them and sworn he'd 'beat the shit' out of them if either twin had the guts to rat him out to their parents.

'He's a jerk,' Mary Theresa had decided.

'Who needs him?' Maggie had preferred to

walk to school on her own anyway. 'He's just a pain.'

Mitch had gone to great lengths to show his disdain of the girls. He'd laughed at them with his friends, shown Maggie's diary to anyone who wanted a peek, and put locks on the door of his room to make sure they wouldn't violate his privacy and sanctuary.

But now things had changed. Mitch's animosity had diminished, and Mary T, as he called her, didn't seem to mind hanging out with him. Maggie secretly thought Mary Theresa had finally figured out that Mitch's heretofore nerdy friends had become hot when they'd started driving, playing varsity sports, and growing serious facial hair where there had once only been severe cases of acne. Whatever the reason, these days Mary Theresa spent more time with Mitch and his friends than she did with Maggie.

Not that it mattered a whole lot. Sure, Maggie missed hanging out with her twin, but it wasn't the end of the world. They were starting to separate finally, their interests weren't the same anymore, and probably the biggest reason they didn't get along was that Maggie refused to be led by the nose by her sister.

Mary Theresa had always made the decisions about what they were going to do, what friends they would share, or where they would go. But Maggie was sick of it. Sick of being a twin. Especially being the paler version of her flashy sister.

When they had started having 'woman cycles' or 'the monthly curse,' as their mother had called their periods, Mary Theresa was the first to get a cramp and therefore able to give Maggie more advice than she'd ever hoped to hear by the time her body had come to grips with womanhood six weeks later. Somehow it made Mary Theresa a know-it-all on all things related to blossoming womanhood and femininity.

A few years back Mary Theresa had gotten into clothes and nail polish and lipstick and listening to music that didn't appeal to Maggie. She'd taken to smoking cigarettes in her room and blowing the smoke out her window late at night, bleaching streaks into her hair, and sneaking out once in a while, never confiding in Maggie about where she was going or what she was doing or whom she was meeting.

'You wouldn't understand,' she'd said once when Maggie had caught her slipping through the window. Mary Theresa had been wearing skintight white shorts and a cropped-off yellow top that showed off her flat abdomen. 'Just cover for me.'

'And say what?'

'I don't know. Use your imagination. You're supposed to be so good at it. All the English teachers say so,' she added with an envious edge to her voice. 'As if you're gonna be a writer or somethin'.'

'Well, I can't *imagine* where you're going or how I'm going to lie to Mom and Dad.'

'You'll come up with something,' Mary Theresa had replied, clutching her pack of Virginia Slims in one hand while holding on to the sill with her other. She flashed her sister a radiant smile, then slipped into the yard, ducking past the pools of lights from lamps placed strategically between the rosebushes that had been in full, fragrant blossom.

Fortunately, their parents had never noticed Mary Theresa's absences, and Maggie had never been forced to lie. Well, not yet anyway.

Now as she skimmed through the water and closed her eyes, concentrating on her breathing and the steady rhythm of her strokes, the unrest in the family ate at her, destroying her concentration.

Whenever Mitch's friends came around, Mary Theresa lit up like a Christmas tree while Maggie felt as if she disappeared into the woodwork. Mary Theresa flirted and giggled, dodging playful pinches, hot-blooded leers, and sensual remarks with an aplomb that left Maggie speechless.

It was bound to happen, she supposed. Who cared anyway?

She sensed rather than saw the edge of the pool, touched it with the tips of her fingers, and tucked quickly into an underwater somersault that propelled her back toward the house where Mary Theresa, disgruntled at the shade cast by the hedge, was shifting in the chaise.

Quickly Maggie swam twenty laps without a break. Her muscles began to ache. One more turn. She saw the edge of the pool near the house and knifed through the water. Stroke, stroke, stroke. Her lungs burned. She stretched and finally her fingers touched cement at the shallow end. She broke surface and gulped in air.

'Done already?' Mary Theresa asked, one eyebrow lifting over the tops of her Ray-Bans. Her body was slick with oil, tanned to a dark tawny shade, her hair piled onto her head.

'For now.' Maggie snagged the white towel she'd dropped at the pool's lip.

Mary Theresa sighed. 'Waste of time,' she muttered under her breath.

Irritated, Maggie patted her face dry, then, spying Mary Theresa basking with conceited calm on the lounge, she reached into the water, and on a whim, flung some cool drips onto Mary's flat belly.

'Hey!' Mary Theresa shrieked and shot out of the chair. 'What do you think you're doing?'

'Nothin'.'

'Nothin',' Mary Theresa mimed in a high-pitched voice, her face pulled into a nasty pout. 'Pulllease, grow up for God's sake, Maggie. Do you know what an embarrassment you are?'

Unperturbed, Maggie placed her hands on the ledge and hauled her body out of the water in a quick, lithe motion. She didn't see how she could be *that* much of an embarrassment because she looked a lot like her sister. Maybe not quite as pretty, but close enough that once in a while people called them the wrong names. Oh, that really burned Mary Theresa's butt. Maggie loved it. 'You're an idiot, a . . . a . . . kid. Why don't you go and ride your damned horse or something?'

'I will.' It sounded like heaven. Anything to get away from this house and all the ill will that seemed to grow as the summer wore on. When had it started to happen, Maggie wondered, thinking back to when she and Maggie were in junior high and Mitch had just started high school. They'd been happier then. All of them.

Maggie didn't remember the muffled arguments behind her parents' bedroom door, or the empty vodka bottles piled high in the trash, or the frigid silence from their mother, an intense, heavy lack of conversation that seemed to radiate from her while quieting everyone else. Bernice Reilly's deadly silence was able to numb them all. One icy look from her furious eyes was capable of bringing conversation and laughter to a standstill at the dinner table or stopping all communication in the car.

As Mary Theresa brushed the offending water droplets from her body, Maggie eyed the long, rambling house set on the crest of the hill. This place had been her parents' dream, and recently, she thought, it had turned into a nightmare. Ancient oaks, olives, and eucalyptuses shaded a well-tended yard and the stucco house where they resided. Painted a soft dun color and resplendent with a sweeping red-tile roof and terra-cotta patio that stretched to the pool — their father's pride and joy — the house seemed cold and empty as a tomb to Maggie, and she longed for their little three-bedroom rambler in the valley.

But with his professional jump to a rival company, Frank Reilly had elevated himself to this house, a new pool and sporty red Mercedes while Bernice had been able to hire Lydia, their Spanish-speaking maid, and for the first time in her life was able to spend hours having manicures, pedicures, and facials between her tennis matches and bridge club.

Maggie wasn't certain the move had been so good. She missed the neighbors and small yard where she could sneak through the broken fence into Jamie Tortoni's vegetable garden. They could share secrets while watching Jamie's father's goldfish swim lazily in a cement pool he'd designed and built. Whenever Maggie had been fighting with Mary Theresa, she'd been able to count on Jamie as a friend and confidante.

But that was a long time ago. When they'd moved, Mary Theresa and Maggie had gone to a different high school. Maggie and Jamie never saw each other anymore.

In the meantime Mary Theresa had changed. At the old house Maggie and M.T. had shared a room decorated with lavender paint, matching twin beds covered with purple-and-pink patchwork quilts and a gold-shag carpet littered with Barbie dolls, stuffed animals, and clothes that never quite made it to the laundry hamper.

Maggie remembered a time when they were about eleven — God, it seemed like eons ago. Late at night, after everyone else in the house had gone to bed, she and Mary Theresa had huddled together, hidden under the covers of Mary Theresa's bed with flashlights to read a dog-eared copy of *Playboy* magazine that Maggie, while searching for Mitch's stash of licorice whips, had discovered buried under his bed along with his crusty old socks and dirty jockey shorts.

'Yuk. Look at that,' Maggie had said, horrified, as she eyed the centerfold where a tanned model with huge boobs and thatch of blond hair at the juncture of her legs was pictured in a sprawled, come-hither position. Long-maned and almond-eyed, the center-fold wore nothing but an endless strand of pearls that, caught between perfect teeth, were draped from her wet lips, past her breasts to nestle deep in the misty blond curls at the apex of her thighs and disappear to God only knew where. Maggie didn't want to consider the possibilities.

'Don't you think she's beautiful?' Mary Theresa, awestruck, had asked as Maggie held the flashlight so that its beam shone straight on the pages.

Maggie had shaken her head, unable to tear her gaze away from the woman's exposed private parts.

But Mary Theresa had rotated the magazine, looking at the model from all viewpoints, pointing out the fact that the naked woman had flawless skin, interesting green eyes, and high, sculpted cheekbones. Maggie only saw her buttocks, boobs with those silver-dollar-sized nipples and . . . well, all that other stuff that made her blush.

'You know this is art, don't you?' Mary Theresa had said with all her eleven-year-old wisdom.

'Then why was it hidden under Mitch's bed, beneath his dirty clothes?'

'Because Mitch is a moron.' Mary Theresa bit at her lower lip and sized up the slick pages. 'Do you think she had a boob job?'

'A what?' Maggie felt something brush against her toes as they hung outside of the sheets. 'Oooh!' She threw back the covers, certain her mother, arms crossed and an expression resembling that of an army drill sergeant, would be standing at the foot of the bed. Instead, Flint, their silvery tabby cat, hopped onto the bed and walked with soft, tiny footprints on Maggie's back. 'Man, you scared me,' she said to the cat, and pulled him under the covers with her. She adjusted her flashlight again and noticed that Mary Theresa's concentration hadn't so much as glitched. 'What were you saying?'

'I was telling you about this kind of surgery to make 'em bigger.' She pointed to the model's enviable chest. 'It's called breast enhancement or something. Linda Stone's mom had it done a couple of years ago.'

'How do you know?'

Mary Theresa tossed her a look that silently called her naive. 'Linda said, and if you look, you'll see that she's a lot bigger than she used to be.' Her eyes narrowed on the picture. 'I can't see any scars.' Mary Theresa's eyebrows drew together thoughtfully as she studied the photograph.

'Ick. Who cares if there are scars?'

'*I* care.'

'Why?'

'I don't know. But it seems important. Boys like big boobs.'

'Would you ever have it done?'

'Maybe.'

'Well, *I* wouldn't.' Maggie shook her head. No way would she have some doctor cut her open and . . . and do what? She didn't want to know. 'Besides, boys are stupid.'

'I know.' Mary Theresa smiled. 'Real stupid. But they like big tits.'

That statement seemed profound today, Maggie thought as the lazy-afternoon sun dried the drops of water on her body. She watched Mary Theresa stretch out on the chaise again, perfect, nonsurgically enhanced breasts overflowing from the top of her neon orange bikini.

Toweling dry her hair, Maggie stood, her shadow daring to cross Mary Theresa's legs.

'Careful,' her twin said. She felt Mary Theresa's restlessness, knew that she was annoyed that Maggie had disturbed her. 'Don't you have something to do?'

'Don't you?'

Mary rolled over and sighed in disgust. 'God, you're pathetic.'

Maggie wanted to chime, *I know you are, but what am I*, then decided that would sound far too childish, only driving Mary Theresa's point home.

She didn't bother to say goodbye, just walked into the cool house, changed, and badgered her mother to let her borrow the car so she could drive to the horse barns where her mare, Ink Spot, was leased. She spent the rest of the afternoon riding through the connecting paddocks of Rio Verde Canyon and relaxing. The sun was hot, heating her crown with lazy rays as it slowly disappeared into the western horizon.

Hours later Maggie stopped at a local drive-in, where she ordered fries and a Coke. She hung out with some kids she knew from school for a while, then, knowing she was late, pushed the speed limit on the way home and parked her mother's car in its spot in the garage.

Her dad's Mercedes was missing, thank God. Maggie smiled to herself as she pocketed her keys because she'd lucked out and avoided a lecture on coming home late. Obviously her parents were gone, out for the evening.

The house was dark, only the exterior lamps lighting the way to the front door, but Mitch's Mustang sat in the driveway, its paint polished to a sheen that looked almost liquid in the lamplight.

Intent on swimming a few laps under the stars, Maggie sneaked around the outside of the house, avoiding the pools of light cast by the exterior lamps. She'd just cool off, swim three or four laps, then call it a night. She was rounding the corner and struggling to pull her T-shirt over her head at the oleander hedge when she heard the noises: the notes of a piano and Elton John's voice singing a song Maggie barely remembered, soft, happy giggles and splashes of water over the gurgle of the hot-tub jets.

Maggie froze.

'Don't!' Mary Theresa ordered, but her voice was playful, teasing.

The hairs on the back of Maggie's neck rose

slowly, one by one, as a deep male voice rumbled in laughter.

It wasn't much of a surprise really. Mary Theresa attracted a lot of male attention; she always had a date.

'Why not?' the guy asked, and Maggie's gut clenched as she recognized the voice.

'I said — oooh!'

Maggie's stomach turned over. Her throat was cotton, and though she knew she was making an irreversible mistake of life-altering proportions, that she would never be able to undo what she was about to see, she peeked through the hedge surrounding the hot tub and stood frozen, eyes locked on the white mist rising from the bubbling water and the two heads that were visible in the muted light. Mary Theresa, her hair piled on her crown, wet tendrils framing her face, was locked in an embrace with a strong, muscular male, one who held her close, his hands splayed over her spine, his face buried in the perfect breasts that she was so proud of. A bottle of vodka — part of their mother's stash, from the looks of it — was opened and sat on the tiled lip of the pool.

Mary Theresa was moving up and down as the man untied the back of her bikini and let it float away. He lifted his head for a minute and Maggie caught a glimpse of Mitch as he started licking and teasing at her twin's chest.

No!

Bile shot up Maggie's throat. She gagged, suddenly on her knees as the contents of her stomach spewed onto the ground. *No!* She couldn't have seen what she'd thought. No way. Her eyes were playing tricks on her. They had to be.

'What was that?' Mary Theresa's voice, slurred.

'Nothin'. Just a dog or somethin'.'

'No . . . stop . . . quit it . . . I don't know what I was thinking.'

'Oh, come on, M.T. Please. You give it away to every other guy — '

'I . . . I can't, this . . . oh, God, what if Mom and Dad came home?'

'They won't. They're at the Kavenaughs. When they do show up they'll both be shit-faced.'

'What about Maggie?'

'Wha' about her? She don't know nothin'. She's out ridin' that damned horse, isn't she? If you ask me, she's havin' a love affair with it. Won't be home for hours.'

'She's smarter than you think. Stop it. Mitch, for God's sake — ' There was splashing as someone climbed out of the pool. Maggie struggled to her feet. She had to run away, to hide, to —

She heard the sound of footsteps, tried to dash behind an olive tree, only to see Mitch looming, his silhouette cast in shadowy relief with the back lights of the ornamental lamps. 'Jesus Christ,' he said, ramming a hand through his hair. 'What're you doin' slinkin' around here and spyin' on people?'

'What is it?' Mary Theresa rounded the edge of the hedge and her eyes collided with

Maggie's. 'Oh, shit.' She was tying the straps of her bikini bra.

'Nothin' happened,' Mitch said, taking a threatening step forward, his foot slipping on the pool of vomit. 'Oh, hell. What's this? Puke? You were *pukin'* here?' Twisted in pure, outraged fury, his face suddenly suffused with bright, burning color. 'How long you been here?'

'I . . . I just got here. Just this minute and I got sick and you . . . you came,' Maggie stammered, wishing she was anywhere other than under his hard stare. She couldn't believe what she'd seen, wouldn't! They both had swimming suits on and though Mary Theresa was disheveled, her hair dripping, mascara running down her face, she and Mitch weren't . . . they wouldn't . . .

'Nothin' happened,' Mitch said again.

'I . . . I know.'

'I mean it, Maggie. No matter what you heard or saw, *nothin'* was goin' on.'

Oh, God, how she wanted to believe him, but the look of sheer terror in Mary Theresa's eyes convinced her otherwise. Her stomach quivered, she turned away and nearly retched all over again. Her head was thundering, her heart pounding, denial pouring through her bloodstream. This couldn't be happening! It couldn't. Not Mary Theresa and Mitch. Oh, God, no!

'Maggie — ' Mitch warned, the hard edge to his voice testament to his feelings.

Emotions roiling, Maggie didn't wait. She pushed past him and started running, through the bushes, down the gravel path, and into the street. She didn't know where she was going, didn't care. She just had to get away. Far away.

The soles of her boots, the ones she'd worn riding, slapped on the cement of the sidewalk. The hillside homes seemed to pitch and whirl as she flew down the street. Somewhere behind an electronic gate a dog barked. Neighboring house lights snapped on. Tears of disbelief and shame filled her eyes. Denial tore at her soul. Racing ever faster, tears streaming down her cheeks, she tried to outrun a vision that was burned into her brain. Gasping, half-sobbing, she tore down the prestigious hill with its stately million-dollar homes and the silent isolated lives within.

Mary Theresa and Mitch! Blood relatives. They were practically brother and sister! Oh, God, no. Ever downward she ran, telling herself that what she'd seen was a mistake, that somehow she'd witnessed something entirely different. It was just her wild careless imagination that was jolting her out of control, that was it.

Above the illumination from the streetlamps, the stars seemed to jumble and collide. Inside, her heart pounded hard. Ready to explode. Her guts cramped.

Reeling, she stopped at a corner, panting, crying, placing her head between her knees, and wondering what in God's name she would do. So her sister and brother were kissing, making out in the hot tub. It wasn't a big deal, was it? So they'd been touching . . . that was part of growing up and exploring and . . . oh, who was she kidding? It was wrong. Way beyond wrong. It was sick. Even if they weren't actually brother and sister. Still, they were related. What Mary Theresa and Mitch were doing violated some deep and primitive moral code.

Nothing happened. Mitch's words rang in her ears, echoed through her mind.

Somewhere in the distance a police siren wailed through the night. A garage door opened and a neighbor dragged his trash can to the curb. *Think, Maggie, think. You've got to go home. Face them. Face Mom and Dad*. Her knees threatened to give way and she clung to the lamppost, taking in deep breaths of air laden with the scents of honeysuckle and roses.

She forced herself to her feet, began running again.

Not far away tires screamed on pavement.

Just pretend it didn't happen, she told herself, *like you didn't see anything, just like you don't see Mother pour vodka into her orange juice in the morning, or that you haven't found bottles stashed in the laundry closet or behind the gardening tools. The hot-tub scene didn't happen. You imagined it. Saw something else*.

Headlights flashed on the asphalt as the sound of a car's engine, Mitch's Mustang, neared. Maggie started running again, faster and faster along the sidewalk that skimmed the edges of brick fences and wrought-iron gates and the secrets they guarded.

The thrum of a bass guitar reached her ears, the rhythmic cadence of drums. Mitch, driving his Mustang slowly, rolled down his window. 'Get into the car, Maggie,' he ordered over the loud music.

'No!' She tried to run again.

'Listen — '

'Go away.' She reached the curb, stumbled, then dashed across a side street as another car caught her in its headlights.

'Damn.' Mitch gunned his engine, and at the far curb, Maggie turned sharply, up the side street. Her lungs burned, her thighs ached so bad they quivered, but she gritted her teeth and kept running. Adrenaline spurred her on. She heard the sound of Mitch's tires screeching as he threw the gearshift into reverse and burned rubber. There was an ominous moment of silence when all Maggie could hear was her own ragged breathing and the thudding of her heart — then the squeal of rubber on asphalt, the sound of an engine being gunned angrily, and the smell of burned rubber hanging in the air.

In a second his car was beside her. Mitch leaned over and rolled down the passenger side window. 'Get in.'

She didn't answer, just kept running, uphill past the houses as her calves screamed in pain.

'Jesus Christ, Maggie, get in the car!'

She was gasping by this time, her lungs on fire.

'Fine.' He slammed on the brakes, threw open the car door, and, while the pounding beat of an old Creedence Clearwater Revival song rocked through the night, Mitch started running. In the best shape of his life, he caught up with her within seconds, grabbed hold of her arm, spun her roughly around, and stared down at her tear-stained face. 'Let's go home, Mag. Come on.'

'No!' She hit him then, her small fist pounding on his chest. 'No!'

'Maggie, please. Oh, Christ.' He pulled her into the circle of his arms and rested his chin on her head.

She heard him breathing, felt his strong heart beating, was aware of the steel-like arms surrounding her. Mitch had always made her feel safe and now he was . . . was . . . she started sobbing again at the horrid thought.

'It's not what you think.'

If she could only believe him.

'Mary Theresa and I were just messin' around. We got into Mom's Smirnoff and got a little carried away. That's all.'

'I . . . I saw.'

'You don't know what you saw. I was stupid, yeah. It was kind of a 'You show me yours and I'll show you mine' thing. Dumb, huh?' Tipping her chin up with one finger he looked down at her and attempted a smile. But his face was pale, his eyes dead and she didn't know what to believe. 'Come on, Maggie. No harm, no foul. Let's go home. Mary cleaned up the mess by the hedge and put Mom's bottle back. No one has to know anything.'

'But — '

He dropped his arms and patted her on the head. 'I'm an idiot, okay? A dickhead. I admit it. I shouldn't drink. Ever. If the coach ever found out, I'd be dead meat, and this thing with Mary Theresa . . . well, it was my fault, I admit it, and we have to keep it quiet, okay? You know I love Sheila.'

Sheila Allman was Mitch's girlfriend. They'd been going together since their sophomore year in high school. A cheerleader who had been homecoming princess and prom queen in the same year, she had been one of the most popular girls at White River High. Along with Mary Theresa.

'Come on, Mag. Get into the car.'

She couldn't shake the bad taste in her mouth, the deep, piercing knowledge that she was being conned, but she had no choice. She had to return to the house. She had nowhere else to go, no one in whom to confide. On shaking legs she climbed into Mitch's car, leaned against the passenger window as he cut a U-turn in the middle of the street. She stared sightlessly out the window as he drove with a little more restraint the short distance back to the house.

John Fogerty's gravelly voice blasted from the speakers. 'I heard it through the grapevine, not much longer would ya be mine . . . '

The music continued to pound as Mitch wheeled into the driveway and stood on the brakes. Maggie threw open the door and nearly fell from the low bucket seat to the pavement. Her legs were like rubber, her mind a kaleidoscope of horrid, ugly, sensual images. She didn't wait for Mitch as she ran to the front door, into the house, and down the long tile hallway to her room. Mary Theresa's door was closed, but a glow of blue light beneath the panels indicated that her lights were out, but she was watching television. Not that it mattered.

Maggie burst into her own room, shut the

door, and flung herself onto the bed. She hadn't seen what she thought she had. She had to believe Mitch. Crawling under the covers, she squeezed her eyes shut, but she didn't sleep a wink and heard, hours later, her parents come into the house, the slam of the garage door over the shout of angry words, and the rattle of a bottle as her mother poured herself a nightcap, probably from the same fifth Mitch had tapped earlier.

It was sick. All of it. And Maggie couldn't wait for the day when she'd be able to leave. Just the rest of the summer, then she could go move out and attend junior college. Forget living here. She wished she could just take off. As far away as possible. Away from this gloomy house with its awful, mind-numbing secrets. Away from her mother's slurred speech and her father's holier-than-thou attitude. Away from Mitch's cocksure jock strut and Mary Theresa's ever-present aura.

No more being a shadow.

Maggie rolled over on the bed, stared at the ceiling and, for the first time in her life, heard the voice, clear as a bell, as if Mary Theresa were in the room with her.

Don't tell, Maggie, please. Whatever you do, don't tell!

'What?'

Mom and Dad would kill me if they found out. Maggie, please, keep this our secret.

6

'How did you do that?' Maggie demanded the next morning. She and Mary Theresa were finally alone, in the kitchen, supposedly doing chores. Mary Theresa, makeup in place but her eyes a little red and puffy, was unloading the dishwasher at a snail's pace before she went to get ready for her vocal lesson and Maggie, not interested in her job of wiping the table, hoisted herself onto the counter and eyed her twin. She hadn't slept well, but decided to hit the problem on its head.

'Do what?'

'You know, talk to me last night.'

'I didn't talk to you.' Mary rinsed off a breakfast plate still sticky with syrup and dropped it into the open rack.

'Yes, you did. I heard it clear as a bell. Like you were in the room. You said, 'Don't tell, Maggie! Whatever you do, don't tell!''

'That's stupid. I wasn't even in your room.'

'I know. So I figured you yelled it through the ducts or something.'

Mary Theresa leveled her with a glance that silently called her sister a million kinds of idiot. 'Why would I do that? Who knows who could have heard me? The ducts don't go just from my room to yours, you know.'

Maggie had thought of that, of course. But couldn't come up with any other explanation.

'Well, you did *something*. 'Cause I heard you.'
'No way.'
'Didn't you ask me to keep this our secret? That Mom and Dad would kill you if they found out?'
'I didn't *say* it. I just thought it.'
'Well, I *heard* it. You said, 'Don't tell, Maggie, please, whatever you do, don't tell. Mom and Dad would kill me if they found out, Maggie, please keep this our secret.''
Mary Theresa's mouth fell open. 'How could you . . . ' She dropped a plate. It landed on the tile floor. Crack! 'You heard that?'
'That's what I'm telling you.'
'But — ' She leaned over and started picking up the bigger pieces of the broken plate. 'I didn't. Damn.' She sliced her finger on one of the shards.
'You didn't what?'
'I didn't *say* anything. Not out loud. You . . . you just imagined it.' Blood dripped from her index finger, and she stuck it into her mouth.
'No way.' With a shake of her head Maggie hopped down from the counter and started helping clean up the mess. She pulled a broom from the closet and ignored the half-full bottle of vodka she spied tucked behind a bag of rags.
'But I . . . I didn't say that. Or anything like it.' Mary Theresa's chin hardened in the same kind of determination Maggie had witnessed all her life.
'Well, I *heard* it.'
'You couldn't have.' Still sucking on her finger, Mary Theresa dug in a cupboard with her free

hand, found a small Band-Aid, ripped it open, and covered her tiny scratch as Maggie swept the broken pottery into the trash. Streaks of egg yolk and syrup stained the floor. 'Oh, crap, Mag. Look what you did. You just made it worse.'

'I'll get it, don't worry.' Maggie had already rinsed out a rag and, on her knees, was polishing the floor to a shine.

Mary Theresa slammed the dishwasher door closed, then, folding her arms under her breasts, stared hard at Maggie.

'What?'

Mary didn't reply, but her eyebrows slammed together in concentration and her lips compressed as if she were contemplating the most difficult problem in the universe.

'What's wrong with you?'

'See.' Her expression changed. 'You didn't hear me.'

'You didn't say anything.' Maggie stared at her sister as if she'd just grown a third eye.

'And I didn't last night, either.'

'But I heard you.'

'You're saying that you heard what I thought,' Mary Theresa said, wiping her hands on a terry-cloth towel. 'I didn't *say* anything last night, but I did *think* some of those things.'

'What?' Maggie stared at her sister in disbelief. 'You just *thought* them. Come on.' Sometimes Mary Theresa was a little far out, but this time she'd really gone around the bend.

'I know, I know it sounds crazy, but last night, after I heard you go into your room, I was so miserable, so embarrassed, and so . . . afraid that you were gonna say something to Mom and Dad that I kind of . . . well, prayed . . . or mentally pleaded with you not to say anything.'

This was too much. After a night of not sleeping a wink, of lying in her bed with visions of Mitch and Mary Theresa, Maggie couldn't deal with this kind of weird talk. She held both her hands up, palms out, and backed up a step. 'I don't know what you're trying to do, Mary Theresa, but — '

'I'm telling you, it's the truth.' She grabbed Maggie's arms in a grip that wouldn't quit. 'So I don't know how or why you heard it. But you've got to understand one thing, that . . . that what you saw last night . . . it, it was nothing.' Sharp fingernails bit into Maggie's skin. Mary Theresa's green gaze was intense, angry. 'You've got to believe me.'

Maggie tossed off Mary Theresa's hands and backed toward the sliding door leading to the pool. 'Look, I'm outta here. You don't have to say anything else. You and Mitch's little secret. It's . . . it's safe with me.'

'It's not a secret,' Mary Theresa insisted, and tears filled her eyes. 'Really, Maggie, you've got to believe me. Nothing happened.'

'Right. That's what Mitch said.'

'I know, but it didn't, not last night . . . '

'And . . . and I believe you,' Maggie lied. She didn't want to think about it. Each time she remembered the scene in the misty hot tub with Mitch's hands on the slick skin of Mary Theresa's bare back, Maggie's stomach turned over and threatened to spew all over again. She slid the door to the patio open and stepped outside, where the sun was blazing and insects buzzed in the bushes. She'd walk the two miles to the horse barns if she had to, but somehow she'd get away from here and all the sickness that seemed to be seeping through the thick stucco walls of the house she called home.

Slipping a rubber band from her pocket to her teeth, she scraped her hair back with her fingers until it felt right, then snapped the band around her clump of hair. Everything in her life seemed a little surreal these days.

Hang in there, she told herself as she headed down the street, toward the main part of town. At the base of the hill, she jaywalked across traffic, then ducked down a shady alley to the main highway. *This craziness will subside. It has to*. At the far end of the alley she made her way around a nest of garbage cans that were beginning to foul the air and startled a black cat sunning himself on the top rail of a fence. Tail aloft, he leaped to the ground and slunk to the protective shade beneath an old Chevy Nova parked near a garage with a sagging roofline.

The alley dumped itself into the heart of downtown, and Maggie appeared at the back parking lot of a McDonald's restaurant. She found enough change in the front pocket of her cutoffs for a Coke, then, sipping from a plastic straw as the late-morning sun beat against the back of her neck, she started walking. Her mother would be ticked off when Maggie called her at the tennis club for a ride home, but too bad. Worse yet, Bernice Reilly probably wouldn't disrupt her massage or bridge hand, so she'd find a way to locate her stepson and send Mitch to pick Maggie up. Great.

Squinting because she'd forgotten her sunglasses, she felt the heat of the sidewalk through her tennis shoes and considered, for one fleeting, wild-hare moment, sticking out her thumb to hitchhike. Lots of kids in school did it all the time, but her parents were death on the idea, so she thought better of it and continued walking though she was starting to sweat.

Heat shimmered in waves rising from the street, distorting her vision of the four lanes of cars that inched through the stoplights in this part of town. The terrain was flatter down here where the markets, fast-food restaurants, taverns, and strip malls lined the road before giving way to cheaper houses than those up on the hill. Telephone and electric wires were strung from huge poles where handwritten signs and printed flyers were posted.

'Lost dog — three-year-old cocker spaniel answers to the name of Roscoe . . . '

'The end is near; listen to the Reverend Bill Ballantine at the New Hope Church Sunday, February twenty-eight, nineteen seventy-eight at eight o'clock p.m . . . '

'Six-family yard sale, Friday, Saturday, and Sunday!'

Ignoring the gum and crud that stuck to the sidewalk, Maggie trudged through the commercial area past shops and storefronts, watching the traffic through eyes that were turned in to her soul. She crossed the streets by rote, waiting until the lights changed, then stepping off the curb. Sweat ran between her shoulder blades, and her mind was filled with images of Mitch and Mary Theresa in various stages of undress. Touching. Kissing. Doing all sorts of disgusting and vile things.

'Hey! Watch out!' A horn blasted, and she jumped back, stumbling on the curb, her drink cup slipping and falling to the pavement, as a canvas-topped Jeep ran a red light and turned the corner, missing her by inches. Coke splashed up her bare legs. She nearly twisted her ankle as she fell backward.

'For Christ's sake, watch where you're going!' The paper cup was squashed by a thickly ridged tire laying down rubber as the driver gunned the engine.

'Bastard,' Maggie grumbled under her breath. She felt sticky, hot and ugly as a toad. What was she doing thinking about Mary Theresa and Mitch? She had to turn her mind to other things. Any other things.

Paying more attention to traffic, she walked through the business district that blended into a residential area where the houses were small and the grass dry and patchy. Chain-link fences kept dogs and kids in the yards while deterring strangers from entering the domain of small stucco cottages with wide porches and planters overflowing with bright blossoms.

Within a few blocks the city gave way to a more rural area where apple and pear orchards competed with chicken ranches. Maggie angled off the main highway to a road that led upward again, through the hills where neatly tended rows of grapes grew in the surrounding vineyards. The traffic lightened, the air seemed cleaner, and the bottom of Maggie's feet burned in her worn shoes.

Trucks, vans, and cars whizzed past as she stuck to the gravel-strewn shoulder of the road and ignored the constant pestering of flies and gnats that swarmed in these last waning days of summer.

She heard the rumble of an engine, a truck from the sound of it, driving on the opposite side of the road, heading in the same direction she was going. She didn't bother to look but couldn't mistake the sound of the tires slowing as it approached, and she braced herself for some kind of catcall.

'Need a lift?' the driver, a man in his early twenties, asked. Positioned behind the wheel of an ancient truck that had obviously seen better days, he flashed her a smile that was a little off center, on the wicked side, and sent a warning to her brain. Whether the grin was sincere or just well-practiced she couldn't determine because of the mirrored sunglasses that served as a shield for his eyes.

'Nah, I can walk.' Her first, natural, do-the-safe-thing response. But she lifted one hand to shade her eyes and squinted to get a better look at him.

'Sure?' He had thick, straight hair, dark brown, streaked with gold, and a day's worth of stubble that couldn't quite disguise the square angle of his jaw. He wasn't all that handsome, well, not really, but there was a rugged edge to him that she recognized, an innate sexual energy he possessed and probably used to his advantage. Without knowing anything more about him, she realized he was trouble, the kind of trouble good girls avoided.

'I'm fine. Really.'

'If you're sure.' He didn't bother to hide his disbelief.

'I am. Really.'

His smile was mockingly amused. 'Your funeral.'

'I doubt it.' Was he flirting with her? This older guy in a faded T-shirt with a few holes around the collar? She felt warm inside, a kind of push-me-pull-you kind of fascination with his devil-may-care attitude.

'Just tryin' to be chivalrous.'

'Yeah, right.' He was about as far from a knight in shining armor as he could get. What kind of con was he running? 'And I'm Joan of Arc.'

'Thought I recognized you.'

Sending him a 'drop-dead' look, she started walking again.

'If that's the way you want it. See ya, kid.' With a glance in his rearview mirror, he stepped on the gas, and the truck shot forward.

Kid? Kid? Her ego deflated. The Coke was suddenly sticky on her legs again, her hair pulled back into an ungainly ponytail, her cutoffs frayed. The guy thought she was a kid? A schoolgirl? Well, she was, she supposed, but seventeen wasn't exactly junior high — and she'd be eighteen in a matter of weeks. And how old was he? Twenty-one? Twenty-two maybe? Well, it didn't matter; she'd never see him again, but still she was bothered, and, for the rest of the trek, she replayed the conversation in her mind over and over again. It wasn't all that great, but it beat the heck out of thinking about her sister and Mitch.

Half an hour later she was walking up the long drive to the stables when she spied his truck, an old beater with primer patches covering the dents of a vehicle that had once been army green.

Great, this day was just getting better and better. She waved to Flora, the owner of the ranch, who stood at the open kitchen window of the old farmhouse. Nearing sixty, Flora had let her hair turn its natural shade of gray, and when the straight wiry tresses weren't hanging down past her shoulders, she wound the strands into a knot that she pinned to the very top of her head, where it was now. From years in the sun her face had a leathery cast, wrinkles, and age spots daring to mar the once-smooth surface, but Flora didn't seem to mind. She never wore any makeup more than a genuine smile. Divorced for 'a million years,' she never spoke of her ex-husband, had no kids, and seemed perfectly content with her life.

'Ink Spot's in the north paddock,' she called through the window as the curtains shifted with a tiny breeze that skipped across the yard. Her dog, a golden mutt named Charlatan or Charlie for short, was positioned under a tree where a squirrel scolded from the upper branches.

'Thanks.'

Bored with the squirrel, Charlie fell into step behind her. His head lolled to one side, probably from the burs that he forever gathered in his ears as he hunted in the surrounding fields.

Chewing the corner of her lip and wondering why the guy in the truck was here, she passed by the rabbit warren where droopy-eared lops peered from their hutches. Their eyes were dark and bright, their noses twitching as she and the dog hurried by on their way to the stable.

She spied Ink Spot, bold black-and-white-patched coat gleaming in the sunlight as she grazed in a field with a couple of other horses — a bay and a palomino — where the grass was little more than dry stubble. The mare lifted her white face to look at her. Snorting, flicking her ears, Ink Spot returned to gingerly pick at the dry blades of grass.

'I can see she's real excited about this,' Maggie grumbled to the dog, who, nose to the ground, wandered off to explore the cracks in the foundation of the garage. Maggie pushed open the door of the stable. Inside the old building the familiar scents of leather and oil, dung and dry straw, horses and cobwebs assailed her as she made her way to a closet of a tack room that was filled with saddles on sawhorses and bridles hanging from pegs, long reins snaking down to the concrete floor.

She set the curb bit and bridle aside, then found a lead rope and halter. Walking out a side entrance, she nearly collided with a man who was about to walk inside.

Of course it was the guy from the truck, she thought with uncharacteristic fatalism. His sunglasses were missing, revealing intense gray-blue eyes guarded by dark, straight eyebrows and spiked lashes. He mumbled a quick ' 'Scuse me' around a dry stalk of grass that was stuck in the corner of his mouth before a flicker of recognition lighted his eyes, and that same arrogant grin she found so irritatingly and blatantly sexual split his face. Rubbing his jaw and smelling of smoke, he looked her up and down. 'Well, well, well, if it isn't the Maid of Orleans.'

'What?'

'Joan? The independent lady too proud to take a lift?' He leaned a muscular shoulder against the doorjamb and effectively blocked her exit.

Embarrassed, she told herself to just shut up, but she couldn't help but rise to the bait. 'And if it isn't the truck driver who thinks it's safe for women to hitch rides with strangers.' Flinging the halter and rope over her shoulder, she squeezed past him, her body brushing his as she edged through the doorway.

'Not just a woman — but a saint,' he mocked, turning as she passed. Laughter followed her outside. Her backbone stiffened, and she whirled to face him again.

'That's right. A saint. Pure as the driven,' she tossed back at him. She didn't know why he irritated her so much, why her skin flushed, and she wanted to slap that damned smile off his lips, but she couldn't help herself. One of his eyebrows lifted in silent amusement. As they stood in the shade cast by the barn, swallows pirouetted and scrambled overhead in a sky covered with gauzy clouds that did nothing to block the intensity of the late-August sun.

'So, Saint Joan, you got a horse here?'

'Mmm.' She nodded; no reason to prolong the conversation.

'Want me to get him for you?'

'Why would you do that?' she asked before questioning what he was doing here in the first place.

'Part of the job.'

Her stomach sank as she started to understand that he might be more of a permanent fixture here than she first thought. 'What job?'

'I work for Flora now.'

'Doing what?'

'Whatever.' Those damned eyes held her spellbound. He shifted the dried piece of straw from one side of his mouth to the other. 'I teach riding and roping, though most people here aren't interested in that. Take care of the stock, that sort of thing.'

'You're a groomer?'

'S'pose ya could call me that.' He winked at her, and she nearly dropped the damned lead rope. 'And a trainer and general do-whatever-needs-to-be-done guy.'

So this wasn't a solitary meeting. He'd be here whenever she showed up. That thought was disturbing. Bothered her. Worse yet, there might be a chance that he would be teaching her how to ride. 'What happened to Enrique?'

'Quit, I think.' He lifted a shoulder, and, beneath the worn T-shirt, a huge muscle moved. For the first time Maggie saw all of him. Wide shoulders, tanned arms where sinew moved easily under his skin, narrow waist, and hips so slim his faded, disreputable jeans, if not for his battered leather belt, might have puddled around his ankles. As it was they hung low. Too low.

'Oh.' She was suddenly embarrassed, painfully aware that she wasn't quite eighteen. Not even old enough to vote. Hadn't he called her a kid? Well, she was. 'Too bad. I liked Enrique.'

His lips twitched. 'You know, if you try real hard, you might like me, too.'

I doubt it, she immediately thought, but didn't say it. If he read the apprehension in her gaze, he let it pass.

'The name's Walker.' He stepped forward a couple of steps, spit out the straw, and thrust a hand, callused and large, at her. 'Thane Walker.'

'Thane?'

'My mother had a lisp.'

'What?'

He chuckled. 'A joke, Joan. It would be smart to leave it at that. Thane's a family name.' His fingers curled over hers in a simple handshake that she felt was way too intimate. 'And when you're not being canonized, I suspect you've got another handle?'

'Maggie Reilly,' she said by rote, as heat seemed to climb up her arm.

'You go to school around here?'

She nodded as he dropped her hand and she backed up a step. 'I did. Graduated last June.'

Why did she feel compelled to answer all his questions, to keep the conversation going?

'Never finished myself,' he admitted.

'Why not?' This guy was a dropout?

His eyes darkened a shade, and Maggie felt a chill. This man, only a few years older than she, had secrets. Deep secrets. 'Other things to do.' As if he decided he'd told her enough, he turned and nodded toward the fields where the horses were penned. 'Which one's yours?'

'The piebald, there, in the north paddock,' she said automatically, and pointed toward Ink Spot. She started toward the field, and Thane fell into step with her.

'You've got good taste.' A new appreciation flickered in his gaze. 'Best horse here.'

'You already know that?'

'Yep.' A big gopher snake slithered out of their way as they walked along the dusty path to the north paddock.

'How?'

'Been around horses all my life. Grew up on a ranch in Wyoming. Now, if you give me that lead and halter, I'll go get your mare for you.'

'I'll get her myself,' Maggie insisted, though why it was so important that she appear grown-up, an adult woman, to this man, she didn't understand. But she did realize that he put her on edge, made her nervous. She swatted at a pesky yellow jacket, then made her way through the gate.

Thane didn't follow her, just leaned on the top rail of the fence with his elbows, while hooking one boot over the lowest board. Maggie could almost feel him squint as he stared at her with unabashed interest, as if she amused him, as if she was some kind of city girl who didn't know up from sideways when it came to horses.

Not that he was too far from the truth.

'Hey, girl. Come on,' she cooed quietly, and reached into her pocket for a bit of apple she'd squirreled away after breakfast that morning.

Ink Spot tossed her head, snorting, her muscles quivering beneath her mottled black-and-white coat. For a second Maggie thought she might bolt, further embarrassing her, but greed won out over independence, and, as the mare's neck stretched forward and her soft lips brushed Maggie's palm, Maggie slipped the lead rope around her neck, then slid the halter into place. 'Good girl,' she whispered, stroking Ink Spot's silky muzzle. Feeling inordinately proud, Maggie turned on her heel and felt an unlikely disappointment. Thane wasn't anywhere near the fence. In fact, he wasn't within sight.

Like a fool, she blushed and tugged on the rope. It was only half an hour later when, astride the piebald, Maggie realized she hadn't thought of Mary Theresa and Mitch since meeting Thane Walker.

* * *

'So, you need a ride into town?'

Thane's voice jolted her, and she nearly dropped the currycomb as she brushed Ink Spot's gleaming coat. 'I'm okay,' she said automatically as she glanced over her shoulder and found Thane returning a pitchfork to the spot where it usually hung just inside the doorway of the stable.

'Well, if you need one, I'm runnin' to the feed store. I could give you a lift.'

'Thanks,' she said. 'But I can call . . . ' Who? Her mother, who was probably already three sheets to the wind? Her father at work? Mary Theresa, who was at her dance lessons? Or Mitch? Inwardly she shuddered. No, she'd walk home if she had to. It wasn't that far, and she didn't want to look like an adolescent who had to phone for rides. 'I'll be fine.'

'Okay.' He wiped his hands on his jeans. 'Just let me know.'

'I will,' she said, surprisingly tongue-tied. There was something about him, an underlying current of electricity, that she sensed was dangerous — a little wild — and though she found that part of him darkly fascinating, she refused to think about it or explore it any further.

Later, she was walking home along the shoulder of the county road when she heard the truck behind her. She'd already tuned in to the distinctive rumble of its engine. 'Maggie?'

She glanced in his direction. One arm was resting on the driver's door, the other on the wheel as he allowed the pickup to slow.

'Yeah?'

'Hop in. I'll give you a ride.'

'I don't need one.'

His smile faded. 'I'd feel better about it.' Through his mirrored aviator glasses he looked at her. Hard. 'I don't bite. Leastwise not usually.'

She hesitated, but couldn't resist. Though he seemed about as harmless as a coiled rattlesnake, there was something she found intrinsically fascinating, a hint of raw masculinity that she wanted to know more about though it frightened her just the same. She sensed that he was a dichotomy, this man, one minute a kind, decent-enough guy, the next a wild man, one who probably smoked and drank too much and had women waiting for him all the way from here to Montana.

He leaned over, opened the door, and, before common sense got the better of her, she climbed inside. She slammed the door shut and saw the ghost of a smile flit across his lips as he forced the rig into first and headed into town. Maggie was sweating, her T-shirt clinging to her back, her hairline damp. Without air conditioning the cab sweltered, and she licked her lips nervously. She didn't know where to put her hands and sat stiffly, looking through the bug-spattered windshield, scraping her mind for some kind of topic, *anything* to talk about.

'You goin' on to college somewhere?' he finally asked as they drove past the McDonald's where she had picked up her Coke earlier in the day.

'Yeah — oh, turn here, up this hill,' she said, and he hung a left, shifting down, avoiding oncoming traffic and gunning the old engine as the street angled sharply upward. With a click of gears he shifted again, and she gave him directions, pointing out where to turn as they wound through the intricate web of hedges, rock walls, electronic gates, and narrow, curved lanes.

He eyed the neighborhood, and, for the first time in her seventeen years, she was acutely aware of her father's station in life, of the status of her address, that to someone like Thane Walker, the very social prestige her mother and father had scrambled so hard to achieve was of no importance. In fact, he might consider it a detriment.

'There — ' she said, pointing to the driveway. Mitch's Mustang was parked near the garage, flanked by long planters filled with petunias. The gate was open. Thane steered his truck into the drive. 'Thanks,' Maggie said as he slowed to a stop. 'I, um, appreciate it.'

'Anytime.' He turned to face her, and one side of his mouth lifted into a smile that, to her horror and surprise, touched a part of her she hadn't known existed — a part that frightened her.

Her heartbeat quickened a bit, and, when his gaze dropped to the wide neckline of her T-shirt, she felt her pulse throb at the base of her throat. 'Uh, yeah . . . ' Oh, God, she sounded like such a ninny as she fumbled for the door latch. Such a *high-school* kid.

'Here. Let me. It's stubborn.' He leaned across her and reached forward. She was suddenly gazing down at shoulders that were strong, muscular beneath his shirt; tanned arms that had ropes of veins running beneath his skin, a T-shirt that was stained and faded, wet with sweat. His head, facedown, was nearly in her lap, and she felt his warm breath against the bare skin of her thighs where her cutoffs didn't quite cover. 'Damned door.'

Her stomach did a slow lazy roll, and her skin prickled. Inadvertently, she sucked in her gut, held her breath, and ignored the warm tingling sensation that started somewhere deep inside her as he gave the door handle a hard shove and, with a metal groan of protest, the door swung open.

'There ya go.' He straightened, and the smell of smoke and male sweat assailed her nostrils as she nearly tumbled out of the truck to put some distance between her body and his. She felt flushed, her skin hot, her legs rubbery. 'See ya around.'

'Y-yeah.' She swallowed hard, and, though she told herself to go into the house, she stood as if rooted to the driveway. Biting her lower lip, she watched his battered truck coast down the street.

'What was that?' Mary Theresa appeared from the far side of the garage. Wearing a short coverup and thongs, she took off her sunglasses and sucked on the part that was supposed to wrap over her ear.

'You mean, 'Who',' Maggie clarified with a lift of her shoulder. For a reason she didn't understand she felt a need to protect Thane from the questions and prejudice shading Mary Theresa's eyes. 'Just a guy who works at the stables.'

'Ahh.' Mary Theresa nodded, as if suddenly wiser. 'So now you're slumming.'

'I just took a ride with him.'

Little lines appeared between her twin's

perfectly plucked eyebrows, and she stared at the open gate as if she could somehow divine exactly why Maggie would deign to ride in the horrid old truck. 'You're lucky it made it.'

'Maybe.'

'No 'maybes' about it. That pickup is on its last legs or tires or whatever.' Turning suddenly, she slid her shades back onto her nose. 'So . . . did you hear any more messages from me today?'

'No.'

'Well, I was sending them like crazy,' Mary Theresa said sarcastically.

'Oh, yeah? Why?'

'Just testing.'

Maggie rolled her eyes to the heavens. 'Look, I don't know why I heard you last night, okay? But I did. Don't do this . . . testing thing or whatever it is anymore.' Hot and tired, she headed for the house. 'I can't explain it.'

'It's a crock, if you ask me. I was just proving it to you. You know, you had me going for a while, but it's all . . . all too weird.'

'Fine. I know. I can't explain it, okay?' Maggie lifted a hand and waved off any more arguments as she ducked under a vine of bougainvillea that draped from the eaves of the house. 'It's whatever you want to think.'

She nearly plowed into Mitch at the door from the garage to the kitchen, and he grabbed hold of her arm. His face was hard; the angles seemed to have lost all of their boyish innocence overnight. 'We're cool, aren't we?' he whispered.

'Wha — ?'

'About last night.'

His fingers dug into the muscles of her upper arm. 'Yeah, we're cool.' The old, smothering feeling that she'd managed to discard while dealing with Thane Walker came down on her full force. Images of the night before played in her mind. She yanked back her arm. 'Leave me alone.'

'Just so we're straight,' he insisted, and then, as if sensing Maggie's mother on the other side of the door, he backed off.

Maggie entered the kitchen and felt the drop in temperature and the breath of cool air, compliments of the air conditioning unit that was blasting away.

'Maggie?' Mom peered around the corner. With short brown hair and freckles she tried desperately to hide, she was a twenty-five-year-older version of her daughters. 'Where were you?'

'At the stables.'

'No note.' Her mother cocked her head to one side and lifted her eyebrows, silently reprimanding.

'I forgot.'

'Remember next time, will you?' She walked into the kitchen from the laundry area, and Maggie was relieved to see that she was steady on her feet. Her words weren't slurred. No glass of 'ice water' melted in her hand.

'I'm sorry.'

'It's all right,' her mother said, but Maggie wasn't sure she believed her, for beneath the soft little smile and the crinkle of her green eyes, there was a hint of worry. The edges of her mouth didn't quite turn up, and her gaze meandered from Maggie's face to the patio. 'You know,' she began, picking up a pitcher and turning on the faucet, 'I think something went on here last night while your dad and I were out.'

'Oh?' Maggie stuck out her lips and lifted her shoulders, as if she didn't have any clue. 'What?'

'Don't know.' Bernice Reilly turned off the tap and began watering the pots of African violets arranged on the counter. 'But I'm pretty sure someone got into the liquor cabinet. I mark the bottles, you know, and I can tell if a bottle has been watered down.'

Damn! Maggie tried to keep her expression completely blank, and when the back door opened, she didn't turn around, just hoped like crazy that her suddenly thundering heartbeat wasn't visible in her throat or anywhere else.

'You know, not only is it just watered down, but sometimes a bottle is missing. Can you explain that?' Her mother didn't look at her, just kept watering the damned plants while Maggie's skin broke out in a horrible sweat.

'Explain what?' Mary Theresa asked as she breezed in. Smelling of suntanning oil and looking the innocent, she glanced at her mother. She plucked a grape from the fruit bowl on the table and winced as she plopped the grape into her mouth. 'Ouch.' Turning, she pulled aside her coverup and craned her neck so that she could see the reflection of her back in the mirror mounted on the wall going into the dining room. 'Damn, burned myself.'

Her shoulders were beyond red; there were actually tiny blisters visible.

'How many times have I told you to be more careful? Let me see.' Their mother eyed Mary Theresa's shoulders and sighed. 'I think I've got some cream that might help. Here.' She reached into the cupboard and pulled out a tube, handing it to Mary Theresa. 'Now about last night.'

'What about it?' Mary Theresa smeared cream onto her lobster-red shoulders.

'Mom thinks someone got into the liquor.'

'I don't think, I *know*.'

'Really?' Mary Theresa seemed to be barely listening as she applied the cream and readjusted her top. 'Well, don't look at us. Maggie and I were together. It was probably Mitch and his friends.' She snagged another grape and tossed it into her mouth innocently.

Maggie nearly choked as Mary Theresa opened the refrigerator door with the nonchalance of an accomplished actress. She pulled out a can of Diet Coke. 'Want one?' she asked Maggie, who, her cheeks burning with embarrassment, couldn't believe her sister was ratting out Mitch — the guy she'd been making out with, her partner in . . . in . . .

'Sure.'

M.T. tossed her a can, grabbed one for herself, and popped the top, wincing a little as if her sunburn was flaring again. 'I think you should talk to him.'

‘I will,’ Bernice said as she replaced the pitcher and wiped a drip of water from her fingers onto the shorts of her yellow jumpsuit. Her lips were compressed into a that-kid’s-gonna-get-a-piece-of-my-mind grimace. ‘Right now.’

7

'I can't believe you did that!' Maggie whispered once she and Mary Theresa were in her bedroom and the door was firmly shut.

'Did what?'

'Threw Mitch to the wolves like that! Mom is gonna kill him.'

'Better him than me.' Mary Theresa dropped onto a corner of Maggie's unmade bed and sipped her soda as if she didn't have a care in the world other than a case of sunburn, as if she wasn't on the brink of excruciating trouble, as if she hadn't done anything remotely wrong.

'But — '

'Don't worry about Mitch. He can handle himself.'

'I don't believe you!' Maggie set down her drink, picked up some darts, and hurled them one after the other at the back of her door, where a dartboard was covered with a picture of her latest boyfriend, Sean, a wingback on the football team. When he hadn't been able to convince Maggie to go 'all the way' even when he'd told her that he loved her, he'd dropped her for a freshman girl with braces, long blond hair, and legs that seemed to go on forever. He'd bragged about scoring with the girl two weeks later, then promptly discarded her for a sophomore on the girls' soccer team. Maggie yanked the darts from the board, stood a few feet away, drew back, and took better aim. She let the first dart fly. It pierced Sean square in the middle of his chest, where his heart was supposedly hidden. She'd have to aim a little lower next time.

'It was all Mitch's idea anyway,' Mary said, pouting a little. 'Let him take the heat.'

'What was all his idea?' Maggie was sick of the vague innuendoes and secretive glances. 'So what's going on, M.T.?' She threw another dart. Bingo. Right in the crotch.

'Oh, just drinking and getting into the hot tub.'

'So he's gonna take the fall.'

'What else can I say?'

Maggie threw the darts. One, two, three. All landed close enough to Sean's head, heart, and other areas to convince her that she hadn't lost her touch. 'Well, just keep me posted, would ya? I'd like to know what the latest secret is. You know, so that I don't blow it.'

'I will,' Mary Theresa said. 'You don't have to get nasty about it.'

'I'm not,' Maggie argued as Mary Theresa drained her can of soda and, standing, dropped it into Maggie's already overflowing wastebasket. 'Trust me. I know what I'm doing.'

Maggie didn't believe it for a minute. Lately, Mary Theresa seemed to be on a collision course with any and all things sensible.

⋆ ⋆ ⋆

That night Maggie flipped through the channels of her small black-and-white television, listened to Johnny Carson's monologue on the *Tonight Show*, then clicked off the set and flung herself onto the bed. Her restless thoughts had slipped to Thane Walker again, and she couldn't figure out why he seemed lodged in her brain. He was kinda good-looking, if you liked the rough-and-tumble cowboy type. He had a sense of humor, irreverent though it was, and there was a touch of mystery to him that appealed to her. But she knew he was way too old for her, way too hard-edged, way too worldly. Still, she couldn't quit thinking of him.

'Give it up,' she muttered as she picked up her large black magic ball, the one Mary Theresa had given her on their eleventh birthday. Mad at herself and the world in general, she shook the magic ball for all she was worth.

What're the chances of me and a guy like Thane Walker? she silently asked, then looked at the answer floating to the surface of the ball. *The answer is unclear*.

Oh yeah? Well, does he have a girlfriend?

There is a good possibility.

Are you full of crap?

My sources say no.

Right, and I'm the queen of England. She dropped the ball onto the bed, grabbed a dart from the bedside table, launched it, and smiled as it landed on Sean's left kneecap. 'Shows you for messin' with me,' she whispered as she turned off the light and closed her eyes.

Thane's face, all tanned angles and planes, swam to the surface of her consciousness, in much the same way as the messages seemed to swim upward in her stupid fortune-seeing ball. She wondered where he lived, who his friends were, if he was with a woman at that very minute. Sighing, she told herself to forget him.

Through the open window, over the sounds of insects buzzing and the hum of traffic on distant streets, Mitch's voice, low and harsh, seeped into Maggie's bedroom. She couldn't believe that he was outside the window, and then with a quick peek through the open pane, realized that he was standing in the shadows, on the far side of the pool, unaware that his voice carried, clarion clear, over smooth-as-glass water. And he wasn't alone.

'What's got into you?' he demanded.

Maggie slithered like a snake onto the floor and clasped her knees, wishing she couldn't hear the damning words as her heart drummed in dread.

'What do you mean?' Mary Theresa asked. Maggie's stomach tightened painfully.

'Oh, come on, you practically sicced Mom on me, didn't you?' Mitch was furious. 'She grounded me, you know. Threatened to take away my car. Shit, Mary T, why?'

'Because it made more sense. She'll believe that you and your friends got into her booze and partied. But if I said that it was you and me — '

'You didn't have to say anything.'

'I did. She *knew*, damn it. And Maggie, she knows.'

There was a moment of silence, and Maggie didn't know what was worse, the accusations or the pulsing quietude that oozed through the crack between window and frame. She closed her eyes, didn't want to think about Mitch and Mary Theresa, wished she could close the window and block out any hint of their conversation.

'Well, at least Mom doesn't know about us.'

'We'd better keep it that way.'

'I know. I know. I, hell, Mary T, I don't know what to say.'

'Don't say anything, okay?'

'It . . . I mean it was great but — '

'Shh! It's over! It . . . it was all a mistake . . . '

'I know, I know.' Mitch's voice was filled with self-loathing. 'I shouldn't have drunk so much, shouldn't have kissed you — '

'Shut up!' Mary Theresa's voice was sharp. Commanding.

'I'm just trying to apologize.'

'I get it, okay?' Irritation flavored her words. 'Just leave me alone, Mitch. From now on, don't even touch me.'

'I won't. Believe me. But — '

'Just don't. We *can't!* God, Mitch, this is *so* sick.'

'You started it.'

'No, I didn't . . . I just wanted to teach you a lesson . . . because of the last time . . . after the prom.'

'That was different.'

'I know . . . but . . . oh, shit, just forget it!'

'I don't know if I can.'

'You have to.' Mary Theresa was emphatic. 'We have to.'

Hot tears formed in Maggie's eyes — tears of embarrassment and shame that drizzled down her temples. She wished she could close her ears as easily as she could her eyes. A sick feeling swept over her and her stomach roiled.

'I'll try.' Mitch sounded like a whipped puppy.

'Okay. So we never talk about this again. Never! And if any of your friends ever find out, if you ever so much as breathe a word of what happened to anyone, I swear, Mitch, I'll kill you.'

'Don't worry.' He sounded sincere. 'Just like I told Maggie, nothing happened.'

'Good.'

Maggie let out her breath.

'But Maggie doesn't believe me.' Mitch sounded worried and Maggie cringed inside.

'Who cares?'

'I do. If she thinks we — '

'She doesn't! Jesus, Mitch, get some backbone, will you?' Despite her harsh words, Mary Theresa sounded frightened.

'I just worry about her.'

'She's a wimp. She won't say anything.'

'Don't believe it.'

'I've talked to her. She's so damned naive that she wouldn't believe anything bad about either one of us. I'm her best friend, and you're, well, believe it or not, you're her hero. She thinks you're gonna help her get onto the swim team.'

'I said I'd talk to the coach.'

'Mitch, forget about her, will ya? Leave Maggie to me. I know how to handle her.' Her voice lightened. 'That's the good part of being a twin; understanding another person inside and out.'

Maggie bit her tongue to keep from saying anything.

Their voices became more distant, as if they were walking away from the pool, and Maggie slowly let out her breath in a soft, nearly silent sigh. Oh, God, what was happening to her perfect little universe? How could she look either one of them in the eye? She didn't know what they'd done together, how far their flirting, kissing, and touching had gone, didn't want to think about it. Ever. So she'd block her mind. That was it. The way prisoners of war did when they were finally released, so that they could survive. She'd read about it once in history class and now convinced herself that if a man could withstand the atrocities of war, then somehow lock the painful memories away once the war was over, she could certainly push aside any thoughts of Mitch and Mary Theresa.

Besides, she really didn't know anything about them, did she? Only suspicions that bothered her. She lifted her head, looked out the window, and saw that there was no one by the pool. The water was placid, the stars bright in the heavens, but deep in her heart, Maggie knew that things were far from calm. As surely as if the wind had picked up and raced into her room, she felt her skin prickle with the knowledge that a storm was brewing — a storm that no one, not even God Himself, could stop.

* * *

‘ . . . and thank you, Father, for the blessings of this family. Give us the strength to hold together during good times and bad. Amen.’ Frank Reilly lifted his head as did his entire family. It was the first meal they’d had together since the night when Maggie had found Mitch and Mary Theresa in the hot tub together, and she couldn’t begin to guess what her father suspected or what her mother knew.

Silently they began passing platters of food around the table. Plates of barbecued chicken, potato salad, sliced fruit, and cold asparagus slipped from one hand to the other. No one said a word, and aside from the purr of the air conditioning system and soft notes of instrumental renditions of old Beatles hits floating in the air from hidden speakers there was no noise but the clink of silverware and an occasional quiet cough.

Maggie’s father, a slight man who at five feet ten kept his weight down to a trim 175 pounds, ‘fighting weight’ as he called it, was the patriarch of the clan. Frank Reilly’s word was, and always had been, law. Rigid and determined, ambitious to a fault, he never gave an inch. His thick brown hair had the audacity to silver at the temples, and his mustache, one he’d had since his army days in the mid nineteen-fifties, was more gray than brown these days.

‘Excellent dinner, Bernice,’ he said, as he always did.

‘Thanks.’ She managed a smile that seemed slightly rubbery. They exchanged glances and Maggie’s guts clenched. Something was up.

Frank slowly set down his fork. 'I think we should discuss something as a family.' He placed his elbows on the table and, as if he were praying, tented his hands together. 'The other night when your mother and I were out, it seems that you, all three of you, had some kind of party. Not only is liquor missing from the cabinet, but there was evidence of someone getting sick on the other side of the hedge by the hot tub and wet towels left in the laundry room.' He cleared his throat as everyone set the silverware down.

Mitch looked guilty as hell, wouldn't meet Frank's gaze, Maggie stared down at her plate and tried to swallow the ball of potato salad that seemed wedged in the back of her throat. In desperation she reached for her glass of water. Only Mary Theresa was able to smile. 'A party?'

'That's what I said.'

'Oh, come on, Dad. Mitch had a couple of friends over.' She glanced across the table at Mitch, who was white as a sheet. 'It was no big deal.'

'If alcohol was served and someone was sick enough to throw up, it is a big deal, Mary. A very big deal. Everyone's underage, and that doesn't even touch the fact that you were stealing from us — your mother and me. We don't want to have to put a lock on the liquor cabinet, do we?'

'No.' Bernice picked up her glass and took a sip. 'Never. We want to trust our children.' She looked pointedly at Mitch. 'All of them. You know, Mitch, we consider you as much our son as the twins are our daughters.' Mitch swallowed hard. Didn't speak.

'So who was here?' Frank asked, slowly looking from one face to the next. Maggie wanted to squirm. Sweat broke out on her palms. 'Some of Mitch's friends, you said.' He paused at Mary Theresa before skewering Mitch with his favorite don't-try-to-con-me glare. 'Who?'

'Just some of the guys,' Mitch mumbled.

'They havc names.'

'You know, the guys. Look, Dad, I'm not going to rat them out so you can call their parents.'

'I'm not calling anyone, but this is my house, your mother's and mine, and we have certain rules. Rules you should understand. Rules that you must abide by.'

'I do. We all do.' Color was returning to Mitch's face, and his pitiful, scared expression was changing into a slow, hard burn. Maggie had seen it before, at every athletic competition Mitch had entered, and whenever he was ready for a fight. The cords in the back of his neck tightened, his muscles tensed.

'But you chose to disobey them.'

'It wasn't a big deal.'

'No?' Frank's eyes sharpened.

'I messed up.' Mitch stole a glance at Mary Theresa, and Maggie wilted inside. He looked like he was ready to kill someone. Anyone. 'I'm sorry,' he said through lips that barely moved. 'It won't happen again.'

'I'll say it won't — '

'Frank.' Bernice held up a hand. 'He said he was sorry, okay? Now, let's let it drop. Everyone here knows what's expected of him or her.'

Maggie's stomach was in knots. She couldn't wait to escape from the table, the house, go anywhere. She thought of the ranch, of Thane Walker, and riding Ink Spot far into the hills . . .

'Is that the way it was?' Frank Reilly demanded, and Maggie snapped back to the present, realized that all eyes were turned on her.

'I . . . I wasn't here most of the time,' she hedged.

'But you came home.'

'Yeah.'

'Yes,' her mother corrected.

'Yes. I came home and Mitch had a couple of guys over, I didn't really pay much attention, just went to my room.' Oh, they had to know she was lying, she was so poor at it. Her stomach rumbled, and her intestines felt like they were suddenly filled with water. 'Can . . . I . . . be excused?'

'May I,' Bernice said automatically.

'Please. I don't feel so hot.' She didn't wait for an answer, just scraped her chair back and dashed down the hallway.

'Now, what's gotten into her?' Bernice asked loud enough so that the question rang in Maggie's ears.

Everything, Mom, everything! This whole family. It's sick. It used to be normal and fun and secure, and now it's just sick, sick, sick! Maggie ran to her bedroom, slammed the door shut, and nearly collapsed on the tile counter of the bathroom she shared with Mary Theresa. She couldn't stand the undercurrents running through the air, didn't want to think that her family, the one she'd depended on for as long as she could remember, was falling apart. Slowly she lifted her head to stare at her reflection in the mirror mounted over one of the twin sinks. The eyes that stared back at her were dark, haunted, and confused. Her skin was pale — no tinge of color in her cheeks. God, she was a horrible liar. Horrible.

She stripped off her clothes frantically, as if in so doing she could tear away all the lies and deceit, then she relieved herself and stepped into the shower. Cool, clear water ran over her, through her hair, down her neck and body, washing away the sweat and the worries, the fear that everything she'd trusted as true in her life had been a lie. She leaned against the tile and refused to cry, tried to tell herself that things would get better.

But she knew in her heart that it wasn't over. Not yet. As much as she hated to think it, she was certain the worst was yet to come.

* * *

For the next few days Maggie spent as little time as possible at the house, with its invisible waves of tension. She worked bussing tables at Roberto's, a local Italian restaurant, four nights a week, part of her father's plan to make his kids learn the 'value of a dollar.' Mitch earned his keep as a lifeguard at the city's one swimming pool, and, as the summer progressed, had gotten more tan by the day. Mary Theresa spent most of her time at the local theater, an old brick elementary school that had been converted into a community center and housed Rio Verde's only performing-arts center.

Mitch had his own car, the girls shared with their mother, and whenever she could get away, Maggie found a ride out to the stable to ride Ink Spot and learn a little more about Enrique's replacement. Like it or not, Thane Walker intrigued her.

He seemed a regular jack-of-all-trades and did everything from giving lessons to novice riders to helping shoe the horses when the farrier visited. He groomed the stock, shored up the sagging overhangs of the stable, straightened the tack room, and mended the fences. She'd heard from Flora that he had grown up in Wyoming on a cattle ranch, spent a few years riding bucking broncos and Brahman bulls in rodeo competitions, and had even done some stunt work for a movie production company.

'Yep. Thane's been a godsend,' Flora had confided to Maggie as she'd sprinkled feed pellets into the rabbit hutches, then added a mixture of carrots, lettuce, and greens that looked suspiciously like the beginnings of the salads Roberto's sold for over three dollars a plate. 'I don't even miss Enrique, and he was with me for six years.' Flora knocked the dust from the bottom of the pellet can and squinted into the lowering sun to the barn where Thane, without his shirt, was fixing the spigot on the water trough. His tanned muscles gleamed, flexing in the lowering sun as he strained with the wrench. His upper teeth bit into his lower lip as he yanked on the tool.

Maggie's gaze was fastened to his bronzed chest, bare save for a few brown hairs that sprang between his flat nipples. Sweat ran down from his neck and hairline, and his faded, dusty jeans, with only a battered leather belt keeping them on his hips, slid low enough to display a slice of white skin just above his buttocks when he leaned too far forward.

'Yeah,' Flora said, her voice a little huskier than it had been as he straightened and her eyes followed the curve of his spine. 'I'm lucky that Thane showed up when he did.' She thought for a moment, her lips pursing a bit. 'You know, he's the first man I ever hired without bothering with references. Probably because I was desperate, and he knocked on my door.' She scratched her head at her own folly. 'Don't know anything about him, but what he told me.' With a lift of her shoulder, she added, 'Good thing he wasn't wanted by the law or something.'

Flora went back to feeding the animals as Maggie headed toward the stable. Feeling the weight of Thane's gaze upon her as she passed, she managed to lift her hand in a small wave while hoping against hope that the heat she felt climb up the back of her neck was hidden by her ponytail as it swung behind her. No reason for him to know that her thoughts were starting to be crowded with him, that each night after swimming her laps before bed, his face was her last vision before dropping off to sleep.

It was crazy, really. Aside from that first day,

she'd only had a few conversations with him — short and one-sided, usually about Ink Spot. He teased her mercilessly, wouldn't give up calling her 'Joan' whenever she got a little high-handed, and was a general pain in the backside. Nonetheless, she thought about him constantly. Way more than she should have. At night when she lay in her bed, looking through the open window to the starry sky, she often wondered where he was and with whom.

She remembered how fluidly his muscles slid over each other, the way his hands held a shovel so firmly, his single-sighted intensity as he went about any job. His jaw was always set, his eyes narrowed against the harsh light of the sun, his determination evident in the lines of his face. She'd spent a few nights even fantasizing about touching him, about the feel of his work-roughened hands against her skin, about the pressure of his lips as he kissed her.

Now as she reached the north paddock, she located Ink Spot, standing head to tail with the palomino and switching flies in the shade of a solitary oak tree. Nostrils quivering, Ink Spot lifted her head, spied Maggie, and snorted. With a toss of her head, she took off, and Maggie gave slow, quiet chase. After a few minutes of the game, Ink Spot trotted up to her and pressed her forehead into Maggie's chest.

'I love you, too,' Maggie said, rubbing the hard spot between the mare's ears and slipping on the halter. 'Let's go for a ride.' She led the mare to the stable, and while Ink Spot shifted restlessly in a stall, snorting into the empty manger and generally seeming ill at ease, Maggie collected her favorite saddle and bridle. The horse gave out an irritated neigh.

'I'm coming, I'm coming,' she said, carrying the tack with her. The light wasn't all that great, just shafts of sunlight piercing through open windows and doorways to an interior where dust and straw covered the floor and the scents of old urine and fresh manure mixed with the warm odor of horses. Cobwebs and the empty, brittle carcasses of dead insects littered the windowsills, and barrels of oats and mixed grain were stacked in a corner.

Ink Spot, true to her nature, flattened her ears and cocked a hoof she would never kick, but always used as a threat to Maggie as she cinched the saddle. A pale blue eye watched her nervously.

'Boy, you're ornery today,' Maggie said to the white-faced horse. 'We're going for a ride. Whether you like it or not.'

'Bossy thing, aren't you?' Thane's voice startled Maggie, and she jumped. She hadn't heard him enter through the open door, hadn't picked up on the sound of a worn leather boot scraping against the concrete flooring.

She threw him a glance over her shoulder. 'When I have to be.'

'Is that often?' He reached for a shovel that was hung on a nail near the door.

'Depends.' Buckling the cinch, she wrapped the end through a loop she'd made in the extra length of strap.

'On?'

Was he baiting her? This time when she looked over her shoulder she met his steady gaze with her own. Blue-gray eyes, the color of the sky at dawn, observed her without flinching. She swallowed hard and felt years younger than seventeen. 'On . . . the situation.'

'I thought maybe it was just your nature, Mag Pie.'

She bit back an instant sharp retort. 'Did you?'

'Mmm.' His gaze moved slowly down her body, hesitating a second in silent appraisal. Past neck, shoulders, breasts, waist, hips, and legs to her feet where her tired-looking boots were half-buried in the straw spread upon the floor of the stall. 'Sometimes you seem angry.'

'Angry?' she repeated, feeling a fool. 'How would you know?'

'The way you ride.' He leaned on his shovel now, lifting his gaze quickly to meet hers.

'And how is that?'

'Hell-bent-for-leather. Like you're runnin' from something.'

'You can tell all that just by the way I sit in the saddle?'

'Nope.'

Uncomfortable with the conversation, she opened the stall's gate and led Ink Spot past Thane and through the door. She thought the discussion was over, but she was wrong. He sauntered through the doorway and leaned a shoulder on the weathered siding.

'It's that you're always in a hurry. Faster, faster, faster.'

'Maybe I just like to ride that way.' She stuck a

foot in the stirrup and hoisted herself onto Ink Spot's back. It was still hot outside, the afternoon heat intense.

'Most people who do smile once in a while.'

'I smile.'

He shook his head, the blond streaks visible in the afternoon light. 'You should though.' This time when he looked up at her, squinting as the sun was to her back, his face seemed a bit more boyish, his expression less harsh. 'Yours is a knockout.' With that he hitched himself upright and carried the shovel to a wheelbarrow. Without giving Maggie so much as a second glance, he pushed the wheelbarrow to a huge pile of gravel. Effortlessly he began shoveling the pea-sized bits of rock. The gravel showered into the metal cart, raining from his shovel like hailstones.

Heart in her throat, Maggie yanked on the reins, and Ink Spot wheeled. 'Hiya!' With a slap of the reins, Maggie urged the mare forward and the once-stubborn horse took off, gathering speed and tearing through the open gates of the paddocks surrounding the stable, nose to the wind, bit in her teeth, heading toward the dry hills surrounding the ranch.

Wind streamed through Maggie's hair and pressed in hot waves against her cheeks. Thane's words chased after her, but she kept her eyes on the horizon and clamped her mouth shut firmly. She'd be damned if she'd smile.

* * *

'So what is it with you and the ranch all the time?' Mary Theresa asked a few days later. She was standing with her back to the bathroom, her head twisted so that she could see the reflection of her backside in the full-length mirror. Elton John was singing in the background, his voice muffled. Clothes were thrown everywhere, including over the speakers of Mary Theresa's stereo.

Maggie, lazing on the small of her back in a director's chair with Mary Theresa's name scripted across the back, propped the heel of one bare foot on the corner of her sister's bed. While waiting for Mary Theresa, she thumbed through the latest edition of *People* magazine. They were sharing their mother's BMW today, which meant that Mary Theresa, because she had 'tons of errands,' would drop Maggie off at the ranch.

Maggie made a point of looking at the clock on Mary Theresa's cluttered night table, then swung her gaze in her sister's direction. From her vantage point she saw Mary Theresa's face reflected in the mirror. 'I like the ranch. I'm supposed to be there in twenty minutes for a riding lesson.'

'I know, I know, we'll make it.'

'I could just take the car.'

'Forget it. Besides, there's more to you running out there all the time than just because you take lessons and seem to like the smell of horses.' Mary Theresa's eyebrows were drawn together, and deep little creases marred the skin between them. 'This hangs all wrong. Doesn't drape,' she said, disgusted with the gauzy pink dress that fell from her shoulders to her knees. 'The designer must be a moron.'

Maggie thought the dress looked fine. 'Maybe you should wear a bra under it,' she offered, as Mary Theresa's breasts and nipples were visible through the sheer fabric.

'I will, stupid, when I go out, but a bra won't affect how the back hangs.'

'Sure it will.' Maggie couldn't help egging her sister on and felt more than a little satisfaction when Mary Theresa, rolling her eyes, let the dress drop, struggled into a bra, and zipped up again. 'See.' She glanced at the clock. She was really going to be late, if M.T. didn't get a move on. 'It's fine now. Let's go.'

'Okay, okay,' Mary Theresa said, sighing. 'So you were right. It looks better.'

'It looks great.' No reason to lie.

Mary sent her a sly glance. 'You know, you could do something a little more feminine sometimes.'

Maggie lifted a shoulder and thumbed through the magazine. 'I suppose.'

'It wouldn't hurt.' She adjusted the neckline again and smiled at her reflection. 'Especially if you're trying to impress some boy.'

'I'm not.'

'Oh, sure, and you're hanging out at the stables just because you're so into horses.'

'I like to ride,' Maggie said without a trace of enthusiasm.

'Uh-huh.' Sighing, Mary Theresa undressed and, wearing only her panties and bra, hung the pink dress on a hanger. 'I think you've got a boyfriend out there.'

'Don't be ridiculous.' Maggie paused to look at a slick, black-and-white picture of Princess Anne astride a thoroughbred sailing over a hedge.

'Just tell me it's not that cowboy who delivered you here the other day.'

'It's no one,' Maggie lied, and hoped her expression didn't give her away. She couldn't tell Mary Theresa about Thane, about how she couldn't stop thinking about him, about the way her heartbeat elevated each time she saw him. No. Instinctively she realized that if Mary Theresa had a hint that she was attracted to him, there would be a price to pay. A dear one. She tossed the magazine aside and found her boots.

'Oh, right.' M.T. slid into a pair of black shorts and a red tank top. As she was stuffing the hem of her shirt into the waistband of the shorts, she said, 'You never asked me any more about Mitch.'

Oh, God. 'Mitch isn't one of my favorite topics.'

'Good. Because there's nothing going on, you know.' Mary avoided Maggie's eyes as she found a rubber band and a couple of clips. With one clip in her mouth, she deftly wound her hair into a French braid that she snapped off with the rubber band and pinned to her head.

'I didn't think there was.' Maggie forced her feet into her boots.

Mary flashed her thousand-watt smile as she sprayed her hair and shoulders with perfume. 'Okay, end of subject.'

Amen, Maggie thought, and wished she believed it. 'Are you ready?'

'Yeah.'

'Good.'

Mary twisted off the radio and they headed outside.

The ride to the stables was thankfully short and silent. Mary Theresa, ten miles above the speed limit, had the radio blaring and drove with one hand; the other, casually holding her cigarette, hung out the driver's side window. She was careful to turn her head and exhale out the window as well.

'Mom knows you smoke,' Maggie observed as they turned off on the lane to the ranch. The BMW bucked and bounced down the gravel lane, its underbelly scraped by weeds growing in the center strip between the twin ruts made by hundreds of tires over the years.

'So?'

'I don't know why you try so hard to hide it.'

Mary Theresa slowed and tossed her sister a look that silently called her an idiot. 'There are lots of things Mom and Dad don't know about me. That's the way I like it.'

'Fine. I was just saying — '

'Okay, I've heard the lecture before.' Angrily, Mary Theresa stood on the brakes, and the car slid to a stop near Flora's garage. 'I don't need to hear it again.'

'I didn't mean that — '

'Forget it.'

'No — '

'Just get out, okay?' Mary Theresa was really

ticked off. 'You know, Maggie, I'm sick and tired of your holier-than-thou attitude.'

'Get real.'

'You know, I'll bet you're out here doing it with some lowlife cowboy!'

'What!' Maggie's jaw dropped open. She gaped at her twin in disbelief. 'I'm not — '

'Well, if you're not, then quit hanging out here. Find a boyfriend and grow up, will ya?'

Maggie's blood started to boil. She held her tongue. No reason to get into it. She reached for the door.

'You could do better,' Mary Theresa said, 'than some piss-poor hired hand who — '

'Who isn't related to me?' Maggie cut in, her temper boiling. 'Sorry. But I think our cousin or brother or whatever-you-want-to-call-him is taken.' She said it without thinking, and Mary Theresa's face drained of color. She gasped and could barely speak.

'I'm not . . . I mean I — '

Maggie climbed out of the car. She was already regretting her sharp tongue even though Mary Theresa had asked for it. 'I'll find a ride home.'

'Oh, God, Maggie, please, it's not — ' A tear started to drip from beneath the edge of Mary Theresa's sunglasses. But Maggie wouldn't listen. She slammed the door shut and stormed down the short hill to the paddock near the stables. Why had she let Mary Theresa draw her into an argument? Why? Why hadn't she kept her damned mouth shut?

Thane sauntered out of the stables. A half

smile was tacked onto his face, softening the contours of his square jaw. 'Bad day?'

'Don't ask.'

He whistled under his breath. 'Okay, I won't. From where I stand, you've got a pretty good life, princess.'

'You don't know anything,' she retorted, then saw a light of amusement fire in his cool gray eyes. That damned self-satisfied smile didn't move an inch. 'And I'm *not* a princess.'

'Oh, that's right. I forgot. You're a saint.'

'Enough!'

He chuckled. 'Whatever you say.' He shoved his hands into the front pockets of grimy, nearly threadbare jeans. 'You're the boss.'

Her head snapped up, and she started to argue. 'I'm nothing of the sort — ' But she stopped short when she noticed the twitch of his lip, the crinkling of the corners of his eyes. What was it today? Something in the air that convinced people to pick a fight with her? 'You ready?'

'Always.' His voice had lowered a bit, and she felt a prickle of anticipation run across her skin, like the breath of the wind touching her intimately, but there wasn't the slightest breeze moving the leaves of the trees.

Thane's gaze shifted just as she heard the crunch of sandals on gravel. His eyebrows lifted a fraction as he stared over Maggie's shoulder and his interest shifted from her. She felt it. As she had a hundred times before. She didn't have to turn around to sense that Mary Theresa was approaching. 'Thought you might need this,' she said, as Maggie looked over her shoulder.

Swinging saucily down the hill, she held out Maggie's oversized suede bag, the one with a long fringe and a shoulder strap.

'Thanks.' Maggie swiped it from her sister's outstretched hand.

Mary Theresa smiled as she looked past Maggie to Thane. 'Hi, I'm Maggie's sister, Mary Theresa.'

'Thane Walker.'

'The horse trainer?' she asked as if she'd listened raptly to everything about him.

'Sometimes.'

She laughed gaily. 'And other times?'

'I do a little of everything.' He lifted a broad shoulder and Maggie wished for once that he didn't look so damned sexy, that his tanned arms weren't visible, that his eyes weren't such an intense shade of gray blue, that he didn't appear so raw and masculine and . . . interested in her sister. Maggie felt, as she had all of her life, as if she had suddenly disappeared.

'So you're giving Maggie a lesson today?'

One of Thane's eyebrows lifted. 'That's the plan.'

'Think you could teach me how to ride?'

Maggie nearly fainted. Mary Theresa wanted to ride a horse, the same animal that she had called 'stinky, obnoxious, and just plain boring'?

'You wanna learn?'

'I might.' A dimple creased Mary Theresa's cheek.

'Then I 'might' be able to teach you.'

'Good.'

'Set it up with Flora.' Thane's interested gaze swung back to Maggie. 'Right now, I think you and I should get to it.'

'Right,' she said dully.

'Bye!' Mary Theresa lifted a hand and wiggled her fingers, then turned and swung up the hill. Thane glanced briefly at her, then back to Maggie.

'You didn't tell me you had a twin.'

'Didn't see a reason to.'

'She's pretty.'

Maggie's heart sank, and she wondered what she was doing here.

'Almost as pretty as you.'

Her head snapped up. 'Sure,' she said automatically before she saw that he was being serious — no smile curved his lips, no flicker of amusement danced in his eyes.

'You don't think so.'

'I don't worry about it one way or the other,' she lied, though she felt a warm glow inside that she would, under no circumstances, let him see. She'd gotten compliments before, plenty of them, but this was different; she sensed Thane Walker didn't hand them out casually. He didn't seem the kind of man to say a kind word just to see her reaction or because he wanted something more from her.

'Just thought you should know.'

'Why?' She couldn't help asking.

Appearing skeptical, he hitched his chin toward the parking lot, where Mary Theresa was climbing behind the wheel of the BMW. She tore out of the lot. 'Because I get the feeling that she might run roughshod over you.'

'No way,' Maggie said, the backs of her ears burning.

He didn't say anything else, just got down to the business of teaching her how to command the horse. Riding bareback, she tried to listen to his instructions as he explained about holding the reins in gentle hands that not only told the horse what she expected but also felt her mount's hesitation or determination. She went through the motions of turning Ink Spot in several different gaits, but her mind wandered, and she was more aware of the back of Thane's neck as he looked downward, how the cords supporting his head stood out, or the way his hair fell over his eyes, only to be pushed aside by an impatient hand, or the sensations he caused when he touched her briefly, fleetingly, when he adjusted the position of her fingers as she held the leather straps. Rough, callused, dirty hands guided hers.

'Just hold like this — no, a little more tightly,' he said, his voice low and commanding as his hands covered hers.

The back of Maggie's throat turned to cotton. 'Like this?'

'Yeah, but don't squeeze the hell out of 'em. Remember, this is how you're communicating with Ink Spot. She has to feel that you mean business without scaring her. Intimidation that earns her respect. Here.' He patted the animal's thick neck and in one swift move swung up behind Maggie.

She nearly jumped out of her skin.

'Let me show you.' Strong arms surrounded her, big hands clasped over hers, and the wall of his chest was pressed firmly to her spine. She couldn't move and tried not to notice that his legs were formed intimately to hers, the fronts of his longer jeans-clad thighs hot against the backs of her bare legs and knees. His booted feet dangled longer than hers, but the hard pressure of his fly rode steady against her buttocks.

New sensations stole through her blood, turning it hot, causing sweat to dampen her skin. Images that had nothing to do with guiding horses galloped through her mind, and she thought as she held her breath that she might pass out.

'Here.' Holding her hands over the reins, he clucked to the horse.

Ink Spot resisted at first, but Thane urged her forward by moving his legs. His breath was hot against the back of Maggie's neck. She swallowed hard as the mare broke into a gallop, and Thane's free arm encircled her waist, holding her close, keeping them both astride and riding in unison. She sucked in her stomach, felt a tingling in the deepest part of her, and tried like crazy to keep her mind on anything but the hardness pressed against the base of her spine and the dizzying images that teased her mind.

'Like this,' he said, leaning forward so that his chin bridged her shoulder and his head was next to hers. His hands moved subtly with the reins, and the horse responded, turning in a smooth arc to the left, dark ears flicking as if searching for more clues from the two riders. 'You try.'

She nearly dropped the reins, but forced her hands to take control, to mimic his commands as he held tightly to her, and the buildings of the ranch, the stables, barn, garage swept by in a dizzying blur. Her heart and head pounded, her blood pumped through her veins wildly, and she wondered what it would be like to kiss him, to feel his hands on her body . . . Oh, God, she was hot.

'There ya go, now ease up a bit.'

Automatically she relaxed and let the reins slip through her fingers.

'Whoa — not so much. That gives her too much head, and you'll have no control.' Again he grabbed hold of Maggie's hands. 'Firm but not hard, see? Show her what you want.'

Maggie nodded, felt his head turn and his eyes study her face. For a split second she thought he might kiss her, might tip her chin with one strong finger, forcing her to twist her neck so that he could capture her lips with his. Her heart thundered, her pulse skyrocketed, and she stared straight ahead, seeing nothing, sensing his gaze lower to her shoulders and chest, rising and falling with each one of her ragged breaths. 'I — I see,' she said, nodding slowly, trying to clear her head, but as long as any inch of his skin touched hers, rational thought proved impossible.

'Good. Whoa.' He pulled gently up on the reins, Ink Spot slowed, and he swung to the ground easily. Maggie nearly lost her balance. 'Now, you try. Yourself.'

Oh, yeah, right, she thought, but managed to

encourage the piebald to a trot, somehow handle the reins though she felt as if she were all thumbs, and guide the horse around the paddock while keeping her seat. Fence posts and clumps of dry grass marked her progress; horseflies hovered in the air.

Thane stood, long legs apart, arms folded over his chest, eyes trained on her every move. His shoulders stretched the seams of his faded blue T-shirt, his biceps bulged, and she thought then that he was probably the sexiest man on the planet.

'Better.' He nodded, his eyes narrowing as he watched, his lips compressed, that blond-streaked hank of hair falling into his eyes. 'Definitely better. Work on it.'

'I — I will,' she promised, and wondered why he made her feel like a schoolgirl. Checking his watch, he flashed her a smile guaranteed to break a young girl's heart. 'Class is over.'

'Good.'

'Wanna do it again next week?'

Yes! 'Probably.'

'Let me know.'

'I will,' she promised, knowing that she'd work extra hard at her job, collect as much money as she could in tips and wages, just to spend an hour this close to him. It was crazy, she realized as she turned Ink Spot toward the open gate and the arid fields beyond. He was too old for her. Way too old. And he was a stranger — a kind of mystery man from Wyoming somewhere. A cowboy who'd probably been kicked out of high school before he'd graduated and had never so much as set one foot inside a university. Her parents would faint if they thought she was interested in this guy — a lowlife from the wrong side of the tracks.

But Maggie couldn't help herself. She found Thane Walker downright fascinating, and, for the first time in her seventeen years, she didn't give a damn what her mother, father or even Mary Theresa thought. This time, she was going to make her own decisions about her life, and the devil could damn well take his due.

8

A few days later, Maggie was still troubled, her mind jumbled with thoughts of Thane and her splintered family. Each day the tension seemed worse, and she sought solace as she rode through Flora's acres alone even though she sensed a storm approaching.

The creek bed was dry, littered with rocks, not so much as a trickle of water or muddy patch indicating that water ever ran through this part of Flora's ranch. Astride a fidgety Ink Spot, Maggie surveyed the chasm that cut through the parched acres and tried to imagine it with water bubbling and rushing over the stones, with insects skipping on the surface and tadpoles congregating in the deeper pools, but all she saw was dirt clods, clumps of dry grass, and dead, dust-dry leaves.

Clucking her tongue to the horse, she tried to shake off her bad mood, but found it wedged firmly in her psyche. As oppressive as the clouds that gathered in the sky, the feeling that something cataclysmic was about to happen weighed heavily in her heart.

Ever since she'd seen Mitch and Mary Theresa together, she'd felt this, the premonition that all hell was about to break loose, and the thick, roiling clouds that had blown in off the ocean hundreds of miles away did nothing to dispel her apprehension. She edged Ink Spot toward the stand of monstrous eucalyptus trees near the northeast corner of the ranch. Once in the shade, she dismounted and dusted her hands. Perching on the edge of a boulder, she looked across the canyon. Vineyards stretched over the rolling hills, row upon row of grapevines interspersed with access roads. The leaves were still lush and green, and soon the grapes would be harvested, crushed, and their juice aged in oak casks. Not that she cared. Not that she really gave a damn. Her blouse stuck to her back, and sweat seeped from her pores. Ink Spot lifted her nose to the teeniest breath of wind and snorted, shaking her head and rattling her bridle as a horsefly hovered near her head.

Biting her lip, Maggie slid off the giant rock and lay back on the prickly dry grass. Through the branches, she viewed the sky, thick with dark and troubling clouds. Her ponytail pulled at her head, and she yanked out the rubber band, then finger-combed her hair and stretched. How many nights had it been since she'd slept well? A week? Two?

Rolling over, she rested her head on her arm and closed her eyes. The drone of insects was interspersed with the squawk of a blue jay hidden in the branches overhead. She felt at peace here, more at peace than she did at home or work. Here she could escape, if only for a little while . . .

* * *

Thane finally caught sight of the piebald grazing, white-and-black tail switching at flies, riderless among a copse of scraggly oak and eucalyptus trees. With a sense of satisfaction he urged his mount, Buster, forward and ignored the spark that fired in his blood whenever he was around Maggie.

He'd known that she'd taken Ink Spot out this afternoon. Hell, he'd sensed her presence the minute she'd shown up at the ranch sometime around noon, and he'd been barely able to concentrate since. There was something about her that he found fascinating, more than that really, she was downright tempting. There were a dozen reasons he should avoid her like the plague. She was too young, a kid, not quite eighteen. She was a princess, lived in the pricey part of town, wheeled around with that snotty twin of hers in a goddamned BMW and sometimes a Mercedes. She was his boss, in a manner of speaking, and she had a smart mouth on her, the kind of girl or woman he usually detested.

Besides that, he had his own demons to deal with. He couldn't get close to anyone and reminded himself that she was way out of his league. If she had any inkling as to his past . . . if anyone did . . . The dark part of his soul opened for a second, let in a little shaft of light, then withered away again. No matter how hard he tried, he couldn't outrun his past. Sooner or later it would catch up with him.

That was the bottom line; he couldn't get involved with a woman, especially a girl who'd been raised to expect the better things in life. It was just too damned dangerous.

And yet he'd found it impossible to stay away from her. As if she were Eve in the garden of Eden, he was tempted. Sorely tempted. To the point that just looking at her brought a stiff erection that was damned near painful as it pushed against the button fly of his Levi's.

Lately his nights had been assailed with images of her and he'd fantasized about her, even while alone in his unmade bed, with only his hand as comfort. He'd thought about the flash of defiance in her eyes, the flush of her cheeks, curve of her mouth, and the way she chewed on the corner of her lip whenever she was nervous. Though he'd tried not to, he hadn't been able to ignore that her breasts would fit snugly into a man's palm or that her buttocks were round, firm, and usually tense.

Now, as he approached the shadowed grove, a black-and-white magpie screeched, its yellow beak open wide in the branches above the ridge where Maggie lay.

She was stretched out on her side, her eyes closed, and his heart seized at the thought that perhaps she'd been thrown, struck her head on a rock, and lay either dead or unconscious. Jaw clenched, he dropped the reins, dismounted quickly, and knelt at her side. 'Maggie? Hey.' He touched her shoulder, felt her warm skin beneath his fingers and the prickle of desire that came with it. 'Hey, kid, are you all right?'

As she roused and her eyes blinked open, he was taken with the depth of her gaze, the green of her eyes, so vibrant and alive, the dark fringe of lashes.

She let out a scream loud enough to wake the dead in the next county.

'Maggie — '

Quickly she struggled to a sitting position.

Both horses spooked, neighing nervously.

'Shh!' His fingers tightened over her shoulder, and he felt the warmth of her seep into his blood.

'Wha — oh, God!' Her hand covered the spot where her blouse closed over a top button and where, he presumed, her heart was pumping wildly. Between her splayed fingers he caught a glimpse of skin, of cleavage where the lapels gaped.

His crotch tightened painfully.

'Damn it, Walker, you scared the devil out of me!'

'I didn't mean to, but — ' He dropped his hand and felt like a damned fool. His jaw hardened, and he forced the desire that had already started burning in his blood to cool. He wanted her. Hell, he'd wanted her from the first second he'd seen her walking at the side of the road in those tight little cutoff jeans. 'I thought you might've been thrown.'

'What? No. Thrown, but why — ?' She looked as if she might be offended; her words seemed to tangle in her throat and her cheeks flushed an enticing shade of pink. 'Where's Ink Spot — ?' Anxiously she scanned the ridge where boulders and lateblooming wildflowers erupted from the dusty ground.

'She's fine.' He hitched his chin in the direction of the two horses who, calming, had begun to pick at the sparse blades of bleached grass. He told himself to back off. They were too close; it had been too long since he'd been with a woman.

'I . . . I must've dropped off.' Maggie, obviously embarrassed, stood quickly and brushed the dirt and grass from her shorts. 'What time is it?'

'A little after three. You need to be somewhere?'

'No.' She shook her head and glanced at the threatening sky. 'Not for a while. I'm supposed to be at work at five-thirty.'

'Then we've got some time.' He heard the words and silently cursed himself.

'For what?' she asked.

'Whatever it is you want, Maggie.'

She looked down at him, still squatted on the ground, and he watched her throat work. 'What is it you think I want?'

'Someone to talk to.'

'Oh, yeah?' She crossed her arms over her chest as if she was about to argue with him, so he slowly rose and stood, regaining the height advantage. 'Why is it you're always telling me what I need or want?'

'You asked.'

'I know but you're always . . . giving me advice. I don't remember ever asking for any.'

'Sit down, Maggie.'

She angled her chin up and stared at him. 'Why?'

He gave no answer, because he had none. Instead he linked his fingers with hers, saw denial forming in her eyes, and ignored it as he pulled them both to the ground again. Refusing to listen to the warning bells clanging in his mind, he stared into those wide, innocent, and oh-so-seductive eyes. 'I'd just like to get to know you.'

She drew her legs up and wrapped her arms around them. Looking at him, she rested her chin on her knees and watched him with thinly veiled suspicion. 'So, what're you doin' up here?'

He thought about lying, making up some excuse as he rocked back on his heels. There were lots of odd jobs that he could claim needed his attention — the fence, downed trees, trespassers — but he thought better of it and tried to keep his gaze from wandering along her legs, up, past the bend of her knee where her thighs disappeared beneath the ragged hemline of her shorts and the tiniest bit of panty lace was visible. 'I came looking for you,' he admitted.

'For me?' She was wary, disbelief obvious in her eyes.

'Uh-huh.'

'Why?'

'You left the stable a couple of hours ago, and I thought it was time . . . that maybe something had happened.' *And I want to make love to you. Damn it, girl, run. Run now!*

'Oh.' Disappointment clouded her gaze. Her lips twisted into a little, crestfallen pout. Her teeth sank lower into her lip, and he wondered how it would feel to kiss her, to touch her, to run his hands along the smooth flesh of her arms and legs and . . . 'Well, you found me. I'm fine. And I really think it's time I should be going.' She started to rise, and he should have let her, just let her climb on that damned black-and-white mare and ride down the trail to the ranch house. But he didn't.

Instinctively he reached out, the fingers of one hand surrounding her bare arm. Her muscles flexed beneath his fingers. Her head snapped up. The pupils of her eyes dilated a bit, but she didn't draw away.

'Stay a while.'

'Why?' He saw her throat work as she swallowed. She was nervous, nervous as hell. So was he. He shouldn't be doing this, talking to her, touching her.

'We could get to know each other.'

'Why?' Again, that damned question.

He hesitated just a second. Thought hard. His fingers tightened over her arm. 'Because, Maggie,' he said, his eyes searching the jade green of hers, 'because I want to.' He leaned forward just a bit, so that his face was closer to hers, close enough to sense her breath catch. 'Because *you* want to.'

Her gaze skittered to his mouth, then back to his eyes, and the innocent desire he saw on her face was his undoing.

'I should be shot for this,' he whispered, then, with a hand to the back of her head, he pulled her forward, slanted his lips over hers, and lost himself in her kiss.

Maggie closed her eyes. She told herself not to

panic as each warm, incredible sensation swept over her. Her blood was on fire, her lungs constricted, and when she felt his tongue press against the seam of her lips, she sighed, parting to him, thrilling to the feel of his tongue as it slid past her teeth, slick, wet, searching, flicking against each sensitive recess.

Warm heat, like tallow running down a burning candle, seeped through her extremities. His breathing was shallow. Ragged as the gust of wind that brought the scent of rain. He trembled as they fell back against the ground, and she moaned, unable to deny the pleasure that rippled through her. She lost sight of what was real and what was fantasy.

Somewhere a magpie cried, and a horse nickered softly, but it wasn't here in this time and place. The here and now was filled with the scents of leather and smoke, the taste of salt on skin, the feel of callused, rough hands reaching beneath her tank top, of fingers grazing her nipples.

He kissed her hard, so hard her head spun, so hard she felt a desperate yearning deep in the most delicate core of her. She didn't protest when he lifted her tank top from her shorts or when he bowed his head and pressed hot, wet kisses to the bare skin stretched over her breastbone. Her chest rose and fell rapidly, and he nuzzled, gently at first, but harder and harder, his tongue dipping along the lacy edge of her bra.

Pulsing and hot, desire sped through her bloodstream. In the back of her mind she told herself that she should stop this now, before it was too late, but the words died in her throat, and all that escaped her lips were soft, anxious moans.

She sighed as he lifted one breast from its lacy cup to run a rough thumb across her already-aching, button-hard nipple.

'I want you,' he admitted, and the words sounded ripped from his throat. 'I've wanted you from the first second I laid eyes on you.'

'No — '

'Shh, Maggie, it's true, and I hate it.' He breathed across her bared breast, and she gasped, then, slowly, his eyes locked with hers, he took the nipple into his mouth and kissed it as if he'd never stop. Deep inside she started to throb. With his tongue, teeth, and lips, he tasted and teased, causing the world to spin and desire to thrum around her. The interwoven branches of the trees overhead became indistinct, the clouds farther up dark and sensual.

With deft, practiced fingers he removed her bra, his hands skimming her skin, his mouth following close behind. She smelled the scent of rain, felt the first drizzling raindrops as he buried his head in her naked abdomen, and she felt his breath on her navel.

'Is it all right?' he asked, slipping the button of her waistband through the buttonhole.

'Is — Is what — ?' She couldn't think, gulped back words, couldn't stop.

He gave a tug. The button fly opened with a sharp report of snaps. She felt moist between her legs and knew somewhere in the deepest recesses of her brain that she was about to step over a line that could never be recrossed, that going any further was more than dangerous, it was playing with fire. But the feel of his tongue and lips caressing her skin, breathing flames across the sheer cotton of her panties, creating a swirling warmth deep in the center of her, made the words of denial die in her throat.

A part of her loved this man. Another part was curious about him. Another part was scared beyond reason, and the last, that very intimate part of her, wanted desperately to break down the walls of girlhood and embrace becoming a woman.

His teeth tugged at the elastic of her panties and she swallowed hard as both the tattered cutoffs that had guarded the scrap of cotton lace and the panties themselves were slipped easily off her body. Cool moist air caressed her skin while skillful hands parted her legs and a man she barely knew, a man she had fantasized about, a man whose mystery and irreverence had touched her soul, began to kiss her as intimately as any lover dared.

She moved against him, moaned at his ministrations, and wanted more. Her fingers curled in the soft ground, the wind sighed overhead, and she began to writhe.

God help me, she thought wildly, perspiration mingling with the dewy rain. A rumble swept over the hills, and, as the first spasm hit her, she cried out, her voice low, guttural, unlike her own. And then he came to her. Shedding his clothes as easily as he had shucked his hands-off persona, he kicked off boots and jeans, threw off his T-shirt, and slipped upward, through the bridge of her knees until he was kissing her on the lips again and his hard thighs pressed hers farther apart.

'Maggie,' he said, looking into her eyes as she felt his erection, hard and thick, brush against her. 'I didn't mean . . . Oh, God . . . I . . . ' His gaze caught in hers. The rain started to fall in fat drops, and before another word was spoken, he thrust. Deep. Hard. To a point that pain blinded her and she gasped.

'Oh, hell, I — '

She moved then. By feminine instinct. And he groaned, the apology that was forming on his lips cast to the wind. His arms surrounded her, and he drew her close, his lips claiming hers in anxious, wild abandon as he withdrew and thrust, over and over again, easing the pain, creating a whirlpool of hot, wet need that surpassed the ache.

And she moved with him. Her body slick with rainwater, her blood on fire, her mind splintering as faster and faster he stroked, pushing her — them — into a place she'd never been. She cried out as the first convulsion ripped through her. A loud primal roar answered her. Thane's face contorted as if in pain. He collapsed atop her spent, sweating, and gasping. She held him tight, tears glistening in her eyes, raindrops collecting on her skin.

He lifted his head and kissed her tears away. A tortured shadow passed through his gray-blue eyes. 'For the love of God, Maggie Reilly,' he said as rain ran down his chin and dripped on her bare breast, 'what the hell am I gonna do with you?'

'Funny, I was wondering the same thing.' She offered a tentative smile.

He laughed then and kissed her again. Despite the rain, the wind shimmering in the trees, and her lingering doubts, she wound her arms around his neck, opened her mouth, felt his body rub against hers and, closing her eyes, she gave herself to him all over again.

* * *

'Okay, so I get it,' Mary Theresa confided a couple of weeks later as she wheeled the BMW into the parking lot of Roberto's restaurant. Olive trees shaded the long low building, and a laurel hedge separated the street from the parking lot. Traffic whizzed by on the busy street.

'Get what?' Maggie grabbed her purse and apron, then shouldered open the passenger-side door of the BMW. A gust of hot air shot through the interior of the car, stealing the breath from the air conditioner.

'Why you're so crazy for the cowboy.' As the radio blasted, Mary Theresa, wearing her favorite pair of designer sunglasses, scrounged in her purse, retrieving a pack of cigarettes and her lighter.

Maggie's heart jolted. The last person she wanted to know that she was involved with Thane Walker was her sister. She remembered Thane's comments about Mary Theresa. *She's almost as pretty as you*. The one man in the universe who thought so. She warmed inside at the compliment, remembered making love to him in the rain, or in the barn, or anywhere they happened to be, then shook her head as she stepped out of the car. 'I'm not crazy about anyone.'

Mary Theresa clicked her lighter shut and drew in hard on her Virginia Slim.

'Oh, yeah, like I haven't seen that look before. You're in love with him all right.'

'In love?' Maggie repeated, upset. How could she have been so transparent? 'That's nuts, M.T.'

'Maybe, but there it is,' she said in a cloud of smoke. Angling the rearview mirror down to catch her reflection, she patted at the edge of her lips where her peach-colored gloss had found the nerve to smudge. She opened her mouth in a perfect oval, then wiped away the excess. How could anyone, especially Thane, think Maggie was prettier than her sister? 'Anyway, I know I put him down, but I figured out what you see in him. He's kind of a bad-boy type, right? A rogue, the kind of guy that if Mom and Dad knew you were seeing him, they'd both shit. Right?'

'No, I — '

'Oh, come on.' Mary Theresa looked over the tops of her sunglasses, pinning her sister with her knowing green eyes as Maggie stood with the passenger door swung wide. M.T.'s voice dropped an octave and was barely discernible over the rush of traffic and the pulsing beat of a tune by Bruce Springsteen. 'We both know about temptation, about being turned on by things we shouldn't, about . . . ' She lifted a shoulder. 'Living a little. My shrink would call it rebelling.'

'I'm not — '

'Sure you are.' Mary Theresa's gaze was steady. 'We both are.'

'Wait a minute — '

'You wait a minute, Maggie. I *know* how you feel. I understand you better than anyone else in the world. We're twins, remember. Supposedly you heard me when I cried out in my mind — though I still can't figure that one.'

'I — ' Maggie tied the burgundy-colored apron around her waist with nervous fingers.

'Somehow you heard me or read my mind or whatever you want to call it.' Mary Theresa shook her head in wonder. 'I don't know how or why, but you did. So, trust me, I can feel things about you, too. And you're falling in love with Thane Walker. Whether you want to or not. So — could you close the door? I'm late.'

Maggie nudged the door closed with her knee. Mary Theresa, cigarette clamped firmly between her peach-tinged lips, threw the BMW into reverse, shoved her sunglasses onto the bridge of her nose with one finger, and turned to look over her shoulder as she backed out of the parking space.

'Don't forget to drop the car off . . . ' Maggie said, but Mary Theresa had already flipped on the blinker and gunned the sports car into traffic. Great. For a reason she couldn't explain, Maggie felt as if the trouble she sensed on the horizon had just taken a giant step closer.

* * *

Maggie, dead tired from her shift, walked out of the restaurant at eleven and, after a quick view of the parking lot, wanted to strangle her twin. Mary Theresa had forgotten her again, she thought, when she didn't spy the BMW parked anywhere in the lot. 'Damn you, M.T.,' she muttered, intent on going into the restaurant and calling the house.

She'd gotten as far as the door when she saw her father's red Mercedes speed into the lot.

Dad was behind the wheel.

Maggie's guts clenched.

Something was up.

And it wasn't good.

Frank Reilly stopped the car by the front entrance and Maggie braced herself. Her father's expression was as dark as the night. His jaw rock-hard, his lips beneath his mustache white with repressed anger.

Terrific.

She slid inside, closed the door, and felt her father's anger radiating in unspoken waves as he jammed his pride and joy into Drive.

'What happened? Where's Mom's car?' Maggie asked, her feet aching from the long hours of standing, walking, and carrying tubload after tub-load of dirty dishes into the kitchen.

'In the garage.'

Something was definitely up.

'My God, what is that odor?' he demanded.

'Garlic . . . spices . . . it gets on my shoes.'

'Well, roll down the window, will you?'

She opened the window, and cool night air raced into the posh interior.

'Is there a reason you picked me up?' she asked, cringing as she reached down, slid one pump off with the toe of the other, and massaged her foot.

'I thought you and I should talk. Alone.'

Uh-oh. Her stomach tied itself in painful knots. This was no good. No good at all. 'About?' She tried to sound calm and nonchalant, as if her father picked her up from work every night.

'About what's going on, Maggie, and don't start denying anything before I start talking.'

Maggie's mind was spinning in circles, and none of the images that flashed by were good.

'Your mother and I . . . we're afraid that one of you girls is involved with some boy, that you're seeing him behind our backs. That you might be getting yourself into trouble.'

She froze. Just stared straight ahead at the taillights of the car in front of them. Well, no one had ever accused Frank Reilly of being subtle.

'So, Maggie, what do you have to say?'

'Nothing. There is no boy, Dad,' she lied, then decided it wasn't really a fabrication. Not really. Thane wasn't a boy. She ran her finger nervously along the window ledge.

'What about Mary Theresa?'

Her throat closed, and she had to force the words out as her father slowed for a red light. The car idled, and Maggie wished she could disappear. 'I, uh, I don't know. She was going with Brad a while ago.'

'Your mother said they broke up.'

Oh, great. For the first time in three years it seemed her mother had been paying attention. 'I, I don't know.' Her palms began to sweat and itch.

'She doesn't talk to you?'

'Not all the time.' Maggie lifted a shoulder as if to deny the topic, but she knew her father wasn't buying it.

'It's the damnedest thing.' Disgusted, he slapped on the blinker and cruised through an intersection as the light turned amber.

'What?'

'That's what I'd like to know. Just a feeling I've got. That little fiasco with the booze and the hot tub a few weeks back was just part of it; there's something going on, I can feel it and' — he slid her a determined glance — 'I want to know what it is.'

'There's nothing, Dad.'

'Fine.' He pressed on the garage-door opener clipped to the Mercedes' visor. 'I guess I'll just have to talk to Mitch. Maybe he'll give me a straight answer.'

Maggie bit her tongue and slid into her shoes. She was out of the car before her father had set the emergency brake. Quickly she walked into the house. Through the kitchen and past the family room where her mother was seated, drink in hand and watching the *Tonight Show*. The host was interviewing some superthin model Maggie didn't recognize.

''Night, Mom,' she said.

'Good night, honey.' No slurred speech. 'See ya in the morning.'

'Okay.' Before her father followed her inside, Maggie hightailed it to the bedroom, where she stripped off her apron and matching tie, tossing them both on her unmade bed. She didn't want to deal with her parents and their suspicions or anything else. She was bone tired and was intent on taking a shower, throwing herself into bed, and falling immediately asleep.

She closed the door behind her, stacked the curled dollars and handful of change that constituted her tips for the evening on a corner of the bureau, and opened the door of the bathroom. Mary Theresa was waiting, sitting on the counter, her eyes wide and round, the smell of smoke hanging in the air.

'Did Dad talk to you?' she asked.

'Yeah.' Maggie unzipped her skirt. 'Oh, yeah.' The black mini fell in a pool onto the tile floor.

'What'd you say?'

'Nothing.'

'Good.' Mary Theresa hopped off the counter and plowed the fingers of both hands through her hair. 'This is such a mess. He suspects something is going on.'

'I know,' Maggie whispered, glancing at the door to her room. What if her father followed her? She turned on the spray of the shower, as much to mute their voices as let the water heat. She flipped on the radio that sat on the counter and turned up the volume. Over a DJ's voice spouting a news update about an accident on the freeway, she said, 'He's going to talk to Mitch.'

'Oh, God.' Mary Theresa sat on the edge of the toilet and buried her face in her hands. 'It looks so bad. Even though nothing happened between me and Mitch.'

'Don't say anything.' Shedding bra and underpants, Maggie stepped into the shower, felt the needles of hot water against her skin, and closed her eyes. All her muscles seemed to melt as she lathered slowly. Mary Theresa hadn't taken her advice and was babbling on, but Maggie couldn't make out her words, didn't care. She just wanted a few minutes of peace.

It wasn't going to happen. Not tonight. The second she twisted off the spray, grabbed a towel, and stepped out of the tub/shower, Mary Theresa started in again. 'You could tell Mom and Dad about Thane,' she suggested.

Maggie nearly fell through the floor. Her hair dripping, the towel half-wrapped around her torso, she stared at her twin as if Mary Theresa had lost her mind. 'Are you crazy?'

'It would be easier to explain.'

'No.' Maggie had, in the past, gone along with her sister on most of Mary Theresa's harebrained plans, but she wasn't going to sacrifice herself this way.

'What does it matter?' Mary Theresa was warming to her plan; didn't seem to think that exposing the fact that Maggie was seeing Thane on the sly was anything close to a problem.

'It matters.'

'He's just a cowboy.'

'That's not the point.' Maggie ran a comb through her hair and winced as the teeth caught in a tangle. With a hand towel, she rubbed a clear spot in the steaming mirror and tried to see her reflection as a current pop artist's voice filled the room.

'Come on, Mag — '

'No!' Maggie worked on her hair, dragging the comb through her wet, wavy tresses. 'Ouch.'

'Just listen — '

Knuckles rapped soundly on the door to Maggie's room. 'Girls?' Bernice's voice was loud enough to be heard over the radio. 'When you're dressed come into the family room. Your father and I want to talk to you.'

'Shit!' Mary Theresa whispered, her face draining of all color.

'Girls? Did you hear me?'

'In a minute,' Maggie yelled.

'Well, hurry up. It's late.'

'Oh, God, what will we do?' Mary Theresa asked, her hand to her mouth. 'If they figure out — '

Maggie was sick inside. The images of the hot tub rolled through her mind. 'You and Mitch, you didn't — '

'No!' Mary was shaking her head furiously. 'Okay, it got close, but we didn't.' Her face wrinkled. 'It was stupid, I know. Just messin' around, drinking too much, and . . . oh, God, Maggie, you've *got* to believe me.' Tears were running down her cheeks, and she swiped them away with the back of her hand. Mascara smudged on her cheeks, and her eyes appeared sunken. In a matter of seconds she seemed to have aged ten years. 'Please,' she begged.

Maggie's fingers tightened around the rattail of the comb.

'I'll do anything for you, if you just tell Mom and Dad that it was you. That you and Thane — '

The plastic comb broke. Maggie knew she was being a fool, manipulated by the master, but she had no choice. If her folks had any inkling, any idea that there was even the tiniest hint of incest . . . Her stomach clenched as the word burned through her brain. 'Okay. Okay.' She walked into her room, found a pair of panties in her top drawer, stepped into them, and let the towel drop onto the floor. She scrounged around on the foot of the bed until she found her bathrobe and slid her arms through the sleeves. Cinching the belt tight around her waist, she looked at Mary Theresa, who stood in the doorway to the bathroom working at scrubbing off the evidence that she'd been crying. 'Let's go.'

Together, their silent evil pact hanging between them, they headed toward the family room. Maggie braced herself, steeling her shoulders, determined to take her parents' wrath rather than have the family torn apart because Mitch and Mary Theresa were morons with the morals of alley cats.

She thought fleetingly of her own actions, of lying about what she was doing at the ranch, of the times she'd been with Thane in the woods, the fields, or the hayloft of the stables. Her skin tingled, and she flushed a little. Her parents would grill her and her father would probably threaten Thane, order him to stay away from Maggie. Forever.

Pain split her heart. How could she do it? How could she sacrifice something so wonderful as the love she felt for this man? Her throat tight, her feet feeling like lead weights, she followed Mary Theresa into the family room and saw the censure in their father's eyes as he stood near the fireplace, his shoulders stiff, his spine rigid, his face the mask of a drill sergeant. 'I want answers, girls. Straight ones.' He motioned to the leather couch. 'Sit.'

'Frank,' their mother said. She was seated in her favorite wing-backed chair, one foot resting on an ottoman. 'There's no reason to be hostile.'

'They're lying and Mitch — ' He rolled his eyes toward the ceiling and nodded as if he were slowly counting off the seconds. 'Where in tarnation is that boy?'

'Who knows?'

'It's well after midnight.'

'He's nineteen, Frank.'

'Well.' Taking a deep breath, Frank Reilly lowered his head and skewered his two daughters with one frightening, determined gaze. 'Maggie. Mary Theresa. Would one of you tell me what's going on here? Who's the boy?'

Maggie sank onto one leather-bound cushion. Inside she was shaking and quivering and her lips were suddenly so dry they felt as if they would crack. Mary Theresa perched on the edge of the couch and stared at Maggie, silently encouraging her.

'Well?' Their father's face was florid, his eyes shining black beads that didn't show a glimmer of empathy.

Maggie swallowed hard. She opened her mouth and forced the hated words over her lips. 'It's . . . It's me, Dad. I have a boyfriend.'

'Oh.' Was there a twinge of relief in his voice?

'You?' Their mother took a sip from the glass that had been sweating on the table and Maggie realized that she'd been above suspicion — the plainer tomboy of a daughter who was more interested in swimming laps and riding horses than being involved with boys.

'Y . . . yes. I have a boyfriend.'

'Who?' Frank demanded.

'No one you know.'

'Someone from the restaurant?'

'No.' Maggie's guts churned painfully. 'He's — '

Brring! The phone jangled loudly. Their mother physically jumped. Frank glared at the instrument. 'Who would be calling at this time of night?' Impatient and irritated, he crossed the room and snagged the receiver, cutting off the second ring. 'Hello?' he nearly shouted, then paused. 'Yes, yes. Frank Reilly.' All eyes in the room turned to him and witnessed the instant deterioration of a strong man. 'You must be mistaken,' he whispered, his face crumpling, his broad shoulders sagging as if suddenly burdened with an incredible weight.

'Frank?' Bernice asked, her voice shaking.

Frank Reilly slumped against the wall. 'No,' he whispered loudly, then more vehemently. 'No! No! No!' His fist pounded on the wall.

'Frank? What is it?' Terror laced their mother's voice. 'Frank, you're scaring me and the girls and . . . what? What is it?'

Maggie's skin prickled and a dull, muted roar, the sound of waves crashing on a distant beach, caused a headache to build behind her eyes. 'Dad?'

'Oh, God.' Mary Theresa began to shake.

'I'll be right there,' he said, his voice cracking as he hung up the phone and stared at his family through eyes that shone with tears, eyes that Maggie was certain couldn't see. 'That was the police.' His voice was gruff with emotion. 'It's Mitch . . . they found him on the beach.' He took in a deep breath, crossed the brown sea of carpet, and wrapped his arms around Bernice. 'He's gone.'

'What?'

'He's . . . oh, God, he's dead.'

'No!' She started fighting then. 'You're wrong, they're wrong, Frank, no. Not Mitch — '

'Shh.'

Bernice gave out a sharp keening wail that screamed through the house, bouncing off the walls, echoing in the rafters.

'No!' Maggie shook her head violently side to side. Tears filled her eyes. 'I . . . I don't believe it.'

'Honey, it's true.'

Bernice, sobbing and screaming, began pounding with small, impotent fists on her husband's chest. 'Mitchell,' she cried, tears rolling down her face. 'No, not Mitchell. He . . . he was a son to me. It didn't matter that . . . that I didn't give him birth . . . oh God, oh God . . . '

Mary Theresa sat stunned, her eyes dry and round, her face as white as death.

'There's some mistake!' Maggie was on her feet. 'Call them back, call them! Whoever called.' She reached for the phone, grabbed the receiver and, with tears streaking down her cheeks, shook the mouthpiece at her father. 'Call them, Dad!'

It's true. I feel it. Oh, God, Mitch is dead.

'What?' Maggie whirled on her sister, who hadn't moved, still sat like a statue on the couch. 'How do you know?' Mary Theresa blinked and didn't say a word.

'How does she know what?' their father asked, his lips beneath his mustache beginning to quiver slightly. Those once beady, suspicion-filled eyes had begun to glisten.

'She just said that . . . ' Maggie let her voice fall away.

'She didn't say a word! Christ, what's got into you?'

Maggie's stomach clenched. 'But — '

It's no mistake, Maggie. Mitch said he was gonna do it. Mary Theresa's body began to shake. Her eyes held her sister's, and without so much as a sound, she said, *I think he killed himself.*

PART III

Cheyenne, Wyoming

November 1998

9

Thane felt no sense of homecoming, just a cold, dark certainty that his life had changed forever. With Maggie asleep in the passenger seat beside him and the gauge of the gas tank nearly on empty, he cranked the steering wheel and turned the truck into the lane leading to the heart of his ranch. Home, if you could call it that. Dawn was just cracking — spreading weak light over the flat, snow-laden acres.

Against Maggie's protests, they'd spent five hours of the past night in a fleabag of a motel on the sagging mattresses of twin beds only a few feet from each other. Thane hadn't slept a wink. Just knowing she was an arm's length away had kept him awake, an erection so intense it was nearly painful, reminding him how much he wanted her. That he'd once loved her.

Hell.

It had been a long, long time ago.

A lifetime.

Now, as the blizzard chased them down and the beleaguered windshield wipers slapped time to a fading country ballad, he shoved any lingering tender thoughts of her aside. He didn't have time for the pain of nostalgia. He'd leave that to lovesick fools who didn't know better.

Bone tired, his bladder feeling as if it would burst from half a dozen cups of coffee, he wheeled the rig down the lane where ten inches of snow smoothed out the ruts that ran parallel to the fence posts that were his guide. No tire marks were visible, no weeds poking above the smooth white surface.

Four-wheel drive kept the wheels moving, snow packing and churning under the tires as the ranch house came into view. This little piece of land had become his sanctuary as it had once in a while been Mary Theresa's.

Christ, what a mess. Damn Mary Theresa. His fingers tightened over the wheel, his knuckles showing white. As if he were choking his beautiful, self-centered and destructive ex-wife.

'Damn it all to hell.'

And still the snow fell.

The outbuildings of the ranch appeared through the flurries and the house, two compact stories of stone and cedar, stood dark, not a lamp lit. It didn't matter; he was relieved to have made it this far.

But for how long? What is all this crap with Mary Theresa? Where the hell is she? For the past few days, ever since he'd come to the conclusion that she really was missing, the same questions had been racing like a brush fire through his mind, powered by caffeine and the slow-burning anger he'd always felt for that woman — the one woman who had been his wife. If it was possible, he'd love to grab hold of her narcissistic shoulders and shake some sense into that calculating, beautiful head of hers.

Whoa, pardner, she could already be dead for all you know.

Again his jaw clenched to the point of

breaking and he eased off on the gas as he parked as close to the house as possible.

'Where . . . where are we?' Maggie asked, yawning and opening one eye. She'd been half-asleep, dozing on and off for hours. Now, with her auburn hair resting against her cheek, her eyes blinking off any lingering bit of slumber, she straightened, squinting through the foggy glass.

He'd hoped she'd aged over the years — put on weight, or shown signs of wear, but the few little lines around her eyes only added a depth to her — a maturity that he hadn't been aware was lacking all those years ago.

God, he'd had it bad for her then. No woman, and he'd had more than a few by that time, had touched him as she had. It wasn't so much her beauty, but her spirit that had reached him. Her razor-sharp tongue hadn't hidden the complexity of her soul, and her sense of humor, even in those tense days, had been his undoing. He'd sensed that she'd been frightened of him, but fascinated, and though he'd told himself to forget her, to leave her alone, to keep his goddamned fantasies buttoned up and his pants on, he hadn't been able to resist.

And it had cost him.

More than he could ever imagine.

She roused and yawned. 'You said something?'

'We're here.'

Squinting, she looked out the window. 'Where exactly is 'here?' '

'My place.'

'Your place?' She was starting to awaken, her

mind clicking into gear — he saw it in the change of her expression, an adjustment from slumberous acceptance to clarified understanding. 'You mean in Wyoming?'

'It's as close as we can get right now.'

'But — '

'Look, Maggie, one of us has got to sleep and piss — not necessarily in that order.' He cut the engine and shoved on the door. Wind, as cold as an arctic blast, filled the interior. He didn't have time for arguments and had to escape the warm confines of the truck.

'I thought we had to get to Denver. ASAP.'

'We are.' He yanked out some of his gear, and she, shooting him a glance that called him all sorts of foul things from a liar to a murdering bastard, grabbed a small bag and her purse. Together they trudged through the knee-deep snow to the porch. 'Make yourself at home.' He unlocked the door, then held it open for her. 'There's a bathroom and extra bedroom upstairs, where you can crash if ya want.' He tossed her a look, and she saw the weary lines around his eyes. 'I need a few hours, that's all. Then we're outta here.' He walked to the hallway and fiddled with the thermostat.

'Fair enough,' she said, though she didn't like being in Thane's house for a second. It was too personal, too close. And though warmer than the outside, it seemed cold and unwelcoming.

'The kitchen is that direction,' he said, pointing down a short hallway as he mounted wooden stairs that led to a landing before curving up to the second story. As his bootheels rang on the steps, she dropped her bag and walked to the kitchen. Small. Sparse. Just the essentials. Butcher-block countertops, cracked linoleum floor, the necessary appliances, and a table with two chairs pushed under a window that looked out across the parking yard to the barn and outbuildings.

The rest of the lower floor consisted of a living room decorated in what appeared to be cast-off or garage-sale furniture; a bedroom that had been converted into a den now equipped with a computer, modem, fax machine, floor-to-ceiling bookcases; and a bathroom.

She heard the toilet flush upstairs and the shower begin to run as she noticed the telephone/answering machine, its red light blinking. With only a slight qualm she pressed the PLAY button and heard three messages from Detective Henderson demanding that Thane phone the Denver police, another folksy greeting from someone named Howard Bailey, giving him a report on the livestock and what had happened on the ranch in the past couple of days, and one from a woman named Carrie, a friendly female voice who just asked Thane to call her back.

Maggie wondered about the woman, but shoved all thoughts of her aside as she made her way back to the kitchen. She heard the sounds of pipes and water running and decided Thane was still in the shower. Good. She needed a break from him. He was too intense, too good-looking, too much a part of her past.

Rummaging in the cupboards, she found a can of coffee on a shelf, located a much-abused coffeemaker on the counter, and set to work. While the coffee perked, she scrounged through the contents of the refrigerator, found eggs, a half loaf of bread that had seen better days, part of an onion, a couple of crisp apples, and a brick of cheddar cheese. Nothing fancy, but it would have to do.

Grating cheese and cracking eggs, she thought of Mary Theresa and her life in Denver. What did Maggie really know about her sister? She'd visited only a few times, once when Mary Theresa had married Syd Gillette, an older man who owned a string of hotels and treated his third wife as if she were one of his possessions. Mary Theresa had been younger than Gillette's son, his only offspring, a boy who had been conceived in Syd's first stab at wedded bliss.

Mary Theresa and Syd's marriage hadn't lasted a year. Since then Mary Theresa had avoided walking down the aisle.

So who else did Maggie know — who were the people associated with her sister? Eve Lawrence, Mary Theresa's secretary, was the first to come to mind, and lately she'd worked out with a personal trainer whose name escaped Maggie. There was a boyfriend, ten years younger and a model of sorts — or had it been a tennis pro? His name had been Wayne . . . no, Wade, and his last name had been the name of a dog . . . Wade . . . Shepherd? No. Pomeranian, that was it. Then there was the cohost of *Denver AM*, Craig Beaumont. He and M.T. hadn't gotten along. Or so she thought, but Maggie couldn't really remember. Truth to tell, she didn't know much about him or the other people who were involved with her sister since Mary Theresa had moved to Denver. Maggie had been wrapped up in her own life, her own problems, and her twin had always been secretive and glossed over her own.

Maggie couldn't believe Mary Theresa was dead. Wouldn't. Someone knew something. People just didn't disappear without a trace. This was the age of telecommunications, for God's sake, where the government and every creditor knew intimate details of a person's life through his social security number, driving record, and credit-card use.

So where was M.T.?

Biting her lower lip, she sautéed onions, added the eggs, stirred, and when the mass had about congealed, threw in a couple handfuls of cheese.

By the time Thane walked down the stairs in clean jeans and a flannel shirt that was still unbuttoned, the makeshift meal was ready.

Maggie glanced at his bare chest, where there were still drops clinging to curling swirls of hair she'd never seen before, then looked away before she lost her train of thought. 'You want some breakfast?' she asked, biting into an apple she'd already cut.

One side of his mouth lifted in a charming smile she would have loved to slap off his face. 'Sure.' He buttoned his shirt and tucked in the shirttails.

'It'll cost ya.'

'How much?'

'Just the truth.' She handed him a plate with a makeshift omelette and a couple slices of toast.

'Thanks.' He set his plate on the table, then poured two cups of coffee. 'So what do you want to know?'

'Everything.' She took a seat opposite him and skewered him with a stare she hoped would seem intimidating.

'That's a tall order.' His gaze darkened and in a chilling moment of déjà vu she remembered loving him years before, yet knowing that he kept secrets from her, that his past was guarded. Some things, it seemed, hadn't changed.

'And you're ducking the issue,' she said around a mouthful of eggs.

He ate in silence for a few minutes, chewing thoughtfully, washing down a bite of toast with coffee, then nodded as if agreeing with some inner conversation he'd had with himself. 'Who called?'

'What?'

While watching her, he took a bite of toast. 'You listened to the recorder, didn't you?'

'No . . . I . . . ' She wanted to lie, but figured there would be no reason. She sipped her coffee, then said, 'Detective Henderson wants you to call him, some guy named Howie — '

'Howard Bailey, owns the place next door.'

' — he said everything was fine, and a woman named Carrie left a message for you to call.'

'Did she?' Again that ingratiating and irritating smile.

'Yeah.' Maggie finished her breakfast and shoved her plate aside. 'So, back to the truth.'

'What is it you want to know, Maggie?' He leaned back in his chair.

'I told you — everything.'

He glanced out the window and rubbed his chin. She knew without his saying so that he was examining his soul, taking stock of the secrets and lies that had made him the man he'd become. 'I'm beat to hell. You know that, so how about I check on the stock, sleep for a couple of hours, and fill you in on all the details.'

'No way. I want to know exactly why you're involved with my sister. Why the police suspect you and — ' She stopped before she crossed a line she'd never stepped over, a line she'd avoided for the better part of eighteen years.

'And?' he encouraged.

'Never mind.'

'Come on, Mag Pie,' he said, using an old, familiar endearment from years before. 'Spill it.' He finished his coffee in a gulp and rolled his lips in on themselves. When she didn't answer, he scowled. 'My guess is that you want to know why I married Mary Theresa. Why, when things were so good between you and me, I took up with her?'

The room seemed to shrink. All the old doubts in her mind crawled out of their carefully locked crates. She felt eighteen again. Young, alone, betrayed. 'It doesn't matter.'

'Like hell.' He stood, tossed his plate into the sink, and reached for his jacket. 'I'll keep it simple for now, okay? It was a mistake. From the git-go. I was an idiot. You were the one I loved. But I was young and randy and didn't think beyond the minute's pleasure.' He slid his arms into the sleeves. 'It started out as a mistake. I'd had a few too many beers and then . . . '

'Then you couldn't stop yourself.'

'Nah.' He shook his head as if to convince himself. 'I could have. I just didn't want to.' His eyes held hers for a moment. 'As I said. Young and foolish.' Snapping his jacket, he walked to the door, grabbed his hat, and squared it on his head. 'You want a more detailed explanation, you'll get one. Just as soon as I take care of things and catch up on a few hours' sleep.'

Maggie watched him disappear through the door, and she mentally kicked herself a dozen times over. What did it matter? The past was ancient history. Mary Theresa had been irresistible, even to Thane. End of story.

Climbing to her feet she ignored the jab of pain she always felt when she thought of those dark days following Mitch's death and Thane's betrayal. It was better to put the past behind her once and for all. Right now she only had to deal with what had happened to her sister. She glanced out the window and watched as Thane struggled through the snow, then, throwing his weight behind his shoulder, forced open the door to the barn.

Maggie's throat closed and she remembered the times they had been alone in another barn, the way his mouth felt on hers, the feel of his work-roughened fingers as they caressed her skin. 'Damn it,' she growled, and tossed her dirty dish into the sink. She walked back to the den and, ignoring the flashing light on the recorder, punched out the number for her sister-in-law in California. Tapping her fingers impatiently, she waited until a groggy Becca answered.

'Hi, honey,' she said.

'Hi.' Becca wasn't known to arise sunny-side up.

'How're things goin'?'

'Okay,' Becca mumbled. 'It's early.'

'I know, but I wanted to talk to you.' *More than you'll ever know, kiddo*. 'So is the ankle okay? Does it hurt you?'

'It's fine, Mom. Really.' There was a hint of distrust in her daughter's voice — the innuendo that Maggie was intruding.

'I'm in Wyoming,' Maggie said, and explained about the snowstorm, though she knew Becca wasn't listening, was just ticking off the seconds, doing time as part of her daughter-duty. When questioned about what she was doing, she was evasive but insisted that all her homework was caught up and that she was having a 'super' time, 'the best.' When Maggie said she loved her, Becca mumbled a 'love you, too' by rote that meant nothing other than she didn't want to make her mother mad.

Sighing, Maggie hung up feeling uneasy and out of sorts. She needed to be with her daughter, hated the separation, even though she felt it might be best for their relationship to have a few days apart from each other.

Disturbed, she walked through the spartan house again. Hardwood floors covered with a few rugs, not a plant in sight, no photographs or mementos of any kind. A chipped hurricane lantern rested on the mantel in the living room where a time-worn rocker, end table, television, and battle-scarred camel-backed couch took up residence around a washed-out braided rug and river-rock fireplace.

She hauled her bag upstairs and found the second bedroom, where a twin bed was pushed into the corner and a simple bureau that had once been painted white stood in the corner. The bare wood floors needed refinishing, and the only picture on the wall was a framed ink drawing of a rifle. The glass was cracked in one corner.

'Home sweet home,' she muttered under her breath and twisted open the blinds. Ice had collected on the exterior of the windows, and snow blew in wild gusts. Past the flurries she watched Thane shut the door of the barn and plow his way through the path he'd broken earlier.

Her heart did a stupid little thump, and she berated herself for being a fool where he was concerned. She always had been, though. There seemed to be no changing that. Disgusted with herself, she closed the blinds, cleaned up in the bathroom, and flopped onto the bed. She heard Thane come in, listened as he made a couple of calls — she couldn't make out the words — then closed her eyes. A small headache that began at the base of her skull and crawled upward nagged at her, and she silently prayed for her sister. Through all the pain and tears, all the feelings of betrayal years ago, she had loved her twin, felt close to her. 'Please, M.T., be safe.'

She heard the sound of Thane's footsteps as he climbed the stairs, held her breath as he walked past her door. He didn't slow a bit, and she told herself that she didn't want him to look in on her, that had he opened the door it would have been an invasion of her privacy, that she needed her space to think this all through. And yet a small and very feminine part of her was disappointed that he hadn't stopped or rapped softly and tried the door.

Furious with her thoughts, she pounded on her pillow, twisted the comforter over her, and squeezed her eyes shut. She needed to sleep, to clear her mind, to wake up refreshed so that she could face the police in Denver and find out what the devil was going on.

* * *

Reed Henderson was on his second cup of coffee. Thankfully the caffeine was beginning to surge through his bloodstream and take hold. He'd already ducked a bevy of reporters, ignored calls from the local news stations, and even evaded the DA, who was demanding answers.

About Marquise.

A fading local star who was starting to become a cult figure. Or so it seemed. She'd never even been that famous in life, but now, with her disappearance, hers was very much the name on everyone's lips. He doubted that anyone else cared much. She wasn't exactly a national obsession; a couple of bit parts in B-movies in her early twenties, a stint as a weathergirl before she ended up as a news reporter for a small station in Sacramento. Then she landed the job in Denver. She'd been an anchor for one news team before jumping to a rival station as a talk-show host of a daily morning program that, according to the demographics, appealed to housewives in their mid-thirties with two years of college and pre-school-aged children.

Marquise wasn't exactly high-profile as far as the rest of the country was concerned, but the local press and viewers had loved her. Until recently. In the past year *Denver AM* had fallen off in the ratings; there was talk of replacing Marquise with a younger, fresher, more with-it face or canceling the show altogether.

So much for her professional life.

However, it was better than her personal one: two husbands, a string of lovers, and a nearly estranged sister. Everyone else who had been close to her was dead. Both parents gone and even the brother — well, if he could be called that — had committed suicide. Maybe it ran in the family — though Mitchell Reilly had been only a first cousin, the son of Frank's deceased sister who had been unmarried at the time of her son's birth. No one had known who the kid's father was, and when Carol had died of a genetic heart defect not long after Mitch had come into the world, Frank Reilly had stepped up to the plate and not only adopted the kid but raised Mitch as if he were his son.

Henderson frowned to himself. Marquise's friends were an odd mix and he was still working on those.

Hannah poked her head around the open door. Behind her, phones rang incessantly over the buzz of conversation, jangle of keys, and hum of computer monitors. Every once in a while laughter erupted, or someone shouted over the din, but the small cubicles and open desks created a sense of barely organized mayhem.

A slow-spreading smile slipped across Hannah's pointed chin, and beneath a fringe of blond bangs her eyes danced. 'Guess what? The elusive ex-husband called last night.'

His head snapped up. 'Walker?'

'One and the same. Called from his ranch in Cheyenne. He's on his way here. With the sister.'

Reed's gut told him something was wrong. 'Isn't she from a small town in Idaho?'

'Uh-huh.'

'Why would they be together?' he wondered aloud. 'I thought the divorce between Walker and Marquise was kinda messy — no love lost — that sort of thing. So why would the twin sister be arriving with him?' Scowling to himself, he spun the seat of the chair and stared out the window for a few long seconds, but he didn't see the face of the building across the street, nor the few pedestrians bundled in ski jackets or long wool coats, wool hats, boots, and scarves huddled against the wind as they made their way along the sidewalk. Now, his vision was turned inward to the case — the damned case.

'Beats me. Something to ask.'

'Are they bringing the niece — what was her name?' He spun the chair again, glanced down at the notes on his cluttered desk, thought about a cigarette, and found a stick of gum in his top drawer. 'Rebecca?'

'Don't know.' Hannah leaned against the doorjamb to his office, her favorite position when they hashed things out. 'Why?'

'Marquise had a lot of pictures of the kid. Almost as many as she kept on herself.' He opened the stick of nicotine-laced gum and plopped it into his mouth as he surveyed the woman who had worked with him for over three years. Attractive, smart as a whip, in good shape and, he suspected, in love with him. A mistake. They both knew it, but didn't ever broach the subject. It was a line he never intended to cross. Too sticky. Affairs had a way of ending and ending badly. He liked this woman too much to mess things up.

And then there was Karen to consider. They were divorced, had been for years, but . . . he still kept her picture in the top drawer with his forty-five and empty flask that still reeked of scotch.

'We'll see if they bring the daughter when they get here.' Folding her arms over her chest and pulling at her right earring, the way she always did when she was thinking hard, Hannah said, 'You know, a lot of people close to Marquise are dead.'

'I thought about that.'

'Good. Don't know if it has any bearing, but it's odd, I think.' She started clicking the deceased off, lifting fingers as she counted. 'First, the stepbrother dies in the ocean, suspected suicide; then the parents split up over his death, try to reconcile, and the mother ends up falling while supposedly cooking dinner in the kitchen, hits her head, and dies with a blood-alcohol level in the stratosphere.'

'Next the father, Frank, bereft and broken, has himself a massive heart attack, and the two girls, barely in their twenties, are on their own. They've only got each other and a couple of husbands, right? Except that Mary Theresa marries quickly and divorces even faster and the other one, Maggie, she hangs in there, has a kid, then when things get rocky, separates, and the guy has a car accident, ends up in a coma, takes a while to die. According to the hospital records, Dean McCrae's bloodstream was pure whiskey — kinda like the mom — when he was life-flighted in.' She wiggled her fingers. 'That's a lot of dead bodies for a small family. Now the centerpiece, the golden girl, is missing, probably dead somewhere.'

He reached for his baseball. Gave it a toss. 'So what're you saying?'

'Just that it gives one pause. Nothing more than that.'

'You think there was foul play involved?' The stitched ball landed softly in Henderson's waiting fingers with Koufax's signature rolled toward the ceiling. He flung it toward the fluorescent lights again.

Shrugging, pink lips protruding thoughtfully, she turned her palms toward the ceiling. 'Probably not. Maybe just a coincidence, but any way you look at it, it's a helluva string of bad luck.'

The ball landed in his waiting palm. 'But these things happen. The brother was a screwup, the mother a drunk, the father a type A who lost it when things got out of control. As for the brother-in-law, he's just another statistic, someone who had a few too many, got behind the wheel, and ended up in the morgue.'

'Jesus, listen to you.'

'It's all true.'

She let out a small cynical laugh. 'That's what I love about you, Henderson. You're so damned sensitive and empathetic.'

He ignored the jab. 'Goes with the job.' He glanced at his watch. 'When are they showing up?'

'Sometime this afternoon according to the message.'

'Good.' He placed the baseball in the chipped replica of the mitt, then opened the thick file on Marquise, and sifted through some of his notes until he found a copy of Marquise's last will and testament. The document was surprisingly simple for such a complex woman. The only beneficiaries were Margaret Elizabeth Reilly McCrae and her daughter, Rebecca Anne McCrae.

Henderson couldn't wait to talk to the ex-husband again. And the twin sister. She should be interesting.

Hannah walked into the room and rested a hip against his desk. Reaching forward, she tapped the polished nail of a long finger on the copy of Marquise's will. 'Where'd you get this?'

'Doesn't matter.'

'Of course it does; we both know it. But, well, forget the legalities of it. Right now this document doesn't mean diddly-squat. No one's recovered a body. The woman might not be dead.'

'Then where is she?' Reed asked, because the thought that he'd been set up, that he might possibly be a pawn in Mary Theresa Reilly Walker Gillette's scheme, stuck in his craw.

'That's a good question, Detective,' Hannah said, as the phone jangled, catching Henderson's attention. 'A damned good question.'

* * *

Somewhere a door slammed. Maggie's eyes flew open, and she focused on an unfamiliar room. Where was Becca? Her heart galumphed in a few unsteady beats before she remembered that she was at Thane's ranch, and they were on their way to Denver. To find Mary Theresa.

She threw off the comforter and marched to the bathroom, where she splashed water on her face, finger-combed the tangles from her hair, and glared at her reflection. She managed to wipe away the smudges of mascara from under her eyes, dab on some lipstick, and toss an if-this-isn't-good-enough-it's-too-damned-bad look at her reflection before grabbing her things and hurrying down the stairs. She dropped her bag and purse on the floor near the front door.

Thane was in the den on the telephone. ' . . . yeah, I know. There're just some things I gotta take care of . . . we've been over this before, Carrie.' A pause. He turned and saw

Maggie standing in the doorway. For a split second their gazes collided, skated apart, then hit again.

For an instant she couldn't move, then gave herself a hard mental shake. This was Thane she was dealing with. Thane. The man who had taken her heart and trampled it with the worndown heels of his damned shit-kicking cowboy boots, the man who didn't seem to have a past, the man who had married her sister and now was a suspect in Mary Theresa's disappearance. 'I said I'd call.' He hung up and surveyed her with an intensity she found unsettling.

'Trouble in paradise?'

One side of his mouth lifted, though the smile didn't quite reach his eyes. 'Let's just leave it at trouble. You ready?'

'As I'll ever be.'

'Just let me connect with Howard. Then we'll take off. There's fresh coffee in the maker.' He turned back to the phone, and she left him alone. In the kitchen, she poured coffee and stood at the window. The snow had stopped, at least for the moment, but already the tire tracks that they'd left only hours before were nearly filled by drifts. Overhead, the first few patches of blue sky were visible.

She shivered as she thought about the hours ahead. What would she find in Denver and where, oh, where was her sister?

She heard the sound of Thane's boots and turned as, shoving an unruly lock of his hair from his eyes, he appeared from the hallway.

'Okay. Howard's on for a few more days.'

'So we can leave?'

'Yes.'

She took a last swallow from her cup, then tossed the dregs down the sink. 'I think you promised me some answers.'

'That I did.' He rubbed the back of his neck. 'Let's load up. On the way to Denver I'll tell you everything you need to know.'

'Everything?' she asked, wondering if she really wanted the truth.

'Whatever your little heart desires, Mag Pie.'

If you only knew, Thane, she thought, swallowing the sudden lump in her throat. *If you only knew*. But this wasn't the time for sentimentality. Too much was at stake.

10

'Okay, Walker,' Maggie said, once they were inside Thane's cold pickup. 'Let's start with Mary Theresa. What did you have to do with her disappearance?'

'I thought we'd already settled that one.' Thane guided his truck onto the main road. The tires slipped, spun, then held as sunlight pierced through the clouds. 'I don't know anything about what happened to her. Period. The cops seem to think otherwise.'

Maggie wasn't convinced he was telling the truth and if the police were questioning him, there had to be a reason. A good one. The police weren't stupid. They were used to dealing with kidnappings, murders, abductions, rapes, and every crime under the sun. 'When was the last time you saw her?'

He hesitated. 'The night before she disappeared.'

'Oh, God.' She felt as if someone had kicked her in the gut. 'The night before?' she repeated, trying to register this information. According to Mary Theresa she and Thane hadn't had much contact after they were divorced. They had gone their separate ways. 'I don't understand.'

His lips pursed, and she felt that same old invisible wall, a shield, rise between them. A muscle worked in his jaw and his eyes narrowed on the horizon as if he were carefully weighing his words. 'We had some unsettled issues.'

'What issues?' Maggie leaned closer to the passenger door and stared hard at this man she'd loved, the one to whom she'd willingly given her virginity and heart, the one who had betrayed her so brutally that she never thought she'd love again. She wasn't immune to him, couldn't ignore his rugged male allure. Chiseled features, harsh as the Wyoming countryside that had spawned him, stretched tight.

'I think we'd better start at the beginning,' he said slowly.

'Always a good idea.'

'I mean at the very beginning.'

She felt a jab of apprehension, a frisson of foreboding, slide down her spine, but she wasn't one to back down. 'Okay.'

'I never did explain to you what happened between Mary Theresa and me, did I?' He sent her a glance that warned her that the conversation was going to travel in painful territory.

'I don't think I wanted an explanation.'

'Sorry, Maggie. You're gonna get one anyway.' He shifted down for a corner, then snagged his sunglasses from the dash. 'I'm afraid you're not going to like what I have to say.'

'That's pretty much guaranteed.' Steeling herself, she decided she could face anything. She'd spent the last eighteen years second-guessing everyone involved; now it was time to hear Thane's side of the story.

'You and I were pretty involved, remember?'

How could she forget? Rather than show any

emotion, she nodded. 'I'd say so.'

'Then Mitch drowns, and all hell breaks loose.'

She couldn't disagree. The pain that existed in her family; the fingers pointed in accusation; the disbelief that Mitchell Xavier Reilly, captain of the Rio Verde High School swim team, could have drowned; the suspicion that he'd taken his own life had infiltrated the house like a disease that gnawed at all of them, eroding the family. There was darkness then, and depression. Their mother drank more heavily, didn't bother to hide her alcoholism; their father took up smoking again and avoided going to the office, which had always been his sanctuary — his bastion of self-esteem. Mary Theresa pretended nothing was wrong, smiling, laughing a little too loudly, wearing more makeup than usual, and avoiding the house, while Maggie turned inward, lying on her bed for hours, staring at the ceiling and fighting the insidious but oh, so real suspicion that her brother's death had somehow been her fault. 'I remember,' she said, her voice husky with the agony of the past. Those days were shadowed, emotions raw and bleeding, the house a bleak, dark tomb.

'And do you remember that you avoided me?'

Sighing, she nodded, not wanting to think about her part in the unraveling of all that she'd once held as good. 'I couldn't face you.'

'Because you threw me to the wolves.'

She nodded and ground her teeth together. She wasn't going to take the blame for more than her fair share of what had happened. 'If you're talking about telling Mom and Dad the truth about seeing you, yeah, that's what I did. But I didn't know at the time that Mitch had . . . had drowned.' After all these years she still had trouble thinking that her adopted brother had somehow taken his own life, couldn't believe it.

He flipped down the visor as the sun began chasing away the clouds in earnest, bright rays dancing on the pristine countryside. The road had been plowed, but the truck's tires still spun once in a while, the truck sliding where patches of ice were hidden beneath the drifting snow. 'Your dad came at me like a hound from hell.'

'He was upset.'

'Oh, no.' Thane's hands tightened on the steering wheel, his knuckles showing white. 'He was beyond upset. Way beyond. Showed up at Flora's ranch, called me every name in the book and swore that if I ever so much as looked at you again, he'd kill me. It's a wonder I wasn't fired.' His mouth compressed in a silent rage that spanned the years and pulsed in the cab. 'I was lucky that Flora took my side.'

Maggie picked at a hangnail. 'What's this have to do with Mary Theresa?'

'That's just it. It didn't start out as anything to do with Mary Theresa. But I figured you and I were through.'

Her heart squeezed at the memory.

'So, imagine my surprise when you called and told me you wanted to meet me, that you didn't care what your folks said, that you missed me.'

She forced her hands into her pockets so she'd

quit fidgeting and stared out the windshield. 'I meant it,' she conceded. At least she thought she had. She remembered stealing into the den, making the call. She'd been so nervous she nearly knocked over a desk lamp, her heart pounding loud enough that she was certain her sister, sleeping down the hall, could hear its wild beat. But she hadn't been able to stop herself from dialing him — hadn't been able to believe that it was truly over. 'Can you pick me up?' she'd asked, scared spitless at the thought that she was openly defying her parents.

Less than two weeks earlier, Frank Reilly, his upper lip quivering in rage, had specifically forbidden her ever to see 'that two-bit rodeo punk' again. 'If I ever catch him near you, I swear, Margaret Elizabeth, I'll break his goddamned neck!' her father had promised her, his gaze steady, his lips compressed into a razor-thin line beneath his stiff, unyielding mustache.

For the first few days, Maggie had accepted her father's edict — she'd never been one to defy him openly — but the week after the funeral, when the oppression in the house felt like a smothering cloak and the air conditioning unit had given out, creating a heat that mingled with the general desperation and malaise within the thick walls, Maggie had needed to get away.

She'd been consumed by memories of making love to Thane that first time, had recalled the smell of rainwater slickening his body as he'd entered her and broken the thin veil of her virginity. She'd remembered looking up into blue eyes that seemed to mirror her own soul as he'd spilled himself within her.

Finally, Maggie couldn't stand another second in the dark gloom of her parents' grief, nor could she bear her sister's fake upbeat attitude. Mary Theresa was forever shopping, buying new clothes, trying out new hairstyles, and painting her fingernails outrageous colors. Her laughter rang down the tile hallways and sounded as phony and out of place as a foghorn in the desert. But she refused to slow down, to face what had happened, and had kept herself in constant motion so that she wouldn't feel the pain that shrouded Maggie as she'd lain on her bed, pinned by the burden of her grief.

'You've got to get out,' Mary Theresa insisted one day as she breezed past the pool where Maggie was listlessly swimming laps. M.T. had lost weight, and there was no vibrancy to her skin, no luster in her eyes.

'I will.' Maggie dragged herself from the water and dabbed at her face with a towel.

'I mean it, Maggie, this place is like a mortuary.' Then she heard herself and let out a brittle laugh that was followed by tears falling from her eyes. 'Oh, God, I didn't mean — '

'I know.' They looked at each other and Mary Theresa's façade of happiness cracked. Her perfectly madeup face crumpled like an empty, crushed can.

'Oh, shit, Maggie, I . . . I . . . ' Her voice broke, and all at once Maggie was on her feet, feeling the hot cement under her soles as Mary Theresa fell into her arms. They clung together, crying, sobbing, holding each other up under the tonnage of anguish, the desperate heartache and guilt they each bore. 'I think I killed him.'

'You didn't.' Maggie held on tighter as Mary Theresa, her gauzy dress wet, her phony energy zapped, sagged against her.

She convulsed, her body racked with horrible sobs. 'I should never have — '

'Shh. It's over. Let's not talk about it.' Maggie couldn't bear listening to any confessions now. Whatever had happened between her cousin and sister was now dead, buried with Mitch.

They rocked gently, their heads nestled in each other's shoulders, their bodies shaking until their tears had run dry, their painful moans of grief finally silenced.

Mary Theresa lifted her head and, spying her image in the reflection of the patio door, cleared her throat and stepped out of her sister's embrace. Swiping her eyes, brushing away tears from her red cheeks, she seemed suddenly embarrassed at her display of emotion. She sniffed and, biting her lip, looked away, as if afraid to see the pain in her sister's eyes. 'Sorry, I don't know what came over me.'

'It's okay.' Maggie blinked and lifted a shoulder. 'It came over me, too.'

Mary Theresa managed a false, wobbly smile as they walked inside and through the house to Maggie's room. 'Let's just forget about all this,' she suggested, clearing her throat and running anxious fingers through her hair. 'It's just . . . too . . . too depressing.'

'Of course it is. Mitch is dead.'

'But we're not.' Desperation and fear flashed in her eyes. All the anguish, compassion, and tenderness they'd shared on the patio vanished. Swallowing hard, she hooked a thumb, jerking it toward her chest. '*I'm* not.' She picked up a brush from the top of Maggie's nightstand and ran it through her hair so fiercely it crackled as if in protest. In the reflection, her eyes found her sister's and for a split second Maggie thought she saw a glimmer of hatred, a dark glimpse of guile that made Maggie's blood turn to ice, but it disappeared in a flash, and she thought she'd imagined it.

'I don't know about you, Maggie,' Mary Theresa continued, 'but I can't stand all this . . . this wallowing in pain and self-pity and grief. It's not that I don't miss Mitch, but . . . but I've got a life to live.' With that she dropped the brush, turned on her heel, and walked briskly out of the room. End of subject. End of grief. End of memories.

Maggie hadn't been able to believe it. She'd sunk onto a corner of the bed, feeling broken and bleeding. If only she could pull herself together as easily as M.T. apparently had. Instead she'd sat motionless for nearly half an hour, the minutes ticking by as she'd reined in her pain, the bottom of her wet bathing suit dampening her quilt.

Two nights later she worked up the nerve to call Thane. She and her sister were alone in the house. Mary Theresa was asleep, their parents were out, but still Maggie perspired at the thought of getting caught. If Frank Reilly guessed his daughter was intent on crossing him, he'd ground her for the rest of her life, take away all her privileges. But Maggie didn't care. Crossing her fingers, she prayed she would connect with Thane as she punched out his number. The phone rang four times before he answered, and her heart was going crazy, her pulse pounding in her eardrums.

''Lo?'

At the sound of his voice, still muffled as if he'd been sleeping, her heart skipped a beat or two. She was desperate to see him again.

Since her parents had decided the ranch was off-limits for a while and she couldn't go anywhere where she might have contact with him, she suggested that they meet after she was finished working the late shift at Roberto's the following night. If she worked things right, they might be able to sneak away for an hour or two.

Her silly heart had soared when Thane, after listening to her plan, had said, 'You're on, Mag Pie. I'll see ya then.'

On cloud nine for the first time since the funeral, she tiptoed to her sister's room and shook Mary Theresa by the shoulder. She had to let her in on the scheme, as M.T. was supposed to pick her up from Roberto's around ten. Yawning, a little grouchy from being aroused, Mary Theresa had agreed to being an accomplice before pulling her pillow over her head and falling back to sleep.

Maggie hadn't slept a wink. The thought of seeing Thane again had been too exhilarating. She'd been up at the crack of dawn, swum laps, and even cleaned her room to keep busy; but still the day had dragged by until she arrived at the restaurant.

Everything was as it should be. Roberto's was busier than usual for a Saturday night; families and couples crowded into the waiting area until tables were available. Maggie flew through her shift, clearing tables, carrying tubs of dishes into the kitchen, replacing silverware, filling water glasses as the hours rolled onward.

Around nine-thirty business began to slow. Nervously, she watched the entrance and at about a quarter to ten, Thane swung through the front door. Dressed in clean jeans and a wheat-colored polo shirt, he sauntered through the vestibule and scanned the connecting rooms until his gaze landed full force on Maggie. She nearly dropped the plastic tub of clean silverware wrapped in napkins she was carrying to the servers' station. He winked, her heart soared, and, cheeks burning, she managed a ghost of a smile.

'Maggie!' Enid whispered harshly. 'Table three. Step on it.'

'I'm on it,' she muttered, embarrassed and feeling all thumbs as she swiped the table clean, set out fresh silverware, checked to see that the condiment jars were filled, then adjusted the placement of wineglasses on the table, a job she could usually do blind-folded. In her peripheral vision she saw Thane walk into the bar and take control of a stool at the corner of the mahogany counter. From this vantage point, he could look over a short wall topped by planters filled with lacy ferns and view the dining area where she worked.

He ordered a beer and waited.

For the remainder of the shift Maggie was so aware of him, she had trouble concentrating. She felt his eyes upon her, anticipated spending time with him, looked forward to kissing him, and blushed when she thought of what they would eventually do together. She wanted to bury herself in his strength; to lose herself in him; and fantasizing of making love to him, she had twice filled a glass to overflowing, nearly spilling ice cubes and water on a wasp-thin woman with a severe expression and too much lipstick. Red-faced, Maggie swabbed up the mess and mentally called herself several kinds of fool.

The clock inched laboriously onward and the dinner crowd thinned. Just after ten, she was pocketing her tips, untying her apron and trying to keep control of her rapidly escaping emotions. She hadn't seen Thane in weeks, and the thought of being with him again caused her throat to turn to sand.

'See ya tomorrow,' she promised Enid and Walter, waving to them as she hurried across the foyer. Thane left some bills on the bar and climbed down from his stool. His heart-stopping smile was just stretching over his jaw when the front door of the restaurant was flung open to bang into the wall.

Maggie nearly ran into her father.

'Dad.'

'Hi, Mag.' Frank Reilly's eyes held no hint of amusement as he stared at his daughter just long enough to tie her tongue, then sent his gaze up the two wooden steps to the bar, where Thane was standing. 'Get into the car,' he ordered his daughter.

'No, Dad. Wait a minute.'

'Get in the car, now, unless you want things to get worse,' he ordered.

'No.' For the first time in her life Maggie stood up to the man who had sired her.

'Maggie — ' Her father's voice was deep, filled with authority. 'Don't defy me. Not here.'

'I'm going with Thane,' she said, and started for the bar.

Thane was down the wooden steps in an instant. 'What's going on here?'

'I forbade my daughter from seeing you, Walker, and I told her that if she ever did, I would make your life a living hell.' Shorter by three inches, bristling with authority and a hot rage, Frank glared upward at the younger man. 'I could ruin you, you know.'

The door opened. Two couples, laughing and talking, smelling of cigarette smoke and booze, careened into the lobby.

'Dad, please — '

'I said, 'Get into the car, Maggie.''

'Not unless she wants to.' Thane reached forward, the fingers of his hand surrounding her forearm, his grip crushing the sleeve of her white blouse as he claimed her. 'She and I are going out.'

'Over my dead body. She's seventeen, Walker. Still a minor.' His nostrils flared in rage. 'Like I said, 'hell.''

'Hey, what's going on here?' The manager, Ted, menus tucked under one arm, shot out of the double doors leading to the kitchen. 'Maggie, is there a problem?'

'I don't give a damn what you do.' Thane's eyes, like those of a hawk finding prey, zeroed in on her father. He tugged on her arm. 'Come on, Maggie.'

'Who're you?' Ted demanded.

'Oh, whoa!' One of the guys in the group of new customers stopped short and held up his hands, palms outward as he started to back away.

'Hey, sister, don't take any shit,' his woman friend advised Maggie, and the other couple laughed nervously. Heads of the patrons at the nearest tables swiveled in their direction, and the soft buzz of quiet conversation seemed to disappear. The clink of silverware became more indistinct as everyone, it seemed, turned to watch the drama unfold.

'I don't know what's going on here,' Ted said, keeping his voice low. 'And I don't really care. Just leave. All of you.'

'I'm calling the police.' Her father started for the pay phone.

'Good.' Ted was in complete agreement. 'You do that, fella. Now — ' He turned. Smiling, he faced the suddenly somber party of four who had just entered. 'May I help you?'

'Let's get outta here,' Thane suggested, but Maggie's eyes were riveted to her father as he reached the pay phone and fumbled in the front pocket of his slacks for change.

'No. I — I can't.' She yanked her arm away

from Thane's possessive grip. She knew her father too well. He would do exactly as he warned — make sure that Thane was ruined, professionally or personally. It didn't matter to him. When Frank Reilly felt backed into a corner, he was ruthless. A poor kid from Pittsburgh who had been a street fighter in his youth and risen to the rank of sergeant in the army, he did what he felt he had to do to survive. He'd stepped on anyone who'd gotten in his way in his climb up the corporate ladder and never once looked back.

'I . . . I'll talk to you later,' she promised Thane.

'No, Maggie, you won't.' Frank, hearing her compliance, shoved his coins into his pocket again and, with a triumphant glare at Thane, shepherded his daughter out of the restaurant. 'You contact that son of a bitch again, and I'll throw you out without a dime.' At the door of the Mercedes his shoulders slumped a bit. 'No, I wouldn't. You know that. But, please, give yourself some time to grow up, will you? Believe me, there are a dozen Thane Walkers on every street corner. You deserve better. It's my job to see that you get the best. Hop in.' He held the door for her, and she felt sick, knew deep in her heart that she'd not only let Thane down, but herself as well. She might never see him again.

'I think I know what's best for me,' she said, staring out the window. Thane had walked outside the restaurant, paused to light a cigarette and stare at the Mercedes.

'How could you?' Her father slid behind the

wheel and paused before starting the well-tuned engine. 'You're just a kid.' Jabbing the keys into the ignition, he paused again, took a deep breath, and in the dark interior cast her a worried look. 'In a few years, you can do anything you damned well please. Your mother and I won't stop you, but right now, you still need some guidance.'

With a flick of his wrist the engine sparked, purring fitfully. Frank backed out of the parking space. 'Look, honey,' he said, the last vestiges of his rage stripped away, 'we've all been through a lot lately. Mitch . . . ' He shook his head. ' . . . let's just take things slow, okay?' He reached over and patted her knee. 'You've got the rest of your life to find the right guy. And I guarantee you in six months, you'll wonder what you ever saw in Thane Walker.'

* * *

Truer words had never been spoken. Within six months she'd learned to hate his name. Or so she'd tried to convince herself. And now she was on the road to Denver with him, trying to work with the man who had betrayed her as well as figure out what had happened to her sister, his ex-wife, the glue that seemed to bring them together, yet was always pushing them apart.

'I remember the last time we tried to get together,' she said as she used one finger to wipe the condensation from the inside of the passenger-door window.

'At the restaurant. Roberto's.'

She nodded.

'You didn't return my calls after that.'

'Wasn't allowed.'

In the dark interior of the truck he scowled. 'You could have done anything you wanted to do.'

'I wasn't like you,' she argued. 'I didn't just take the bull by the horns.'

'You know, Maggie, it's more than taking the bull by his horns. Once you've got him, you have to dig your bootheels in the dirt, stop that sucker dead in his tracks, and twist hard, throw your back into it so that the curve of his neck forces him to the ground.' He slid her a look that spanned a lifetime of making it on his own. 'That's when you win. When you survive. The way I remember it, you were pretty tough for a city girl, ready to spread your wings if not tackle bulls. But you weren't afraid to speak your mind. Oh, hell.' He eased on the brakes and guided the truck around what appeared to be an abandoned vehicle with snow piled high on its fenders, hood, and roof. 'What's this?'

Thane parked the pickup and, with Maggie following in his footsteps, made his way to the snow-covered sedan. The air was bitter cold, a stiff breeze slicing through Maggie's jacket and stinging her cheeks.

'Anyone in there?' Thane yelled, banging on the car and shoving off the snow with his gloved hands until they could peer through the glass to the dark interior. It was empty, no sign of life within. Thane scanned the terrain of flatland, sagebrush, and fence posts covered in a thick layer of icy white powder. 'Hey!' he shouted, squinting at the horizon as Maggie did the same. 'Anyone out here?'

Using her hand as a visor, she scoured the sparse terrain and caught sight of several antelope dashing off in the distance, startled by the sound of a human voice. Otherwise, she saw no movement, not so much as a rabbit disturbing the stillness. The sky was gray again — the color of a dove's soft underbelly, thick clouds blocking the sun.

For a few minutes they shouted and searched the area around the car. No other vehicle passed, and they found no sign of life anywhere nearby. 'Come on,' Thane finally said. 'No one's here.'

'At least no one who's alive,' she muttered, again thinking of her sister.

'No one dead, either. Whoever was driving obviously got a ride.' He took her elbow in his big hand and propelled her toward the truck. 'I think it's time to crack open the thermos. Coffee, crackers, and cheese. What d'ya say?'

She rolled her eyes. 'You sure know how to make a girl feel pampered.'

'Always aim to please.' He offered her a wink as he held her door open, and that one small gesture lifted her mood a bit. There was a part of Thane she remembered as being charming in an irreverent, rebellious way. Along with his wicked smile and tough-as-old-leather exterior, there had once been a man with a heart. That part of him had gotten to her then, and she was afraid, if she wasn't careful, it would get to her again, and she might forget about the darker, secretive side of him that had always given her pause. The man he never let shine through.

As he drove ever south, she poured them each a cup of coffee from the thermos and handed him a mug. 'You haven't explained the situation with Mary Theresa,' she reminded him, sipping from the hot, strong coffee.

'It began as a simple case of mistaken identity, you know that.'

She'd heard this much but never had believed it.

'She showed up at my place, that old barn converted into living quarters just out of Rio Verde.'

She remembered, though she'd only visited him once.

'I'd been drinking — hell, that's putting it lightly — I was on a bender. Decided that you and I were through after the scene in the restaurant, so I went out and tied one on. Nearly passed out on the bed, then she — though I thought it was you — let herself in.'

'And you couldn't tell the difference?' Even after all these years, Maggie still felt a stab of betrayal that sliced deep into her heart.

His lips tightened until they showed white over his teeth. 'Nope.'

'Thanks for stroking my female ego.'

'You wanted the truth.'

Amen, she thought, *no matter what the cost*. 'Am I getting it?'

'In spades. It was late. Dark. I didn't bother locking the door.' He snorted, his face a mask of self-derision. 'So I'm passed out in the bed and she shows up smelling like you, tasting like you, looking like you. As I said, the only light was the moonlight streaming through the open blinds.'

'And you couldn't help yourself.'

'I thought she was you, damn it,' he admitted, remembering waking up to find Maggie next to him, her body warm and willing, her lips and tongue hungry. There had been something different about her, something he'd sensed, but she wore her hair in a ponytail and in the poor light he saw no hint of makeup, no trace of the pinup girl Mary Theresa was always trying to portray. 'At least I did at first.'

'Maggie?' he'd whispered, his body already responding, his erection hard and stiff, his mind still groggy.

'Shh. I'm here,' she'd answered, and kissed him with wet and wild abandon. That had been the end of any resistance on his part.

He'd stripped the rubber band from her hair, started touching her breasts, thrilled that they seemed larger in his hands. The kissing was different, more anxious and desperate. At the time, his brain still soaked in scotch, he was vaguely aware that there was a slight change, but he chalked it up to the length of time they'd been apart, the ache between his legs that had kept him up at night. Her touch had ignited him. His erection had been hard, his blood instantly white-hot.

He'd made love to her, not once, but over and over that night. Somewhere in the back of his mind he'd convinced himself that they would never be together again, that by the light of dawn, Maggie would leave him forever.

It wasn't until she slipped from the bed that he sensed his mistake. 'What's this?' she'd asked, rubbing a finger over the scar he bore on his left shoulder.

'You remember, I told you about it . . . my old man did that the night that I nearly — '

'Oh, right.' She slid quickly off the bed, and Thane sensed the change in her.

With one eye open, he watched her dress, and a sick realization needled through the painful clouds in his mind. The scotch had worn off and aside from a blistering headache, he was able to think again. As she wound her hair into a ponytail, he noticed the difference and, at first, telling himself he was out of his mind, he lay on the wrinkled sheets, opened both damned eyes and stared up at her.

She zipped her shorts and the tiny prickle of apprehension he felt turned to a needle of dread. With bone-chilling certainty he watched as her left hand adjusted the zipper tab and slid the button through its hole.

'What the hell do you think you're doing?' he asked, his voice dead and filled with all of the suspicions that were suddenly racing like fire through his brain.

'What do you mean?' So innocent. Had he been wrong? She reached for her purse. Maggie's fringed suede bag.

'You're not Maggie.'

She paused, then shook her head. 'You're drunk.'

'Nope.'

She glanced at the opened bottle of scotch on his bedside table. 'Whatever you say.'

'What kind of game are you playing, Mary Theresa?'

She flinched a bit, bit her lip, then slowly extracted a key ring from her purse. With her *left* hand. The keys jangled over the soft hum of the alarm clock and the muted songs of morning birds that filtered through the open window. 'I'll see you later.'

'Not until you explain yourself.'

'There's nothing to — '

He leaped out of the bed and, bare-ass naked, pushed her up against the wall. Her back and shoulders flattened against the plaster.

'Oh! Damn it, Thane! What the hell do you think you're doing?' she demanded as his fingers gripped hard.

'That's what I asked you.' Nose to nose, eyeball to squinted eyeball, they glared at each other. 'I know you're not Maggie,' he said, disgusted with himself and the fact that even though he knew the truth, with her pinned against the wall, her perfume teasing his nostrils, the hard muscles of her body flexing defiantly against his weight, he was beginning to get turned on again. His brain was pounding, his eyes burning, the impending hangover parching his mouth as the thought of what he'd done dehydrated his soul. 'You goddamned slut.'

'Careful, Thane,' she warned and Frank Reilly's threats echoed through his pained head. If anyone found them here, him naked and strong-arming her, she playing coy, fragile, and underage, what would happen? The police would be called in and he had a record, a bad one . . . if they located it in Wyoming . . . Slowly he let his arm drop and stepped away from her.

'Get out.'

'Gladly.' She flashed him her thousand-watt smile, and he had the distinct impression that he'd been set up. Big-time. By a master.

'This is between us.'

'Believe me, I won't say a word.' She walked out of the bedroom, and he followed her as she made her way past a pile of dirty clothes and a few lawn chairs that he used for furniture. She wrinkled her nose and shook her head at the sorry state of his home. Not that he gave a good goddamn. Any money he didn't use, he saved and invested. He intended to buy a spread of his own someday. Furniture and the amenities could wait.

'Maggie will never know,' he said as she reached the door.

Her hand paused over the doorknob. 'Unless you tell her.'

'What's this all about, Mary Theresa?'

She looked over her shoulder, her eyebrows raised, her face as beautiful as that of her sister. Thane's guts ached with the depth of his betrayal. 'It's personal,' she said, and breezed through the door in a cloud of Maggie's perfume.

He heard the sound of a car's engine being fired, then the chirp of tires. 'Good riddance,' he muttered, sick at what had transpired between them. But it was over. He'd never have to face her again.

Or so he'd thought.

But he'd been wrong. Dead wrong.

A month later she turned up pregnant.

11

'So you couldn't resist making love to her.' Maggie had settled down in the seat, her head propped on the backrest as the city of Denver came into view. Sprawled at the base of the Rocky Mountains, concrete and glass skyscrapers stretched far and wide, rivaling the snow-covered peaks in their ascent to the sky.

Thane's eyebrows slammed together. 'I couldn't resist making love to *you*,' he said, and the interior of the cab seemed suddenly close. 'Remember?'

All too well. Her heart ached with old, never-forgotten pain. 'Mary Theresa wasn't me.'

'I said, I made a mistake.' He shifted down as he approached the traffic-snarled city. 'If it's any consolation, I paid.' Glancing at Maggie, he added, 'Being married to your sister wasn't a picnic.' A shadow flickered through his eyes and she sensed it was concerning the child he'd never seen born. Silent memories were ghosts between them, dark spirits of distrust and deceit.

'I don't know why she impersonated you that night,' he admitted as he turned onto a side street. 'I asked, of course, more than once, but she always just lifted a shoulder and said she really didn't understand it herself, that she just wanted to see if she could fool me.' He shifted down and slowed as a stoplight turned from amber to red. Pedestrians wrapped in thick coats, scarves, and hats crossed in front of the truck, their booted feet moving quickly. 'But I've always suspected it was something more . . . something deeper.'

Maggie shivered inwardly. 'No one understands why Mary Theresa does anything,' she whispered, ignoring the frigid sense of dread determinedly crawling up her spine. She had an inkling of something dark and sinister, a facet of Mary Theresa that she'd never known and a side that Thane, as M.T.'s husband, had seen more often than not. Wrapping her arms around herself, Maggie added, 'I hate to say it, but I think Mary Theresa understands her motives less than any of us do.'

The light changed, and Thane stepped on the accelerator. 'Anyway,' he continued without much inflection, 'she showed up, stripped, got into bed with me, and I made the mistake of thinking she was you. In the morning I figured out that I'd been duped, but by that time it was too late. The damage was done. She called me a few weeks later and told me she was pregnant. She laid the choices out to me. Either I married her or she would get an abortion. I picked the first option. But I did think I owed you an explanation. That's why I drove to your house that night. Remember?'

Oh, yeah, she remembered all right. In vivid Technicolor. As she gazed through the windshield to the snow-covered streets, Maggie didn't see the bustle of the city, the pedestrians or traffic or high-rises; instead her sight turned inward and she recalled that night as if it had happened just this past week.

She'd been swimming laps in the backyard pool, cutting through the water, strong and steady. The day had been warm with the heat of late summer. As she reached the edge, she slowed, stood, and, gulping air, had pushed her hair from her face. As she caught her breath, she recognized the distinctive rumble of an ancient engine without much of a muffler attached. Her heart jolted. Thane! His truck was chugging up the drive. *Dear God, what is he doing here?* Her father would kill him!

She scrambled out of the pool.

The engine died.

Grabbing her towel, she ran past the hot tub and oleander hedge, her bare feet scraping on the gravel path. As she rounded the corner to the front of the house, she realized she was too late. Thane was already inside.

Her stomach clenched.

Cutting through the garage, she rounded the Mercedes and flew through the door to the kitchen.

'What the hell are you doing here?' she heard her father demand. Oh, God. Had Thane bullied his way into the house?

'Where's Maggie?' Thane's voice. Hard. Demanding.

Her heart tore into a thousand pieces. She was through the kitchen like a shot. 'Thane?'

'Get out, Walker,' her father ordered. They were standing, toe-to-toe, glaring at each other in the wide foyer on the other side of the living room. Shiny-leafed philodendrons and prickly cacti were clustered near the door to soften the austere plaster walls and tile floor, but now the air was charged, the smell of a fight destroying any sense of warmth or ambience.

Beneath his neatly pressed pin-striped suit, crisp white shirt, and spotless tie, Frank's muscles were coiled, and he was itching to throw a punch.

'I just want to talk to your daughter.' Thane's gaze traveled past the older man's shoulder as Maggie entered the living room. He looked like he'd been to hell and back. Three days of growth shadowed his jaw, and his cheeks were hollow. Worse yet his eyes — those gorgeous blue-gray eyes — were haunted, as if by Satan himself.

Her heart squeezed so hard it ached, and she nearly stumbled as she stared at him. Something was wrong. Horribly and undeniably wrong. In a split second she understood that she didn't want to know what had changed, what demons gnawed at Thane's soul.

'Are . . . are you all right?' she asked in a worried voice that wasn't her own. Her insides were shaking, her stomach roiling.

His jaw slid to one side, and he nodded, but the pain in his eyes, the denial, was all too visible. Maggie thought she might get sick.

'We need to talk.'

'About what?' Her heart was a drum, her palms itchy with sweat, denial screaming through her brain. 'What's wrong?' She was dripping, her hair wet, her face scrubbed free of all makeup. Scared beyond anything she'd ever felt before, she started across the living room.

'I think you'd better go to your room,' Frank

flung over his shoulder. In polished wing tips, he'd rocked to the balls of his feet. His arms were rigid but flexed, his fingers curled into fists. When Thane shifted, Frank was his shadow, blocking his way. 'And you, Walker, take a hint and leave before things get ugly.'

'This'll only take a minute.'

'I don't have a minute to give you.'

'I do.' Maggie swallowed back her fear.

'Good. Meet me in the truck.' Thane's gaze held hers. His fists were clenched until his knuckles showed white, his face etched in determination, though she sensed there was an underlying edge of defeat in his expression, something she didn't understand, something that scared the hell out of her.

'You'll do no such thing, Margaret,' her father interjected, though he was still staring at Thane, sizing him up, squaring off for battle. Maggie had seen that intense expression before whenever he and Mitch had gotten into it.

'It's important.' Thane's jaw tightened to the point that the skin was stretched over his cheeks, hollows pronounced. Bloodless lips barely moved. 'I want to talk to you alone.'

'Leave her alone, Walker,' Frank ordered. 'Take whatever it is you're peddling tonight and leave. Stop sniffing around my daughter. Maggie — go to your room.'

'No!'

Her father's head snapped around. His face was beet red, his eyes malicious slits. 'Don't argue with me.'

But Maggie intended to stand her ground.

'I'm going to talk to Thane, Dad, and you can threaten me up and down, say you're going to throw me out, ground me for the rest of my life, but I want to hear what he has to say.' She inched her chin up a notch and looked at Thane. The desperation in his eyes warned her that whatever it was he wanted to discuss had caused a piece of his soul to chip away.

'This man's a criminal, Maggie. I had him checked out.'

'I don't believe you.' She was suddenly cold to the marrow of her bones and barely noticed the beams of headlights that flashed through the window of the living room, didn't really hear the clank and hum of the garage-door opener as it engaged.

'He put his father in the hospital a few years back, nearly killed him, isn't that right, Walker?'

Thane didn't say a word.

'So you stay away from my daughter, or I'll sic the police on you so fast your head'll swim.'

'Frank?' Bernice was walking into the house from the garage. In one arm she carried a sack of groceries, in the other her purse. 'There's a truck outside. Mary Theresa says it belongs to — oh.' She stopped short. 'I see.'

Two steps behind their mother, Mary Theresa appeared. Her face was pale as death, but there was a little spark of triumph in her eyes. Her gaze skated over Maggie to land full force on Thane.

In that second, Maggie understood.

Her heart plummeted.

Blood thundered in her head. *No, no, no!* she

silently screamed as she caught the intimate, aching glance between Thane and M.T., the type of look exchanged only by lovers. Her stomach turned inside out, and her legs felt like rubber.

'What's going on?' Bernice asked.

'For the love of Christ.' Frank's face had turned the color of ashes.

A dull roar, like the sound of the surf through a cavern, rushed through Maggie's head. She was hot and cold all at once, and she started denying the confession before it passed Thane's lips. 'No — '

'There's something I need to tell you.'

'I . . . I don't want to hear it.' She started from the room, but Thane, quick as a snake striking, sprang past her father and reached forward. Strong, angry fingers captured her arm, whirled her around, forced her to meet the sheer agony etched in the lines near his eyes.

'Just listen to me, Maggie.'

'No, leave me alone — '

'You heard her, Walker! That's it; Bernice, call the police!'

'No,' Mary Theresa whispered. 'Mom, don't.'

Their mother's face slackened in painful realization. 'Would someone please tell me what's going on here?'

'Mary Theresa and I are getting married,' Thane said.

'*What?*' Bernice demanded, her voice low and aching.

'You'll have to kill me first!' Frank advanced, only to be stopped dead in his tracks by a look from Thane that would halt an advancing army.

Married? Maggie shook her head. Had she heard wrong? *Married?* All her own silly fantasies of loving Thane, of sleeping with him, of marrying him and bearing his children shattered as surely as fragile china on stone. Her throat was hot, tears filled her eyes, and with more strength than she thought was in her body, she yanked and pulled, trying to wrest free from his grip. 'I — I don't want to hear this. I don't believe it.'

'Believe it.'

'I — I can't.'

The fingers on her arm grasped harder, inflicting the same amount of pain reflected in Thane's eyes.

'Leave me alone.'

'You heard her,' Frank said, but some of the starch had left his spine; his shoulders slumped as if he realized for the first time the weight of what was happening.

'There's a baby, Maggie,' Thane admitted. 'My baby.'

A squeal of pure, animal agony ripped through the house, and only when Maggie's legs gave way did she realize that the horrible cry came from her own throat. Thane caught her and held her close as tears rained from her eyes.

'I'm sorry, Maggie,' he said in full view of her twin and parents. His lips whispered against her wet hair. 'Jesus Christ, I'm so sorry.'

'Let go of me.' She started to struggle, sick with herself for the feelings of love that still lingered in her heart and tortured her soul. She should hate him. Detest him. Spit in his face.

'Just listen.'

'Go to hell.' She broke free, and, feeling like a fool in her bathing suit, her chest rising and falling in fury, her towel dangling from her neck to the floor, she managed to lift her chin and glare at him. 'Don't ever . . . ever touch me again. Ever!'

Stumbling, feet leaden and unsteady, she scrambled out of the room, and when her gaze swung to Mary Theresa's, she thought she saw a glimmer of satisfaction beneath the shining veneer of her sister's regretful tears.

Stomach threatening to upchuck, she managed to grab hold of some rags of her dignity and, with her back ramrod stiff, hustled down the hallway to her room, shut the door slowly, and headed for the bathroom, where she locked both doors and somehow managed to splash cold water over her face before the abdominal pains hit.

Gale-force cramps struck. Maggie doubled over, becoming so sick she threw up and shook, heaving, crying, feeling that she was about to die, and not really giving a damn either way.

Thane and Mary Theresa? Oh, God. Let me die right now and end this, she silently prayed. *A baby? Mary Theresa is going to have Thane's child?*

She heard the sound of shouts from the living room, then running footsteps as, presumably, Mary Theresa raced to the sanctuary of her room. Within seconds someone was pounding on the bathroom door. Bam! Bam! Bam!

'Let me in, Maggie,' Mary Theresa begged. 'Oh, God, I made a mistake. A horrible, horrible mistake.' Her fist thudded against the door. 'Let me in. Please.'

Maggie ignored her. Whatever happened to her sister wasn't any of her concern. Soon she'd leave Rio Verde for good, and she vowed never to return.

'If I could do it all over again, I swear, this would never have happened!' Again the pounding, resounding through Maggie's brain, echoing in her heart. 'Maggie, please, let me in!'

Never, Maggie thought, flushing the toilet as her stomach, emptied of dinner, heaved again. This time nothing but bile spewed from her throat.

'Go away!' she cried.

Thane and her sister. Oh, Jesus.

I'm sorry. I don't even love him, Mary Theresa cried, and for the first time Maggie heard the difference between the words that passed over her lips and tongue to the 'voice' that only she could hear. *Maggie, please. I love you. Oh, God, I'm so sorry, I love you!* Sobbing erupted from the other side of the door, and the pounding became more feeble.

Maggie curled into a fetal position on the cold tile of the floor, closed her eyes and her ears. The world spun, and the words of an old Beatles' song, 'Yesterday,' reeled through her mind.

That was the last time Maggie had seen Thane for a long while. He and Mary Theresa had married the day after she and Maggie had turned eighteen and the ceremony had been private, just the two of them, in Reno, Nevada.

Now, so many years later as they wound through the heart of the city of Denver, Maggie thought it strange that she and Thane were together again, looking for the woman whom they had both once loved, the very woman who had torn them apart.

'Mary Theresa made it sound like you and she never saw each other again.'

'We do. Just not a lot. In fact the last time wasn't all that pleasant.' His lips compressed as he drove around a car that was attempting to park on Larimer Square where redbrick warehouses and buildings built before the turn of the century had been incorporated into shops, galleries, and restaurants. Maggie barely noticed.

'Why not?'

'We had a fight.'

'About?' she asked, incredulous.

'Money, for the most part. The argument got out of hand. We were at her house and a neighbor overheard it. That's why the cops think I have something to do with her disappearance.'

'Did — did you threaten her?' Maggie asked, still disbelieving.

'I might have.'

'Might have? Are you crazy? *Might* have?' She shook her head. 'Listen, Thane, you've got to be straight with me. What the devil was this about?'

He hesitated a split second as he edged his truck around a minivan that had decided to stop in a loading zone. 'Mary Theresa wanted to borrow money from me. It's not important.'

'If the police think you're a suspect, I'd say it

was damned important.'

'Didn't you ever fight with your husband?' he asked suddenly. 'You were separated, gonna get a divorce, right?' She nodded, some of the wind stolen from her sails. 'That's the way it was between Mary Theresa and me.'

'But you kept seeing her.'

'Not like you'd think. It usually was a case of Mary Theresa just showing up. No notice, no phone call beforehand. She just appears. Most of the time at the ranch in California when she needs to get away. Sometimes I'm there. Once in a while she comes up to Cheyenne, but not often.' He glanced at her and added, 'It's never been romantic between Mary Theresa and me, Maggie. Never. Even when we were married. There was lust at first, yes. Lust and guilt, but once the lust wore off, it was just regret. We didn't have much in common. Still don't.'

'But she's still in contact with you. I don't understand.'

One side of his mouth lifted in a cynical smile. His eyes darkened a shade. 'That makes two of us. Your sister is a complicated and screwed-up woman, Mag. She . . . ' He shook his head. 'She always plays both ends against the middle.' He hesitated, as if searching his own dark soul. 'It's hard to explain, but there are times when she needs something — a place to hide, I guess. Sometimes she's just broken up with a boyfriend, or there are problems at work or whatever. She just has to get away.'

'So she runs to you?' Maggie asked, incredulous. Could she have been fooled for so long? True, Mary Theresa was an actress, but why would she keep Maggie in the dark?

'Not to me. Usually to the ranch outside of Sonoma.' He lifted a shoulder. 'For some reason she thinks of it as kind of a sanctuary.'

'I didn't know.' But there was so much she didn't understand about her twin, so much she never would.

'She has a room there,' he admitted. 'It's the same one she had when we were married.'

'When you were married?' she repeated and wondered why he was trying to con her. Her temper, always at ready, kicked in. 'Do you expect me to believe that you didn't sleep with your wife?'

'Not after she lost the baby. We were still renting the place then, before I scraped together enough money for a down payment. Mary Theresa moved out of our bedroom and usually locked the door. Sometimes . . . she'd change her mind, for whatever reason, probably to keep me on a short leash. Hell, who knows with that woman, but then she'd come knockin' on my bedroom door, and I always opened it.' His jaw tightened, and his eyes narrowed a fraction, as if he was disgusted at his own particular brand of weakness. 'Intimacy, if you could call it that with your sister, was always on her terms.' He lifted an eyebrow. 'I take it she didn't tell you.'

'No.' *But then I didn't ask. I didn't want to know anything about your life with her*. Folding her arms over her chest, Maggie glared out the window and refused to be saddened by something that had happened years ago.

'Believe me, there's a lot she probably didn't let you know about her life and you might not like it. She had a dark side, Maggie.'

'Don't we all?' she tossed back, unable to stop herself.

'Not like her. Brace yourself. You might be about to find out things about your sister you didn't want to know.'

'I think I already have.'

The police station loomed before them, and Thane, his countenance grim, his expression harsh and unforgiving, parked the truck in a parking lot that had been cleared of snow. With a glance at her, he reached for his hat. 'It's now or never.'

'Let's go.' She didn't want to waste another second.

They walked together along the snow-crusted street, past people dressed in anything from business suits to Western jeans and denim jackets to ski coats and stocking caps. A television van was pulling up as they climbed a few steps. Thane held the door to the station open for her, and, within minutes, they were ushered upstairs to Detective Reed Henderson's office, two Styrofoam cups of coffee warming their hands, the detective himself seated behind a battered metal desk overflowing with files, notes, and scattered papers. If there was any rhyme or reason to his method of doing business, Maggie couldn't figure it out.

He'd been gentleman enough to introduce himself, shake her hand, offer her a chair, and order coffee from an underling, but the eyes in his hound-dog of a face didn't show the slightest bit of warmth.

'So you still haven't heard from your sister?' he said as Maggie, cradling her cup in fingers that were still cold, noticed a picture of Mary Theresa on the bulletin board behind him. Her throat constricted. Despite all the pain, they were still blood kin — twins. So where was her sister? What had happened to the flamboyant and wild Marquise?

She licked suddenly dry lips. 'No. Not a word.' Well, aside from that one desperate nonvocal plea for help. But she didn't mention that. Wouldn't. If she did, Henderson would probably have her evaluated by some kind of criminal psychologist on the force. Avoiding the detective's eyes, she took a sip from the weak coffee in her cup.

'And you?' He lifted one eyebrow in Thane's direction.

'Nope. Stopped by the ranch on the way here. No messages.'

Nodding as if he expected no more, Henderson tented his hands and looked over the tops of squared-off fingers. 'So you went all the way to Idaho to pick up your ex-sister-in-law.'

'Yep.' Thane lifted a shoulder. 'Didn't want her to have to face you alone.'

'Any other reason?'

'Nope,' he drawled. 'Just here for moral support.'

'So you're a do-gooder, Walker?' Henderson said skeptically, his expression doubtful.

'Nah.'

'Didn't think so.'

Maggie felt the tension in the air, the antagonism between the two men. Obviously neither trusted the other. Nor, come to think of it, did she.

'So I take it you don't know any more than when you called me,' Maggie said, her spirits sinking. She hadn't realized until this moment that she was expecting good news upon her arrival in Denver, had hoped that Mary Theresa would have shown up, flustered, tired from a hastily planned trip to who-knew-where, but pleased and amused that she'd caused a stir.

No such luck.

'Nothing more,' the detective admitted. 'She's still missing, as is one of her cars — a Jeep Wrangler, so we think she went somewhere. This could all be a mistake, I suppose, but the fact that she didn't show up for the taping of her talk show; stood up Ambrose King, her agent, who had flown here from L.A. to talk to her about her career; and has been incommunicado since last Friday, suggests that something might have gone wrong.'

'What?' she asked, her temper flaring again. She was tired, hungry, and angry that there wasn't any more information than before.

'That's what we intend to find out.'

'Have you talked to all her friends? Her . . . her boyfriend? Her boss? Her hairdresser, her personal trainer, her . . . ' She let her words fall away.

'Everyone we know of. I was hoping you could come up with some other people she might have contacted.' He glanced over Maggie's shoulder and, using two fingers, motioned to someone hovering on the other side of the door to come in. Maggie glanced behind her as a petite woman with platinum-blond hair and an upturned nose sauntered into the room. 'This is my partner, Hannah Wilkins. Maggie McCrae. I think you and Mr. Walker have already met.'

Thane tilted his head and started to climb to his feet, but Hannah waved him back into his chair. Her eyes hadn't left Maggie. 'So you're the twin sister. I guessed as much.' Hannah shook Maggie's hand, glanced at the picture on Henderson's bulletin board, and shook her head. 'You're a dead ringer for her.'

'Not quite,' Maggie replied, a little uneasy at the woman's intense scrutiny.

'I doubt that many people can tell you apart.'

Not even the man I loved. Maggie sensed Thane's gaze touch hers for a heartbeat, before he took a swallow from his cup.

'Let's bring in another chair,' Henderson suggested, but Hannah shook her head.

'I'm fine. Been sitting all morning.' As if she anticipated Thane offering her his chair, she sent him a steely glance. 'Really. Thanks.' She leaned against the filing cabinet. 'This is perfect.'

'Whatever.' Henderson shuffled through some of the mess of papers on his desk. 'We were hoping you could fill in some blanks for us, Ms. McCrae.'

Maggie leaned back in her uncomfortable chair. 'Sure . . . I mean, whatever . . . ' There was no reason to fight these people, at least not yet.

Though Henderson might not care as much as she for Mary Theresa's safety, he appeared thorough, earnest, and though probably overworked and cynical, had a wealth of information, manpower and technology at his fingertips. So what did it matter if his desk looked like a three-year-old had done his filing?

'Good. Now tell me about your sister and your relationship with her.' The most gossamer of smiles touched his lips. 'I think we've already established the fact that you're twins.'

She glanced at the picture of Mary Theresa pinned to the bulletin board. Yes, they were twins, but she was a pale, washedout version of the vibrant woman smiling in the slick publicity shot. Maggie's head pounded; she was tired and worried sick. 'Yes, we're twins. Identical, but mirror image. Mary Theresa — well, Marquise — is left-handed and I'm right. There are other characteristics as well, nothing quite as obvious. Anyway, she and I lived with our parents in Rio Verde, California; that's about an hour or so north of San Francisco, not too far from Sonoma.' Maggie explained about growing up in their family, about her parents' and Mitch's deaths. Once in a while Detective Henderson broke in with a question or comment and even more rarely Detective Wilkins did the same, clarifying a point here and there.

They didn't ask about her affair with Thane. She didn't mention it. There didn't seem to be any reason to bring up the painful topic, and she never said a word about her means of silent communication with her sister. Henderson and

Wilkins wouldn't believe her if she did, and anything she might confide in them would be taken with a very jaded grain of salt.

Henderson listened, eyed them both, and once in a while reached for a baseball buried under a manila envelope on his desk, only to ignore it. Hannah Wilkins scratched a few notes on a pad she'd taken from her pocket and small dents appeared between neatly plucked eyebrows as she concentrated. Once in a while she tugged at an earring. All the while Thane didn't offer a word, just sat in his chair, one booted foot propped on the opposing jeans-clad knee, his rawhide jacket open, his arms crossed over his chest, his hat resting on the floor. His face was a mask of patient disinterest, but the flicker of anger in his gaze belied him. Thane Walker was doing a slow, steady burn, one that would eventually ignite like a powder keg.

'So after Mary Theresa married Mr. Walker, here, you and she went your separate ways?'

Maggie's heart beat a painful tattoo. She avoided the detective's probing gaze. 'That's right.'

'You went to the University of California, Davis.'

'Yes.' She nodded. 'Eventually, after two years at a junior college. I studied literature and journalism.'

'And met the man who would become your husband . . . Dean McCrae?'

'Yes — I met Dean at junior college and we both transferred.' Why this embarrassed her, she didn't understand, so she looked up and sighed.

'I finished my B.A., Dean went on to law school, and I worked with a private investigator for a while.'

'Before writing true-crime stories?'

'Yes.'

'One child?'

Maggie nodded and wondered what Becca was doing now. 'A daughter. Rebecca Anne. She was born in April of 1985.' Maggie gave the information out by rote, knowing that it was probably all in the files on the computer as well as buried somewhere in the mess of papers and folders on Henderson's desk.

Henderson checked his notes. 'Your husband died in a car accident about nine months ago?'

She nodded, her heart growing heavy. 'Yes.'

'Single car? He swerved to miss a dog, ran off the road, and down a hillside, where the car hit a culvert.'

Maggie felt her skin crawl at the memory. A sheen of nervous sweat broke out on her back. She couldn't stand to think about the dark days surrounding Dean's death or the guilt that nagged at her when she considered it. 'Yes.'

'You were living in Southern California at the time.'

'Laguna Nigel, yes,' she admitted, clearing her throat. 'We moved there right after Dean got out of law school.'

'I don't see what this has to do with anything,' Thane finally cut in. Tiny brackets surrounded his mouth and he couldn't hide his irritation and impatience.

Henderson ignored him. 'You visited a

psychiatrist after your husband's death?'

'Yes,' she admitted, suddenly more nervous than she had been. Though it had been only natural to visit a grief counselor and psychiatrist, Dean's family had disapproved. Connie had pointed out that Maggie had visited the doctor *before* Dean's death — that she'd been battling depression for months, perhaps years, and that there might be something deeper, a more insidious form of mental illness. Jim had been outwardly suspicious of Maggie's fortitude as well as her morals — what woman, after all, would be insane enough not to want to be married to Dean, no matter what his faults? They hadn't said too much but had quietly disapproved, silently insinuating that Maggie might not be a stable influence for her daughter, which was downright ridiculous. Maggie suspected that their concern for Becca was rooted in a deeper worry about her inheritance, the trust fund that sat gathering interest in Becca's name.

'So you have a history of . . . '

'I had a case of slight depression, that's all.'

'That's all?' Henderson asked, clearly skeptical.

'Wait a minute. What is this?' Thane's boots hit the floor, his pretense of disinterest falling away as quickly as if it had been stripped.

'Just trying to get the whole picture.'

'What does Maggie's marriage have to do with anything?' Nerves strung tight, Thane stood slowly, placed his hands on Henderson's desk, and leaned forward, thrusting his face so close to the detective's that there was hardly any space of daylight between them. 'Listen, Detective, Mary Theresa is missing. We came here to give you information. About her. To help you find her. Maggie doesn't need her life ripped apart in the process.'

Henderson's smile held zero warmth. 'Sit down, Walker.'

Thane hesitated, ground his teeth, and slowly returned to his seat. Eyes narrowed on Henderson, his lips blade-thin, his manner was silently combative.

'I've got a job to do here.' Henderson riffled through his papers. 'But don't worry. We're gonna find your ex-wife. Did you have any contact with your sister recently?'

The muscles in the back of Maggie's neck tightened.

'Not for a few weeks. Five or six,' she said, refusing to think of that one silent cry for help only she could hear.

'Did she mention anything that was out of the ordinary?'

'She was always a little out of the ordinary,' Maggie said. 'That's why she was Marquise.'

'But more than usual? Was she depressed or angry or worried about anything?'

'Just the ratings of her show, I think. We mainly talked about my daughter. Mary Theresa and she were — are — very close.'

'When was the last time she saw your daughter?'

Maggie thought for just a second. 'Last summer. Beginning of July. That's the only time she came up to our place in Idaho.'

'Why?'

'Look, Detective, if you know anything about my sister, you know that a cabin in the woods in the panhandle of Idaho isn't exactly her style. Mary Theresa was never one for . . . roughing it. She's a city girl.'

'But she was married to you?' His gaze swung to Thane, and Maggie sensed the wheels of curiosity were cranking overtime in the detective's mind. Cowboy boots, battle-scarred rawhide jacket, jeans, and a work shirt — Thane wasn't the kind of man Marquise would deign to marry.

'We were young,' Thane explained.

'Opposites attracted?'

'Something like that.'

Maggie felt her cheeks flame. She bit her tongue. There was no reason to discuss what had happened so long ago. It was over. Ancient history. Or was it? Why had Mary Theresa kept in contact with her ex-husband if there was nothing between them? Why had they fought? And why did Thane seem like he was hiding something, a secret that he couldn't confide in her? Somehow she knew that Detective Henderson would ferret it out, one way or another. Though she knew she wasn't under suspicion — well, at least she thought she wasn't — the conversation seemed like an interrogation. Henderson wasn't convinced either she or Thane was telling the truth.

'When was the last time you saw Marquise — er, Mary Theresa?' He glanced at Thane as he rummaged in the top drawer of his desk.

'We discussed this the last time I was here.' Thane's eyes were thunderous.

'I know about the fight at her house,' Henderson said. 'We'll get to that in a minute. But she'd come to see you before then, hadn't she?'

A muscle worked in the corner of Thane's jaw. 'About three or four weeks ago. She'd come up to my ranch in Wyoming.'

'Not far from Cheyenne?'

'Yep.'

Maggie's spine stiffened.

'Any particular reason?' Henderson asked, retrieving a pack of gum and shaking out a stick.

Thane hesitated and rubbed his chin. 'It was unusual, even for her. I think I told you that she sometimes went to my spread in California, but this time she came up to see me. She was having trouble with her job. Ratings and arguments with the guy she worked with.'

'Craig Beaumont?'

'Right.'

'Anything else?' Henderson unwrapped the gum and plopped it into his mouth.

'Nope,' Thane said, and again Maggie felt as if he was hiding something from her. From the detective. Something vital. She couldn't imagine what it was, but she was determined to find out.

'So,' Henderson said, wiggling his pencil and frowning, 'the last time your ex-wife came to visit you, how long did she stay?'

Thane's nostrils flared. 'A while.'

‘How long of a while?’

Maggie sensed something was going on here, something important.

Thane rubbed the back of his neck. ‘Three days,’ he said, his face dead serious. ‘She stayed three days.’

12

Three days?

Thane and Mary Theresa had been alone in his house for three days less than a month ago?

Maggie's heart began to ache, though she didn't understand why. It was as if she'd been lied to, betrayed, all over again. She couldn't help swing her incredulous gaze in Thane's direction. Mary Theresa had been in Cheyenne — in that stark house, sleeping in the small bed in the second bedroom? Or . . . had she been with Thane?

'Were you lovers?' Henderson asked.

'A long time ago.' Thane didn't miss a beat.

'But not recently?'

'No.'

'Yet she came to see you?' Clearly the detective was suspicious. He exchanged a glance with his partner, who scratched another note on her pad.

'Sometimes.'

Henderson reached for his baseball as if he didn't know he was doing it. 'Who else did she go to?' He gave the ball a toss.

'Beats me.'

'Oh, she must've told you something.' Catching the ball, he frowned and set it back in the scratched holder that was molded in the shape of a tiny mitt.

'Nothing that you haven't read in the papers.'

'And you have no idea what happened to her?'
Thane's gaze was rock steady. 'None.'

Henderson said to Maggie, 'I assume you'll be staying in town for a while.'

'Yes. I haven't booked a hotel yet, but when I do I'll call. I want to know what's going on.'

'Then we'll talk again.'

'Wait a minute.' Maggie wasn't through. She hadn't shipped her injured, estranged daughter to Dean's relatives in California, spent the last few days driving through a near blizzard, dealt with the one man who had nearly ruined her life, worried herself sick with her stomach in knots, her life out of kilter, only to show up here without getting a few answers of her own. 'So what're you going to do about finding my sister?'

'Continue the investigation.'

'How?' she demanded. From the corner of her eye she thought she caught the ghost of a smile whisper across Thane's mouth.

'Through diligence, resources, leads . . . it's what we do here, Mrs. McCrae.'

'Diligence?' she said. 'You're checking her credit-card receipts — right? The phone, and bank cards and gas cards? And you've got an APB out for her Jeep as well as her? You've let the radio and television stations know that she's missing and have asked for their help?'

'She works for KRKY. Believe me, the media is informed. They called us when she didn't show up for work and they couldn't get through to her.'

'Are you watching her house? And she has a place . . . near Aspen, where she goes to ski.'

'It's covered, Mrs. McCrae.'

'How about her psychiatrist? She was seeing someone — a woman, I think. Kelly . . . '

'Dr. Michelle Kelly.'

'She might have some idea what was going on in Mary Theresa's mind.'

Henderson stood. 'Trust me, we're doing everything possible to find your sister. Talking to anyone who knew her. We'll find her. The last person to see her that we know of was Mr. Walker here. She had a blowup after taping her program on Thursday, went toe-to-toe with her cohost, then blew off a meeting with her agent, who had flown here from L.A. just to talk to her. Even so, because she's flighty and has a history of being a hothead and a flake, the station wasn't in an out-and-out panic, but they were concerned, sent a news crew out to knock on her door to find her, then started digging. That's when we were contacted. By this time KRKY was all over the story, and the other stations picked up on it. I'm surprised they or Marquise's secretary didn't call you.' He glanced at Thane. 'Ms. Lawrence contacted you, right?'

Thane nodded.

'And the newspeople?'

'They had just started nosin' around when I met with you and decided someone should inform Maggie, face-to-face.'

Henderson motioned to Maggie. 'No one called you but me?'

'No.' Maggie shook her head. 'I don't think so. I was away for the weekend, shopping with my daughter, and my answering machine wasn't hooked up.'

Henderson's eyebrows beetled, as if he didn't quite believe what he was hearing. 'Well, the upshot is that after the station manager, Ron Bishop, down at KRKY got worried and couldn't find her, he and the executive producer for *Denver AM* called down here; we asked him to come in and file a missing-person report and have been investigating ever since.' He riffled through his notes. 'The last person who thinks she recognized your sister was the cashier at a convenience store/gas station where she bought a tank of supreme, a bag of Doritos, and a Diet Coke — all bought with cash from a woman who resembled Marquise. The clerk doesn't remember for certain, thinks there might have been two people in the car — a man and a woman — and she *thinks* it headed west out of town. And there's nothing to prove it. Someone bought those items, but the receipt doesn't show who it was and the clerk might just be jerking our chain, trying to get some publicity or advertising for the mini-mart. There are all kinds of nuts out there. In my opinion, it just doesn't mean a helluva lot. The clerk could be mistaken, or your sister could have pulled a U-turn at the next block, but we're checking every lead.'

'Good.'

'So far we're treating your sister as a missing person, nothing more.'

'You're not concerned with the possibility of foul play?' Thane asked.

'We're concerned, but don't have enough

evidence to prove it.' Henderson's serious mask didn't crack. 'We haven't ruled out homicide or even suicide — '

'Suicide?' Maggie said. 'Mary Theresa would never take her own life. What is this?'

'How well did you know your sister?' Henderson asked, and for the first time in her life Maggie didn't know how to respond.

She and Mary Theresa had grown up so close, but even then they'd been on different paths, and as they'd become adults they'd drifted further and further apart. There were so many secrets, so many lies, so many betrayals. The truth of the matter was that she didn't know Mary Theresa very well. Marquise even less.

'I just don't believe that she would take her own life. Why would you even think such a thing?' She turned worried eyes to Thane.

'She tried once before,' Hannah Wilkins said. 'A year and a half ago.'

'No . . . I don't believe it.'

Henderson lifted a shoulder. 'Her stomach was pumped at Pinehurst Memorial.' He shuffled through the papers on his desk. 'She had enough sleeping pills and antidepressants in her to do the job. But she called nine-one-one in time.'

'Oh, God,' Maggie whispered, then eyed Thane. 'Did you know about this?'

'After the fact.'

'Why didn't anyone tell me?' She was horrified. This was her twin sister; aside from Becca, her only living relative.

'She wanted it kept a secret. From everyone.

Somehow she pulled it off. Hard to do when you're a quasi celeb.' He glanced at Hannah. 'Must have paid off people at the hospital to keep it quiet.'

Maggie shivered. It seemed that almost everyone she held dear to her was gone. Mitch, her parents, and her husband were all dead. Her sister and daughter were both somewhat estranged from her and as for Thane Walker . . . well, he too was lost. Rubbing her arms, she pulled herself together. Right now she had to find Mary Theresa. If she was alive, then they could begin to mend their emotional fences. *If*.

'As I said, your sister wasn't the most stable person around,' Henderson reiterated, and stared at her long enough for Maggie to suspect that he was considering the fact that she, too, had been under psychiatric care at one time. Not that it was a crime or rare. Unless your name was McCrae. 'Then there was the note.'

Cold dread grasped Maggie's heart in icy fingers. 'What note?'

'We found it in the wastebasket by her computer.' Henderson produced a scribbled piece of paper, sheathed in plastic, and Maggie recognized her sister's backhanded loopy style.

I can't take this any longer. No one understands me. No one cares. I should just end it all.

Maggie nearly dropped her half-empty cup of coffee. She couldn't believe it, not Mary Theresa. Never. She was too full of life, too full of herself. 'Anyone could have written that,' Maggie whispered, her voice husky as she stared at the damning note.

'It looks like her handwriting, though.'

Maggie nodded, stunned. Was it possible? She glanced over at Thane, saw denial in his eyes, and remembered her sister's desperate plea. She'd heard it when she'd been alone in the barn. Or had she? Her head began to pound, and she was suddenly exhausted.

Henderson rounded the desk and she thought he was about to escort her out the door; but he paused, swung a leg over the corner of the littered surface, and looked her squarely in the eye. 'This wouldn't be some kind of sick publicity stunt of your sister's, would it? You know the kind, to stir up some interest for her failing show, get her some national media attention, maybe help revive her career?'

The question once would have stunned her, but no longer. An hour ago she would have denied the accusation vehemently, but an hour ago she didn't know nearly what she now did about her sister. Mary Theresa Reilly. Marquise. Thane Walker's ex-wife. Once-upon-a-time Hollywood hopeful. Doting aunt. Twice-married has-been talk-show host who had previously attempted to end her own life. 'I — I don't know,' Maggie answered honestly.

'She has a history of storming off sets, of riling up the public, and pulling this kind of disappearing stunt.'

'I know, but she's always come back.'

'Just before the police were called in, usually.' Henderson flipped open the file and ran his fingers down a typed list. 'When she was acting, she held up production of one of the movies she made by pouting and locking herself in her dressing room, all over a minor scene being cut.'

'That was a long time ago.'

'It cost her a contract.'

'I know.'

'So she took some courses, became a weathergirl, managed to work her way up on the local television-news circuit, then took a job here. Since she's been in Denver she's failed to show up for work on two separate occasions, both times claiming health problems, though the consensus was she was in some kind of contractual dispute and was holding out for more money.'

'I don't know about those.'

Henderson glanced at Thane, who gave a grudging nod.

'She also has a history of drug use.'

'What?' Maggie was out of her chair. Shaking, her head thundering with all this new painful knowledge, she said, 'I don't believe it.'

'Prescription medications. A painkiller for her back, a series of different antidepressants, and something to help her sleep. The same ones she used in the suicide attempt.'

'Dear God.'

He flipped the file closed and tossed it back on the pile covering his desk. 'As I said, your sister has more than her share of problems.'

'We all do,' Maggie said, refusing to be intimidated. 'And Marquise is an actress, a — '

'I don't buy into the sensitive artiste bullshit,

Mrs. McCrae. The way it looks to me, Marquise is a spoiled brat. A beautiful, pampered, emotional basket case.'

Maggie bit back a hot retort. She wanted to argue and shout, to call the detective an ignoramus and an insensitive lout, but she didn't want to aggravate him. Truth to tell, in light of what she'd learned, his description of Mary Theresa wasn't too far off base. 'Do you need anything more from me?'

'That's about it for now.' Henderson focused on Thane for a second, then managed a professional grin that held no warmth whatsoever as he stood and offered Maggie his hand. 'But I might want to talk to you again.'

'Good. Because I'll want to talk to you, too. I expect you to keep me abreast of the situation.'

'Wouldn't dream of anything else. Let me know where you're staying.'

'I will,' she said brusquely, then realized that she was on the defensive though she had no reason to be. Slightly galled, she shook his hand. 'Thanks.'

'You, too.'

Instantly on his feet, Thane squared his hat on his head and gave a curt nod to each of the detectives.

Maggie was out the door in a flash, zipping up her jacket and yanking on her gloves. Thane was right behind her. She walked through the maze of desks and general hubbub of people, officers in uniform, plainclothes detectives, office personnel, and lay people as they found their way to the main lobby and walked outside where the air was cold, the sky a brilliant blue, the sunlight dazzling.

Three reporters hung out on the steps, smoking cigarettes and talking, their breath fogging in the air.

One woman glanced at them. 'Hey — isn't that Marquise?' she heard one whisper to another. Maggie's heart leaped and she turned, looking over her shoulder, hoping to spy her sister when she realized the reporter was staring directly at her. 'Marquise? Where have you been?' A petite Asian woman, bundled in a heavy wool coat, gloves, and a scarf, thrust a microphone in Maggie's face. The cameraman was right behind her, balancing a huge camera on one shoulder and pointing it in her direction.

'I'm not Marquise.'

'No?' The reporter smiled and winked. 'Are you going by Mary Theresa again? Look, everyone at the station has been worried sick — '

'You don't understand,' Maggie cut in. 'I'm not Mary Theresa.' She felt Thane's fingers on her elbow.

'Let's get out of here,' he growled into her ear.

But Maggie stopped short and sensed the other reporters approach her. 'I'm Mary Theresa Gillette's sister. I came to Denver to help locate her.'

'You mean Marquise. You're her sister?' The woman paused, then as if remembering something, 'You're not from around here.' She glanced at a cameraman. 'Tess said something about a twin sister, but no one had tracked her down. You lived in California but moved north

— Montana or . . . Idaho.'

Maggie was stunned. It had been only a few days, but the resources of the press were incredible. So they should be used to find her sister.

'Do you have any idea where she might be?' the Asian woman asked.

'No.'

'She's disappeared before, hasn't she?' This from a tall, thin man wearing a ski parka. Another microphone was shoved under Maggie's nose. 'Do you think foul play was involved?' he asked, eager eyes searching for a story. 'Could she have been kidnapped?'

'No comment,' Thane insisted loudly, then said into Maggie's ear, 'Let's not get into this now.'

'Who're you? The bodyguard?' one reporter demanded as Thane tugged on Maggie's elbow and passersby on the street slowed or craned their necks at the commotion.

'The ex-husband,' another reporter clarified.

'Is she a dead ringer for her sister or what?' Ski Parka asked.

'Please, I'd like to set up an interview with you,' the first woman said. She shoved a business card in Maggie's gloved hand. 'I'm Jasmine Bell. I work at KRKY with Marquise.'

'Later,' Thane said.

The woman leveled Thane with a cool I'm-used-to-men-trying-to-push-me-around gaze. 'I was talking to . . . what's your name?'

'Maggie McCrae.'

'I was talking to Ms. McCrae.' Her dark eyes

found Maggie's while the other reporters inched closer. 'Give me a call.'

'If you'll help me find Mary Theresa.'

'I'd love to. Everyone at KRKY is concerned for your sister's well-being. I'm sure Ron Bishop, the station manager, would be more than willing to get our people and resources more involved.'

'Hey, wait a minute — ' The tall reporter was trying to wedge himself between the two women.

'That's it,' Thane said, his expression unforgiving as he shepherded Maggie toward the truck. 'We're out of here.'

She pulled her arm out of his grip but managed to keep up with him. His stride was longer, but her boots pounded the sidewalk in quick time. Anger coursed through her veins. Damn it, she was sick and tired of his high-handed tactics, as if he knew what was best for her.

Fortunately, the reporters didn't follow, and Maggie did a slow, steady burn. By the time they reached his truck, she was ready to explode. 'You and I better get something straight, Walker.' She jabbed a gloved finger at his nose. 'Just because we're both trying to find out what happened to Mary Theresa doesn't give you the right to tell me what to do, or manhandle me, or embarrass me. Got it?'

His eyes narrowed, and for a second, as he stared down at her, she didn't know if he intended to shake some sense into her or kiss her. For a heartbeat the city seemed to melt away. He reached forward. Her breath caught. She swallowed hard but focused on the thin line of his mouth. His arm grazed her shoulder as he forced a key into the lock and opened the pickup's door.

In a second, the magic moment evaporated.

'Don't hold your breath if you're expecting me to say, 'yes, princess.' The way I see it we're in this together. Equally. I'm not about to take any orders, got that?'

'Equally?' she repeated, flabbergasted. 'You think you've treated me equally with those Neanderthal tactics back on the steps of the police station?' She glared up at him. 'Well, let me tell you something, cowboy, ordering a woman around might work on your ranch or in some outpost in the-middle-of-nowhere Wyoming, but not with me.' She hooked her thumb at her chest. 'Don't push me around.' Climbing into the cab, she added, 'I'm not the kind of woman who wants to be placed on a pedestal or put under some man's thumb, and I never have been. You got this, Walker? I *never* want to be told what's best for me, because I think I can figure it out for myself.'

'Right on, sister,' he mocked, and she nearly came out of her seat. 'Now, Ms. McCrae, is that all?' His expression was unforgiving, his eyes as gray-blue and stormy as a raging sea in winter.

'For now.'

'Well, praise be!' He slammed the door shut and strode to the driver's side, where he slid behind the steering wheel, twisted on the ignition, and pumped the gas pedal. When the truck started, he eased out of the parking lot. 'Where to?'

'Marquise's house.'

'Don't you think it's off-limits?'

'Maybe, but the detective didn't say so, and I just happen to have a key.' She pulled out her key ring and flashed it in front of his eyes.

'You didn't ask.'

'Because I didn't want him to say no. This isn't exactly a game of 'Mother, may I?' So if Henderson has a fit, I can plead innocence or at the very least ignorance.' She wiped some condensation from the passenger side of the windshield with her glove. 'Besides, my sister gave me the key 'in case of an emergency.' I think this qualifies.'

Thane nosed the truck into a slow line of traffic heading for a bridge that spanned Cherry Creek. 'You know, lady,' he said as they eased over the bridge, 'you're more like your sister than I thought.'

She felt an unwarranted jab of disappointment. The more she knew about Mary Theresa, the less she felt she had in common with the woman who had become Marquise. 'From you, I'll take it as a compliment,' she lied.

'Exactly how it was intended.'

'Oh, right.' Unable to hide her sarcasm, she opened her purse, found a pair of sunglasses, and forced them onto the bridge of her nose. She didn't believe him for a moment.

In her estimation, Thane was hiding something. Something big. And she was bound and determined to find out what it was.

* * *

From his viewpoint at an upper-story window, Detective Henderson sipped his coffee around the wad of gum that had grown stale in his mouth. Squinting, he noticed Thane Walker's black pickup meld into the steady flow of traffic. A few seconds later an unmarked police vehicle followed suit, and he felt a little better. He didn't trust Walker, and, if his gut instincts were right, Marquise's twin sister was holding something back, some piece of information.

But then everyone involved was tight-lipped — from Syd Gillette, the second husband, to Wade Pomeranian, Marquise's latest lover — they all seemed to hold a secret. Even Eve Lawrence, Marquise's secretary and a woman who seemed genuinely worried, wasn't anxious to talk to anyone associated with the police department. The same could be said of Craig Beaumont, the cohost of *Denver AM*, who appeared to hold more than his share of grudges against his partner.

Sooner or later, Henderson knew, the truth would come out. It always did. It just took the right amount of digging and a lot of patience and perseverance.

Of all the people associated with the case, Thane Walker bothered him the most. Probably because he'd been in trouble before. Then there was that little domestic dispute that Marquise's neighbor, Jane Stanton, had reported. Too bad the woman had heard only bits and pieces of the conversation, but Walker had threatened Marquise according to the woman. 'If this is one more of your bullshit lies, Mary Theresa, I swear

I'll kill you.' Or so the neighbor who lived alone with six cats was willing to testify. What was that all about? And why was he so damned secretive? His I-don't-give-a-good-goddamn attitude settled like lead in Henderson's gut. 'But why would he want his ex-wife dead?' he muttered to himself.

'That's a good question. He really doesn't have much of a motive, does he?' Hannah had finished scribbling her notes and tucked the pad into a voluminous purse she forever carried with her.

'She does owe him money.'

'How much?' Hannah's head snapped up.

This was news he'd just learned from the county records, news he hadn't yet shared with her.

'A couple of hundred thousand. Closer to two-fifty.'

Hannah whistled low. 'Secured?'

He nodded. 'Second trust deeds on both her houses. About the only collateral the woman had. She was in debt to her pretty neck. If Marquise is dead, he can force a sale against the estate and collect.' Seeing that the tail was neatly and discreetly in place as the unmarked Jeep rounded the corner, he turned and shoved his hands into his pockets.

'Couldn't he do it if she was alive?'

'Oh, yes. But she could fight him; make it messy. Lots of bad publicity and lawyer fees.'

'Does he need the money?'

'Doesn't look that way. The guy has a knack for investments, it seems. Self-made. Worked hard, put money away, got lucky on a couple of real-estate deals. He bought a lot of land in California when the market went bust a few years back. Now that it's turned around, it looks like he's a wealthy man. But who knows?'

'You think he'd find a way to kill her for two hundred grand?' Hannah was skeptical. 'He doesn't strike me as the type.'

'Walker's hiding something. And, unless the convenience store clerk really did see Marquise, Thane Walker was the last person who saw her alive. So, I'll want to talk to Marquise's neighbor again, find out if she remembers anything more about that argument.'

'It'll have to wait. Jane Stanton is visiting her daughter for a couple of days.'

'What?'

'Her daughter had a skiing accident, or something,' Hannah said, flipping the pages of her notebook. 'Jane wanted to see that she was okay. But she should be back by the weekend.'

'Great.' Sometimes it seemed that nothing went right.

Hannah clicked her pen. 'So what do you think Walker's hiding?'

'That's the quarter-million-dollar question, isn't it?' Henderson spit his gum into the trash and still hungered for a cigarette. 'But now at least we know that he's got motive.'

'Still no body.'

That was the good news. Maybe Marquise was alive somewhere. 'Yeah, there's a chance we still could get lucky. She might turn up fit as a fiddle.' But as each day passed, he thought that chance was less and less likely. 'This could be an elaborate publicity stunt, or she could've holed up. Maybe she's hiding somewhere and licking her wounds for some reason. Could be she just needed to get away, or she might have had a bad case of amnesia.'

'The Jeep will turn up.'

'Mmm.' *Unless it's already in a chop shop*. He rubbed a knot out of the tight muscles at the base of his neck, the same damned muscles that always tightened up and gave him a headache whenever he was stressed out. 'What did you think about the sister?'

'I liked her.' Hannah nodded and clicked her pen again, as if she were agreeing with herself.

'Why?'

'Smart. Honest. Down-to-earth. Concerned about Marquise. She handled herself pretty well.'

'You think so?' He usually respected Hannah's opinion, even when it didn't jibe with his own.

'Yeah. Him, I'm not so sure about.'

'Me neither, but tell me, as a woman, what do you think about the guy?'

'Oh, you want the female perspective.'

'That's right. Shoot.' Henderson picked up his now-cold cup of coffee.

A small smile played upon Hannah's lips and she tugged thoughtfully on her ear. 'Well, for one thing, he's sexy as hell. Too damned male for his own good. He's almost a cliché, you know. Tall, ranch-tough, chiseled features, irreverent. A cowboy with an attitude. Every American woman's secret fantasy.'

Henderson snorted.

'Even your remark that he's hiding something holds some kind of appeal; women are curious, they like a man who has a dark side. Don't ask me why. There's a thrill to it, I suppose. The element of not knowing. Danger.' She was obviously looking for a reaction. Henderson gave her none.

Hannah cocked her head to one side as she always did when she was thinking. 'Walker's used to having women fall all over him, unless I miss my guess. Probably Marquise never quite got over him.'

'So that's why she ran to his ranch every time she got into trouble?'

'A good guess.'

'What about the sister, Maggie? How does she fit in?'

'Now, there's an interesting glitch,' Hannah said, her eyes narrowing thoughtfully and the tip of one polished nail tapping her front teeth. 'Woman's intuition tells me that she's in love with him.'

'With Walker?' He'd sensed it, too, didn't like that particular kink in this already-tangled case. He preferred things more straightforward. Trouble was, they never were. Christ, he could use a cigarette.

Hannah nodded, her smooth brow creasing at the implications. 'Yep. Unless I miss my guess, Ms. McCrae's got it bad. Real bad. For her twin sister's ex-husband.'

13

Leaning against a counter in the small storefront, Becca eyed the tattoo artist warily. The woman was so skinny she looked like a walking skeleton. With frizzy bleached blond hair, tanned skin, and too much eye makeup, she didn't come across as the kind of person to trust with your body. But she believed in her art because she had hearts and flowers decorating one arm and a flaming cross with a banner that said *Jesus is Love* on the other.

'Okay, doll, what'll it be?' the woman asked around a wad of gum as a cigarette burned unattended in an ashtray. There were other artists as well, seated in cubicles with their clients, gloves on their hands as they used equipment that looked like electric pens to trace patterns on different body parts. The place was clean enough, the floors gleaming, the walls decorated with pictures of tattooed bodies.

'Get one of those Chinese suns,' her cousin Jenny said, urging her on as a paddle fan slowly turned, moving the stale air typical of greater Los Angeles. Jenny was fairly beaming. Dressed in the short skirt and sweater of her cheerleading outfit, she looked as out of place as Becca felt. 'The ones that mean something. Or your sign of the zodiac, that would be cool.'

'When were you born?'

'In April, but . . . I was thinking more like a hummingbird.'

'No problem.' The woman took a drag from her cigarette and reached upward to the wooden shelves where there were stacks of books. 'Let's see . . . birds, I got birds here somewhere . . . ' She found a thin-leafed book, flipped through it, then frowned. ' . . . nope, oh, here it is.' She pulled down a pattern book that had seen better days and placed it on the desk in front of Becca. Refusing to be intimidated by the woman or her cousin, Becca riffled through the pages. 'This one,' she said, pointing to a ruby-throated hummingbird hovering in midair.

'Nice. Where d'ya want it?'

'Umm. I was thinkin' on my ankle.'

'Awesome,' Jenny said. 'I wish I had the guts to get one.'

'Do it,' Becca urged. It would be so much cooler if Jenny did it with her.

'I . . . I can't. I *hate* needles.'

'Not much pain involved.' The woman leaned forward, eyed Becca's bare legs, and nodded. 'That'd work.'

'Great.' Jenny was more enthusiastic than Becca. Her brown eyes glinted with mischief. 'How much?'

'Depends on the size and the difficulty.' The woman thought long and hard. 'We'll discuss price when your mother gets here.' She straightened, frizzy blond hair falling back into place.

'My mother?' Becca's heart dropped.

'Or your dad. Or a legal guardian. Whatever.

You know that I can't do this without your guardian's permission.'

'Why not?'

'Oh, honey.' The woman smiled sadly. 'You're gonna hafta do some big talkin' to convince me you're eighteen.' She popped her gum, took a final drag from her cigarette, and shot smoke out of the side of her mouth. 'Don't suppose you've got a driver's license or a passport or some kind of document with your age?'

'No, but — '

'Didn't think so.' She offered a kind smile. 'Well, unless you come back here with your guardian, I can't help you out.'

'But — '

'Hey, I don't need that kind of trouble.' She pointed a long finger at the sign over the cupboard holding her books — a sign clarifying age restrictions — then she jabbed out her cigarette in a tin ashtray and flipped the pattern book of birds closed. 'Come back with your mom, or when you're older, okay?'

'Oh, come on,' Jenny begged, and Becca was surprised that her cousin was so interested in Becca's doing something that could land her in big trouble. Maybe there was more to Jenny than met the eye. Becca was already beginning to suspect that her older cousin might rat her out at a moment's notice. Jenny had already demonstrated that she adhered to the CYA — cover your ass — mentality.

'Really, girls.' The woman shook her head. 'I have a couple kids of my own, and if they did anything to their bodies behind my back, I'd give

’em what for, believe me.’ Her overly madeup eyes were sincere. ‘As I said, next time, bring your mom.’

Since they had no other choice, Jenny and Becca walked outside, where the November sun was warm and bright, sparkling off the dusty sidewalk. No trees lined the streets in this part of town, and litter blew in the dry wind that followed the cars through the alleys and around squatty buildings.

‘Bummer,’ Jenny said. ‘I thought if we came down here, they’d do it. My friends go to nicer places. You know, they’re almost like doctors’ offices, but I knew they wouldn’t do it without a parent’s signature.’ She unlocked the driver’s side of her silver Jetta, crawled inside and flipped a switch to unlock Becca’s door. As Becca took her seat, Jenny folded up the dash guard that she’d placed on the inside of the windshield to protect the interior from the heat. It didn’t help much. The car was pretty warm even though it was early November. But it felt good to Becca.

Leaning her seat back as Jenny eased into traffic and turned on the radio full blast to the sound of a song by Jewel, Becca smiled and told herself she didn’t miss her mother. Lately she had been such a pain. This was much better. Though hangin’ out with Aunt Connie and Uncle Jim wasn’t all that great. Connie was always sighing and complaining, and Jim was a tight-ass. Everything had to be just so.

But Jenny. For the most part, aside from her need to protect herself, she was beyond cool. Becca dragged a pair of sunglasses out of her backpack and slid them onto her face. Jenny fumbled in her purse for cigarettes and a lighter. 'Want one?' she asked her younger cousin.

Becca grinned and took the offered filter tip. Jenny handed her the lighter and laughed when she couldn't get the flame to hold steady. 'Like this,' she explained, and flicked the lighter with expertise.

She held the flame to Becca's cigarette and Becca drew in hard. Too hard. The smoke burned all the way to her lungs. She ended up coughing wildly, and Jenny laughed as she lit up and rammed her car into gear. 'I wish I had a convertible,' she complained, but Becca didn't mind. She didn't even care that she couldn't get the stupid tattoo. Rolling down her window, she took another puff, coughed, and was determined to get better at this smoking thing.

She leaned her seat way back and held her hand out the window with the cigarette burning. Oh, yeah, this was the life. She loved L.A.

'I overheard Mom and Dad talking last night,' Jenny said, as Becca watched a scraggly looking palm tree flash by.

'About what?'

'They were talkin' about you coming to live with us permanently.'

'Really?' Becca coughed on more smoke. 'Mom's thinkin' about it?'

'I don't know. I . . . um, I don't think I was supposed to hear — they were on the patio and the window was open, so I kinda just hung out and listened.' Jenny bit her lip. As if she'd revealed too much and was suddenly regretting it. She glanced over her shoulder, gunned the engine, and beat out a boy in a red Kia to the next light. ‘So, Becca, don’t say anything to your mom, okay? She probably wants to surprise you about this L.A. thing.’

‘Cool,’ Becca said, inhaling on the cigarette again. And it was — really cool. Maybe her mother was finally coming around.

* * *

Marquise’s home was no less than a mansion. Maggie had always thought so. Built of red brick and stone and guarded by ancient maple and aspen trees, the house rose three stories to a sharply pitched, snow-covered roof. Leaded-glass windows winked in the bright sunlight as Thane and Maggie trudged a path through the melting snow to the front door.

‘She has an alarm system,’ Thane reminded Maggie as she stuffed the key in the door.

‘I know.’

They entered; the electronic beeper started ticking off the seconds; and Maggie, yanking off her gloves, walked unerringly to the broom closet near the kitchen, opened the door, and deactivated the security system, pressing a series of buttons just as her sister must have every day. A sense of desperation caught hold of her and she tried to shake it off, but entering Mary Theresa’s empty house gave her a small case of the creeps, made her feel as if she were walking on someone’s grave.

That’s crazy, she reminded herself. *Just*

because M.T. isn't here, doesn't change a thing.

But being with Thane didn't help; there was just too much she didn't know — couldn't trust — about him.

For all its stately outward appeal, the home's interior was eclectically decorated — some of the furniture and art pieces a little offbeat. The living room, study, and library were all conservatively decorated in tones of hunter green and tan that reminded Maggie of a stuffy men's club. Occupied by oxblood-leather couches, wing-backed chairs, antique tables, brass lamps, and leather-bound tomes reeking of snobbery, those rooms were at odds with the rest of the house, which was decorated without any common theme and filled with whatever caught Mary Theresa's wild eye. Period pieces were interspersed with modern posters and artwork that was little more than junk, but somehow appealed to M.T.

A dour-faced mannequin dressed in Roaring Twenties attire, complete with beaded, fringed flapper dress, feather boa, and long cigarette holder, stood near a suit of armor in the entry hall. The kitchen was festooned with hanging pots and pans, a sturdy knife rack, baskets of dried herbs, marble counters, and bouquets of wilting flowers. Zebra-striped chairs were scattered near a faux leopard couch and a large table with a ceramic chess set was placed near a cherrywood-faced fireplace.

But for all its personality, there was a sense of lifelessness throughout the rooms. Without Mary Theresa the house was dead inside. No laughter.

No sounds from the television or stereo. Just the soft hum of a hidden furnace and the ticking of a cuckoo clock.

Maggie unlocked French doors that opened to a wide brick patio. Outside, the air was brisk and cold. Planters, filled with last fall's dead blossoms, were buried in snow. The yard, a field of white, rolled toward a lake where the smooth glasslike surface was occupied by a flock of Canada geese and the late-afternoon sunlight glinted in sharp, vibrant rays. A copse of leafless cottonwood trees stood near the opposite shore, and, far in the distance, the peaks of the Rocky Mountains rose like cathedral spires to touch a blue, cloudless sky.

'Not a bad place to live,' she said, her breath fogging in air that chilled her hands and cheeks.

'If this is what you like.' Thane squinted into the sun.

'Did she?'

He lifted a shoulder. 'Who knows with her?'

'No one.' Together they walked back inside, and Maggie locked the door behind them.

'Nothing simple for Marquise,' Thane observed, running a finger along the back of a leather couch.

'Mary Theresa,' Maggie said automatically as she eyed the kitchen. She'd always hated her sister's stage name; thought it sounded so uppity. One name for God's sake. 'But, yeah, this is overkill for one person.' She walked into the dining room, where a table with twelve chairs stretched beneath a chandelier resplendent with fragrant, half-burned candles rather than electric lights.

In the living room a concert grand piano gleamed ebony and reflected the sunlight from a bank of windows overlooking the lake.

'Why would she leave this place?' Maggie wondered aloud, and started up a curved staircase to the second floor.

Mary Theresa's bedroom was a study in femininity. Decorated in varying hues of rose and pink, it housed a king-size bed covered in shimmering white silk, a grouping of tables and chairs, and an armoire that hid a large television and stereo system. On the walls were professional photographs of the woman who had evolved from Mary Theresa Reilly into Marquise. In subtle black-and-white or startling color, Maggie's twin was visible from every possible angle. There were a few pictures of Maggie and more of Becca, her school and sports pictures propped on the night table and bureau top. Exotic stuffed animals from a life-sized llama to a coiled snake occupied the corners and crannies of the suite. Silk flowers offered color.

And yet the room seemed empty. Barren.

Thane glanced at the pictures without comment and Maggie wondered how often he'd seen them before, how many times he'd visited Mary Theresa's bedroom.

She closed her mind to those thoughts and stepped into the bathroom, where a sunken marble tub was framed by huge windows screened by flowering orchids. Mirrors covered the walls and ran along a marble counter, where bottles of perfume, cologne, and cosmetics were strewn in haphazard fashion. Candles and potpourri scented the air.

Maggie picked up a bottle of cologne and wondered again where Mary Theresa was, what had happened to her. 'Do you think she would try to take her own life?' Maggie asked as she replaced the bottle, picked up an atomizer, and smelled the tip, only to be reminded of her sister.

'Nope.' He met her gaze in the mirror and loosened the buttons of his jacket. 'The woman I knew was too selfish to end it all. Too vain.'

'So you think she was kidnapped?'

'Nah.' He shook his head. 'Ransom demands would have been made by now. It's been over a week since she stormed off the set.'

Maggie opened the closet door and stepped into an expansive cedar-lined closet, where hundreds of pairs of shoes were kept neatly in their boxes, and dresses, skirts, evening gowns, blouses, and slacks, encased in plastic, hung perfectly. Sweaters were folded in drawers; T-shirts, shorts, and jeans were folded and tucked onto shelves.

'So what happened to her?' Running her fingers over a soft green angora sweater, Maggie tried to imagine what Mary Theresa had been thinking, where she could have gone. 'And why do the police think you're involved? Don't try to deny it; you said yourself that Henderson considers you a 'person of interest' in the investigation, and I saw the way he looked at you today.'

'Like I was a criminal.'

Maggie inclined her head.

'It's probably because we were married, divorced, but still saw each other once in a while,' he admitted as they walked down a hallway. 'And the fight.'

'You said it was about money?'

'Mostly it was about lies. Mary Theresa was jerking my chain. I'd caught her in a lie.'

'About?'

'Something that happened a long time ago.'

She let it drop. Sooner or later he'd confide in her.

They opened the doors of the first of two guest rooms, an exercise room, and two more bathrooms that completed the second floor. The closet was filled with men's clothes — suits, slacks, silk shirts, and several pairs of shoes. 'Looks like Marquise's boyfriend stayed over a lot,' Thane said.

'Boyfriend?'

'With an emphasis on the boy part. Wade Pomeranian. Her latest.' Thane scanned the contents of the closet with a jaundiced eye.

Mary Theresa had mentioned him in passing during their last phone call. He was younger, a model, Maggie thought. 'You don't like him?' she asked.

'The feeling is mutual.' Thane shut the closet door and walked into an adjoining bath, where shaving paraphernalia and men's toiletries were arranged perfectly on the tile counter. Thane sneered at the half-filled bottles. 'For the record, I think Pomeranian's a snot-nosed kid who doesn't give a damn about her but is hanging on because she has connections in the entertainment industry. He's self-serving, vain, and a royal pain in the ass, but other than that a helluva guy.'

'Oh, come on, Walker, don't hold back, what do you really think?' she teased.

'That she'd be better off without that leech. But, as she was fond of telling me whenever I offered her advice, it was her life.'

'Is her life,' Maggie clarified. '*Is.*' A long, sable-colored robe with a hood hung on the back of the door. Matching slippers were tucked by a scale positioned near the shower. Maggie fingered the robe's belt. 'Looks like something a monk might wear.'

Thane snorted. 'Don't look for a rosary tucked in the pocket, okay? Pomeranian isn't exactly a saint.'

'No one is,' she observed, as they made their way up another set of stairs.

On the third floor, the attic had been converted to a dance studio, complete with sound system, ballet barre, and shining hardwood floors. Mirrors covered the walls, and the sloped ceiling was broken up by dormer alcoves.

'Any other reason you and Mary Theresa don't get along?' Maggie asked, sensing something more, as if Thane had never quite disconnected from his ex-wife, as if there were ties that bound them together, ties Maggie had never known existed.

His jaw slid to the side. 'You mean other than that she tricked me into marrying her, we got a divorce, and she's been a pain ever since?'

'Yeah,' she prodded.

'She does owe me money,' he admitted.

'Ahh . . . ' Maggie said. 'How much?'

'Enough.'

'This is no time to be coy, Walker,' she said, pointing a finger at his chest as they walked down the stairs to the main level again.

'Okay. She owes me two hundred thousand dollars, plus interest. All told, it's closer to two hundred and fifty.'

Maggie stopped dead in her tracks at the base of the stairs. 'You're kidding.'

'Nope.'

'Why?'

'She needed it.'

'I question that,' she said, eyeing the foyer with its marble floor, polished cherrywood staircase, and chandelier. The flapper and medieval knight stood guard. The piano was visible behind French doors that closed off the living room. 'For what?'

'Taxes. Your sister forgot to pay for a few years, and the IRS doesn't like that much.'

'So you bailed her out?'

'I loaned her some money.'

'A lot of money.' She walked into the den and sat down in Mary Theresa's chair, as her legs were a little less steady than they had been. Picking up a pencil, she tapped it nervously against the edge of the desk as Thane stood near the window, staring out at the expanse of snow-covered lawn. The sun was lowering in the western sky, the November night fast approaching. 'You haven't been leveling with me,' Maggie finally ventured.

'How's that?'

'You didn't tell me about seeing Mary Theresa fairly regularly, and my guess is you knew that I didn't think you two had any contact.'

'I only saw her when she was in trouble.'

'You should have told me,' she insisted, more than a little hurt. An old sense of wariness stole into her heart.

'I did. When you asked.'

'Give me a break.'

'Maggie — '

'And you didn't mention the loan,' she pointed out, her blood starting to boil. Who was he to keep things from her? Weren't they in this together?

'It wasn't the issue.'

'Good Lord, Thane, are you crazy?' she snapped. 'Don't you know what's going on here?' She pushed back the chair, shot to her feet, and crossed the distance between them. 'Weren't you in the police station with me today? Detective Henderson thinks that either Mary Theresa is pulling some elaborate publicity stunt, or that she might have holed up and killed herself, or that you were somehow involved in a kidnapping or worse! That fight you had put you right up at the top of the suspect list!' Exasperated, Maggie threw her hands up in the air. 'I mean, I thought you came to my place to drag me back here because you wanted my help. That . . . that you thought that we, together, could find Mary, that . . . I don't know, that we could help the police clear this up.'

He stared at her long and hard, the way he had years before, and she swallowed with sudden difficulty, her anger evaporating a bit as she sensed a shift in the atmosphere in the room.

'Did it ever occur to you that I might have used all this as an excuse to see you again?'

Oh, sweet Jesus. His words rippled over her heart like a brook over stones, smoothing out the rough, painful edges.

'I don't think so, Thane,' she said, refusing to be seduced by words she'd wanted to hear so many years ago. 'I think you showed up because you needed my help. Period.' She walked back to the desk and plopped down in the chair, then caught sight of Mary Theresa's Rolodex. 'Who did the detective say was the last person to see Mary Theresa?'

'A cashier at a gas station. But that doesn't seem to have panned out. Anyway, Henderson also said something about the guy making a mistake and being someone always on the lookout for cheap publicity. There were some time discrepancies as well.'

'Whether the clerk saw Mary Theresa or not, the last person to really talk with her was you, right?'

'That we know about,' he allowed.

She stared hard at him. 'And, before she met with you, she saw the people she worked with, right? Craig Beaumont and the other people at the station. Maybe her secretary.'

'As I remember it.'

'Me, too.' She flipped through the well-used

cards and as she did, the names she'd heard from Mary Theresa jumped out at her: Craig Beaumont, Syd Gillette, Robert Inman, Dr. Michelle Kelly, Maggie and Becca McCrae, Wade Pomeranian, Thane Walker . . . along with names she didn't recognize at all.

Eyeing the telephone and answering machine, she pushed the play button and listened to several hang-ups as well as calls from the television station; her agent, Ambrose King; Eve Lawrence; Detective Henderson; and the first of her own desperate telephone messages. 'Mary Theresa, this is Maggie. If you're there please pick up . . . Mary Theresa? . . . Oh, okay, Marquise, are you there?' A pause. 'Look, I, um, I got a message from you — you know, the kind you used to send — well, at least I think I did, and I need to talk to you, so please call me back. I'm still at the ranch in Idaho . . . '

'What kind of a message?' Thane asked as the recorder clicked off and Maggie felt like a fool.

'Nothing.' She shook her head.

'No, you said that you received a message.' He crossed the room to the desk and pushed the play button again. To Maggie's mortification, they heard her desperate plea all over again. 'What did you mean?'

'It doesn't matter.'

'Like hell, lady. I think you just made the point that we were in this together and we shouldn't keep secrets, so what kind of message?'

'Let it go. You wouldn't believe it if I told you.'

She tried to breeze past him, but his fingers locked around her wrist and he spun her to face him. 'Try me,' he suggested, his face so close to hers she could feel his heat, smell that same particular scent that was uniquely his.

'Drop it, Thane.'

'Not on your life.' His eyes held hers — steely blue and calculating. The fingers around her wrist tightened.

'All right,' she said, ignoring the fact that her breath seemed to disappear deep in the back of her throat. She hesitated, but her heart was pumping, adrenaline surging through her blood. 'Try this on for size, cowboy. Every so often — well, more like once in a blue moon — Mary Theresa and I . . . we communicate, I guess that's the only way to say it, but we do it without speaking.'

'Without speaking?' His eyes narrowed as if to see deeper into her mind and find out if she was lying to him. He was studying her so closely she wanted to move out of his line of vision, but she was trapped, her arm held fast.

'That's right. And I'm not talking about letters or e-mail or sign language, Walker. This is mental telepathy.'

'Bull.'

She raised a knowing eyebrow. 'You asked.'

'Yeah, well, try again.'

'It doesn't work often and it only works one way.'

'How's that?' he said, skepticism deepening the craggy lines at the corners of his eyes.

'Mary Theresa can throw some kind of inner voice and I . . . I can hear it.'

'Just you?'

'Just me.'

He snorted in derision.

'It doesn't matter how many miles we're apart, I can still hear her.'

'Sure.'

'You asked,' she reminded him.

His smile was cold as deepest winter. 'So what have you been 'hearing' from her lately?'

'Not enough.'

'But something.'

She licked her lips nervously and his gaze skated to her mouth before returning to her eyes.

'Tell me, Mag Pie.'

She swallowed hard. 'Okay. I heard from her about an hour before you showed up at the ranch in Idaho.'

'Convenient.'

'The truth, damn it!' She yanked hard on her arm, but his fingers surrounding her wrist only tightened their manacle-like grip.

'Since then?'

'Nothing . . . well, I did hear from her when I was sleeping but . . . ' She shook her head. 'But I'm pretty sure that was just a dream.'

'Jesus H. Christ.'

'It's true, damn it. Believe it or not.'

'Okay,' he drawled, 'just for the sake of argument, let's say I believe you, then what about before? When did you hear or whatever you want to call it . . . uh, receive messages from her?'

She took in a long breath and wished she could call back all the words. No doubt he'd think she was a loony. But it was too late. 'The first time it happened was the night Mitch . . . Mitch and Mary Theresa were drunk, um, in the hot tub and then again the night he died. Another time was when you came to the house and announced that you and she were going to get married, and, then, the last time, after years of silence, believe it or not, I heard her again. Just a little while before you showed up at the cabin. She was desperate and scared and pleaded with me to help her.' She tilted back her head, lifting her chin in challenge, blatantly defying him. 'Go ahead, tell me I'm lying or that I'm crazy.'

'Either you're lying or you're crazy.'

'Wrong. It's what happened,' she insisted, finally able to pull away from him and rub her wrist. Oh, God, this sounded so lame, so damned lame. 'But the last time . . . the last time she threw her voice at me and . . . and it had to have been after she was already missing, after the police found the suicide note, after her disappearance, so you see, she isn't dead. Couldn't be. Or else she couldn't have sent the message!'

'If she did.'

'Why would I make this up?'

'I don't know.' He stared at her as if he thought she was insane, as if she didn't have a rational thought in her head.

'And what did she say in this message?' he asked.

'Just that she needed help,' she lied, unable to accuse him of a crime she didn't understand.

His jaw clenched. A muscle worked near his

temple. Disbelief registered in his eyes.

'Say it, Walker.'

'You're making this up.'

'Why?'

That was a damned good question. Thane didn't want to trust her, had learned long ago never to believe a woman, any woman; but with Maggie it had always been different. As it was today. 'Because it doesn't make sense.'

'Does anything' — she made a wide, sweeping gesture with her arm, encompassing the entire house in that one motion — 'anything about this make sense? You know, Walker, if you want me to trust you, you'd damned well better trust me!'

Her green eyes snapped with fire, her cheeks were flushed a bright, indignant hue, and the corners of her mouth drew down into a small pout that he found fascinating. 'Do you, Maggie?' he asked, trying to ignore the fact that she still got to him. As no other woman ever had. 'Do you trust me?'

'No.' The answer was quick. Emphatic. Cut like a knife. 'But I'm trying, damn it. I don't know about you, but I'm not gonna sit around and let the police do this in their own sweet time.'

He felt the first warning of a new kind of trouble. 'What do you mean?'

'I worked for a private investigator for a few years, learned the ropes, and I think it's time I figured out what happened to my sister. Whether you believe me or not, she called out to me, Thane, and it was after she was supposed to be missing.'

'That's crazy.'

'So I've been told. The police, if they dig deep enough, are going to find out that I saw a psychiatrist, not once, but twice. The first time was years ago, after Mitch died and you and Mary Theresa got married; I went to college, but was treated for depression.'

He was surprised. Maggie was one of the sanest, most down-to-earth people he'd ever met in his life.

'And the second time was about a year ago; my marriage was failing, my daughter was becoming estranged, and I felt like I'd fallen into a deep, black hole. The harder I tried to climb out, the farther down I seemed to sink. I clawed until my fingers bled, but I just couldn't get to the top, wasn't able to smell fresh air or able to reach the light at the top, so I had to go under a doctor's care.' She hesitated and he saw a fresh, desolate pain in her eyes.

'And then your husband died?' he ventured, knowing he was prying, probing into painful areas, but unable not to ask a question that had been bothering him ever since he'd seen her again.

She managed a thin smile. 'That's not exactly how it went. Yes, I was depressed, and I was on medication, but the cause of the depression was my marriage. Dean and I had mentally separated, disconnected years before; we were living different lives, completely divided. He was seeing another woman, though he denied it vehemently, and I couldn't stand it. I filed for divorce.' She rubbed her arms and looked away. 'The day he was served, he drank nearly a fifth of Jack Daniel's, drove outside of the city, and lost control of the car.' She shuddered.

'And died.'

'Not for a while.' Tears gathered in her eyes, and she swallowed hard. The tip of her nose turned red. 'No, not Dean McCrae. He hung in there, in a coma, for eleven days, while the rest of us, me, my daughter, his parents and brother and sister-in-law held a vigil, praying for him, talking to him, begging him to survive.' She blinked and wiped the moisture from her eyes. 'In the end he gave up. Everything started shutting down, and the doctors told me he was brain-dead. We — well, I — pulled the plug. At the time, his family agreed, but then . . . ' She cleared her throat and took a deep breath. ' . . . anyway, the upshot was that his parents and brother blame me, my daughter blames me, and we're all working through a truckload of guilt.' She angled her face upward defiantly, her gaze boring into his so deeply he was certain she could see each and every one of his sins. And there were many. More than anyone would ever guess. Anguish twisted her perfect features and tracks from her tears glistened on her cheeks. 'Any further questions, cowboy?'

He didn't answer. Couldn't. All his resistance cracked, and as he'd wanted from the first time he'd laid eyes on her again, he dragged her into his arms. She gasped, her eyes widened, and he pressed his anxious lips to hers.

A million reasons to stop this madness crashed through his head. She couldn't be trusted, she was Mary Theresa's sister, he'd broken her heart once before, she hated him . . . but he didn't care, didn't give a good goddamn about anything but the touch and feel of her. It was comfort. It was lust. It was heaven.

God, it had been so long. Heat sang through his blood, and his tongue slid past her teeth, searching, touching, mating as she moaned softly, opening to him as if she had no resistance. Thoughts of bare, fragrant skin, rain-washed hair, and hot sex flashed through his mind. He remembered the first time he'd made love to her, how her back arched upward in the rainstorm, how warm and tight she'd been as she'd so willingly offered him her virginity there in the woods, how she'd trembled, just as she did now, fully dressed, in his arms.

In Mary Theresa's house.

That thought was a dash of ice water.

As if she, too, suddenly realized that they were trespassing, violating a woman who could be dead, her sister, his ex-wife, the very woman who had stood between them before, Maggie struggled to pull away from him. 'I don't think this is a good idea.'

'I know it isn't.' But he didn't release her, held her fast, and kissed her again. Hard. She seemed to melt for a second, only to push against him again.

'Really, Thane. I — you — we've got a job to

do. We have to find Mary Theresa, and I can't be confused about it.'

'Are you?'

'Yes.'

Silently cursing himself, he dropped his arms.

'*You* confuse me. And it can't happen. I — I won't let it.' She seemed to gather strength as she put some distance between them. But her breathing was ragged, her eyes glazed with the unique passion only they had shared. 'Let's just find Mary Theresa.' She walked to the desk again and picked up her sister's Rolodex. 'I think I'll borrow this.'

'What?'

'And, while we're here — ' Sitting on the edge of her sister's chair, she stared into the monitor, flipped a switch, and waited for the computer to hum to life. Once the screen was glowing, she typed with agile fingers and was somehow into Mary Theresa's calendar.

'How do you know how to access all these things?'

'Mary Theresa isn't exactly a computer wizard. She's always used her birth date as her access code. It just so happens to be mine, too.' She managed a fragile smile. 'Remember I worked for a — '

'Private investigator, I know. I think it's starting to haunt me.'

She was still typing, scanning private files, and sending commands. Within a few minutes the printer was spewing out information about the past month of Marquise's life, addresses and phone numbers of her nearest and dearest, even information on projects she was working on. '*Voilà*,' Maggie finally said, scooping the pages from the printer. 'What is it they say — a little knowledge is a dangerous thing?'

'Amen.'

Thane watched as she folded the printed pages and dropped them, along with the Rolodex, into her voluminous purse. As she started to rise from the desk, Thane heard the clank and rattle of the garage door as it engaged. 'Listen.'

Maggie's head snapped up. A huge, relieved grin widened the lips he'd so recently kissed. 'She's home!'

'Maybe.' The sound of an engine rumbled from the area of the garage, and the throb of the bass notes of a heavy-metal tune nearly shook the foundation. The music and engine stopped. Maggie tore down the hallway. She reached the door to the garage as it was flung open.

Wade Pomeranian, his long dark curls tangled and wild, his smile as eager as Maggie's, strode into the house in five-hundred-dollar snakeskin boots, a long black-leather coat, and a cloud of marijuana smoke.

'Baby!' he cried, a grin cracking his sober features. He wrapped his arms around Maggie and twirled her off her feet. 'Oh, God, it's good to see ya! The police, everyone . . . they told me . . . I mean, shit, they all acted like you were dead or . . . somethin' . . . ' His smile faded, and he set Maggie onto the floor. Looking down the hallway, he demanded, 'What the hell is he doin' here?'

Thane, irritated at the younger man's display, felt one side of his mouth lift. 'You know, that's funny, Pomeranian,' he drawled, sizing up Marquise's latest lover. 'I was just about to ask you the same thing.'

14

'I'm not Mary Theresa.'

'Oh, shit, baby, are you fucked up again?' Wade's dark eyes were suddenly serious. He stomped a foot and turned up one hand, clawlike, shaking it toward the ceiling. 'I told you to quit takin' those damned pills.'

'I said I'm not Mary Theresa. I'm her sister. Maggie McCrae.'

For a second he didn't say a word, just stared at her. Then it finally hit; he recognized the differences. 'Oh, fuck!' He took a step backward and looked from Maggie to Thane and back again. 'Shit. You . . . you're a dead ringer for Marquise!'

'What're you doing here?' Thane asked.

'I just came for some of my things and I saw your truck outside and then I saw Marquise . . . well, Maggie . . . oh, fuck!' He shook his head, and the long curls that fell past his shoulders gleamed under the light. 'Jesus. You look so much like her it's . . . cosmically weird. Wow.' Slightly recovering, he realized he had no place being in Marquise's house. He held up his hands as if in surrender. 'Look, I'll just run up and grab my things.'

'Wait a minute.' Maggie hitched her head toward the kitchen. 'I want to talk to you.'

'Me?' He was instantly wary. 'Why?'

'Because I want to know what happened to my sister.'

'So do I,' he said readily. 'But I don't have a clue. Really.'

'Let me be the judge of that. Come on, let's talk.'

She flipped on a switch at the entrance to the kitchen. Through the windows dusk was crawling across the land, the sky turning to lavender and the ground, where the snow still covered it, a pale shade of gray.

Though he was reluctant, Wade took a chair at the round, glass-topped table. Maggie ignored the thin layer of dust that had collected on the surface and, as she sat in a chair opposite Pomeranian, moved a crystal vase of dead irises and roses to one side, leaving a trail of faded petals and pollen that scattered over the glass.

'Why are you two' — Pomeranian motioned vaguely toward the cooking island where Thane stood, leaning against the attached eating bar — 'y'know, like together?'

'We knew each other a long time ago.' Maggie was more interested in asking the questions than answering them. 'Look, please, tell me about Mary Theresa. The police seem to think that she was suicidal — ' One of his dark eyebrows arched a little as he sank in the chair, settling low on his back, long legs stretched out, hands folded together, but visible through the glass. His nails were manicured, his hair shiny, his skin swarthy and dark, but flawless. Compared to Thane he was reedy, but he probably photographed well.

'I don't think Marquise offed herself if that's what you're asking.'

'What do you think happened to her?' Thane asked.

'Shit, man, I don't know. Don't you think I want to find her?'

'Do you?'

'Yes!' Wade's smooth face twisted into a mask of frustration. 'I love her.'

'Is that what it is?' Thane obviously wasn't convinced.

Maggie shot him a look to shut him up. 'When was the last time you saw her?'

'The Wednesday night before she left.' He sighed and glanced out the windows. 'We had a fight. Something stupid. I wanted to be interviewed on her show, always had, and she put me off again.' His lips tightened around the corners. 'I got pissed, really pissed, and told her we were through.' He snorted, and though his fingers remained laced, his thumbs moved nervously. 'So . . . anyway, she kinda threw me out, and I left. It was about ten, I guess. I went back to my apartment, felt like shit, couldn't sleep, and called in the morning about six-thirty, but she didn't pick up, so I figured, 'fuck it, she knows my number,' and didn't even try to reach her for a couple of days. I had a photo shoot in Salt Lake that day, and I looked like shit, because I hadn't slept a wink, but I got through it and stayed in Utah until Sunday.'

'You didn't hear from her?'

'No.'

'Didn't try to call again?'

'The ball was in her court. I figured I'd give her some time to cool down and figure out what she wanted.'

'But you love her,' Thane remarked, his voice bland.

He nodded, his curls bouncing. 'I do.'

'I'll handle this.' Maggie sent Thane a glare guaranteed to make lesser men tremble, and the irreverent son of a gun had the gall to smile at her, turn his palm toward Wade Pomeranian, and lift his eyebrows as if to say, 'Your witness, counselor.'

Wade checked his watch. 'I'm running a little late.'

'Okay, okay, just bring me up to speed,' Maggie said, irritated and rapidly coming to the conclusion that Thane was correct in his opinion of Mary Theresa's lover. The guy seemed like a flake. 'What do you think happened to Marquise?'

'Shit, I don't know.'

'As I said, the police seem to think that she might have had some kind of suicide wish.'

He barked out a laugh. 'Right, and I told you what I thought. Marquise? No fuckin' way. She loved life. Always wanted a little more from it, always hatchin' some scheme to make more money or promote herself, but she wasn't about to end it. Not her.'

'Then do you think she might've been kidnapped?'

'Hell, I don't know.' He shrugged his slim shoulders. 'Don't know why anyone would do it.'

'Money,' Thane said.

'Or attention,' Maggie added.

'Or maybe some psycho. There are always nutcases runnin' around. Beats me.' He looked sincere. Well, as sincere as he could in the black getup and professionally coiffed hair.

'Look, I'm outta here. I'm already late.' He flashed a killer smile, one that made him his money modeling. Scooting his chair back, he dropped his feet to the floor, slapped his thighs, and without another word strode out of the room at a sharp clip. His coat billowed behind him, and Maggie was reminded of Batman's cape.

'How long has Mary Theresa been with him?' she asked.

'Six, maybe eight months.' Thane lifted a shoulder. 'Too long.'

She heard Wade stomping around on the second floor, then rapid-fire footsteps as he hurried down the stairs. He didn't bother to step into the kitchen again, though Maggie, from her position at the table, watched him fly through the door to the garage. His coat sailed behind him as he carried a bundle of clothes toward a sleek navy blue BMW. The door to the garage slammed shut before Maggie saw much more, but she heard the sounds of the garage door cranking open, a keyless lock beeping, a powerful engine firing, loud music blaring, and then everything receding as Wade and his sports car made tracks.

'How was that for a breath of fresh air?' Thane asked, still staring at the door.

'Different,' she said, but realized that Mary

Theresa didn't really have a 'type' where men were concerned. None of the men in her life had fit into any kind of mold. Including Thane.

'Come on, I'll buy you dinner,' Thane offered.

'I'll take you up on that, but first I need to check into a hotel and rent a car.' She grabbed her purse and headed for the broom closet. Expertly she activated the security system. As the alarm beeped softly, she and Thane hurried outside. The air was frigid, the stars bright, and the few streetlights glowed against the snow-covered terrain.

'Why rent a car?' he asked. 'I'll drive you wherever you need to go.'

'Don't you have a ranch or two to run?'

'I have foremen who can handle whatever comes up.'

She hazarded a glance at him as they trudged in the melting path they'd broken earlier. He didn't belong in this neighborhood of sprawling mansions and tended acres. He looked as out of place as a mustang in a paddock of thoroughbreds, a man who belonged on the windswept plains of Wyoming where he'd been bred. She told herself to stay away from him, that he was dangerous, at least on an emotional level, maybe more. And yet there was something about him, a subtle sexual aura that seemed to smooth out the rough edges, something that caught hold of her and wouldn't let go. His hawkish nose, deep-set eyes, and untamed hair seemed more appealing than ever. She had only to think of the kiss they'd shared, the kiss she'd wanted so desperately in Mary Theresa's study, to realize that she wasn't the least bit immune to him. 'I think I need my own vehicle, Thane.'

She reached for the handle of the truck's door, but he placed a hand near her head, holding the door closed. 'Do you? Why?'

'I want my independence.'

One seductive eyebrow raised. 'Why?'

'Because I don't want to depend on you.'

'I'm pretty damned dependable.'

'But not honest,' she said, turning and leaning her buttocks against the pickup's dirty fender.

'You don't think so?'

'Call it feminine intuition, or a gut feeling, or even say that it's because I believe in the old adage of once burned twice shy, but the bottom line is this: I think, no, I suspect would be a better word, that there's still something you're not telling me, Thane. Something important. And it has to do with my sister. You didn't leave your ranch in Wyoming, drive all the way to Idaho to shanghai me back to Denver unless you had a reason, a stronger one than that you wanted me to vouch for you with the authorities.'

'No?' He didn't deny it.

'So spill it.'

'You won't believe that I just wanted to see you again.'

Her heart caught. But only for a second. 'Don't even start that with me, okay?' She held her hands on either side of her head, as if in surrender. 'You've been divorced a long time. If you wanted to see me again, you could have called.'

'You were married.'

She shook her head. He wasn't going to fool her, sweet-talk her, or, God forbid, seduce her into believing a lie. 'That wasn't it, either. There's something else going on with you,' she insisted, her eyes searching the ranch-tough blades of his face. 'Something big.'

'You're such a damned skeptic.'

'I wonder why?' she tossed back, only to have his arms surround her and his lips crash down on hers again. Hot. Wet. Demanding. She should have been ready for the onslaught to her senses, should have expected him to kiss her, but even if she'd been forewarned, she wouldn't have stopped him. As his tongue plunged into her mouth, she opened it eagerly. The thrill of his touch, the mystery surrounding him, the fact that he wanted her again was all so damned heady that she couldn't stop. She kissed him back, her arms winding around his neck as if of their own accord, her heart pounding, her skin tingling, her own tongue tasting and dipping.

It's just because it's been so long since a man has kissed you, touched you, held you as if he couldn't help himself, she tried to tell herself, but despite the fact that it had been over a year since she'd made love to a man and that was only because Dean had been so insistent, she knew that there was more to her reaction than pure physical lust.

This was Thane who was holding her, Thane who was kissing her, Thane who was acting as if he couldn't resist her. Thane's face pressed feverishly to hers, his lips moving far too sensually against hers. She trembled.

Groaning, he settled into the juncture of her parted legs, his jeans-clad thighs inside of hers, his erection hard against her lower abdomen.

God, she wanted him. Here in the cold night air, her spine pushed up against the door of his truck, her breasts flattened against the pressure of his chest, she wanted him. Heat throbbed deep inside her, and her blood tingled as his hand slid inside her jacket to cup her breast. Beneath her sweater her nipples hardened, and her knees grew weak. If not for the support of the truck, she would have sagged into the snow, drawing him with her, wanting nothing more than the feel of his naked body driving into hers.

'This is insane,' she murmured into his open mouth.

He lifted his head, and she stared into eyes as dark and dusky as the night. 'It's always been this way with you, Maggie. Always.'

'Oh, right.' Her head was starting to spin. 'Even when you were with Mary Theresa. You know, Thane, she always came between you and me.'

'Not true,' he said, his gaze focusing on her lips again. 'In fact she used to say the same thing about you.'

'What? That I came between you and her?'

His gaze lifted to hers, and the lust she saw burning in their midnight blue depths caused the breath at the back of her throat to stop. 'Not only that you came between us, but that I fantasized that she was you.'

'No — don't even say it.' She didn't believe him. Wouldn't.

His mouth tightened, and he released her slowly, stepped away. 'The damned thing of it was that she was right. Every night when we went to bed, I thought of you, Maggie.' He stared up at the shimmering heavens and shook his head as if at his own folly. 'Every damned night.'

'I — I don't think we should be discussing this. Not here. Not now.' She didn't dare believe him.

'Not ever,' he agreed, reaching around her and opening the door. White lines of irritation edged his lips. 'Get in the truck. We'll grab something to eat.' When she started to protest, he amended, 'Yeah, yeah, I know. Right after I get you checked into a hotel and you find yourself a goddamned rental car.'

'And I talk to Becca.'

'Whatever.'

As she climbed into the truck, he swung the door shut behind her and, muttering under his breath about 'mule-headed, stubborn, pain-in-the-ass women,' found his way to the driver's side. He fired up the engine, threw the truck into reverse and managed to crank up the radio in one smooth motion. By the time the pickup rolled into the street and he'd jammed the gearshift lever into first, Maggie was finally able to breathe again.

He glanced in the rearview mirror. 'You know that we're being followed, right?'

She hadn't noticed, but wasn't surprised. A glance over her shoulder confirmed his suspicions. 'The police?'

'Probably.' He drove out of the gated community and watched as an undistinguished Jeep followed suit. 'I noticed them on the way over here. Just wasn't sure.'

'If it's not the police, it could be someone involved in Mary Theresa's disappearance.'

'Or the press.' He slid her a glance and a crooked daredevil smile crossed his lips. 'Want me to lose them?'

She laughed. 'In this?'

He patted the dash. 'What was it Han Solo said about the *Millennium Falcon* in *Star Wars?*'

'I hate to think.' She rolled her eyes.

'Something like she may not be pretty, but she can jump to hyperspace in . . . oh, I don't remember the quote. Anyway, trust me, this truck can haul ass when asked.'

'Oh, right.' She couldn't help but smile even though she was experiencing a case of nerves. Being this close to Thane was unsettling, kissing him was tempting but perilous and having someone following them bothered her. But she couldn't let it. Not until she found out what was happening with her sister. She glanced in the rearview mirror. The Jeep was several cars back, but still in pursuit. 'Let 'em follow us,' she decided. 'We might just learn something from them.'

Thane's smile was without a drop of humor. He didn't bother to speed through the amber light, but let the Jeep lag behind them. 'My thoughts exactly.'

* * *

'This is a place I stay when I'm in town,' Thane said as he wheeled into the reserved parking area of the Brass Tree, a hotel located not far from downtown. 'The kicker is that our friend Syd Gillette owns it.'

'Mary Theresa's latest husband.'

'That's right. Ironic, I think,' Thane said without a smile.

Maggie had known that Gillette was a hotel magnate, but hadn't paid any attention to which of the 'few independent and elegant' hotels he'd owned, even though Mary Theresa had mentioned it in the short span of time she'd been married to the guy.

Thane left the truck with a valet, and liveried bellboys helped them with their bags. Built before the turn of the century, the Brass Tree's redbrick charm rose eight stories and had once towered over the surrounding buildings. A grand hand-carved staircase, polished to a deep cherry sheen, rose off a marble-floored lobby where stained-glass windows and crystal chandeliers vied for attention. Antique chairs and lamps clustered around a three-storied fireplace in a reading room at an angle from the front desk.

Earlier in the century the Rocky Mountains had been visible from the Brass Tree; now steel and glass high-rises were the focal points of many of the old rooms. But the interior was charming, the rates not in the stratosphere, and Maggie was thankful for a place to call home for the night.

The suite she and Thane agreed upon was roomy enough, with two bedrooms flanking a central living area complete with fireplace, love seat, and couch. Complimentary brandy and chocolates were waiting on the marble-topped table.

Maggie dropped her bag onto the end of her bed, reached for the phone, and dialed her sister-in-law in California. Connie was polite but cool and informed Maggie that the girls were 'out' for a while. She'd have Becca return the call when they got back. When Maggie made the mistake of asking how Becca was doing, she was frostily informed that her daughter was 'having the time of her life.' Connie's voice lost some of its sarcasm as she confided, 'You know, Maggie, you didn't do her any favors by uprooting her and taking her to the edge of nowhere.'

'Despite what you may believe, Connie, Settler's Ridge isn't one of the seven levels of hell. In fact it's kind of charming, quaint, and wholesome. I like it. I like it a lot.'

'Maybe it's just your cup of tea. You're a loner by nature, Maggie, don't deny it. But think of Becca. She's only thirteen, for God's sake. She belongs here with her friends.'

'That's why she's visiting.'

There was a hesitation on Connie's part, and Maggie sensed there was something deeper going on. 'I, um, I'm taking her to a specialist for her ankle.'

'Why? Is it worse?' Maggie's guilt jumped into hyperdrive.

'No, she seems fine, but you never know. I want her to see an orthopedist — as well as Jenny's pediatrician. She's just skin and bones.'

'Connie, don't overreact.'

'I'm just concerned. She's Dean's only child. The last of his line.'

'I know.' *Oh, Lord, how I know.*

'Jim and I are concerned. That's all. And the folks, they are, too.'

Another jab of guilt. Dean's parents were aging, his father recently confined to a nursing home, his mother living close to Jim and Connie. The only McCrae standing in the way of Jim inheriting all his family's wealth was Becca.

'But if you don't want her to see a specialist . . . ' The innuendo was impossible to ignore. Once again, without saying a word, Connie was implying that Maggie put her own needs over those of her child.

'Just have Becca call me, okay?' Maggie couldn't get off the phone fast enough. She gave Connie the number of the hotel and replaced the receiver. She'd been dealt a deck of grief from Dean's family in the past; she didn't need any more now. Even if Connie's intentions were good, they were certainly misguided. The sooner Maggie found Mary Theresa and got this mess behind her and returned to her home in Idaho, the better.

And what if you don't? What if you can't find Mary Theresa? What if she really is dead? Or kidnapped by some lunatic? It happens to women all the time, especially famous ones.

Her heart sank, and depression nagged at the edges of her consciousness. Suddenly, everything seemed impossible.

Thane rapped on the French doors separating

her bedroom from the living area of the suite, then poked his head in. 'I don't know about you, but I'm starved.'

'Me too,' she admitted, needing to clear her head from the snare of her dark thoughts. 'I'll be ready in ten minutes.'

'Fine.'

She threw herself together, put on black slacks only slightly the worse for wear from being packed in her bag, a cream-colored angora sweater, black belt, and shoes. Touching up makeup that needed major repair, she settled on a fresh swipe of lipstick, a little mascara, and blush, then gave up. Her hair was unruly, she hadn't packed any jewelry, and she didn't much care. She wasn't in Denver for dinner dates with Thane or anyone else; she was here with a purpose.

'Good enough,' she told her reflection, and ignored the lines of worry at the corners of her eyes. Grabbing her purse, she hurried into the living room and found Thane, in dark slacks and a long-sleeved shirt, pacing in front of the small couch. He looked up at her entrance and a smile tugged at one side of his mouth. 'You clean up nice, Ms. McCrae,' he said.

'Ditto.'

They were out the door and down the elevator without much ado, and a maître d' seated them at a corner table in a dining room divided by dark wooden panels topped with beveled-glass windows that glittered seductively in the glow of dozens of candles.

Thane recommended prime rib, Maggie

ordered brook trout, and they sipped wine as the courses came and went. Small talk was the order of the day, and they spent some time eyeing the other patrons, wondering if any of them were with the people who had been following them. 'It's weird,' she admitted, feeling warm inside from her second glass of Chardonnay.

'What is?'

'This whole case, if that's what you want to call it. Mary Theresa's disappearance and now being here with you. I just never would have expected it to happen.' She looked up at him for a split second, then glanced away, afraid she might get lost in the intensity of his gaze. 'As I said, weird.'

'Could be fate.'

She nearly laughed. Thane Walker believing in kismet. That would be the day. 'Sure.' She took a swallow of wine and winked mischievously. 'That's what it is.' She noticed a few of the patrons at nearby tables turn to look at her, their expressions puzzled as they talked to the other members of their party.

'They think you're Marquise,' Thane said, as if reading her mind. 'But they're not sure, and if you are, then why haven't the newspapers and television stations reported the fact that you're alive and well? Why aren't you hosting *Denver AM* with Craig Beaumont?'

'I know,' she admitted, and the seed of an idea that had been planted in her brain while she was searching through Mary Theresa's house started to sprout. 'Why aren't I?'

'What?'

'Why aren't I Mary Theresa?'

Thane's expression changed, his smile fading. 'I don't understand.'

The sprout was taking hold, and she was beginning to see the possibilities. She leaned over the table. 'Why don't I step into Mary Theresa's shoes? Literally and figuratively. If I go through her life step by step, so to speak, well, at a faster pace, for the last week or so, maybe I can figure out what happened to her.'

'Wait a minute, I don't get what you're saying,' he argued, setting down his glass and shoving his plate to one side.

'Sure you do. What do you think would happen if *I* became Mary Theresa — no, I mean, if I became Marquise? You know, lived in her house, walked through her daily routine, re-created her life so I could get the real picture, or at least a blueprint of what she was going through before she vanished.'

'You're not serious.' He looked stricken.

'As serious as I've ever been about anything in my life.' She was warming to the idea, and Thane was obviously growing cold as death. 'I might be able to learn what happened to her and that's why we're here, isn't it? You want to find her.'

'Everyone does.'

'But it's more than that with you,' she said, seeing the storm clouds brew in his eyes.

'I'm concerned.'

'You want to find her, of course, we all do.' The glow from the wine, the seduction of looking into Thane's eyes again, the feeling that she could trust him nearly overtook common sense. 'You know what, Walker? I'm going to do this. I'm gonna be Marquise.'

The waitress, a pert girl with short red hair and an easy manner, cleared their plates and offered dessert and coffee.

'We're fine,' Thane assured the girl, and once she'd stepped away from the table, he pinned Maggie in his glare. 'I didn't drag you all this way to tempt fate. Hell, Maggie, this is crazy. You're playing with fire.'

'Then why did you 'drag me here'?'

'We've been over this.'

'But I'm not buying it. Level with me, Thane.'

'I have.'

'Not completely.'

The waitress returned and slipped them the bill, which Thane signed to their room. Maggie started to reach for her purse and protest, but he held up a hand. 'We'll square up later, okay?'

'Just try not to bully me.'

'Wouldn't dream of it.'

They returned to the suite, and, once there, Maggie found the folded pages of Marquise's diary with the addresses and phone numbers of the people she was closest to.

'It'll be simple,' she said, as Thane lit the fire. Kicking off her shoes, she sat on the edge of the couch. 'I'll just call everyone with whom she had an appointment and interview them.'

'Interview them?' he repeated skeptically, straightening as the gas fire hissed quietly and flames licked ceramic logs. 'So now you're a pro?'

'With my background, in a way, I am.'

'And you feel no qualms about donning Marquise's persona and life?' He wasn't amused.

'No. Someone on this list' — standing, she held the pages and shook them under his nose — 'knows something. If not where Mary Theresa is, then what was happening in her life. You can't tell me that her shrink doesn't have some idea as to her mental state. The police think she might have committed suicide, by — well, how? I don't know. Possibly driving over a cliff or holing up somewhere and giving herself a lethal dose of drugs or whatever? But if she was in that frail a mental condition, shouldn't her psychiatrist have had some clue? And what about the people she worked with, her personal trainer — Laslo . . . Laslo . . . ' She looked through the pages. 'Laslo Rolf. Wouldn't she confide in him, or her secretary? Or someone she worked with?' More agitated by the minute, the wheels turning in her mind, she paced in front of the fire as she studied the copied pages of her sister's diary. 'So, no, I wouldn't mind becoming Marquise for a while. Not at all. It's to help.'

'I'd be careful when you start interviewing her psychiatrist, especially if you're serious about walking in your sister's shoes. The shrink might think that you're doing it for other reasons — that you have some need to become Marquise. From the outside it could appear more than a little incestuous.'

She froze at the word. Mitch. Mary Theresa. Thane. Memories of that heart-wrenching time of her life burned through her mind, the same hurtful recollections that had haunted forever and were part of the reason that she had, years before, been under psychiatric care. 'I think we'd better leave incest out of this,' she suggested.

'It's behind us now.'

Never, she thought with the same bitter realization that had chased after her for the better part of two decades. *It'll never be behind us*. 'You know, Thane, you don't have to get involved.'

'Of course I do.' He rubbed his chin angrily. 'I don't have any choice.'

'The police won't — '

'I'm not talking about the police, and you know it, Maggie.' In a heartbeat, he grabbed hold of her wrist. Strong fingers wrapped possessively around the small bones of her arm and pulled her so close that she could smell the pure male essence of him, see the pores in his skin, watch his blue eyes dilate until they were nearly black. 'I always have been involved,' he said in a voice that was low and rough. 'With you.'

Oh, God. She swallowed hard, met the questions in his eyes with those of her own. So much time had passed, so much anger, so much agony. She licked suddenly, dry lips, and the pressure on her arm increased. The pads of his fingers were hot against the soft flesh on the inside of her wrist where her pulse was jumping wildly.

Be careful, Maggie, don't read too much into his words. She'd heard his lies before. 'You don't have to say — '

'I know. I don't *have* to say anything. But this

is just you and me, Maggie. Alone. The way it should have been.'

Her heart screamed to believe him, to trust the words she so desperately wanted to hear, but she hadn't spent the last eighteen years healing only to rip open the scars herself. 'Don't do this, Thane, not now.'

'Why not?' His gaze moved to her lips, and she had to fight to keep from staring at his mouth, at wondering what it would feel like to kiss him here, away from the world, in this intimate hotel room.

'I — I came here because you asked me, but I probably would have anyway, so . . . so, let's not make more of this than there is, okay? We've been thrown together, true, but we should keep things in perspective. Just because I came here to help clear your name, you don't owe me anything.'

'I didn't think I did.' He stared into her eyes for a second, and she saw the clouds in his gray-blue gaze, the torment that only he understood. 'This isn't about obligation.'

'No?' she asked, refusing to focus on his mouth, which seemed suddenly so close.

'It's about want.'

She swallowed hard, thought about stepping away, but didn't. Her pulse, beneath his fingertips, was throbbing, her mind spinning in erotic circles that were dangerously seductive. Firelight flickered against the far wall and high ceiling.

She licked her lips again and his gaze caught the motion. 'What is it you want, Thane?'

'What I always have.' He took her other hand, and the typewritten pages of Marquise's life drifted to the carpet. 'I want you, Maggie. I think I told you that before.'

'And . . . ' Oh, God, she was getting lost in his enigmatic gaze. He was the devil, a demon sent to curse and vex her, a man whom she couldn't resist but wouldn't trust. He'd only bring heartache; only cause pain, and yet, when his head lowered and his lips found hers, just as before, she didn't draw away, didn't push him aside.

No, as his one hand held her wrists and the other wrapped around her shoulders, dragging her close, she didn't resist. Caught in the wonder of his touch, the pressure of his tongue, the glory of the taste and smell of him, she relented, as easily as if she'd planned this seductive moment all of her life.

'Let me love you, Maggie,' he whispered against the side of her face, his breath tickling her ear, her skin prickling with anticipation.

The words should have cleared her mind. He'd never loved her, never would. What had existed between them was passion — raw and primal, sex in its purest, most animal form. She should have walked away, but didn't. Instead she kissed him with all of the fever in her blood, with the vital and primitive need that was building deep in the most private parts of her.

The room seemed to fade, shadows in the corner closing in. His hands reached under her sweater and she didn't protest. He kissed her face, her neck, her eyes and she moaned, feeling the angora being tugged over her head, then cool air caressing her bare skin. He threw the unwanted garment toward the door, and Maggie's legs threatened to give way. Thane's mouth was everywhere, kissing, touching, hungrily feeding a desire that had been building for years. Her fingers found the buttons of his shirt, slid them through the holes, then scraped past the scar on his shoulder and moved anxiously down his sinewy arms as she shed him of the unwanted garment.

Don't do this, her mind screamed. *Maggie, this is only asking for more heartache. Be smart! Think of Becca! Remember Mary Theresa! Remember how much he hurt you*.

But reason fled. It had been too long since she'd made love to him, and memories of their heat, the special passion that they'd shared, burned through her brain.

His lips found the curve of her neck and moved lower still to the circle of bones at the base of her throat while his fingers searched inside her bra, kneading her breast, toying with her nipple until need, hot and pulsating, seared deep in her soul.

Don't! Don't! Don't! she screamed at herself, but didn't listen. She, too, was exploring with anxious fingers, touching the rugged muscles of his chest beneath a mat of thick hair that hadn't been there years before.

He sucked in his breath as her fingers skimmed his nipple, and she felt a washboard of muscles in his abdomen: hard, tight, rigid.

He unhooked her bra, and one long finger

trailed the length of her spine as the lacy bit of clothing fell away. His mouth caressed her skin, nuzzling the tops of her breasts, lowering slowly until his tongue found her nipple and licked it in dizzying circles. Maggie's knees crumpled, and he caught her. As easily as if she weighed nothing, he lifted her from her feet, carried her into his bedroom, and laid her on his bed. Cool silk caressed her bare skin as he settled against her and, stroking her breast, kissed her as if he'd never been with another woman, as if any other female was long forgotten, as if she was the only woman on the planet.

Her slacks and panty hose were removed quickly, rough, persuasive fingers stripping her of any scrap of clothing. He pressed his face into her abdomen, and she turned liquid inside. His tongue rimmed her navel as his fingers touched and teased her nipples. Perspiration dotted her skin.

Maggie closed her eyes, the room swayed, and she gasped as he kissed her even lower, in the most intimate of places. She couldn't help the movements of her body as she writhed with anguished desire. It had been so long . . . she was so hungry and this . . . this was Thane . . . the only man she'd ever truly loved. The only one she wanted.

'Trust me, Maggie,' he said, reaching upward, taking her smaller hands in his and gently placing her palms over her own breasts. He shifted, breathing against her thighs. She tried to remove her palms, but he laced his fingers in hers and forced her hands to move in strong, circular motions on her body. Her nipples were hard buttons beneath her palms, her breathing shallow, desire causing her to writhe. 'Come on,' he whispered, and he caressed with his fingers, stroking, feeling, playing with her nipples, encouraging her to do the same.

'But — '

'It's all right, Maggie. Touch yourself. Feel good.' And then he slid into position, one hand cupping her buttocks, his fingers digging into the hard flesh. With his free hand, he opened her, gently delving and withdrawing until she thought she'd go mad. She wanted more. So much more. His breath fanned her, his tongue found that special spot that only lovers discover, and he touched and tasted of her slowly at first, then with more fervor, his breathing ragged, her body arching as the need increased. The room faded away; she was alone with him, moving to his rhythm, lost to everything but the feel of him, aching for anything he would give her.

'Thane . . . oh, no . . . oh, God . . . Thane . . . '

The first spasm hit.

She bucked upward.

He held her firmly, refusing to let her go, giving more and more, fanning the fires of desire to a new height, and again she was forced into a wild, wanton vigor that caused her to convulse and the world to shatter behind her eyes. She cried out, her voice hoarse, her arms reaching for him, and he pushed himself through the valley between her legs, wrapped his arms around her and kissed her as if he would never stop. Tears burned hot behind her eyelids, but she didn't care, clinging to him, her naked, sweating body enveloped in his.

She expected to satisfy him as he had her, knew he, too, needed a release, and reached for the zipper of his slacks, but he stopped her hand with his own. 'Later,' he whispered into her hair.

'But — '

'Shh. This was for you.'

'Don't patronize me, Walker,' she tried to protest, the room still muted and soft.

'Wouldn't dream of it. Trust me, I'll expect to be repaid in kind.' He kissed her tousled hair. 'Soon.'

'And what if I refuse?' she teased.

'You won't.'

'You think you're that irresistible?'

'Sure of it, Ms. McCrae,' he said with a smile. 'Sure of it.'

'Of all the egotistical, self-serving . . . '

He seemed doubtful, daring her to continue, and she blushed at the recent memory of their one-sided lovemaking.

'I, um, stand corrected.'

'Good.' He kissed her temple and yawned. 'Now, go to sleep, Maggie. If you're serious about this plan of yours, which, for the record, I'm still dead set against . . . '

'Too bad.'

He sighed and twisted a lock of her hair around one finger. 'It is, isn't it? Anyway, tomorrow you're gonna have some pretty big shoes to fill, and I, Ms. McCrae, am sticking to you like glue.'

She started to protest, but he silenced her with

a kiss. 'Enough,' he said, 'before I change my mind and have my way with you.'

'Promises, promises.'

'Careful.'

'Never, Walker.'

'I know. And that, darlin', is the problem.'

No, Maggie thought with heart-piercing clarity. *The problem, Thane Walker, is that I'm falling in love with you*. Oh, God, no. No! She couldn't love Thane. She didn't even trust him! She rubbed her arms, as if she could erase the premonition of doom that had settled like lead in her gut. But she couldn't. From this night forward the course of her life would be changed forever.

Nothing would ever be the same.

15

You're playing with fire.

The words seared through Thane's brain, and he winced as he slipped out the back door of the hotel and huddled against the wind that swept through the well-lit streets. That was the trouble with the city; it was never dark, and this morning he needed all the cover of darkness he could find. Checking his watch, he frowned. Four-fifteen. Denver hadn't started to awaken yet.

Turning up the collar of his jacket, he jaywalked, ducked through an alley where snow was still packed against the old buildings, then zigzagged his way on foot about eight blocks to an all-night restaurant with a pay phone in the lobby. He had a pocketful of change that he used for the long-distance connection. He dialed swiftly, the number burned into his brain, and as he did, he eyed the customers in the coffee shop through the second set of glass doors. They were mostly truckers, he guessed from the looks of the men huddled over their black coffee and platters of ham and eggs.

The phone rang three times before a groggy voice answered. ''Lo?'

'It's Walker. What have you found out?' No reason to mince words.

'Hell, what time is it? It's not even light out,' Roy DePres grumbled, his voice gravelly. Thane had known DePres since grade school in

Laramie. At fifteen they'd been caught stealing cigarettes and beer from the local mom-and-pop grocery just out of town. Both boys had been kicked out of high school and worked swabbing the floors and cleaning the rest rooms of the store to avoid being prosecuted by the owners. Roy had gone on to become a Green Beret in the army. Thane had avoided being sent to prison for nearly beating his old man to death. Not that his dad hadn't deserved it. He'd been drunk and hell-bent on hitting Thane's mother with a tire jack. Thane still bore a scar where the jack had grazed his shoulder.

'Jesus H. Christ,' Roy said around a cough. 'Give me a minute, will ya? I gotta take a leak.' For another full minute Thane waited, watching as an old guy in a Dodgers hat flirted with a reed-thin waitress who, from the bone-weary look of her, must have already put in most of her shift.

Through the long-distance wires Thane heard the sound of water running, a hacking cough, the toilet flushing, then fumbling hands on the receiver. 'Okay, I've been checking on everything you told me,' his friend said, the words muffled a little as, Thane suspected, he rammed his first cigarette of the day between his teeth. 'If what your damned ex-wife told you was true, I can't prove it. Yet.'

'You think it was a lie?' Thane asked, the quiet fury that had been his constant companion for more than three weeks surging through his veins again. 'That she set me up for a wild-goose chase?'

There was the sound of a lighter clicking and a deep draw of breath. Thane felt the urge to break down and light up. Hell, he deserved it. 'Wouldn't be the first time she gave you the runaround, would it?'

'Nope.'

Mirthless laughter barked through the lines. 'You never got over her, did you?'

If only you knew. 'Doesn't matter. Just find out if she was tellin' the truth.'

'Surprised you're not doin' it on your own.'

'And have the police and press all over my ass?' Thane thought he'd explained this. 'Remember. This is all under wraps.'

'Covert Op. I know.'

'I'll call back tomorrow.'

'By then, I might have more info.'

'Good.' He hung up, feeling empty inside. *Damn Mary Theresa and her games*.

He thought about going into the restaurant and having a large cup of black coffee. He could use a jolt of caffeine, but decided against it. He didn't want anyone to check the records of this particular pay phone, and if the police suspected he'd used it, they'd find out way too much.

Checking the street, he slipped out of the diner and hiked back to the hotel, where he planned to pick up his truck and his tail. He smiled grimly to himself. If Detective Henderson or the press had any idea what he was doing, they'd be all over him.

And what about Maggie? What would she do?

He gritted his teeth and shoved his hands farther down in the pockets of his jacket as he thought about her and the fact that, sooner or later, he was going to make love to her. Together they were like fire and paper — ready to ignite. That's the way it always had been between them. It wasn't gonna change. It had taken all of his willpower last night not to go through with the one act that seemed to bind a man and a woman together whether they wanted it to or not. Damn, but he'd wanted to claim her for himself, thrust into her, and feel the warmth of her body surround him.

'Christ you're a fool,' he chided. 'A goddamned romantic moron.' Maybe he should have done it. Hell, he'd come close. Too close. The smell of her skin had been his undoing. Even now, thinking about her trembling beneath him as he touched her with his hands and mouth made him so hard he ached.

He ignored a DON'T WALK sign and strode across an intersection after a sanitation truck had eased around the corner.

Doesn't Maggie deserve the truth?

No, he decided. Not yet. Maybe not ever.

So you're just going to bed her and keep her in the dark?

The way he saw it, he didn't have much of a choice.

* * *

'You need your head examined,' Maggie told herself as memories of the night before curled seductively through her mind. 'Oh, God.' What had she done? Hadn't she warned herself a million times over about him? And yet last night . . . 'Oh, Maggie, wise up!' She shoved her lank hair from her eyes. Naked, embarrassed, and alone in Thane's bed, she scooted to a sitting position and glanced to the windows, where sunlight was streaming past the gauzy curtains. From the hallway she heard the sounds of doors slamming, footsteps, and conversation. Other guests were up and about. And Thane was gone. Where? He didn't leave a note, and there wasn't a message light flashing on the phone. 'Great.' She considered the night before all over again and told herself she was a fool of the highest order. So what if she hadn't actually and technically made love to Thane? 'Close enough.' *Just like in grenades and horseshoes*. 'Come on, girl. Get a move on.'

She showered, changed, and decided it was time to be independent. Within forty minutes, she'd ordered coffee, fruit, and breakfast rolls from room service as well as charged a rental car to her Visa card, and checked with Detective Henderson only to find that there weren't any new leads or breaks in the case. Finally she dialed Becca in California and woke her grumpy daughter up for the second day running.

'Don't you know it's early here?' Becca complained.

'I just wanted to see that you were okay. I called last night, but you were out.'

'Yeah.' She heard Becca yawn and presumably, from the sound of it, stretch. 'Aunt Connie told me to call you today. Is something wrong? Did you find Marquise?'

'Nothing's wrong and no, I haven't located her yet.'

'What do the police say?' Becca, for the first time in weeks, actually sounded interested in what her mother was doing.

'Nothing more than the last time I talked with you.'

There was a minute's hesitation before Becca said, 'She's all right, isn't she? Marquise? She's okay?'

'I hope so.' Maggie wished she could give her daughter more encouragement, then decided she needed to lighten the conversation. There was no reason for Becca to worry. 'So how's Jenny?'

'Okay, I guess, just pissed off — I mean ticked off — that I don't have to go to school and she does.'

'It's only temporary. Until your ankle's healed and I've found Mary Theresa.'

'I know, but it still bugs her.' Maggie thought she detected a small note of triumph in Becca's voice, which was unusual. For as long as Maggie could remember, her daughter had worshiped the ground that her older cousin walked on. Jennifer McCrae could do no wrong in Becca's estimation.

'So how is the ankle?'

'A lot better. Don't even need crutches.'

'You're sure? Aunt Connie said something about a specialist.'

'Aunt Connie's just paranoid. She's always talkin' about doctors and lawyers and all that stuff. You know, she's kinda weird, Mom.'

Maggie smiled. Becca was definitely mellowing.

They talked for a few more minutes, and Maggie hung up feeling relieved, that there might be a chance she and her daughter could bridge the seemingly ever-widening gap that stretched between them.

'Room service.' A deep male voice accompanied a sharp rap on the door.

Within minutes she was eating a scone, washing it down with coffee, and making a list of everyone she wanted to interview, starting with the people at the television station and Eve, Mary Theresa's secretary. Eve had been with Mary Theresa for years, ever since she'd moved from California to Denver. Twice divorced and fighting her expanding figure, she was a workaholic who was 'the most organized person you'd ever want to meet,' Mary Theresa had told Maggie once. Eve had known Mary Theresa longer than anyone, aside from Thane, in the area.

Next, Maggie wanted to speak to Mary Theresa's psychiatrist and doctors, or at least the ones she'd seen in the weeks prior to Marquise's disappearance. She also put Syd Gillette, Mary Theresa's second husband, near the top of the list. According to M.T.'s calendar, she'd met with Syd the night before she'd disappeared.

'Curiouser and curiouser,' Maggie whispered, tucking her bare feet beneath her as she sat in a corner of the couch while sipping a cup of strong coffee. The gas logs sizzled and through the gauzy curtains sunlight was streaming into the room, lifting her spirits. It felt good to be doing something and compiling a list of the people in Mary Theresa's life was a start.

A key turned in the lock, and she felt her cheeks burn with embarrassment as she glanced up to watch Thane let himself into the room. His jaw was black with a day's worth of whiskers and he'd donned jeans, a flannel shirt, and his jacket — as if he'd just come in from a wintry ride on the range.

His gaze touched Maggie's and all her newfound determination faltered. Without saying a word, he replayed the scene from the night before with just one studied, intense look. Her spine stiffened and she reminded herself that she wasn't going to make the mistake she'd made last night again.

Oh, right, her mind threw back at her.

'Mornin',' he drawled as a slow-spreading smile offered the glint of not-quite-straight white teeth.

'Don't try to peddle any of your country-boy charm on me,' she grumbled. 'I'm not in the mood.'

'No?' He had the gall to look surprised. 'Why, Ms. McCrae, I thought I'd come back here and find you singing and laughing and ready to face the day.'

'And why is that?'

His mouth twitched as he unsnapped his jacket. 'Because, darlin', you sure were enjoyin' yourself last night.'

She cleared her throat, and the back of her neck heated. 'Well, yes. About that. I don't think we should . . . well . . . ' *Come on, Maggie. A confident modern woman wouldn't beat around the bush like this. Oh, Lord . . . even her private thoughts were part innuendo*.

'Don't think we should what?' Tossing his jacket over the back of a chair, he leaned one jeans-clad hip against the back of the couch.

She folded her arms over her chest. 'Okay, wise-ass, I don't think we should have sex, okay?'

'*We* didn't.'

'That's just a question of semantics, Walker. I'm not ready to play word games with you, okay?'

He lifted a shoulder, sat down in the chair opposite hers, and, after pouring himself a cup of coffee, plucked a green-tinged strawberry from the fruit cup and plopped it into his mouth with maddeningly little concern.

'I think it would be best if . . . we kept to our separate rooms. Maybe the idea of this suite isn't such a hot idea. We could have regular hotel rooms or even separate hotels — now there's an idea.'

'Or we could stretch a blanket across the middle of this room, like they did in that movie years ago — you keep to your side and I'll keep to mine to protect our respective virtues,' he teased.

'Knock it off. I'm serious about this.'

He lifted one dark eyebrow in skeptical disdain. 'Are you?'

'Very.'

The look he sent her fairly sizzled, and her heart thumped crazily, but she nodded stiffly.

'Whatever you want,' he drawled, and she couldn't stop the flush that warmed her cheeks. He knew what she wanted. They both did. That was the problem. Was sleeping with him worth the emotional risk or damage?

'No,' she said out loud, then felt like an idiot.

'I don't think I asked you a question.'

'Private, one-sided discussion.'

'Let me know if you change your mind.'

'I won't.'

His smile was downright wicked. 'I'm countin' on it, darlin'.'

'And don't call me — '

'I won't.' But his eyes glinted in pure devilment. She didn't know whether to kiss him or strangle him, so she did the next best thing and ignored all the heated innuendos that seemed to thicken the atmosphere in the room.

Resting the heel of one boot on the cushion of a nearby chair, Thane tossed her one last don't-bullshit-me grin, then picked up the folded newspaper and scanned the headlines. 'Your sister's still page one.' He looked over the article before handing the section to Maggie, who read it with interest but learned nothing new.

Thane found the sports page and snapped it open, then glanced at her notes. 'You've got a list,' he observed. 'Don't tell me. People you plan to interview.'

'That's right, but the first person on the list is you. Where did you go this morning?'

'Miss me?' he taunted.

'About as much as I'd miss a coiled rattler,' she retorted, then settled back in the couch and shook her head. 'Sorry. I didn't mean to snap at you.' Sighing, she studied the depths of her coffee — dark and opaque. 'I'm just worried.'

He set the paper aside. 'You're not the only one. Since you seem hell-bent to do your own investigation, I decided to jump-start it.'

'How?'

'I did some checking.'

She was surprised. 'And what did you find out?'

'That Wade Pomeranian was out of town, as he said.'

'How do you know?'

'I called around, found out who his agent is, and phoned the guy at home. He wasn't too happy, but I got the name of the photographer who did the shoot, then gave him a buzz. Our boy Pomeranian was, indeed, in Salt Lake on the day Mary Theresa disappeared.' He yanked open his paper again, but Maggie snatched it from his hands.

'Wait a minute,' she said. 'Last night you were dead set against me snooping around, and now you've taken up the cause like it's your new life's goal.'

'Maybe it is.'

'What's going on, Walker?' she asked, narrowing her eyes at him and wishing she could read his devious and untrustworthy mind.

'A simple case of employing the 'if you can't beat 'em, join 'em' theory. It's obvious that you're not going to give this up, so I decided I'd rather work with you than against you. Though

I'm sure the police will do a more-than-exemplary job, they seem to think I might have somehow been involved in Mary Theresa's disappearance. Maybe I should take a more active hand in finding out the truth.' He took a long swallow of coffee, his eyes appraising her over the rim of the cup. She wanted to trust him. And she wanted her sister home again and her child to reach out to her.

If wishes were horses, then beggars would ride, she reminded herself, even though it would be so much easier to have Thane on her side rather than harbor all these doubts. Just because she'd received a silent message from her sister — or had she? now she wasn't certain — she was second-guessing herself, but it didn't mean that Thane had anything to do with Mary Theresa's disappearance. So what if the police thought he might be involved; they always looked to family first, especially estranged ex-husbands, didn't they? And just because he'd shown up in Idaho, on her doorstep, protesting his innocence, didn't necessarily mean that he had another agenda, a secret ax to grind.

He reached for a scone, and a small smile tugged at his lips. 'So what's on the slate for today, *Mary Theresa?*'

'Very funny.' She eyed her list. 'And the name's Marquise.'

'I keep forgetting.'

'Try to stay on track,' she teased, knowing that he was sharper than cut glass. 'What I need from you is to drive me to the car-rental agency.'

'I thought I'd drive you — '

'We discussed this, Thane. I already ordered the rental. So either take me there, or I'll call a cab, or have the car delivered. Your choice.'

His smile disappeared. 'Not so fast. What if Mary Theresa was kidnapped? What if this is more dangerous than you think? Don't you think you might be the next target?'

'Why?'

'Who knows? That's just the point.' He was dead serious. He finished his scone, brushed his hands, and stood, his boot heels making impressions in the thick mauve carpet. 'I don't know what we're up against here. Do you?'

'No.'

'Then let's sign up for the 'better safe than sorry' plan.'

'I'll be careful.' He looked about to argue, so she added, 'I'm a grown woman, Walker. Lived my life without you for most of my years. I think I'll be fine. Now, I plan to visit KRKY about the time the show airs, then talk to her secretary, her other ex-husband, and her psychiatrist.'

He scowled, but put whatever argument that was brewing aside. 'I'll check with her attorney, the yard-work people, her trainer, and some of her neighbors and friends.'

'Good. We'll meet back here tonight.'

'Take my cell phone.'

'I don't need it.' She wanted his help, but didn't need to be treated like a baby.

'Unless you want me stuck to you like glue, you'll take the damned phone.' His eyebrows had slammed together and his expression was suddenly harsh as a Wyoming winter. He wasn't going to budge.

For once she didn't argue. They didn't have much time. Marquise's program was set to air within the hour, and Maggie was determined to check out the dynamics of KRKY.

* * *

After picking up a late-model Ford Taurus, she wheeled into the parking lot of the television station. The studio was located beneath the ground level of a red-brick tower bearing the station's name. She was greeted by an open-mouthed receptionist, who stared at her as she gave her name. 'Maggie McCrae.'

The receptionist was dumbfounded. 'Forgive me,' she said, flushing to the roots of her short brown hair, 'but . . . you look just like one of our staff, the cohost of *Denver AM!*'

'I'm Mary Ther — Marquise's sister. Her twin.'

'Oh. Jeez. I didn't know. But it doesn't surprise me. Well, sign in here — line thirty-six.' She scribbled in the time, then slid a logbook under a protective glass window. After the formalities, including a name tag, she was escorted by a petite woman who walked almost as fast as she spoke on their way to the station manager's office.

Ron Bishop was waiting. A portly man who smelled faintly of cigars and whose hair had given way to a neatly clipped horseshoe that ringed his head, he rounded a battle-scarred oak desk and extended a hand. When she clasped his fingers, he placed another over the top and gave her palm a vigorous shake. 'Ron Bishop. God, you look just like her. I . . . we . . . none of us knew about you. I mean we knew that she had a sister of course, but not a twin. Would you like to go on the news with a plea to her or whoever's holding her hostage?' he asked, as the thought entered his head, and the wheels, oiled by the idea of soaring ratings, started turning.

'I'll think about it,' Maggie said, eyeing the surroundings. A stuffed marlin shone and arced above the desk, and the other three walls were adorned with awards and eight-by-ten glossy pictures of the manager shaking hands with celebrities he'd met over what appeared to be a span of thirty-odd years in the business. A television was mounted in the corner. *Denver AM* was already in progress.

She glanced at the set where Craig Beaumont, all blond hair, tanned skin, and blue eyes, was interviewing a local Martha Stewart wanna-be. Wearing jeans, a plaid shirt, and a know-it-all expression, the petite woman was explaining about making bird feeders out of things from the kitchen cupboard. Peanut butter, seeds, and other grains were molded into various shapes and displayed on a table for the camera to pan.

'Hell,' Ron said, showing off teeth that glinted with gold fillings as he considered all the implications of Maggie's resemblance to her sister, 'you could even co-anchor her program, at least for a segment, or so.' Behind thick glasses his eyes started to gleam in anticipation. He reached into a humidor for a cigar, though he didn't light it. 'We'd advertise it on the five o'clock and eleven o'clock evening news, then again in the early morning at six.'

He was pushing too hard, too fast, and Maggie didn't like the feeling. She didn't trust this man, though she'd barely met him. She was starting to feel like Thane — unable to trust anyone. 'I'll have to think about it,' she said, sizing the station manager up and wondering whether he had a sincere bone in his body. 'I'm only here because I'm looking for my sister, trying to find out what happened to her.'

'Of course, I understand, and you have the station at your disposal. No one would love to find out what happened to Marquise more than I,' he added, seeming sincere. He leaned back in his chair, letting his suit coat drape open, his fingers still running over the smooth surface of the cigar. 'I won't lie to you, Ms. McCrae, there was a little trouble — well, not really trouble. Let's just call it a difference of opinion between Craig and Marquise on which direction their show should take, but I can assure you that everyone here at KRKY is only interested in your sister's welfare. We were the first to start looking for her, you know, and rival stations might make a bigger story than there is about some disagreements between the two hosts, but that was mainly just industry gossip and envy. *Denver AM* has been consistently at the top of the ratings.'

'Until recently,' Maggie prodded, and the large man lifted a dismissive shoulder.

'It's true, there had been a bit of a slump this past year, but we're taking care of that.'

I'll bet, Maggie thought callously as, after a quick commercial, Craig Beaumont explained to the audience again that the reason he was hosting the program solo was that Marquise was missing. A still picture of her was flashed onto the screen as he asked anyone who had any information as to her whereabouts to call in. The following segment was dedicated to her and showed clips of the few movies she'd been in and a few of the most humorous or poignant moments of Marquise with her guests on the Denver show.

Maggie, silent, watched the screen, and a million memories washed over her. Her eyes misted as she saw her sister laughing, talking, or flirting with a guest. A huge lump formed in her throat and she bit her lip as Mary Theresa as Marquise winked into the camera or tossed back her head and laughed. *Where are you?* Maggie wondered, and had to clear her throat. Marquise had hosted the show alone for the first four years — she'd been the pioneer behind it. Craig had come along two years ago and had, over time, become more and more important, and, according to Mary Theresa, more demanding.

'He wants it all, I tell ya,' Mary Theresa had confided in one phone call. 'Blondie would like it if I just disappeared.'

'Ms. McCrae — ' Ron Bishop's voice brought her back to the present, and she had the uneasy feeling that he'd asked her a question.

'Oh, sorry — what did you say?'

'That I'd give you a tour of the station if you want one.' He glanced at his watch. 'I think we just have time.'

'Sure.' She needed as much information about her sister's life as she could amass.

They talked a while longer and he showed her the newsroom, where desks were joined together in a hub, with only soundproof panels separating them. Reporters typed stories on their computers, researchers collected data, a news board was everchanging, and televisions tuned in to every station in Denver were suspended overhead. Another soundproof room was the studio where the news was filmed. Computer-directed cameras faced a curved, bleached desk where the news team worked each shift. In another room several computers were hooked up to the news department's web site.

Bishop introduced her to several people, including J.R. Alexander, the assistant news director. An energetic, quick-witted man of about forty, with steel-rimmed glasses and a smile that was as quick to flash as vanish, he moved from one computer station to the next, answering questions, giving advice, and generally riding herd over the hubbub.

'Want to cohost the show?' J.R. asked, giving Maggie the once-over. 'I bet the viewers would never know the difference.' Behind his glasses, his brown eyes gleamed as he thought of the possibilities. 'Ever done television?'

Before she could answer, he was called away.

Ron guided her into a maze of back hallways. 'J.R.'s been with us a little longer than your sister and was the executive producer of *Denver AM* before we promoted him into management. Here's where we do our film editing . . . ' He gave her the grand tour, introducing her around.

With each new person Maggie met, curious glances were cast her way. She heard the whispers behind her back, though she ignored them.

'My God, I thought she was Marquise!'

'Can you believe the resemblance?'

'It's weird. Creepy. I wonder if she's the same kind of self-serving, raving bitch.'

'Oh, Jesus, let's hope not. One is enough for a planet this small.'

Laughter and sniggering followed her, but she ignored it. After *Denver AM* had finished taping and the studio audience had filed out of the building, Ron led her down a labyrinthine hallway to a small office occupied by Craig Beaumont.

Marquise's cohost was reaching for his coat, which hung on a hall tree near the door to his tiny office. He did a quick double take at the sight of her. 'Marquise! My God, you nearly gave me a heart attack. Where the hell have you been? You . . . you look great.' He hesitated, as if he sensed something different for the first time, and he glanced at the beaming Ron Bishop. 'Wait a second — '

'This isn't Marquise. It's her sister. Maggie McCrae, Craig Beaumont.'

'Hey, is this some kind of joke . . . ' he said before realizing the truth. 'For the love of Jesus.

Look at you. You and Marquise — you two are identical, right?'

'Nearly.' She nodded, and his blue eyes took in every inch of her, as if validating what his ears were being told.

'I can't believe it.' Still holding his coat, he sat down on the corner of his desk. 'Wow.'

'My thoughts exactly.' Ron Bishop was all business. 'Now, listen. J.R. was half-kidding when he brought this up, but I think it would be a nifty attention-getting angle to put her on your show, you know, act like she's Marquise during the lead-in, something like, 'Is this Denver's most celebrated missing person?' We'll check with Tess O'Shaughnessy' — he turned to face Maggie — 'she's now the executive producer of the show — '

Maggie wasn't going to be bullied into anything. 'Wait a minute.'

' — but it would be something along those lines, then you start interviewing her, not as Marquise, but as her twin. Wouldn't that generate a helluva lot of interest? People are already curious, and the viewing public has a fascination with twin stories — they're all over the miniseries and soaps. And here we've got it all rolled into one. A bona fide mystery *and* a twin deal and, of course, it could help us all find out what happened to her. That's the most important facet, the real reason for the impersonation. The more people who watch the show, the more likely someone will call in with information.'

Craig was starting to warm to the idea. 'Later

in the show, we could have other twins come on — or twins separated at birth, that sort of thing. Explore what they have in common, why with different parents they still have the same mannerisms and interests and tastes.'

'Exactly.'

'Hey, slow down.' Maggie couldn't believe what she was hearing. 'I'm not interested.'

'What?'

'I just came to Denver to find my sister, not exploit her.'

'But you'd be doing her a favor. Maybe even help find her. One of our viewers might have seen her.'

'Wouldn't they have called by now? Surely they'd recognize her.'

'But we could do some special advertising, draw a bigger audience. What do you think, Ms. McCrae?'

Maggie wasn't going to be drawn into this ratings-driven, testosterone, winner-take-all mentality. 'I'd just like to talk to you,' she said directly to Craig Beaumont.

'Mr. Bishop?' A rail-thin woman with doe-shaped eyes and a smart black suit poked her head round the door. 'You wanted me to remind you of your meeting with Mr. Danvers at the Brown Palace at eleven-thirty.'

Bishop checked his watch, mumbled his apologies, and reminded Maggie that she'd be doing her sister a favor if she agreed to be interviewed on *Denver AM* or the news, then hustled out of the tiny room.

'Sorry about Ron. He's . . . well, he's just

Ron,' Craig said. 'Always thinking ratings.'

'The nature of the beast,' she said with a shrug.

'All of us are geared to improving the quality of the show as well as improve our market share.'

'I understand, but as I said, I just want to find my sister, and I thought you could answer some questions for me.'

Craig eyed her for a second, then nodded, and for the first time Maggie saw a deeper side to this man whom her sister had once referred to as 'a poster boy for ex-surfer dudes.'

'Sure. But let's talk outside the station,' Craig suggested. 'There's a restaurant two blocks down the street where we might have a little privacy.'

Maggie agreed. Here, in Marquise's workplace, she felt everyone's eyes upon her. 'Lead the way.'

* * *

Thane drew blanks. Anyone he talked to had little or nothing to say. The convenience store clerk had a faltering memory and the people who worked for Mary Theresa thought she was an angel — that was the word used by Raoul, who handled the yard work. 'An angel sent down from heaven.' An elderly man with six children, two of whom still lived with him, he was devoutly religious and thought that the last five years of his life working for Marquise had been the best.

Her personal trainer, Laslo Rolf, was a surprise. Because of his own prejudices and

Marquise's usual taste in friends, Thane expected the guy to be a major flake. But he'd been wrong.

At twenty-eight Laslo had the body of an Adonis, a mixture of good genes and a healthy exercise-and-nutrition-driven lifestyle. Laslo spent his days working with different women and men, all wealthy, some as newsworthy as Marquise, but none quite as flamboyant.

'Who knows what happened to her,' he said between sessions in the gym with which he was affiliated. They stood at a broad bank of windows looking toward the Denver skyline, where bright sunlight was reflecting on the steel-and-glass towers and the snow was melting as the temperature climbed.

The clank of bodybuilding machines echoed as weights were hoisted and dropped. Muted music was barely audible over the hum of stationary bikes, stair machines, and treadmills.

To his credit, Laslo actually sweated, and he wore a jogging suit over his well-honed body, a white towel draped around his neck. 'With Marquise, you could never tell what was going on. One minute she was on a serious health kick taking vitamins, living on lean meat, vegetables, and fruits; the next thing you knew she was poisoning herself with liquor and drugs.' His nose wrinkled in disdain. 'The trouble with Marquise is that she doesn't have any dedication, no loyalty to her body or the ability to stick to any kind of regimen.' He lifted his broad shoulders. 'But she's not alone. It's a problem in this country.'

'She ever talk about takin' off?'

'All the time.' Laslo dabbed at the perspiration on his forehead with the end of his towel. 'She had dreams, thought she'd end up in New York or back in L.A. doing something in television. That seemed to change week to week — all those problems at the station. Her cohost is a real prick, always out to get her. If you ask me, she was confused and pressured. Either work or, well . . . personal issues.' His mouth pursed, as if he'd said far too much. 'Maybe I shouldn't be talking to you,' he said. 'After all, the way Marquise told it, you were a major part of the problem.'

The muscles in the back of Thane's neck tightened. 'What did she tell you?'

Laslo hedged. 'You know, Walker, half the time I thought she still held a torch for you.'

'And the other half?'

'The other half tells me that she was afraid of you. That you were the only person that frightened the bejeezus out of her. Why's that?'

'Hell if I know,' Thane replied, though that wasn't exactly the truth. Mary Theresa had half a dozen reasons to distrust him — all of them valid. 'You know what they say about ex-husbands.'

'The only good ones are dead ones.'

Thane grinned. 'I've heard that before.'

'Kind of like ex-wives, I suppose,' Laslo said, his eyes drilling into Thane's as an announcement for the next step class was broadcast. 'Look, I've got to go. My next appointment's here.'

A short woman, decked out in expensive workout gear and jewelry, beamed at the sight of the much younger man. Laslo rained a smile on her, and the slightly pudgy woman melted.

Thane got the hell out of there. The gym with its weight machines, rowing machines, ever-moving steps, and sweating bodies all staring at televisions mounted high on the walls or instructors with bodies most of the soft-bellies who walked through the door wanted to duplicate, made him uncomfortable. He believed in staying in shape by simple hard work. Physical labor.

He unlocked his truck, noticed that the Jeep that had followed him here was gone, and felt a bit of relief. But as he drove out of the parking lot, he spied a Plymouth four-door pull away from the curb, and he knew Henderson was still watching him. Adjusting his rearview mirror, Thane nosed his truck toward the heart of Denver again and wondered how Maggie was doing.

Being away from her made him restless and edgy. Though he told himself it was insane to worry — she was a grown woman, for God's sake — he couldn't help the frisson of concern that cut into his brain when he thought of her walking in her irresponsible twin's shoes.

Like she's safe with you. Guilt burrowed deep in his soul. He was using Maggie. Plain and simple. And she didn't know it.

'You're a miserable son of a bitch,' he growled at himself, but it didn't do any good. He'd step on anyone who got in his way. Including Maggie.

Leveling a curse at himself, he flipped his visor down, squinted into the sunlight, and wished the whole mess with Mary Theresa was over.

And when it is, Maggie McCrae will hate the sight of you. Well, so be it. He gunned the engine and set his jaw. No one ever said that life was fair.

16

'I'll admit it,' Craig Beaumont agreed as he downed his second Bloody Mary. 'Your sister and I didn't see eye to eye on which direction our program was heading.' He swirled his drink with a stalk of celery and ignored the bowl of red bean and rice soup he'd ordered. The tiny restaurant was decorated with a Southwestern theme. Lariats, spurs, longhorns, and even a pair of bronzed chaps covered the walls, while the booths were constructed of bleached oak and Formica, topped with lanterns and softened by cushions in muted golds, pinks, and lavenders — the colors of a western sunset.

The food was Tex-Mex, the atmosphere quiet, the waiters seemingly discreet.

'You fought with her the day she disappeared.'

He nodded, waving one hand. 'It was a big scene in front of the assistant producer and crew. A mistake.'

'Tell me about it.'

'It seems so silly now,' he admitted, shaking his head. 'Marquise had been adamant about adding a segment about local celebrities — people in the Mountain States with star power, I guess you'd say. She wanted to dress things up, give the show a 'makeover,' I think her words were. Make it look more like something out of L.A. Sleeker, more sophisticated.'

'And you opposed this.'

'Our demographics showed us that our average viewer is a homemaker with a couple of kids who holds down a part-time job. Some college. Twenty-five to thirty-eight . . . well, anyway, we were going for a homey-folksy feel. We've always had a local chef make a dish during one segment, and you can write to the station, or e-mail for the recipe. We have gardeners, makeovers, local authors, the high-school football heroes, health tips, and artsycrafty things to spruce up the house. Every once in a while we'd have a celebrity who was passing through, either filming a show in town, or hawking his biography, or whatever, but Marquise wanted this to be the new thrust.'

He drained his drink. 'And to be truthful, she wanted me out.'

Maggie wasn't surprised. She picked at her taco salad and asked, 'Why?'

'Because she wanted to run the show. As she had from the minute I came on board. She always resented that, you know — that I was hired behind her back. Never really thought I contributed. So, when ratings started falling again, it was *my* fault.' He flashed her a false if-ya-get-my-drift smile as he reached for a slice of bread, started to butter it, then thought better of it. 'There had been some talk of canceling the show altogether — or going with an entirely new format. The upshot is that Marquise wanted to revamp it — well, excuse my little pun — and handle everything herself.' He munched on his bread and thought for a second. 'Your sister was a prima donna, you know. Saw herself as a queen bee.'

'How did you see her?'

'As a major pain in the ass.'

'She seemed to think the same of you.'

He snorted. 'She would.'

'So you have no idea what happened to her?'

'None.' He blew across a spoonful of his soup. 'I don't wish her any harm, you understand, but I'm not sorry she's off the set. And the reason I can say that is that it's common knowledge at the studio. Anyone will tell you the same thing.'

'Why didn't you like her?'

'Because, Maggie, Marquise was unprofessional. She was always showing up late, demanding everyone listen to her views, threw the worst tantrums I've ever seen, and was totally and irrevocably out of line. Professionalism isn't in the woman's vocabulary.' He ate two more bites. 'She blamed everyone but herself for her problems. Now, don't get me wrong. I really do hope she's okay — she's not a bad woman, just screwed up. And I don't have any idea what happened to her.'

Maggie was warming to Craig whether she wanted to or not. He was self-serving and vain, but seemed honest enough. He made no bones about the fact that he didn't like Marquise and though Maggie wanted to defend her sister to the hilt, to rail against anyone who dared utter a disparaging word against her, at least she understood Craig's motives.

From the restaurant she drove to the outskirts of town and an unobtrusive cinder-block building housing Lawrence's Executive Options, where Eve Lawrence, as president of the company, oversaw and managed ten or twelve accounting and secretarial underlings who, combined, did the paperwork for several small businesses in the Denver area along with handling Marquise's accounts, fan mail, and correspondence.

No-nonsense and dogged, Eve shook her head at the sight of Maggie. 'I know you hear it over and over, but you look so darned much like Marquise, it's spooky. I mean because she's missing and all. I knew you two were pretty close because I'd seen pictures of you, but I didn't realize how much until just now. Mary, Joseph, and Jesus. Spitting image doesn't begin to cover it. Oh, well.'

She clapped her hands together, and Maggie noticed that she wore a ring on nearly every finger. Her makeup was perfect, not one red hair out of place, and her fingernails were painted a deep red and didn't have the slightest chip. In a dark brown suit and boots, Eve Lawrence presented herself as the quintessential business-woman. 'Let's get down to it. What can I do to help find her?' She escorted Maggie into a boardroom and sat next to her at the table. A secretary brought coffee and several files that were filled with information.

'This is all the most recent stuff,' Eve said, as the girl slipped through the door and closed it behind her. Eve poured cream into her cup and watched as clouds swirled to the surface of her coffee. 'If you want copies, I'd be glad to show them to you — well, except for her private papers — tax returns, financial statements, that sort of thing.'

Eve, after a painful second divorce, had followed Marquise to Denver from Los Angeles and built her own business when she realized that she could expand and take care of more than one client. Marquise had given her letters of recommendation and spoken to prospective clients on Eve's behalf. In return, Eve Lawrence seemed to give Marquise her undying respect and trust. As Eve told it, theirs was a near-perfect relationship except that Eve's business was off, and there were a couple of hitches in her dealings with Marquise.

' . . . personally, and this is just between you and me,' Eve confided as she sipped from her cup, 'your sister was going broke. Couldn't control her spending. I shouldn't say anything, but it's all going to come out as she's going to be sued for the money she owes.' Eve shook her head. 'I tried to warn her, but she wouldn't listen.'

'Mary Theresa always played by her own rules.'

'The IRS doesn't take that lightly,' Eve said.

'No, they don't.'

'And, worse yet, your sister had horrible taste in men.' She held up a hand as if she expected Maggie to argue with her. 'I know, I know, I shouldn't make any comments. I don't have a stellar track record myself, and for the most part I stay out of her private life altogether, but she's made some questionable choices. You've met her first husband? Thane Walker?' Maggie's heart froze. Eve rolled expressive eyes. 'Outwardly, he seems fine, you know, the laid-back cowboy type, and sexy as all getout, but there's something about him I don't trust. He's not as much of a roll-with-the-punches kind of guy as he appears, too secretive for my taste. For some reason, and God only knows what that is, Marquise never could quite sever her relationship with him.' Eve sighed.

'Is that right?' Maggie said, a sense of dread seeping through her.

'It's as if he wanted something from her — maybe he'd never stopped loving her, I don't know.' Maggie's throat tightened, and she ignored the painful *I told you so* that echoed through her heart. 'And then there was Syd, the second one. More bad news. I don't mean to sound like a man-hater — I'm not, really — but the ones around Mary Theresa are either conniving or weak. Syd's smart and rich as hell, but he treated Mary Theresa like she was a piece of jewelry, you know, what they call a 'trophy wife,' one who's supposed to come out when she's asked, then stay in the box where he put her and be a good girl the rest of the time. That didn't sit well with your sister, let me tell you. Syd tried that garbage one too many times, and Mary Theresa showed him.' Her eyes glinted as if she knew more than she wanted to share. 'Hit him where it hurt, then gave him his walking papers.'

Maggie sipped coffee and listened while Eve talked freely about the men in Mary Theresa's life. 'It's like she could never really settle down. Between Thane and Syd there were a few boyfriends and after Syd quite a string. No one special, though, all more or less the same — mindless pretty boys. It seems that she was throwing it in Syd's face that she could date younger and better-looking men — ' Eve waved a finger in Maggie's face ' — including his ex-son-in-law, oh boy, did that one tick him off.'

'What was his name?'

'Let's see.' Eve snapped her fingers, and her eyebrows knitted thoughtfully. 'Oh, crap.' She leaned back and sighed, her face pulling together thoughtfully. 'Now, I know it. Let's see. Inman, that's it. Robert Inman. He's not quite thirty and he and old Syd used to play golf together, until he tossed Syd's daughter over for another woman.'

'Mary Theresa?' Maggie asked, feeling sick.

'Mmm.' Eve nodded and smiled a bit, as if she extracted a bit of pleasure in the Gillette family's pain. She took a gulp from her cup. 'Marquise should never have done it, I know, but Robby — that's what she called him — was a real lowlife, always running around. If ya ask me, Marquise did his ex-wife, Tanya, a big favor.'

'I don't suppose Tanya saw it that way.'

''Course not. She was pregnant at the time. It broke up the marriage.' Eve's expression darkened. 'Syd had to find himself a new golf partner.'

The coffee soured in Maggie's stomach. She set her near empty cup on the table.

'Anyway, eventually Mary Theresa gave up on

Robby and found someone else. Her latest boyfriend, that Pomeranian kid, only wanted to ride her coattails and hoped she would get him into films or television with her connections. Fat chance. That new agent of hers, Ambrose King, was always, well, at least in my estimation, pushing her in the wrong direction. So that leaves her slime of a cohost. In my book Craig Beaumont is a snake.' She frowned into her cup. As if she finally realized that she sounded as if she was gossiping, Eve waved off anything else she might have thought. 'Well, I'm the kind of person who believes in calling 'em as I see 'em, and I'm worried about your sister, Maggie. This isn't like her — well, it is, but she hasn't pulled a vanishing act like this for a while. And never for this long. It's . . . unnerving.' She finished her coffee and set the cup aside. 'I just hope she turns up alive and well, and we can all get this behind us.'

'So do I,' Maggie said, though she was feeling more ill at ease with the passing of each day. 'Do you think she was bothered by anything in particular?'

'Besides her life in general?' Eve laughed. 'No, don't think so.' She wagged a finger at Maggie. 'Now, before you start asking me if she was suicidal, the answer is an emphatic 'no' again. The police seem to think she might have gone off somewhere and done herself in, but I doubt it.' She looked directly into Maggie's eyes. 'That wouldn't be Marquise's style.'

They talked for a while, and Maggie left feeling frustrated, learning little more than she had already known, sensing she was no closer to finding out what happened to her sister than she ever had been. The snow was melting under a bright southwestern sun, and the air was clear and fresh, but Maggie couldn't help the sense of foreboding that clung to her like a shadow.

⋆ ⋆ ⋆

'You're sure?' Thane hugged the receiver to his ear and ignored the country-western music and loud conversation that emanated from the bar.

'That's right,' Roy said, his rough voice as clear as if he'd been in the next room rather than some tiny outpost in California. 'It took a little diggin' but I got lucky. Seems as if your ex-wife spent some time in a small private hospital called Our Lady of Sorrows, not far from the Mexican border. The nearest town is miles away. It's for mental patients, and a lot of celebrity types go there on the q.t. to pull themselves together or dry out or to get off drugs. Mary Theresa checked herself in about six months after your divorce was final, pal.'

Thane's gut clenched, and if Mary Theresa had been anywhere near him, he would have grabbed her and throttled her for her deception. 'Hell,' he ground out.

'I guess congratulations are in order,' Roy said, laughing without much mirth. 'It's not every day a man discovers he's got a seventeen-year-old son.'

Betrayal burned through Thane's soul, and he remembered the way Mary Theresa had thrown it in his face just last week. She'd called him in Cheyenne and she'd been sobbing, swearing she was going to kill herself, out of her mind with her latest emotional trauma. She'd begged him to come to Denver. He'd pushed the speed limit and straightened corners the entire distance.

When he'd arrived at her house, he'd found her in the kitchen, dressed in a black silky bathrobe and offering him a drink as she led him to the kitchen. He should never have followed. She'd been three sheets to the wind, and when he'd refused the bourbon, she'd gotten right to the point and asked to borrow money from him. He'd refused, and she'd fallen into a million pieces, first trying to seduce him and then crying.

She'd tried all her tricks on him. First she'd kissed him, opening her mouth and licking his ear, telling him he was the only man who had ever satisfied her.

'Give it up,' he'd told her, pushing her away. She'd stumbled, falling against the kitchen counters. Tears had sprung to her eyes, and she'd started sobbing again, as if she were broken-hearted.

Of course it had been an act. Just one of the many masks of Marquise that she donned with such agility.

'Don't even think about it, Mary,' he'd told her when she'd wound her fingers in the lapels of his jacket and turned her face up to him. Her eyes had shone with tears. Her cheeks and nose had turned red from booze, tears, and effort. He hadn't budged. 'I'm not buyin' it, lady.' Slowly, he'd pried her fingers from his coat.

She'd flown into a rage. Her beautiful eyes had flared with green fire. 'You have to help me.'

'No, Mary Theresa, I don't have to do anything.'

'But you . . . we . . . '

'We're nothing. Ex-spouses who never loved each other.'

'Bastard!'

'Absolutely.'

'God, you're cold.'

'Learned from the master.'

'How can you be so heartless, so cruel?' she'd asked, pouring herself another screwdriver and swirling the vodka and orange juice in a tall glass. Her eyes glistened with tears, mascara ran down her cheeks, and she looked like hell. 'You know, Thane, I gave you everything. I was only seventeen when you seduced me — '

'This won't work either,' he'd said. 'I don't feel guilty.'

'But — '

'And for the record, you seduced me. Pretended to be Maggie.'

Her lips had curled into a sneer. She set her drink on the counter. 'It was always Maggie with you. Even when I was pregnant with your child, you pretended I was her. You're sick, Walker.'

'Probably.'

Sniffing loudly, she'd hung her head and taken on the pose of the wounded. Another mask. Staring at the floor, she'd whispered, 'I need your help, Thane. You're the only one I can count on, the only one who — ' She caught herself, bit her lip, and a tear fell to the floor.

He nearly buckled but held firm. 'Forget it, Mary. I'm through with this — with you. It's gone on long enough. No more.'

'You can't do this to me.' Her voice was but a whisper, and she ran a finger over the tile of the counter.

'You've done it to yourself.'

'So now you're preachy.'

'I'm outta here.'

'Just listen, Thane. I'll pay you back. Please. I owe back taxes, and God, the credit cards are immense, and there's talk of canceling the show and . . . oh, shit, what am I gonna do? Thane — '

'No way.'

'But I need — '

'You can't keep coming to me. Every time there's a problem, you call me. It's time you stood on your own two feet or leaned on that pretty boy of a boyfriend of yours.'

'Wade?' she said, wrinkling her pert little nose before taking a swallow. 'He's useless.'

'Then find someone else, damn it, Mary Theresa. It's what you're good at. You and I — we're through.'

A bubble of laughter escaped her throat. 'Silly boy,' she said, though tears were still drizzling from her eyes, and she stopped her runny nose with the cuff of her robe. Her eyelids lowered to the same seductive half-masts he'd always found so damned alluring. 'We'll never be through. Don't you know that?'

'What I know is that it's finally over.' He opened the French door leading to the patio.

Cold air, promising winter, raced into the room.

'Don't think so.' She lifted her glass and drained it of vodka and orange juice. Then slowly, her gaze never leaving his, she started crunching ice between her beautiful teeth.

'As I said, I'm outta here.' He was through the back door and taking in deep gulps of air. Dry leaves scattered and scratched across the bricks, and the lake, with naked branched trees standing guard, was a cold dark mirror.

'Don't you wanna know why it's not gonna be over? Why it never can be?' Following him outside, where the evening air was brisk and clear, the first few stars flung high in the purple sky, she hurried to catch up with him. The hem of her bathrobe dragged in the brittle yellowing grass, but she didn't seem to notice.

'No.'

'Sure you do — '

He made it to the gate and unlatched it. Somewhere in a neighboring house, a door slammed. 'Forget it, Mary.'

'Can't do it and neither should you.'

He didn't listen, made his way toward the front of the house, but she caught up with him, grabbed hold of his shirt. 'I've got a secret,' she taunted, her face white in the thin moonlight.

'More than one, I'll bet.'

'But this one's a doozy. It's about you.'

'Not interested.'

'Oh, I think you should be.' Her voice had taken on a singsong quality as he approached the edge of the garage and the front of the house. 'You were the one who was so keen on being a daddy way back when.'

'What does that have to do with — ' He spun on a heel and took hold of her wrist. His heart slammed in his chest as he began to understand. 'What are you saying?' he demanded, his voice low. From the corner of his eye he saw a cat slinking through the shadows.

'Don't you get it?' She laughed, the tinkling sound of victory. Somehow she thought she'd won.

'Get what?'

'We did have a baby, Thane. A boy.'

'No way. You told me you miscarried.'

'After the first one . . . I found out just about the time we split the sheets.'

'It's a lie.' His head hammered.

'If you think so.'

His short supply of patience fled. 'I mean it, Mary.'

'Oh, well, you're not interested.'

He slammed her up against the side of the garage. 'Don't mess with me.'

'I'm not, Thane. It's true. You've got a seventeen-year-old son.'

'You're drunk.'

'Not drunk enough.'

'I swear if this is another one of your bullshit lies, Mary Theresa, I'll kill you!' His fingers tightened roughly over her shoulders, and he shoved his face so close to hers he smelled the perfume in her hair, the nearly odorless scent of vodka on her breath.

'You don't have the guts.' In a heartbeat he realized how easily he could crush her bones or

. . . take her into his arms and make love to her until . . . Oh, Christ, no! He dropped his hands and stepped backward, nearly tripping on the damned cat. It yowled, then hissed, scrambling under the fence. 'Where is he?'

'Don't know.'

'You're lying.'

'Nope. I gave him up.'

'Where?' Thane demanded. 'Where were you?'

'Write me a check. Then we'll talk.'

'You miserable, self-serving bitch!'

'There was a time when you didn't think so.'

'There was a time when I was trapped,' he'd said, but felt the noose that kept him tied to Marquise tightening. Anger churned through his blood. 'But no more. No more!'

'Then rot in hell, Thane Walker.'

I am, he thought, driving away.

Now, as he hung up the phone knowing that he'd missed seventeen years of his son's life and that he'd never really fallen out of love with Maggie McCrae, the sister of his ex-wife, he knew more than he ever had that Marquise had cursed him as surely as if she'd cast a spell. She'd been right. He'd never be rid of her.

* * *

Driving through the sun-washed, crowded streets of Denver, a city she'd visited only a few times, Maggie felt isolated and alone.

A few years ago there had been so many people in her life; but her parents had died, her in-laws turned their backs on her when she'd decided to divorce Dean, her daughter didn't trust her, and now her sister was missing. Glancing at a map on the front seat, she slowly maneuvered the rental car to the hotel, where a valet parked it, and she took the elevator to the suite she shared with Thane.

'Home sweet home,' she said, dropping her purse into a chair. Kicking off her shoes, she checked Thane's bedroom. It was empty, the bed freshly made. Sighing, she leaned against the French doors and thought a second too long about falling asleep with his arms around her. How safe it had seemed. 'Get over it, Maggie,' she mumbled, remembering that what she and Thane shared was lust, not love.

She placed a call to Marquise's agent in Los Angeles but was snippily informed that 'Mr. King is out of town for the rest of the week,' so she gave her name and was promised that Mr. King would call her 'ASAP.'

'Dream on,' she grumbled, dialing Michelle Kelly, Marquise's psychiatrist. On the third ring a recorder answered, and Maggie left a message requesting an appointment.

Frustrated, she looked at the clock and wondered when Thane would be back. Even if he was gone only for a few minutes, this might be her chance to try and find out more about him — the secrets she sensed he hid.

It was Thane. He did this to me. Don't let him get away with it.

Did what, Maggie wondered. Ignoring the ridiculous sense that she was trespassing, she wandered into Thane's bedroom and looked around for his bag. She found it in the closet, and, straining to hear if a key were inserted into the lock announcing Thane's arrival, she rifled through the contents. Jeans, slacks, sweater, shirts, socks, and underwear. A small shaving kit. Nothing more. No papers, no address book, no clues as to what he was hiding.

'So much for being a master detective,' she muttered, replacing his things and pushing aside the fear that she was spinning her wheels, that no matter what she did, she wouldn't be able to help her sister or unlock the secrets surrounding Thane Walker.

In the one day of walking in Mary Theresa's shoes, she hadn't gotten far — probably barely out the door. But what had she expected? To 'crack the case' in twenty-four hours when the Denver police had been working for days? Rubbing the kinks from her neck, she walked into the bathroom and twisted on the gold faucets of the sunken tub.

'You're a ninny,' she chided, catching sight of her reflection in the full-length mirror as she stripped out of her clothes. It was strange seeing herself through eyes that compared her to Mary Theresa. Stark naked she walked to the mirror and lifted her hand, pretending the image staring back at her was Marquise, who, raising the opposing arm, was the very mirror-image twin she was labeled at birth.

'Where are you?' Maggie asked, resting her head against the glass, forehead to forehead with her reflection. Marquise's reflection. Mary

Theresa's reflection. Oh, Lord, it was all so confusing.

She took a seat on the edge of the sunken tub and massaged her aching feet. She wasn't used to wearing heels or pretending to be her sister. Steam rose, filling the room as she wound her hair into a knot that she clipped to the top of her head and again caught sight of her image in the mirror.

How much did she really look like Marquise? Enough that Thane had been able to fantasize about her last night?

Don't do this, Maggie. It's dangerous. Dark. Creepy.

Settling into the tub, she let the hot water envelop her and replayed the night before in her mind. In retrospect, the lovemaking with Thane seemed almost surreal, and oh, so sinfully tantalizing. Her skin tingled at the thought of what Thane had done to her, how his touch had driven her to heights of ecstasy she hadn't scaled in years. He'd been her first lover and was still the best.

'Oh, sure,' she growled, snapping back to reality. The reason she was still interested in him was because he was forbidden fruit, the great taboo of her life. His secrets fascinated her; his badboy charm seduced the hell out of her and reduced her to the state of being just another foolish woman. Disgusted, she refused to think about how he could drive her crazy with desire, or how with one glance from those stormy eyes he caused her to fantasize about him. *And him to fantasize about Marquise?*

What was it Eve had said, that Thane had never severed his ties to Mary Theresa? That she suspected that he still loved her — that they were still connected? Why? What was the link that kept them bound?

A headache started to pound with the questions that haunted her. She washed herself, closed her eyes, and let the soothing water grow cool around her. She tried to concentrate on her sister's whereabouts, attempted to piece together what little she knew, but thoughts of Thane and the magic of his hands and mouth kept getting in the way.

She dozed for a second and woke up to cold water and shadows filling the room. She couldn't forget she was here with a purpose, that Mary Theresa was the reason she was in Denver. She climbed out of the tub and was reaching for a robe when she heard the door to the suite open. Quickly she threw on the short robe and hurried to the living room.

'Well?' she demanded, as Thane yanked off his gloves. He'd been striding into the room but stopped when he caught sight of her, and she was suddenly embarrassed, aware that she was barely dressed.

He tossed his gloves and jacket onto a chair. 'I didn't learn much.' His gaze strayed to her throat, where the neckline of the robe overlapped. 'The convenience store clerk was a bust. Not even sure if Marquise did stop by. Laslo seems on the up and up, and the gardener and housekeeper worship the ground she walks on. I stopped by Syd Gillette's hotel, but he wasn't in, and he and I never did get along.' Abruptly he met her eyes again. 'How 'bout you?'

'Not . . . not much better,' she admitted, and had to clear her throat. He brought with him the smell of the outdoors and his hair was ruffled, falling over his forehead in a boyish manner that reminded her of a summer long ago. 'But I still want to talk with her agent and psychiatrist. The people at KRKY seem to care about what happened to her, but who knows?' She looked him squarely in the eye and couldn't forget making love to him. 'You know, I've been fooled before.'

'Cheap shot, Mag,' he said, then walked to the bar, found a bottle of scotch, cracked it open, and poured himself a drink. 'Want one?' he offered.

She was tempted. The muscles in the back of her neck were tight, her head still ached a bit, and being around Thane made her edgy; but she'd never been one to rely on alcohol, had seen too much devastation in her own family to be much of a drinker. 'Make it small.'

One eyebrow lifted as he poured. 'Whatever you want, darlin'.'

'I thought I told you to stop calling me that.'

He shook his head and grinned. 'Testy today, aren't you?' He crossed the room and handed her a glass. 'To you, Maggie,' he said, touching the rim of his glass to hers.

'To Mary Theresa,' she said automatically, and took a long swallow as one of his eyebrows inched upward. Smoky scotch seared a path to her belly.

'Whatever.' Sipping his drink, he turned on the fire and glanced into the mirror over the fireplace. In the glass he stared at her for a long, uncomfortable heartbeat. Maggie took another quick drink. Being this close to Thane was a bad idea. He knew her too well, was too familiar, too damned irresistible. 'I think I'd better move into another hotel,' she said, surprised that her voice had grown husky.

'Why?'

'You know why. This' — she shook her head — 'this is crazy. Last night . . . '

'What about last night?' Turning, he leaned a shoulder against the mantel and finished his drink in one long gulp.

She tried not to stare at his throat as it worked or notice the crow's-feet that fanned from the corners of his eyes when he looked at her or how long his legs seemed to be in the shadowy room. She didn't want to think of his touch or how he smelled or the fact that no one had ever kissed her with the same intensity as Thane had. Not even Dean.

A needle of guilt pricked her heart. She'd married Dean McCrae on the rebound, told herself that she would learn to love him, that what she'd felt for Thane had only been child's play, first love, the thrill of experimentation and exploration. Nothing more.

But she'd been wrong.

The love she'd felt for this solitary cowboy had never died, damn it, and even now, years later, trapped in a romantic hotel room, it didn't seem to matter that they were here because of Mary

Theresa, that the woman who had once broken them apart now drew them together, that all the pain of the past could oh-so-easily be relieved.

'Don't be dense, Thane,' she said, finishing her drink and casting caution to the wind by padding barefoot to the bar and pouring herself another stiff shot. 'We both know that we can't ever . . . that you and I . . . it'll never work, and I'm not up for just a quick fling, okay? I've got too much on my mind.'

When she turned he was beside her, and though he didn't touch her, didn't so much as brush a hand against her shoulder, she could feel him as surely as if they were naked and lying entwined, skin to skin, body pressed against anxious body.

The scotch was already warming her blood.

'I think we should talk about something.'

His tone stopped her cold. 'What?'

'There's something you've got to face, Maggie. Something important.'

She took another sip before asking, 'And that is?'

'The fact that Mary Theresa may be dead.'

'What?' She nearly dropped her glass. 'No way.'

'Think about it. She's been gone almost a week now without a call or note or word of any kind. No ransom note, no demands, nothing.'

'I don't believe it,' she said, shaking her head. 'I can't. What — what about her Jeep? Where is it?'

'Maybe stolen. Or with her body.'

'Don't even talk like this! I won't believe it. I can't.'

'Maggie — be reasonable, something's happened.'

'No.' She shook her head, walked to the windows and stared out at the night. 'No.'

'Maggie, listen, you've got to prepare yourself,' he said, his voice rough. 'She could be gone.'

Tears touched the back of her eyes and she was suddenly angry. At Thane. At Marquise. At the whole damned world. 'I know she's okay.'

'How? Just because you're twins — '

Whirling, she nearly spilled the remainder of her drink. 'You wouldn't believe me if I told you.'

His eyes narrowed. 'You *know* something? And you didn't tell me?'

'I couldn't.' Dear God, could she confide in him now — tell him all the truth? Did she dare? The scotch made her bold, the intimate room engendered the sharing of secrets.

'What?'

'Remember when I told you about the mental telepathy?'

'Not something I'd easily forget.'

'I suppose not.' She fortified herself with another swallow of fiery liquor.

'Something else?'

Oh, God. 'You could say so.'

He set his glass on the bar and shoved both hands into the front pockets of his jeans. Leaning his hips against the counter's edge, he said, 'Don't tell me she's been sending out messages again.'

'No — I, um, haven't heard from her since the

last time — in the barn.'

'Before I showed up at your ranch in Idaho.'

'Yes,' she said, suddenly as cold as she had been on that very day. She wondered if she could trust him and decided it didn't matter. It was now or never. Her hands were shaking as she crossed the room, forcing some distance between her body and his. She finished her drink and set her empty glass on the mantel. 'The message she sent me that day was horrifying.'

'She asked for your help,' he prodded.

'But there was more to it than that.' She shoved both hands through her hair, dislodging the clip that had held it pinned to the top of her head. 'I know you're having trouble believing this — I did, too. I've been told by professionals that it's impossible, that I've imagined it, that in all the cases they've studied of identical twins, they've seen nothing like this and since it's so . . . erratic, I can't prove it.'

'We've been through this part before, Mag Pie. Why don't you quit stalling.' His voice was low, nearly threatening.

She froze. Oh, Lord, why had she opened her mouth in the first place?

'You said she contacted you. What did she say?' he repeated.

'The truth of the matter is that she said you were involved.'

'Involved? In what?'

'In whatever happened to her.'

'What?' he whispered.

'She . . . she said that you did it to her. Whatever she was talking about.'

‘Is this some kind of joke?’

‘Of course not.’

‘You believe that I . . . oh, hell.’ His fingers curled into fists. ‘Son of a bitch. Son of a goddamned — ’ In three swift strides he crossed the room and grabbed her shoulders. ‘Listen to me, Maggie, I don’t know what you or Mary Theresa are trying to pull here, but I didn’t do anything to harm her. You understand?’ His fingers dug deep into her shoulders.

‘Pull?’ she replied. ‘You think I’m trying to put something over on you?’ She couldn’t believe her ears. After all the time they’d spent together, after kissing and touching and . . . Dear God, how could he possibly think she would lie to him? *But you don’t trust him, do you? Not completely. Be honest, Maggie.* ‘That’s . . . that’s ridiculous.’

‘Any more ridiculous than trying to make me believe that you and your sister, from whom you’re practically estranged, are involved in some kind of mental telepathy and that she . . . she is trying to blame me for her disappearance?’

‘I know it sounds crazy but — ’

‘Holy Christ, it *is* crazy, Maggie.’ He stared at her with harsh, unforgiving eyes. ‘What the hell is this?’

‘You tell me, Thane.’ She glared up at him. ‘You’re the one with the secrets.’ Shadows shifted in his eyes and she sensed a lie. ‘Damn you, Walker, why can’t you be straight with me?’

‘Probably for the same reason you can’t with me.’ His gaze drifted from her eyes to her lips. ‘You never said a word about Mary Theresa pointing some kind of mental finger at me. And now all of a sudden — '

'It's true, damn it. Why would I make it up? Why? You think I want you to think I'm a loony? For God's sake, Thane, for once in your life, trust me.'

'Why?' he demanded, and she nearly slapped him.

'Go to hell.'

'Too late, darlin',' he said roughly as he dragged her so close she could smell his heat, ''cause I'm already there.' With that his lips crashed down on hers and kissed her long and hard, sucking the breath from her lungs, causing her blood to ignite. One hand slipped beneath the lapel of her robe to cup her breast.

She closed her eyes as rough fingers grazed her nipple.

Don't do this, Maggie, she warned herself. *Don't. Don't. Don't!* But she couldn't stop, and when his tongue pressed against her mouth, her lips parted willingly. One hand worked the knot of her robe, the other shoved the terry cloth over her shoulders and suddenly she was naked, sagging against him, and he was on his knees, kissing her breasts, touching, suckling as goose bumps rose on her flesh. Her fingers plowed through his hair as he kissed her navel, his tongue rimming the small indentation, his hands lowering to her buttocks, where they held her fast against him.

She melted inside and moaned and he kissed her intimately before she sagged into his waiting arms and he carried her to the bed. *Stop,*

Maggie, she told herself as she looked up at him looming over her, a dozen questions in his gaze. But the warning fell on deaf ears and she turned off the denials racing through her brain as she found the buttons of his shirt, pushed the cotton fabric off strong shoulders and down long, sinewy arms. She tossed the shirt to the floor. Anxiously her fingers found the button fly of his jeans and with one tug, the fasteners gave way. She should stop, right now. Before things went too far. But she couldn't. Deep inside she felt a yearning, a need that pulsed between her legs and pounded in her heart.

'Maggie,' he whispered as she, scooting lower on the bed, forced the jeans over his slim hips and down long, rock-hard thighs. His skin sheened with perspiration, and, as she ran her fingers along the length of his spine, he sucked in his breath. She kissed the soft hair on his thighs, traced the dark line of down that arrowed from his waist to his crotch, then gently, looking up at him with eyes she knew were luminous, touched his erection with the tips of her curious fingers. 'God, Maggie . . . ' He kicked the Levi's to the carpet, dragged her upward, and spread her legs with his knees. 'You make me crazy,' he growled, propped on his elbows, staring down at her with lust-glazed eyes. 'You know, woman, you always have.'

'That . . . that works two ways, cowboy.' Oh, Lord, she wanted him, more than she'd ever wanted a man, more than any woman should want a man. She trembled with the wanton need that awakened in the deepest center of her womanhood and licked, like flames on dry kindling, through her blood.

He glanced at her mouth, leaned down to kiss her again, and then, as his arms entrapped her, he closed his eyes and swore under his breath. 'Maggie, I just don't want to hurt you.'

'Then don't,' she said, desire throbbing through her. 'Don't — ' *Just love me, Thane. For once, love me. Not my sister, but me!*

'Christ, I should be hung for this,' he growled, before his lips claimed hers again, strong arms held her hard and possessively. His entire body tensed and he groaned savagely, thrusting deep, penetrating the deepest part of her. She gasped, he withdrew, then delved again with a desperate surrender that brought tears to her eyes. 'Maggie, sweet, sweet . . . oh, God.' His voice was ragged, his breathing raspy, his hair dark with sweat. Eyes held hers as his tempo increased, and the veins on his neck bulged. She moved with him, danced the intimate dance of lovers, her fingers digging into the flesh of his back. She couldn't breathe, couldn't think, saw only the man above her in a cloudy haze. Faster and faster — the room spun wildly until she bucked upward, convulsing, hanging on to him as he tossed back his head and stiffened, pinning her to the bed, claiming her as his own, joining with her as man and woman have joined for millennia.

'God help me,' he breathed, spilling into her before collapsing and drawing deep, irregular breaths.

God help us both, she thought, as he held her.

Exhaustion and frustration had taken their tolls. She closed her eyes and told herself it didn't matter that she'd made love to him, that whatever happened they needed this time together, and she refused to give in to the dark doubts that crowded around the corners of her mind. Instead she snuggled against Thane and relaxed, sighing as he drew the cover over her. Snuggling close, she listened to the steady, comforting beat of his heart. There was enough time for recriminations tomorrow.

* * *

'Cover for me, would ya?' Jenny begged as she pulled her hair through the neck of her turtleneck. The lights were out, Uncle Jim and Aunt Connie had gone to bed, and Jenny was planning to sneak her car away from the house to meet her boyfriend, Kevin, a twenty-two-year-old with hair dyed black, several nose rings, a goatee, and a permanent scowl. Becca thought Kevin was cool, he even played drums in a local band, but she didn't like having to do the lying for her cousin. From the moment Becca had dropped her duffel bag in Jenny's closet, Jenny had been asking her to do a lot of 'covering' for her, and Becca had the vague suspicion that she was being used.

Jenny's clock was a wooden Elvis, painted to look like the King. The face of the clock was inserted into Elvis's torso, but his hips swung free, keeping time to the seconds that were ticking away. Right now, the clock didn't seem quite so whimsical and cool, but it did tell Becca that it was nearly midnight. Uncle Jim, a businessman who woke up at 5 A.M. so that he could jog five miles before driving to work, had been in bed since ten. Aunt Connie had rattled around the kitchen and had been on the phone until nearly eleven, then she, too, had turned in. No doubt they were both sawing logs, but Becca didn't want to be left holding the bag if they woke up. 'Let me come with you,' she suggested.

'Oh, yeah, right!' Jenny rolled her expressive eyes. Along with the black turtleneck sweater, she was dressed in tight black jeans. A huge belt with a gold buckle accentuated her tiny waist. She straightened the buckle, then reached into her top drawer and pulled out a few bills from a jewelry case she kept beneath her bras. Her secret stash of money — over two hundred dollars that she'd saved from her allowance. Tucking the bills into a pocket, she said, 'Haven't you ever heard the expression 'three's a crowd'? Kevin and I don't need a baby-sitter, if ya know what I mean.'

Becca got it all right. But it bugged her. 'So what am I supposed to say if your mom comes in?'

'I don't know. That . . . that I got restless and went out to take a walk, or to get something to eat, or something. Anything but that I'm with Kevin, okay? Mom would probably have a coronary, right here in the middle of the room. She thinks Kevin is a . . . wait a minute, I think the direct quote is, 'a low-life punk who's probably on drugs and will never get anywhere.' '

Jenny wrinkled her nose and pursed her lips in an impression of her mother's persnickety expression that was dead on. Becca couldn't help but giggle.

'Don't worry. I'll be back in a couple of hours. Okay?'

It wasn't, but Becca muttered, 'I guess.'

'Good. Tomorrow we'll go to the mall, I promise.'

Becca hated the mall.

Biting her lip nervously, Jenny carried her black shoes in her hands, and Becca slid lower in the bed. 'Here.' Jenny picked up the remote control that had been left between the brushes and CDs on her dresser, then tossed it to Becca. 'You can watch Letterman.' Opening the door a crack, she gnawed on her lip and scouted the hallway; then, with one final glance at her cousin, she slipped through the opening, closed the door softly behind her, and slid noiselessly down the hall.

Becca was sweating. She strained to hear any sound through the open window. A cat mewed quietly from a hiding spot in the backyard, a few cars passed on the road in front of the house, and far away a horn honked. Then she heard it, the sound of an engine turning over as Jenny, who always parked her Jetta on the street, started the car and, without the tiniest squeak of tires, took off.

Becca ran to the window and peered through the slats of the blinds in time to see the red taillights of the Jetta disappear around the corner. The night was eerie, blue light from the streetlamps glowing through the palm-tree fronds and branches of the grapefruit trees that shaded the garage. Becca's heart was thudding, pounding so loudly she was certain Aunt Connie, three doors down, could hear it.

Swallowing hard, Becca wondered why she'd ever wanted to come here. At this moment she hated L.A. and couldn't help but feel alone, betrayed, and abandoned. Jenny was a turd, and Aunt Connie and Uncle Jim acted funny, always asking her questions about her life in Idaho, about her mother, about how she *felt* about living so far away, about how her mother spent their money. There had been a few quiet inquiries into her mother's health and job, and Becca got the feeling something was up — something she might not like. When she'd asked Jenny about it, her cousin had just shrugged.

'They're always uptight, and with Grandpa in the nursing home, it's been worse. They're gonna drag you to see him, you know, because he's about a goner and they're all worried about his will. Something about trust funds, I don't really get it.' She'd rolled her eyes and gone back to filing her nails.

Now, Jenny and her Jetta were long gone, and Becca turned away from the window to flop down on the bed and fight the stupid feeling that she was going to cry. Here in L.A., where she was supposed to be having so much fun, she felt miserably alone. And scared. If Aunt Connie found out that Jenny'd taken off, she'd have a stroke. And probably blame Becca somehow. In the few days she'd been here, Becca had already sensed that she was not just a guest, but kind of a burden. Aunt Connie not only resented her, but was blaming her for any kind of trouble that happened.

The seconds ticked by, and Becca's heartbeat finally slowed. The house remained still. Throat dry, Becca finally let out her breath, clicked on the television, the volume muted and low. As she switched through a billion stations, she caught a glimpse of her mother's face — no, wait, it was Aunt Marquise. She stopped channel-surfing and caught the news out of Denver, that her aunt was still missing, and the police were beginning to suspect foul play.

What? Foul play?

Her heart hammered. What exactly did that mean? Foul play? Murder? Oh, man, she hoped not. Kidnapping? Rape? All those horrible things that she saw on the news or in those police-drama shows? Jeez, not Marquise. No way. Anxiously, Becca listened to the report, learned nothing new, and was suddenly worried sick. Something big was going on, more than she had ever imagined. She snapped off the set and pulled the covers over her head. Where was Marquise? Nobody could really hurt her, could they? Hadn't Aunt Connie said that Becca's mother had called earlier, when she and Jenny had been at a movie? Had she been calling about Aunt Marquise? Oh, man, oh, man, this was bad.

It was just a dumb news report. She couldn't let herself get freaked out by it.

And yet she started to shake. She thought

about her favorite beautiful but wild aunt, who looked so much like her mother but was ten times cooler.

Becca blinked against a sudden, stupid wash of tears. Swallowing hard and feeling a thick lump clog her throat, she realized how badly she missed her mom and her dad. Tears threatened her eyes, and she set her jaw to combat them. Why had her mom decided to divorce her dad? She'd never really gotten a straight answer on that one. And, crap, why had he ended up dead? That old dull ache, the one that throbbed in her chest for months after her father's accident, started up again, and she hugged her pillow close to her body. She missed him. So much. And now she missed her mother. Something she'd have sworn was never possible.

Sniffing loudly, she thought of the last few months when they had been living in Idaho. Maggie had wanted to get away from L.A. and 'all the memories, all the pain.' Becca had fought the move tooth and nail, had refused to speak to Maggie, had even wished she could die, and hadn't been afraid to tell her mother just how she felt.

Now, Becca cringed at the thought. At the time, Maggie had been seeing a shrink and had insisted that Becca visit him, too. Maggie McCrae had been a basket case — well, they both had been. Thinking back on that painful scene, Becca was embarrassed that she'd laid so much guilt on her mother and, though she hated to admit it, she had decided that living in

Settler's Ridge wasn't all bad. In fact, some of it she actually liked.

Like riding Jasper through the woods at night with that stupid, ugly, Barkley loping on three legs behind the horse. That one-eared dog had turned out to be her best friend in the world. Barkley slept on the end of her bed and followed her everywhere she went, just like he would have if she'd raised him from a pup. Yeah, he was dumb.

Then there were the kids in school. Lots of 'em were geeks — country bumpkins who didn't know anything about L.A. or surfing or beach volleyball or anything other than what they saw on MTV, but some of the girls seemed okay, and there was one boy in her class, Austin Peters, who was pretty cool. He had shaggy blond hair, cut kinda long, and he was on the shy side; but he smiled at Becca sometimes, and when he did her heart went kerthunk. Austin Peters had the greatest blue eyes she'd ever seen.

Oh, man, why was she thinking of Austin now, when she was a million miles away from him, her mom was in Denver, and her Aunt Marquise was possibly the victim of 'foul play'? Becca cleared her throat, sniffed back her tears, and told herself not to worry about Marquise. Hadn't her mother always said Mary Theresa always landed on her feet? So nothing could possibly be wrong. Nothing. The news had just screwed something up. That was possible, wasn't it?

She squeezed her eyes shut and, for the first time since the day of her father's funeral, Becca McCrae prayed.

17

Brrring! The phone jangled, jarring Maggie from a fitful sleep. Where was she and who — oh, God, she was with Thane in the hotel room and she'd just . . .

Again the phone blasted.

Becca. Or Mary Theresa.

Still half-asleep, she scrabbled for the receiver of the telephone, her heart hammering as if she expected bad news. It was morning, sunlight seeping through the cracks of the curtains, the noise of traffic from the street and water running in nearby rooms sifting through the walls.

'Hello?' she called into the mouthpiece as she sat up and scooted to the head of the bed, where her pillow was pressed to her back. Thane propped himself up on an elbow, his naked skin gleaming in the morning light, his mouth set in a hard, worried line.

'Ms. McCrae?' a male voice she recognized asked.

'Yes.'

'This is Detective Henderson.'

Her heart nearly stopped. The man's voice was toneless. 'Yes?'

'Listen, you'd better sit down. Your sister's Jeep's been located. Off the highway near Turkey Canyon. Single-car accident.'

'What?' Tears sprang to her eyes. Denial screamed through her brain. 'I — I don't believe it.' She was shaking violently.

'Maggie, let me — ' Thane reached for the receiver, but she wouldn't let go, held on to the damned phone as if it were a lifeline to Mary Theresa.

'Are you still there?' Henderson asked.

'Yes,' she said, her voice the barest of whispers. She began to shiver as the words sank in. 'But I don't believe . . . I can't believe that my sister . . . ' Her voice failed her altogether.

Thane's eyebrows slammed together, and he stared at her hard, his naked body close, his eyes filled with questions.

'I'm sorry, Ms. McCrae, but there's no doubt about it. The license plate and description of the Wrangler match,' Henderson said. 'It's hard to miss your sister's vanity plate. It reads 'Marquise.' '

'Oh, God,' she whispered, her fingers holding the receiver in a death grip. A million images of her sister swirled in a blurred kaleidoscope through her mind. Mary Theresa as a blond tot, as a preteen hiding under the covers and reading her brother's *Playboy* magazine, as an adolescent smoking and sneaking out of the house, as a young woman pregnant with Thane's child and scared to death . . . Maggie swallowed hard, had trouble finding her voice. 'Mary Theresa. Is she — ? Is she alive?'

Thane reached for the phone again, but Maggie shook her head, pushed him away.

'We don't know yet. A state trooper found the rig as the snow began to melt. The Wrangler's pinned beneath the top of a pine tree that must've split on impact and there's nearly a foot of snow on top of that.'

'Sweet Jesus,' she whispered, her throat catching, tears drizzling from her eyes.

'The trooper called in for backup, and a team's dug deep enough to see someone — a woman — in the front seat, but it'll be some time before they can get her out and look for identification.'

She let out a little squeak of protest. Her stomach clenched, but she couldn't let the fear get the better of her. 'I'll — we'll — be at the station in twenty minutes,' she said into the phone, her blood turning to ice, her heart cold as death. She was shaking so violently she could barely hang up the phone.

'That was the police.'

'I gathered that much. Are you okay?' Concern darkened his eyes.

'Yes . . . no . . . yes, I will be.' She tried to pull herself together. 'They . . . they think they found her,' she said in a voice that sounded distant and distraught, not at all like her own. 'And . . . and there was some kind of accident.' She blinked and drew in a quivering breath. 'Detective Henderson didn't say it, but I could hear it in his voice. He thinks Mary Theresa is dead. Dead! Oh, God, Thane she can't be, she just . . . can't be.'

'Wait a minute, slow down.' He tried to hold her, but she edged away.

'Don't you understand?' she whispered, her voice dry, her soul black as the darkest corner of hell. 'They found her car and a body, a woman's body. It — it could be her, Thane.'

Reaching forward, he dragged her into his arms and, despite her protests, held her close. Tears rained from her eyes and she wanted to fall into a million pieces. Pain and desperation clawed at her heart, ripped through her soul. It couldn't be true. It couldn't. Mary Theresa was still alive. She had to be. And yet Maggie was sobbing, clinging to Thane, her fingers curled into fists.

'Shh,' he whispered. 'Maggie, darlin', it'll be all right.'

'No! No! Oh, God, no!' she wailed. 'It'll never be all right.'

His fingers twined in her hair, and he rocked her gently, pressing her head into his shoulder as his other arm held fast to her waist. 'Slow down, Maggie. Tell me what Henderson said.'

She tried. Through the blinding pain, she managed to repeat most of the conversation.

'We don't know anything yet, then. Nothing's certain.' But his voice was dead, as if he were lying. 'Come on, let's get a move on.'

'I can't believe it,' she whispered over and over as she dressed as quickly as she could, throwing on jeans and a sweatshirt, not bothering with makeup or jewelry, just barely able to slip into running shoes.

Thane, too, yanked on his jeans and wrinkled shirt before finding both their jackets.

They were on the road in five minutes.

* * *

The police station was a madhouse, as the press had already gotten wind of Marquise's accident. 'I've got to call Connie and warn her before Becca turns on the television and sees this,' Maggie said, horrified at the swarm of reporters who were collecting at the station. She didn't ask, just reached for Thane's cell phone, gave her sister-in-law a quick rundown of what was happening, then spoke briefly to Becca.

'Hi, honey.'

'Have they found Aunt Marquise?' Becca demanded. 'I saw something on the news last night.'

'All I know for certain is that they've located her car,' Maggie hedged, upset that Becca was getting information from other sources. She had to level with her daughter and give her straight facts — just as soon as she had them herself. Fingers tightening around the phone, she said, 'But we're at the police station and going to talk to the detective in charge of finding Mary Theresa. The minute I know anything I'll call.'

'Promise?' Becca, the tough kid, sounded scared.

'Scout's honor. I already told Aunt Connie the same thing. Now try not to worry.'

There was a hesitation, and Maggie's heart broke. 'Okay,' Becca finally said, her voice breathless as if she was fighting a losing battle with tears. Maggie felt horrible. She wanted her daughter with her, should never have let her go to California. 'Look, honey, I'll call you back once I get to the hotel. Do you have the number?'

'Yeah.'

Maggie's heart tore. Becca was too far away. Mary Theresa was missing. She'd made love to Thane and her entire world was tilting badly, her life falling apart. 'Love ya.'

'Me too,' Becca said meekly and hung up, leaving Maggie holding the receiver and wishing she could reach through the wires and hug her daughter. Becca was usually a pretty strong kid, but all the worries about Marquise seemed to be getting to her as well.

'Let's go,' she said, clearing her throat as she handed Thane the phone and reached for the handle of the door.

Together they walked toward the front of the police station, where the crowd of reporters swarmed. At the sight of Maggie there was a stir. Several cameramen advanced toward her.

'Hang in, this might be rough,' Thane said. One arm surrounded her shoulders as he hustled her up the steps. Three microphone-wielding reporters accosted them, shouting questions, following them up the few concrete stairs to the double doors of the station.

'Marquise? Is that Marquise or her double?'

'Please, just one word.'

'It's the sister — '

Maggie ducked her head. Thane was more forceful, helping her up the steps and shouting, 'No comment, we don't know anything yet,' over his shoulder.

'This is a nightmare,' he whispered once they were on the second floor and were being ushered into Henderson's office. Upon spying them through his open door, the beleaguered detective waved them in. 'What the hell's going on?' Thane demanded.

'As I told Ms. McCrae, we found Marquise's Jeep. Sit down,' he invited, waving them to the worn plastic chairs in which they'd sat on their earlier visit. He ordered coffee, but Maggie couldn't take a swallow from her Styrofoam cup. Her stomach was churning; her intestines felt as if they were waterlogged.

'What about Mary Theresa?' Maggie asked, dreading the answer.

'Not sure yet.'

Thane drank his coffee and looked as if he'd rather be any other place in the world. Even through the closed door, the buzz and excitement of the other offices seeped in. Henderson's phone rang twice, and he had short, terse conversations with whoever was on the other end.

Hannah Wilkins rapped on the door, then slipped into the tight little room. 'The ME is allowing them to remove the body soon,' she reported, and Maggie's heart shredded. 'To the morgue. And the press is all over this. We've already had calls from all the stations and papers.' She handed a list to Henderson. 'So far the official word is 'no comment.' '

'Good.'

Maggie didn't think it was good. Not good at all.

'And we've been getting calls from everyone who knew her.' She handed Henderson a list.

'Pomeranian, King, Gillette . . . ' Henderson

nodded. 'We'll call them back.'

'Wade Pomeranian is demanding answers.'

Henderson's expression didn't change. 'So are we.' He swung his gaze back to Maggie. 'I'm sorry for the wait — '

A uniformed officer poked his head into the room. 'The fax you were waiting for came in,' he explained.

Henderson waved him in and accepted a couple of pieces of paper that Maggie was certain would change the course of her life forever.

Henderson scanned the pages as the officer left the room. Maggie's brain was screaming with dread, her pulse thudding. She felt sick and silently sent up prayer after prayer for her sister while Thane didn't say a word, just sat grim-faced, his eyes trained on the detective.

Henderson's hound-dog face drooped even farther as he scanned the fax. Maggie's heart plummeted. She gripped the edge of her chair and felt her head pounding.

'No positive ID yet,' Henderson said quietly, 'but your sister's purse was in the Jeep and — '

Maggie thought she might be sick.

' — the woman in the driver's seat is about the right size.' His voice was toneless, his gaze on the damning sheets of paper. 'The victim's pretty mangled up. Lacerations, contusions, broken teeth, as she wasn't wearing her seat belt and was thrown into the windshield.'

Bile screamed up Maggie's throat, and she had no choice but to scramble to the wastebasket and retch.

'Ms. McCrae — ' Henderson was on his feet.

'Leave her alone,' Thane ordered. 'Maggie — ' He was beside her in an instant.

'Don't — ' Maggie lifted a hand, afraid someone would try to touch her, comfort her. She didn't want anyone, not even Thane, to offer any consolation. Not yet. 'If . . . if I could just have a few minutes in the rest room.'

'I'll take her.' Detective Wilkins helped Maggie to her feet, and together they made their way through the maze of offices to a women's room with pale green walls and a tile floor layered in years of built-up wax. The urge to vomit had passed and Maggie huddled over a sink, where she washed her mouth and splashed water on her face.

Get a grip, she told herself as she eyed her sorry-looking reflection in the mirror. She was pale as death, her eyes sunken and shadowed, her lips bloodless, her unbrushed hair falling lankly around her face. *You can't lose it; not now. Not until you find out the truth and then, damn it, not even then*.

'Better?' Hannah asked.

'Marginally.'

'Can I get you anything? Coffee or a glass of water or . . . a cigarette, maybe?'

'No.' Maggie yanked out a paper towel and wiped her hands, then her lips. 'I'll be fine. This is all so scary, all . . . just a shock.'

'I know.' Hannah offered her a thin, patient smile. 'You and your sister were very close.'

'Are,' Maggie corrected. 'We *are* close.' She tossed the paper towel into the waste barrel and, with as much dignity as she could muster, made her way through the hallways and large rooms crammed with desks to Henderson's office.

' . . . so until we make a positive ID, I'm not sure how we're gonna handle this.' Henderson was chewing gum to beat the band, and his eyes were mere slits as they narrowed on Thane. He looked up as Maggie entered. 'The body's been transferred to the morgue. Are you up for an identification?'

'You don't have to do this,' Thane said. 'I'll handle it.'

'No.' Maggie was firm. 'She's my sister.' Dry-eyed, she nodded at Henderson. 'I'll do it.'

Thane looked as if he was about to argue but didn't. For the first time in his life that Maggie knew of, he did as he was told, following Henderson's instructions to the letter. Numb, her heart as cold as the bottom of the ocean, her mind screaming all kinds of denials, Maggie, too, took the detective's lead. Within minutes they were in the morgue, standing behind a large window, watching as a man in a lab coat lifted the sheet from a naked body.

Maggie's hands curled into fists so tight that her fingernails dug into her palms. She stood next to Thane, not touching him, but knowing that he was nearby, that if she needed to lean on him, he would support her. Throat too tight to swallow, she stared through the window as the sheet was pulled down and the face of the battered woman came into view. Cuts and bruises, discolored skin and swelling destroyed her features. Her hair was red-brown, the same mahogany color as Mary Theresa's.

Maggie thought she might be sick all over again. She could barely look at the body, though she'd seen corpses before; in her previous line of work she'd viewed a few. But never before had it been anyone she'd loved, and she never had really been comfortable viewing death — especially the victims of a violent end.

But this . . . could it be?

'It's not Mary Theresa,' Thane said, his eyes as harsh as an eagle's as he glared through the viewing window.

'He — he's right,' Maggie said, relief washing over her as she grasped Thane's words. She couldn't explain it, because there was no rational reason, but she knew that she wasn't looking at her sister's body.

'This woman weighs more than Mary Theresa,' Thane said as the sheet was completely stripped away.

'And Mary Theresa had . . . has . . . freckles on her shoulders, from being badly sunburned when she and I were about seventeen,' Maggie added. 'She'd tried to have them bleached, but they were always there . . . '

'This isn't Marquise,' Thane said again, his countenance harsh. 'This woman's name is Renee Nielsen.'

Henderson had been reaching into his breast pocket for a nonexistent pack of cigarettes. He froze at Thane's words. 'You know her?' Cocking his head toward the viewing window, he glared at Thane. From the corner of her eye, Maggie saw

Hannah Wilkins withdraw a notepad and pen from her pocket.

'Yeah,' Thane said. 'I knew her.'

Maggie's throat went dry. *Renee Nielsen*. Why did the name ring bells?

'Who is she?' Henderson prodded, as his partner began to scribble furiously in her notepad.

'A woman who used to work for me.' Thane's lips barely moved as he stared at the battered figure through the viewing glass. 'She did odd jobs at my spread in California a long time ago.'

'She knew Marquise?'

'Yeah.' Thane's eyes narrowed. 'Renee kept the house up when I was away — ran into Mary Theresa a couple of times, I think. As I said, I hired her years ago.'

'Were you married at the time?'

'No, after that. Mary Theresa had moved to L.A., and I'd started spending most of my time in Cheyenne. My foreman, Tom Yates, he did the actual hiring.'

'But she doesn't work for you anymore.'

'No — moved away from the area about two years ago.'

'And went where?'

Thane lifted a shoulder. 'I can't remember. Seemed like somewhere in the Northwest, Portland or Seattle. Tom would have her forwarding address, social security number, and the like.'

'Would he know her next of kin?' Hannah asked.

'Maybe. She was divorced, I think. No kids

that I know of, but I'm not sure.' Thane's lips curled over his teeth. 'Jesus,' he whispered. 'What was she doing in Mary Theresa's rig?'

'We'll give your foreman a call. What's the number?'

As he gave Hannah the phone number of his California spread, Thane glanced at his watch. 'He should be at the ranch now, but he might not be near the phone.'

Hannah Wilkins scratched out the number as she marched toward the door. 'I'll call now and be right back.'

'Get all the info you can on Ms. Nielsen.'

Hannah sent Henderson an oh-sure-like-I-haven't-ever-done-this-before look over her shoulder as the door closed behind her.

Henderson turned his attention back to the viewing window and stared for a few long minutes through the glass to the body. The lab assistant stood ready to cover the dead woman. 'So why would she' — he pressed the tip of an index finger to the glass — 'be driving your ex-wife's Jeep?'

'Beats the hell out of me.' Thane shook his head slowly, and Maggie stared at the corpse before looking away. *Thane had known this woman? She'd worked for him? Mary Theresa had known her as well?* Maggie didn't recognize Renee, and yet her name was familiar. Why? Nothing made any sense. The headache that Maggie had been fighting for days thudded painfully behind her eyes.

'You remember if Ms. Nielsen had any relatives?' Henderson asked.

'No.' Thane shook his head. 'But Tom might know.'

'Let's hope. We'll need all the information you've got.'

Thane's eyes narrowed a fraction. 'You've got it.'

'Did your sister ever mention Renee Nielsen to you?' Henderson asked Maggie, then motioned to the assistant behind the glass to cover up the body.

'No . . . I don't think so,' she said truthfully, yet there was something familiar about the name. 'Maybe. I can't really remember.'

'But you didn't know her?'

'We'd never talked or met, no.' Maggie shook her head and was grateful that the dead woman was draped again, her battered face hidden. 'Why would she be in Mary Theresa's Jeep?' she asked, echoing Henderson's question.

'That, Ms. McCrae, is exactly what I intend to find out.' He sent Thane an unfathomable look before guiding them out of the room and hitting the light switch. The room was suddenly dark, and Maggie shivered as they walked into a hallway that seemed garishly bright in contrast. 'Believe me,' Henderson assured her, 'we'll find your sister.'

Someone has to and soon, Maggie thought. *Before it's too late*. 'I . . . I'd like to call my daughter again, just in case she sees or hears something on the news. I want her to know that the dead woman isn't her aunt.'

'You can use one of the phones upstairs.'

'Good.' As they walked toward the elevator,

she said to Thane, 'Then I want to see the wreck.'

'It'll just upset you,' Thane said, as Detective Henderson punched the call button.

'You can't get too close,' Henderson said. 'We're treating the accident as a crime scene.'

Because you think Mary Theresa's dead, Maggie realized as the elevator bell rang, and the doors whispered open. Well, she wasn't going to give up. Mary Theresa was somewhere — she just had to be found. *So why hasn't she contacted you again — thrown her voice and told you where she is?*

Henderson pushed a button to an upper floor and Thane settled next to Maggie as the elevator groaned and the car began to move upward. His jaw was set, and he looked mean — as if he could spit nails.

For a split second she had the creepy sensation that he knew more than he was telling, that true to Mary Theresa's desperate call to her all those days ago, Thane was somehow involved to his damned sexy eyeballs in his ex-wife's disappearance, that his seduction of her was planned — a distraction to throw her off track.

So why then would he drive all the way to Idaho only to bring you back here? Why let you get so close?

Maggie didn't know, but she damned well intended to find out.

18

'No one could have survived that,' Maggie whispered, her stomach curdling as she stared through the bare, broken limbs of chokecherries and aspen trees. Marquise's red Jeep, a tangled mass of twisted metal and broken glass, was barely visible in the melting snow, mashed against the red rocks and the thick trunk of a pine tree. The rig had been partially dug out from the snow. Its license plate was visible but crumpled — the first three letters, MAR, a painful reminder of who owned the wrecked vehicle.

Several detectives searched the vehicle and the surrounding area for clues. Other officers measured skid marks. Yellow crime-scene tape roped off the area, and a few curious passersby had stopped their cars and climbed out to rubberneck at the scene in morbid fascination.

'No one did survive.' Thane scanned the surrounding area. Sparse trees, deep canyons, red boulders peeking out of snow that was melting under the brilliant rays of sunshine.

'Why did Renee have Mary Theresa's Jeep?'

'Who knows?' Thane lifted a shoulder and rubbed his jaw. Another car parked along the road, and he scowled at the man and woman who'd obviously decided to stretch their legs while viewing the accident scene.

Wearing sunglasses, a baseball cap, and a

heavy jacket with the collar turned up, Maggie hoped not to attract any attention. The excitement of stepping into her sister's shoes, of being Marquise, had faded, and, like every other reclusive celebrity, she knew what it felt like to want to blend into the crowd, to avoid recognition, to guard her privacy. Maggie McCrae was already tired of being Marquise — she just wanted to find her sister.

The wind was fierce, though the day was clear, and she had to hold on to her hat as gusts tried to snatch it away from her. Detective Henderson had donned boots and a parka and was trudging through the snow, snapping orders to the men who were on the detail of searching the area. Dogs on leashes barked madly, trying to pick up a scent, as officers held them in check. Maggie crossed her fingers that Mary Theresa wasn't dead, that her body wouldn't be recovered from this desolate canyon. 'Please let her be safe,' she whispered under her breath, and shivered as she glanced up at the sky.

'Pardon?' Thane stood beside her, mirrored aviator glasses hiding his eyes, his head bare, his sun-streaked hair ruffling in the wind.

'Nothing.' She stuffed her hands into her pockets and heard strangers' voices filled with idle curiosity, but no sense of despair or fear.

'Wonder what all the fuss is about?' a female voice, raspy from years of smoking cigarettes, asked.

'Someone died. A woman.' Her companion, maybe her husband, wasn't into conjecture. 'From the looks of it, she might be that newswoman — look at the plates.'

'Must be why there are so many cops here . . . uh-oh, here come the vultures — damned press.'

Maggie craned her neck and spied the white van with KRKY splashed in blue letters across the door. A satellite dish and other equipment were visible, and, as the van rolled to a stop, a cameraman and Jasmine Bell in a full-length blue coat climbed out. Her shiny hair, perfectly coiffed, fell victim to the wind. She scanned the crowd, spotted Maggie, and waved.

'I think we should leave now,' Thane said, noticing the news crew.

'It's just the press.'

'But they're gonna want an interview.'

'So we'll give them one,' Maggie said, and without waiting for his response, wended her way through the crowd to Jasmine.

The reporter flashed her toothy smile. 'Thought you might be here. What's going on?'

The cameraman stood at the ready, and Maggie frowned. 'Not yet, Phil,' Jasmine said.

Maggie gave her the rundown, and Jasmine told her that KRKY was giving the story number one priority. 'We're very concerned, you know,' she said, 'and there's talk of KRKY putting up a reward for anyone who has information about Marquise. No questions asked. When she's discovered, the person who gave us or the police the lead that led us to her will collect ten thousand dollars.'

'Whose idea was this?' Maggie asked, mentally checking off Craig Beaumont.

'Ron Bishop and Tess O'Shaughnessy came up with it.'

'Figures,' Thane muttered.

Jasmine ignored him, her attention centered on Maggie. 'Would you mind answering a few questions?'

'Not at all. In fact, I'll even make a plea to anyone who might have information about my sister.'

'That would be great. How about you?' Jasmine asked, her dark eyes moving to Thane. 'As an ex-husband, someone who was once married to her, would you like to make a statement?'

'No.' Thane's jaw was rock hard. 'Don't get me wrong, I'd like to find Mary Theresa, but I'm not gonna be part of some media circus.'

'It could help. This is going to be relayed to the network and will probably be on cable news within the next hour or so.'

'Maggie can do what she wants, but count me out.' He was firm, his lips a thin, resolute line, and Jasmine was intuitive enough not to push. Phil filmed the crash site, then zeroed in on Jasmine before turning the camera on Maggie, who took off her shades, answered a few questions, then looked directly into the lens. 'I would just like to say if anyone has any information about my sister, please contact the police.'

'Would you look at that,' the smoky-voiced woman said from somewhere behind Maggie. 'Put a little makeup on her and she could be that missing woman . . . the one whose car is down in the gulch.'

'Shh. She's not.'

'But — '

'Just hush, Sally.'

Maggie slid her sunglasses onto her nose again and ignored the curious stares cast in her direction. A few more cars stopped, another news team and tow truck arrived, and Henderson — with the help of other policemen — insisted that everyone back up, allow the police to do their jobs, and, unless they had data that would help the investigation, be on their way. He was interrupted by several phone calls and underlings, but managed to keep things moving along. Eventually he motioned Thane and Maggie to meet with him beside his car.

'We haven't found anything yet,' he admitted, chewing on a stick of gum and squinting against the afternoon sunlight, 'but we've got tracking dogs and the best men in the state, who will help canvass the area here. If your sister is anywhere near, we'll find her.'

'KRKY is offering a ten-thousand-dollar reward,' Maggie ventured.

'I heard.'

'Will it help?'

Henderson spit his gum onto the side of the mountain road. 'I'd like to say it won't hurt, but what will happen is every nutcase in the country who needs some extra cash will come up with some kind of scam.' His lips twisted into a sardonic smile. 'Let's just say it's gonna take a lot of manpower to wade through the shit.' He shrugged. 'On the other hand, it might just be the incentive some greedy son of a bitch needs to sharpen his memory.' He frowned as the tow-truck driver maneuvered his truck to the side of the road and released a long cable attached to a winch. 'We can only hope.'

* * *

' . . . and so, the mystery remains unsolved,' the reporter, an Asian woman from a Denver news station, reported via satellite to L.A., where Becca lay sprawled over a beanbag chair in the middle of her cousin's room. Eyes riveted to the screen, Becca, fascinated but horrified, watched as a publicity photograph of her aunt was flashed onto the screen, followed quickly by pictures of a wrecked Jeep twisted in a clump of trees on the side of a canyon. 'Mary Theresa Gillette, known as Marquise and cohost of the popular morning program *Denver AM*, is still missing. The identity of the woman driving Marquise's Jeep is being withheld pending notification of next of kin, and no one knows what happened to the Denver celebrity, but the investigation into Marquise's disappearance continues — '

The slap of thongs heralded Connie's arrival from the vicinity of the spa. She walked into the room, grabbed the remote control from the nightstand, and aimed it at the television.

'KRKY is offering a ten-thousand-dollar reward for information as to the whereabouts of — '

Click. The set immediately went dark. 'I don't

think you should be watching this.'

'Wait!' Becca launched herself off the bed and slapped on the television. Her mother stood talking with the Asian woman. ' . . . so please, if anyone has any information about my sister, please contact the police — '

'That's Maggie.' Connie was flabbergasted. 'What's she thinking?'

'Duh! She's trying to help find Marquise!' Becca said, tired of her aunt's bossing her around.

'Don't speak to me — '

'Shh!' Becca didn't care about being polite. She had to find out what her mother was saying, but it was too late. Connie aimed the remote control, and the screen went dead.

'Why'd you do that?' Becca demanded.

'It's too upsetting for you to watch.'

'It was my mother!'

'But she already called and explained about the accident. There was no need for you to — '

'Marquise is my aunt! Like you are. I want to know what happened to her!' Becca was sick of being treated like a little kid.

'We all do,' Connie assured her. She pasted on that saccharine smile that Becca had come to loathe. 'As soon as I hear from Maggie again, I'll let you know.'

'But I want to talk to her now.' Something was going on, and Becca was more scared than she'd ever been in her life. A woman was dead. Even though her mom had called and explained about it, Becca wasn't satisfied.

'We will. I'll call her later.' Aunt Connie was getting pissed.

Becca wasn't going to wait. She hopped to her bare feet, winced a bit as her ankle still gave her a little trouble, then walked stiffly to Jenny's bed and picked up the receiver of her princess phone. But she didn't dial. There was no reason. She'd just talked to her mother a little while ago. Still, she was scared. Scared to death. Her throat closed, and she fought tears. 'But someone's dead. *Dead*. And they can't find Marquise.' She dropped the receiver.

'I know, Becca, but everyone's doing the best they can.' Sighing loudly, Connie sat on the edge of Jenny's bed and shook her head. She placed a hand on Becca's shoulder, and Becca had to fight the urge to cringe. 'Try not to worry, okay? I'm sure your mother will call the minute she knows anything else. She's probably not even in her hotel room right now and' — she looked pointedly at Jenny's clock, the one of a fake wooden Elvis where his hips swung like a pendulum — 'look at the time. Remember, you've got a doctor's appointment in an hour.'

'I'm not going.'

'Of course you are, dear; your ankle hasn't healed, and Dr. Orem is the best orthopedic man in all of Beverly Hills.'

'My ankle's fine.' Becca was tired of her aunt's platitudes, sick of being treated as if she were a stupid nine-year-old.

'Now, don't argue, okay?' Connie's face, though set in a kind expression, was hard as granite, and Becca had learned over the last few days that the woman ran her house with an iron fist covered in a doeskin glove. As much as she had loved L.A., Becca was beginning to want to leave. Connie was a big reason; and her Uncle Jim, what a weenie he'd turned out to be. It was always 'Yes, dear' this, and 'Of course, honey' that. He didn't seem to have a mind of his own. Even Jenny, for all her rebellious streak, had to toe the line and do exactly what her mother asked or she was browbeaten for hours as Connie would walk around the house with a wounded look, dabbing at the corners of her eyes, like she couldn't believe that her daughter could be so cruel. What a crock. It was amazing that Jenny had the guts to sneak out.

'Get ready while I change, and try to wear something nice.' She eyed Becca's cutoff jeans as if they were poison. 'You know, a shorts set or a skirt would be appropriate. If you didn't bring something of your own, I'm sure Jenny has something you can fit into.' Connie's smile was patronizingly patient, and Becca realized that her concern of a few moments before had all been fake. 'We're not just going to the specialist. I want you to visit your grandfather.'

'But — '

'He's in a care home, honey, and he'd love to see you.'

Becca had never been close to her father's father, but nodded. She couldn't get out of this one.

'And then we have to stop by the lawyer's office.'

Becca's shoulders stiffened, and she felt

instantly apprehensive. 'Why?'

'Legal papers — I'll explain later.'

'Can't you explain now?' Becca asked, suspicion her newfound companion.

'It's complicated.'

'Which means you don't want to tell me.'

'Oh, sweetie.' Connie sighed dramatically, and Becca folded her arms over her chest, then plopped onto the bed.

'Well, you are thirteen; I suppose I should tell you. I know that you've been really unhappy in Idaho. Uncle Jim and I are very worried about you.'

Becca didn't like the sound of this.

'The schools up there have to be atrocious.'

'They're all right.'

'But all your friends and family are here and . . . well, you know Uncle Jim and I would love to have you come and live with us permanently. I'm willing to give up my office and move into Jim's so that you could have a place to stay.' She smiled brightly. 'We could be one big happy family.'

'What about Mom?'

'Oh.' Aunt Connie cleared her throat. 'All this would have to be run by her, of course, and well . . . she could move back to L.A. anytime she wants. That would be even better. She . . . she could be closer to us and Grandma and Grandpa, and there are doctors here who would help her.'

'Doctors?' Becca's heart was pounding. 'Is she sick or somethin'?' Maybe her mom hadn't told her the truth, maybe she was fighting some deadly illness. After all, she *was* old. Thirty-seven. And she was on her knees in the barn, looking pale as death on that day that they found out about Marquise. Becca swallowed a suddenly huge lump in her throat.

Connie walked across the room and placed a comforting hand on Becca's small shoulder. 'Your mom hasn't really been okay since your dad died, sweetie. And that's understandable. It . . . it was a shock to us all. So, anyway, we'd better get going.'

'So why are we gonna see a lawyer?' Becca didn't get it.

'Just in case you decide to stay with us. There will be legal papers to sign. Guardian stuff.'

Becca studied the rug for a second. 'I think I better talk this over with Mom.'

'Oh, we will. We all will.' Connie flushed bright red, and when Becca looked up at her, Connie glanced away and fiddled with the neckline of her cover-up.

'I want to see her first.'

'Well, you can't, not now — '

'I think I should go to Denver.'

'Oh, sweetie, that's just not possible.' Again the phony smile, and in that instant Becca knew Aunt Connie was lying to her. Scamming her. The way Jason Pennicott, a boy in her class, tried when he wanted her to do his homework or trade something good like a Twinkie or a Ding Dong from her lunch for some lousy carrot sticks or a crappy peanut-butter-and-jelly sandwich. 'You know, Maggie's a little fragile.'

'Fragile?' Becca repeated, the niggling suspicion that Aunt Connie was implying more than she was saying boring deep in her brain. 'Mom's not fragile.'

Her aunt's smile was placidly patient. She sighed — that same old sigh that meant 'you're just a girl, Becca, you couldn't possibly understand.' But Becca did. More than Connie knew. Yeah, her aunt was trying to pull a fast one. And Becca knew just how to handle her.

'Okay,' she said meekly with a lift of one shoulder, as if she'd really bought her aunt's line. 'I'll call her later.'

'Good idea.' Connie was instantly relieved and stupid enough to think that she'd won. Fat chance. 'Now,' the older woman pointed a professionally manicured finger at her niece, 'try and wear something presentable, okay?' Connie's façade slipped, and the look she sent Becca was a mixture of pity and disgust. 'We'll call your mother later. I promise. But we don't want to upset her. Now come on, sweetheart, we've really got to get a move on.' Connie tapped one finger on the face of her watch. 'Hurry up.'

Becca waited until her aunt left, then quickly called the airline that she'd used to get to L.A. Within minutes she'd ordered her ticket for a night flight to Denver. Before Connie became suspicious, Becca threw on a decent-enough outfit, opened Jenny's top drawer and, feeling guilty, slipped out some of the bills from Jenny's emergency fund. She didn't have enough money for the airline ticket and cab fare, so, after calculating what she needed, she took $150 from the drawer and cringed as she stuffed the bills into her purse. She'd pay Jenny back, but she couldn't tell her cousin what she was doing; Jenny would either rat her out or end up getting in trouble herself.

'Ready?' her aunt called, as Becca slammed the drawer shut. Connie, her expression vexed, threw open the door. 'Come on, Becca. We're late. I swear you're slower than Jenny and you haven't even brushed your hair.' Exasperated, she picked up Jenny's brush and handed it to Becca. 'You can do it in the car on the way.'

Becca followed her aunt and swallowed a smile as Connie's high heels clicked out a quick tempo to the garage. She and Jim were scheduled to go out tonight, and Becca intended to be on a flight to Colorado.

⋆ ⋆ ⋆

Shaken from the sight of the wreck, Maggie huddled against the passenger window in Thane's truck as it sped south toward Gillette's home. She felt cold inside. Empty. And her heart squeezed in fear for her sister. Where was Mary Theresa? Was she alive? How was she connected to Renee Nielsen, and why was the woman driving her car? There was a connection — something she should know about Renee Nielsen, Maggie thought, but she couldn't figure it out, couldn't remember where she'd heard the name. Certainly not from Mary Theresa.

From Thane's cell phone, they'd called Tom Yates, who was faxing as much information as he had not only to the Denver police, but also to the hotel for Thane. 'He didn't know much,' Thane admitted. 'Just that Renee had moved away a few years back, up to Beaverton, which is a suburb of Portland, Oregon. She didn't have a lot of friends and no relatives nearby, but he'll send everything he's got on her to us.'

It wasn't a lot of information, but all they could get for the moment, so as she stared out the window, Maggie had to content herself with the hope that her sister was still alive. The countryside, brown patches of ground showing through the melting snow anchored by dead grass and weeds, flashed by.

'So tell me what you know about Renee Nielsen,' she suggested as she adjusted her gloves and tried to forestall the sense of doom that seemed to be forever chasing her. Maggie was more determined than ever to find her sister and she wasn't about to stop checking out everyone who had seen her sister in the past couple of weeks.

'Not much to tell,' Thane replied. As his hands tightened over the wheel, Maggie was reminded of the cryptic message she'd gotten from her sister. 'I knew Renee a long time ago, but she was just an employee who worked part-time. She just did odd jobs. Worked as a waitress at a local deli part-time, house-sat, took care of pets when people went out of town, and did housework on the side. Tom hired her to keep the house up, and when I was in California for any length of time I saw her. She was friendly, quiet, and pretty much kept to herself. I can't begin to guess what kind of a relationship she had with Mary Theresa. I didn't know her all that well. Seems to me she was married, but separated from her husband or some damned thing. Never did divorce him that I know of. But I didn't know she was close to Mary Theresa.'

'Maybe she wasn't close,' Maggie said, chewing on her lip pensively. 'Maybe she just saw an opportunity.' She glanced at Thane, and her forehead wrinkled in worry as Thane wheeled the truck into a gated community spread around an exclusive golf course. A security guard in a gatehouse stopped the truck, asked whom they planned to visit, made a quick call, then waved them through.

'Looks like the hotel god has deigned to see us,' Thane said, driving across a bridge spanning a lazy creek. Patches of snow covered well-tended lawns of homes that were as expensive and elegant as the one Marquise owned. Thane pulled into a curved driveway that ended in front of a five-car garage. 'Let's go see what the second Mr. Marquise has to say for himself,' Thane said darkly, and Maggie didn't comment.

As they reached the front door it was thrown open, not by a servant as Maggie would have expected, but by Marquise's second husband himself. Syd Gillette oozed success. Nearing seventy, his girth had started to expand, despite his avid interest in golf and tennis. His once-dark hair was now shot with silver. A big bear of a man, he was tanned, dressed in golf shirt and slacks. He eyed Thane with suspicion.

'Maggie,' he said without a trace of warmth.

'It's been a long time. Come in, come in. I was just watching the news.' He walked them down a marbled hallway toward the back of the house and a private atrium that overlooked the golf course. 'A shame about Marquise. God, I wonder what happened to her — Annie, would you bring us drinks? What'll it be?' He motioned toward his guests.

'Anything — tea, if you have it,' Maggie said.

'Scotch straight up.' Thane didn't crack a smile, just leaned a shoulder against one wall as Maggie, upon Syd's urging, sat on the edge of a wicker couch beneath a skylight. Broad-leafed plants grew around a fountain that splashed noisily as the maid carried in hot water and coffee. Syd mixed drinks from a bar around the corner.

Once they were all settled, she sipping tea on a soft cushion, Thane nursing his drink while staring through the glass windows to a snow-covered fairway, and Syd taking up residence in a recliner, he finally asked, 'What do you know about Marquise's disappearance?'

'We were hoping you could shed some light.'

Syd scowled. 'Don't know how. She and I weren't on the best of terms, didn't see much of each other.' He looked pointedly at Thane. 'You know how that goes.'

'Enlighten us.' Obviously Thane wasn't going to pull any punches. Sitting in a club chair, he turned his eagle-sharp gaze on Gillette.

'She and I were civil.'

Why was he talking in the past tense? As if Mary Theresa was already dead?

'But that was about it. I was just getting over Ellie when I met your sister. In retrospect, it was probably just a rebound thing on my part. Hell, who could resist that woman?' He threw a knowing glance at Thane, who didn't comment, just sipped his drink. Maggie gritted her teeth. He was right, of course. No one, not even Thane, had been immune to M.T.'s charms.

'Anyway,' he continued, 'we got married, and about the time Marquise finished saying 'I do,' she was already into 'I don't.' ' He took a long swallow from his gin and tonic, and his face clouded. 'We didn't get along, and there were some . . . other issues.'

'She got involved with your son-in-law.'

Gillette froze. His expression turned thunderous. 'I didn't know that was common knowledge, but yeah. She and Robby got together.' He scowled into his drink. 'Ruined my daughter's marriage.' Thick eyebrows lifted. 'Well, it's all over and done with now, and there's no love lost between me and Marquise, but I don't wish her ill. Don't believe in dwelling on the past.'

'What about your daughter?' Maggie plunged on.

'Tanya? She'll get over it. In time.' But the corners of his mouth tightened, and his jaw clenched, showing a muscle that twitched.

'She had a baby.'

Gillette swore under his breath. 'A boy. Chad. And he gets to grow up without his dad. Thanks to Marquise. Jesus Christ, what a mess.' Syd tossed back his drink and ran a hand over his face. Clean-shaven and robust, he hardly looked his age. 'The divorce was hard on my daughter, and it will be for a long time. She loved Robby, probably still does. Hell, he turned out to be a prick, didn't he? And Marquise was just playing with him. Didn't even care for him.' Syd sighed.

'You think she did it to get back at you?' Thane asked, as if he understood his ex-wife's motives.

'Definitely. Sounds egocentric, I know, but I'm sure Marquise was making a point.'

'Because — ?' Maggie asked.

'The prenup I had her sign. She wanted to change it from the git-go.' Ice cubes rattled in his empty glass. 'Oh, well, time will take care of everything, I suppose. Tanya and I will get over it. Chad . . . well, it's tough for a kid to grow up not knowing his dad.' Syd ran a hand over his jaw. 'I should know. I never knew my old man.'

Thane's jaw slid to the side, and his fingers drummed impatiently on the arm of his chair, but he didn't comment.

'But your grandson has a father,' Maggie ventured.

'You think so?' Gillette threw her a look that silently called her naive. 'This is the same guy who tried to talk his wife, his *wife*, mind you, into an abortion because he didn't want a kid. Robby couldn't be bothered, because he was already involved with his father-in-law's bride.' Gillette walked to the bar and poured himself another stiff drink. 'So you can understand why I don't see a lot of my ex-wife anymore.'

'End of story?' Thane asked, as if he didn't believe it for a minute.

'End of story. Marquise and I ran into each other once in a while, as we're part of the same social scene.' He swirled his glass, stared into the clear depths. 'But we pretty much avoided each other. Let the lawyers haggle it out between them and moved on. I married Yvonne, and Marquise . . . well, she got into younger men. Not just Robby.' He tossed back his drink. 'She doesn't like men with children — 'extra baggage' — that's what kids were to Marquise. She wasn't too happy when she found out Tanya was pregnant. But then neither was Robby.'

The muscles in Thane's face tightened perceptibly. He set his barely touched drink on a glass-topped table.

'What do you think happened to her?' Thane asked. 'You had an argument with her according to the police.'

'Anytime I talked with her, it turned into a fight. That's not exactly a news flash.'

'What was the fight about?' Maggie asked.

'What it always was. Money. She wanted more. Thought she got screwed on the divorce because she didn't end up with any of my hotels. So she always came around, wanting to borrow from me. This time I said 'no,' and from there things went downhill.'

Maggie tried to delve further and asked a few more questions, but Syd was vague. Yes, they'd fought, but that was to be expected. They'd been divorced, after all, and Marquise wasn't known for her even temperament. As he ushered them to the door, he'd made one last comment. 'What can I say? You know your sister. Marquise is

Marquise.' As if that explained everything.

'I don't think so,' Maggie replied. 'The way I see it, Marquise is really Mary Theresa.'

* * *

'What do you want first?' Hannah asked as she slipped into Henderson's tiny office. He'd just returned from the site of the accident and was tired as hell. This case was going to drive him into early retirement, back to Camel straights, or both. Right then, he didn't really give a damn. 'The bad news or the good news?'

'Didn't know there was any good.' Henderson reached for his baseball. 'Let's have the bad.'

'Guess who's lined up to be the next guest on *Denver AM?*'

He gave the ball a quick toss, caught the damned thing, then, only slightly calmer, set it back in its holder. 'Okay, I'll bite — who?'

'Wade Pomeranian.' She offered him a cat-who-just-swallowed-the-canary grin.

'Is that so?'

'Uh-huh. It isn't a secret that he's wanted to be on the show for a long time. He even stormed down to the station one day and fought with Marquise about it in front of witnesses, including Craig Beaumont.'

'So now he gets his shot.'

'Yep. And here's the kicker. Beaumont and the executive producer were opposed to Pomeranian being on the show, didn't like his connection with Marquise. Even when they had a fashion show last spring and Wade could have modeled men's clothing, Craig Beaumont put the kibosh on the idea. Nixed Pomeranian specifically, but now that Marquise is missing . . . *voilà*, Beaumont and the executive producer have changed their collective tune.'

'Now they want Wade.'

'To interview him as a friend of Marquise's.'

'Jesus H. Christ.'

'Ron Bishop insists that they're helping locate Marquise, as opposed to exploiting the situation.'

'Maybe they are.'

'Maybe. Anyway, they're not stopping with Pomeranian. The producer wants other people who know her as well; they're dedicating at least one segment to her and going to remind the viewers that there's a reward for information that leads to finding her.'

Henderson leaned back in his chair. 'So who else are they inviting to be Beaumont's guest?'

'First of all, they've approached Maggie. Want her to dress and act like Marquise.'

'Shit. Don't tell me they want the ex-husbands, too.'

'Possibly. But who knows if they'll agree.'

Henderson shook his head. 'I don't like it.'

'Maybe it'll help.'

He couldn't disagree, and at this point he was frustrated. No lead to the whereabouts of the missing celebrity, no body, no ransom note, nothing but a suicide letter that might or might not be fake. Another woman was dead, and the sister and ex-husband were running around trying to do Henderson's job for him. The press was on his neck and the D.A. was demanding answers. Reed Henderson thought the clues leading to Marquise were drying up faster than the Colorado River on its way to L.A. He'd kill for a cigarette.

'There's more.'

'Pile it on.' He motioned with his fingers, encouraging her to tell him everything.

'It looks like Marquise's Jeep wasn't involved in a single car accident after all. We just got some reports back and the boys who checked out the accident scene think another vehicle was involved. Hit-and-run. Black paint on the back fender of the Jeep seems to indicate that it was forced off the road.'

Henderson's back stiffened and his pulse elevated a bit, the same way it used to when he hunted and caught a glimpse of a buck in the undergrowth.

'Walker's got a black pickup,' he thought aloud, mentally clicking off the possibilities. His mind was already spinning ahead. This was unexpected news, that Marquise's rig might've been forced off the road. A whole new twist. A clue that might break the damned case wide open.

'Walker's truck doesn't have any damage. We already checked. It was at the site today.'

'Damn.'

'You really hate the guy, don't you?'

'I just don't trust him,' Henderson admitted. 'He's got his own agenda. Lying. Nothin' I hate worse than a liar.'

'And nothin' you like better than nailing one to the cross.'

'Amen.' He managed a thin smile. 'What else do you have?'

'Not a lot more. We'll know the make and model once the paint tests are finished and some of the glass is analyzed to see if there was damage to the other car's headlights.'

'We can only hope.'

'You're sick, Detective.'

'Just practical. We could use a break. Solve the case and get the D.A. and the press off our asses.' Henderson reached into his drawer for a pack of gum, but came up dry. Back teeth grinding together, he spun in his chair and thought. Hard. 'So was it a case of someone losing control, hitting the Jeep and then, scared, taking off? Or — '

'Was it intentional?' Hannah asked. 'I guess that's what we have to find out.' She walked into the room and leaned her hips against his desk. 'This case gets more interesting all the time, doesn't it?'

'If you say so.' Henderson clasped his hands behind his head and leaned back in his chair. 'So, if that's the bad news, what's the good?'

Hannah's lips twitched into a half-smile. 'You wanted to talk to Jane Stanton, the next-door neighbor who overheard the fight between Marquise and Thane Walker.'

'I called over there and she was still out of town.'

'Well, the good news is that the daughter's recovering from her skiing injury and Jane's back.' Wilkins had the audacity to wink at him.

Henderson was out of his chair like a rocket and reaching for his jacket. 'What're we waiting for? Let's go.'

* * *

Tucked under the eaves of a remodeled turn-of-the-century manor that had been converted to individual business suites, Marquise's psychiatrist's office was lit by soft lamps that glowed in the coming night. Dr. Michelle Kelly welcomed Thane and Maggie into the cozy room, smiled, offered herbal tea, and asked them to sit on a long leather couch reserved for her patients. Decorated to put people at ease and make them comfortable, so that even the most reticent patient would speak freely, the corner room smelled faintly of incense and herbs. Surrounded by ferns and jade plants growing profusely in glazed ceramic pots, an unlit fireplace graced one corner. Shelves of books lined the walls. *Definitely designed to inspire confidence*, Thane thought sarcastically.

Not much older than thirty, slight and thoughtful, the doctor studied Thane with inquisitive golden brown eyes magnified by thick glasses. Though her manner was meant to put people at ease, Thane decided the tiny woman dressed in layered sweaters, long skirts, and heavy sandals didn't miss much.

Of course she was interested in them. Thane could only guess what self-serving and twisted lies Mary Theresa had told her shrink about her sister and ex-husband. Dr. Kelly, if she wanted to, could probably write volumes on Marquise's personality and mental state.

However, she had one major flaw. As far as Thane could tell, despite Dr. Kelly's stellar reputation, she had been unable to propel his ex-wife to better mental health even though Mary Theresa had been her patient for three and a half years.

But then Mary Theresa was the head case to end all head cases.

Maggie asked questions, and Dr. Kelly skillfully dodged most of them. 'I'd love to tell you more,' Michelle Kelly explained as she sat in a rocking chair and sipped the foul-smelling tea, 'but because of patient-client confidentiality, I really can't.'

'Do you think Mary Theresa is suicidal?' Maggie asked.

'She suffers from depression. Sometimes it's worse than others, but . . . no . . . I wouldn't classify your sister as suicidal.' She set her tea down on a tiny table near her chair, removed her glasses, and carefully polished the lenses with the corner of her cardigan sweater.

Obviously, Maggie was relieved and about to end the conversation, but Thane had questions of his own. 'Did Marquise ever mention to you that she had the ability to talk to people through mental telepathy?'

Maggie stiffened, and the psychiatrist stopped rubbing her glasses. 'You mean without speaking?'

'Right. I'm talking about the ability to throw

her voice to someone else.'

Dr. Kelly's smooth brow furrowed. 'No. I don't think so. And I would remember it if she did, I'm sure. Why?'

'Just something she'd said to me once, a long time ago,' he lied, seeing Maggie turn ghost-white from the corner of his eye. 'It probably doesn't mean anything. She was always rambling on. Just something I remembered.'

Slipping her wire-rims onto her nose, Dr. Kelly asked, 'Did you ever see or hear of her doing this?'

'Never. But then she was always saying something outrageous,' he admitted, ending the interview and surviving Maggie's silent treatment for the half hour it took to return to the hotel.

'I can't believe you brought up the telepathy thing,' she finally exploded, once they were alone in the hotel room again. She threw her purse and bag on the couch and turned on him. Anger flashed in her eyes, and she planted her fists firmly on her hips. 'I told you that in confidence.'

'Don't you want to find your sister?'

'Of course — I do. You know it!'

'Then we'd better use every means possible, don't you think?'

'I don't see how this helps.'

'Everything helps.'

'I'm not sure. Besides, you're not being honest with me.'

He felt his neck muscles stiffen. 'I'm not?'

'No. There's something you haven't told me.

Something to do with Marquise. You neglected to mention that she'd stayed in your house for three days not too long ago. You never mentioned that you and she still saw each other fairly regularly, and you're holding back. Now, what is it, Walker?'

He opened his mouth to protest, but the look she sent him warned him not to try and con her. 'Respect me enough to be honest, Thane. Considering the circumstances, I think you owe it to me.'

He thought for a long, hard second. How much could he trust Maggie? How would she react to the truth? Hell, he never wanted to tell her this. But it was bound to come out sooner or later. Slowly he unbuttoned his jacket, reached into the inside pocket, and took out his crumpled pack of cigarettes along with a battered book of matches.

'I thought you quit smoking.'

'I did.' He shook out the last filter tip and lit up quickly, drawing in a deep lungful of smoke, then took off his jacket and tossed it over hers on the chair. Crumpling the empty pack of Marlboros, he walked to the fireplace. 'Okay,' he said, wondering if he was about to make the worst mistake of his life. He felt the unaccustomed rush of nicotine and watched as she mentally steeled herself.

'You're still in love with my sister,' she whispered so faintly he barely heard the words. Her face was ashen, her eyes haunted, agony evidenced in her expression.

'Oh, no, Maggie. It's not as simple as that.' He

plowed stiff fingers through his hair and took another deep drag.

'Then what?'

'It's that the last time I saw Mary Theresa she dropped a bomb on me.'

'What kind of bomb?' Maggie asked.

It's now or never, he thought angrily as he stared down at the tortured face of the only woman he'd ever loved. 'Mary Theresa told me that she and I have a son.'

19

'What?' Maggie felt her face drain of color. Her legs wobbled and she dropped onto the arm of the couch. This was a lie. It had to be. If Mary Theresa had ever had a baby, she would have said something. Wouldn't she? 'No . . . wait a minute — '

'That's right. He's a teenager now. Conceived before we broke up; a boy I didn't know existed until the last time I saw her.'

'But Mary Theresa wouldn't have kept this from me. From you.' Her throat was dry, her palms itched.

'No? Come on, Maggie. This is Mary Theresa . . . Marquise we're talking about.' His lips compressed with nearly twenty years of raw emotion, nearly two decades of deception. 'You know she's lied to us both.' His eyes found hers and she saw the naked pain — the torment he'd dealt with for years.

'And that's what your fight was about?' she guessed, feeling sick inside. The expression of pure hell on Thane's face convinced her that he wasn't lying, wasn't making this up just to gain some kind of misguided sympathy. His mouth was tight, his eyes dark and narrowed on the fireplace, but she was certain he didn't see the marble façade; Thane's view was turned inward to a murky nightmare only he could see.

'Sixteen years,' he said as the cigarette burned

forgotten between his fingers. 'Sixteen years of my boy's life. Lost.' His eyes found Maggie's again. Guilt, hurt, and a quiet, seething rage burned deep in his gaze.

Maggie shuddered, knowing in an instant that she was going to hear something she'd rather not, a deep secret that Thane had kept hidden to the world.

'You don't know much about me.'

'I think I know enough — '

'No, Maggie. You don't understand. I grew up in a small town in Wyoming with an old man who drank too much and, when he wasn't screwing other women, beat up on my mother. Fine guy, hard worker when he was sober; a mean son of a bitch when he drank, which he did a lot.'

'I can't tell you how many times Mom would have to drive into town and pull him out of a tavern, and when she did, she was repaid with a fist to her face.' Thane's eyes turned black. 'But she always forgave him. Because of me. She didn't even have an eighth grade education; couldn't afford to leave the bastard, because of me and my brother.'

'Brother?' she repeated, her voice so soft she wasn't sure he'd heard her.

'He's dead. Car wreck. Had the same problem with alcohol Pa did.' Thane's nostrils flared and one hand curled into a fist that was so tight it shook. 'I swore that when I had a kid of my own, I would do it right. Nothing, and I mean nothing, would stop me from being the best damned father on this planet. I'd raise him the way he was supposed to be brought up, knowing a father's love, a mother's nurturing, a parent's sacrifice, but I didn't get the chance. Mary Theresa made sure of that.'

'Dear God,' Maggie said, her heart bleeding for the pain this man had borne, the secrets that had ripped at his soul, the demons that tortured his brain. He sucked hard one last time on his filter tip, then squashed it in a planter. Smoke curled out of his nostrils and mouth.

Dropping her head into her hands she tried to think, to remember a time her sister could have hidden the fact that she was pregnant with Thane's child. 'So that's why you married her. The first time when she was pregnant.'

He didn't reply. His jaw slid to one side and he stared at her as if he would never stop.

'And now you have . . . she has . . . a son.' Maggie shivered inside. 'And she never told you?'

'Not a word. Until that last fight and that, Maggie, is why I threatened to kill her.'

Tears burned behind Maggie's eyes and she rubbed her arms, trying to keep the chill of betrayal at bay. 'Why? Why would Mary Theresa do this . . . keep something like this from you?'

'Because it would interfere with her career! For Christ's sake, Maggie,' he said, advancing on her. 'Haven't you learned anything about your sister? Don't you know how low she'd sink, how many people she'd manipulate just to further her damned career?'

'But . . . but I would have known about it. She

would have told *me*.'

'Like the way she told you that she had seduced your lover?'

The words cut cruelly, bringing back old, raw wounds that had never quite healed. 'Don't,' she ordered. Marquise was missing, could possibly be dead, she couldn't, *wouldn't* think these horrid, sick thoughts —

'Give it up, Mag Pie,' he said as if reading her thoughts. His voice was so low it startled her and her head snapped up.

'Marquise was pregnant seventeen years ago, Maggie. You were in college — you didn't see her. She managed to stay away from anyone who knew her during the last months when her condition was undeniable.'

Denial swam through her head. 'I — I think she would have confided in me. She wouldn't have kept something as big, as important, as a pregnancy a secret,' Maggie said, but even as the words passed her lips she knew she was kidding herself. What did she know about her chameleon of a sister — Mary Theresa who had turned into Marquise? Didn't she have a past history of deception? In the past few days Maggie had learned so many devastating facts about the woman who was her twin, the sister with whom she shared so many physical characteristics and yet from whom she seemed to have an opposite soul.

'As I said, the last time I saw her, the night I wanted to strangle her, she threw it in my face that she'd had our boy, given him up for adoption, and that I'd spent all of his life not knowing one damned thing about him.'

'So you haven't met him?'

'Haven't found him yet.'

'Then how do you know he exists?' She could hardly trust her own voice. 'If Mary Theresa is such a liar, how do you know?'

'I hired a private detective. He found the birth records at a small private hospital in Southern California, not far from the Mexican border. Now he's tracking down the adoptive parents. I expect to hear from him anytime.' His smile twisted without a trace of humor. 'He's got some leads.'

'So your interest in finding Mary Theresa is for more than clearing your name,' she said, finally understanding why Thane seemed so totally and irrevocably tied to her sister. 'You want her to help you find your son.'

'Obviously now that I know she wasn't lying, yes. I have questions for her; questions only she can answer.'

'So do I.' Maggie considered the past week, the hours of being alone with Thane, the days spent driving in the truck, or searching for clues in Denver, or the few precious minutes of making love to him. All that time she'd fought her feelings, telling herself that she wouldn't let herself fall for him again, that she wouldn't allow him to walk all over her, that she was smarter than she was when she was seventeen and she wouldn't let any man, Thane Walker in particular, use her.

Because of Mary Theresa.

Because of the betrayal.

Because, deep in her heart, she'd never really let go of him.

It looked like she'd been wrong about so many things. So very wrong. But she couldn't trust Thane, for even though he'd bared his soul, he'd revealed the all-too-painful truth that he'd searched out Maggie, that he'd spent time with her, that he'd seduced her, as always, for his own purposes. Because of Mary Theresa and their son. His life was and would forever be entwined with her sister's. Just as it had always been. Before they had been lovers. Now, Maggie thought, aching inside, Thane and M.T. had a son together, shared a life.

Help me. Maggie, please. It was Thane. He did this to me. Maggie, please. Don't let him get away with it. Mary Theresa's painful plea echoed through Maggie's memory. She plucked at a piece of lint on the back of the couch. 'Why . . . why would Mary Theresa have sent me the message?' she asked. 'The one I heard in the barn?'

His glance was filled with skepticism. 'I don't know that she did. The psychiatrist said that Marquise had never mentioned it.'

'That's a lot different than saying it didn't exist. Just because Mary Theresa didn't confide in her.'

'She was Marquise's shrink. Why wouldn't she tell her?'

'Why didn't she tell me about the baby?' Maggie shot back. 'Look, Thane, I can't explain it, all right? But it happened.' She stood and felt her spine straighten until she was meeting his cloudy gaze with her own. 'And it's true.' She angled up her chin with renewed determination. 'I'm sorry about you not knowing your son. Really. And . . . and I wish things were different.' *Oh, God, Thane, if you only knew, had any inkling about how much I loved you*. 'But I can't change anything. I would if I could, but I can't. So now I've got to concentrate on finding Mary Theresa.' She struggled to keep her voice steady.

'Believe me, no one wants that more than I do,' he said, and she couldn't help that little snag of disappointment that tore at her heart. For as much as she'd never stopped loving him, the same could be said of his feelings for his ex-wife. Though he denied it vehemently, she couldn't trust herself to believe him. Wouldn't. He'd lied too much already, kept far too many secrets. He started to reach for her, but dropped his hands when she slid away from him and refused to give in to the urge to fall victim to him all over again.

'Don't even think about it.'

'You don't believe me.'

'To tell you the truth, Thane, I don't know what to believe,' she said. 'I . . . I just don't want to be confused any longer and I can't afford to make another mistake.'

'Another one?'

'With you.' Clearing her throat, she walked across the room. 'Now, if I remember right, we've got things to do.' *Even though I would love nothing more than to melt into your arms*. Setting her jaw against such wayward thoughts, she added, 'Let's start with Renee Nielsen.' With fresh intent, she strode to the table where she noticed the message light was blinking furiously on the phone. 'First I want to see if Becca called.' She dialed the message center and scribbled down the recorded missives.

The first call was from Tess O'Shaughnessy, the executive producer of *Denver AM*, asking Maggie to be a part of a program dedicated to Marquise; the second was from Craig Beaumont, reiterating the request. The third was from Howard Bailey, who asked Thane to call back.

Maggie handed Thane the message and their fingers touched briefly. In that instant Maggie felt the connection she'd always had with him, the same tiny spark of electricity that hadn't dulled despite the years, despite the lies, despite the dark cloud of betrayal that had been with them both. She thought he might kiss her, wanted desperately to feel his lips pressed intimately against hers, silently begged that what they shared wouldn't be destroyed.

And yet she couldn't forget that he still loved Mary Theresa. No matter how hard he denied it, the connection that existed between him and his ex-wife was far stronger than the tenuous link between them. 'I want to go over Marquise's diary again — I have this feeling I'm missing something, that there was a reference to Renee.'

The phone rang again and Maggie snagged the receiver, half-expecting to hear from her daughter. Instead, it was Detective Henderson.

Maggie froze. Her gaze locked with Thane's.

'Sorry for calling so late, but I thought you'd want to know,' he said, and Maggie experienced the cold fingers of dread crawling up her spine.

Her hand clenched the receiver in a death grip. 'It's about your sister.'

'What?'

'Well, we're starting to think that your sister's Jeep might have been forced off the road.'

'What do you mean?' she whispered, questions rushing through her head. 'Are you saying someone intentionally tried to kill Mary Theresa?'

What the hell was Henderson insinuating?

'Don't know for sure. Could be. Could have just been an accident or road rage or, yes, it could be someone who wanted to harm either your sister or Renee Nielsen.'

'Dear God.' Maggie's soul turned to ice.

'As I said, it might have been a hit-and-run accident where the driver had panicked — '

'But that's unlikely.'

'Or a goddamned coincidence.'

Maggie's voice sounded far away even to her own ears. 'Come on, Detective. Neither you nor I believe in coincidence. The most likely scenario is that someone tried to kill my sister.' He offered more platitudes, and she hung up more scared than she'd ever been in her life.

'Tell me,' Thane demanded.

She briefed him on the conversation. 'I guess you were right.' Her eyes met his and locked.

'Damn!' He grabbed hold of her arm. 'I knew this was going to be dangerous. Son of a bitch! Son of a goddamned — '

'Hey, slow down.' She pulled away from him, nearly falling backward when he unexpectedly let go.

'We need to leave.'

'And go where?' she demanded.

'Out of Denver. I never should have brought you here.' Furious with himself he let fly a blue streak.

'And where will we go? Think about it, Thane. We've got to find Mary Theresa. Now more than ever. Her life is probably in danger!'

'I know, Mag Pie, and that means yours is as well.' He snatched her wrist, dragged her into the bathroom and forced her to look in the full-length mirror. 'It doesn't take a genius to see that you're in danger. If someone *is* trying to kill your sister and even went so far as to kill Renee, thinking she might be Marquise, what do you think will happen when he gets a good look at you, huh?' She stared into her own haunted eyes and swallowed hard. It was true. She and Marquise had been mistaken for each other all their lives. Her gaze met Thane's in the mirror and in his steely blue eyes she saw fear, pure and primal.

'We can't leave,' she said despite his punishing grip. 'Not until we find my sister.'

'What if it's too late, Maggie?'

'It isn't. I won't believe it.' She rotated toward him and he surrounded her with steel-strong arms.

'Okay,' he said, his lips brushing against her crown. 'We'll try to find her, but you've got to promise me that you'll be careful.'

'And what about you, Thane? Can you promise me the same?'

His muscles flexed and he lowered his mouth

to press his lips to hers for one single tantalizing instant. Then he rested his forehead on hers and said with unerring certainty, 'What I can promise you is simple, Maggie. I'm gonna get the son of a bitch who's behind all this and when I do, believe me, he's gonna wish he was dead.'

* * *

Henderson sat at his desk and stared out at the night. His coffee was cold, his stomach rumbling, and he was sick to the back teeth of Marquise or Mary Theresa Reilly or whatever the hell her name was. He'd called Maggie McCrae out of some sense of duty as sooner or later the press would find out that another vehicle had been involved in the accident and they would be swarming on the story like yellow jackets at a backyard barbecue.

He twirled his pencil, glanced at the photo of Marquise pinned to his bulletin board and thought about the other cases under his command. They paled in public interest and, he had to admit, in his as well. Like the rest of the viewing audience he was half in love with the foolish, egotistical celebrity. Yes, she was vain, a liar, a woman who stepped on those who got in her way, a flamboyant personality who obviously didn't know the first thing about getting her shit together, but there was something enigmatic and dangerously fascinating about her.

Since her disappearance, she'd garnered media attention from as far away as Chicago and Tampa. Once nearly forgotten, a dull dying has-been, she'd suddenly gained that unique luster of a tragic heroine — a woman lost; a beautiful female in the throes of some mystery. And even he wasn't immune. 'Christ,' he growled, disgusted with the turn of his thoughts. It was time to wrap this thing up — long past.

He glanced at the manila folders haphazardly stacked on the corner of his desk — a pile of other investigations that he couldn't ignore. Yet here he was, late at night, still trying to figure out what the devil had happened to a woman who was fast becoming Denver's most famous celebrity. Mary Theresa Reilly Walker Gillette had, by becoming mysteriously invisible, made herself more well known than ever. A household word.

Was the accident a coincidence?

A planned publicity trick gone awry?

Some heinous plot?

'It's sick,' he grumbled to himself, and hated being a part of the media circus and speculation that were a party to anything that had to do with Marquise. If only he thought he was making some kind of headway, but the investigation seemed stalled, log-jammed, and it made him irritable and cranky.

Somewhere in the outer offices another midnight hero, some detective working late, coughed. A second later a phone rang in another part of the building.

Henderson spun his chair to stare at her glossy photograph full in the face and felt his stone of a heart chip a bit at the sight of her bright smile and mischievous green eyes. Almost as if she were pulling a fast one over on the photographer and anyone else even remotely associated with her.

Rubbing the stubble on his jaw, he thought about recent stalemates in the case. His interview with Jane Stanton hadn't gone well. A neighbor of Marquise's, Jane was pushing eighty, and though she was spry, her memory sharp enough, her hearing, apparently, wasn't always dependable.

'I was looking for Precious that night, you see,' she'd said, blue eyes cloudy with cataracts as she'd offered the detectives tea that tasted like it had been made from some bitter weed. She'd sat in a rocking chair with an afghan and the cat in question on her lap. Precious had blinked his yellow eyes slowly as if he enjoyed being the center of attention while other felines — five in all — took up various perches in the stately old home.

An orange tabby had viewed them from the top shelf of a bookcase, a Siamese had peered from a crack in a cupboard door left slightly ajar and the other three strolled around the room, hopping onto the furniture or staring through the window at winter birds fluttering in the bare branches of a copse of saplings planted near the back deck.

'He's such a naughty boy,' the old woman confided, 'always trying to stay outside, aren't you, dear?' With a smile she continued to stroke the cat. 'Anyway, I was looking for this little imp, here, when I heard a commotion on the other side of the fence. I couldn't see through the bricks, mind you, but I recognized the voices and though they were muffled, I'm sure I heard Marquise call that Walker man by his name . . . at least I think so. But I heard, clear as a bell, him threatening her. Warning her that he'd kill her.' She nodded curtly, as if agreeing with herself. 'Usually I try not to eavesdrop but that night . . . ' She shrugged her thin shoulders as if to say, 'what can you do?'

'You couldn't hear what they were saying?' Hannah clarified, and the woman's wrinkled face drew together like a tiny purse.

'Not really, but I thought they said something about money or a child . . . oh, I don't really know.' She smiled sadly and sighed. 'I usually keep to myself, you know. Just call for a ride down to the center once in a while.'

'Do you know Marquise?'

'Only just to wave and say 'hi.' I saw the young men come and go — the latest one, the fellow with all the hair and the flashy car . . . ' — sparse gray eyebrows rose over the rims of her glasses — 'I think he's a little rude. The ex-husbands are a nicer lot.'

'Did Marquise leave with anyone that night?'

'Now, that I can't be sure.' She'd pressed the tip of one long, bony finger to her lips and thought for a second. 'It seems that I saw her Jeep leave and there were definitely two people in it. A man and a woman, I think . . . but . . . ' she shrugged, ' . . . it was dark, except for the second or two they were under the streetlights, and I can't be certain.'

Judging from the clouds in her eyes,

Henderson had silently agreed.

He and Hannah had somehow managed to force down most of the strong tea without the benefit of gleaning more information, then left in frustration. Now, hours later, Henderson felt backed up against the wall. He'd read the accident report on Marquise's vehicle over and over again, hoping to find some new clue that he'd overlooked, perused the faxed documents on Renee Nielsen until he could recite them backward and forward and barked at underlings to find any and all information on the dead woman.

There was nothing out of the ordinary about Thane's employee — except that she'd been on his payroll and had ended up dead in his ex-wife's mangled vehicle. Had Renee borrowed Marquise's Jeep? Stolen it? No — Marquise's handbag had been in the backseat. The contents were as expected: wallet, brush, mirror, six tubes of lipstick, mascara, tampons, credit cards and sunglasses. A few receipts for gas. An address book that was battered and, from the number of crossed-out names, should have been replaced a while back. Most of the people had moved long ago. He knew. He'd called them all and come up dry. So, unless Renee had stolen Marquise's purse as well as the Jeep, the natural assumption was that Marquise had been with her.

Or had she? Maybe she'd left her bag in the car and forgotten it when she'd handed Renee the keys.

Nah.

Henderson's head pounded with unanswered questions.

Marquise's Jeep had been examined by the best detectives in the department, men who were trained to search for clues, if there were any; but the vehicle looked normal aside from the traces of black paint on the mangled rear fender.

The paint was the one bright spot in the otherwise dark case. Already the analysts in the lab had discovered from paint scrapings taken from the wreck that the paint was a blend used by Chevrolet; the glass from the headlight, again from a Chevy product. A pickup or Blazer had helped nudge Renee Nielsen's vehicle off the road.

But why?

Who had wanted to kill Renee? Or Marquise?

The answer was in the missing vehicle, and Henderson had communicated with all the law-enforcement agencies in the entire southwest to be looking for a dented black Chevy. DMV and dealership records would be scrutinized.

It was late, the department quiet. If he had any brains at all, he'd drive home to his apartment and put in a call to the kids. Instead he shuffled through his notes again. From the looks of it Marquise didn't have much of an estate, and everything she did own would be left to her niece, Maggie's kid. Marquise had two insurance policies. One named Maggie and Becca McCrae; the other was to a company that Marquise had helped found, MER, Inc., a local business-development company that didn't do diddly as far as Henderson could see. Marquise was the CEO, what a joke, and Eve Lawrence handled the books, which showed a negative cash flow. Frowning, he shuffled through his notes, searching for more information on MER, Inc.

Before he could locate what he wanted, the door to his office flew open. Bang! It hit a file cabinet.

Hannah, her face flushed, her eyes sparkling, marched into the room.

'You've got something,' he guessed, sensing her excitement, the kind that comes only with a break in a stagnant case. He shoved the papers into his briefcase and turned his full attention to his partner. She was a pretty woman anyway, but when she'd figured something out, her cheeks flushed, her eyes gleamed and she was more attractive than ever.

'Could be.'

'What?'

'Okay.' She plopped down on the corner of his desk and he ignored the fact that her skirt hiked up a notch. She swung one leg and leaned closer to him. 'What we've got is that of all the people connected with Marquise, several own late-model black Chevys.'

'Who?' Henderson asked.

'It's an interesting list. Let's start with Ron Bishop, the station manager at KRKY. He owns a Mercedes and a black Chevy pickup. His wife usually drives the Mercedes.'

'Check him out,' Henderson said, though he

doubted Ron would kill off one of his stars, no matter how much of a prima donna and pain in the butt she was.

'Will do. Now there's also Gillette.'

Henderson sat up straighter in his chair. This was interesting. 'He did own a black Blazer a couple of years back, but he gave it to his daughter, Tanya Inman.'

'Whose husband dumped her for Marquise?' Even better.

'Bingo.'

Henderson's old chair squeaked as he leaned forward, riffling through the files on his desk, flipping through the pages, trying to find some kind of information on Tanya Inman. 'Check them out, too.'

'Will do. But here's the really interesting one,' Hannah said, a teasing smile on her pale lips. 'A black late-model Blazer was recently purchased by one Renee Warner.'

'Warner?' That sounded familiar. He turned to the information they'd collected on the victim.

'Mmm. Renee Nielsen's maiden name. Seems she decided to take it back a few months ago, then went out and bought herself a two-year-old Blazer. Apparently found one in the paper, contacted the guy, and paid him with a cashier's check. Just registered through DMV six weeks ago, listed her address as an apartment on the north end of town.'

Henderson couldn't believe this sudden turn in luck. He was already on his feet, snapping his briefcase closed. 'And?'

'And nothing. I already checked it out.

Furnished, but for the most part empty. The place hasn't been lived in for weeks. It was, as they say, clean as a whistle. None of the neighbors had ever seen anyone fitting Ms. Nielsen's description.'

'So where was she living?' Some of his excitement ebbed.

'Don't know yet.'

'Think she's connected somehow to Walker?'

'Seems unlikely, as he's the one who came up with the ID.'

'He didn't have much choice. We would've found out anyway.'

'Give up on him, would ya? Just because he threatened his ex-wife, who owed him some money, and now a woman who worked for him is dead, doesn't mean that he's guilty of anything other than having poor taste in women and being an easy mark.'

'Ya think?' He reached for the baseball, but left it in its holder. The heating system rumbled, blowing air and stirring up dust.

'I do.'

'So how is Renee Warner Nielsen connected to all this?'

Hannah winked at him. 'I'm working on that one. Between the bank where she got the cashier's check, the previous address and references she gave the landlord, and information on the insurance on the vehicle, we might just come up with something.'

'If we're lucky,' Henderson said, reaching into his top drawer for a stick of gum.

'Come on, Reed,' she said, tossing her hair

back and laughing. 'The day you believe in luck is the day I give up coffee.'

* * *

With a soft bump, the jet touched down at Denver International Airport, and Becca grabbed her backpack from under the seat in front of her. She'd listened to her CDs for the two-hour flight, eaten the stale peanuts, and downed a 7UP, all the while trying not to get into a conversation with the plump fiftyish woman next to her. Her name was Gladys and she would tell anyone who showed the slightest bit of interest about the birth of her first grandchild — like it was the biggest event since the last Rolling Stones tour, which, unfortunately, she'd managed to attend. To listen to her you'd begin to believe that Mick Jagger was the greatest singer to ever grace a stage. Obviously Gladys had never seen Beck on MTV.

Not that she really cared. Becca had more important things on her mind, but she kept them to herself and even refrained from rolling her eyes when the old lady made some joke about throwing a bra onto the stage at Keith Richards's feet. Sheesh. Old people! Head cases!

Besides, Becca's guilt was eating at her and she didn't give a rip about the baby *or* the Stones. She was already feeling like a sneak, a thief and an ingrate, but it was all too bad. Once she hooked up with her mother again, everything would work out.

If Marquise is okay.

'She has to be,' Becca said as the plane taxied along the runway and she saw the distinctive illuminated peaks of the roof over the main terminal.

'Who has to be?' Gladys asked, smiling and showing off teeth that had been filled with gold. She was touching up her lipstick, trying to keep a steady hand as she squinted into a tiny mirror on her compact while the plane's engines wound down. Becca glanced out the window over the wing, saw the flaps raised, and felt her stomach clench. 'Has to be what?' the woman insisted.

'Nothin'.' The less said, the better.

'Are you going into the city? Is someone going to pick you up?' She smeared her lips together, spreading the maroon color, then dabbed at the corners of her mouth with her finger.

'Yeah, my mom's gonna be there.'

'Good. Good.' She wasn't really listening, and she twisted her lipstick back into the tube. Winking at Becca, she said, 'Grandma's got to look good, y'know. Don't want to scare Baby Charlie right off the bat.'

She chuckled, and Becca managed a thin, barely-patient smile. The woman was completely out of it. Baby Charlie probably couldn't care less if his grandmother resembled a gorilla, but rather than roll her eyes and tell the woman to get a life, Becca stared out the window as the plane eased into its position near the jetway. If this lady had any idea that Becca had lied to Aunt Connie, stolen from Jenny, then hitchhiked to the L.A. airport to save some money, the woman would probably fall into a dead faint. That would be too bad for Baby Charlie because from the looks of the packages stowed under the seat, the kid was gonna be outfitted with enough Beanie Babies to fill his nursery.

The plane rolled to a stop and Becca crossed her fingers that a cab to the Brass Tree hotel wouldn't cost her more money than she had. If it did, well, she'd probably just have to stiff the driver. That thought settled like lead in her stomach, but she didn't worry about it too much. She couldn't. She had to connect with Mom before Aunt Connie found out she was gone and the 'you know what' hit the fan.

* * *

I give, Maggie thought as she stared at the wrinkled pages she'd copied from Marquise's diary that she'd found on the computer. Her plan of becoming her twin and walking through her life hadn't helped her find her sister. All it had managed to do was make her aware of a darker side of Marquise, convince her that she hadn't known her twin at all, and bring her closer to a man she should never trust, a man whom she was certain she still loved, a man she should still avoid.

And scare her to death. Ever since the report of Marquise's Jeep being run off the road, Maggie had been more determined than ever to locate Marquise.

If only she could. She'd called Marquise's housekeeper at the house in Aspen, dialed every friend and neighbor she could find in Marquise's Rolodex and ended up with nothing for her efforts except a huge phone bill and an aching head.

Thane, too, had been on his cell phone most of the night, calling people in California about Renee Nielsen, connecting with Howard Bailey and Tom Yates about his ranches, and had finished by making a call to Carrie Edgars, who had left him a voice-mail message on his cell phone earlier.

Maggie didn't eavesdrop, but the French doors separating his bedroom from the living area of the suite were open and she couldn't help but hear snatches of the conversation.

'You knew how I felt . . . no, Carrie, that's not the way it was or is . . . we talked about this last summer . . . okay, in September . . . so it's time for both of us . . . yes, you, too, to move on . . . of course. Hey, that's just the way it is. Well, hope it works out . . . '

He hung up and she, seated on the couch, had watched him surreptitiously. Closing his eyes, he rotated his neck as if trying to crack his spine and relieve some tension.

His cell phone jangled loudly. Grumbling something under his breath, he answered tersely, as if he expected Carrie to be calling back.

'Walker.' A pause. His lips flattened over his teeth, and through the glass panels of the French doors, his gaze met Maggie's. In a heartbeat she knew that something was wrong. *Mary Theresa. The police have found her and wanted to break the news to Thane before talking with me.*

Maggie's heart plummeted. She was hot and cold all at once. Fear congealed her blood as she stood, the papers in her lap forgotten and fluttering to the floor.

'Where are you now?' Thane demanded as he walked into the living area and spoke into the handset.

Maggie's heart was a drum. Another long pause and the conversation was again one-sided. He checked his watch. 'All right,' he agreed, snagging the jacket he'd flung carelessly over the back of a chair. 'I'll meet you there in half an hour.' He hung up and shrugged into the short rawhide coat. 'That was Roy,' he explained, his expression a mixture of worry and excitement. 'He thinks he's found my son, and he's flying through Denver. Waiting for a connection, so I'm meeting him at a bar in Denver International. Why don't you come along?'

Relief chased away her fears though she knew the feeling was only temporary.

The invitation was tempting, but she shook her head. 'No, Thane,' she said, knowing this was something he should do on his own. 'I've got a million and one things to do here. I *know* there's some connection between Mary Theresa and Renee Nielsen — something I've seen somewhere.' She motioned to the rumpled stack of papers that represented Marquise's life. 'I'll go through these again.'

'I don't like leaving you here alone.'

'I'll be fine.' His concern was touching, but ludicrous. 'I'm a big girl.'

'There might be a nut on the loose.'

'The doors here lock and hotel security seems pretty tight to me. Really.' She placed a hand on his arm, ignored the protests forming in his eyes. 'I'll be safe.'

'I'd feel better — '

'When you find out about your son.' She felt a painful little tug on her heart; the knowledge that Thane and Mary Theresa had conceived a child was a new stumbling block, one more tie that bound them together forever and reminded her of their betrayal.

Get over it, Maggie, this boy is your nephew. M.T.'s child. Thane's son.

'Go,' she encouraged. 'If you're gonna meet your friend between flights, you don't have a lot of time.'

He found his keys in a pocket of his jacket. 'Promise me you'll be careful. Don't take any risks. And stay put. I'll be back in a couple of hours.'

'I should be right here. Go on. I'll go over these notes again.'

'You think it'll do any good?'

'Don't know. Won't hurt.'

He stared at her for half a second. Fire ignited in his eyes. 'Oh, Christ, Maggie, you take care of yourself,' he whispered, grabbing her fiercely under the arms and forcing his mouth to hers. He smelled of smoke and leather, tasted of coffee. His kisses were warm, hard, and filled with a new desperation that caused her heart to pound. There was something different about him. About them. She couldn't breathe, could barely think, and the room seemed to spin.

Dear God, help me, she thought, knowing that she was foolishly trapped in a one-sided love. His tongue was insistent, and his voice cracked when he lifted his head. 'What you do to me should be illegal,' he admitted, stroking her hair.

'You'd better go — '

He cut her off with another kiss, the pressure of his lips anxious and wanting, the heat from his body quick to spark. It was as if he was kissing her for the last time, she realized, as if he sensed the same aura of despair that had been boring a hole in her soul for the past few days.

'I'll be back soon,' he promised, his voice gruff as he lifted his head and touched the tip of his nose to hers. 'And then, darlin', you and I, we have to talk.'

A lump filled her throat. 'I know.'

'Maggie, Maggie, Maggie.' Sighing, he let his arms fall and strode to the door.

'Good luck.'

As he glanced over his shoulder, one side of his mouth lifted in that smile she'd loved all of her life. 'Why do I feel like I'm gonna need it?'

'Don't know.'

With a wink, he was out the door, his boots echoing dully down the carpeted hallway before the door slammed shut.

Maggie touched her lips with her fingertips, refused to give in to the urge to cry, then picked up the scattered pages of her sister's life and sat down on the edge of the couch, her eyes scanning the computer printouts sightlessly. She gave herself a quick, hard mental shake because her thoughts drifted back to Thane, who was on his way to find out about his son.

'Now listen, Maggie,' she told herself, shuffling through the pages. 'Think about Mary Theresa. You have to find her, and the answer to what happened to her is here.' She shook the damned printouts. 'Here. Somewhere. You just have to be smart enough to find it.'

Maggie. Where are you?

Maggie froze. The voice echoed through her head. 'Mary Theresa?' she whispered. Oh, God, was it Marquise? Maggie spun as if she could see her sister, though she knew the act was foolish.

I need your help. Oh, God, I counted on you.

'Where are you?' Maggie asked, blinking rapidly, the pages in her lap forgotten.

Please come . . . I . . . I need you. I've made such a horrible mistake.

'Where are you?' Maggie screamed to the four walls, relieved that her sister was alive, convinced that she was sending her messages again, angry and frustrated that she couldn't reach her. 'Mary Theresa! Where the hell are you?' Her throat was rough, her eyes filling with tears. 'Can you hear me?' Closing her eyes, she tried, as she had over and over again through the years, to throw her own inner voice. *Where are you, damn it! M.T. — I'll come to you, but I don't know where you are . . .* She waited. The seconds ticked off. Tears began to fall from her eyes.

She thought she'd lost her again and, in exasperation, her fingers crumpled the pages still in her hands. 'Damn you, Mary — Damn you, I can't help you if I don't know where you are!'

Maggie? Can you hear me? I'm going home . . .

20

In the bustle of the airport bar, seated at a corner table, Thane ignored his drink — a bourbon on the rocks. The ice was melting, the drink becoming weak. He didn't give a rip as he stared at the pictures of the teenage boy, snapshots Roy had taken. The kid was good-looking, with dark hair that waved a bit, green-blue eyes, high cheekbones, and a jaw that promised to become square as the years rolled by and he reached manhood. Pride pulled the corners of Thane's mouth up a bit, bitter reality caused his eyes to narrow in anger. Mary Theresa, the bitch, had kept this secret to herself, only leveled with him when she was backed into a corner, when she wanted the upper hand.

'His name is Ryan,' Roy said. 'His phone number and address are here.' He pointed to the manila envelope from which he'd extracted the photos. 'You can call him if you want.'

'You're sure he's mine?'

'Not without a DNA test, no.' Roy, his short, clipped beard beginning to show signs of gray, took a swig from his beer and tried to catch the waitress's attention. The bar was filled with travelers talking and laughing, drinking, snacking, and just killing time between flights. Carry-on bags, backpacks, laptop computers, and briefcases littered the floor under the tiny tables. 'What I'm sure of is that he's Marquise's, er, Mary Theresa's — she was still using her given name back then.'

The waitress, a freckle faced girl who didn't look old enough to serve alcohol of any kind, glanced in Roy's direction and he took advantage of the situation, holding up his near-empty bottle of Coors and wiggling it, silently asking for another.

'I'll be right with you,' she promised.

Roy grabbed a handful of popcorn and motioned toward the picture. 'But look at that kid, would ya? If he's not your son, he should be.'

'You think he takes after me?'

'Not now. But when you were a kid. Damned straight. The spittin' image. Ahh, here we go.' He grinned up at the waitress, whose lack of expression didn't invite conversation or, Thane guessed, many large tips. 'Thanks, sweetheart. You're a love,' Roy said with a playful grin.

She barely smiled. 'Anything for you?' she asked Thane in a toneless voice.

'No, I'm fine.' He couldn't take his eyes off the glossy snapshots.

'He's preoccupied,' Roy explained, as she scribbled on a notepad, slapped the tab onto the table, then moved onto the next group of thirsty patrons. Roy drained his first bottle before starting on his second. 'Here's the scoop. The kid is the only son of Vera and Bill Brown. The old man — well, he's only forty-five, not exactly ancient, I suppose — is a firefighter, his mother a travel agent who works four days a week. They think this boy is God's gift and the kid hasn't given them a lot of grief. Yet. Plays soccer and baseball, doesn't have a steady girlfriend as far as I can tell from what I managed to dig up.'

'He's held down two jobs, one scooping ice cream — that one lasted about three months. Later he signed on at the local car wash and took a turn polishing fenders. Right now he's not working.'

Thane nodded, staring at his son. *His son*. Ryan Brown. A boy he had yet to meet; a kid he hadn't known existed until just recently. Damn Mary Theresa.

'Since I've given you the phone number and address along with a hefty bill for my services,' Roy said with a smug, self-deprecating grin, 'I figure from here on in, the ball's in your court.' With a glance at his watch, he scowled. 'Oh, shit, I gotta run. Got a plane to catch. Finish that, will ya?' he asked, pointing to the long-necked bottle that he'd barely touched. 'And pick up the tab. This one's on you.' He grabbed the overnight bag he'd stuffed under their small table and started for the door.

'Roy?' Thane said, realizing his friend was leaving.

'What?'

Thane stood and stuck out his hand. 'Thanks.'

Roy's grin showed off teeth that were beginning to yellow. 'Any time.'

* * *

Heart thundering, Maggie wheeled into Marquise's drive and felt like an intruder as her sister's home loomed in the watery blue glow of street lamps. The house, usually warm and inviting, was dark, a massive structure with all the warmth of a tomb. But this had to be right, didn't it?

The message she'd received didn't make any sense. Why would Marquise be at her house? Or did she mean that she was going to . . . 'Don't even think it.' Maggie cut the engine and tossed her keys into her purse. Just because Mary Theresa had supposedly written a suicide note, one that the press, thankfully, hadn't mentioned anywhere, didn't mean that she was actually going to take her life.

Maggie was out of the car in a second and flying up the front walk. She banged on the front door and poked the doorbell with an insistent finger, but she knew no one was inside; the house looked cold and empty. Using her key, she unlocked the door, stepped inside, and nearly jumped out of her skin as the security system started beeping softly and for a second she thought a man was lurking in the shadows.

Then she remembered the suit of armor and forced herself to remain calm, to try and settle her erratic pulse and the feeling of doom that seemed to seep from the walls. Her boots slapped against the floor as she snapped on lights along the hallway to the closet where she disengaged the alarm system. 'Mary Theresa?' she called, knowing deep in her heart that she was alone in the behemoth of a house. She walked back to the base of the stairs and again called to her sister, but the house was silent.

'Great,' she said under her breath, and glanced at the suit of armor and mannequin as if they could hear her. She felt goose bumps rise on her skin and rubbed her arms through her thick jacket.

Maybe coming here was wrong, maybe Maggie hadn't interpreted Mary Theresa's message correctly, she thought as she crossed the living room and spied the piano, black and gleaming near the bank of windows that viewed the still lake. The water was smooth and dark, only a ribbon of moonlight illuminating the surface. The snow had completely melted away, and the grass shimmered silver and cold in the night.

'Come on, M.T., where are you?' she whispered, a feeling of dread settling like lead in her heart. Where was her sister? She passed by a hallway mirror and jumped at her own image — her sister's image.

You're losing it, she told herself and set her jaw. *Just wait. M. T. said she'd be here*.

Or did she? Maybe you didn't hear a message at all. Maybe it's all in your mind, just as the shrink told you a long time ago, or maybe it's just wishful thinking.

'Damn.' She sat on the piano bench and sighed. 'Where are you, Mary?' she wondered aloud, running a finger along the keys of the concert grand and listening to the tinkling notes as she stared into the vast darkness of the night. Dread squeezed her throat, and just being alone in Marquise's house started stretching her nerves as tight as the wires of this piano.

Maybe this was a wild goose chase. A mistake.

She walked to the den. Switching on Marquise's computer, she waited for the machine to boot up, then dialed Connie in L.A. in the hopes of connecting with Becca. The computer went through its start-up procedure, the monitor glowing as the phone rang several times only to be answered by a machine. Rather than leave a message, she hung up. 'So far you're batting a thousand,' she told herself, trying to fight an overwhelming sense of disappointment.

She missed Becca terribly. But it was probably one-sided. Though Becca was starting to come around, it seemed, and though the seductive luster of L.A. had begun to fade, even a bit, in Becca's eyes, the ravine between mother and daughter seemed impossible to bridge at times.

'Pull yourself together.' The cold dark house was beginning to get to her. She *had* to pull herself together. Glancing at her watch, she bit her lip and prayed that she and Mary Theresa would connect, the mystery surrounding her disappearance and Renee Nielsen's death would be solved, and she could return to Idaho where she and her daughter could resume their normal, if very dull, lives. Right now, dull sounded like heaven.

And what about Thane? she asked as she sat in a desk chair and stared at the monitor where the few icons of Marquise's programs decorated the screen. *What are you going to do about him?*

'Nothing.' But she dialed the number of the hotel and left a message in their suite telling him where she'd gone and that she'd be back soon.

She didn't want him to worry about her, then decided she was a fool of the worst order. Oh, he cared for her a little — but not enough, not the way she loved him. She closed her eyes for a second and tried to deny her feelings, but she'd only be lying to herself. She loved Thane Walker. Pure and simple. She always had. Even during the duration of her stormy marriage to Dean McCrae.

Guilt crowded into her mind. 'Fool,' she muttered. Thane would never love her. He didn't have the capacity, and there was always Mary Theresa; like a ghost she came between them, even when they were pressed together, naked body to naked body. Mary Theresa had been in the bed with them.

'Stop it!' Her case of nerves was getting to her. 'Sheesh, Maggie, you're a head case,' she chastised, opening a program and eyeing Marquise's address book.

Now Thane had a son, a boy he'd never met, Mary Theresa's child . . . why that thought hurt so badly, she didn't understand. She told herself to get over it. Aside from his on-again/off-again relationship with Mary Theresa, he also had a girlfriend in Wyoming — Carrie Whatever. Even if that was truly over there was the other issue.

And he's never stopped loving your sister.

Maggie's throat ached and she refused to think of Thane and the emotions that burned so bright in her heart. She couldn't love him. Wouldn't. It served no purpose whatsoever and would only cause her heartache. So she'd kissed him again. So she'd touched him. Made love to him. So what? People did it all the time. There wasn't anything special or magical about it.

Get over it, she told herself as she began going through Marquise's files again, although the sense that she was trespassing gave her pause.

She scrolled down the address list, viewed the tax file and financial statement. With a sinking feeling she realized just how horribly in debt her sister was, how desperate her financial situation had become. Back taxes, credit-card bills, overdue lease payments, foreclosure notices on her place in Aspen and this very house.

'No wonder she ran away,' Maggie said, playing with the computer, cross-indexing — trying to find any match for Renee Nielsen. No Nielsens whatsoever. But there was another Renee. Renee Warner. Maggie felt a tingle at the nape of her neck, the sense that she was about to find something, something she didn't want to see. With deft fingers, she scrolled down, double checked, did a file search and found no checks made payable to Renee Warner. But there were a couple of checks made payable to herself for cash and noted on the computer as RW.

'Could mean anything,' she told herself. '*Rear Window*, for example, or right wing or anything and Renee's name is Nielsen . . . ' Her neck ached and she glanced at the clock. It had been an hour and a half since the last 'message' from her sister. Since then nothing. Maybe she was having a nervous breakdown, just like Dean's family always insinuated. Fat chance. Connie and Jim were always looking for ways to prove that she, even if capable of being Becca's guardian, at least was too mentally unbalanced to handle the trust fund Dean's father had set up for her child. It was all so sick. She'd been crazy to let Becca spend any time with them, but she'd had no choice. And she wasn't crazy! Mary Theresa had contacted her.

So where is she? Her heart leapt to her throat as she thought of the car accident and the fact that some other vehicle had edged M.T.'s Jeep off the road. Had something happened to her since the message? Could the person responsible for Renee's death have found her sister?

'Come on, Mary. Come on,' she said nervously. Rubbing the strain from the muscles in her shoulders, she stood.

Thump!

She froze.

Outside, from the direction of the thud, a cat screamed.

Maggie started for the kitchen.

Click.

A lock gave way and Maggie's heart, fueled by adrenaline, pumped wildly. With a squeak, a door opened. Maggie felt a cool rush of outside air creep into the house.

'Mary Theresa?' she called, praying it was no one else.

* * *

Henderson had just turned off the answering machine in his apartment and was sorting through the day's stack of bills and junk mail while deciding whether to heat up a TV dinner or just roll into the sack and ignore his rumbling stomach. The phone jangled and he snatched up the receiver, answering quickly, by rote. 'Henderson.'

'Officer Bates, Colorado State Police.'

Henderson's mind clicked into gear.

'You put out an APB on a black Chevy Blazer, and I think we found it.'

'Where?'

'Off an old mining road near Crested Butte. It's a wonder we found it at all. Got a crew on it already.'

'Anyone inside?' he asked, feeling a niggle of anticipation. This might just be the break they were looking for.

'Don't know yet, but it looks bad.'

'Single car?'

'Far as we can tell.' The officer gave specific directions to the spot; Henderson asked to be kept posted and then he hung up. Walking to the desk in the second bedroom, he opened the top drawer and, cussing himself all the way, opened the cellophane around a three-month-old pack of Camel straights — the pack he'd saved for an emergency such as this.

'Damn you, Marquise. Where the hell are you?' he asked, poking a cigarette between his teeth as he rummaged in the drawer for a match. He found a lighter that refused to spark and thought it a grand irony if tonight, when he was finally going to break down and have a smoke, he couldn't come up with a damned match.

'Shit,' he grumbled, and opened his briefcase on the off chance that an old book of matches was in one of the pockets. Instead he found the copy of the legal documents for MER, Inc. There was something about the holding company that bothered him, the same way he felt when he woke up on a camping trip in the desert a while back and found a scorpion crawling up his arm — that if he didn't do something and quick, think fast, he was going to get stung. *Some*thing was wrong with the damned corporation.

Sitting in the desk chair, the unlit cigarette wedged between his lips, he started reading, flipping through pages and pages of Articles of Incorporation, lines of legalese that sometimes blurred before his tired eyes. 'Hell,' he thought, finding nothing, when finally, buried deep in the text, a name came to light — the third name involved in the corporation: Renee Warner.

'I'll be damned.' How could he have missed this?

Three women linked together.

Marquise.

Eve Lawrence.

And Renee Warner a.k.a. Renee Nielsen, a woman lying dead on a slab in the morgue. 'Well, I'll be damned,' he whispered. 'I'll be god . . . damned.'

The cigarette fell from his mouth and he shot out of his chair, grabbing his wallet, keys and gun. He was through the door in a heartbeat.

⋆ ⋆ ⋆

Thane had been edgy from the time he'd left the airport. He'd driven back to the hotel like a madman, trying not to blame himself for leaving

Maggie alone, consoling himself with the fact that she was a smart woman, a woman who knew how to handle herself, and yet he was impatient with the traffic and the elevator in the hotel. The closer he got to her, the more nervous he became.

Because you love her, you idiot. You always have. From the first second you saw her walking along the side of the road, her spine stiff, her eyes straight ahead, her cheeks flushed as she headed to Flora's ranch.

For years he'd denied the depth of his emotions to himself as well as the rest of the world, but the truth of the matter was that he loved her.

'Damn,' he ground out as the doors to the elevator opened and he strode down the hallway to their suite. But the minute Thane unlocked the door and walked into the hotel room, he knew something was wrong. Maggie wasn't in the room, but it wasn't empty. Her daughter, Becca, had plopped herself in the middle of the couch and was staring up at him with wide, distrustful eyes.

'I thought you were in L.A.' He glanced around the suite and saw no trace of Maggie, just Becca's backpack.

'I was.'

'Where's your mother?'

'At Marquise's house. I just listened to the messages. She left one for you.'

Thane had a bad feeling about all this. The muscles in his back tightened. 'She didn't say anything about you coming here.'

'She doesn't know,' Becca said, her eyes, so like Maggie's, full of challenge. 'I came on my own.'

'What happened in California?' he asked, walking to the phone.

'Nothin' good,' Becca said as he listened to the message that Maggie had left. 'I decided I needed to be with my mom.'

'And your aunt and uncle agreed?' he asked skeptically as he hung up. It was nearly three in the morning and, from the looks of her, Becca hadn't been here long.

'They didn't know,' she said. 'I just called and talked to Aunt Connie.'

'Holy shit.'

'That's what she said.'

Thane didn't have much practice dealing with in-your-face teenagers, but he wasn't going to take any lip from any kid. Even Maggie's. 'I think you'd better talk this over with your mom.'

'No shit, Sherlock. You drive.'

'And you watch your mouth.'

Becca's eyes thinned. 'I will. Just as soon as you watch yours.'

'We'll talk about this in the car. I'll call your mom from the cell phone.'

'I *don't* need a lecture.'

'Well, kiddo, you're gonna get one.' She grabbed her backpack and headed for the door without any sign of a limp. 'And I doubt if you're gonna like it.'

She opened her mouth to smart off again, thought better of it, and snapped her jaw closed. As far as Thane was concerned, that in and of itself was a major victory.

* * *

'Maggie?' Mary Theresa, devoid of makeup, wearing dirty jeans and a sweatshirt, her hair all tangled and unwashed, stumbled through the back door and into the darkened kitchen.

'Oh, God!' Relief flooded through Maggie at the sight of her twin. Hot tears filled her eyes. 'Mary Theresa!' She dashed across the room, stumbling slightly as she bumped into a bar stool, knocked against the knife rack, ignored the jab of pain in her shin and flung herself at her sister. 'I was so worried, so damned worried,' she choked up as Mary Theresa crumpled in her arms. 'I thought . . . oh, you don't want to know what I thought.' She held her as if she couldn't let go and all the bad feelings she'd harbored over the years — the jealousy, envy and distrust — melted away. This was her sister, her twin. And she looked like hell.

Mary Theresa was crying, her slender body racked with sobs, her fingers digging into Maggie's shoulders. 'Oh, God, Maggie, I — I've been such a fool. Such a damned selfish fool.' She sniffed and pulled back long enough to wipe her nose with the back of her hand. Tears tracked from her eyes. 'I'm sorry,' she squeaked out, hardly able to speak.

'You're sorry?' Maggie said, fighting the urge to break down altogether. 'Oh, God, I'm just glad you're alive. I thought you were dead. I — I've been so worried. I got your message, but

I couldn't understand what happened.'

'No one would believe it,' Mary Theresa said as she disentangled herself and sagged against the counter. She wiped a hand over her forehead and Maggie noticed that she'd lost weight, was barely more than skin and bones.

'What happened?'

'This was all a mistake. A horrible mistake. I — I read the papers today, saw that Renee is dead.' Even in the dark room, she paled and Maggie flipped a switch. The kitchen was suddenly awash in light. Mary Theresa, as if she'd been shot, looked wildly around the room. 'Don't!' She turned off the lights and then, with Maggie on her heels, walked quickly through the rooms and snapped off light after light. 'Does anyone know you're here?' she asked, fear strangling her words.

'No, but . . . well, I left a message for Thane.'

'Shit.'

'What's going on?'

'Nothing good. We've got to get out of here. I just need a minute to clean up and grab some clothes and money and . . . '

'What're you talking about?' Maggie followed Mary Theresa upstairs. For a woman who was so weak she'd practically fallen into the kitchen, Mary Theresa had found a reserve of strength. She dashed up the final steps and walked unerringly into her bedroom. Pulling the shades and the drapes, she said, 'Close the door behind you.'

'Mary Theresa, what the hell's going on?'

Maggie asked, but did as she was told. The door shut with a click.

Mary Theresa turned on a small lamp near the bed. 'Is it true? Is Renee Nielsen dead?' she asked, but from the haunted look in her eyes, she already knew the answer.

'We thought it was you.'

'Oh, God.' Mary Theresa ran two sets of stiff fingers through her hair and her face was chalk-white beneath smudges of dirt. 'I didn't mean . . . I had no idea . . . ' Her voice squeaked and she placed a hand over her mouth. 'It was a single-car accident, right?' she asked, obviously skeptical.

Maggie shook her head as she stood near a table laden with framed photographs of Mary Theresa. 'Hit-and-run according to the police. The press just doesn't know about it yet.'

Holding a fistful of hair and squeezing, M.T. asked, 'Why would anyone want to kill her?'

'An accident . . . no one intended to . . . '

Mary Theresa wasn't listening. 'No, no, no! Don't you get it?' She was on her feet in an instant and inside the cedar lined closet. 'It had to be Eve.'

'Eve?' Maggie repeated. 'Hey, what're you talking about?' But she was starting to feel a needle of understanding pierce her brain.

'This was all her idea to begin with.' Inside the closet Mary Theresa was throwing clothes into an open designer bag. Jeans, slacks, shirts, blouses, all flung in with abandon. Maggie was reminded of a person on speed. M.T. was so thin and yet jazzed up, her movements quick and jerky.

'What was Eve's idea?' she asked as M.T., stripping off her dirty clothes, hurried into the bathroom.

Maggie followed, stepping over sweatshirt, jeans and bra as Mary Theresa turned on the shower. 'I shouldn't take the time, but I want to wash off all this . . . this filth.' In the shadowy mirror, Maggie saw her reflection — dressed in slacks, blouse, and vest; M.T. stark naked, her breasts firm, her ribs evident. So much the same. So different.

Mary walked through the shower, taking less than three minutes to clean up. She was toweling off, her hair wet as she stepped into a clean warm-up outfit. 'We've got to get out of here,' she said, not bothering with makeup and yanking on her running shoes.

'What was all Eve's idea?' Maggie asked again as M.T. leaned over to tie her laces.

'The disappearing act, of course.'

Maggie's heart sank. This was all a publicity stunt that had taken a bad turn? And a woman was dead.

'Slow down.' She reached forward and took hold of her sister's arm. 'You *planned* this?'

'What'd you think?'

'But — '

'As I said it was Eve's idea. We were short of cash and I'm borrowed to the hilt.' She zipped up her bag and wide, haunted eyes, so much like Maggie's, stared straight into hers.

'It was all just a setup, for publicity to hike up

the ratings. The show was in trouble and we needed to do something, *anything*, to boost the market share. The dullards calling the shots at the station weren't listening and I knew we were either gonna be canceled or I would be replaced. Trust me, Maggie, the writing was on the wall.'

She said it without too much emotion, as if she'd had no choice but to deceive everyone.

'Eve knew of a cabin owned by one of her clients that hadn't been used for years, so I went there and hid out. The only people who knew where I was were Eve and Renee.'

'Renee?' Oh, God, this was beginning to sound bad. Really bad.

'That's what I was talking about. Douse the light, will ya?'

Maggie switched off all the lamps as Mary Theresa hiked the strap of her bag to her shoulder.

'So Renee was in on this, too,' Maggie guessed, sick inside. As relieved as she was that her sister was alive and seemingly healthy, she couldn't stand the callous way she spoke of their plot of deception.

'Because Eve had to stay here in town and make sure everything went according to plan, Renee did the running back and forth because no one knew she lived here or who she was. She even changed her name back to Warner to try and keep a lower profile. Anyway, the plan was that after there was a big stir and my name was a household word again then I . . . I was supposed to escape from my 'captors' and there would be this massive manhunt and no one would ever find out that Eve was behind it.'

'The police aren't that stupid.'

'Sure they are.' Mary Theresa was heading down the stairs, her feet tripping rapidly over the familiar steps. 'I'm an actress, for God's sake, I could have convinced them that some mountain men had grabbed me and since I would be fine, the manhunt would slowly disintegrate.'

'But people would believe that there were men who . . . '

'So what? As I said, no one was supposed to be hurt.' She was walking toward the kitchen again. 'I need a drink.'

'Why would Eve agree to do anything of the sort?' Maggie asked as they reentered the kitchen.

'Because I owed her money.' Mary Theresa reached into a darkened cupboard and pulled out a glass which she filled with water from the sink. 'I'm in bad shape, Mag,' she confessed. 'I owe everyone money and things were falling apart by the minute. Do you know what would have happened if the station changed the format of the program and I lost my job? Holy Christ, I'd be ruined! That would have been a disaster.'

'But — ' Maggie's head was swimming. 'Renee's dead, Mary Theresa. *Dead*.'

'I know.' She took a gulp of water. 'Like I'm supposed to be. No wonder she insisted I write that suicide note and leave it in the trash to throw the police off. Can you believe it? Eve just left me up there. No phone. No electricity. A million miles from civilization. And I'm sure I was drugged. Eve was probably going to give me enough to kill me once she'd done away with Renee,' Mary Theresa said before taking a long swallow from her glass, then reaching into another cupboard and retrieving what, in the poor light, Maggie assumed was a vial of pills. 'Christ, I've got a headache. The drugs weren't part of the deal, you know. I was so damned tired all the time. I should have been suspicious, but I wasn't. I think Eve had Renee give them to me so I wouldn't get smart and try to escape. She even got rid of my car, the car that Renee and I took up and hid there.'

'The Jeep.'

'Yeah, no one could drive it because of my plates, so Renee used her black rig, but one day, because Eve supposedly had some kind of car trouble, she took the Blazer. When she didn't return when she was supposed to, Renee decided to risk taking the Jeep. She took off and never came back.'

'There was black paint on the Jeep,' Maggie said, horrified. Eve Lawrence, a murderer? Over money? It didn't seem to fit.

'Figures.' Mary Theresa, shaking, tossed back a handful of pills and swallowed them.

'What about those — the ones you're taking now — if you've been on drugs, isn't that a bad idea?' Maggie said, trying to keep up with her sister's explanation.

'Aspirin, Mag. Don't worry. Shit, I bet this headache is because of the damned pills I was given. I was getting pretty tired of being up there, let me tell you, but Eve kept telling me that each day I stayed away would only make my reappearance all that more newsworthy.' She laughed mirthlessly. 'Guess who was played for the fool?'

'All of us.'

M.T. took another long swallow from her glass before tossing the rest of the water into the sink.

'You think Eve would kill two people for money? I met her . . . ' Maggie shook her head. 'That's way too drastic.'

'She's nuts, obviously.'

Maggie remembered the cool businesswoman she'd met with the other day.

'Okay — let's assume for the moment that Eve's back was against the wall and she . . . killed Renee to cover her tracks or because . . . because she thought you'd somehow escaped,' Maggie said, not believing her own words. 'What happened then?'

'I'll tell you on the way to the car. You have one, right?'

'A rental.'

'Good. Don't want to use mine. Not yet. Not until I know what's going on for sure.' She started for the front of the house. 'When Renee didn't come back after a couple of days, I got worried and started hiking out. My head was clearing up and I knew something was wrong. Really wrong. I was really pissed because I was in the middle of no-goddamned-where. Fortunately some kids were snowmobiling and they found me, took me to the road, and I walked until I found the highway where some trucker out of Salt Lake picked me up.' She sighed. 'The worst part of this is that no one recognized me.

Here there was supposed to be this massive manhunt for me, and Eve was certain I'd catapult myself into instant fame — become a goddamned American icon — and the three people who saw me didn't know who I was. The trucker left me off at a restaurant outside of town — that's where I saw the newspaper and learned about Renee. I took a cab here and even the stupid cab driver didn't figure out who I was.'

'I don't think that's the worst part,' Maggie said, remembering all too vividly her sister's egomania. 'I think we'd better call the police,' Maggie added, walking toward the phone.

'Later. When I get my story straight.'

Maggie was thunderstruck. 'What's to get straight? You've got to tell them the truth. Period.'

'And blow all this? All the work? All the built-in publicity?' Mary Theresa asked, shaking her head. 'Are you crazy? Maybe we can say this was all Renee's idea and — '

'Stop it!' Maggie stopped dead in her tracks, and yanked hard enough on Mary Theresa's arm to whirl her around. 'It's over. All over. Don't you get it?'

'Don't you?' Mary Theresa asked, dropping her bag. 'I can't give up my life. My career.'

'You don't have to give it up . . . just change the course.' She met her sister's gaze in the half-light, the only illumination the weak light from the street lamps that pierced the windows. 'You've done it before. Often,' Maggie pointed out, then couldn't keep from blurting out the question that had been nagging at her since she'd first seen her sister again. 'Why did you throw your voice at me — why did you blame Thane for all of this?'

Mary Theresa sucked in her breath. She eyed her sister and shook her head slowly. 'You really want to know?'

Maggie wasn't certain. There were so many emotions, so many years, so many lies and deceptions all tangled up in Mary Theresa's life with Thane, and yet she had to know the truth, hadn't come all this way to close her eyes and bury her head in the sand. 'Yes, M.T. I want the truth. All of it.'

21

'There's activity at Marquise's house,' Hannah said, striding into Henderson's office in the middle of the night as if she did it every day. Which she often did. Her lipstick had faded, her eyes were weary, but she was still pretty, even when she was all business. 'Jane Stanton, Marquise's neighbor, called, said there's a car in the driveway. Jane's certain that she saw a few lights when she was trying to get one of her menagerie in for the night.'

'Let's go.' Henderson had been waiting for the report on the Blazer, but he was on his feet in an instant. 'Where's Walker?'

'According to his tail, he took a side trip to the airport, but didn't catch a flight.'

'So he's still in town?'

'Appears as so.' Hannah fell into step with him. 'You know, we probably should have kept a stakeout at Marquise's house and forgotten keeping Walker in our sights.'

'The verdict's not in on that one.' Together they walked through the station and headed to the parking lot. 'Got a weapon?' he asked Hannah as they climbed into the department's rig.

She patted her shoulder. 'Just like American Express,' she said without a smile. 'I don't leave home without it.'

* * *

'I'm listening,' Maggie said to her sister. 'Either you tell me everything that happened or I call Thane — '

'Thane?' Mary Theresa spun around and shook her head. 'We're not calling him. Not ever.'

'Why not?'

'Because . . . because I don't want to face him.'

'I think you'll have to. You have a son by him.'

Mary Theresa had been reaching for her bag. She froze. 'He told you.'

'Yes.'

'Oh.' She let out a long breath. 'Look, we don't have time for this.'

Maggie knew she was right, but couldn't resist asking, 'Why did you try to blame him? Why, when you contacted me, did you say he did this to you?'

'It's complicated.'

'Try me.'

'Because he wouldn't bail me out, damn it. I needed help and he didn't care.'

'You're talking about the money?'

'Yes! It's all about money! Wake up, Maggie. Maybe you . . . you can run away to some dilapidated ranch in the middle of nowhere but the rest of the world needs decent lives. It costs so much — '

'You implicated Thane in your disappearance because you wanted to get back at him?' Maggie said, seeing red. 'You lied to him about having his son and yet when he wouldn't loan you some more money you threw your voice and insinuated that he had something to do with your disappearing act?'

Maggie was horrified. Who was this complex woman with whom she'd shared so much, so little?

M.T.'s chin inched up a knot. 'It got you here, didn't it? I figured you'd rush down here to save him and put some more pressure on the police — so that we didn't have to drag the scam out any longer than necessary.'

'This is so sick,' Maggie whispered, leaning against a bar stool.

In the glow from the clock on the microwave, Mary Theresa fiddled with the zipper tab of her warm-up jacket. 'I knew you never really got over him.' She bit her lip and looked away for a second. She swallowed hard. 'I guess I owe you an explanation.'

'What do you mean?' But Maggie sensed what was coming, realized that she really didn't want to know the source of her sister's betrayal all those years ago.

'You know why I did it, don't you?'

'Did what?'

'You know.' She lifted a shoulder and licked her lips. 'When I went to Thane the first time — to his apartment.'

'You mean when you slept with him,' Maggie clarified, her heart beating dully, the pain that had been hidden away for so long emerging fresh and bitter. She gripped the counter and waited.

'Yeah, well, it was because of Mitch.' Mary Theresa's face contorted in pain.

'Mitch?'

Mary Theresa glanced away, to stare out the window to the inky night. 'I got pregnant. That night in the hot tub — it wasn't the first. Mitch and I . . . well, he helped me one night when I was out on a date with Carl Janovich — he was an older boy and I . . . I teased him, I guess, and he started getting rough. We were at a party and Mitch showed up in the nick of time. Carl had already started slapping me, calling me a slut and a whore and all sorts of horrible names.' Mary Theresa swallowed hard and her eyes shone with unshed tears. 'Anyway,' she said, her voice cracking a bit, 'Mitch hauled me out of there, started giving me a lecture, and I . . . I broke down. I was crying and upset and he . . . he just held me. I clung to him, he kissed my hair and one thing led to another and . . . ' She closed her eyes. 'Before I knew what was happening, we were making love. And again on prom night. And . . . '

Bile rose in Maggie's throat.

'We both tried to break it off, but couldn't. Then you caught us in the hot tub and that was the end of it.' She wrapped her arms around her middle. 'Except that I was pregnant. That's why Mitch killed himself, Maggie, because I was pregnant with his kid.'

'His?' Maggie repeated, stunned.

'Yes. I, um, needed a father for my baby, so I dressed up like you and went over to Thane's. He was all too easy to fool as he'd been drinking.'

'Oh, God.' Cramps spasmed in Maggie's stomach. 'But why? Why Thane?'

'He was available. And I wanted to get back at you because deep down, I blamed you for Mitch's death. I knew it was wrong, but there it was. I tried to break it off with him and then you caught us in the hot tub and things went from bad to worse. Mitch got paranoid, swore you were gonna tell Mom and Dad. He started talking crazy and then . . . told me he was going to kill himself. I didn't believe him . . . ' Her voice faded away.

'And then he drowned,' Maggie said, not wanting to hear this side of Mary Theresa's story and yet unable not to listen with morbid fascination.

'Yeah.' She sniffed. 'I, um, thought it was because he was scared. Of you, and I wanted to get back at you. Revenge.'

'Oh, Mary Theresa — ' Maggie lifted a hand, cutting off any more of the horror.

'Don't. It was wrong. I was messed up, I know it.' She buried her face in her hands, her fingers digging through her hair. 'But I couldn't stop myself and then I got pregnant again. Oh, shit, what a mess. I never loved Thane. Never. But I was jealous of you.'

'Of *me*? Oh, Mary, why? You were the popular one, you had everything going for you.'

'But Thane loved you. I mean really loved you. I could see it in the way he looked at you, the way he flirted with you, how you two joked. And he never once looked at me. No matter what I did. He was the first boy who wasn't interested.' She lifted her head and met Maggie's disbelieving gaze. 'No one has ever loved me the way Thane loved you. No one.' She swallowed hard. 'No one ever will.'

'Enough. I can't hear any more of this. We've got to get out of here and whether you like it or not, you've got to call the police.'

'No way.'

Maggie had heard enough. In two swift strides she was across the room, her nose pressed to the identical one of her sister's. 'Come on, Mary. It's over.' She wanted to slap some sense into the woman who still wanted to play at being Marquise. 'You have a son! A son!'

'That was a surprise.'

'Thane's boy. And you didn't tell him. I can't believe it!'

'I — I didn't know what to do, but I didn't want to be tied down with a kid, especially after losing Mitch's — and I wanted out of the marriage to Thane. I don't have to tell you that you're never more alone than when you're married to the wrong person.'

Maggie couldn't argue; she'd felt the same way during her years as Dean McCrae's wife. 'Come on. Let's go.' She picked up Mary Theresa's bag; somewhere in the distance she heard the plaintive wail of a siren.

Swiping tears away with the back of her hand, Mary Theresa wrested her bag out of Maggie's fingers. They started walking toward the front door.

'So why didn't you just call me and tell me you were in financial trouble?'

'I couldn't. I was the one with the fantastic career, the men, the money. I couldn't admit that I'd failed, Mag. Not to you. And so when things got really bad a few weeks ago, Eve hatched this scheme for me to disappear and boost the ratings and the like. If things worked out at the station because of viewer interest, I could name my own price, or go somewhere else, maybe revive my movie career and, of course, write a book. I, um, even thought you could help me with that one. But I was angry with Thane, really angry. And I wanted you to come here to be a part of my triumphant return.'

'I was scared to death.' They reached the front door.

'I know, I know, but if I hadn't thrown my voice and communicated with you, you might have thought I was dead. This way you knew better.'

'So why didn't you communicate with me again?' Maggie demanded, angry. 'You still put me through hell.'

'I had to keep up the façade.'

'I didn't know you knew how to throw your voice at will.'

'I don't. I just got lucky. It's . . . it seems to work best when I'm scared, when I'm on some kind of adrenaline rush. Jesus, I don't know. Come on. We've wasted enough time already.'

Maggie agreed. She couldn't get out of Mary Theresa's house fast enough. They hurried outside and climbed into the car. 'You've got to face Thane whether you want to or not,' Maggie said as she slid behind the wheel.

Everything Mary Theresa had told her had turned her blood to ice. Her sister was so calculating, so self-centered, and yet they were twins. Outside, alike; inside as different as night and day.

She twisted on the ignition. Nothing. 'What the devil?'

'What's going on?' Mary Theresa said, her eyes scanning the darkened neighborhood where sprawling mansions stood on large plots, windows glowing warmly in the night.

'Don't know.' She tried again.

The car didn't even sputter or cough.

'This is ridiculous.'

'Come on, come on.'

'I'm trying!'

Again she tried the ignition but the car was dead.

'I don't have time for this. We'll chance taking one of mine,' Mary Theresa insisted, but Maggie sensed a trap. The rental car had been running fine, no hint of problems during the days she'd used it.

'I think we should go to the neighbors' — '

But Mary Theresa wasn't listening. She'd grabbed her bag and was already storming into the house, opening the unlocked door and rushing inside. Maggie, warning bells clanging in her head, took off after her.

'Wait, M.T. — '

She ran inside and this time Mary Theresa

had snapped on the kitchen lights. 'I'll just be a minute,' she explained, when Maggie blinked against the glare. 'No one will notice and even if they do, we'll be gone in a flash.' She opened a cabinet where keys were hung on the inside of the door. 'Here we go . . . oh, shit, the keys are gone.'

'What do you mean, 'gone!' '

'The spare sets, they were all here.' Her forehead puckered and fear crossed her features. 'Oh, God, I'll bet Wade took them!'

'Where're yours — ?' Maggie asked, then remembered Mary Theresa's purse had been in her Jeep.

'Let's go — uh, I'll call a cab.' She reached for the phone, but as she did Maggie heard the scrape of a shoe behind them. Whirling, she spun and found Eve Lawrence, big as life, in the hallway leading to the garage. 'Oh, God — '

'Eve!' Mary Theresa's voice was hushed.

'I figured you'd show up here.' Eve wasn't smiling; in fact, her eyes reflected a sadness and she clucked her tongue as she shook her head. 'Put down the phone, Maggie.' Sighing, she said, 'I was hoping it wouldn't come to this.'

Maggie started to step forward until she spied the small pistol tucked discreetly in Eve's gloved hand. 'You should have stayed where you were supposed to, Marquise.'

'You left me for dead.' Mary Theresa was moving now.

'I was coming back.'

'Sure.'

Eve sighed. 'You had to have more pills,

Marquise. Otherwise the suicide wouldn't look real.'

'It wouldn't anyway — there . . . there was evidence that other people had been there. You couldn't have gotten away with it.'

'No one could connect me.' She frowned thoughtfully. 'It would have worked. Especially if Renee had kept a cooler head.'

'You killed her,' Mary Theresa said.

'I didn't have much of a choice.'

'But why?' Maggie asked. 'You killed a woman for money — '

'For money. Is that what you think?' She wasn't looking at Maggie now, but Mary Theresa.

'What else?' M.T. asked, but there was a flicker of worry in her eye.

'Take a wild guess.'

Mary Theresa swallowed hard.

'Thane wasn't the only man your sister stole from someone, was he, Mary Theresa?' Eve took a step forward.

'Oh, Eve, don't — ' Mary's face was the color of chalk.

'Oh, no, and it wasn't only Robby Inman who fell for you. You remember him, don't you, Maggie, Syd Gillette's son-in-law, I told you about him.' Eve's voice had risen an octave and her eyes were bright, shimmering with tears.

Maggie's heart froze. Suddenly she understood.

Eve nodded. 'My second husband, Scott.' She sighed and leveled her pistol at Mary Theresa. 'Scott adored me. Thought I was God's gift.

Until he met your sister.' She was in the full light of the kitchen now and she seemed older than her years, world-weary, as she aimed the gun at Marquise. She leaned one hip against the counter and glanced at Maggie. 'The worst part of it was, the affair didn't mean anything to you. Scott was just someone to play with, someone to steal. I should have quit then, told you to go take a hike, but I couldn't. You were the only client I had — the celebrity draw. Do you know how long I've hated myself for my weakness, for still being at your beck and call while you stole my husband from me, then tossed him over?'

Maggie felt sick inside. Mary Theresa's eyes were round, her skin white. 'Don't listen to her, Mag,' she insisted.

'Forming that company afterwards, MER, was just to salve your guilty conscience,' Eve said. 'You know, I think I've got an idea how to end all this.'

'What?' Mary Theresa asked nervously.

'A way to clean up the mess that you and Renee made.'

'No — ' *Maggie, we've got to do something. She's gonna kill us both. Grab the knives!* 'Eve, this is foolish. We've got to work something out. Come on — ' As Marquise tried to reason with her, Eve glanced her way. The rack of knives was only a short distance away. Heart drumming, Maggie edged closer to the counter.

But the wheels were turning in Eve's mind. 'It's gonna work out, all right. My way.'

She raised the pistol.

Stop her! Now!

Maggie lunged forward.

Eve twisted the gun, pointing it at her own left arm. Crack! The little gun went off. Eve screamed in agony.

* * *

'You stay here,' Thane commanded Becca as he stood on the brakes in front of Marquise's house.

'No way.' Becca wasn't going to be pushed around.

'Don't argue; it could be dangerous.'

'So?' She didn't seem the least bit intimidated but he understood her reasoning. This was a kid who had lied, stolen, and hitchhiked to get to her mother from California. Thane's paranoia wasn't going to hold her back.

'I don't know what's in the house. Stay put. I'll be back for you.'

'Liar.'

'Do it, Becca,' he ordered as he climbed out of the truck, wishing there was a way to lock her safely inside. Obviously his lecture about being mature, responsible and doing what your elders say had had no effect on her whatsoever.

He started up the walk, turned on his heel and pointed at the truck with one authoritative finger.

A pistol cracked.

A woman screamed in agony.

Maggie!

He burst through the door and ran blindly through the hall. His head pounded with fear.

He'd lost her. Come all this way only to lose her. Dread and rage thundered in his heart. 'Maggie! For the love of Christ! Maggie!' His voice was raw, his heart pumping, hell-raising fury and blind-ass fear driving him on.

'Thane — stay back!' Maggie's terrified voice.

She was alive.

'Get the hell out.' Another voice, one he didn't recognize. He kept running.

He heard footsteps behind him. Sirens screaming outside.

'Mom?' A small voice.

'Becca? Oh, God, no!' Maggie yelled. 'Stay back! For the love of God — Thane, get her out of here! *NOW!*'

'Shut up!' The woman's voice again. Boots thundering, he rounded the corner and saw a woman with blood running down her arm and a gun in her hand. She turned, her face ashen, and leveled the weapon at him.

'No!'

'Mom!' Becca ran into the room and started to push Thane, but he grabbed her.

'Becca, get away!' Maggie screamed, vaulting toward the bloody woman, who rounded, her hand wobbling. As Maggie reached her, the barrel was pointed at Becca and Thane.

'Oh, God, no!' Mary Theresa threw herself between Thane and Eve, just as the gun spat fire.

Bam!

With an agonizing scream, Mary Theresa hit the floor. Thane pushed Becca into a chair.

The shooter took aim again.

Thane sprang through the air.

Crack! The pistol exploded with a burst of fire.

Pain, white hot, burned through his gut. He wrestled the woman to the ground, fighting a blackness pressing against his brain.

'Thane! No! No!' Maggie cried.

The world swam before his eyes but he held onto the woman who was clawing at him, trying to aim her damned gun again. He blinked, hearing footsteps, sharp male voices. Orders.

'Stop! Police!'

He was being pried from the woman, but she managed to turn the gun on herself. *Bang!* Becca screamed. Maggie vaulted to the couch where Becca sat, white-faced and shaking and crying. 'It's okay, baby, it's gonna be okay.' She held her tight, rocked with her child and saw Detective Henderson's face through a haze. Her head was pounding; the air smelled of blood and hot metal.

'Shit, it's a goddamned war zone in here,' Henderson said. 'Call the paramedics!' he ordered a uniformed man.

'They're here.'

What seemed like dozens of uniformed men and women, weapons drawn, burst into the room. Immediately they set about helping the injured, and Maggie was torn between holding her child, her lover, or her sister. Tears ran down her face and she trembled inside. *Please God, let them live. Let them all live*.

'I need oxygen over here.'

'This one is still alive — who the hell is it?'

'Eve Lawrence,' Maggie said woodenly, seeing

Eve's body oozing blood, her eyes behind broken glasses staring up at the fluorescent lights. 'She . . . she was the one behind it all. She even shot herself . . . so that you'd think we did it, I suppose.' Was that possible? Had Eve been so desperate that she would wound herself then try and kill both Marquise and her?

'She saved my life,' Becca said, looking at Marquise, who lay, blood pumping from her chest. The floor was sticky and purple with a spreading stain as a paramedic worked feverishly over her, trying to staunch the blood, applying an oxygen mask. Policemen and women were everywhere. Maggie, holding Becca, inched toward Thane.

'Get the kid out of here,' Henderson barked.

'I've got her,' Henderson's partner said, offering a tentative smile as she embraced Becca. 'I'm Hannah. You must be Becca.'

'Mom — '

'It's all right, honey.'

'Let's go into the other room.' Hannah helped Becca out of the crime scene and toward the front of the house.

'I'll be right there,' Maggie promised.

Maggie! I love you. You know that, don't you?

They were placing Mary Theresa on a stretcher. 'Christ, it's that television woman!'

'I need to talk to her,' Maggie demanded.

'She can't hear ya. Get her into an ambulance!'

Goodbye, Maggie . . .

'No!'

I'm so tired . . . I . . .

'We're losin' her,' one of the paramedics said.

'NO! NO!' Maggie wailed, throwing herself at the stretcher, feeling strong arms pull her back. 'You're going to be fine. Mary Theresa, can you hear me? Hang in there!' She was sobbing, choking with the knowledge that Mary Theresa was dying. Pain tore through her and she felt a rending in her soul, as if part of her had been ripped away. 'Oh, God, no!'

'Shit, she's going.' Running, two men carried Mary Theresa on the stretcher out of the room and to the waiting ambulance, but Maggie knew in her heart that she'd lost her sister forever.

'Get her out of here,' Henderson said. 'Have her checked at the hospital for injuries and shock.' They were talking about her!

'I'm not going anywhere!'

'Lady, please — '

'Just wait. Thane?' She dropped to her knees where Thane was being worked on by a paramedic.

'He's lost consciousness.'

'Get him to the ambulance.'

Fear, as cold as death, scraped over her heart with steely nails. 'I have to be with him.'

'He won't know it.'

'Don't care. Let me ride with him. Thane, can you hear me, love? Thane . . . I love you . . . ' She thought she saw a twitch of his lips, but she couldn't be sure . . . he was pale and bleeding and . . .

She felt someone place a blanket over her shoulders and started praying like she'd never prayed before in her life.

She couldn't lose Thane now. Not ever again. But it was out of her hands.

* * *

Somewhere deep in the void he heard her voice. 'Thane, can you hear me? Love?'

Love? Was that Maggie's voice? Pain screamed through his body and as he opened one eye, light, white and blinding, flooded his senses.

'Thane? He's trying to open his eyes! Oh, God, Thane, we thought, I mean . . . ' She was crying, her voice cracking. 'Mary Theresa is dead . . . but you . . . oh, please.'

He forced his eye open again and her face, a blurry image, came into his line of vision. She was smiling and crying, her tears raining down on him. 'You scared me to death,' she said, sniffing and laughing and sobbing. 'I thought I'd lost you. Again. I couldn't bear it.'

He felt her hand, warm as opposed to the cold steel of the hospital bed rail. He tried to speak and his voice failed him. 'Maggie — ' he croaked out.

'Yes, love.'

'Would . . . would you . . . '

'Would I what?'

'Stop . . . crying . . . '

'I can't.'

'Long . . . long enough to tell . . . tell me you'll . . . marry me.'

'What?' She gasped, then started crying harder. 'Marry you? Are you nuts? I'm not leaving this hospital until I do.' She let out a half-laugh and a sniff. 'The way I figure it, you can't very well run away from me.'

'Wouldn't do it. Love you,' he said, and as he drifted off again, he heard her swearing her undying love for him as well.

'I love you too, cowboy, so don't you do anything as stupid as dying on me, y'hear. I love you!'

Epilogue

Christmas Eve
Settler's Ridge, Idaho

' . . . let it snow, let it snow, let it snow . . . '

The radio played softly while Maggie tucked a special present under the tree. She smiled as she saw the reflection of Christmas lights on her wedding band. Who would have thought? She'd never expected to marry again, never thought she and Thane would become a family, but she'd been wrong.

She walked to the window and spied Becca and Thane trudging through the snow. They'd fed the horses and were returning, with Barkley yapping and bounding behind them.

Mary Theresa was dead; Eve had made sure of that. Now Eve Lawrence was behind bars, awaiting trial for not only Marquise's death, but Renee Warner Nielsen's as well. Maggie's publisher was screaming for her to write the book of Marquise's life and death, but Maggie couldn't bring herself to do it. It was sad, she thought, how her sister had found in death the fame that had eluded her in life. Now her picture was flung across the tabloids; speculation as to her private life ran high. The American public and press couldn't get enough of her.

As for her, Maggie was happy to be back in

Idaho, away from Dean's family. Jim and Connie had given up their quest to become Becca's guardians and Becca was finally settling into school here. She even had her first boyfriend, a cute quiet boy named Austin Peters.

The door opened and Barkley flew into the room, only to shake the snow from his coat and dampen the presents that were piled beneath the boughs of the little pine tree.

'We could be celebrating in Cheyenne,' Thane had teased.

'Or Rio Verde,' Maggie had reminded him.

But they decided to live here while Thane, still recovering from the shot that had cracked two ribs and destroyed his spleen, healed. In the spring, they would decide whether or not they would move.

A lot depended on his son, Ryan, whom he'd met once. The boy's adoptive parents, Vera and Bill Brown, realizing that Thane had no intention of stealing him away from them, had allowed their son to meet his biological father. There were plans for the summer. Fishing trips and backpacking.

Yes, life had settled down. Even Becca and Thane were getting used to each other, though they still clashed. 'Both bullheaded,' Maggie had informed them on many an occasion.

Becca headed off to her room to call Austin, and Thane, seeing they were alone, dragged Maggie into his willing arms. 'What say we do it tonight under the tree?' he suggested in her ear.

'You — the cripple? On the floor?' she teased, looking into the eyes of the man she loved and feeling just a moment's sadness, for she missed Mary Theresa, would never feel that special bond between herself and her sister again.

'Try me?'

'Should I?'

'Definitely.' He kissed her long and hard, stealing her breath, heating her blood, and she wondered if she'd ever grow tired of this man — or even just satisfied and content.

Not a chance. He was and always would be too exciting. From the bedroom she heard Becca's happy laughter. Obviously she'd connected with her new boyfriend. 'I have something for you, Mr. Walker,' she said, reaching under the tree and retrieving the tiny box. 'Open it.'

'Now?'

'Umm.'

With a lift of one eyebrow, he watched her as he untied the ribbon and removed the lid. Inside were a small pair of red and green bootees. He didn't move. Didn't say a word.

'We'll need those next year.'

His smile was wide. He glanced down at his own bare feet. 'Don't think they'll fit.'

'No?' she teased. 'Well, you don't know until you try, cowboy.'

He placed a hand over her flat abdomen. 'You tryin' to tell me something, darlin'?'

'Only good things.' His arms wrapped around her waist, and he kissed her again. 'Merry Christmas.'

'To you, too,' he said with a positively wicked grin. 'Now . . . about you and me under the tree . . . you're not gettin' out of that one.'

'In your dreams, cowboy.'

'Most definitely.' He winked down at her. 'And in yours as well.'

A GIFT FROM SEBASTIAN

A GIFT FROM SEBASTIAN

BOXTREE

To all the other babies

A donation from each copy sold will go to the Sebastian Diamond Sleep Laboratory at St Michael's Hospital, Bristol. This unit, which continues to research into the causes of cot death, was funded by the Diamond Cot Death Appeal.

Published in Great Britain in 1995 by Boxtree Limited,
Broadwall House, 21 Broadwall, London SE1 9PL

1 3 5 7 9 10 8 6 4 2

ISBN 0 7522 0515 3

Cover designed by Robert Updegraff
Typeset by SX Composing, Rayleigh, Essex
Printed and bound in Great Britain by Butler & Tanner, Frome, Somerset

A CIP catalogue entry for this book is available from the British Library

Introduction

Dr Stanley Rom picked our little baby up in his hands, and looked him straight in the eyes. Our little boy, who at just two weeks old had already fought so hard to live. Now he was well enough to come home to meet his brothers – and truly become a part of the family. His eyes shone with the milky innocence of brand new babyhood as he nestled in those hands, those huge physician's hands which had delicately and intricately performed the tasks necessary to save his life, and which now cradled him completely within their span.

Mike and I looked on in awe and relief that the tense weeks of special care had ended, and he was now ours again, to love and nurture without tubes, drips and monitors. I longed to take off his hospital robe and dress him in our baby sleepsuit, and wrap him in the same shawl which had warmed our other sons.

'Your baby is quite well,' said Dr Rom, with an affectionate smile. Then he turned back to Sebastian and lifted him closer to his face. 'Now, young man, you go out and make your mark in the world!'

Tears welled up in my eyes. I was already so proud of my little boy. How could I possibly have known then what would happen to Sebastian, and quite how he would make his mark?

Like all babies, he seemed to radiate love and light. He was a beautiful child. But then I would think that – I am his mum. He was wise, diplomatic, clever and loving. And above all, Sebastian knew something the rest of us didn't know. I cannot describe it better than that, because I do not understand it.

A friend of a friend of mine lost his ten-year-old daughter in a road accident. He said she had always been a different sort of child from others. He had always thought, long before she died, that she had 'a mature spirit'. She had been a loving, laughing, spontaneous little girl like all others, but there was always something else – an unfathomable maturity. I understand now what he meant – because Sebastian had that, too. My family know that I'm not just clouding my memory with sentimentality. We all felt it. A maturity of spirit.

It was a chance remark – but I caught my mother-in-law saying it to Mike in the kitchen one day. She'd just finished giving Sebastian his bottle, and had been staring deep into his eyes and cooing at him, enjoying the special closeness you get when you're feeding a much loved baby. She wouldn't have said it if she'd known I was near. But I'd been upstairs fetching something, and was returning down the steps to the basement area. She was talking about Sebastian.

'I don't know why I feel it, but he's only on loan to us, this one,' she said. And Mike agreed.

Silently, so did I. Or rather, I knew what they meant – though I wouldn't have dared articulate it. Our children are only ever 'on loan' to us. We are there to love, teach and guard them for as long as we can – but one day, we know they will fly. Sebastian somehow knew it, too.

A wonderful letter arrived at my door one day, from a lady in Eastbourne, a Mrs Rylands, who tried to explain that Sebastian would indeed have known his destiny. 'We all have to work out our own "karma", and put right whatever we may have missed in a previous life,' she wrote.

She said Sebastian would have sat down with God, and worked out his final task on earth, before reaching Heaven. 'Sebastian already knew he would only be with you for a short while. God chose him especially for a purpose – but because he was an experienced and fulfilled soul, it was not necessary for him to spend very long here.'

'If I had lost a baby in the same way it wouldn't have got the same publicity,' she said in her letter. But, she said, Sebastian chose his parents, the time and the place wisely, in order to get something done. Of course you'll grieve, she said. But also remember that through you, Sebastian has achieved his karma.

I like that.

Of course, you probably know now what did happen to him. Four months after we celebrated his homecoming from maternity hospital, and on the morning of his brother's birthday, I found Sebastian dead in his cot. The pain of losing him is still like a constant living laceration in my body. And my heart will never accept it.

I have my wonderful photographs, though, and they help me through the worst days. But so many of my shots of Sebastian are of him lying down, on his tummy, fast asleep. The only moments when I had enough time, and hands free, to pick up a camera were, ironically, when he was sleeping. On his tummy, always on his tummy. It stabs at me now, like a fresh wound every time, the sight of him sleeping so cosily on his tummy, arms up, his perfect little fingers almost caressing his nose, his eyes tight shut but edged with long black lashes.

If only I had known, my dear little Supi. I would have turned you over. If only I had known.

Chapter 1: July 1990

It was a picture-postcard start to a perfect holiday – the sun was hot, the sea blue, the hotel was perfect and there was a cosy little spot by the baby pool which we adopted as our own. Like cats coming in from the cold, we slowly unfurled in the heat, watching the children run, jump and splash in a frenzy of new-found freedom. Mike ordered Brandy Sours, the traditional cocktail of the island. I leaned back and closed my eyes, knowing I could trust our nanny, Alex, to keep hers on the blur of fluorescent armbands and floppy sunhats which was our kids. This was real relaxation. Heaven. This was Cyprus as we knew it.

At lunchtime the parasols went up, and an olive-skinned waiter in cool, crisp cotton brought the customary poolside snack of Greek meze and Village Salad – with the ever-present Coke. Mike and I escaped upstairs to the silence and seclusion of our suite, looked down on the pool scene below, and thought how lucky we were, and how happy. Here, in cool, air-conditioned luxury, stark contrast to the human barbecue below, you could feel your skin tingle with goose-bumps.

Mike drew the curtains, and in the gentle shade, we made love. We made Sebastian.

I know the exact day only because we had joked about it at the time. The night before, Cyprus Airways had lost one of our bags. It had gone to Athens, or stayed in London, or done the round trip – we never found out quite where it had gone, why it had been separated from the others, nor why it took two days to trace and recover.

It was one of those flights which sounds sensible when you

book it, but lands you at the inhuman hour of one in the morning on a foreign piece of tarmac, arguing with Jobsworth airport officials who don't speak your language. All suitcases had been unceremoniously dumped on the runway, because the baggage handler had gone home to sleep. So there was a mad scramble while the stalwart passengers found their own luggage, and dragged each piece to the customs hut. Mike's was the one case missing. Another passenger said he thought a young boy had taken it. By the time we found that a young schoolboy had already passed through customs and been collected by his Army parents and taken off home to the British military base, an hour had gone by.

Cypriot tempers were rising. The Jobsworth officials couldn't understand why Mike was so unimpressed, and was using words their dictionaries did not explain. When I saw the clock reach 3 am I had had enough. Alex was almost asleep, holding our toddler, Jamie – who appeared comatose and was dribbling down her blouse. Oliver, just three years old, was sitting astride his suitcase, moaning in dismay. The novelty of staying up late had long expired. Mike and a man in a peaked cap were embroiled in a heated exchange about whether or not you could be forcibly deported from a country if you hadn't actually got as far as immigration.

There's only one thing for it, I thought, slightly ashamed of my decision. I would have to play the little woman. I would have to cry. I started to sob loudly, clutching Oliver for dramatic support. He immediately augmented my image of despair.

It worked. They all apologized, and I was offered several grubby handkerchiefs. Mike withdrew his flowery insult, made several hours earlier to a stewardess who'd long since gone to her bed, and the whole ugly matter was forgotten. We managed to find our extremely patient, and by now very rich, taxi driver outside the airport arrivals gate, and we were off. On our hols at last. Thankfully intact, except for one bag.

But it had been Mike's suitcase – with the all-important toiletries. And I wasn't on the pill. So we should have known the risks of making love that day. 'It'll be Cyprus Airways' fault!' we quipped, never thinking for a second that another baby could possibly be on his way. Not just like that.

It was the happiest holiday I have ever had – and I delight now in thinking that the little cluster of cells which became Sebastian's life was busily dividing and subdividing inside me while I was so content. And, of course, blissfully unaware that I was pregnant. Because the reality hit me weeks later like a sledgehammer. The time simply wasn't right to be enlarging the family again. Too much was going on. Life had suddenly become very complicated and job security was at an all-time low. Things were going wrong at work – in fact they had been going awry almost since I had transferred from the daily routine of presenting *Good Morning Britain* to the Sunday current affairs slot.

It hadn't been my idea – it was the opportunist brainwave of TV-am's managing director, Bruce Gyngell. He had rung me in Australia, where I was spending maternity leave following the birth of son number two, Jamie, to suggest I think of retiring from the high-profile daily show to Sundays. Until then, David Frost had occupied the slot, filling it with politicians and other headline makers. He never failed to get an interview with a prime minister or two when he wanted but, somehow, I felt – along with other production staff at TV-am – that the programme lacked friendliness and warmth. So, I was excited when Bruce told me that David was leaving TV-am to host a new current affairs show in America. I was thrilled – for David, and for myself.

Bruce seemed almost angry that Frost had left him, but was pleased he had found a solution which would mean hanging on to me. He had been conscious that I might want to leave, now that I had two young children. 'Now I'm left with a load of Sunday shows and no-one to present them. I think it's a great time for you to move in.... What do you think ? You can't go on getting up at three every morning with two young children.'

He was dead right. This was the perfect answer to my problem – the ideal job for a working media mum. I said yes almost before Bruce had asked the question.

'Right,' he bellowed, deal done. 'We'll fax a contract out to you – and my advice is to sign fast in case David's show flops and he comes back for his old job.'

We laughed – but I didn't realize then that his words were based on a real fear and that just a few weeks later, and before I was due to receive that fax, David Frost would be returning.

For some strange reason, that fax never reached me. Whenever I rang TV-am to ask why, the only answer I ever got was 'lawyers'. Bruce couldn't figure it out either. Things weren't progressing as he had wanted. And all the time stories were abounding in the press about Frosty's 'flop' programme in New York. Already, the rumour machine at work was speculating that he would soon return and want his Sunday shows back. Eventually, Bruce came out to Australia himself, on holiday. I was summoned to meet with him at Kerry Packer's sunshine home on Palm Beach, north of Sydney.

The Packers' tame kookaburra was being fed scraps of meat, perched on the wooden balcony, as I walked into the family living-room and was greeted with a hearty slap on the back from Kerry and a tearful hug from Bruce. Emotion always played openly on Bruce's face – and he was genuinely happy to see me. I think he'd always had a soft spot for me and always will.

They ushered me over to a quiet spot on the gigantic verandah, which had breathtaking views of the bay, the sand and the surf, now and then eclipsed by swaying eucalyptus trees. Bruce took a pen out of his shirt pocket – as ever in pale pink and embroidered B.G. – and scribbled a list of dates on a sheet of white paper.

'We still don't know about Frost,' he said in a quick,

businesslike manner, 'but for the moment we want you to present Sundays from the week you get back, through to the summer. Then we'll leave thirteen weeks free during the summer for...er...other projects – I might want to try out some new talent – and then you'll come back on in the autumn through to Christmas. As for 1990 – we'll have to see about dates later. Because David might well be back by then. But you can take it from me that you'll have at least half the year – we may just have to sort out dates between you and David.'

It sounded great news to me. So what about a formal contract ? I had learned long ago that nothing counts in TV unless it's written, preferably in blood.

'We'll have that ready for you to sign as soon as you get back. I promise,' said Bruce. And he and Kerry sealed it with a drink, a long cocktail on ice, dreamed up by the bronzed, half naked male housekeeper who was flitting about in the open-plan kitchen. This is the life, I thought. But I had to decline the offer of lunch because husband, children, in-laws and my mother and sister, who had all joined us on our three-month Australian holiday, were waiting on the beach below.

Mike and Bruce had been sworn enemies since the days of Mike's sacking from TV-am, so I thought I ought to make a hasty exit lest the two men should meet. I needn't have worried. Bruce spotted Mike strolling along the sand and walked up to him, arms outstretched. There was sincere delight on the part of both men to talk again. But they carefully avoided professional banter. Instead, the talk was of Australia and how we didn't really want to go home.

Bruce later became the boss of Channel Nine in Sydney, and more recently the Chief Executive of Yorkshire Tyne Tees Television back in Britain. How I'd love to work for him again. There never was a more colourful boss, nor a less predictable. His moods could change faster than the wind. But if he loved you, deep down, he would never forget.

The show was called *Diamond on Sunday*, the title sequence

featuring scenes from topical events all whizzing round within a revolving diamond shape. And it was once surveyed, by the industry's *Broadcast* magazine, to have a higher proportion of ABC 1 female viewers than any other programme on TV. In truth, that simply meant that, although the audience never reached more than two and a half million – not much bigger than Frost's – the viewers were mostly thinking women. And I was rightly proud of that at the time.

Presenting the programme was a happy time. It gave me the chance to interview the people who really interested me, at their most fascinating times. Everyone from David Owen, as he announced that he was leaving the SDP, to Nigel Kennedy, whose *Vivaldi's Four Seasons* album had hit Number One in the charts. And one programme was a live outside broadcast from the Berlin Wall, on the weekend it fell.

At home, life was splendid. My only other regular TV commitment was a Thursday afternoon programme on ITV called *TV Weekly*. Every Thursday I would leave our house in North London at six in the morning and travel to TVS in Southampton, returning about eight in the evening. It meant that I didn't see the children for a whole day, but compared to the lot of most working mums, it was perfect.

And then, during the summer, it became clear that my dream routine was about to be wrecked by a formidable force known as David Frost.

Frosty wanted his shows back – if not exactly all of them, he wanted the best dates. Which would inevitably leave me with the summer weekends – the so-called 'silly season', when there was always a dearth of journalistic stories and when the celebrities were away. So there was, for a topical programme, nothing very much to talk about, and no-one to talk to.

It was put to me in a variety of phrases, by a very awkward and embarrassed Bruce Gyngell, that I would have to do what I was told, because David Frost was a founder member of TV-am, and a Very Big Cheese indeed. I was also told that the company's board had discussed the matter, and that the directors had concluded that Frost would be better for them on the high-profile Sunday programme than I, because he could attract a greater amount of serious politicians. And that all the power of politics was needed to ensure that TV-am regain its franchise, coming up for renewal in the following year.

I was dumbfounded. The man who had been almost dismissive of Frost and his image just a few months before (and, significantly, half a world away from London) was now speaking a different, and almost deferential language. I pointed to the dates, phrases, promises in my contract. They would honour it as far as they could, Bruce promised. No-one was putting me on the streets – I would still get about fourteen or fifteen programmes to present, at some stage during the year. I had seen that stubborn look on Bruce's face when he was dealing with others, but never with me. It was almost like method acting – you just knew that it was not natural to him and he had perfected that steely stare in front of a mirror. It was method business behaviour – all the more cruel because he was working at it. And then he said something I'll never forget, because it completely betrayed the very real joy he had shown when I had become a mother.

'Those babies of yours cost us money,' he barbed. I muttered something in return about the fact that I'd been entitled under my contract to full maternity rights, and that I'd taken hardly any leave at all. But it was pointless. He'd hit me where it hurt.

And so it was over the next few weeks, while my *Diamond on Sunday* programme was being aired, live, every weekend, that Bruce became a stranger to me. Where once he would dart out of his glass office if he saw me walk past, to engage me in conversation, he would stay behind his desk, raising his papers to avoid eye contact. He had used to pop into my office for a chat, to ask how the children were, or to tell me about his. But now my office was quiet. It was the lull before the storm – because, pretty soon, he started to communicate by memo, or – worse still– by allowing his junior ministers to send me memos.

We had always prided ourselves, since the very beginning of the TV-am era, that we had almost invented a new kind of TV current affairs – based on an interview technique which defied the coldness and confrontational style of TV journalists like Brian Walden or Jeremy Paxman. We called it sofa television – and in its way it was every bit as dangerous as *Weekend World* or *Newsnight*, because many interviewees could be easily caught off-guard, relaxing into the cushions, the coffee and apparently easy chat, only to be floored by a simple but incisive question. Nick Owen and I had worked hard at perfecting the technique, over years of early morning interviews with mining boss Arthur Scargill, party leaders David Steel and David Owen, Labour supremos Michael Foot and Neil Kinnock, any number of Margaret Thatcher's cohorts, one momentous exclusive with Princess Michael of Kent about her alleged SS father and a memorable knockabout with Denis Healey.

The great and the good had gained a firm respect for breakfast TV, in much the same way that they had become convinced, in the previous decade, of the importance of the *Jimmy Young Show* on Radio 2. Breakfast TV was how you got to the voters – but it wasn't the 'easy ride' it somehow pretended to be. One slip-up, and you were headline news.

So I was shocked to receive, as my star within the political firmament of TV-am started to flicker, a memo from the Head of News, telling me that there would be serious repercussions if I was ever seen again on air, holding a TV-am coffee cup in the middle of an interview. Even if that exchange was merely with another TV-am journalist. (I had, in fact, been holding a cup while talking to our correspondent, Martin Frizell, who was doing a live broadcast from outside Strangeways Prison, where the inmates had been rioting the night before.)

It wasn't the cup which was important, of course. What was

significant was that the Head of News, Bill Ludford – a man who had been brought in to TV-am by my husband Mike because we had both thought so much of him – felt he could now write me stupid, petty memos. That in itself meant that my days at TV-am, the company I loved so much and for which I had worked long, dedicated and hellishly antisocial hours, were numbered. You can tell these things when your mini-fridge disappears overnight from your office – and mysteriously re-materializes behind the desk of some junior executive who was still at school when you made your first appearance on breakfast TV.

I went to my agent, who went to a lawyer, who went to a barrister. I decided that I wouldn't give in to TV-am's drastic alteration of my working schedule without a fight. And, contractually, right was very much on my side – though it was interesting to note that, by the time I had received the contract in Australia, many of the phrases which would have further protected my position had been uncannily left out.

You'll remember, though, that on that sunny morning on Kerry Packer's verandah overlooking Palm Beach, Bruce had had the sense to write down his promises. I still had that piece of paper. Maybe, although he couldn't admit it, he had been looking after me all along, as best he could. I like to think so. But there was no avoiding confrontation – and in the end, my agent, Jon Roseman, and I agreed to a showdown meeting, with Bill Ludford and TV-am's lawyer, Paul Vickers.

Not since the earliest days of that television station, when the likes of Anna Ford and Angela Rippon were fired, had there been such a high-profile, emotive showdown. But Bruce chose to delegate the unpleasantness to Bill. Show-business was not Bill's strong point – he was generally a man of few words, a red-wine-and-curry man, an ex-Fleet Street hack with a flair for news instinct rather than man-management. Woman-management was possibly his greatest weakness. The company had lost several talented girl presenters, notably after confrontations with Bill. I always thought that, like a great many male executives in the world of TV, Bill seemed happier with female employees when they were in a junior position, and eager to please. Once they were rewarded with any degree of authority or position of power, he appeared less comfortable, and it was only a matter of time before they left, amid whispers that they had become too difficult, too demanding, too big-headed.

Strong women in TV are generally unloved. You'll find that many of the big female names have, on the face of it, bad or difficult reputations. But scratch the surface, and you'll inevitably discover that those bitching about them are the insecure, anonymous men whose simple lack of talent ensures that they remain unknown.

And so it was that, while still turning up for work every weekend, and enjoying great camaraderie with my small and loyal team, I issued a writ against TV-am for breach of contract.

It was an extraordinary situation. On Friday and Saturday afternoons, I would walk through the rotating glass door (with the little buttons on it which you were meant to press to promote inner peace and communal spirit – a Bruce Gyngellism), up the central staircase, and endeavour to find my office. It kept being moved, further and further away from Bruce's. Other employees didn't know whether they should even acknowledge me. The secretaries, parked obediently outside each executive suite, shot me sympathetic half-smiles. But mostly, people buried themselves in their work. I hadn't had much time to get to know the weekend workers. It was the army of journalists, producers, directors and researchers who worked on the main weekday programme that I knew best. They phoned in their support to my home phone. There were even two private calls from directors of the TV-am board, incredulous at what had been allowed to happen.

Indeed, my writ had made headline news – but it was,

ironically, a favourite adage of David Frost's which I decided to stick to during those uncomfortable days, when newspaper reporters tried every trick in their repertoire to get me to talk: 'Never complain, never explain.' And, by and large, though it was terribly tempting to put my point of view publicly, I managed to say very little about why I was suing TV-am.

Many of the papers made up their own reasons, and there were several stories about 'the worm turning' on the TV company which had made her a star. Some of the nastier writers made the ridiculously simplistic deduction that I wanted to be on TV all the time. One cartoon showed my face as the ever-present TV-am clock-face, in the corner of David Frost's show. 'There,' a viewer remarks, 'that should keep her happy!'

No-one thought, at least in print, that it was merely a case of a company going back on its word. Or of the younger, female, TV presenter losing out to the muscle of the older male. And throughout the whole nasty business, David Frost himself made no comment, no appearance nor involvement. So to this day, I could conclude that he, personally, knew nothing of it. I could... On the other hand, I remember that in 1983, when the station nearly folded just weeks after its launch, Frost took himself off to America while his fellow founder members of TV-am, Anna and Angela, were fired. He then calmly sent Anna Ford a plant – which she threw on to the compost heap where, typically, it thrived as if to mock her!

The horrible letters continued between their lawyers and mine. And it was clear that I would never return to work at TV-am. It was, therefore, a question of how much money they owed me, from a contract which they had failed to honour. It was now up to the lawyers. I was sure I had right on my side, but that doesn't stop you sweating when your solicitor rings up every so often with their latest unkind retort – and his latest estimate of how the legal fees are totting up.

The only good news on the horizon was that ITV had decided to commission a show which I had piloted for TVS, under the command of an old friend, Chris Riley. Chris was a wiry, hyperactive talent – he'd been a teacher, appeared with his mum on *The Generation Game* and got the TV bug. Just a few years later, he'd become one of the brightest TV producers in the industry. I met him at TV-am, where he was an Editor of the Day. His programmes were always fast and furious – bordering on mayhem – but well constructed and fun to present. And he had an instinct – one I've found to be surprisingly rare – for knowing how to handle TV performers, and give them the help and support they need.

Chris was now working for TVS in Southampton, having got fed up with the exhausting overnight shifts, and exasperated with Bruce, a boss with whom he couldn't reason. He'd formatted a TV show about television, a mixture of entertainment gossip, production news and behind-the scenes location filming. He'd contacted me while I was in Australia to ask if I would present the pilot.

I was only too happy to be involved – and thrilled when it was successful. Presenting *TV Weekly* would involve me in one long day's work a week. Combined with my TV-am weekend work, it was a perfect schedule for a new mother, who still wanted plenty of time to be with her children. Oliver, the elder of our two sons, was just three and starting nursery school. Jamie was hardly a toddler. They were every bit as challenging, rewarding and draining as I had expected children would be. But back in my carefree, single, childless days, I had never dreamed that I would want to be with them so much that I almost resented having to go to work.

I'd found what many mums dream of – a highly paid, challenging job, with hours that suited me and the kids. But as the legal wrangling dragged on through the late summer weeks, I started to get cold feet about the money this lawsuit was costing. And I was almost too busy, too preoccupied, too tense about things to notice that my period was late. Very late indeed. But once I thought about it, I just knew: 'Cyprus!'

I rushed to the calendar, tore it down and flicked back to July, where the word 'AWAY' was written large in black felt-tip. I did my sums. Yes, it was entirely possible that I was six weeks pregnant. How would I tell Mike? Another baby was the last thing we wanted right now. In fact another baby was the last thing we wanted full stop. Oliver and Jamie were quite enough, thank you. We'd never have planned a third.

Why is it that we women so often feel guilty when it comes to breaking the news about a surprise baby? Why do we feel as if we should apologize for the bombshell? After all, it takes two to make a child.... Armed with that thought, I slipped the newsflash in between courses at dinner that evening. Mike nearly choked. 'But how?' he spluttered.

'Cyprus...' I said. 'Don't you remember...'

'The lost baggage...' he recalled. 'But that was just once. No-one gets pregnant that easily....'

So that was it – no champagne, no fireworks. No ringing around our families to tell them they were going to be grand-parents again. We were having a baby – but neither of us was happy about it. We were both surprisingly silent. Mike smiled ironically, turned to me and said, 'What are we going to do about it?'

I shrugged my shoulders. 'I dunno....'

It was almost too big a subject to go into that night. We'd both had enough of a shock just taking in the facts. We were two people who'd always been very much in control of their lives. Until now.

'I suppose I ought to confirm it first....'

So I rang my girlfriend, Shirley. When you're well known – and particularly when you're tabloid newspaper fodder – you just cannot pop into Boots and buy yourself a pregnancy testing kit. It would be asking for trouble. And if your husband is pretty well known, too, you can't get him to buy one, either. Next morning I left the children with our nanny, Alex, and dashed round to my friend's flat. Shirley and I had been best friends since we were little. We'd shared everything together. Now we sat like secretive schoolgirls on the floor of Shirley's bathroom, staring at the test tube and waiting for the indicator paper to change colour.

Blue. There was no doubt about it now. Oh, my God, I was pregnant again. Shirley threw her arms around me – but I was weeping with panic, not delight. 'Oh, what am I going to do?' I wailed.

Shirley was shocked. She couldn't have children – and here was I, newly married with two adorable sons and moaning about adding to that joy. But you only know if you've been there yourself, how after two births in fairly quick succession you have to fight hard to recover. I was only just beginning, physically, to feel normal again after Jamie's birth. I had ballooned in size, followed and failed one diet after another to regain my figure, but at last, after hiring a highly expensive personal trainer, I had slimmed down to my normal nine stone. Jamie was only just getting the hang of sleeping through the night. From birth he'd been colicky and even at night he would wake every twenty minutes – reducing Mike and me to zombies.

I was scared about cot death – a colleague at TV-am had lost her baby daughter that way – so I had insisted on attaching Jamie to an apnoea monitor. It was a square-shaped sensor pad which you put underneath the child's mattress – and the alarm goes off if the baby stops breathing. I'd heard about these monitors from our GP, Peter Wheeler. He'd recently attended a family who'd had a cot death. He was profoundly shaken by the experience, and had told me all about the horror of what had happened that morning, when the family nanny had found the child dead. To make things worse, the parents were abroad, and had to be contacted by relatives who were all frantic with shock and grief.

I asked Peter what caused cot death. I didn't know very much about it, though I'd done at least two interviews about it on TV-am. One with the *Dr Who* actor, Colin Baker, whose daughter had been a cot death victim.

'They just don't know,' he said, sadly. 'The babies just seem to forget to breathe....'

The baby who had died had been one of twins – and they had had to put the other twin on constant surveillance, and a monitor. So, when I was expecting Jamie, I went back to Peter, and demanded that he tell me how to buy a monitor.

'But what would you do if the alarm went off?' he'd asked.

'I don't know – pick the baby up and shake him, I suppose,' I offered. The truth was, I hadn't even countenanced that it *would* go off. If cot death was caused by a baby forgetting to breathe, then I would simply remind it. At least that was better than finding your baby dead hours later.

So I got my monitor – and I used it, without being specially trained. No-one told me that some models were prone to go off all the time – and this one seemed to wait until Jamie was peacefully asleep and you had gone down three flights of stairs. Then, as your foot touched the last step, or you'd just made yourself a cup of tea, you would hear the shrill screech of the alarm – your heart would miss a beat, and you would race back up all those stairs again, dreading that your precious child was dying. When you got to his room, Jamie would be shaking with fright at the noise, and it would take another half hour to get him off. It drove us all nuts – and Lord knows what it did to the baby. Was every alarm a false one? Or did he stop breathing, only to be jerked back to consciousness by that devastating screech? I shall never know.

So when, months later, he was still waking ten or twelve times a night, I started to worry that he might be ill. Luckily, I had a friend who was a paediatrician at University College Hospital. I begged my first favour – and he invited Mike and me down to his unit in London's West End. 'Come on Thursday afternoon,' he said. 'It's usually pretty quiet then – that's when I do my bereavement clinic....'

As we were ushered down the corridor by a nurse, I remember noting that it was so very quiet it was almost sinister – even though there were treatment rooms and a large waiting area stacked with toys. And then, sadly, I remembered what he'd said about it being the time for his bereavement clinic. How sad, I thought, that as a paediatrician he doesn't only save little lives. He has to deal with death like any other doctor....

Did our baby have a problem? He gave Jamie a thorough check-up. 'No,' he concluded. 'But you two have. You both look tired. Tell me exactly what you do with Jamie at night. Because I'll bet a pound to a penny it's nothing to do with his health – it's more likely behavioural.'

He smiled sagely when I mentioned the apnoea alarm. 'But what would you do anyway if you found he wasn't breathing?'

'Shake him?' I tried.

'Look,' he said, sitting back. 'If you take my advice, you'll take the monitor off him and put it away in a cupboard.'

So we did. I'd become convinced myself that the wretched machine was wrecking our lives – I just hadn't found the courage to stop using it, afraid that Jamie might die without it. And it worked. I put the monitor away – and within days, Jamie was sleeping for longer periods. Soon, he was sleeping right through. We never looked back.

Like I said, everything at home was getting better. Oliver was starting nursery school – and we had found a brilliant new nanny, in whom I was gaining more and more trust. She was called Alex, and the kids adored her. That meant I could go to work without feeling guilty. We could go out in the evenings again, without worrying. Mike and I were just starting to feel like a couple again, rather than a pair of over-exhausted babysitters. That was why another baby seemed like bad news. We agreed to decide the fate of this next pregnancy over dinner at one of our favourite restaurants, Mosimann's.

It seems odd now, looking back, that we should go somewhere so plush, so luxurious, so romantic, to discuss such a thing. And, indeed, romance was very much on our minds. Though neither of us treated the subject of abortion lightly, we weren't so much discussing a baby's life as the survival of our marriage and our family. We both knew our partnership had been through a great deal of stress. We both understood the danger of yet more.

By the end of the evening I knew what I wanted to do. And Mike agreed. We took what we thought was the most sensible decision for the four of us. We would go for an abortion.

I am so very, very glad that I just couldn't go through with it.

Chapter 2

We had a smashing playroom in our London house. It was down in the basement, next to the kitchen. It had a frightful red carpet, and was dominated by a monstrous red velvet sofa – both of which we'd inherited from the previous owners. When they lived there, the woodwork was painted red, too – and the wallpaper was dark. I remember that when we'd first looked around the house, and gone down the stairway to the basement, it had seemed like descending into the flames of hell.

But we couldn't afford to change everything straight away – so we painted all the woodwork bright white, and washed the walls with primrose yellow. Suddenly it looked like a delightfully colourful children's room – and that's the way it stayed. Eventually it gathered adult clutter, too, like the fax machine, the satellite system, the video and the music centre, and so it became the heart of the house – and it always seemed to be bursting with children.

When you live in London, and you have a nanny, your house becomes part of the nanny circuit – which means that your kitchen is always alive with girls drinking coffee, organizing tea parties and outings for your youngsters. At three and eighteen months, our children had a far more active social life than us. They were always visiting the zoo, going on open-top bus rides around London, feeding the ducks in Regent's Park or seeing Postman Pat at the theatre.

This is a home which welcomes children, I thought one morning, as I was listening to them play in the garden. How could we reject one now? Slowly but surely, the little baby forming inside me was triggering hormones which were changing my mind. He was determined to be born.

Well! If I was going to have another baby, go through more bouts of morning sickness, lose my figure all over again, get all over-emotional again – then could I really cope with the legal mess I'd got myself into at work? For some time, Mike and I had wondered if we should now stop the legal proceedings. It was fast turning into one of those situations where both sides lose out and only the lawyers get rich. Like a divorce.

Mike was usually the one to insist on fighting injustice to the bitter end. In the past, he'd issued libel writs against newspapers – and continued the battle long after I would have backed away. In the face of horrendous newspaper threats, and even more vitriolic headlines, he'd had the temerity to dig his heels in. And, always, he'd been right to do so. But this time, even Mike felt that things had got out of hand. One morning, before he left for work at the satellite station, Music Box, where he was managing director, we had a shouting match about it. He said I'd been stupid to run up such a massive legal bill. It was clear TV-am were going to resist all the way, either out of spite, or to make me spend myself penniless.

I reluctantly picked up the phone to my lawyer, Ian Bloom, to tell him to back off – and to find a way to extricate me from the lawsuit and save as much money as possible. He wasn't in – his secretary promised he'd get back to me. Just two hours later, while I was changing Jamie's nappy and planning the children's lunch, Ian rang. He didn't wait to ask me why I'd phoned him. 'Great news!' he trumpeted. 'They've offered a settlement – and I think you're going to like it....'

I was to be paid every penny due in what was left of my two-year contract – and they didn't want me back to work for it. They must have thought I'd balk at that, since the original argument had been about airtime being taken from me. But in these new circumstances, the deal couldn't have been more suitable. Rather like a highly-paid, two-year term of maternity leave – albeit with no job waiting at the end of it. Still, I could live with that!

I rang Mike. 'My God, brilliant news,' he whistled. 'But you'd better get the deal sorted quickly – before they find out about the baby. Or they'll probably try and find all sorts of reasons to withdraw the offer....'

There was, also, the small matter of how my divorce from TV-am was to be announced. Tony Fitzpatrick, a long-time friend who ran his own public relations and press agency, advised that we talk to Bruce about how things might be done with dignity. 'After all,' he told me. 'You were the Queen of TV-am for six years. You can't just disappear into the night – especially when the press know that you were actually suing the buggers. You've got to say goodbye to your viewers properly.'

Mike and I laughed at the suggestion. We were sitting now in Tony's plush office in London's Docklands, furnished with plush black leather and chrome. He poured us champagne and handed round the Twiglets.

'Bruce will never let me back on that sofa!' I retorted.

'Don't be so sure,' wiled Tony. 'Bruce knows that you made that sofa famous. He knows how important it is to keep the audience happy – and he knows how fond those viewers are of you. 'You should be allowed to sit there, be given flowers, talk about how sad you are to leave – and then wave goodbye. Out of courtesy to your viewers.'

Mike and I shook our heads in unison. 'He'll never agree to it!' But Tony knew. He knew Bruce. His life partner, Jason Pollock, had been TV-am's show-business editor since the start of the station. They both knew Bruce almost as well as I – in some ways better.

And so, within days, Tony came back to us with the astonishing news that Bruce had agreed – and that I would be a guest on *Good Morning Britain* that very Friday. I would be able to say my goodbyes to the station I'd helped to build, and the viewers who'd liked, loathed and supported me since Day One.

I wore a black polo neck sweater, black pencil skirt, and my new Paul Costelloe red hunting jacket – an outfit I'd only recently slimmed into. But this morning I had to suck my tummy in. I daren't let them see what was already a less than flat stomach – or they might suspect.

Bruce had come to see me in the hospitality area, as I waited to go into the studio. 'You look fabulous,' he said. 'How are the children? And Mike?' And then he walked away, without waiting for my reply. I guess he felt awkward. But it made me sad that he seemed so cold.

So I went ahead with the niceties. Lorraine Kelly and Mike Morris, now the main presenters of my old show, did me proud – and were genuinely thrilled that I had been able to leave in style. As I left the building which had been my home from home for most of that decade, dubbed 'Egg Cup Towers' by the tabloid press, I felt it was the end of a wonderful period of my life. Bruce must have felt it too. He wrote me a note. It said:

> And so we come to the end of an era. I cannot let it pass without writing to thank you personally for the great contribution you made to TV-am. Your dedication, commitment and professionalism was the hallmark of the time you spent with us. I do not underestimate the toll this took on your family life. I do want you to know how much we appreciated your presence.
>
> Love Bruce

I owed a lot to that place and to the characters who'd peopled it but I'd also given a great deal, I hoped, towards its astonishing success. I would never forget it – and I can honestly say that I have never since worked anywhere so dangerous, exciting, so exhausting, and so very rewarding.

I felt I'd won a moral victory. I had made them honour their contract. Now I had things to do at home. After all, there was a new baby coming.

Chapter 3

One Monday morning, just as we were about to go on air with Frankie Howerd, the 'Oooooh! Missus!' comedian who was regularly brought on to the programme to cheer us all up, he turned to me and said sadly: 'You know, Anne, it's no fun being famous any more....' He'd just been savaged by the Sunday newspapers – and I remember thinking how terribly sad it was that his mood should match his celebrated hang-dog expression. After a lifetime of hard slog, working his way up the show-business ladder, and then a career spent making people laugh, did his talent really deserve to be rewarded with humiliating headlines and malicious words?

But the press in the Eighties were having a field day at the expense of anyone well-known. They were already regularly shredding Princess Diana's image with stories of anorexia; it seemed to the rest of us that one particular tabloid wouldn't be happy until they'd driven Elton John to suicide; and their alleged disclosures about *EastEnders* star Leslie Grantham made Frankie Howerd's moan appear sadly prophetic.

And, since I had 'risen from nowhere' on this precocious and notorious breakfast TV station, I automatically became press fodder. Everything I did seemed to make news. Even when I broke my toe one morning, bashing it on my briefcase on the way into work, it resulted in a story on the front page of the *Sun.* That was one of the few times in those days that they wrote anything nice about me.

Pressmen say that the public 'want to know' about celebrities' private lives – and that's how they sought to defend their most appalling tactics. On several occasions, I had reporters posing as policemen, delivery men, florists, and even doctors – just to get inside my front door. And it's very frightening. One started rifling through my dustbin – what on earth could he have been looking for?

The pressmen say you have to put up with it – it's part and parcel of being famous. And if you do nice interviews for *Hello!* magazine, you cannot moan about uninvited press intrusion. Well, I did once do a feature and photo spread for *Hello!* magazine in its early days – so I suppose I had it coming to me....

I was almost eaten alive by the press in those days. My worst enemy was the *Sun*, closely followed by the *News of the World* and the *People*. The other tabloids seemed to be fair and unfair in equal measure. But it was the journalists on Britain's best-selling popular paper who really went for my throat, with a determination that felt like deliberate destruction.

My biggest mistake was having a private life at all. My next mistake was having a less than conventional one. Unfortunately for my press image, I was already in love by the time my name hit the headlines. And my love was already married – to someone else. I don't seek to defend what some would still consider an indefensible situation. But sometimes life doesn't hand you everything on a clean plate. I'm not the first girl who has found herself hopelessly in love with the wrong person. And I certainly shall not be the last.

Whatever the rights and wrongs – as a human being, you need time to sort these things out. Time and privacy. But when you've got at least three newspaper reporters, photographers at their heels, standing on your doorstep – you have neither. Your own emotions, and the hurt and sensibilities of others – including children – take second place to the newsmen's 'right to publish'.

In effect, that means that when the man at the door is shouting through your letterbox 'Are you in love with Mike Hollingsworth or not?' you know that you cannot win either way. If you speak to them, you are fuelling their story. If you don't, they'll run with their own version and defend their inaccuracies by citing your unwillingness to co-operate. If you go to the door, they'll snap you looking strained, worn and defeated. Unless, that is, you make yourself up, in which case you'll be described as looking brazen. So you don't answer the door at all – in which case they use a file picture of you, smiling all over your face. Whatever happens, tomorrow's headlines will only make the private anguish worse, on all sides.

But the real malice which they reserved for me dated back to one incident over which I felt I had no control. Mike and I were very much together – though he was not yet divorced – when I found I was pregnant with our first baby. We decided that this was a baby we very much wanted. My GP, Peter Wheeler, was delighted for me. But he advised me to wait until I was at least twelve weeks pregnant before telling anyone. As we all know with babies, you can never be absolutely sure that all will go well in the first few weeks.

Mike and I hadn't even thought how we would break the news to our respective families, when I thought I was miscarrying. It was almost Christmas, and we were just about to go shopping in Harrods one evening. As I walked up the steps to the Hans Crescent entrance, I collapsed on Mike's arm, bleeding heavily. Luckily we were only steps from the car, and just half a minute from Peter Wheeler's surgery. He was there as I staggered in. By this time I was in tears, and both Mike and I were panicking at the thought of losing the baby. Peter arranged for me to have an immediate ultrasound scan at a nearby private hospital – and, within the hour, we were relieved and comforted to see the little blip on the scanner screen which showed that Oliver was still alive. I had a placenta praevia. I had to go home, put my feet up for a few days and rest – or we could still lose the baby.

We'd been home just a few hours when the phone rang. It was a reporter from the *News of the World.* They had been tipped off that I was pregnant. Could I please confirm or deny?

I was stunned. How could they possibly know? I hadn't even told my parents yet. And anyway, I couldn't safely think that I was pregnant. I could still have a miscarriage.

The reporter must have sensed my shock. 'We have very good sources,' he said, contemptuously. 'We know it's true.'

'You can't possibly know,' I stumbled.

'Well, are you pregnant, or not?'

I hesitated, and then plumped for it: 'No,' I said, and put the phone down.

Later that evening, the TV-am press officer rang us to tell us that they, too, had received a call from the *News of the World*. They were going to run a story all over their front page with a headline saying 'Baby for TV Anne' and the first line of the story: 'Anne Diamond last night denied reports that she is pregnant. But....'

No time, nor privacy to even consider the little baby inside me – nor how we were going to cope, whether we would marry, where we would live. The most important thing at that moment was ringing round the family – so that they wouldn't read it in the papers first.

Little did I know that, from that day onwards, the *News of the World* and its associated papers would never forgive me for denying what they saw as a true story. Several times later in my history with them, they would brand me 'Liar'. The press in the UK has altogether curious double standards. On the one hand, they pester you to do interviews and photo shoots with them. Then they decry people who seek publicity.

It's difficult now to understand the media interest I attracted when my pregnancy was first confirmed. It's an extraordinary thing, but even in the modern 1980s, it was unprecedented for a woman to be on TV, as regularly as every day, while she was pregnant. Women simply shied away from the camera during the fat months. Most jobs in the TV world would allow you to do just that. But I couldn't take five or six months off. And, anyway, I didn't want to. So I, unwittingly, became the first female presenter in the UK to be on air, live every morning, throughout the pregnancy. Some critics later described me as 'flaunting my pregnancy'. I didn't. Actually, I refrained as much as I could from mentioning it. But mums-in-waiting up and down the country wrote to me, saying they were going through exactly the same experience.

On the day it was announced, Michael Aspel was our guest. He made a huge fuss of me – and later talked about me in the introduction of his prime-time talk show. Jasper Carrott, too, made me his first gag that night in his show. And Terry Wogan invited me on to his chat show to talk about it.

So, on the night I went into labour, Mike wasn't surprised to learn that, while we were still in the delivery room, the press had been tipped off that the baby was about to arrive. And they all wanted a photograph.

We sent out a message, via the hospital's administrators, that mother and baby were doing fine, but that we would not be doing any interviews or photocalls for a few days at least. But for one particular publication that was not good enough. I was still drinking tea, and looking forward to a bath, Mike holding the baby, when the matron knocked on our door and came in.

'I just thought I should warn you,' she said. 'I don't want to alarm you – but our porters have just had to deal with a man who was found wandering down the corridor looking for you. He was dressed in a white coat and was pretending to be a doctor. He was apparently from the *Sun*....'

And that was why, just six hours after I'd given birth, Mike, Oliver and I went home. We were smuggled out of the hospital via the service lift and in a laundry van. Once we were in our own car, we made for home. But our own entrance was surrounded by pressmen, so we went into the adjoining block of flats, up to the roof, and walked across the roof and down the stairs to our own flat. When I look back on it now, I go weak at the knees, but we'd have done almost anything then for a few days' absolute privacy.

Once the press realized we were inside, they pushed letters through our letterbox, pleading and offering money for exclusive first shots of the baby. The *News of the World* sent a big bouquet and a letter bidding £50,000. 'I'll bet there's a bug in these flowers,' I laughed, as I arranged them. And then I grew cautious. In those days, it was entirely possible that they could have bugged them. 'How would you like them, Kitty?' I asked my housekeeper, a dear old lady who was married to the caretaker of the flats. 'Why don't you take them home?'

Kitty gave them a peremptory glance. 'Well, they're too good to waste – but I'm not taking them home so's the papers can listen in to me and my Les. I'll take them to the church. And then if the *News of the World* are listening in, all they'll get is hymns.'

Every time a florist arrived with a new bouquet, the waiting reporters would rush at the door, cameras already flashing. Several beautiful posies got squashed because we were too afraid to open the door further than the security chain would allow it. One reporter, from the *Today* newspaper, offered the florist £15,000 if she could snatch a Polaroid snapshot of the baby.

When we eventually did agree for shots of Oliver to be printed in the *Daily Star* we were accused of hawking our son around Fleet Street in order to make money. This is rubbish – but the other newspapers printed the accusation so often, it became perceived as being true. Even *Spitting Image*, the satirical puppet programme, featured me in a sketch. I was seen pushing a supermarket trolley, with Oliver in the baby seat. When I got to the till, and the checkout girl asked for money, I got out a Polaroid camera, took a picture of Ollie – and paid for the shopping with it!

Then, of course, they went for our nanny....

Debbie had come to us from her last job as a nurse at

London's famous Great Ormond Street hospital for children. She'd written to me at TV-am – a lovely letter saying that she'd like to look after a healthy child after so many years nursing sick ones. First she was interviewed by my lovely loyal secretary, Gay – who was a mum herself and knew the ropes of working motherhood – and then she came to see me. I liked her straight away. Her experience with babies was fantastic – but her ability to whip together a tasty Caesar salad and her skill at mixing a gin and tonic made her outstanding!

I thought we'd got it right with Debbie. But what I forgot – or rather, I didn't know it would be significant – was that Debbie's training was as a nurse, not a nanny. Mike and I began to feel that we were being treated like unwelcome visitors – and that Ollie was a patient. He was always spotlessly clean, well turned out, routinely aired in his pram, and promptly put to bed in his own room. But we never felt that he was a member of the family. In fact, we started to feel that we were all outsiders in an efficiently run ward.

One morning I'd popped out to Mothercare and come back home with a baby carrier – one of those sling things which you tie in unfathomable knots around your body, and which holds your baby against your chest in a papoose. 'Look, just what we need for carrying Ollie around the house!' I said proudly, as I unwrapped it. 'Now, how does it go?' I looked to Debbie for help.

She took the carrier from me, slipped it around her shoulders and waist, popped the baby into it and looked up, smiling. 'That's great!' she smiled, and then at Oliver: 'You like that, don't you?'

I stood there , looking at the nanny wearing my baby. I had bought the carrier for me, not her – and I was reduced to looking on, rather like a visitor who'd brought a gift for a new mum and baby. In one insensitive, uncaring gesture, she had robbed me of a simple delight.

What's more, as the end of my eight weeks maternity leave

loomed, Debbie was licking her lips at the prospect of my return to work. She even admitted to it, when we had our upsetting but inevitable 'little chat'. We agreed that it wasn't working, and that she would leave as soon as she could. She said she needed to go off and arrange things. I thought she meant she was looking for another job, or somewhere to stay. I was glad she had taken it so well – and I hoped we would be able to remain friends. It was still morning, and I fed Ollie and played with him until he fell asleep on my bed. For once, Debbie wouldn't fly in and whisk him away to be tucked neatly into the crisp white sheets of his own cot.

It was probably about three hours later that I got the phone call.

'Hello – is that Anne Diamond? It's Kevin O'Sullivan, from the *Sun*.'

My stomach churned. It always did when one of those guys rang. And how had he found our phone number? But I'd had brushes with this one in the past. He was a well-known Fleet Street terrier. Once he had his teeth into you, there was no letting go. What on earth could he want?

'I just thought you'd like to know, Anne, that I've just had lunch with your nanny. She's told me a lot of very interesting things... How do you feel about that?'

There were no words to describe it. After a short silence, thankfully I went on to automatic pilot. It's something I had come to learn – before you say anything you may later regret, you should always buy yourself time. And it's always better than slamming the phone down, because that gets reported, too, as a sign of horror or hostility.

'Can I get back to you?' I stammered, trying to sound cool.

'Please do,' he cooed, and then gave me his number. But I didn't phone him back – I called Mike. By now, my heart was beating fast. Surely not our most private moments with our wonderful new baby, surely not our intimate thoughts – shared with a trusted employee – surely not our personal family photographs all over pages of the *Sun*? Surely she hadn't dealt us such a betrayal?

'Get Shirley to come over and be with you,' advised Mike, always organized even in the most prickly predicament. 'I'll be with the lawyers most of the afternoon.'

Sure enough, Shirley dropped what she was doing and rushed around – though she could barely believe what had happened. While we were sitting in my living-room, still in shock and trying to drink tea, I heard the key in the lock of the front door. It was Debbie. She made straight for her room, but I followed her, and asked her in as calm a voice as I could muster why she had done it, though a lump kept coming to my throat. She was stuffing clothes and personal belongings into a black plastic bin bag. Others – already stuffed – were by the door.

She couldn't look at me – she just muttered: 'I've got nothing to say....' I remember thinking immediately that it was an odd sort of thing to state. It was a phrase well used by people familiar with handling the press.

She shuffled her bin bags out of the door – and left on the hall table the door keys and the two credit cards which she used on my account at Mothercare and Marks & Spencers. Limply, I watched her go. She'd performed her exit quite well.

I rang Mike again – and got him on his mobile phone. He was sitting in a lawyer's office. 'Debbie's just come back and taken her things away,' I whimpered. 'She wouldn't listen to anything I had to say....'

Mike mumbled a few hurried words to the lawyers at his side and then came back with: 'Go after her, and ask her to retract. It's worth a try....'

I looked outside. Debbie was packing the bags into a car, being driven by a man I thought could be her brother. I rushed out, and immediately became aware that a photographer was standing on the opposite pavement – snapping me as I hurried towards Debbie. Was he there to catch me throwing an hysterical tantrum? Was he after shots of a cat-fight?

By now, Debbie was in the front passenger seat. 'Debbie, please – don't do this,' I entreated. 'Even if you want to hurt me and Mike, don't betray little Ollie. I thought you really cared for him....'

She looked up at me – this time right in my eyes. I could see that she was confused and upset. 'Don't worry,' she snapped. 'I haven't said anything horrible about you. I'm not even sure I'm going to go ahead with it anyway.'

With that, the car pulled away. I turned back to the doorway. The photographer was snapping away, but I resisted the temptation to throw something at him. That would have made a great picture.

Mike spent most of the night at the lawyers. They had eventually been forced to contact a judge in chambers who had granted an injunction, ordering the *Sun* to stop the story. Their presses were already rolling – and it was almost unheard of to stop them once they were printing. It caused unbelievable mayhem at the *Sun* – and they weren't to forgive us for it.

Debbie rang later in the evening. She was sorry. She told me the reporter, Kevin, had met her in a pub, and offered her £30,000 in cash for her story. 'That's more than most people earn in a year,' she gasped at me. I could almost see her point.

'So did you agree to tell them anything – did you sign anything?' I asked her.

'They said I'll get the money later....'

'But did you tell them anything?' I asked again.

'Well, he did get out his notebook and write down quite a lot,' she admitted. 'But I'm sure they won't print anything if I ask them not to....'

Well, that's what you might think, if you'd never handled the press before.... 'Oh, Debbie,' I sighed. 'Don't you see? You've already given them what they want. They'll simply open the quote marks and say what they like. And I'd be surprised if you ever get your money, either.'

She went silent at the other end of the phone. And then she promised: 'I'll phone them and tell them I don't want anything to do with it....'

An hour later she rang again, this time in tears. They had more or less told her to get stuffed. They had their story, she said, and claimed they had never discussed money.

Of course, the *Sun* had lawyers as wily as their journalists. They could not print the story in the *Sun*, so the magnates at News International decided to print it in *Today*, a sister publication. Debbie had said some pretty hurtful things. Like how I apparently treated Oliver like a new toy. How I was terrified he would be kidnapped. How Mike and I argued – and how he was annoyed by the baby crying. To me, the real hurt was the fact that she'd gone to the newspapers at all. If you read it, you could quickly see that she was merely describing the private tensions which must happen in any family when the first baby arrives. Maybe she was surprised that life at home with a TV couple wasn't more like the *Mary Tyler Moore Show*.

(A year and a half later, Debbie died. Although a trained nurse – and a skilled one according to her nursing qualifications – she had succumbed to an eating disorder and had destroyed herself through massive laxative abuse. Of course, because she had once made headlines, the press reported her death, and the coroner's inquest findings – something which must have been dreadfully hard for her family to bear. And I apologize to her relatives if mentioning her here has added to their grief. But I think that she, too, was a victim of the press's misguided belief that any information, however private and confidential, was theirs to print.)

I hadn't even got back to work yet – and both Mike and I started to doubt whether we'd ever find a nanny we could trust. But we had good friends. Shirley was thrilled to help – and luckily, she had some time free. She relished looking after Oliver, but it couldn't be permanent. And neither Mike nor I felt we could trust another outsider. That's when Paula Yates stepped in with a unique gesture.

We'd known each other on and off for some time – mostly because we had come to know Bob Geldof, Paula's rock star husband. He'd appeared on TV-am many times during the making of the Band Aid record, to raise funds for famine victims in Ethiopia. Bob had planned, as a follow-up, a live version of the phenomenon – he planned to call it Live Aid, and to have it broadcast live throughout the world. It had sounded impossibly ambitious to us in the television industry. Getting TV companies in Britain to agree to do anything simultaneously was nearly impossible – let alone his dream of reaching the entire world. But he was a fascinating man – and he might just do it. So Mike, who was then the Director of Programmes at TV-am, agreed to support him as much as he could – and the company agreed to send Bob, with a film crew and me as a reporter, to Ethiopia, to see for himself what needed to be done, and how the charity money could be best spent.

As a result we came to see more and more of Bob and Paula socially. They were a close family – at that time they had just one daughter, the notoriously named Fifi Trixiebell. But it was clear they wanted more. We had been with them, in fact, on the very day I went into labour. Bob had been stuck for a celebrity to open the fête which was held annually at his Kent mansion, and he'd asked me if I would help out. I was so bored with waiting for the baby to come, that I agreed. By my reckoning, I was almost nine and a half months pregnant. When I look back at the photos now – I don't know how I even had the nerve to go out, let alone be photographed at a public event. Even more amazing was the fact that I wasn't jostled into labour by the journey along country roads to their house, by the intense heat, or by the wonderful summer pudding Paula had made for tea. Or maybe I was – because by the time we headed for bed that night, my head hit the pillow and my waters immediately broke.

So now Paula's act of friendship came as a welcome act of Live Aid. 'I've thought about it, and there's only one thing which would be truly useful to you right now,' she said.

'Yee-e-e-es?' I wondered.

'I'm going to lend you my nanny for a while. She's been with us for ages – she's fantastic – and she'll get you all sorted out. But mind – I want her back. OK?'

Now Paula's nanny was legendary. She was called Anita, and she strode into our home with a sense of purpose and confidence that restored our faith in human nature, and, in particular, the belief that we might find someone who would look after our child, fit into the family, and become the godsend which Anita was to the Geldofs. 'Give me time – and I'll find you the nanny of your dreams,' she told us and proceeded to interview us about the nanny we would like to have – what sort of people we were at home and what our expectations were of life, and of our child. She stayed with us a couple of weeks – and showed me what it was truly like to have the best in professional child care. I'll never forget her's – or Paula's – kindness.

Anita couldn't find anyone for us straight away – but I'd been lucky. Nanny Sue walked into our lives at just the right moment, though she only stayed with us six months. She was from the famous Norland College – but more importantly, she was the daughter of old friends of mine. Her mother and father had been stalwart members of my home town's operatic society, where I'd been an ambitious junior. Tom and Sally Rollins were the nicest of people, and thoroughly down-to-earth. Their daughter could be nothing less – and here she was, applying for our job. She was a brilliant nanny, and Oliver was lucky to have her during those first few infant months. When she left us – as nannies do – I was bereft. I rang Paula's house – and spoke to Anita.

In the meantime, I hired Carol. Again, it just didn't work. I worked in breakfast TV. Carol didn't get in from her nightclubbing until the early hours – often just moments before I left for work. And once I heard her arrive by the crunching sound outside as the car bumpers hit the street bollards. When I got home, at about midday, the house would often be silent. I would gingerly go upstairs, wondering why. More often than not, Carol was fast asleep in bed, with Oliver, at nine months, still in his night-time sleepsuit, lying in her bed beside her, staring at the ceiling.

Carol and I agreed we were animals from different time zones. It was her boyfriend, whom I'd met for only thirty seconds at the front door, who sold his story to the *News of the World*. In it, among the other scathing remarks about how I expected nannies to be slaves, he said he'd never ever seen me change a nappy. That in itself was true. Like I said – thirty seconds at the front door was all I'd ever seen of him. But it rankled – the idea of me never changing a nappy. I would still like to sock him in the face with one.

Nanny Sue was on the phone that Sunday morning. 'Do you want me to ring up the newspapers and stand up for you?' she almost sobbed.

Just as Mike and I were seriously considering which one of us should now give up work, and become a house-parent – Anita rang. 'I've found you the nanny of your dreams!' she proclaimed.

And she had.

Anne Waterman wafted into our lives like a breath of fresh air. Oliver adored her – and we came to trust and love her. She came all over the world with us: she fell in love with Australia when we did, potty-trained in Los Angeles, wheeled a buggy around Manhattan, took Ollie on the rides in Disneyworld, and taught him to use chopsticks in Hong Kong. In Sydney, where we lived for three glorious months in a millionaire's house overlooking the Harbour Heads, she would take Oliver swimming or playing on the beach every morning before breakfast – while I nursed the newly-born Jamie. She was exactly what we needed. And when she left us – because, dammit, she fell in love – once more Anita helped us.

'I don't suppose you ever get two nannies of your dreams, do you?'

'Of course you do!' said Anita. 'I'll find you the next dream person.' And she did – Alex.

Alex came for her interview on a particularly difficult day. Oliver was being an obstreperous toddler – and Jamie had kept me up all night, and was now screaming for his latest bottle of milk. I was sitting in the upstairs living-room of our terraced house in North London. I thought it would look better than the *Steptoe and Son* junkyard downstairs. But Alex took half a minute to figure us out. She just sort of scooped up the children – and they were immediately captivated. Within fifteen minutes and over our third cup of tea, when the boys seemed more content and the atmosphere less frenetic, I knew Anita had done it again. Suffice it to say Alex is still with us. And every one of our children has been the better for knowing her.

Because if you cannot look after your children yourself all the time – and few of us can – then the person to whom you entrust that task must either be grandma, auntie – or otherwise a professional who's very special indeed. I simply cannot understand those who belittle the jobs of childminder, carer, nanny or teacher. To me, next to parenthood, those have to be the most important jobs of all.

Chapter 4

By contrast to the circus which surrounded Oliver's and Jamie's births, Sebastian's arrival was of little interest to the media. By then, we were married – and I had given up the high-profile business of broadcasting every day from TV-am. Indeed, my only TV committment was *TV Weekly*. The furore over my departure from TV-am had long ceased, and on the personal front, life had never been quieter nor more peaceful.

I had been invited to appear on a BBC morning programme about celebrities and their mums – and had chosen that as an opportunity to announce the pregnancy. It resulted in a single paragraph in the next day's papers: 'Baby Number Three for TV Anne'. 'My goodness, what a difference,' I thought. 'We must be respectable nowadays!' Oliver and Jamie were looking forward to having a baby brother. They had even given him a name – though we couldn't figure out exactly why they had decided to call my bump 'Supi'. At any rate, it stuck so firmly that, by the time his birth loomed near, our family were worried that we might actually christen him with that name. Eventually, we chose Sebastian with Patrick as his second name. I reasoned that if he ever needed to explain his nickname to anyone, he could say it was simply the running together of his two initials, S and P. So his nickname led to the choice of his real Christian names, rather than the other way round.

The pregnancy itself, however, was not particularly easy this time. Towards the end I had a condition known as polyhydramnios – which means I had too much amniotic fluid – and I was uncomfortably large and breathless. Four weeks before Supi was due, I started to suffer from chronic backache.

Our nanny, Alex, reminded me she was going away to her grandmother's house in Devon that weekend. 'Perhaps I'd better stay,' she volunteered. 'Maybe you're going to have the baby sooner than you think....'

'No, there's another month to go yet,' I panted. 'Don't worry.'

'I don't want you going into labour while I'm away – I don't want to miss any of the action!' Alex laughed as she brought me a cup of tea that Saturday morning. I was still in bed. But the pain seemed better. Perhaps it had just been backache after all.

But Alex couldn't have been on the train more than half an hour when my twinges became painful – and I rang my obstetrician, Maggie Thom.

'You'd better come and see me.' She sounded worried. 'I'll meet you at the Wellington at ten.'

Mike rang Alex's best friend, Sandra, who was also a nanny but with a husband and child of her own. Could she pop around and mind the children while we went to the hospital?

'But where's Alex?' she asked.

'Hurtling towards Devon,' answered Mike. But Alex's family had already assured him they would turn her right round as soon as she arrived in Exeter. They knew she would want to be with us.

'Typical!' laughed Sandra – and she came round. Which was just as well, because I was well into premature labour.

It was not a painful labour – since by child number three Maggie Thom and I had agreed on the wonders of epidurals. But I did start to get worried when, much later into the evening, a paediatrician entered the room, and started kitting up the little special resuscitation trolley at the other end of the delivery room. Maggie caught my concern. 'It's just routine – because the baby's coming early,' she said.

My perfect little boy, our third son, our special Supi, was born shortly after five o'clock that Saturday evening. There was a lot of suctioning noise going on at the 'business end' of me – he wasn't placed straight on to my stomach, as the others had been. The paediatrican was busily doing something with him. The midwife wrapped him in a towel as they cleared his airways. Then they cut the cord.

'He's having a few small problems with his breathing – but nothing to worry about. It's just because he's a bit premature. But you can hold him for a few minutes.' They handed him to me. He had a pinky-grey little face, still covered in greasy vernix but unmistakably the likeness of his brothers. Mike took a quick snap with the camera. But the baby shot me a glance which smacked of panic – and then went quite blue. I turned to the midwife: 'He can't breathe!' and handed him back hurriedly. I was still being stitched up – and felt quite helpless while my little son was rushed to the warming unit again and more suction sounds began.

Mike hovered, sensing their concern. Our little boy was a good size, and appeared perfect. But he was definitely having problems with his breathing – and was struggling to live.

'We'll just take him to the special care baby unit for a few minutes,' they said, wheeling him away. 'Please don't worry – he just needs a bit of oxygen....'

The midwife came back a few minutes later. 'Don't worry – they'll just keep him for twenty minutes or so. Have a cup of tea, and try to relax – he's absolutely beautiful.'

Her next bulletin informed us that they might keep him in intensive care for a couple of hours. But again, nothing to worry about. I still couldn't walk, because of the epidural. So they wheeled me, flat on my back on a patient trolley, in through the doors of the special care baby unit to see him. Now he was washed – and quite pink – but laid out, flat on his back, like a laboratory specimen, under a warming light. There were wires to his chest and toes – and several machines were flashing red numbers and blipping green lights. He was almost encapsulated in a clear perspex hood, which had a long tube leading to an oxygen cylinder.

It was then I first realized that our little Supi was seriously ill. And – though he'd been the baby we hadn't expected and we'd joked that he would have to 'be a good baby' and he'd 'have to fit in with the rest of us and be no trouble' – his life was suddenly just as important as Oliver's and Jamie's. I didn't want him to die. I reached out my arm, and caressed the tiny heel of his dainty little foot – the only bit of him that wasn't under the oxygen box.

I felt unnervingly out of control. Here was I, helpless on a hospital trolley, drips still taped to my hand and arm, and there was my little child, pathetically clinging on to life, his chest almost collapsing with the effort of every breath. I wanted to grab him, and make a run for it. But instead I meekly listened to the professionals telling me not to worry, and wheeling me back to my own room.

I calmed down when Doctor Stanley Rom, the senior hospital paediatrician, came to visit. He had been called in to see Supi, and his manner was quiet and composed, almost soothing.

'Your little chap is not too well,' he started. Thank goodness he was not going to tell me not to worry. He could see I already was. 'He is having some problems breathing – and we're going to find out why. Now it could be that his oesophagus is incomplete, in which case we may have to talk about an operation. But we're going to have to do an X-ray first – to see what's happening.'

The champagne you always get at the Wellington with a new baby was waiting on ice. Mike had gone back home to organize Sandra, Alex (who had just returned from her day on the railways) and the boys – and he would be back soon.

The X-rays showed Supi's oesophagus was, thankfully, completely developed. They had been able to pass a tube into his lungs. There was nothing wrong with him that time, and careful nursing, wouldn't heal.

I had a bath, more tea and something to eat. And then one of the midwives offered to wheel me in a chair, around to the special care baby unit that was to become so familiar over the next two weeks. Because, although they had said Supi would be there at first for just twenty minutes, then two hours, then overnight, he would end up staying there for two weeks. And now I started the long process, as all parents do when they have babies in SCBU, of learning which tubes go where, and which machines do what.

'That one tells you his oxygen saturation,' the sister said. 'And that one is his heart rate.'

And all the time, while other little lives fought in incubators besides our own, I could not take my eyes off the little mite I already felt was part of our family, his little rib cage, puffing out bravely with each breath, and then collapsing so dramatically that I could have sworn I could almost see his spine through the skin. He was foaming slightly at the mouth but his little arms and legs lay motionless. At the bonny weight of 5lb 13oz he was bigger than the other babies in SCBU – but he seemed to have worse breathing problems. Apparently that had something to do with my excess amniotic fluid.

I stared at him, gently stroking those little feet, until the sister thought I should get some rest myself. And, when Mike returned, I had a lot to tell him.

It was a lonely night, without my baby. The midwives kept popping in with bulletins – and I went to see him myself once, walking slowly along the corridor on legs still wobbly from the epidural. They said he was doing well. But he didn't look any different to me. His breathing still looked critical.

'Should he be here?' my husband asked Doctor Rom, in as tactful a manner as possible. 'Or should he be in a children's hospital, like Great Ormond Street?'

Dr Rom smiled wryly. He knew exactly what we meant. You book into a luxury hospital like the Wellington for just that – luxury. But when it comes to life and death – maybe the best place to be is down the road, at one of the big teaching hospitals in London.

'I understand what you're getting at, and yes,' he said, 'Sebastian needs to be where he'll get the finest medical care there is. If for one second I believe we should move him to another hospital, I will do just that. But right now I have absolute confidence that this hospital has everything he needs. You were right to ask. You love your little boy and you want the best for him. And I'll make sure he gets the very best.'

We started to relax. We visited Supi again. He still didn't look any better – but we began to understand that he needed time. He had been born too soon, and would have to go on 'cooking gently' inside the incubator instead of inside me. We coudn't hug him, cuddle him or welcome him properly into the world, because he hadn't really been born yet. The Special Care Baby Unit, dimly lit and quietly throbbing with machinery as it was, was almost like an extension of the womb. Only when he came out would he be properly with us.

Mike came again in the afternoon, this time with Alex and the boys. Sister Chan, whose meticulous manner I mistook at first for officiousness, allowed the boys in to see their brother, but barred Alex because she was not a blood relative. She stood outside the SCBU door, her eyes welling up with tears as she watched Oliver and Jamie walk in. At three years old and eighteen months, they could hardly understand that this tiny pink baby, whose face was all but obscured by tubes, was their little brother.

We stayed for a few minutes while they admired the machinery, Mike shot some video, and then we all headed back to my room, where we opened the champagne and drank a toast to Supi's health. The boys had made me some cards – and they had brought flowers.

Supi, meanwhile, was moved to a more permanent special care cot, and was laid out on his tummy, which helped his breathing. Not only did it make him more comfortable, but it wasn't so distressing to look at, since you couldn't see his sad little rib cage crumple with every respiration.

And so, over the next few days, new words appeared in our vocabulary – as they must with every parent who goes through the experience of having a child in special care. Words like 'Skiboo' and 'intubate' became commonplace. I learned how to change a nappy without dislodging the drips and sensors. I found that he loved having his spine gently stroked – his face would visibly relax. And I would discover that, after sitting for a while by his cot, caressing his little toes, or patting his bottom, hours would have passed by.

And, all around me, other babies were coming and going, their anxious parents running the full spectrum of human emotions. And I realized how very lucky we were.

Chapter 5

Anyone who was in the same maternity wing at the same time as me would remember me as the strange, almost obsessive person in a tartan dressing-gown, pushing a wheeled object up and down the corridor between my room and the Skiboo (the nickname for the Special Care Baby Unit).

Shrouded in a white blanket, its identity wouldn't have been immediately obvious to the outside world. It was the electric breast pump. This time I was determined to succeed at something I'd failed to do with my first two sons – breastfeeding. It was a skill that had passed me by when God had handed out natural talents. I'd seen – in fact I'd interviewed – all sorts of baby experts from Hugh Jolley to Michel Odent, extolling its virtues. I'd witnessed friends of mine – ex professional models with figures that could grace a catwalk just days after giving birth – almost drowning their gurgling offspring in cascades of milky goodness.... But me, with natural assets large enough to generously fill a 'medium' size Mothercare nursing bra, I couldn't produce enough to keep a fairy alive.

When they were new-born, both Oliver and Jamie had taken one look at me and opted for the Cannon Babysafe and SMA Gold. My breastfeeding history was a sorry tale of personal torture followed by guilt and tears. I'd had one-to-one tuition from a La Leche League counsellor and I'd tried the Sheila Kitzinger twenty-four-hour 'peak production plan'. But nothing worked.

When you write or say anything publicly about child care, you have to be seen to beat the drum for breastfeeding. And I know that breast is best – for everyone concerned. I accept that new research even suggests that it's positively beneficial for the mother, and could help reduce her risks of developing breast cancer.... But if you can't do it, you can't do it – and feeling guilty as hell doesn't help you or your baby.

But this time, I thought, I'd got help on my side. Supi could not make many demands on me, since he wasn't allowed any milk yet – and I was surrounded by a huge team of midwives, all of whom were trained in teaching women to breastfeed. If I cannot do it now, I thought, I never will. But because I couldn't even hold Supi yet, let alone put him to the breast, I did my best without him. I became intimate with the Skiboo breast pump.

Day five – and Dr Rom said that Supi could have his first milk. One millilitre – to be put down his nasal gastric tube, and siphoned into his stomach. They would then see how he reacted, and whether he could digest it properly. I went back to my room with a challenge. Could I produce one millilitre of milk? It's not a huge amount, by any standards, when you think that five millilitres fill a teaspoon. But it wasn't easy. Squeezing blood out of a stone would have been simpler. It must have taken half an hour – but I got there. A milky white drip of colostrum, a mother's first 'supermilk', hovered on the edge of the sterile feeding bottle which I'd brought with me.

The midwife looked at my offering, and giggled. 'Well, there's not much of it – but it's power-packed!' she said, taking it up into a syringe. 'Let's go and give it to him....'

Supi was doing well. I'd entered Skiboo one morning – and my heart missed a beat. He wasn't there. Or, rather, he wasn't in his usual place. There was a plastic cover on his heated cot, and all the wires and tubes were folded away. Luckily, the nurses saw me before I had time to think the worst. 'It's OK – he's over here in the incubator!'

At first, I took this as a sign that he was worse. But, actually, it was a mark of his progress. He now didn't need constant supervision, and could sleep happily in a safely enclosed environment where they could gradually reduce his dependence on oxygen. When he'd done well there for a few more days, he was allowed out into the air. Now he was in a conventional transparent hospital cot, still wired up to bleepers and monitors, but breathing ordinary air. And all the time, his respiration was becoming more normal. His little chest didn't cave in the way it had at birth.

But he was losing weight. Now he needed food. He was fast asleep. The midwife undid the end of his gastric tube, and injected his first feed down it. Then she held it up, and we watched the little dribble go down, and then inside him. What an extraordinary business, I thought. I watched in awe. Even more when, an hour later, the sister suctioned up, again through the gastric tube, the contents of his stomach to see if he'd digested that little drop of milk. He had – so Dr Rom decided he could have another in another hour's time.

'Let's not rush things,' he said, calmly. 'He's growing slowly but surely....' Let's not rush things, I agreed, seriously worried about whether I could manage any more milk.

Meanwhile, in a special fridge in the nursery next door, other women were refrigerating spare bottles of their produce. Pints and pints of the stuff, all carefully labelled – ready to provide overnight feeds for their bouncing babies. I felt totally inadequate. Thank goodness Supi wasn't expecting too much of me. Come to think of it, he hadn't even noticed he'd been fed at all. Soon, as with all healthy babies, he did need more – and luckily, I was able to provide it. I was proud that I could.

As I used to sit at his cotside, spending hours holding, changing and feeding my little baby amid all his wires and tubes, I watched the other players in this strange, gentle soap opera. I chatted to and listened to the other mums and dads, and all the support cast of relatives who passed through – some just for a few hours, others for weeks, like me. And for the first time in my own experience of motherhood, I learned that parenting can be about death, as well as life.

One morning, I walked in, full of the joys of spring, wheeling the breast pump before me, when a tragic sight met my eyes. A baby had come in the night before – and I'd seen him in his incubator before they pulled the screens around. He (it might have been a girl, I never knew) had been so white. That's what struck me hard. His little body was so very white. No colour at all. While I had quietly fed Supi, in the corner of the unit, several doctors had been talking in hushed voices over the little baby's incubator. The tone of their voices had been very serious and sad. That baby must have something terrible wrong with him, I thought – and didn't dare to ask anyone more.

Now, as I opened the Skiboo door, I heard a sound I'll never forget – the heartrending sound of a mother's pitiful wailing. I never saw her face. She sat with her back to the world, but I could see that she was holding her little white baby in her arms. She was rocking backwards and forwards, with her baby tight against her chest, her long, black hair draped down her back. Backwards and forwards, rocking, and wailing at the wall. Her baby was dead.

My eyes shot to my little Supi, sleeping in the corner. From the doorway, I could see his monitors bleeping and flashing as usual. A nurse came up to me: 'Can you come back in a few minutes?' she asked me, softly. I nodded, meekly, and went back to my room silently, suddenly aware of the savage, primitive cruelty of childbirth and motherhood. Until then, I had known only the joy. There, but for the grace of God, I thought...

Another incident sticks out in my memory, from those days in special care. It was the morning that we all heard on the news that Eric Clapton's son had died. He was called Conor – and he'd been with his mother, staying in a high-rise apartment block in New York. By some dreadful freak accident, a large window had been left open in their apartment. Conor, a typical little rascal of six, had been rushing around the room, and had fallen out. He fell fifty-three floors to his death.

It was in all the papers. The morning TV programmes were discussing it. The whole maternity wing of our hospital was subdued. Everyone seemed to be in a state of shock. Mothers held their new babies closer to their breasts. In corners, people were whispering: 'Isn't it dreadful? Did you hear? He was such a lovely-looking child....' And we were all asking the doctors: 'Surely he would have blacked out before...' No-one wanted to finish the sentence. All day, nurses, doctors and patients were shaking their heads in disbelief and sorrow. I vowed that we would put bars on our windows as soon as we got home.

I meant to write to Eric Clapton. Mike and I had known him when he was married to Patti. They were a smashing couple, mainly because they were so normal, despite their legendary status to anyone who'd lived through the Sixties. We had once, at a party, talked about our mutual liking for Gucci leather-ware, and I'd told Eric that Mike had bought me – as a birth-day gift – a briefcase from Milan. I joked that what I really wanted next was a vanity case to match. But that it could only be bought in Milan.

Several weeks later, and totally out of the blue, Patti rang me and said that Eric had just come back from touring in Milan, and had brought back a Gucci vanity case for me. I was stag-gered, because it had only been a chance remark. But he'd remembered, and even got the colour right.

Now, years later, I wanted to tell him that, though none of us had ever known his son, we all cared so very much. Conor's death had affected everyone in the hospital very deeply. I meant to write, but I never did – afraid that I might intrude upon his grief. I learned myself, later that same year, that such letters are very important. And that expressions of regret, or sympathy, never intrude. They really help.

I was ready to leave hospital well before Supi – so when the team from *TV Weekly* rang to see how I was, I told them I was fit to present the show. They sent the car to the hospital to collect me, and I left Mike at Supi's cotside in the Skiboo. When I reached the Southampton studios, I proudly showed off my Polaroid snaps of Supi. I missed him dreadfully – and it seemed strange, being made-up and dressed for live TV just four days after giving birth, but I knew Supi was doing well, and couldn't be in a safer place. The *TV Weekly* team – Chris, Peter, Roy, Tony and Jane – were all so supportive. Later that year, I was to learn the blessing of their friendship. Then the car returned me to hospital – where I got back to the breast pump.

One evening, Mike and I went out to dinner at a restaurant just around the corner. The nurses had promised to ring on our mobile phone if there was any emergency – but it was our first night out in a long time, and I longed to enjoy a comfortable meal again – one where I could bend in the middle, eat without heartburn, and have a glass of wine. At the rate of one millilitre every two hours, I couldn't see how a drop of wine would be harmful to the baby!

I had promised Supi I would be back later to feed him, and I'd reminded all the midwives, because I didn't want them to think I was away, and so feed him themselves. The sister made sure of that. When I came back, Supi was still fast asleep, next to his Wellington teddy. And, like a little parcel, he had a stick-it note on his back:

> '18th March, '91. DEAR EVERYONE. MY MOTHER PHONED AT 2030HRS AND WILL BE IN FOR MY NINE PM FEED. SO PLEASE DON'T FEED ME, BUT KEEP ME HAPPY IF I WAKE. LOVE, SEBASTIAN.'

I took my camera out from the cupboard underneath his cot, and snapped a picture.

Shortly after that, Supi was allowed out of Skiboo and into the nursery for half an hour – so that he could be cuddled by his brothers and Alex, who'd been impatient to hold him. It became a family photo session, with everyone having the long-awaited chance for a hug and a pose. The boys sat in one of the large nursing chairs, and held him between them. They beamed with pride. What fun they were going to have together – what mates they would be. Oliver at three, Jamie, just two years old, and Supi, who was still three weeks short of his due date – but looking bigger and stronger every day.

The midwife who delivered him looked in. 'Quite a handful,' she laughed. 'It won't be long before they're all following you around like three little ducks!'

I was relieved that they were at last all together. My three boys.

A few days later, I agreed to do a short questionnaire for a regular feature in the *Daily Express*. They said it would only take two minutes, as they were set questions which they asked all the celebrities.

'What's your proudest achievement?' asked the girl reporter at the other end of the phone.

'Having three healthy sons,' I replied.

I don't know why the next question came next, but it did.

'And what's your greatest fear?'

'Losing them,' came the automatic response.

I couldn't have known how awfully ironic that simple comment was to be.

Chapter 6

He seemed so tiny when we brought him home – but he already had a great character. He seemed to know exactly what he wanted, but he wasn't a howler or a screamer – he just insisted, with a quiet determination which led us later to think that he would become the family diplomat. It's astonishing how little babies can very quickly impress you with the depth of their character. Supi would sit in the middle of the floor, in his baby bouncy chair, and run things. If his two brothers were arguing, he would gurgle or coo, immediately grab their attention, and so prick the bubble of tension.

Oliver had been awaiting, with some degree of understanding, the birth of his baby brother with impatience. He now revelled in his company, helping to feed and change him with excitement and curiosity: 'Why does his tummy button stick out?'

Jamie, on the other hand, was feeling a little displaced as baby of the family. He still had a bottle (of water) at night. But now he wanted to carry it around with him during the day, too. There was no doubt he was jealous – or at least anxious. But he only showed his worries to the adults, by wanting more cuddles, more loving. And, of course, he hated us holding the baby. Sometimes, while I was feeding Supi, happy that the other two were busy with Alex, or building something out of Duplo or Sticklebricks, I would catch Jamie out of the corner of my eye. He would be looking at me, with just a hint of resentment. He'll get over it with time, I thought. But he never showed any hostility towards Supi himself. As long as Supi wasn't actually in our arms, he was OK. In fact, Jamie became a dab hand at helping to feed him. He loved and understood bottles, after all. And, on car journeys, Jamie would help plug Supi's dummy in, if it fell out!

But two weeks home – and Supi caught a cold. With his prematurity, and his history of breathing problems, it was a difficulty he could have done without. But, I suppose, having two older brothers – both of whom played daily with other children at nursery school – it was hardly surprising that he succumbed to a virus. It was a tense time for me, though. I slept Supi in a Moses basket next to my bed. Now I tipped it up, so that he was almost sleeping uphill – and I steamed the room until the wallpaper came off the walls.

During the worst snuffly period, I stayed awake most of the night, holding him upright against a pillow. But as soon as he was a little better I propped him up on a cushion in his own basket, and under a makeshift tent made of sheets – to try and minimize the damage being done by the steam to the walls. Despite trying to watch him every moment, I dropped off to sleep myself. When I awoke, several hours later, Supi was sleeping happily inside the tent. But he'd slid down the tipped basket, and was in a quaint sitting position at the bottom, with his knees bent over the side, and his feet dangling in mid-air.

In the bedside cupboard above our heads was the apnoea alarm, packed away after our traumas with Jamie. Even in the worst of Supi's cold, I never once thought to get it out.

The cold almost over, I now needed some sleep, so we called in an old friend, the maternity nurse who had helped us with Jamie nearly two years before, Nanny Anne Robinson. Anne had a wonderful, soft and gentle way with babies. A very quiet person herself, she would rock and sing to them for hours on end. Supi loved her – and she stayed with us for several weeks.

With such a great deal of professional help – and both sets of grandparents happy to come round and lend a hand – we were determined that Supi should join in everything the others did. We travelled to the Lake District for a short holiday, we wheeled along the Mall to join the crowds watching the Trooping of the Colour, we had a day out at Thorpe Park, where the bigger boys delighted in petting the animals at the Farm. Everything they enjoyed, Supi did too. And, because my TV commitments were over – and Mike, being the managing director of his station, could schedule his time his own way – we kept ourselves very busy indeed. The boys were thirsty for new and exciting experiences.

But it was also time for a rethink domestically. I was no longer working – and didn't know whether *TV Weekly* would be recommissioned in the autumn. It was a difficult decision – but we began to realize that we no longer needed, nor could afford, a nanny. The two big boys were spending most mornings at nursery school. Soon, Oliver would be there all day. Looking after three little ones under four years of age would not be easy – it isn't for anyone – but I relished the prospect.

Alex understood completely – and promised she'd always stay in touch. She agreed that she'd start looking for another job. I didn't want her to go until she was totally happy with her next position.

You don't give away gold lightly.

Supi's health was generally fine, though we kept in touch with Dr Rom, especially throughout that first cold. Private doctors are expensive, however, and we decided that now we would make far more use of our National Health GP's practice, which was excellent, although always hellishly busy.

Our health visitor was one of the best. Her name was Anne, too. (At one point, we had three Annes in the house, all weighing Supi together!) She had helped us with Oliver and Jamie – and was delighted when she was called around to our home again. 'This house is always a happy place for children,' she said once, which made me very proud. We were a little worried because Supi had a touch of oral thrush inside his cheeks and on his tongue – and he wasn't feeding (now on bottles – I hadn't been that successful at the breastfeeding!) with his usual enthusiasm. The doctor gave us the antibiotic Nystatin – a yellowish liquid which smelled of almonds and which tasted sweet and sticky. We had to squirt one dropper-full in his mouth four times a day. He hated it, but it cleared the infection very quickly.

He also had a slight problem with one testicle. It occurred to me slowly, over a few days, but soon I was sure that his left testicle was slightly swollen. I mentioned it to Anne, the health visitor, who agreed that it might need medical attention. Off to the doctor again. Yes, it was a hydrocele, a swelling usually caused by excess fluid. It wasn't painful, I was assured. And, indeed, Supi didn't seem concerned about it at all. It wasn't usually harmful in any way, the doctor continued. But she said she would refer Supi to a specialist. Did I want to go private, or NHS?

'Is it urgent?' I asked.

'No,' she replied. 'He's not in any pain, and it's not harmful in any way – so you don't need to see a specialist quickly....'

'In that case, let's go with the National Health Service.'

'Right,' she said. 'I'll make the arrangements, and you'll be notified about your appointment within the next few days, I should think.'

The letter came the following week, as we neared the end of May. It was for 15 August. I had a flicker of doubt. Where the children were concerned, I always liked to be on top of any health problems they might have, no matter how trivial. This would be the first time I would wait so long to get anything done. Still, if Supi was in no pain, and it wasn't dangerous... I decided to wait.

Our bedroom looked dreadful. I hadn't liked the wallpaper much anyway, but now it was curling up and dying. Corners were coming away where the steam from Supi's humidifier had strayed. And over my side of the bed, one piece was falling off.

We'd been wanting to redecorate, and redesign the room for ages. Now it was crying out for attention.

Supi's own bedroom was ready for him – I had prepared it while I was pregnant. It was covered in a Habitat wallpaper, a balloon pattern in bright primary colours. How did I find the time in those days? I had painted the wardrobe and cupboard knobs to look like balloons, and even given them tiny, dangly strings. I'd made big fabric balloons to hang in the top corner, to hide the damp patch on the ceiling, and the centrepiece was a hot-air balloon lampshade, which we'd bought in Australia. The big boys had used the room as an upstairs playroom while we were expecting Supi. Their toys were now shoved back under their beds, and Jamie's old cot brought out of the attic.

I'd also made cot bumpers, and a duvet cover, out of the balloon material. I'd bought a new mattress because I'd read something in the papers about cot death and old mattresses – and I didn't want to take a risk. I deliberately bought one made with cotton fabric on both sides, because the article had said there was something suspect about PVC. I went to John Lewis in Oxford Street, because ours was a particularly big cot and it wasn't easy to find the right size mattress in the ordinary high-street baby shops.

I bought new cot bedding, and a new sheepskin for Supi to lie on. I'd always been quite a fan of sheepskins for babies – since our first nanny, Debbie, had suggested we buy one for Oliver, to help him through his colicky nights. She said that they had used them at Great Ormond Street for babies who needed the extra feeling of security and comfort.

It was a trend which had started in New Zealand and Australia. Some say it was a cynical move by the sheepskin industry, to improve sales. But anyway, the belief grew that babies liked the feel of sheepskin, and thrived when sleeping on them. You couldn't go anywhere in Sydney without seeing a baby on one – in a pram or buggy. Even when the sun was at its hottest. Everyone said that as it was a natural skin, it breathed – so your baby couldn't get too hot. Toddlers still carried bits of sheepskin with them, as comforters.

Supi seemed to like his. In fact, he loved his room. Whenever I carried him in there, his eyes would light up and he would smile. A little teddy bear mobile, made from coloured plastic like stained glass, dangled over his changing mat. There were white bars on the window, thanks to Eric Clapton's Conor, so we could safely have a breeze. The weather was getting warmer. We were going to have a good summer.

Alex was away on holiday. It gave me a taste of what life would be like as a full-time mother of three, without the help of a nanny.

The afternoons were the busiest. The trick was to get lunch down the big boys and their school tracksuits on while Supi was still asleep. Then there was the marathon task of making it past the front door. Our problem was that, living in central London, we were restricted to residents' parking spaces, which were few and far between. It was a miracle if you could ever park near the house. Then, if you did, you were loath to lose that space, but you had no choice if you had to do the school run. Keeping control over two little boys while trying also to hold a baby car seat, complete with baby, open car doors and negotiate the horrendous straps on two more car seats, and I was ready for a nervous breakdown. And that's before I'd even made it to school. Once I'd found an equally rare parking space outside St Mark's Nursery, the whole process would have to be reversed.

Then quickly home – because 2.30 was time for Sebastian's afternoon feed. That would take at least half an hour, plus a nappy change, and then it would be time to collect the boys again at 3.15pm.

Luckily, despite the fact that St Mark's was in the middle of trendy Camden Town, most of the other mums at the school gate were surprisingly normal – and usually looked as harassed as me. One notable exception was Catherine Bailey, wife of photographer David Bailey, who was there most days to collect Paloma and Fenton, their daughter and son. Even if she was in everyday clothes and no make-up, she looked as though she had just stepped off the Milan catwalk. He, by contrast, looked almost sinister, in a greyish-black duffle coat, and he always seemed to lurk in the shadows or behind trees until the school door opened. If you didn't know his famous face, you would probably think he was a spy or a secret agent! When we all turned up for school nativity plays and sports days, snapping away at our children with our Polaroids and Instamatics – he would be there, too, a doting dad like any other. But his snaps were probably infinitely superior.

If afternoons were hectic, then bedtime was mayhem. But now that Mike was busy redecorating the main bedroom, I would park Supi in his car seat, in the middle of the bare floor – and let him talk to his father while I bathed the big boys upstairs. He loved it, watching Mike move the ladder around the room, stripping wallpaper and chatting as he went. Often the radio or TV would be on, with a newsreader's piping voice in the background – and Supi seemed to enjoy the hive of activity. His eyes would bulge with enthusiasm and he would kick his socks off as he chortled.

By the time I had put the big boys to bed, with their musical box jingling out the mind numbing dirge of Brahms's Lullaby, Mike and Supi had gone downstairs to the kitchen. I would come down the stairs to the bottom level and hear Mike chattering away to his youngest son as he applied all his culinary skills to a packet of Marks & Spencers fresh pasta, a pot of tomato and mascarpone sauce, and a green salad with hazelnut oil dressing. It was one of our favourite quickie dishes – and tasted as mouth-watering as if Mosimann had served it up himself. Now Supi, his car seat balanced carefully on the kitchen bench, would watch us as we ate, and gurgle along with the adult conversation.

He was so easy to love, such great company. And those little eyes at time seemed so wise. I had never seen Mike so relaxed with a baby. He loved all his children, I know. But he had always appeared to be one of those men who gets on best with them once they're older, can do things, and can hold meaningful conversations. Here, with Supi, he seemed to have found a mutual path of communication which belied the baby's age.

It seems so fanciful to describe it now – as if we might be accused of wishful thinking, or retrospective sentimentality. But I remember him saying, on one of those tomato and mascarpone evenings, as he nodded towards his miniature sous-chef in the bouncy chair: 'He is amazing, this one....'

I felt it, too. Not that we loved him any more than our other sons. I could never be one of those mothers who have a preference between her children. To me, that seems terribly cruel. Every child has a right to be loved individually, and loved completely. They may each be entirely different characters – but they all have endearing qualities, and it's your job as a parent to find them – and offer the love that will help them grow.

It's just that Supi felt different in a unique way. He drew you to him, like a warming light. He exuded happiness – and his laugh was infectious. Maybe it's because we had witnessed his fight for life during those days in the Skiboo. Maybe that's why his survival seemed so magical to us – and his existence so precious. It made him hard to put to bed at night. But such was his delight at the balloons in his room that I never felt guilty about leaving him there, even if he wasn't yet asleep. He had a favourite toy – a wind-up Babar musical merry-go-round. I would place it in the top corner of his cot. He would lie on his tummy, arms above his head, eyes wide, and watch the little elephants go round until he fell asleep. I would hear his breathing on the baby listener, and know that he was peaceful. And at three months, he slept right through the night, often for ten or eleven hours. No trouble at all.

Always, as prompt as the best alarm clock, he would wake at

ten to seven in the morning. Five ounces of warm milk, then a short break for a bath with mum, two more ounces, and then an hour's nap. That was his routine in the morning. I knew it well, and fitted my life around it. And while he slept, I would get the big boys up, and breakfasted.

Life as a family of five was beginning to take shape. Alex had found herself a new job, and was working with us for just a few more weeks. Right, we thought – time for a holiday.

We decided to go to Düsseldorf to visit Mike's old nanny. After the war, Mike's father – who was a soldier – had been stationed in Germany. One of the few perks for the family had been a German nanny. She was called Maria, and remained a dear family friend.

Mike drove over to Europe – and I and the children followed on by plane, with Mike's parents, who were going to stay with Maria. Maria and Mike had already met up, and they came to the airport to collect us. We left the Hollingsworths with Maria, and packed the children into the car for the drive down the autobahn to Strasbourg. We were going to stay for a few days with my younger sister and her husband.

Louise and Colin had met while they were both working at Marks & Spencers. Louise had been training as a personnel manager, and Colin as a manager. Just a year before, Colin had been offered the post of manager at the store in Strasbourg, France. They both saw it as a tremendous challenge – but it meant that my sister, whose own career was very important to her, would have to give up her job. She still missed working, but very much enjoyed the life in Strasbourg. And, indeed, it was a fascinating city – and the suburb where they lived, Mundolsheim, very pretty.

You could tell that, as a couple, they were beginning to think about having a family, too. Colin took expert charge of feeding Supi while the rest of us kept the bigger boys entertained, unpacked the car, settled ourselves in the spare bedrooms, and made tea. Louise and I stood quietly at the living-room doorway, secretly watching Colin cradling the baby.

'He's very good with him, isn't he?' I mused.

'Oh, yes...' agreed Louise. 'I think he'd really love children of his own.'

I suspect that, over the next few days, Supi revelled in his aunt and uncle trying out their child-rearing instincts. When I look back now at the video I made of that happy visit, Supi is always being held by one or the other of them. But my shots are so fast and furious. The pace of our life was quick, and my camera work as fleet. It seems I never held on to the shots for long enough. As soon as the camera has focused on Supi's little face, it's panning off again. I didn't seem to stay and savour the close-up. I didn't know how important it would be. Now it's so frustrating to watch that video. I find myself physically reaching out, to grab the image, to tell the TV to stop. I want to freeze-frame those moments, those fleeting seconds which were so short-lived, and sense them again.

It was time for a proper summer holiday. Where better to go than our old friend, Cyprus. Back to the land of Supi's conception!

Chapter 7

We were really enjoying our holiday in Cyprus. We thought we had everything – in particular three wonderful sons, less money or job worries than most people – and lots of love. That holiday revolved, as all good family holidays do, around the children's routine. Most of all, around Supi's because he was the smallest – now four months old. His feeds and naps dictated when the rest of us swam, ate and slept. I can see him now in a gloriously milky haze, either fast asleep in the shade while his big brothers played with Sticklebricks by the side of the pool or sitting up in his buggy, sunbonnet akimbo and a splodge of sunblock on his nose as he watched us eat meze in a seaside taverna.

But we did have just one business meeting to drive to – an hour up the Cyprus motorway to the capital, Nicosia. We'd be back in time for the afternoon swim. The children would hardly notice we'd gone. Alex would feed them, rock one to sleep with her foot while craftily assembling a Lego spaceship with her hands, nap them and have them changed into their swimming trunks by the time we'd returned.

But just a few minutes out of Limassol town, I was crying. When I'm in the car, the distance between me and my children is too great, and grows too fast. Mike calls it my 'blues', and wipes away the tears with comforting words and practical advice. Many fathers understand how it must feel – but they have never had the umbilical tie. Mothers don't lose it with the cutting of the cord.

I always think of my children when I'm in the car – especially if I'm being driven, and have time exclusively to think.

Ten minutes into the journey, and I'm often crying.... Always thoughts of them, at first happy, gradually becoming morbid. By the time I've reached the motorway, on my way into work – and especially if I pass the scene of a notorious crash or pile-up, the thoughts have become frightening – even more so if Mike is with me....

What if the children need us and we're miles away? What if we have a dreadful accident? Who would break the news to them? How would they cope? And I break my heart imagining them growing up without their parents. I want to be there for all that.... Many, many times I have nearly turned the car back, but never quite have. The sensible voice in my head tells me that all mothers think these thoughts – and that every parent must learn to let go.

Our appointment was with the owner of a firm which manufactures beautiful children's clothes. He was a typical Cypriot – he loved children and spoke proudly of his own. We inspected his designs and samples – we were hoping that we could start an 'Anne Diamond' range of children's outfits. Mmm. Oliver would look nice in that one, I thought. And Jamie will grow into this one. There was nothing quite right for Supi, though. I asked if I could have samples for my boys.

All the way back, I wished the miles away, aching to see the boys again – who, of course, had hardly missed us. They had new outfits to try on – except Supi who was happier anyway in just a T-shirt and a nappy. When he took his tea-time nap, I took the video camera out of its case and shot some relaxed scenes of us all drinking Coca-Cola and changing into warmer evening clothes. I fixed the mosquito net over Supi's pram, and we went for a slow walk, dodging the sprinklers which were watering the hotel's thirsty grounds.

We went to the Bunch of Grapes for Sunday lunch. High up on a mountainous ridge, overlooking the sea, is a village called Pissouri. You have to know it's there, but word of mouth is the most effective method of advertising on an island like Cyprus – and so Pissouri enjoyed a regular influx of visitors, and boasted two or three large tavernas.

The Bunch of Grapes was a particular favourite with the British forces families who were stationed nearby at the RAF base of Episcopi. It was built of stone, and so was very dark and cool inside, but its main delight was the walled courtyard, canopied with vines, which allowed a gentle, flecked light to dimple the diners below. Mike and I had come here since our first visit to Cyprus in 1980 – well before we knew that we would marry and have children.

It was also a favourite haunt of an old mate of ours, Gordon Honeycombe, the ITN newsreader, who had joined TV-am in the early days to add a much-needed air of authority. He had discovered Pissouri and the Bunch of Grapes years before – and had been so impressed that he'd written a novel about it, *The Edge of Heaven* (a perfect description of the place), about a young Cypriot boy and a British officer's wife. Practically everyone in the village had a signed copy. And most of the young men swore that they were in fact the passionate male lead.

Though the Bunch was now owned by a Dutchman, the manager was a Briton. Over the years we had come to know John quite well, and always looked forward to the annual opportunity to meet up with him again, and with his German partner, Roswitha. They were always surprised when they saw us – because for the last few years we had turned up each time with a new baby. Now they met little Supi, and toasted his health in Brandy Sours – the best on the island.

We sat at one of their larger tables, covered with the customary red and white gingham cloth, clamped down against the wind with tableclips and weighted down with baskets of bread, bowls of hummus and taramasalata and tzatziki dips with village bread – and we talked. Once the gossip was out of the way, the conversation turned again to news from the

Middle East. Being in the restaurant business, John and Roswitha were a focus for news and reports. They also had close friends in all the neighbouring countries. The hostages in Beirut were big news. Rumour and counter-rumour suggested that something was going to happen – and soon. We talked of John McCarthy, and Terry Waite. Were they still alive? Roswitha said she'd heard that McCarthy was alive, but that Terry Waite had died long ago.

And so the hours went by. The children began to tire of eating, flicking flies out of their drinks, and playing with their father's sunglasses. We decided to go back to the hotel, where they could have a swim. We said goodbye. We knew that we would probably not return this holiday. We were flying back to Britain soon. Back to Luton airport.

Roswitha kissed the children goodbye – and planted a peck on Supi's nose. We walked out through the archway, festooned with scarlet and mauve bougainvillea, and made for the car.

'Hold it!' called Alex, who was slightly ahead of the rest of us. 'Go back a bit, under the arch, and I'll take a picture of you....' And she took a quick snap. That's the only picture I have of the five of us together. And even though you cannot see Supi's face – I was holding him against my shoulder because he was getting tired and a bit crotchety – I treasure it. The next time we would get our cameras out would be for Oliver's birthday, which was in just a few days' time.

We flew back with Monarch – one of the nicest airlines I've ever travelled with – because they had it just right when it came to looking after families with small children. I've been on so many planes where the cabin staff boast that they have 'baby-changing kits' and they know how to warm up a bottle for you. What they mean is that they used to have one or two nappies, but cannot find them now. That one loo, down at the very farthest end of the cabin, has a baby changing table – but there's no room to breathe in it. And somebody must have taught them that babies like milk boiling hot.

But Monarch seemed to know their business. Maybe they did a bit of research with travelling mums and dads. And they found out that you need to feed your children before yourself, and without your own lap-table being piled high with food. That children like sausages, sandwiches, burgers and chips – otherwise they don't feel they're on holiday. And that mums need help with boisterous two-year-olds – not scathing looks and disapproving glances.

Luton airport turned out to be a much nicer place than Heathrow, too. It's funny how your perception changes once you've got little ones....

We had tons of washing when we came back – and we seemed to spend the next two days dealing with it. I went supermarket shopping for the birthday party. The invitations had gone out long ago – it was to be a teddy bears' picnic. I knew that our local Sainsbury's had most of the required goodies – teddy biscuits, chocolate teddies, even teddy crisps. We had teddy pastry cutters – and we could use them to cut sandwiches, too. I came home burdened with boxes of teddy plates, cups and jelly dishes, paper tablecloths, and teddy bunting. I'd checked out the party shop in Camden Lock. They had big foil teddy balloons which they would fill with helium on the day, and I would have to collect them in the Range Rover.

And I had friends who had hinted that they would be sending around something very special. They worked for a public relations firm and Oliver, Jamie and I had helped them launch a charity fund-raising event, sponsored by the toy firm Fisher Price. Oliver and I had visited the toy factory in Peterlee, Yorkshire. One of the PR team, a woman called Paddy, had confessed to me, in a quiet moment during our visit, that she, too, had had three children. But one, a boy, had died of cot death. At the time, I hadn't known quite what to say – and she'd apologized to me for mentioning it. She was afraid it would make me fearful.

Everything was set for a great birthday for Oliver. It was 11

July, and the weather was warm and sunny. Alex went out to buy a present which she knew Oliver would want. A big scooter, with large black tyres and alloy wheels which made it look a bit like a BMX bike. And she also bought a little red, smaller type – as an un-birthday present for Jamie.

We had to wait until the big boys were in bed that night, before trying to assemble the large scooter. Alex sat in the middle of the red carpet in the playroom, and tipped out all the bits, along with the nuts, bolts and Japanese instructions.

'Oh God!' she wailed. 'This doesn't make any sense!'

We laughed, as Mike offered to fetch his tool kit from the garden shed. I was feeding Supi his regular evening taste (it was never enough to be called a meal) of mashed banana. Then, as Alex appeared to be getting more successful, I sat on the red couch and gave Supi his evening bottle. He would usually polish off all eight ounces, and burp magnificently before bedtime.

'There!' announced Alex, triumphantly, a shiny black and chrome scooter in her hands. 'That's it. Now how can I wrap it up without it looking like a scooter?'

Supi stared at it – and started to coo contentedly. His eyes shone. He looked as thrilled as the rest of us. I bounced him gently on my knee. 'It's a scooter, Soops,' I whispered in his ear. 'Play your cards right, and you'll inherit that when you're older!'

And then I took him upstairs to bed. I remember that evening so well – because everything seemed perfect. When I carried him into his bedroom, he was snuggling into my shoulder – but I could sense his usual 'perking up' when he saw the balloons. It was quite warm, so I pulled down the top sash window about eight inches, to let in more fresh air. And then I laid Supi down, on his tummy, on the sheepskin. I wound up his Babar merry-go-round and watched him as he held his head up high and gurgled at the little revolving elephants.

He was wearing just a T-shirt (one we'd bought in Australia

with little koalas and hot air balloons) and a nappy. Should I put a shawl over him, I wondered? No, he was probably warm enough. Anyway, I would come and check on him again soon, and I could decide then.

So I said goodnight to him, and left the door ajar. He was accustomed to getting himself off to sleep, he never cried – he was what lots of mums would call a 'good baby'. At any rate, I knew he was happy in his own cot, and his own room.

I went into the other boys' room. They were sound asleep, too. Then I returned downstairs, where I switched on the baby listener. I heard the last strains of the merry-go-round jingle, and then could quite clearly hear Supi's gentle breathing.

I checked them all a couple more times that night, before Mike and I went to bed ourselves at about 11pm. I took the baby listener with me and plugged it in by my bedside, where I also had a bottle warmer, with which to warm Supi's morning feed.

I was adjusting the volume control on the listener. Downstairs among the bustle of the kitchen, it was turned up high. But in the bedroom, I needed to reduce the volume, so that Supi's movements could be heard without the hum of the receiver keeping us awake.

'He's breathing a bit heavily tonight,' Mike remarked. I listened more closely. Yes, he did sound a little more snorty than usual, but nothing alarming. Maybe he was brewing another cold.

Chapter 8

It was a lovely, warm, bright summer morning. I looked at my clock. Ten to seven. Supi would be waking soon. Mike had been downstairs making an early morning cup of tea. He handed mine to me, and also a cold bottle of baby's milk from the fridge. I popped it into the bottle warmer, and switched it on.

'It's a wonderful day,' I said, delighted that the weather should smile on our teddy bears' picnic. Discarded sandwiches and sausages on sticks might be acceptable when squashed into the lawn. In the carpet, they're a nightmare. I dreaded the thought of having to do the party indoors, as there were about thirty small children and as many adults. Maybe we'd be lucky.

'Don't be so sure,' warned Mike. 'It looks almost stormy. It could rain. I wonder if we should think about hiring a marquee? There's bound to be someone who'll hire one out at short notice....'

Ours was a London garden – I'd never thought of it as big enough to take a marquee.

'How small do they come?' I asked.

'No idea,' said Mike. 'I'll go outside and pace it out...Ollie up yet?'

We both pulled on our clothes and headed upstairs – straight for the big boys' bedroom, where I could hear them talking excitedly. Oliver beamed as we all burst in and sang 'Happy Birthday to You'.

'Your presents are downstairs,' I told him. 'So hurry up and get dressed....'

I went to check Supi. I was a bit surprised he hadn't woken yet. The bustle and banter behind me were all happiness as I opened the door to the balloon room. I could see Supi fast asleep in his cot, his left arm dangling out through the cot bars, his face away from me and the top of his head jammed against the cot side. He had wriggled his way off the sheepskin, towards the top left hand corner of the mattress. He often did nowadays. He was trying to crawl.

Maybe I'll leave him for a few more minutes, I thought. Then I can have a quick bath on my own. I'll just check he's OK....

I walked over to him and lightly touched the dangling arm. It was cold. But then, arms which dangle out of cots, over the sides of beds, or out from under duvets, are often a bit cold. I leaned forward and touched his other arm. It was cold, too. Ice cold. I lifted his little hand – and my heart stopped.

His whole body lifted up with it. His head, shoulders, chest – everything. He was stiff. Like a little marble statue of a baby lying in a bed. He was stone cold. I rested his hand back down on the sheet, and backed away, drawing breath as I stepped.

I could hear the other children coming into the room, behind me. I backed up to the doorway, and turned to Alex. 'The baby's dead!' I heard myself saying – and then, louder: 'The baby's dead!'

Alex stood, incredulous. The two little boys looked up at me. They didn't understand.

'Oh my God, the baby's dead,' I said again. And now I knew it must be true, because I heard myself quite distinctly saying it. I wailed : 'Where's Mike?'

'He's in the garden, I think...' Alex faltered, and then Oliver and Jamie let out piercing screams.

I ran back into Supi's room, to the window, which overlooked our back garden. I could see Mike below, pacing out the lawn for that marquee. I screamed his name, louder than I've ever screamed in my life, and pulled at the bars of the window. One bar came clean away in my hand. I rapped furiously on the window-pane – and I saw him look up, his face at first curious, changing within a split second to horror. I saw him start to run.

I turned back to the cot. I'd never seen a dead person before. But I knew death – I'd seen dead pets, long ago, in my childhood. I recognized the hopeless, despairing, numbing certainty of rigor mortis – now terribly reproduced here in my own precious son. I picked him up, and held him to my chest. The cold of his body was chilling – the back of his head, where I always put a steadying hand, felt like a ball of stone, but with a sad little dent in it, where he'd pushed it against the cot bars. I leaned his body back slightly in my arms, so that I could look at his face. It was cruelly squashed, where his face had rested on his cheek. And it was white, dead white, except for purple blotches, where the blood had gathered.

My Supi, my little boy. I hugged him tighter. My little Supi, dead....I sank into the white wicker nursery chair by the bottom of the cot. I couldn't believe it, and I felt somehow removed from reality. It felt as though I was in a film. It's at moments like this in movies, or in books, that the character faints or collapses in shock. But it doesn't happen like that in real life. You just go on, reeling at the gathering pain and growing realization.

I heard Mike bound up the stairs. Outside, on the landing, I heard a breathless: 'What's happened?' and Alex replying, still in shock, 'The baby's dead.' And the boys still screaming, whimpering and sobbing.

Mike ran in, panting. I looked up at him. I was still holding Supi close, but his little arms, so stiff, did not return my embrace. Mike later said that the sight which met his eyes, of me absurdly rocking this little statue, with those arms sticking out on each side, is one he'll never forget.

'He's dead,' I cried. 'Oh, Mike, he's dead....' And then the tears came, in final recognition of the truth.

Mike's face still registered shock. 'Can we...? Is there nothing we can do...?'

'No,' I wailed. 'He's dead, Mike...he's been dead for a long time.'

I don't know how long we just clung to each other, with our dead child between us, before Mike said he must call the police. I heard him tell Alex to take Oliver and Jamie downstairs, and try to give them breakfast. I just clasped Supi tighter – and the cold was burning into my chest. I stroked the fine down on his head – he was losing his new-born dark hair and growing into a blond – but the head beneath it was frigid, although the flesh still soft.

And the feeling of being in a film continued. Everything went into slow motion – things happened around me in a blurry haze. And I could almost see myself and my child, confused and helpless. Mike appeared again and again, constantly checking on me whilst trying to organize the boys, Alex, and call the police, the doctor, and my friend Shirley.

He hadn't spoken to Shirley for about two years. Long ago, they had got along extremely well, but after a terrible argument Mike had decided he didn't want anything to do with her. It had been very painful for me, since she and I were so close. So we met away from Mike, and often during the day when he was at work. Now, on this dreadful morning, one of his first instincts was to call her. But he didn't know her phone number – and the only one he had in his Filofax was out of date. So was the number in our family phone book. Mike was distraught – he knew he must find her. I think he was afraid that I might go to pieces.

He phoned the police, who said an officer would be around straight away. And then he phoned Peter, our private GP, who had become a friend. His wife, Gilly, answered the phone. Peter had already set off for the practice. But, ever the professional doctor's wife, she wasted no time on tears and sympathy. 'I'll get him to call you straight away,' she promised. And within two minutes, he was ringing from his car.

It was a call Peter must have dreaded returning. He had been so badly affected by the cot death which had happened to him just two years before. Being a loving father of four children himself, he had told me once that he could imagine nothing worse than cot death.

'You know there's nothing I can do,' he warned Mike.

'Yes, but please – come for Anne's sake...' Mike pleaded with him.

And then, just as Mike put the phone down, it rang again. It was Shirley, slightly nonplussed to have got Mike, and a bit embarrassed. 'Oh, er...hello, Mike,' she stammered. 'Can I speak to Anne, please? I just wanted to wish Oliver a happy birthday....'

Nothing could have prepared her for Mike's distressed response. 'Shirley, Shirley – thank God you've rung! Please come, please come round. Shirley, our baby's dead!' She blurted out the only remark that was needed: 'Mike, I'll be there in half an hour!' She had a taxi waiting outside her front door. She had been going to a meeting, and wanted to speak to Oliver before she left – but now she was on her way to help us. And we needed her.

The doorbell rang. It was a policeman. He asked to go straight upstairs. Mike brought him into Supi's bedroom. I was still sitting in the little white chair, cradling our baby. The young policeman stood in the doorway for a second, taking in the scene. Then he removed his helmet, and I could see that his eyes were brimming with tears. He held out a hand to me.

'I'm so sorry,' he started – and then took his hand back, to wipe a tear from his cheek. 'I'm so terribly sorry. You see, the same thing happened to me, too....' And then tears overcame him.

This time, I held out a comforting hand to him. I didn't know what to say, and nor did he. His name was Ken Wake and fate had cruelly sent him to attend to us, not long after he had endured the agony of his own child's cot death. Mike stood back, almost unable to take this all in, and then he put an arm around the policeman's shoulders.

Later, when he had gone back downstairs, Shirley came in, hesitant at first, and then rushing to me with her arms outstretched.

I had put Supi back in his cot. I longed to lie him on his back, so that I could see him in a more natural position. But it only emphasized his terrible stiffness. And I couldn't bear his little squashed face – it was just too awful to look at. So I put him back down in the only way I could – in the same position in which he had died.

Our doctor, Peter Wheeler, came. He stood quietly at one side of the room, leaning awkwardly against the changing table. He muttered something again about babies forgetting to breathe – and asked if I wanted sleeping pills. I said no. I felt a strange mixture of pity for him, and impatience at his helplessness. For the first time I realized that doctors were not the gods I'd always assumed them to be. They do not always have the answers. And, faced with a situation for which they're untrained – death – they are as ineffective as the next person.

Mike's sister, Sue, came to sit with me. We both sat on the floor near the cot. I was stroking Supi's hand. I wanted so badly to hold him – but it was such awful agony when I did.

'I know it seems stupid,' I confided in Sue, 'but I want to put socks on him – his feet look so cold.' His feet and hands were purple. It looked ghastly on such a helpless little baby. My instinct was so strongly telling me to wrap him up, and make him warm.

'It's not stupid,' said Sue. 'If you want to put his socks on, then do.'

I went to the drawer where I kept his tiny, beautiful clothes. Together Sue and I silently pulled the little white socks on to his feet. Still, he looked so cold. So I took a white shawl – the one I'd wrapped him in when he left Skiboo – and draped it around his body. Now he looked comfortable and warm. Sue and I sat back on the floor – and just cried.

There was another knock on the bedroom door. Mike came in and introduced another policeman, a plain clothes detective inspector. He was kindly, offered his sympathy, and looked around the room. 'Was it this warm in here overnight?' he asked.

I suppose it was quite warm. The sun was shining, though not directly into the room, since it was south-facing, and didn't get direct sunlight until afternoon.

'The window has been open all night,' I murmured. Only later did I think that he must have seen Supi, now wrapped up in a shawl, and may have assumed that he had been dressed like that all night, too. I could clear up any confusions later, when I presumed I would be asked lots of questions.

Mike came back to me, and persuaded me to leave Supi for a short while and come downstairs. I grabbed his arm: 'Could we...? Is it possible...? Could we donate any of Supi's organs?'

It was something I'd always felt strongly about. Now I remembered an interview which Esther Rantzen had done on *That's Life*, with a woman who had lost her son in an accident. He was about ten years old, and he'd fallen off a wall. Just a distance of about eight feet – but he had been killed. She said the decision to donate all his useful organs had helped her through her grief – since she felt that part of him had lived on, had benefited other children. And it helped make some meaning of his death. Now I wondered if, somehow, Supi could help other little babies like him. Maybe he could help a blind child to see. Or his little heart could save another baby's life. I thought of our tense days in special care – and how I would have wanted such help, if we'd been told that only a transplant could save Supi's life.

I was worried that my suggestion might offend Mike – but he was pleased I'd broached the subject. 'I'll ask...' and he went off to find the policemen. Minutes later, he came back, shaking his head. 'It's too late for his organs to be used – and anyway, they won't allow you to donate if there has to be a post-mortem. And they are going to have to do one, I'm afraid.'

I would have loved Supi to have had the chance to help another baby. Now, as well as having his life snatched away from him, he was to be denied that, too. It seemed even more cruel.

I wanted a bath. Still with the feeling of being in a movie, somehow distanced from reality, I went to the main bedroom, and had a bath and washed my hair. Shirley stayed with me, her face a tortured blend of her own grief, and concern for me. It was only when I found myself drying my hair with the hair-drier, that I suddenly felt revolted by myself, doing something so trivial and selfish when my baby had just died. I turned to my friend: 'Oh, Shirley... My baby is dead, and here I am drying my hair!'

I dropped the hairdrier down on the bed where I was sitting. It was such a small, insignificant act. Yet I was shocked that I could be doing it. But it was the first awful realization that life was to go on. It seemed like a hideous insult to the sad little body in the cot upstairs.

After my bath, and when I'd changed into clean clothes, I went on downstairs to the kitchen. I noticed it the second I entered the room. The large, yellow plastic Milton sterilizer, which dominated the sink area, had gone. One of Alex's first jobs in the morning was to do the baby's bottles. She had asked Mike what she should do now – and they had agreed to put all the bottles and baby-feeding paraphernalia away. They thought the sight of it all would just upset everyone. It hurt me that it had so quickly vanished. There was a gathering crowd of relatives and friends already, making gallons of tea. I accepted a cup, and reeled at my ability to drink.

Sandra, Alex's friend, who had helped out on the day of Supi's birth, had come round. Mike had met her at the front door, and she'd fallen into his arms, saying: 'Oh, Mike – it's every mother's nightmare....' Sue was still there, Shirley, and two policemen. Soon we were joined by Mike's parents. And Mike told me that he'd phoned my parents in Bournemouth, and my mother was already on her way, on a train.

Now Mike, his face lined and strained with concentration, set to work on the phone. He had made a list of those who needed to hear the news from us first, rather than on the TV or radio. The policeman had warned that there was a reporter outside the door already, and there would be more. That reporter, a girl from the *Daily Star*, had got Mike. She asked if what she'd heard was true. Mike said yes. And then she asked the classic: 'How do you feel?' He just looked at her, and quietly and calmly shut the door. From that moment onwards, neither of us went to the door again.

My agent, and our friend, Jon Roseman, arrived to help. He said the news had been on the radio bulletins as he'd driven up from his home in Sussex. He added that there was now a large crowd of some twenty reporters and photographers in the street outside. He turned on the TV in the living-room, and switched to *Sky News*. I watched in disbelief and horror as I saw shots of Mike and me laughing and chatting at some celebrity event, and heard the newsreader's voice-over about a baby being found dead.

I wanted to go back upstairs to Supi. Mike came with me, and we took Oliver and Jamie with us. I sat down on the floor again, and the two boys stood, curious but silent.

'Supi is dead,' I said to them gently, and they nodded, meekly. But I knew neither of them really understood what 'dead' was. I needed to make them understand that Supi had not disappeared in the night. I didn't want their last awareness of him to be my screaming and panicking.

'Look.' I motioned them gently towards the cot. They could see their baby brother inside, his head turned away to the wall, his left arm extended, a shawl covering him. 'You can touch his hand. See? It's cold, very cold...and that's because there is no life in him any more.'

Oliver felt Supi's hand, and then Jamie followed. They both looked serious, but calm.

'And see, if you put your hand on his back, you'll feel that he's not breathing....'

They both patted him lovingly on the back. Such a lot to take in. Such complexity to absorb when you're only two and four.

'That's what happens when you're dead. You don't breathe any more, and your body goes cold. And there's no life anymore. Supi won't be with us ever again.'

Then I grasped at something I knew both of them had heard of, since we'd talked about it so much over Christmas. 'He is going to Heaven, and he'll be with baby Jesus.'

Oliver looked from the cot, up to Mike and me. 'Why are you crying?' he asked, softly.

My eyes started watering again, and I was suddenly aware of how sore they felt. 'Because it's sad, Oliver. It's so very, very sad. We love him so much, don't we?' And they both nodded. 'We love him so much. And Mummy and Daddy are sad that he cannot stay with us any more.'

I asked them if they wanted to say goodbye to him, and they both said yes. Oliver went back to where his baby brother lay motionless in the cot. He stroked Supi's hand again. 'Goodbye, Supi,' he said, almost in a whisper, as though he wanted to keep that moment private.

Jamie copied him. His touch seemed, like the toddler he was, rather more robust. I could see the white flesh of Supi's hand dimple as Jamie pressed it. 'Goodbye, Supi,' he chirruped.

I was sure that, one day, they would be glad they had said a proper farewell.

Chapter 9

'Do you want a priest?' Mike asked me.

It jolted me out of the feeling of suspended animation which was almost cushioning me from the harsh facts. But, yes, I knew that I would like someone to come and give Supi the Last Rites. We agreed that I should ring the local Catholic Church. I was brought up a Catholic – and one of the traditions which stayed with me still, and often provided great comfort in times of need, was the lighting of candles.

There was the most beautiful and bustling Catholic church in the next street. Coincidentally, its entrance was opposite the back door to our local Marks & Spencers.

Whenever I went shopping, the children and I would pop into the church on the way – and light a candle. They loved the place, its peace, and the gentle faces of the saints in the statues. Whenever we had lost something, and needed to find it, we would light a candle to St Anthony. He always came up trumps. But since Christmas, and the stories of the Nativity at school, the boys had particularly come to like the statue of the Madonna and Child. They always lit several candles to her, using all my small change to buy them.

I had never met the priest – but I knew from the church, and the way it was always busy that he must be one of the more enlightened of the Catholic flock. After all, it was an inner city church, with a large Irish and Portuguese community – and the Church often sent their best young priests to such postings.

I sat down at the dining table, with the plain-clothes DI at my side, and prepared myself to make the call. I rang the number. A brisk voice answered: 'Yes, can I help?'

'I wonder if someone can come,' I stammered. 'I live just up the road, and I come into your church quite often. You see, my baby has just died...and I wondered if...'

'What's that?' said the voice. 'You say your baby has died? Well, I'm sorry, both our priests are out.'

'Ohh,' I quavered. 'When will they be back?'

'Well, not for a while...' said the voice. 'What did you want them to do?'

'Well, I just hoped that they could come round,' I ventured. 'And maybe say the Last Rites, or something...'

'Oh, no!' said the voice, 'you can only perform the Last Rites if someone is still alive – not if they're already dead...I'll just go and ask the old priest, he's upstairs. Hold on a minute....'

The DI turned to me and asked what was going on. I relayed to him what I'd just been told. He rolled his eyes skywards, impatiently.

The voice came back, after just a few minutes. 'I've spoken to the Father upstairs,' he said. 'He says you can only perform the Last Rites if it is still alive. There's nothing we can do if it is already dead...'

From being stunned, I was catapulted into outrage. 'My baby is not an it,' I blurted into the receiver. 'He's a he!' I burst into tears, and slammed the phone down.

The DI was absolutely incensed. He banged his fist on the table. 'That just about confirms everything I've ever felt about the Church!' he spat, then put a comforting arm around my shoulders.

Once I'd calmed down, Mike suggested we have one more try for a priest. The only other church with which we had any ties was St Mark's, where Oliver and Jamie went to nursery school. Mike rang Sheema, the nursery school headmistress, to ask for the vicar's phone number. She was so shocked at the news that she couldn't hold a practical conversation. We found the vicarage number in the phone book, instead, but all we got was an answering machine. I was exasperated, although many people might consider that I had no right to be. We had never actively supported any church. Why should we deserve their help now?

'Let's not bother any more,' I said, resigning myself to the belief that the Church was really only interested in its own.

One of Shirley's best friends was a priest. He was called Peter, and we'd both known him from our teenage years, when he'd been the new curate in our home town of Malvern. Now he was the chaplain at Harrow School. We both knew he was abroad at the moment.

'But he has a friend who might help,' said Shirley, thoughtfully.

'No, don't, Shirley,' I said. 'I really don't want someone we don't know....'

I looked around, at the room full of anxious faces. It struck me that we all looked so desolate. It was one of those times when, even if you spend most of your life ignoring the Church and its doctrines, you desperately need the sort of guidance and spiritual comfort only ritual can give.

'Please...' entreated Shirley. 'I've got an idea. Let me have one last try.'

With that, she disappeared downstairs to the privacy of the kitchen phone. Five minutes later, she emerged, looking slightly more pleased. 'The other chaplain is coming,' she said. 'You will really like him, he's lovely. And he wanted to come! Harrow is only just up the road. He'll be here in about half an hour.'

We had never met James, but no sooner had he been told the news than he offered to jump in his car. In fact, he had left home in such a hurry that he'd forgotten the white bit of his dog collar. He only remembered it when he was parking the car outside our house. As he reversed into a space, he caught sight of himself in the rear-view mirror. Since he was going to have to run the gauntlet of Fleet Street massed outside our front door, he thought he should look right. So he tore off a scrap of paper from his *A-Z* road map, and fitted it into his collar. No-one would ever have suspected.

If there is a Heaven, if there is a God, then James was sent to us that morning on direct orders. He was everything we needed, and more. He strode in quietly – and if he felt awkward or distressed by his task that morning, he never showed it. Mike and I took him upstairs and showed our little boy to him, as proudly as you would show off a newborn baby to a visitor.

'We've been told that you can't do the Last Rites if he's dead,' I said to James.

'Strictly that's true,' he answered, softly. 'But I can say prayers. We could have a little service here, around his cot. Would you like that?'

We nodded, and all three of us gazed quietly down on the little sleeping figure.

'He's not there any more, is he?' I said to James. 'That's just his body. What was Supi has gone, hasn't it? I've never been so sure of anything. He's just not there any more....'

Mike and I had both thought it, earlier that morning, when we had held him so tightly between us.

'No,' sighed James. 'He's not there any more. But this was his body, in which he lived, and so it is still very, very special.'

My mother still hadn't arrived – and Mike was told that the coroner wanted to take Supi's body soon. In the back of my mind, I knew that they must take him away – so that they could start their investigation into why he had died. I knew that was important. So, reluctantly, I accepted that we would have to go ahead with James's service without my Mum. I knew she would have wanted to be there, but we could not wait any longer.

Everyone came up to his little room. Mike and the boys, Shirley, Alex, Nana and Grandad Hollingsworth, Mike's sister Sue – and we stood in a semicircle around the cot. Supi, still apparently sleeping peacefully and unaware of the fuss going on around him, became the focus of our heavy eyes. At the end, we all said the Lord's Prayer together. Then they all left Mike and me alone with him.

'He's not here, is he?' I said again to Mike. We both leaned over the side of the cot, looking down at Supi's body, and stroked the shawl on his back. The tears were running down Mike's cheeks, as he agreed.

I looked up at the window. It was still magnificently summery outside, and the sun was beginning to come around to shine directly in on us. It must be nearly midday. I looked again at the top sash, which was still open about eight inches, as I'd put it the night before.

'Then where has he gone?' I asked. 'Where is he? He couldn't just disappear... He had such life, such a spark. That can't just evaporate, can it? It must be somewhere...'

'I don't know,' Mike sobbed. He put his arms around me, and we clung tightly to each other.

Finally, he wiped his own, and then my eyes. 'Come on. They want to take his body away. You don't want to see them taking him, do you? Come downstairs and sit in the bedroom for a bit.'

We both braced ourselves to say a last goodbye to our little boy.

I leaned over and kissed his upmost cheek.

I heard him breathe... Oh, my God! I heard him breathe!

'Mike...' I gasped. *'I heard him breathe....'*

But even as I said it, I knew I was deluding myself.

'Oh, God, Mike...' I wailed. 'I thought I heard him breathe... I thought I heard him breathe.' I wanted to collapse. I wanted to die. I wanted my baby back. *I wanted my baby back.* My arms felt so empty. Where had he gone? We had been robbed of our child just as cruelly as if someone had stolen into our house in the middle of the night and murdered him.

I sat in our bedroom, shaking in disbelief, and I heard the

steps of the people from the coroner's office go up to Supi's room and then down again. I heard the front door close behind them. They had taken him to the mortuary. I lay back on the pillow, and there, by my bedside, was Supi's morning feed, still standing in the bottle warmer. It was beginning to curdle.

Mike came in. 'They took him away in a really nice little carry-cot,' he said. 'I thought you'd like to know.'

I hadn't even thought about how they would carry him away. Mike had obviously been dreading the sight of a body bag.

The second policeman, the DI, had brought a leaflet with him from the police station. It was a photocopy of a factsheet published by the Foundation for the Study of Infant Death, and it had two holes punched in it, where it had, presumably, been in a file. Now it lay on the ottoman, in the centre of the living-room. Everyone had read it. It had given them something to do – there was a dreadful feeling of being in suspended animation, and of being besieged. Now I picked it up, and read it.

'Information for Parents following the unexpected death of their baby' it read, and I drank in the matter-of-fact, sensible words. That leaflet became our bible for the next few days. Its advice, on everything from how to arrange your own funeral service, to how to deal with children's questions, became invaluable as we coped with one of the worst tragedies any parent has to face.

My mother arrived. We fell into each other's arms. I could feel the double burden of grief in her embrace. She was breaking her heart for Supi, but also for me. And she looked so terribly betrayed by what had happened. She said afterwards that you simply don't expect your grandchildren to die before you.

Jon Roseman said we should agree a statement for the press. More reporters were clamouring outside, and needed some sort of quote from us. We put together a simple confirmation of the facts. Just as Jon was about to go to the door and deliver it, I stopped him. 'I think we should put the word "beloved" in there,' I added. 'I want them to know that he was loved.'

So the statement read 'their beloved son, Sebastian...' It seemed better but so terribly final. To me, it was a gravestone word.

I turned back into the room. Oliver was wearing the policeman, Ken Wake's, helmet. He and Jamie had melted into the background so tactfully all morning. They had been quiet and watchful – and the adults around them, particularly the policemen and James, the priest, had been delving in the Lego box with them. Now Oliver's face turned up to mine, and he said, not impatiently, but quite firmly, 'Mummy, can I open my birthday presents now?'

Yes. I had forgotten. It was Oliver's birthday. He was four years old.

We hurriedly made a few sandwiches. Shirley dodged through the reporters to buy a birthday cake from Marks & Spencers, and we huddled around the ottoman to light the candles. We sang Happy Birthday, and Oliver blew out the candles with as much delight as if the day had turned out the way it had been planned. We even took pictures with the camera I'd loaded especially for scenes of children, balloons and party games. Now I look back, I cannot think how we even smiled, let alone sang and posed for pictures. But we were in a haze of disbelief.

Later Oliver put on his helmet and knee-pads – all matching presents – and went to Regent's Park with Alex, to try out her gift to him. It was the scooter, the gift I had promised Supi that he would one day inherit.

I turned to James, who saw my despair. 'Don't ask me, because I don't know why, either,' he said, anticipating my question. 'God sometimes does awfully cruel things. I don't know why he should take the life of a little baby like Supi. I am angry, too.'

We were sitting quietly in the garden. I see-sawed between

phases of crying until there were no more tears left, and periods of total immobility. Suddenly, Jon Roseman appeared, and gently but firmly put his arms around James and me, escorting us inside. 'Don't look around,' he said. 'But there's a very large, long lens trained upon you both from a building over there.'

A particularly intrepid photographer had clambered upon the roof of an overlooking building. He had the sort of lens on his camera which I'd seen at polo matches, trained upon a distant Princess Di. We shut the French windows, and drew the net curtains across, and wept in private. The warm July sun, which should have been the icing on the cake of a jolly birthday celebration, was beating instead on an empty garden.

At about five o'clock it was clearly the end of the journalists' day. The reporters left. Already, our little boy's death was yesterday's news. But we were only just beginning to live it.

Chapter 10

It felt so strange that night driving with only two child seats in the back of the car. I couldn't get over the feeling that I was abandoning my baby, leaving him behind with total strangers. I had to keep shaking off the vision of his little body on a cold slab – or the nightmarish thought of a knife cutting into him.

But on another level of my mind was the nagging need to know what had happened to him. Why had he died? Was it a 'cot death', as the TV bulletins had already decided? Or had I done something stupid – something which I hadn't realized – to cause his death? Had I missed some vital sign of illness, or disease? Had I failed to hear him choking, perhaps?

It must be my fault, I was sure of that. Babies don't die unless someone does something wicked or negligent to them. I worried all the way down the motorway to Bournemouth, where we were going to stay with my parents, as Mike drove and the boys dozed, one gnawing his muslin comforter and the other sucking his bottle.

'Oh, no...' Mike groaned, as his eyes darted between the road ahead and the rear-view mirror. We were near our destination. 'I think we're being followed....'

It was nearly midnight. A pair of headlights was pursuing us, wherever we went. Mike took a few odd turns. The headlights persisted. We were only streets away from my parents' home.

'We don't want to lead him there,' said Mike. 'Or we'll never get a moment's peace. Can't they just leave us alone? Today of all days, couldn't they just leave us alone?'

Mike stopped the car. The other one overtook us, and

motored on ahead. Maybe we were wrong. Maybe they hadn't been following us. At any rate, they'd gone now. We turned down the road to my Mum's house. There, outside my parents' driveway, was our pursuer.

'So he already knows where we're going,' sighed Mike again. He turned the car around.

'Where are we going?' chorused the children, dismayed.

'I don't know,' answered Mike, angrily. I could see that he had been strong for long enough. He was near to breaking now, weighed down with the exhaustion of the long drive, on top of the shock, grief and disbelief which was oppressing us all.

We rang my parents from the car. My mother had returned earlier by train so that she could prepare rooms. 'We can't come,' I wailed at her. 'There's a reporter parked outside your door. They'll never let us alone. They'll be crawling in through the windows.'

My mother was alarmed. She could hear that both of us were panicking. 'Where are you going to go?' she asked.

'I don't know,' I cried. 'I don't know. Anywhere. We'll find somewhere.'

My elder sister, Sue (both Mike and I have sisters called Sue) was there too, waiting for us. She grabbed the phone. She could see that someone had to take charge. They were worried about our state of mind.

'Look, you've got to come here,' she said, almost angry with us. 'Think of those two little boys. They need to be put to bed. You need to rest. You need to be with people who love you. *You come on in, now...*'

By now, I was sobbing again. The children were wailing. Mike was agonized and exhausted at the wheel. Our pursuer had clearly decided not to sit it out – he had disappeared. When we reached the front door, we almost fell in. Sue grabbed us both, with a powerful grip, and steered us towards the sitting-room. My parents scooped up the children, their toys and clothes – and we all sank into the sofas, hurt and weary. Then, as Sue poured tots of whisky, we talked into the night, my father shaking his head in sorrow and disbelief. My mother put the children to bed – and Mike and I, now almost in a dream, went in their room to kiss them goodnight.

'Mummy,' called Oliver, as the lights went out. 'Mummy...?'

'Yes?'

'Mummy...?'

'Yes, Oliver?'

'Mummy... Why... Why, when a baby dies...?'

'Ye-e-e-s?'

'Why, when a baby dies... do you phone everybody?'

Mike and I didn't exactly go to bed at all – we lay on it, hugging each other and alternating between dozing and weeping. It was the longest night – and, as dawn broke to a cold, cloudy morning, we felt raw and frail. It was our first day without Supi – we had already made it to Day One, and our sheer survival felt like a betrayal of the little boy we loved. Oliver and Jamie were still asleep. I hadn't even thought to be afraid for them. Though the news bulletins had mentioned 'cot death' in their reports, I hadn't properly grasped the concept.

I sat in the dining-room with my mother, drinking tea, and staring out of the window at the drizzling rain outside. Mike said he was going out.

'Don't worry if I'm gone for a while, I just want to walk,' he said.

I sat like a zombie at my mother's dining table, and as I poured my second mug of tea, I realized that life was going on – even though I didn't want it to. Every sip felt like a disloyalty to Supi. As his mother, how could I go on living without him? How could I nourish myself, knowing that he was dead? How could I attend to the stupid trivia of life, like getting dressed, or eating food, when he had gone? The toast cloyed in my mouth, yet I still ate it. I went back to the bedroom, washed and dressed – and then got the children up, too.

They were overtired and anxious. But Oliver had new toys – especially the scooter – and Jamie had un-birthday presents to play with. Sue had suggested they spend the day at her house, with her husband, Dave, and her two sons. Adam and Stuart were teenagers, and absolute heroes to mine.

The morning newspapers clattered through the letterbox. My parents always had the *Daily Telegraph* and the *Daily Mail* delivered. Dad picked them off the floor. I don't think any of us were prepared for the shock of those front pages – particularly the size of the tabloid headline. 'ANNE DIAMOND BABY TRAGEDY,' it screamed.

'They say it was cot death,' read Dad. 'But how could they know? How could they possibly know?'

'What is cot death?' asked Mum. 'We didn't have it in my day... or at least I never heard of it. Why do they talk about it so much nowadays?'

The doorbell rang. I watched as my mother opened it. There on the doorstep, his clothes soaked through, with water cascading down his face, was Mike. He was totally drained of colour. He looked like a ghost. He must have been walking in the rain for three hours.

'I'm sorry,' he said quietly, when he had changed. 'I went down to the little church where your sister got married, and I just sat in the graveyard. It's easier in the rain – people can't see that you're crying...'

All Saints' Church, West Parley, is a tiny but beautiful medieval village church, set in glorious countryside, near a river with ducks and swans. It is so old that it still has box pews which had once been owned by local wealthy families. Though we were a family of lapsed Catholics, my mother sometimes went to services there and my sister, Louise, had chosen All Saints' for her wedding. One of the reasons was undoubtedly because of its picturesque quality. But another was because its vicar, Fred Rason, was such a lovely man. He was a former businessman who had received a 'calling' and he was refreshingly open-minded about ministering for anyone, not just regular worshippers.

The following morning, a Sunday, Mike and I left the children with my parents, and drove down to All Saints', just to sit quietly inside. We thought we might stay for the morning service. When we got there, the door was open. We read on the noticeboard that the service would be in half an hour – so we sat in the pews for a while, holding hands and thinking. Then we walked in the grounds.

People were beginning to arrive. There were a lot of Sunday best suits, and plenty of large hats. As we made our way towards the main entrance I was aware that we had been recognized by several ladies, who were talking worriedly. One came over, and held my arm. 'I'm so sorry,' she said. 'About what happened to your baby. It's simply dreadful... I shall say a prayer for you today.'

And then another woman beckoned us to one side. 'Are you sure you want to go in?' she asked, her face concerned. 'Did you know that this morning's service is a baptism? Maybe you shouldn't...'

Suddenly I was aware that there were a lot of little babies going into the church, held proudly in their parents' arms. So that was why there were so many posh hats. The woman was right to warn us. We did not belong there that morning. We turned and walked away, through the procession of churchgoers, and up the path to where we had parked. At the car, our brave faces collapsed, and we hugged and wept again. A car drove past slowly. It was our pursuer from the first night. But at least he had the good grace not to stop and ask us how we felt.

We drove on and on, round and round the New Forest. Mike usually enjoys driving – and on this day it became therapeutic for us both. Several times we stopped for an hour or more, and talked. It was dusk when we found ourselves outside the vicarage. We both knew we would have to address the business of a funeral – and we had simultaneously thought of Louise's vicar, Fred. We were both worried that we might be turned away, since we were neither locals, nor churchgoers.

'Well, let's try him, and see what he says,' said Mike. And we rang the doorbell.

It seemed like ages before we heard the tread of his feet, and then the sound of the doorcatch being fumbled. Fred stood in the doorway, his kindly face bathed in warm light. I saw immediately that he had a hole in the toe of his socks.

'Yes?' he said. But we didn't have to say anything. He knew us. His face fell sad and he held out his arms wide. It was as though someone had sent us.

'Come in,' he welcomed. 'Excuse my socks, won't you?'

To us, Fred was an extremely practical man. He was compassionate, sympathetic and warm. But he did not offer us any reason for Supi's death – and we did not ask him why his God had done it. Instead, he gave us vital advice on what to do next, how to arrange a cremation (I couldn't bear the thought of Supi being buried), and he agreed to do the funeral. He sent us away with a list of things to do – from arranging transport to choosing hymns.

Chapter 11

Jon Roseman was on the phone as soon as we were back in our London home. 'The papers have all been on to me,' he said. 'They all want to know where and when the funeral is going to be. What do we tell them?'

'We tell them it's private,' said Mike, firmly.

But that didn't satisfy them. Later Jon returned, this time in some distress...

'They say if you don't tell them where the funeral is, they will make it their business to find out. And it sounded more like a threat than a promise.'

'Who is doing the threatening?'

'The *Sun*,' said Jon. 'And I think they mean it.'

We remembered that the media had almost ruined the funeral of Eric Clapton's little boy. In their frenzy to get a close-up picture, they had pushed and jostled the mourners, and trampled on other graves. We dreaded that. Mike consulted a friend who had once been a Fleet Street editor. He advised us to write personally to every editor, and plead with them to stay away, stressing that we wanted privacy. He said they would be bound to comply in the present climate. They were worried about the increasing likelihood of the government passing a privacy law.

So we wrote to every editor – and it's fair to say that every editor duly concurred. Except that, at the *Sun*, our plea was like a red rag to a raging bull. They weren't going to let that stop them. They would find a way to get what they wanted.

Mike was on the phone to the coroner's office, asking them what was going on. We were shocked to find that, though they had taken Supi's body away at the end of Friday morning, they had not performed the autopsy until Monday. I had thought they had rushed his body away, so that they could immediately perform a post-mortem and find out what had killed him. But they had left him on a cold slab all through the weekend. Surely some vital evidence of disease or illness might have disappeared by then?

This was just the start of my anger, an anger which was to stay with me through the busy months ahead. Why had no-one come to inspect his bedding, his cot, his bedroom? Why hadn't we been asked detailed questions about his health, and his demeanour? Or the health of the rest of us? Why hadn't someone come to take temperature readings? I hadn't even been asked whether he was breast- or bottle-fed. Was no-one interested in why he died?

'We should hear from the pathologist later today,' said Mike.

By early afternoon, the pathologist rang again to confirm that it was Sudden Infant Death Syndrome – that is, that the child has died suddenly and unexpectedly of no known cause. It is a diagnosis of exclusion. It tells you what they know he didn't die from. It rules out murder, and obvious illness or disease. My old friend, Dave Edwards, the paediatrician who had helped us with Jamie, came over to our house – and told us everything he knew about cot death. 'Which is very little,' he admitted. His work was mainly with premature babies – his particular expertise did not stretch to the fortunes of the baby once it had been home for four months.

'Very little is known about cot death at all,' he said. 'There is a fair bit of research going on, but it's making slow progress. We do know that overheating may have something to do with it. And God knows whether there's anything in this theory about cot mattresses.'

I made a mental check on those points. Yes, it had been a hot night, but Supi had been wearing only a T-shirt and a nappy – and his bedroom window was open. It was hardly what you'd call too hot. And yes, I'd bought a brand new mattress. So what could have caused Supi to die? What about this theory that babies simply forget to breathe?

'I don't think it's that simplistic,' said Dave. 'But I'm sorry. I feel useless to you. I don't know why he died. I just don't know.'

Friends came to visit. Neighbours brought notes and posies of flowers. My sister Louise came over from France. At one point, we had so many people – all good friends – in the house, that several of the men got together and went out to buy a Chinese take-away meal. We sat in a group in the playroom, eating with chopsticks from the foil cartons. Before long, someone said something funny and we all laughed. Then, a string of jokes, some of them quite grim. The doorbell rang. Tony, the PR adviser, and Jason – whom I'd worked with at TV-am – came in. I remember the look of shock on their faces. They had come to pay their deepest respects to a family who had just lost their son. And they were greeted with hoots of laughter and the clattering of chopsticks. I felt instantly ashamed – and then realized that we were all too tired, too exhausted, too cried-out to care. And that in the midst of grief, there truly is plenty of laughter, albeit slightly hysterical.

On Day Four, something happened which was to trigger my impatience with the medical world, and its apparent conspiracy of complacency. It was the day when I thought we were all going to die. Mike's parents had come over, and we were playing with the children in the garden. Mike had started to build a fence at one end of the lawn. It was a job he'd been meaning to do for years. I sat in the shade.

Jamie trotted over to me, his face pale.

'Mummy, I feel sick.'

I sat him on my knee and felt his forehead. He was very hot. Suddenly, he vomited all over the grass. He fell back into my arms, and went limp.

'Mike!' I screamed. 'There's something wrong with Jamie!'

We were tending to Jamie when Oliver, in a ghastly copy of his brother, did the same thing – vomited, and almost fainted in a heap on the lawn.

I could feel my heart thumping with panic. 'Oh, my God. We've all got some terrible disease. Whatever killed Supi is going to kill them, too. We're all going to die...'

I raced for the phone, and called Dave Edwards (our paediatrician friend). Luckily his hospital was near – and he was with us quickly. I was still shaking with fear when he summed up.

'Look, I've given them both a thorough examination,' he said, slowly and firmly. He knew now that he was dealing with two very frightened people. 'They are not going to die, all right?' he paused, and clearly saw in our faces the need to say it again. 'They are not going to die. What they've got is ordinary, plain, straight-forward chicken-pox. A bit of Calpol to keep their temperatures down, and they'll be as right as rain in a few days – and then you'll just have the spots to contend with...'

By now, that was not enough for me. I wanted to know more. What exactly was chicken-pox? How did it spread? What did it do to you? And what could it do to a tiny baby, if a tiny baby caught it?

'Now, don't go getting the idea that chicken-pox is the cause of cot death,' said Dave, almost laughingly. 'It is not. Chicken-pox is a virus – and cot death isn't.'

But could a virus play a part in cot death? Already the germ of impatience was beginning to grow inside me. Why did everything the doctors say beg another question – which they were almost reluctant to answer or investigate?

If he'd wanted to get away quickly, I'm afraid Dave didn't that afternoon. He stayed several hours, and ended up on the floor, drawing on scraps of paper diagrams of viruses, hearts, lungs and blood circulatory systems.

When he'd gone, I turned to Mike. 'Shall we ring up the pathologist tomorrow, first thing?'

Mike nodded. 'And ask if there was any trace of chicken-pox in Supi's body? Absolutely!'

While our old friend and GP, Peter Wheeler, had found it hard to cope with the tragedy, our NHS doctor came around several times, to check up on us. This time, she came to see how the boys were progressing with the chicken-pox. Sure enough, the spots were now coming through in an unsightly and very sore rash. I told her that we'd been speaking to the pathologist, and asked him to look for evidence of chicken-pox in the baby.

I had expected her to be supportive. Instead she seemed angry with me. 'What are you doing talking to the pathologist direct?' she railed. 'You'll just upset yourself. You really mustn't do that. It's not good for either of you to go probing about in such matters. You're just torturing yourselves.'

I couldn't believe my ears. It was our child who had died. And I wanted to find out why. In my business, journalism, there was only one way to find the truth quickly – and that was to speak directly to the people concerned. Why shouldn't we speak to the pathologist?

'Don't you think it might be important?' I asked her.

'Chicken-pox has got nothing to do with cot death,' she said. 'And, anyway, all traces of virus will have disappeared by now. That will have gone some six or seven hours after death.'

I was stunned. How could a medical mind be so closed? And why had they left Supi's autopsy until three days after his death, and until vital evidence, like viruses, were untraceable?

Mike rang the pathologist again. He was told that our NHS doctor had been in touch, and they now thought it unwise to speak directly to us. We didn't persist. What was the point? They had ruled out infanticide, obvious disease or illness. That was their job done. There was no 'protocol' for them to search any further. Verdict – Sudden Infant Death Syndrome. In other words, we don't know what killed your baby. As long as we know it wasn't murder or negligence, that's all right by us. SIDS effectively stands for Hard Luck This Time. Cheer Up And Have Another One. It is, quite literally, an excuse for a verdict.

Nowhere, it seemed to us, was there a doctor who was in the least bit curious, let alone caring about what had happened to our baby. And there was another thing: it had said in one of the newspaper reports about us that four or five babies died from SIDS every day. Did that really mean that, on the morning our world turned upside down, the same mind-numbing tragedy had hit the hearts of four or five other families?

It was barely believable. Because that meant over twenty a week. Over 2,000 a year. Healthy, bonny babies. (Because by the very definition of cot death, it happens to lively, healthy babies.)

Two thousand? How come we had never heard about it? How come there wasn't an enormous government inquiry? How come there weren't questions asked in the House? How come it wasn't a national scandal?

How could we simply accept it? What was wrong with us all? How come so many people had patted us on the back and told us to go away and have another one? Is it because he was a baby?

If, every year in this country, 2,000 young adults were found mysteriously dead in their beds from something called Sudden Adult Death Syndrome, wouldn't there be a national emergency declared? What the hell was going on in this civilized country of ours?

With Shirley, I went down to the headquarters of the Foundation for the Study of Infant Deaths, to thank them for the wonder of their leaflet, which had been so helpful. And to ask them what had killed my baby. We met Joyce Epstein, the director, who had been in her job only about six months. With her was Dr Shireen Chantler, a scientist and secretary of the Foundation's scientific advisory committee.

They were kind and sympathetic, and offered coffee. They told me how the Foundation had been set up, after a cot death twenty-one years before. The child's mother had found that nothing was being done to investigate the cause of SIDS, and vowed to do something about it. As I sat in their lofty office, drinking their tea, it seemed to me, perhaps unfairly, that very little progress had been made in the last twenty-one years.

'The government does next to nothing about cot death,' said Joyce in her clipped Canadian accent. 'The Foundation raises millions of pounds, and funds masses of scientific projects. Progress is being made – but we're still a long way off finding the cause.'

For the first time, I was talking to someone who knew about cot death. And yet it kept nagging me how little was known. They told me that they were worried about the future. Fundraising was becoming more and more difficult. And if the Foundation ran out of money, the research projects would have to stop.

'I hope you don't mind my saying,' said Dr Chantler. 'But you're the best thing that's ever happened to cot death.'

Joyce Epstein shot her an angry look. But it was all right. I understood what she meant. She was, after all, a research doctor and not a bereaved mother.

'Tell me,' she asked quietly, as I was preparing to leave. 'Was your baby sleeping on his stomach?'

I responded immediately – lest there be any doubt he was in the safest position of all. 'Yes, all my babies have slept on their tummy,' I said. 'Why?'

'Well,' said Dr Chantler, looking concerned. 'There has been some research into sleeping position – but we don't know very much about it yet...'

We left, armed with a couple of videos and a handful of books.

'It's good to talk to someone who understands,' Shirley said.

'Yes, but they can't bring Supi back, can they?' I replied. In truth, I had found the pair of them a bit creepy. And, somehow, it had annoyed me that they were running an organization about cot death when neither of them had any personal experience of it. Their professional calm had irritated me. This was not a calm situation – it was raw, stinging torture – and I needed the solace of other mums who really did know how it felt.

Mercifully, they were already putting pen to paper.

Chapter 12

Every morning, from Day One, letters came tumbling through our letterbox. I don't know how I would have got through the day without them. We heard from friends we had almost forgotten, old colleagues in TV and radio stations all around the world, and celebrity names who offered their status to help raise funds for cot death research. But in an even greater number came the long letters from total strangers. Yet now we had more in common with them than the others, because, they, too, had lost a child to cot death. They were the people who could say 'I know how you feel' and really mean it. In their hundreds, they wrote to 'Anne Diamond, LONDON,' to tell us both that they understood the agony we were enduring, the sense of hopelessness, of betrayal, the feeling that life was no longer worth living.

But there was one particular letter I was waiting for. I almost sat by the front door willing it to come. It didn't materialize on the first day after Supi's death, nor the second, nor the third. But it came on the fourth – and I drank in its every word, trembling as I read it.

It was the letter from Clare Richards. I just knew she would write. Clare had been a producer at TV-am when I was working on *Good Morning Britain*. She was a highly intelligent, bright bubbly girl, full of drive and enthusiasm for her job. I didn't know her particularly well, but I remember the office buzz when she started to bulge, and then announced to everyone that she was pregnant. Everyone was delighted for her and her husband, Hugh.

Clare left work to have her baby, and expected to take her

full six months' maternity leave before coming back. So it was a shock to find her back at work just a couple of months later. Her beautiful, and totally healthy baby, Harriet, had died of cot death.

Clare had taken the baby to see her mum. She had laid Harriet down on her mother's bed, and the two women had left the baby sleeping peacefully while they made lunch downstairs. Twenty minutes later, when Clare went to check, she found Harriet dead. They tried everything – shaking her, mouth to mouth resuscitation, all to no avail.

The whole office was talking about it, in hushed tones. I don't think I had the courage even to go up to Clare and offer my sympathy. At that time, I didn't understand babies, let alone the agony of losing one. But when Clare later asked me to support a fund-raising event for cot death research at her home town, I gladly agreed.

Now, I knew I needed Clare's advice. And she wrote a long letter. Later I visited Clare at her home. It was good to see her again, though desperately sad. Where we had hardly known each other as colleagues, we were now united in our separate experience of grief.

Harriet had been just one month old – and a girl. Fairly unusual for cot death, Clare explained. The 'classic' cases of cot death tended to be boys, often with a history of prematurity, and the most common age was four and a half months. So Supi was a 'classic'.

Clare had only two pictures of Harriet – and they were quite distant shots of her, taken by a neighbour. Everything they had belonging to her, including their own personal pictures of her, had been burned in an accidental fire at their house.

'But that's all right, I have my memories,' said Clare. She said that she, too, had wanted to know more about cot death, to ask why Harriet had died. 'But,' she warned me, 'be careful not to become obsessed with his death. I was advised from the beginning not to make Harriet's death bigger than her life. And it's her life I now remember.'

Clare had gone on to have another child, a boy. 'I look upon him as my gift from Harriet,' she said. 'Because, if she had lived, I'm sure we would never have gone on to have him.' She now has two gifts from Harriet.

Many, many letters came from Ireland. And Mass cards. It seemed that on the Sundays immediately following Supi's death, hundreds of masses were said for him, especially throughout Ireland.

One letter was from a couple who had lost their baby daughter, Sorcha, on exactly the same day one year before. They had been suffering their own private agony, marking the first anniversary of her death, when they heard on the news that Anne Diamond, the British TV star, had lost her baby son to cot death.

And this one, from my old TV-am mate and footballing star, Jimmy Greaves, gave us quite a shock:

Dear Anne and Mike,

Our deepest sympathy to you both for what has happened.

Irene and I suffered the same fate in 1958. I can only say time heals but in the meantime our thoughts are with you,

Yours very sincerely,

Jim and Irene Greaves.

It was a fact about Jimmy Greaves that even his greatest football fans hadn't known. Their first son, little Jimmy, had died of cot death. He, too, had been a 'classic' case – a four-month-old boy.

Just a few weeks before Supi died, we had taken all three of our children to a favourite annual bash – Esther Rantzen's birthday party. Esther often held a large gathering in the rambling grounds of her country home in Hampshire. Most of the BBC and half of ITV would be there – famous faces and infamous names, together with some of the most influential producers, directors and controllers. It was always a good afternoon. So, even with a small baby and all his paraphernalia in tow, we joined in the fun. Now we received letters from many people who had been there, and who had met him:

> Dear Anne,
>
> I am Esther's cousin. And I had the pleasure of meeting you and your sons at her birthday party last month. My daughters were in the swimming pool with your boys.
>
> I was very sorry indeed to hear about the death of your baby. He gave me a lovely smile that afternoon and even made me feel broody. No doubt he gave a lot of pleasure to many people in his short life.

It was a lovely letter to receive – because it spoke of Supi's life, not just of his death. Months later, when Mike and I were at a party given by Jeffrey Archer, the millionaire novelist, I remembered a conversation I had with a prominent politician's wife. 'I was so sorry about your baby,' she said to me. 'He looked absolutely beautiful.' It mattered so much to me that she had added that last comment. I knew he was gorgeous – but now I needed to hear it from others, too.

We even got a letter from the people who used to live in our house:

> Dear Anne,
>
> As a mother of two baby boys myself, I cannot imagine how you must feel – but I feel even more appalled that such a wonderfully happy house could allow this to happen, because I lived there with my

family for sixteen wonderful years, and am deeply shocked.

With very best wishes,

Vicky Isow

Claire Rayner sent a lovely letter, and offered her unique help, should we want to talk. Jilly Cooper immediately sent us a letter of sympathy, entreating us to eat properly and take lots of Vitamin C – 'it sounds banal, but it does help because the flip side of a shock like this is utter, numbing exhaustion.'

A short note came from the Wirral. It said:

Just to say we're all thinking of you up here. Love, Mike McCartney and family.

I had met Paul's brother a few years before, and all we'd talked about then was kids.

From Cyprus, a fax from John and Roswitha at the Bunch of Grapes:

Words are nothing. They cannot express our feelings. Please understand that. We don't want to elaborate in words. But we all want to tell you 'God bless you all' and give you the strength to accept his will.

'My heart aches for you,' wrote Gay, who had been my wonderful and faithful secretary during my years at TV-am:

Only parents could begin to know the despair and sorrow you feel. Poor loveable little Supi – and poor Ollie and Jamie. How they will miss him and not understand and ask painful, heartbreaking questions.

I wish so much that I could comfort you. What a

terrible sadness for everyone.

But I know that you are both strong and devoted loving parents and you will find some way to carry on in spite of the terrible ache you feel inside.

I'm thinking about you all the time and hoping and praying that you may find a way to lessen your pain.

Many of our friends had learned the news from reporters, who'd phoned them to ask for their reaction. My old sofa-mate, presenter Mike Morris, wrote:

Sometimes words fail even a so-called communicator. I first heard about your tragedy when a man I'd never heard of phoned me at home. 'Who do you work for?' I asked. 'The *Sun*,' he said.

T'was ever thus. I gulped and said : 'Hold on a moment... I can't gather my thoughts.' For some reason one phrase crossed my brain: 'She's a fighter.' I knew the phrase was right but in my tiredness (you know all about that!) I was terrified that it was inappropriate. I still don't know the answer. I know that you're brave and I hope to God that helps.

No honeyed words of assurance will fill the vacuum or erase the vision you must have suffered. Even the comforting arm around the shoulder will make you temporarily weaker. Even time itself will not heal. It will, however, make the scar less vivid.

All I can say is that if you ever want a temporary haven or a quiet afternoon or even complete silence, please regard my home as a possibility. When you have lived through madness sometimes only a fellow madman can begin to comprehend. Please give my regards to Mike as the two of you search for strength over the next few months.

Yours, with love and admiration,

Mike Morris

I had always known he had a heart of gold, but I had never thought him quite so eloquent. I read his letter and cried. It just proved to me how close a team we all had been at the breakfast station, particularly the original few who had kept the station going in its first few turbulent months. Many of them sent wonderful letters, including Greg Dyke – the man they called the station's saviour. And delivered to our door by special messenger came a heartfelt note from Bruce Gyngell. I knew he would be hurting badly for us.

So many people sent poems, I could have compiled an anthology. Many were overtly religious – or offered philosophical explanations I was not ready for.

Anne Robbins, a TV-am viewer from Yorkshire, must have started composing as soon as she heard the news:

The crib that held your little one
Is empty now – your child has gone
And yet he's but a breath away
His love's around you every day.

He chose to spend his life with you
He knew that time was precious too.
He gave to you a lifetime's love,
Now he lives with God above.

Just be thankful for all the joy
Brought to you from this little boy.
Some never know a baby's smile
You were blest for a little while.

So dry your eyes and weep no more
Love the ones that were born before
You and the babe will never part
He lives forever in your heart.

Ed and Amanda Watkins wrote from their home in Belper in Derbyshire:

Words cannot express the feelings that we share with you. I have heard that so many times, and by now, so must you have done.

We lost our daughter, Stephanie, in May this year, although still very recent and at times, painful, we have found that we can carry on. Given time, I promise you both you will smile again, you will laugh, and you will not feel guilty. If you want to speak to somebody who is not famous, not an expert, but who is going 'through it', don't hesitate to ring or write or just turn up. Others have helped us so perhaps we can help you, just a little.

Take care and love each other.

So many people seemed to be frightened that the intensity of our grief might drive Mike and me apart. It happened to one woman, who wrote an anguished letter:

Dear Anne and Mike,

I feel compelled to write to you, firstly to say how sad and helpless I feel for you both and secondly to tell you of my experience in the hope that perhaps if you read this letter you may not suffer as much as I have.

My first child, a daughter called Amy, was born on 17 October 1980. I was twenty-seven years old, I was married to my second husband and everything seemed rosy.

We had three months with my darling Amy. Then it happened. 14 January 1981. That date will be engraved on my memory for as long as I live. Amy was fine that morning but by 4pm she was dead. I had been out in the car with her, and then I carried her carrycot indoors. Amy was sleeping peacefully and I put her into the bedroom while I wrote a letter. By about 4pm I thought I'd wake Amy for a feed. I picked her up (mumbling something about her being a little lazy-bones, as you do!) and I knew instantly. The look on her face will be with me forever. I had lost my Amy and there was nothing I could do about it.

I know you will feel grief, pain, guilt, frustration, hate and all the other negative emotions. In some ways I think the fact that Amy was our first child may have been a blessing. I was completely incapable of giving love to anyone, and my husband suffered dreadfully.

He tried to comfort me through those awful first weeks, but I felt so bad I didn't want comfort. I did not want to feel better, so I shunned his attention. I refused to let him help me.

We contemplated suicide, things got so bad. I can remember one evening, I'd been crying all day. We were just about to go to bed and I told my husband I could not face another day. I didn't want to wake up in the morning. We actually discussed ways we could do it.

I spent my days swallowed up in grief. I wouldn't speak to anyone. My friends would phone but I wouldn't answer the phone and my husband had to cope with all of that.

Thinking about it now I suppose I was pretty selfish. My husband was suffering, too, and I was probably making things worse. I shut myself away with memories of Amy and there I stayed.

Thankfully I became pregnant the next month and that pregnancy was what kept me going. I still felt the same but I had to keep going for the new baby. I desperately wanted another girl.

My relationship with my husband had deteriorated, I continued to go it alone. Of course, I never realized what I was doing at the time.

Lindsay was born in November 1981. Although at the time we were overjoyed, her birth brought new problems and pressures. As you can imagine, we watched her like a hawk. Took it in turns to watch her twenty-four hours a day.

After the three months hurdle had passed, things got a little easier, although I became pregnant again – so physically I was shattered and probably mentally, too, as I still hadn't come to terms with Amy's death.

Ten years on, I have two beautiful healthy children who are very special to me. Sadly I am divorced from my husband because the gap between us could not be overcome.

This morning, the children have gone on holiday with their father and I am very tearful.

I've made so many mistakes. Things could have been so different. I hope you will share each other's grief. Give each other the comfort you so badly need and accept it gladly. Most important of all, don't bottle anything up inside. Tell each other every thought and feeling, however bad. Cry and grieve, talk about Sebastian but don't forget your love for each other and your children. You might think it couldn't happen to you, but take it from someone who let it happen to her.

Time is the greatest healer. I remember someone saying that to me, and thinking they don't know what they're talking about. I'll never get over Amy. Never feel better. But it is true I'll never forget Amy. I love her dearly and always will. I still weep for her especially on her birthday. I fill the house with flowers and find it hard to cope that day.

Her pictures are around the house and I can now look at them and smile – something I thought I'd never be able to do.

I hope very much that this letter will bring you some kind of comfort. It will be a long, long road back to any kind of normality, but you will get there eventually – and together, I hope.

Yours sincerely,

Helen Hill

PS. Life is eternal and love is immortal
and death is only an horizon,
and an horizon is nothing
save the limit of our sight.

'Dear Anne and Mike' [wrote Vivienne Richardson from Northern Ireland]:

My heart goes out to you. I know exactly how you are feeling. David and myself have lost four children – all boys. Three just after birth, and one miscarriage at twelve weeks. Please don't forget about your other sons, they need you also – don't be afraid to cry with them. Mike will feel a bit left out because people always ask how mum is – forgetting that dad had any part at all.

I believe my sons were taken for a reason only God knows. I know we will meet them again some day –

even though I would rather have them here now. We have a six-year-old daughter, Victoria, whom we treasure. We can't have any more because my womb burst, lung collapsed and I had a clot on my heart. I ended up with my womb being removed.

I know you'll never get over this but the pain gets easier, and as someone said to me – Heaven would be a very lonely place without children!

He is being well looked after and we will meet our sons again.

I am not a Bible thumper but I do believe in God and in Heaven. I do hope your family will find peace soon, Love and God Bless...

After my abortive conversation with the voice on the phone at the local Catholic church, I was surprised but very comforted to receive a note from the priest who had been out on the morning of Supi's death:

Dear Mr and Mrs Hollingsworth,

May I just give first and foremost my deepest condolences on your tragic loss, and assure you of my prayers.

I am very sorry that neither Father Tom nor myself were here when you called. I returned only this afternoon (I am a school chaplain) and I came round and discovered a considerable number of press people camped near your door. Rather than publicly intrude on private grief, I felt that it would be better to write than to in any way add to the pain.

Please find small comfort in faith, and believe that God does not create to destroy. Your child, though taken from you, is alive and well and with Him, in whom all hope and faith is founded...

I was pleased that he'd written. And glad that he had put two and two together (because, I realized, I'd never told the voice who we were or where) and come around. Of course, by then, James had reached us. But I was sad, too, that he hadn't knocked on our door. Because we might still have needed him. Maybe even priests, as well as doctors, policemen and other officials, need more instruction on bereavement care.

One letter was a small parcel. It contained a book called *Coping with Cot Death* (Sheldon Press). In it there was a short letter from the author, Sarah Murphy:

Dear Anne and Mike,

I have hesitated about sending you a copy of my book for fear of intruding. But remembering how isolated we felt following the cot death of our three-month-old daughter Elizabeth, even though we were surrounded by friends, I've decided to risk sending it and hope that you won't feel offended.

I was so very sorry to hear about Sebastian's sudden death. I help to run our local support group in Brighton and Hove and I remember you coming to the James Bond première, Anne, to help raise funds for research into cot death.

Having tried actively to prevent such deaths, the irony of what has just happened to you is not lost upon me.

Please accept my very best wishes to you all, and I hope that my book may be of some help to you.

It was. I took the book back to bed with me that morning, and read it from cover to cover within two hours. It is the best, and most constructive, book I have ever read on the subject of cot death and bereavement. I immediately felt some small sense of recovery. As though, one day, there might be light at the end of this painfully dark tunnel. And I also felt some strange kinship with this extraordinary woman who had been through what I was going through.

Several months later I was opening a dolls' house fair in Brighton, to raise funds for research. On my way out of the hall, a slim woman came up to me in the crowd. 'I'm Sarah Murphy,' she said. I wanted to fling my arms around her. At her side was her daughter Mary, almost a teenager – the twin sister of the baby who had died. The emotion of meeting her was almost too much to bear, in front of such a crowd and with my best 'personal appearance' suit on.

Sarah's book is a must for anyone who has lost a child. I regularly lend my copy to people who are bereaved, and not just by cot death. She, too, wrote a poem shortly after Elizabeth's death:

Elizabeth

I thought I could swim but I find I can barely tread water.
I relive that morning – no warning, so well and so real:
I bathed you and dressed you and fed you, no danger in daytime –
The thought of you gnaws at a rawness that time does not heal.

At lunchtime, your pram in the sunshine, the radio talking.
I went out to check you and saw you were sleeping, content.
The phone went – a friend: could she visit? I hastily tidied,
She came and we chattered and frittered the half-hour we spent.

The binmen came, clattering lids, and I went out to check you –
Dead . . . you were dead . . . you were dead, oh dear God, you were dead.
How could our cord have been cut with no slice of the knifeblade?

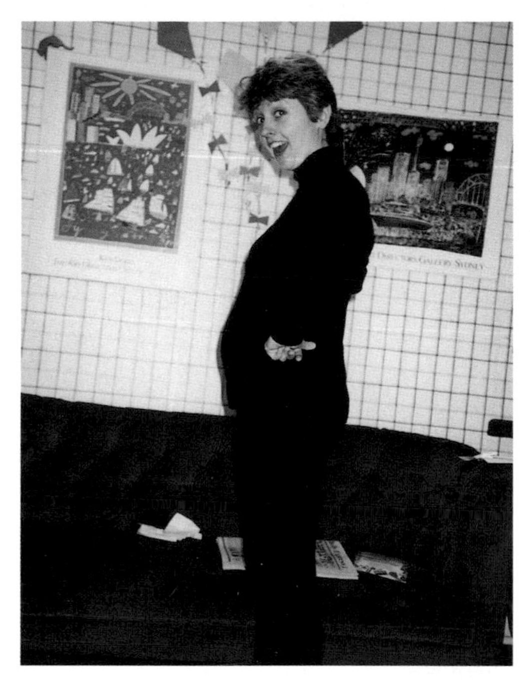

Me seven months pregnant with Supi – and just before the problems of polyhydramnios set in, causing me to go into labour four weeks early.

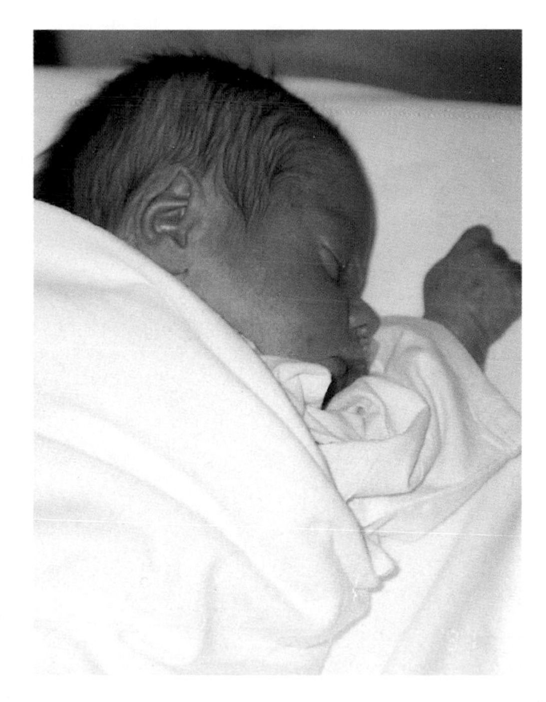

This was the shot we used on the front of Supi's birth announcement. Ironically, he is of course, happily asleep on his tummy.

Oliver and Jamie were thrilled to hold their younger brother for the very first time, as soon as he was allowed out of special care.

Some people think that cot death babies are weak little things. This picture of Supi with Oliver proves that he was a loving, living member of the family and full of character.

Mum and Sebastian at the Bunch of Grapes in Cyprus. He was beginning to get a bit tetchy, so we set off home.

Just as we were leaving the Bunch of Grapes, Alex stopped us and took this photo. It's the only shot I have of the five of us together as a family. I will always be grateful she took it, even though I didn't think to turn Sebastian round, so we could see his face.

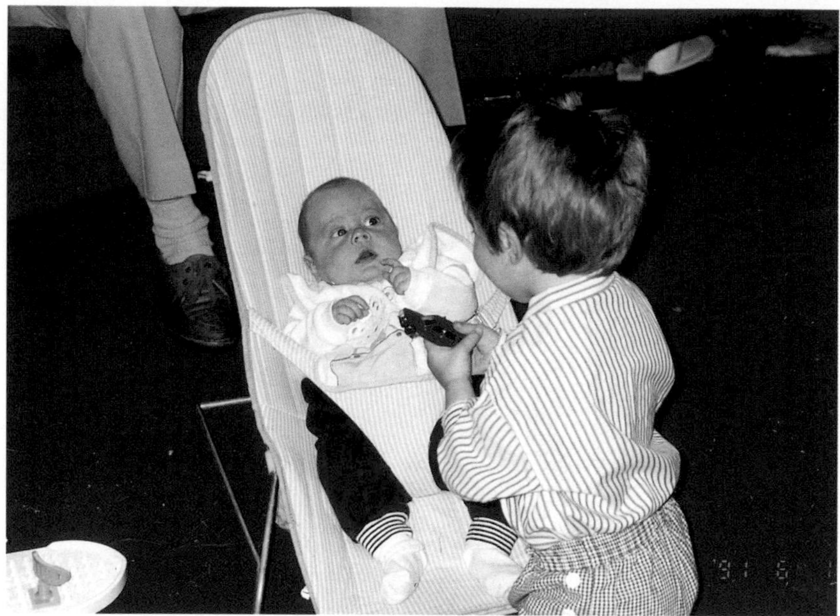

Jamie with Supi. Supi was usually the centre of attention, ‘chairing’ events from his bouncy chair in the middle of the room.

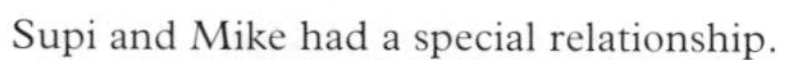

Supi and Mike had a special relationship.

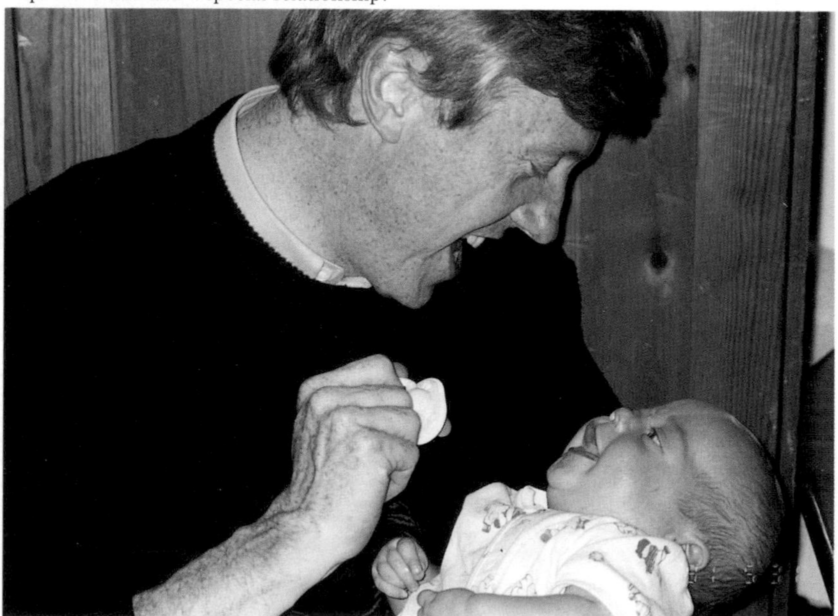

THE Sun

Friday, July 19, 1991 25p

TV star says sad farewell

OUR LITTLE LOVE

ANNE'S PLEA

The *Sun's* front page on the morning after the funeral. Contrary to some reports, we had asked every newspaper to stay away – with no exceptions. But the *Sun* still managed to get this shot.

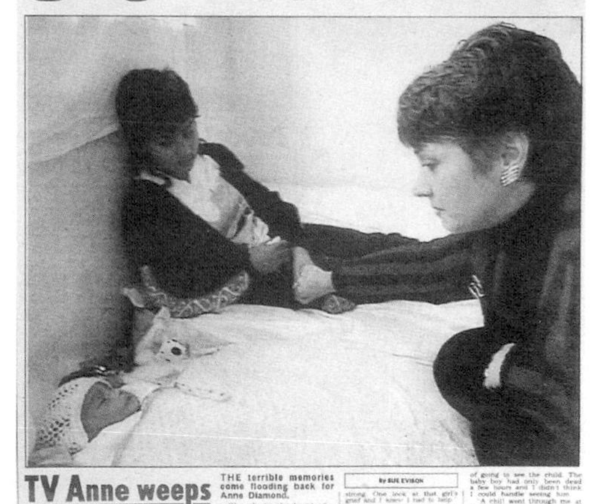

SO BRAVE

TV Anne weeps with mum over cot death baby

THE terrible memories come flooding back for Anne Diamond.

By SUE EVISON

Continued on Page Two

The morning I met another cot death mother – a 16-year-old Maori girl and her tiny dead son. This picture came from the documentary and was released to the press.

The New Zealand expedition team – Alex, Shirley, me, Oliver, Mike and Jamie. The boys felt they were part of the mission to find out what had killed their baby brother.

Mrs Virginia Bottomley, then Health Minister, and me on the day the Back to Sleep campaign was launched – 'the most successful health campaign ever'. (© *Express Newspapers*)

The 'Back to Sleep' poster. A great slogan, but the artwork was rather confusing and some people read it as 'ack to Sleep' and wondered what it meant!

The launch of the Health Education Authority campaign highlighting the dangers of smoking to babies (© *Peter Trievnor/Times Newspapers Limited*)

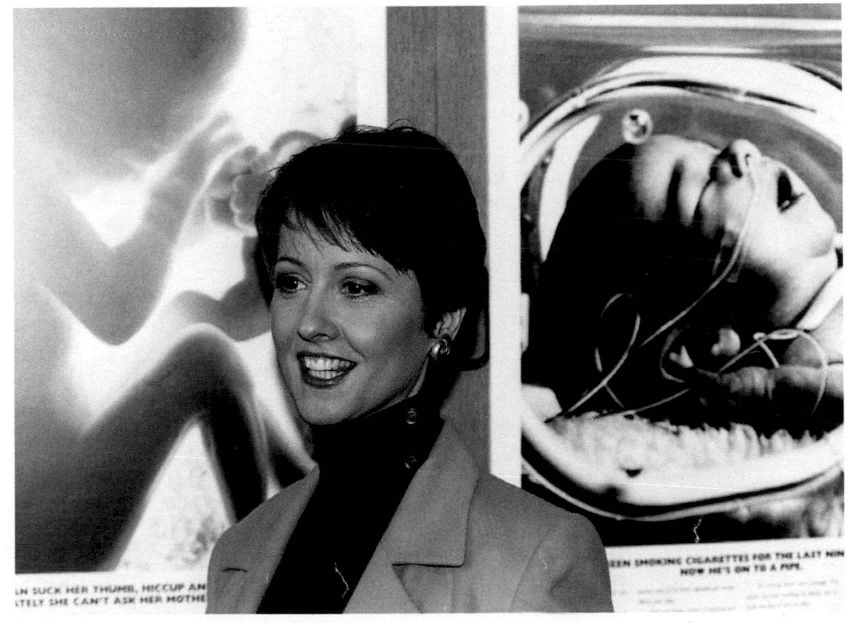

At every month of Jake's life we felt another milestone had been passed – so we celebrated each month with a birthday cake. This was his sixth!

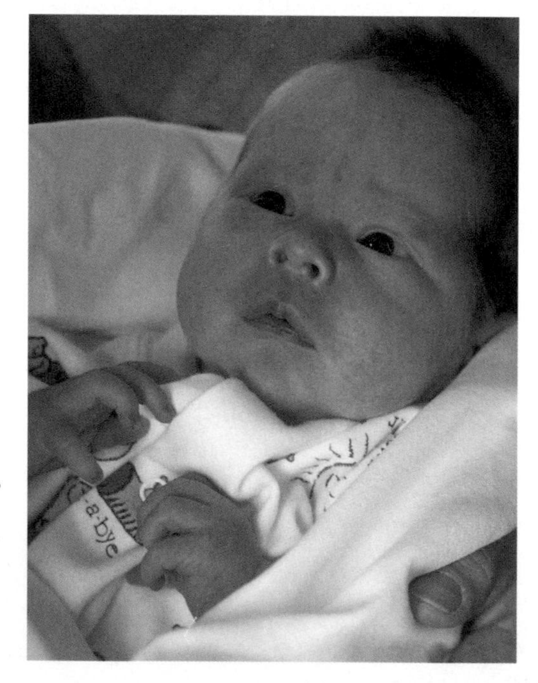

And finally, the fifth son, Conor Joe, who was born four years after Supi, almost to the day. Now, as everyone joked on the congratulations cards, we have our five-a-side football team – though one member will always be missing.

Life doesn't end at three months when your whole life's ahead.

You died so alone yet so near and it buffets like breakers.
I should have been with you, it drags at me, tugging me down.
I'm only afloat with the rafters of friends and my family –
It's hard to stay surfaced when part of you's wanting to drown.

The binmen are clattering lids and the radio's talking.
Thursday, the day that you died, and a year has gone by.
Groundless, I'm floundering, wounded yet walking – in water
That thwarts with the not-knowing-how and the not-knowing-why.

Acceptance will come, there's so much that we can't understand.
In the grief of this world what's the measure of one baby daughter?
I still have belief, the sea's calmer; I know I'll reach land.
But I thought I could swim and I find I can barely tread water.

As Sarah's letter had made a dramatic impact upon me, so Mike was deeply moved by a letter he received from another bereaved father. He was called Anton Simon – and he told Mike how he and his wife, Tess, had lost their baby son, Harry, only a couple of months before. He described how every subsequent action, every mouthful of food, every trivial chore of everyday life now felt like a betrayal of Harry. Like us, they couldn't conceive of how life could possibly go on.

His words struck such a chord with Mike that he wrote back, and within days, Tess and Anton phoned us. We all talked on the telephone for what must have been hours, crying, comparing anxieties, worries, feelings of guilt. They sent us an extract from Charles Dickens's *The Old Curiosity Shop*. I keep it in my purse – so that it is always handy. Because if anyone understood children, and fought to turn our society into one which cared more for little ones, then it was Dickens. As a loving father, he, too, knew the pain of losing a child. He wrote this after describing the death of little Nell:

> Oh! it is hard to take to heart the lesson that such deaths will teach, but let no man reject it, for it is one that all must learn, and is a mighty, universal Truth. When Death strikes down the innocent and young, for every fragile form from which he lets the panting spirit free, a hundred virtues rise, in shapes of mercy, charity, and love, to walk the world, and bless it. Of every tear that sorrowing mortals shed on such green graves, some good is born, some gentler nature comes. In the Destroyer's steps there spring up bright creations that defy his power, and his dark path becomes a way of light to Heaven.

Tess and Anton, although we have never met them, stay close in our hearts. We still write occasionally – but they are more often in my thoughts. And Harry's name is one of the many in my heart, whenever I do something in the fight against cot death. Or when I light a candle.

A friend once told me that he didn't know what he felt about religion – but he was sure of one thing: 'If there is a Heaven – then to a child it must be some sort of giant Disneyland. And if that is so, then Sebastian is already on the rides!' I like that. And there's another thing. If Supi is there, then he is with a lot of little friends.

Chapter 13

Supi came home in a little snow-white coffin. Mike carried him upstairs to his own room and laid the casket in the cot. We both wanted him to stay there one more night, before the funeral the next day. But the sight of him, waxen-faced and doll-like, dressed in his summery Cyprus outfit, lying on his fleecy sheepskin, in a white coffin, in a white cot, served to underline the illogicality of his death. That he should be lying dead among so much softness, comfort, baby-whiteness, seemed an affront to nature.

Alex asked if she could see him. I took her into his room and lifted the top off his coffin.

'He doesn't really look like Supi,' she said quietly. And she was right. He didn't. Although the funeral parlour had been very sensitive with the make-up, his face was quite the wrong colour. And to try and hide the purple lips, they had lightly dabbed him with orangey lipstick. In a way, it helped. It emphasized to me that our child, our delightful little gurgling baby son, was not there. This was simply his body – and we had to 'do right by him'. But his spirit was no longer there.

My eyes always looked up to the sash window whenever I thought of where he had gone. Do spirits soar, as I had been taught in my Catholic teachings? Had he flown into the warm, summer night? Or had his energy been absorbed into the very fabric of the walls around us?

'A coffin in a cot,' I said to Alex, shaking my head. 'I hope you never see such a sight again.'

I did not lift him out. I was too frightened of discovering on his body, on his head, the marks of the pathologist's knife.

Besides, I had held him so long on the morning of his death, I didn't think I could again bear the unnatural feeling of a cold baby. I wanted to remember him warm with life.

We had resolved not to tell the children any more than the very simple explanation that Supi had 'gone to Heaven'. We sensed that, at just four and two years old, they would accept that for the present. We wanted them to come to the funeral service – so we had to explain the casket, which we said was a box of messages and flowers which we were sending to Supi in Heaven. We were careful not to let slip any remark that might betray the truth that Supi's body was in there. I thought that the truth would be too awful for them to comprehend, especially since we were opting for a cremation afterwards.

Planning a funeral service certainly helps concentrate the mind. It's undoubtedly a ritual designed to get you through those first few awful days when you are beyond comfort – and have not yet achieved acceptance. Should we have music? Both Mike and I wanted simplicity, and something childlike. So we chose 'The Lord's My Shepherd' and 'Jesus, Good Above All Other', a hymn I had loved since primary school.

Should we have a choir? Again, I wanted things kept simple – so my first reaction was no. But one of Mike's favourite pieces of music was the 'Nunc Dimittis' by Geoffrey Burgon which was sung at the end of the TV series, *Tinker, Tailor, Soldier, Spy.* We wondered if we should have the record played in the church. But Shirley, herself a former singer with a great many influential musical friends, thought she could do better...

'Please, *please* let me try and find a choirboy!'

I laughed. *Yes, you do laugh even though you're planning the funeral of your own son.* 'You'll never find one who can sing that. It's a pretty obscure piece of music. And it's got all sorts of difficult orchestral bits in it, too...'

'Just give me a chance,' insisted Shirley, and she hit the phones. Several hours later, she came to find us, looking very pleased with herself. 'You'll never guess who lives in Bournemouth,' she started.

We looked puzzled.

'Only the runner-up to Choirboy of the Year!' she smiled. 'I've spoken to his dad, who will accompany him, and they do know Mike's favourite 'Nunc Dimittis'. What's more, they want to know if you'd like a trumpeter, because they know one who can do it...'

Mike and I sat down at the dining-room table, and together composed a letter to Supi. We cried, and hugged, and made endless cups of tea – none of which we drank – and we worked into the small hours. This was the letter which we then placed with him:

Dearest Supi,

Today is the day of your funeral and we would like to stand up in church and say how proud we are of you. Neither of us believe we will be able to say anything out loud – so we are writing it down in order that you may at least understand how we feel.

We have to say something. Once we could have expected to sing at your birthday, to applaud at the Nativity Play, to read you bedtime stories, to help and advise, cajole and encourage ...

I thought I would be able to write it all down here, but I can't. It is still too painful to read right through. Maybe it should remain totally private, between Supi and us.

Oliver and Jamie scrawled a note and a picture for him and Alex, too, gave him a special message with a tiny, dried rose-bud, tied with a blue ribbon.

So many people said to us afterwards: 'I don't know how you did it. I wouldn't have been able to cope' but Mike and I knew that we *had* to cope. To collapse in shock, as the papers had described me doing, or to lock yourself away in grief, would have been to abandon our parental duty. Now, as much as our duty to nurture our living, healthy children, we felt a responsibility to our little dead son. He badly needed us to help him leave this world with dignity and a vital expression of love.

We also knew, as Fred the vicar had told us, that we would have to live with this day for the rest of our lives. And we should do whatever we felt was needed, so that we could look back upon this day with affection and the knowledge that we did right. So we invited our close family, and friends who had known Supi. Gay, my former secretary, came – and so did Nanny Anne Robinson, who had helped care for him in the first few weeks of his life, my colleague and great friend Nick Owen and his wife Jill – and of course, Shirley.

One morning the phone rang – Mike answered it, and then burst into tears. It was Becky, his daughter from his first marriage. He loved her very much, but she had not spoken to him for two years, after a small row, which had exposed the sensitivities of her feelings after her parents' divorce. She had, therefore, never met Supi. But she had read in the newspapers of his death – and decided to ring her dad. She sent the most beautiful posy of flowers – and later wrote her little lost brother a poem. And she and her father became close again.

Everyone gathered at my parents' bungalow before the service – so when we arrived, the assembly was complete. We put Supi in a bedroom – and those who wanted to could see him. I went in with my sisters. We sat silently around him, on the bed, and stared at his little face, his tiny fingers permanently frozen in a delicate clasp. My sister Sue had written a poem. Her hands trembling as she held the card, and her voice quivering, she read it out to him, then gently placed the card at his side.

It was time to go to the church. The police had been warned that we might have some unwelcome visitors from Fleet Street, but when we arrived there was no sign of anyone. We sighed with relief. Our letters to the editors must have worked. Mike carried the coffin in, past the baptismal font, and down the aisle, past our friends and family in the box pews. He laid it at the altar, among the flowers.

A blonde choirboy, aged about twelve, was sitting near by. I shot him a smile, and he smiled back. It must have been a terribly upsetting experience for him, that day. There was also a man I didn't know at all, sitting in the choir stalls. I had a suspicious mind, borne of many years of trying to anticipate Fleet Street tricks...Could he be a reporter?

Mike and I joined Shirley and Oliver in the front box pew. Alex sat with Jamie behind us. Both boys were quiet and controlled – though I think Jamie's calm was helped along by Alex and a nifty supply of Polo mints.

Through breaking voices, Shirley read 'Suffer Little Children To Come Unto Me' and Nick the poem 'Above the Bright Blue Sky' by Albert Midlane:

There's a Friend for little children
Above the bright blue sky,
A Friend who never changes,
Whose love will never die;
Our earthly friends may fail us,
And change with changing years,
This Friend is always worthy
Of that dear name he bears.

There's a home for little children
Above the bright blue sky,
Where Jesus reigns in glory,
A home of peace and joy;
No home on earth is like it,
Nor can with it compare;
And everyone is happy,
Nor could be happier there.

The choirboy stood for the 'Nunc Dimittis' – and his bright treble voice pierced the heady, almost suffocating atmosphere of overpowering sadness. And then the mystery man stood up – and blew his trumpet. Of course! He wasn't a reporter – he was the trumpeter for the 'Nunc Dimittis'! Shirley and I glanced at each other. She had done well. The music was beautiful.

As we left the church, Mike carrying the coffin and me gripping his arm, Fred whispered in our ears: 'I'm sorry – but there does seem to be a photographer outside...'

We were beyond such matters. By now, with our emotions heightened by the readings and the music, we were in another world, unaware that our grim faces were being snapped on a long lens, and that even small details, such as loading the coffin into the car, were being captured on film.

We followed Fred in his car to the crematorium. And there, as soft organ pipes played in the background, the three of us watched his little casket, crowned with our posy of country flowers, descend to the depths.

My sisters say I was white when I returned to my parents' home. We were both drained. 'Our little Supi had a trumpeter,' I repeated again and again, to anyone who'd listen. 'Our little boy had a trumpeter...'

We laid out all his flowers on the lawn. My sister Sue took flowers from each posy and bouquet to make a dried flower basket for us to keep.

'Whose flowers are those?' Mike's mother asked, pointing to one posy.

'They're from Becky,' I said. 'She's back.'

Mike's mother dabbed her eyes. 'That's Supi at work,' she said. 'He's reunited Mike with Becky.' And she glanced at the sofa, where Mike was sitting with Shirley. 'And Supi has brought them back together as well. He's done such a lot of good in his little life.'

Chapter 14

Later that same afternoon, and while we were still wondering how we could live through such pain, Jon Roseman took a phone call. It was from the *Sun.*

'They say they've got a very powerful picture from the funeral and they're going to use it on their front page,' he relayed to us. 'They're asking – will you give them permission to use it?'

Permission? Since when did the *Sun* ever ask for permission to print something about you? Our answer was blunt. 'No,' said Mike. 'We asked everyone to stay away. Tell them no, we most certainly do not give our permission.'

Jon passed the message on – but within half an hour, they had rung him again on his mobile phone. Apologetic at having to discuss the subject at all at such a time, Jon took Mike and me aside again. 'I'm so sorry to have to put you through this,' he said. 'But they insist that I give you the full facts. They say they didn't intrude on your funeral – that they were offered the pictures by a freelance photographer. They say it's a very dramatic and poignant picture of you both carrying the coffin, and they're going to use it to appeal for funds for cot death research. They say they're going to use it anyway – but they would rather do it with your permission.'

Mike snapped. He had been brave and controlled all day. Now his patience was breaking. He turned on Jon and almost shouted: 'They must be bloody worried about being seen to invade our privacy, mustn't they? Yes, I bet they would rather have our permission. That would get them neatly off the hook, wouldn't it? No – they do *not* have our permission. We asked everyone to stay away – and everyone else did. It would be completely wrong for us to sanction them just because they say they're going to do it to raise funds.'

And that's how it was left. We didn't hear from them again. But at least we had been prepared for the shock of seeing the next day's newspaper. Because our picture wasn't just on the front page. It was the front page. The headline, in huge type, read: OUR LITTLE LOVE. There were few accompanying words. Simply, and at the very foot of the page, they had printed: 'All donations to the Foundation for the Study of Infant Death, 35 Belgrave Square, London W1.'

It was indeed a very poignant picture. Outrageously intrusive, yes, but undeniably powerful. Together, Mike and I looked at it with mixed feelings. As the people involved, the parents of that child in the little white casket, we were incensed, and tormented, at the invasion of our most private moment. But as television journalists we immediately recognized the impact of a powerful image.

'I'm glad we didn't give them permission, though,' said Mike.

But it wasn't as simple as that. Within twenty-four hours we had become victims of the sniping circulation war within Fleet Street. Again, poor Jon Roseman was fielding calls, this time from an angry *Daily Mirror*, charging us with complicity. They were accusing us of doing a deal with the *Sun*. They assumed we had asked all the other newspapers to stay away, and all the time we had planned to give the *Sun* the exclusive rights to be there at the funeral.

We could barely believe it. We had hardly survived our own child's funeral than we were being accused of something so cheap and tawdry that it threatened to sully his name. We charged Jon with getting back to both newspapers. The *Daily Mirror* were told that they were seriously wrong. The *Sun* were told that they would be quickly and sensationally reported to the Press Commission if they didn't make it clear in the next day's edition that they had acted against our will, and had never received our permission to print. They acquiesced – and made the point clear. In a very small paragraph. At the bottom of a different page.

But, they were right about the impact of that picture. The publicity prompted a flood of calls to the switchboard of the Foundation in London. The Samaritans up and down the country reported that they were deluged with calls from panicking mothers. Bereaved parents were unable to get through to the helplines, which were jammed instead by parents frightened that their babies might suddenly stop breathing.

'We cannot really reassure them,' a spokeswoman told the national newspapers. 'Cot death can strike at any time and cot death babies are healthy right up to their death. There is no known cause for cot death. Parents must trust their instincts and common sense and see a doctor if they are worried. It's a pity it takes a celebrity's baby to die to raise the issue.'

One lady wrote to me when she saw the *Sun*'s front page. It brought home to me how long my grieving might take:

Dear Anne and Mike,

Just a line to say how sorry I was at the tragic death of your little boy. I saw Mike with the little white coffin in the *Sun* paper, and I just burst into tears. It brought back memories of when I carried my little Robert of nine weeks to church to be buried, only he died in his pram instead of his cot. Perfectly well when I put him down.

They do say time heals but believe me, Anne, you never forget. My Robert would have been fifty now. I always have a little weep when I go to his grave. I am nearly seventy-seven years old.

All good wishes to you and Mike and your sons.

Sincerely yours,

Betty Davies
Andover
Hants

In one way, we had to admire the appalling cheek and steely nerve of the man running the *Sun*. Its editor, Kelvin MacKenzie, was a legend in Fleet Street – though not a pleasant one. His name was spoken in soft tones, not out of any reverence, but because everyone was frightened of him.

He it was who was responsible for headlines like 'Gotcha!' when British forces sank the Argentinian ship, the *Belgrano*, during the Falklands war, or 'Freddie Starr Ate My Hamster!' He's the man who printed a picture of a skull all over his front page, claiming it belonged to the man Leslie Grantham murdered. And he's the editor who approved the victimization of Elton John, only to be forced ultimately into paying the superstar a million pounds in damages.

He boldly went, bearing a large, red and not always justified 'exclusive' banner, where other editors feared to tread. On top of that, he had, and enjoyed using, a vocabulary which would make a dockyard navvy blush.

Now, after betraying us at our most vulnerable time, he rang to ask us to a friendly breakfast meeting – to discuss setting up a fund-raising campaign for research into cot death.

The message we received from his office was short and clear: they had had an enormous public reaction to the front page. They wanted to start a *Sun* campaign. Last time they raised money, they had amassed hundreds of thousands of pounds within a very short time. And, again – the old, very effective threat: 'We will do this without you but it will be more effective if you endorse it. But, make no mistake, we will do it anyway without your help.' In legal circles they call it blackmail. In Fleet Street, it's everyday business.

We balked at the thought of being manipulated in this way. But on the other hand, we liked the idea of raising money for research. Through our letters, we were just becoming aware of the magnitude of human suffering caused by this killer known as Sudden Infant Death Syndrome. We still wanted to know what had killed our baby. And if this was the only way to push things forward ... We reluctantly agreed to meet Kelvin MacKenzie, along with one of his lieutenants, Neil Wallis.

We met at a West End hotel for breakfast – though I don't think anyone ate. We sensed that Kelvin was one of those pressmen who likes to keep a distance between himself and the people he preys upon. It's very easy to victimize, to tear a reputation to ribbons, to lambast and lampoon when you don't know the person you are destroying. But once you see the whites of their eyes and realize that they're a fellow human being, it takes a lot more courage.

We both felt that Kelvin seemed a little awkward. He got down to business quickly. 'The *Sun* doesn't do fund-raising,' he said brusquely. 'In fact, it's only ever done it once before in its entire history. But, when it does it, it does it well. And, having the biggest circulation in the country, it raises one hell of a lot of money.'

'How much?' we wanted to know.

'Well, last time it was well over half a million,' he said.

We sat back, and drank our coffee. I tried in vain to hide my shaking hand.

'Last time we did it, it was at the time that they were phasing out the halfpenny, so we appealed for everyone's halfpenny pieces. People in the East End called it the tiddler – so we called the campaign 'Save a Tiddler for a Toddler – and it worked. Instead of giving them in at the bank, they sent them to the *Sun*.'

He leaned forward, across the crisp damask tablecloth, where his coffee spoon had dripped a large puddle of coffee. He nearly put his elbow in it. 'So we thought we could do another Tiddler campaign. It will work again, because everyone hates these little coins...'

He held up a tiny 5p coin. They were becoming well-known as a nuisance, too small for their value – and too easy to lose. 'Well, we can do the same thing all over again. This time it will be for cot death. And we want you to give it your name. Bear in mind, we'll do it without your help. But I think it would work even better if you endorsed it.'

It was almost impossible for us to refuse. We weighed up the conflicting advantages and disadvantages. Some people might not wish to support a campaign which was so closely identified with a down-market newspaper. It might attract criticism from the others, too. But there were a great many *Sun* readers – some twelve million – and they were the very sort of people who could be highly motivated by an emotional issue, particularly one concerning children. Aesthetically, we might have preferred to run a campaign in the *Daily Telegraph* or the *Sunday Times* – but it wouldn't reach as many people.

We agreed. But first there was a rather sticky matter to sort out. We were still deeply in litigation with the *Sun*, over their publication of the interview with our nanny, Debbie, four years before. No way were we just going to abandon our legal case against them. Kelvin dug his heels in, too. No way was the *Sun* going to say sorry and admit its culpability.

But, out of respect for Supi, both sides conceded that there had to be a compromise. We all agreed that the terms of settlement would be private and confidential, but that the *Sun* would pay £10,000 into the new charity, to kick it off. And that this sum would be described as a donation given jointly by the *Sun* and us.

It just shows that disputes, no matter how bitter, can be resolved if the willingness is there. On this occasion, even the hardest man in Fleet Street saw the greater objective.

Mike became engrossed in long discussions with lawyers and accountants from both sides about the setting up of the charity. In fact, it involved reviving the old 'Tiddler' charity and changing its directors, one of whom was Michael Heseltine, the Tory MP and cabinet minister. This all had to be done in consultation with the Charity Commissioners. I, meanwhile, wrote a short piece for publication in the *Sun*, to launch the appeal. It was the first time, too, that Supi's picture would be publicized. I had read so much about his death in the newspapers of the past few days – but no-one had asked for a picture of him. Now I thought it was about time I showed the world how beautiful he was.

When we handed the photos to Neil Wallis, he looked at them long and hard – and then gulped. He told us that he, too, had known the anguish of watching a child fight for life. His baby daughter had spent weeks in an incubator, and had nearly died. He looked again at the snaps of Supi in his bouncy chair, Supi with his brothers the day he was allowed out of Skiboo, Supi with Mike, enjoying a laugh, and Supi with me underneath the vines at the Bunch of Grapes. 'Christ,' he sighed at us. 'You two have got balls.'

My piece was headlined 'Why Did My Baby Die? – Anne Diamond Launches a Fund for You to Give Just a Tiddler to Save a Toddler Like Her Sebastian.' Again, it took up the whole front page. In it, I wrote:

> At ten minutes to eight on Friday morning, July 12, I found our little boy Sebastian dead in his cot. He was four months old.
>
> My family are still in deep shock. I don't think I can yet believe it. The coroner later told my husband Mike and myself that Sebastian had died from Sudden Infant Death Syndrome – or cot death.
>
> What no-one has been able to tell us – either then or now – is why he died. We keep asking why and we are told to stop torturing ourselves with the question. But surely it's the only question we should be asking – again and again, until someone finds out the answer.

We now know that four other babies in Britain died from cot death on the same day we lost Sebastian. I bet those four sets of parents are also asking 'WHY?' just like us.'

Inside – the bold strap: 'Help Us End the Evil of Cot Deaths', and those happy family snaps.

'Weeks after these pictures were taken, this happy group was torn apart when laughing little baby Sebastian died from cot death syndrome,' wrote Neil in his editorial:

> 'Four other families, all of whom probably have similar happy snaps, were devastated when exactly the same thing happened to them that day.
>
> All are victims of an appalling syndrome that kills 2,000 such lovely, laughing babies a year.
>
> It has got to be stopped. Which is why these pictures are on loan to the *Sun* from Anne and Mike's private family album.
>
> And which is why Anne and the *Sun* today launch the Diamond Cot Death Appeal with a joint £10,000 donation.
>
> Now we are asking you to match that with just one tiny 5p piece.
>
> If every one of our caring family of twelve million *Sun* readers contributed just one 5p coin, it would raise £600,000.'

Readers were asked to organize office collections, start swear boxes, do sponsored events – all for 5p coins.

> 'Is it worth it?' Neil ended.
>
> 'Does it matter? Can your little 5p coin really make any difference?
>
> Look at those pictures again. As Anne and her husband Mike promise you from the bottom of their broken hearts – the answer is yes.'

As I read the words, before they went to print (that was part of the deal), I knew that it was brash, tabloid, sensational journalism. It was written in ‘Sunspeak’. I also knew it would work. And they had promised to back up their coverage with a helpline phone number. I strongly believe that if the media creates a scare – and there was no doubt that we were airing a subject which was, however justifiably, bound to cause mass fright, then you had to address that reaction. At the very least we could provide counsellors at the end of a phone line.

The money started rolling in from that day. The paper did constant updates. One day, they held a telephone auction. Stars such as George Michael and Elton John donated items for inclusion. On that day alone, we raised £35,000.

Sebastian was beginning to make his mark. But I still had no idea of how immense and far-reaching that mark was to be.

Chapter 15

We needed to get away – so Mike, me, Shirley, and the boys went back to the hotel in the Lake District where we had spent a few glorious, yet rainy and windswept, days with Supi. It was, maybe, a sort of pilgrimage for Mike, since his childhood friend, John Chapman, lived there. I already had the love and support of my best friend, Shirley. He needed to talk, too, to a friend he'd known and trusted since schooldays. When you are bereaved, you can tolerate no pretence. You need the sort of love that is understood – because you are already vulnerable. John and his wife, Sue, sat and listened to us for hours.

They were a lovely couple, with two grown daughters, both of whom would undoubtedly leave home within a few years. John and Sue spoke of their plans to buy a house with enough land to keep horses. Sue was excited. It was something she had always wanted to do. It was the first time I had met them both, and I liked them immediately.

But in Carlisle I first experienced a feeling of loss which was to haunt me for months. Mike and I, Shirley and the two boys, were shopping in the central pedestrian precinct. We had been there just a matter of months before and I had popped into the various baby shops to buy a baby-carrier for Supi. Now, all I could see were babies in buggies. Little, laughing, gurgling babies being pushed towards me, past me, away from me. Every time I saw a pair of chubby little legs in a buggy, I scanned the baby's face to see if it was Supi. If a buggy went past before I could see the child's face, I found my eyes following it, my legs almost chasing it, until I could satisfy myself that it wasn't him. When we were driving along in the car, my eyes would fix upon every pushchair in the street. And then I would realize what I was doing, and break down.

Why was I searching for him? I knew he was dead – I'd seen his body. And yet I felt an obsessive urge, a compulsion, to just make sure he wasn't in that stroller, or in that one...I was bewildered. Was I going mad? Was I one step away from taking someone's else's baby? Was this what turned ordinary women into baby snatchers?

Yet I didn't want anyone else's baby – I only wanted mine. I wanted him so much that my arms ached. My breasts, even though we had long abandoned the breastfeeding, almost burned with the desire to feed him. I could hear his chuckle around every corner. I could see his little legs kicking their socks off in every buggy around me. And the disappointment, when I found that the face wasn't his, was driving me insane. In the middle of the busy precinct, I just stopped and tears started streaming down my cheeks. Mike, Shirley and the boys clasped themselves around me in one big human pyramid.

We must have seemed a strange sight, but no-one commented. If they recognized us, they probably understood. The tenderness of many strangers was very comforting. After we had popped into town once for some errand, a London cabbie had refused to take his fare. We hadn't even exchanged words – but he instantly recognized us. 'I couldn't take anything off you, mate, not after what you've been through,' he said to Mike. 'I've got kids, too. Put it towards your cot death fund...'

While total strangers often knew how to handle us, some friends and acquaintances would cross the street rather than meet us face to face. One old colleague from Central TV saw us coming towards him in the middle of a shop. I could see his eyes dart around for an escape route. But he couldn't avoid us. Instead he bounced up, thrust his hands into his raincoat pockets and said the first thing that came into his head – something

I knew he would rather have not said: 'Hi! Long time no see! So... how's life?' We could see that he wanted a trapdoor to open up and swallow him.

Down at the Catholic church, we were swamped with well-meaning hugs, hand-clasps and slappings on the back. 'The next one will be a girl,' so many of them said. Or: 'You've got a little angel in Heaven.' I lit my candles – but I didn't really have faith that anyone up there was watching me. The statue of the Virgin Mary, holding the infant Jesus in her arms, looked down upon me, through her vast pile of floral offerings (still with the Marks & Spencers price-tag on them). How could Christ's mother, with whom I was always told I shared a birthday, allow my son to be taken from me? Surely she knew the pain of such a loss? And yet I still prayed to her. You can erase the Catholic from your head, but never from your heart. I still felt that maybe if I prayed hard enough she could bring Supi back to me.

I prayed and prayed into the night as I lay in bed next to a sleeping Mike. Occasionally he awoke to find my face wet with tears, and me unglamorously blowing my nose to cover up. He would comfort me – but he thought I was simply mourning my son. I wasn't. I was praying so damned hard that I thought my brain would explode. If miracles can happen, then I want one now, I demanded silently of God. I'll be the first mother in the whole history of mankind who will simply refuse to accept a child's death. I won't tolerate what fate has doled out to me – I simply won't have it.

I prayed and prayed. I'll test them, I thought. If God and his Son can work miracles, then let's see them do it. But in the morning, nothing had changed.

Following our visit to John and Sue Chapman, we travelled back down the motorway from Carlisle to London on the day that John McCarthy, British hostage in Beirut, was released. It was wonderful news. But I kept thinking – Jill Morrell, the girlfriend who fought so hard for his release, has had the answer to her prayers. I'll never get mine. And I felt ashamed for begrudging her such joy.

Two days after we'd returned home, and while we were having a quiet Sunday morning with Oliver and Jamie, Mike received a phone call from Sue in Carlisle. It was shocking news. John was dead. He'd been walking the dog early that morning, and had simply dropped down dead on the pavement. It was a massive heart attack. And so, within days of organizing his own son's funeral, Mike found himself attending the funeral of his best friend. Hundreds of people turned out for the service. John was a very popular man, a church usher and a member of the local rugby club.

Sue and I rushed into each other's arms. I barely knew her, but I knew her pain. John's funeral was a large affair – a demonstration of feeling from everyone who had known him. Supi's funeral had been tiny in comparison – but the emotion as strong. It made me realize that, in human terms, the only real difference between the two people we had just lost was the size of their coffins. Because although Supi had lived just four and a half months (plus another eight months inside me) his effect on those who knew him was just as strong as if he'd lived fifty years.

Several people, notably those who didn't have children, remarked to me: 'Aren't you lucky you didn't really have time to get to know your son? He was with you such a short time.' It was an agonizingly insensitive thing to say – though clearly a great many people think it, when someone loses a baby. But what they'd never understand is that our child was with us for a whole lifetime. The moment we knew of his existence, he became part of the plot which was our family story. He was immediately built into the computer programme which mapped out the rest of our lives. At six months, he was going to sit up. At nine, to crawl. From now on, we'd need a house with an extra bedroom. And more money for school fees. Another seat on the airliner for holidays. Would he want to go to university? Would I like his girlfriends?

We hadn't just lost a baby of four and a half months. We'd lost a schoolboy, a teenager, a pimply adolescent, a college student, a young man, a father with children of his own – our grandchildren. And there was nothing in that computer programme which allowed for his sudden cancellation. I was still the mother of a four-month-old baby boy. All the maternal instincts, the inbuilt reactions, even the way I was physically (still overweight, but hardly caring), were part of a programme which had been dramatically interrupted. No wonder I was feeling wretched. And it was while I was almost drowning in a quagmire of hopelessness that Mike took a call from a woman named Linda McDougall.

'Who's she?'

'Well,' said Mike, who knew her but only vaguely. 'She's quite well-known as a film producer and documentary maker. Used to work on *The Cook Report* and such like. She's also the wife of the Labour MP Austin Mitchell. '

'What does she want?'

'Well, that's just it... she wouldn't say. Very secretive. She wants to meet for lunch. And she particularly doesn't want you there...'

He came back from the lunch strangely excited, and almost scared to tell me what he'd heard.

'She's from New Zealand,' he started.

Yes, yes, I thought. Very nice to hear about her birthright. But what did she have to say?

'Well, she really wants to tell you all about it herself. It's to do with cot death. It seems they're experts on it in New Zealand – and they might have found an answer.'

So I agreed to meet Linda, too. She had approached Mike first, because she was afraid I might be too upset to handle what she had to tell us. I have to say that this was the first and last time I have ever known Linda be sensitive to anyone's feelings, particularly mine. I met her at a small restaurant in Hammersmith, near the hospital, and opposite LBC, the capital's talk radio station, where I had been standing in for Michael Parkinson on his morning show. Mike had thought it would be a good way to gradually rehabilitate me to everyday life.

Linda was a remarkable woman, I could tell that from the moment she started to speak. She was about forty, medium build, and with a stack of blonde, short hair. She looked the part – a shrewd, hard-nosed journalist – more interested in 'the story' than the glamour of TV. She was probably the sort of producer who usually looked down with contempt upon people like me, who become 'celebrities'.

It's difficult to find words to describe Linda that won't immediately invite a writ. To say she is brusque would be a serious understatement. She would consider it her duty to truth and honour to call a spade a bloody shovel, and to expose bullshit at any cost. To say she was cold would be to deny the humanity which motivated her journalistic instinct. She was, as the Americans would say, a tough cookie, who sometimes forgot to be pleasant. Today, though, she was as gentle as a lamb. But she delivered a punch.

'My old mum regularly sends me newspapers from New Zealand, so I can keep up with home news,' she started. 'And in one of them, I read a remarkable thing...' She leaned forward, and stared me in the eyes. 'The Kiwis have been doing a huge campaign against cot death. Did you know anything at all about this?'

I shook my head, eager to hear more.

'Well, apparently they've found a way to prevent it. And they've had incredible success. It's something to do with the way babies sleep – and overheating, and smoking. But they've been telling mothers in New Zealand to do certain things – and it works.'

I had that feeling again, of my heart wanting to explode out of my chest. I could feel its beat thumping through my rib-cage. Like the morning I'd discovered Supi dead.

'What position did your baby sleep in?' she asked me

bluntly. It was the second time I'd been asked that question.

'On his tummy,' I replied. 'That's the way you're meant to do it – it's better for them.'

'No, it isn't,' said Linda, ominously. 'Apparently that's what's killing them. Or, rather,' she corrected herself, 'that is what is making them *susceptible* to cot death.'

I sat for a moment, trying to take in what she'd just said. And then came a thousand questions.

'Look, I don't know the answers to any of this,' Linda said. And then she threw her arms upwards. 'But don't you think someone should be asking those questions for all the other mums out there who don't want their baby to die like Anne Diamond's?'

I knew immediately what she meant. We journalists needed to ask what was going on. We needed to go to New Zealand and find out what they had discovered. *Was there really a cure for cot death? What was it? And why didn't we know about it in this country?*

And then, a question which seared through me like a lance: *Could I have saved Supi?*

Chapter 16

And so we found ourselves, one cold, rainy morning, 12,000 miles away from home, on a dank, miserable beach in North Island, New Zealand.

'This is one of our greatest tourist attractions,' said Linda, disappointed. 'This is Waihi beach. It's usually bristling with people surfing and barbecueing. I'm afraid I'm not going to get the shots I really wanted with this weather...'

This was the first day of filming – and Linda had even rented a beach house so that we could shelter from the sun in between takes. But it was October – and this was an example of a damp Kiwi spring day. Shirley, Alex and the boys were with me. We were only eight weeks from Supi's death, and still very raw. I couldn't leave the children behind, half way across the world. So I had brought them along. Besides, if we were going to find out what killed Supi – then it was a crusade which involved the whole family. Oliver already understood that much, and had told his friends at nursery school that he was going to find out why his baby brother had died.

Mike had commitments, and couldn't come straight away. Unbelievably, another friend of his was close to death. Alan, a highly respected TV producer and director (he directed the notorious BBC Royal *It's A Knockout!*), had cancer. Since the diagnosis at around Supi's birthday, Alan's health had rapidly deteriorated. Mike, so practical in crisis, was doing everything possible to support Alan and his girlfriend, Karen.

Many, many evenings, we had debated long and hard with Karen whether Alan should continue with traditional treatments, or try a less orthodox dietary approach. Mike had helped get them a Macmillan nurse. But now Alan was in hospital – literally on his deathbed. And it was Mike who helped the couple achieve their dearest wish – to get married.

'I can't leave Alan now,' Mike had said to me, just days before we were to fly to New Zealand. 'I don't think he has many days left. I want to be here for Karen.'

I understood. But Mike was worried about how I would cope with the fearsome Linda McDougall, without protection. We were anxious that this documentary should remain tightly controlled, as we were inevitably going to expose our grief on TV. We knew that, as well as investigating the medical angle, we would have to tell our own personal story. But the Revd Fred Rason's words rang in our ears: *What you do now, you will have to live with for the rest of your lives*. So Shirley was recruited as my bodyguard – with strict instructions to keep an eye on Linda.

But things went wrong almost immediately. As soon as we had arrived, limp as wet lettuces from the twenty-six-hour flight to Auckland, I was called to a meeting with Linda, and the co-producer, Jan Euden. 'The story has changed quite considerably from what we thought it was going to be,' they announced to me.

What was that? The hackles on the back of my neck started to rise. 'What do you mean?'

'Well,' said Jan, who had spent the last three weeks researching all the major medics on the New Zealand cot death scene, 'this is no longer about what causes cot death. It's no longer about the mechanics of death – because they still don't know that.'

But that's what I'd come all this way to discover, wasn't it?

'What they've found, is a way to reduce the risks of cot death.'

It didn't sound madly exciting to me. I wanted to know what cot death *was*. I'd read so much about it by now. There were theories that the baby stops breathing because it is in too deep a sleep. I had heard ideas that it might be due to stress – that we left our babies alone in cots for too long, almost in a state of sensory deprivation, with empty stomachs because we expected them to sleep through the night, without constant feeding. I had felt guilty about that one, though I clung to the fact that according to the pathologist's report there was still milk inside Supi's stomach when he died. So he hadn't been hungry.

What about the theory that it might be an allergy to cows' milk? Or biological washing powder? Or a reaction to electrical fields, or even ley-lines? Those were the theories I was anxious to investigate. Now Linda and Jan were going on about something called risk reduction. What on earth was that?

Over the next few days, I began to learn that this thing called 'risk reduction' was what was going to save hundreds and thousands of babies. And not just New Zealanders, but *our* babies. *British* babies. And Australian babies, and Tasmanian babies, and Dutch babies, and French babies, and Belgian babies, and Irish babies, and German babies and Canadian babies, and American babies. In fact, it was going to save the lives of babies wherever it was tried.

So we waited on windy Waihi beach for my first interviewee.

'You'll really love her,' promised Linda. 'She's Mrs Cot Death of New Zealand. There isn't anything about cot death which she doesn't know.'

Shirley Tonkin blew on to that beach like the strong force she was known to be in her country. Small – only about five feet – petite and mousy, you would never guess that this was a woman who had dedicated her life to the study of children, and whose work would have world-wide consequences. She was a paediatrician – and had become increasingly concerned over the years at the number of cot deaths she had witnessed. In fact, New Zealand had the highest cot death rate in the world, and no-one knew why.

Linda took me to one side and whispered gleefully in my

ear: 'She's also the mother of Heather Tonkin – Bonkin Tonkin, the girl who had the affair with Captain Mark Phillips!'

Up and down the beach I strolled with Shirley Tonkin, while Linda and her cameraman searched for the right shots. Mrs Tonkin had been told my history – she knew all about Supi – and she was worried for me: 'You know you shouldn't be here,' she said to me, quite sternly. 'You should be at home. Are you sure you want to do this?'

I told her about my anguish at seeing other people's babies – and how I looked for Supi in every pram.

'That's because you haven't accepted his death yet,' she said. 'You're still searching for him. '

We must have walked miles, trudging up and down that soggy beach, as the soundman recorded our conversation. I told Shirley Tonkin how I had found Supi, on his tummy, up against the bars of the cot. I mentioned the little dent on his head, where he'd pushed himself against the bars.

'That's exactly how we're finding a lot of these babies,' she said. 'So many of them have wriggled into a corner and then got themselves wedged into a position they cannot get out of.'

She looked at me again, concerned. 'Are you sure you're going to be all right doing this documentary?' she asked. 'I think you should be at home with your husband, and starting the long process of learning to live with your grief. You cannot avoid it, you know.'

I did know. But even stronger than my grief right now was a feeling of vengeance. I wanted to avenge my son's death. I wanted to kill what had killed him. Only then could I embrace the grim luxury of mourning.

We were deep in conversation, and I was warming greatly to this small woman with the big heart, when Linda came bounding up to us. 'That's great!' she said. 'Now I just want you to go down to the far end of the beach again, and walk through that rainbow...' A huge arc of coloured light had formed in the distance. It seemed to be growing out of the wet sand at the water's edge. Linda saw a shot worth having – and we duly trudged down to the rainbow's end.

When we'd finished with the visual poetry, we were cold and windswept. I needed to talk with Linda about our return tickets, which she was supposedly organizing. I had only a very short window in my diary to shoot the New Zealand footage, because I was due to do *TV Weekly* live the following week. It was imperative I get back to Britain on time, and Linda had promised to arrange the flights. But she hadn't mentioned them yet.

'Linda, I need to make sure those flights are booked.'

'Oh, for God's sake,' she sighed at me. 'How can you go on about flights at a time like this? Can't you see what we're doing here is important?'

'I just need to make sure. If I'm not back in time to do *TV Weekly*...'

This was the wrong way to tackle Linda. The notion that another programme might be as important, or even have priority over hers, was beyond her comprehension.

'*TV Weekly* is my job – I'm under contract to be there to do it,' I sighed. 'And you did say you'd arrange it...'

'Oh, my God,' she sighed again, melodramatically. ' I think you're got the wrong priorities here...You've got totally the wrong attitude to the job!'

At that, I saw red. 'Don't you dare accuse me of having the wrong priorities!' I yelled at her. The camera crew backed away, uncomfortably. They sensed a duel. 'I don't need to be told about priorities! I lost my baby just eight weeks ago – I think I know how important this all is!' And I stormed off.

Looking back, she had been tactless and I oversensitive. But then, I probably had every right to be. Alex, Shirley and the children were inside the beach house, sorting out sandwiches, biscuits and tea. They saw me run off, obviously in distress. Linda stormed in, and up to Alex.

'Does your boss usually go off the deep end at the slightest word?' she spat.

My bodyguard, Shirley, came after me.

'So help me, I cannot stand that woman,' I wailed at Shirley. 'She's had us waltzing up and down a bloody beach all day. What's she doing? Making a travel film?'

Shirley put her arm around me. 'Come on, let's go back to the hotel and we'll ring Mike.' But Mike was already on his way to us. Alan, his friend, seemed to be better, and Mike was confident enough to leave Britain. He was expected at Auckland within the next twenty-four hours.

The next day we filmed at Shirley Tonkin's office – and she showed us videos, which she'd recorded with an infra-red camera, of babies as they slept during the night. They were mostly babies of about four months, the 'classic' cot death age. They were put down to sleep on their stomachs, and during the night, while they were still deeply asleep, they wriggled and writhed their way up or down the cot. She was particularly interested in babies with breathing problems, or who had once had breathing problems because they had been premature births. They were high in the cot death statistics. Shirley reckoned that they got themselves in positions in which it would be difficult for them to continue breathing.

'Many of them get stuck in one corner of the cot,' she said. 'And, although they can effectively wriggle one way, they seem to be unable to go into reverse. So they seem to be getting themselves into a fix.'

She said it was particularly worrying where the cots had 'bumpers' or pads along the side of the cot. 'So many babies seem to bury their faces into these bumpers,' she said.

So the ones who had died from cot death – had they in fact suffocated themselves?

'It's difficult to say,' said Shirley Tonkin, shaking her head. The wall behind her was covered with snapshots of babies – many of them babies who had died. 'But one thing started to nag me, as I questioned all the parents after they'd suffered a cot death,' she went on. 'When I asked them to describe how they'd found their baby dead – it started to occur to me that they all started their terrible story using the same words...'

What were they, I asked.

'They all said... *"When I turned the baby over..."*'

Yes? What of it?

'Well – it began to strike me that *all the babies had been on their tummies*. Hardly ever did we seem to get a baby who didn't need turning over for the parents to see its face. By far and away, the babies who were dying from cot death were the babies who were on their tummies.'

Chapter 17

The next day I brushed away my growing disquiet with Linda's attitude. I was eager to get on with the job, and find out more. We were set to go to Auckland's biggest hospital and meet Ed Mitchell, a consultant paediatrician and guardian of the computer files which were processing the world's newest cot death information.

He was a friendly, bearded man. British born and married to an English woman, he had worked in New Zealand for many years, and he had headed New Zealand's cot death study, set up to find out why this little country had the highest cot death rate in the world. It was almost a national scandal. If you were a mum or dad in New Zealand, you had either had a cot death yourself, or you knew someone who had. It was that common.

'We couldn't understand why,' explained Ed. 'New Zealand has one of the best records in the world for child care – and yet we were losing more babies to Sudden Infant Death Syndrome than anyone else...We simply had to find out why. So we all got together and set up the first, and most comprehensive, cot death study in the world.'

When was this, I asked.

'Well, it started in 1988.' Right. I logged the date in my brain. That's three years ago, I thought.

Ed went on: 'It's what we call an epidemiological inquiry. Not a laboratory study or series of experiments – but an investigation into every cot death that occurred.'

So if you were the parents of a baby in New Zealand, and you had just found your baby dead, as we had with Supi, you would immediately be visited by Ed Mitchell or one of his team. They were trained in handling newly bereaved parents, but also wise to the fact that most parents were keen to co-operate. They wanted to know what had killed their baby.

You would be asked about everything that could conceivably be relevant. Boy or girl? How old? Breastfed or bottle-fed? Brothers and sisters?

Was your baby unwell in any way? Had he behaved any differently from normal? Was he 'himself' that day? Had you recently changed his routine?

Had he been immunized? Recent coughs and colds or viral illnesses? Did he suck a dummy? Did his parents smoke? Or drink? All these questions, and hundreds more, had to be agreed as part of the 'protocol' of the investigation, so that direct comparisons could later be made.

'And we built into the protocol some questions about sleep position,' said Ed. 'Because the theory about sleep position had been circulating in medical circles for some time – though the whole world pooh-poohed it. We built it into our questionnaire so that we could successfully prove it one way or the other.' Other factors, too, were built into the protocol for the study, which was designed to continue for three years.

Then, as one expert was asking these questions of you, another member of Mitchell's team would find two more families living in the same neighbourhood, with a child of the same age, and ask exactly the same questions of them. These were called 'control' cases. By comparing the data of the dead children and their 'controls', the computer could start to build up a picture. Effectively, it might then tell you why one baby had died that night, and two others had not.

'And what did the computer say?' I asked.

'Well, at first we were just logging the information in,' explained Ed. 'It was some eighteen months before reliable data started coming *out.* But when it did, we were staggered. The babies who were dying were generally the ones who slept on their tummies.'

I was numb. Ed Mitchell took me by the arm. 'Are you all right?' he asked. 'Maybe you shouldn't be doing this. You can't run away from your own grief – this is bound to be hitting you hard.' I made him go on. 'Well,' he continued. 'We found that we were also losing babies who were put down to sleep on their backs or sides. *But when they were found dead, they were on their stomachs.* They had rolled over in the night.'

Ed explained that this discovery threw the doctors and the scientists into turmoil – and conflict. The doctors thought it would be immoral to continue the study without telling New Zealand's mothers what they had found. They felt sure that they could save lives if they told mothers to avoid sleeping their babies on their stomachs. The scientists, proud and excited by the data, insisted that the three-year study must go on for the full three years. To interfere with the way mothers treated their children throughout the country would ruin the data they had already amassed.

'Morally, we could do nothing else but tell the mothers,' said Ed. 'We knew that doing so might ruin other, and possibly more vital, data. But we had to give mothers a chance to save their babies' lives.' So the cot death experts got together and agreed that they should actively campaign with the new message – turn your baby over.

'You can see how difficult it was,' said Ed. 'We didn't really know what we were advising – or the effect it would have. We had no idea at all why it might save a baby from cot death. We just knew we had to try.'

So, looking at all the research data emerging from the first eighteen months of their study, they figured out the main areas of advice. Seventy-three per cent of the cot death babies had been lying on their stomachs, sixty-three per cent had mothers who smoked and over a third were not being breastfed. If the child was lying on his stomach, was not breastfed and had a mother who smoked, he was ten times more likely to die from cot death.

This needed a mass media campaign. Shirley Tonkin knew that there was only one way to reach a large number of people quickly, efficiently and dramatically. Television. She was adamant that they must make an advert to be shown on TV, so she recruited the best known female news presenter in New Zealand to present a thirty-second message, telling mums to lie their babies on their backs or sides.

In New Zealand, it was huge news. Within days, there wasn't a parent, grandparent or babysitter who didn't know the new advice.

1. Lie your baby on his back or side to sleep. If you lie him on his side, make sure that the underneath arm is well forward, to stop the baby rolling on to his stomach.

2. Don't smoke.

3. Breastfeed if you possibly can.

'We put everything we could into the message,' said Ed, as he flashed through the computer graphs which backed up the advice.

And Shirley Tonkin took up the story: she knew it was a message that must reach not just mothers but every member of the family. 'It's not just mum who looks after the baby in any household,' she said. 'There are brothers and sisters, grandmas and grandpas – even the girl next door who does the babysitting. We had to reach them all. There's only one way to do that – TV. We didn't just want prime-time advertising, we needed to put out the ad in the middle of the daytime soaps and quiz shows.'

They even borrowed the British idea of a Red Nose Day – not for Comic Relief as in Britain, but for cot death awareness. Politicians of both parties joined together, red noses touching, to proclaim the news that New Zealand had found an answer to cot death.

I was breathless just to hear the story. 'And what happened?' I asked.

'Our cot death rate fell by fifty per cent within six months,' said Ed, matter-of-factly, but with the hint of a smile under his moustache.

And *when* did this all happen, I urged.

'Almost a year ago,' he replied.

So while this had all been going on, at the other end of our planet, I had been happily putting my baby to sleep on his stomach, safe in the knowledge – or so I thought – that it was the best thing to do. I hesitated, and then asked almost in a whisper: 'Why didn't you tell anyone in Britain?'

Ed shook his head sadly, knowing that what he was to say would hurt me badly. 'Everyone knows about what we're doing. We told your government about it, and the Foundation for the Study of Infant Deaths in your country has even funded part of it. We *did* tell Britain. We *did.* I don't know why they didn't do anything.'

Chapter 18

Who could go to New Zealand with two little boys and not pop along to the All Blacks shop to buy them mini-versions of the full rugby strip? Oliver and Jamie were enjoying their trip – they didn't see much of their mummy, but I felt that at least we were all together at night, when I was at my most fearful.

As soon as Mike joined me, he took me to meet a friend of his, who was now the Director General of New Zealand Television, a man called Julian Mounter. Mike knew that Julian Mounter had once worked with Linda McDougall. We were now so anxious about her that we decided to ask Julian his advice. He met us in his glass-walled office on top of a hill overlooking the city of Auckland. And while we drank coffee and munched biscuits, he told us what he thought.

'I'm not in the least surprised you're finding it hard going with her,' he said, his eyebrows laughing. 'She is well-known for it. But, frankly, she's a bloody good journalist and I don't think she's ever turned in a bad film.'

So we decided to grimace and bear it, and go on with the next stage of our filming schedule. Alex, Shirley, Mike and the boys were to fly to Christchurch. Meanwhile Linda, Jan, the camera crew and I were to do the same journey by car, but also visit Dunedin, Linda's home town, where she'd met Austin, her husband. At the university, a doctor called Barry Richards was researching the effects of overheating on babies. They were experimenting in their laboratories with piglets, warming their bodies very slightly, to see what effects this had on their sleeping physiology.

One theory they were investigating was the thought that, under certain stressful conditions, babies exercised a primitive instinct to 'shut down' their systems. There were stories of how, in the Mexico earthquake and other disasters, babies had been rescued alive and well for up to ten days afterwards, though they had had no food, nor even water. Some cot death experts reckoned that babies who died from cot death had inadvertently – maybe because of being too hot – set this 'shut down' reflex into action, but had been unable to bring themselves back to consciousness. But this still didn't explain why New Zealand should have the highest cot death rate in the world. And why should there be more deaths in the South Island than the North?

'It may be because it gets so cold down here,' said Barry. 'Mothers look at the cold weather outside and wrap their babies accordingly, forgetting that they're indoors in a heated house. We've tried wrapping our piglets in the same clothes and covers that a typical Dunedin mum would use – and it's sent the piglets into distress. Now we're telling mums to clothe and wrap their babies in exactly the same amount of layers that they themselves would be comfortable in. We're also telling them to put away those sheepskins. They may be doing more harm than good.'

In the evening, we visited one of the mothers under his care – a girl, Penny Gray, who had already lost one child. Her new baby was now at the vulnerable age – four months. She showed me how she put her to bed under the new guidelines. 'On her back, and near the bottom of the Moses basket so she can't wriggle down any further under the blankets,' she recited, as though she had learned it by heart. 'And we don't use cot bumpers or duvets, just old-fashioned sheets and blankets.'

Then she put a breathing monitor on an elastic strap around her chest – and a green light blipped every time she took a breath.

'Sometimes the alarm goes off in the middle of the night,

and we nearly have a heart attack,' she said. 'And we log every time that it goes off, so that we talk it over with the doctor next time we see him. Because if it goes off too many times, either we're doing something wrong, or she's having trouble with her breathing.'

She looked at me, and I could see that she was being brave for us, for the camera. 'So far, so good,' she sighed. Cot death was almost an expected hazard in her family. She'd lost her own daughter, her husband had lost a brother and they had both lost cousins to cot death. At the family funeral of their daughter, Christie, there had been fifteen families who had lost a baby to cot death. With four or five babies dying in every thousand (with a population of only three million), it was hardly surprising that cot death had touched nearly everyone in New Zealand.

But the little girl I met the next morning was hardly out of childhood herself before she was plunged into the loss and bereavement of her own baby. We had stayed overnight in a motel in Dunedin – and the crew, Jan, Linda and I ate breakfast as we decided on the best route up to Christchurch. Linda was engrossed in the local paper. I looked to see what was engaging her – and noticed that she was scanning the classified adverts section, and particularly the Births, Marriages and Deaths.

'I'm looking to see if there's been a cot death recently,' she said. 'Of course, it's relatively rare nowadays, but you never know...'

We went on eating our toast and butter. Full cream butter, and full cream milk in the tea. Every meal in New Zealand seemed to be oozing with dairy products, and bathing in a sea of cholesterol.

'Aha! This looks like one...' And she read out:

> BIDDLE, baby Jesse Rangiora, Mihaere. On October 1, 1991 (suddenly at his home)

> treasured son of Cecilia and Shane, much loved grandson of Moana Biddle and Robyn Wilson, and his many relatives and friends; aged three and a half months.

'Right. I'm going to phone them.'

The cameraman and I looked at each other in disbelief. Surely Linda wasn't going to barge in on a family which had just suffered a cot death? Surely she didn't intend for us to go and film them? Surely she didn't expect me to go?

She bounded back, enthusiastically. 'Yep, it is a cot death. The child died yesterday. They're a Maori family, so the baby is still with them, with the relatives all around. Come on, I think I know where it is. Let's get going.' She turned to me. 'Do you want to come? I shall understand if you don't...'

I didn't know what to say, or what to think. 'Yes, I'll come. But I might stay in the car.'

We drove uphill, and turned into a housing estate. At the end of a small cul-de-sac was our destination, a cheap, tatty house built in the sixties with shoddy materials which hadn't stood the test of time.

'Linda,' I asked, still uncertain that I wanted to go in. 'How did the baby die, do we know?'

Linda shook her head. 'The family elder who I spoke to said that the baby had been in bed with his grandmother. It's not clear exactly what position he'd been in, or anything.' She turned to the crew. 'Right, we all need to make a gift,' she said brightly. 'When you enter a Maori house, you have to take a small offering – usually silver coins. It's a tradition which I think we should respect since they're allowing us in...'

We all felt in our pockets for loose change. Jan put it all into an envelope, and they went forward to the front door. Linda looked back at me.

'I'll come,' I said, and brought up the rear.

The family elder opened the door. He was a huge man, tall

and round, dressed in shabby old clothes and still wearing slippers. He accepted our gift, and led us in. His face was hang-dog with melancholy. We were shown into a large room, bare except for mattresses on the floor. There were no curtains, only a couple of white sheets stretched over the window, and someone had sellotaped six or seven family photos on to them, so that they were silhouetted against the light.

On the floor, sitting dejectedly on one of the mattresses was a young Maori girl. She looked all of fifteen. The skin on her face was blotched with pink and purple patches, and her eyes looked as though they had been crying for ever. And next to her, like a tiny china doll, was her baby boy. He was lying on his back, with his arms crossed in front, wearing a knitted cardigan and bonnet, and his tiny body wrapped in a shawl. His little eyes were tight shut and his delicate mouth pursed, almost in a Cupid's-bow kiss. He was dead.

There were 12,000 miles, an entire culture and at least twenty years between this young mother and myself – but I had more in common with her at that moment than anyone else in that room. I walked over to her instinctively, knelt down on the mattress, and clutched her hand.

'I'm so sorry. I lost my baby, too, just eight weeks ago. I know how you feel. I'm so terribly sorry.' And then I looked down at her dead child, and stroked his little cheek. I recognized that deep, chilling cold of dead flesh.

And I thought of what I had liked to hear people say. 'Poor little mite. He is beautiful, absolutely beautiful.'

Various of her relatives were making cups of tea. Others were visiting because they'd just heard the news, or read the notice in the paper. A Maori baby stays within the family for three days after death, because they believe the spirit can still be there for that time. The family elder started praying aloud, and chanting. He cannot have been a very close relative, we thought, because he kept getting the sex of the baby wrong. It was a boy, and yet he kept saying prayers for 'her' and 'her short life'.

We thought we should leave. The crew shuffled out, and I followed. Linda came up to me with a bunch of flowers which she'd bought at the motel. 'I thought you might like to give her these,' she offered. I took them from her, impressed at the kindness of the thought.

I went back in, and saw the young mother now standing in the doorway of the mattress room. We walked towards each other and hugged – and I gave her the flowers. She was starting to cry again. As I closed the front door behind me, and made for the path, I was aware that Linda had the camera trained on my face. She had been trying to film the whole episode.

'Oh my God,' I sighed, and rolled my eyes upwards in despair. At least that would make the shot unusable. I was beginning to have the same respect for her that I had for Kelvin MacKenzie, the editor of the *Sun*. They were both extremely good at their job, but that didn't mean you had to like their tactics.

Maybe Linda prided herself, and still does, on her ability to shock, or surprise you. At any rate, she had her tender moments. She was always lovely to the children – and when the trip was over, she gave me a still-frame from the film, printed as a photo and framed. On the back of the frame, she wrote: 'To Anne – to prove that even nightmares have their good times!' The photograph was of me and Jamie choosing an All Blacks cap, with Oliver looking on. It was a beautiful picture, not the least because it had been carefully composed by an artful director. Later, when the children were buying souvenirs of their New Zealand trip, Jamie bought a big, fluffy penguin and christened it Linda. She was really touched!

At Christchurch airport we met the family so that we could all travel onwards to Queenstown, in the southernmost part of South Island. Queenstown was the country's most beautiful resort – high up in the mountains, it was famous for its ski-ing and snow-sports. This was where Linda wanted her scenic shots for background illustration to the main story of the documentary. So now we could relax a little, and unwind, even though the weather was biting cold. The boys wanted to go and see a sheep station – and there was a touristy one across Lake Wakatipu, where the boys could pat baby lambs and nibble lamb chops for lunch in the restaurant.

On the way back, aboard the steamship *Earnslaw* which spluttered to and fro across the lake all day, we were nearly swamped by a coach-load of Japanese tourists. As soon as they had all ordered their glasses of Coca Cola, they gathered on the main deck and a pianist started belting out an array of singalong tunes. We had to pinch ourselves to make sure we weren't hallucinating. We were in New Zealand, aboard a steam ferry, with hundreds of Japanese tourists singing 'Roll Out the Barrel' and 'Maybe It's Because I'm a Londoner'.

Then the pianist segued into 'Daisy, Daisy', which was my sons' party piece. Oliver and Jamie stood up, and joined in the singing. At once, the Japanese tourists stopped, and let the little boys sing alone. It was the high point of the whole trip for them. That, and the kiwi-burgers you could get from McDonald's in Queenstown. They were basically a hamburger with a slice of kiwi fruit on the top. Ugh. But the boys liked them.

There was also a large restaurant on the top of a high cliff, which you could only easily reach by ski-lift. The children called it 'the restaurant at the top of the world', because you could see its lights from our hotel rooms, twinkling in the middle of a black sky. After one magical meal there, we walked back through the darkness to the hotel. There, Mike had a message. It was from Karen, telling him that Alan had died peacefully in his sleep. We drank a toast to him, to John and to Supi – and wondered if they had all three reached the same destination.

We returned to Britain via Los Angeles, where we stopped off for two nights to take the boys to Disneyland. I thought we needed to get away from all talk of cot death, away from hospitals and research laboratories. And away from Linda and her crew. I hadn't seen very much of the boys during the fortnight we were away, except at night, and I wanted to be with them. But while we were sitting in an open-air restaurant at the end of Mainstreet USA, in the 'Magic Kingdom' of Mickey Mouse, busily chomping into the most enormous hot-dogs, Oliver looked up quizzically.

'Daddy,' he started... 'What is cot death? Did we find out?'

'No,' said Mike, truthfully. 'No, we didn't find out exactly. But we did find a way to prevent it happening to other babies.'

'So what are we going to do now?'

'We're going to go home and find out why we didn't know about it sooner, that's what.'

And that is exactly what we did. The moment we set foot again on British soil, we would start lobbying in every way we knew possible. We would thump on the front door of the Department of Health so loud they couldn't fail to hear the din. *'Look again at the evidence you have so negligently ignored,'* we would rail at them, until they were sick of us. *'Then tell us why it cannot save British babies, too.'*

Chapter 19

I only just made it home on time. I had flown alone on Virgin Airways from Los Angeles to Heathrow, and then caught a light plane from London to Southampton in order to be in the TVS studios with enough time to rehearse, and to make the usual live transmission of *TV Weekly*.

Chris Riley, head of the team, knew why I'd been to New Zealand, and must have realized that I was very preoccupied during those days – but instead of being annoyed by this, the whole team did all they could to make life a little easier for me. After all, they had known Supi. They had all met him when he was just four weeks old. After that first broadcast, just days after I had given birth and I had had to leave Supi behind in Skiboo, I had always taken him to work with me, and he had been looked after in my dressing room by Nanny Anne.

Now they all showed tremendous compassion as I felt the need to talk, to talk endlessly about what had happened. Over a long lunch, they all sat with me in the staff restaurant, as we picked at the food and drank orange juice and coke, and listened as I poured out my heart. If they were uneasy, they never once showed it as I told the tale of Supi's death, the funeral, the press, the Diamond Cot Death Appeal, and the New Zealand trip.

Later, Chris took me aside. 'Of course, your friend Clare is right,' he said. 'You mustn't let Supi's death become bigger than his life. But look what you've been able to find out. Now what you can do is help make some *meaning* of his death.'

I got home that evening quite late. Oliver and Jamie were already in bed, and I was about to fall into mine, when the phone rang. It was my accountant, Russel Tenzer, the proud father of baby twins. 'I'm sorry to bother you – I know you've only just got back from New Zealand. I just wanted to know how you'd got on...'

So I told him. I was surprised I could condense it into thirty seconds – but there was really only one thing to tell the parent of young babies.

'So are you saying all babies should be put on their backs to sleep?' he double-checked with me.

'Yes.'

'And they could die if they're on their fronts?'

'In a word, yes.'

'My God! I won't keep you a moment longer.'

'Why – where are you going?'

'Upstairs, to turn the twins over.' And he put the phone down.

That's when I knew that our message could be *that simple, and that quick.*

Linda rang with the filming schedule for the next week. The documentary was scheduled for 30 October – just two weeks away. We still had the British side of the story to cover. First, we contacted the Department of Health to ask for a full statement on the truth behind what Ed Mitchell had told us – that the government had known all about their work. Then we asked for interviews with the ministers responsible. Then Austin Mitchell, Linda's MP husband, asked a question in the House of Commons about the New Zealand evidence. And finally, Linda released to the *Sun* a freeze-frame of me and the Maori baby, to keep up the media pressure.

Meanwhile, our next filming location was down the M5 in Bristol. Our New Zealand cameraman had flown over specially so that he could complete the documentary, rather than have a British cameraman take over. He had offered to continue the work free of charge because he was so committed to the subject – as long as we could pay his expenses.

Linda was driving. She had already arranged that we should interview a man called Dr Peter Fleming, a consultant paediatrician at St Michael's, the maternity hospital. At that time, as we were hurtling down the motorway at breakneck speed, I didn't think I could possibly meet anyone more inspirational than the New Zealand cot death experts. But here was a man whose quiet determination and stubborn courage had already saved hundreds of babies' lives.

Rather like the New Zealanders mysteriously finding themselves with the highest cot death rate in the world, Peter Fleming was practising medicine in an area – the county of Avon – which had the highest cot death rate in Britain. No-one knew why. But to a leading paediatrician, it was clearly a matter of great concern. So Peter found himself investigating the cot death problem with more vigour than many doctors elsewhere. Maybe it also had something to do with the fact that this caring man, slightly built with a shock of grey-white hair and a beard to match, was the father of four children. It must have worried him on a personal level that the area in which he was living with his doctor wife, Jo, had such a nightmare reputation for baby deaths.

He, too, set up a long-term study, investigating the children who had died and making direct comparisons with their 'controls' – similar children living nearby who had not died. This study had been funded mostly by the Foundation, though he was also supported by a smaller, locally-based charity, Cot Death Research.

The theory about sleep position had first been broached by an Australian paediatrician called Susan Beale, he explained, as we set up the camera and lights in his tiny, cramped office. 'She pestered me about it way back in May 1987, because she'd heard that I was about to start a big cot death study in Avon, and she wanted me to include a question about sleep position in my protocol of questions. Both she and Shirley Tonkin in New Zealand were becoming more and more convinced that sleep position had some sort of sinister importance – but, frankly, I was very doubtful. In the end, they nagged me so much that I agreed, so that I could investigate it and dismiss it.'

So no-one was more surprised than he when the evidence became startlingly clear. As in New Zealand, the babies who were dying were the ones on their tummies. And even those babies who had died, and had *not* been placed on their stomachs, had been *found* on their stomachs.

'It was overwhelming, I'm afraid,' Peter said. 'Maybe you can imagine my horror. Because the official advice to all mothers in this country was that babies should be put to sleep on their stomachs. It's in the government's official Baby Book, which is given to all new mums while they're in hospital. I had even been one of those doctors to recommend it to my own patients. I had even done it to my own sons. What I had discovered suddenly proved that we doctors had been wrong – and that advice was the cause of many needless deaths.'

Such an admission requires a great deal of honesty and courage, which is perhaps why Peter was booed off stage when he first delivered his message to cynical and even hostile medical audiences in lecture halls throughout the world. 'They thought I'd gone mad,' he said. 'But in actual fact, we in Avon had exposed a madness which was masquerading as medical fact. *There never was any proper medical reason for lying ordinary babies on their tummies. It was simply a fad – and unfortunately a dangerous one for some children. The idea that it saved some babies from choking on regurgitated milk is a myth put about probably by doctors seeking to justify their beliefs. There was never any medical basis for it.*'

So we mums had been sold a pup. My mind flashed back to a moment four years before, when my mother had stayed with me just after I had had Oliver. She had been shocked to see me put him down in his cot, on his tummy. 'I would never do that with a baby,' she said. 'I was always told to put babies on their backs, or sides...'

'Oh, no!' I'd said, confidently. 'This is what you're meant to do – it's better for them.' If only I'd been the sort of girl who listened to her own mum, and hadn't read so many books.

If only we'd lived in Bristol. Because, by September 1989, Peter Fleming was so convinced of his data, and so depressed at the reaction of the rest of the medical fraternity, that he decided he would actively 'intervene' in the way Avon women brought up their babies. He would harness the local army of midwives, community nurses and health visitors, GPs and practice nurses, and he would start a local campaign telling mothers four vitally important points.

Number one was about sleep position. At first, he told mums to put their babies on their sides. He thought they would reject the message if it seemed too radical – and he knew many would be frightened to place their babies on their backs, the exact opposite of the official government advice. But within months, the incoming data on deaths convinced him he could go ahead with his 'back is best' message. Armed with a grant of several thousand pounds from the local cot death charity, he printed a hundred thousand leaflets. From autumn 1989 onwards, whenever a woman gave birth in the Avon district, she was told the new advice. Rarely did she ignore it, because it was backed up from every medical source, from her paediatrician to her family doctor.

Within six months, the cot death rate in Avon had almost halved. But still the rest of Britain ignored what was happening...' In fact, I was attacked,' said Peter. '*The Lancet* refused to publish my data and I was told by other scientists and doctors that my research work was unethical and unreliable because it dealt with people who had been newly bereaved. The reaction of the medical establishment was astonishingly blinkered.'

In the first quarter of the year, when they would normally

expect around sixteen or seventeen cot deaths, they got six. They knew then that they had quite literally hit upon a revolution in the history of cot death. That was in the first three months of 1990. It would be another nineteen months before mothers in the rest of the country would share such privileged information. God knows how many babies died in the United Kingdom in that period of time. Some three thousand? I was swaying on my feet. If the New Zealand story had been an emotional brickbat, then this dealt an even harder blow. While I was still only two months pregnant with Supi, Peter Fleming, just one hundred and twenty miles away from my front door, had upgraded his new advice to a full-blown local campaign, convincing mothers in Avon of an entirely different way of looking after their children. A simple piece of advice which was saving children. Though no-one knew which babies were being saved from cot death, it was obvious that some would have otherwise died.

Could Peter Fleming have saved the life of my little boy, had we lived in Avon? I cannot help but think yes, because it was particularly the 'classic' cases of cot death which were the first to almost disappear. As the picture built up over the ensuing months, and now years, there were fewer and fewer cases of four-month-old boys dying suddenly and unexpectedly, compared with the time before Peter's campaign. The cot deaths that were still happening tended to be the cases which were always the more unusual – children rather older than three or four months, children who were old enough to choose their own sleeping position.

What did Peter think of the New Zealand campaign? 'It absolutely reinforces everything I had found true of Avon,' said Peter. 'And while our area is relatively small, the New Zealand data covered a large area – and a whole country...'

That meant another thing to me – and to any doubters who might still exist after our documentary had gone out. If it worked in Avon, and it worked in New Zealand – how could it possibly fail to work in the whole of Britain? You didn't have to be a scientist or a doctor to know that, if we could mount a national campaign here in Britain, it *must* work. And that if we put all our efforts behind it, logically we should be able to follow the same pattern. We should be able to *halve* the cot death rate.

I took Peter to one side as the camera crew cleared up their things. 'What does this tell me about my baby?' I asked him quietly. 'Are you really telling me that my baby died simply because he was lying on his tummy – because I find that difficult to believe...'

Peter shook his head – and for the third, fourth or maybe even fifth time, a cot death expert took me by the arm and asked me if I really thought I should be doing all this, so soon after my baby's death. But I think Peter could see the desperation in my eyes. He recognized it from all the other newly bereaved mothers he'd met. We had to know why our babies had died. We just *had* to know. There would be no peace, no peace at all, until we knew.

'I cannot tell you exactly why your baby died,' he said sadly. 'We still do not know precisely what causes these babies to die. I only know that, for some babies, lying on their tummies is a huge risk factor. We know other risk factors – like overheating and parental smoking. But I cannot tell you much more than that – everything else is just theory. What we can do now, though, is give new babies a better chance than your baby had – a much better chance. We can reduce the risks. It works. But I cannot tell you how or why it works. *I just know that it does...*'

We said goodbye – and as we were turning to go, the phone rang from inside Peter's office. We left him as he returned to answer it. Minutes later, and while we were still loading our equipment on to a trolley, Peter came out to us, quietly smiling. 'I just thought you'd like to know...' he started, and then his voice sank to a conspiratorial whisper. 'That was the Chief

Medical Officer. He's asked me to join a special experts working party to urgently review the latest cot death data.'

My mouth dropped in amazement. So things were going to happen! 'Do you know who else he's asking?' I said.

'I know most of them already,' replied Peter. 'After all, there aren't many of us about. And you can be sure of one thing, it won't take us long to review research which we already know...' There was a look of confidence and sheer determination on his face.

Shortly after that meeting, I had a dream. It still haunts me, though less often now. In it, I am in a huge room, surrounded by hordes of men in white coats – so I presume they are doctors. Suddenly, the door opens and in rushes a man, also in a white coat, and he's waving a piece of paper. He's wildly excited, and he shouts: 'I've got it! I've got it!' And I know that he means he has found the answer to cot death – and it's on that piece of paper.

So I grab the paper from his hands, and run down the corridor with it. At the end of the corridor there's another room, an office, with a grey carpet, and a huge mahogany table. Sitting behind the dark table is an old man, with a very stern face. I flourish the piece of paper at him, and bring my fist down upon the table. 'Now,' I hiss at him. *'Now can I have my baby back?'* And that's where the dream ends every time. I've got to solve the mystery of cot death, so that I can have my baby back. That's what I kept thinking. There *will* be an end to this nightmare.

Chapter 20

'Let's make no bones about it,' said Linda. 'there will be one main reason people will watch this documentary – and it will be to see Anne Diamond cry.' She certainly had a way with words, did Linda. So when she set up the cameras and lights in our own living-room to shoot the final stage of our documentary, I was steeled against every trick she might play. I had done every other interview in the programme – but, of course, I couldn't interview Mike and myself. Now Linda turned the tables on me.

The crew, Jan and Linda hadn't actually heard the story of Supi's death. Not from our own mouths. Now we told them, as calmly as we could, while they recorded it. The house was hushed. We got to the end, and Linda patted us both on the back. She may not have got tears, but she knew she had some powerful material.

'If this documentary doesn't change things, I don't know what will,' she said. They turned off the lights, put the furniture back, and I went downstairs to the kitchen to make tea for everyone.

Linda turned the TV on. It was a big day in the television industry. The franchise awards were about to be announced. This was the ten-yearly fiasco where the ITV companies competed for the right to broadcast in their regions. For the first time, in true Thatcherite style, the franchises had been auctioned. They were to be awarded to the highest bidders. As I returned to the living-room with a trayful of tea and biscuits, the newsreader on *Sky News* started to deliver the bombshells. Thames TV had lost its franchise. So had TVS. So had TV-am.

Mike and I shot each other a look, and smiled ironically. That was the company for which I was making this documentary, the company for which I made *TV Weekly*, and my old employer! Oh dear! I wasn't doing too well!

Linda was whooping with delight. She was closely associated with one of the winners. My phone started ringing. All the people (and there were plenty of them) who had ever been fired by TV-am suddenly seemed to know my phone number. Henry Kelly, the TV presenter and game show host, rang. He had suffered under the ever-changing whims of Bruce Gyngell. 'So at last there is some justice in this world!' he crowed.

I thought of an old friend, Caroline Righton, who had also been fired after a contretemps with the Head of News, Bill Ludford. At the time, she had been very confused and upset. Though in a calmer moment she'd said: 'Ah, well... They do say that if you stand for long enough on the bridge, you will see the body of your enemy floating by...' I thought, with some satisfaction, how Caroline could now come down off her personal bridge.

Although the *Today* newspaper put me on the front page the next day, alongside former TV-am boss Greg Dyke, and called us 'The Avengers', I felt no satisafaction in watching TV-am lose its franchise, nor in seeing TV pictures of a shocked Bruce Gyngell and a disappointed David Frost. It had been a terrific company to work for, and I didn't regret a single minute I'd spent there. I was just sorry that I hadn't left on happier terms.

But all that seemed so unimportant now. It was, after all, only television. Supi's life and death had put things into proportion. The work I was doing now was possibly the greatest challenge of my career and my life. For Supi's sake, I had to get things changed.

In 1984, a Home Office pathologist made an unforgivable statement which he's lucky didn't get him lynched. He said that, in his opinion, most cot deaths were cases of parents smothering their own children. Remember his name – Dr Donald Wayte, just in case you ever meet him at a party. Throw a glass of red wine over him for me. His remark caused so much pain and nearly set cot death research back years. Coming from the lips of someone who was supposedly a caring and careful health professional, it also said a lot about the complacent attitude and harmful backwardness of establishment thinking.

The country's Chief Medical Officer at that time, Sir Donald Acheson, didn't exactly bend over backwards to remedy the harm, either. In fact, the situation was saved almost single-handedly by Princess Diana, who made a point by being seen very soon after at a function organized by the Foundation.

I just thank goodness that a more modern brain was in charge of the country's corporate health when we came back from New Zealand and Bristol. I strongly believe that if we hadn't had a new Chief Medical Officer – and the government had not been vulnerable in the run-up to a general election – nothing would ever have been done to change the official advice in the government's official *Pregnancy* and *Birth To Five* handbooks, babies in Britain would *still* be lying on their stomachs, and dying at the same appalling rate. Because there was almost a conspiracy of complacency in Britain about cot death. It was almost as though someone somewhere had decided that 2,000 deaths a year were somehow acceptable – a terrible tragedy, to be sure, but probably inevitable. After all, one prominent scientist had said to me, babies are very fragile. Throughout history, women had many babies, expecting only a few to survive. Maybe, he said, modern women had expectations which were too high.

Even the one big cot death charity in Britain, the Foundation for the Study of Infant Deaths, which had done such sterling work for the bereaved for the past two decades, had seriously failed when it had come to the crunch, because the Foundation had known about the sleeping position theory since the end of 1989. And from July 1990 they had convincing data, some would call it proof, from both New Zealand and Avon, that turning our babies on to their backs would save thousands of lives. By autumn 1990, they had had the new advice – telling us mothers to turn our babies over – printed up in draft leaflet form. It must have been sitting somewhere on a desk in Belgrave Square all through the spring and summer of 1991, while I had Sebastian.

We had been in constant contact with the Foundation. Indeed, they'd been one of the very first organizations which Linda and Jan had rung when we first planned the documentary. They were aware from the beginning that we were going to New Zealand, and why. While we were still there, and particularly after Ed Mitchell had spoken to us, we had rung the Foundation and asked for an interview upon our return. And while we prepared to go to their Belgrave Square offices to ask them some serious questions, they made an announcement which stopped us in our tracks. Linda went nuclear.

'I don't believe it, I simply don't believe it!' she ranted when she heard. 'The Foundation have suddenly decided they're going to hold a press conference to announce the risk reduction rules! I can hardly believe their nerve. They've had this information for the past two years, and suddenly while we're making a documentary about it, they decide to go public. And they're going to do it next week, would you believe? Just days before our programme goes out...'

There are, of course, two possible explanations for their behaviour. First, there's the one they asked us to believe. That it was a complete coincidence and they were going to announce the risk reduction rules at this time anyway. The second is that they had been embarrassed into action, and they didn't want to be shown up, in their very field of expertise, by some upstart of a bereaved mother and a nosey documentary crew.

All I know is I lost my baby while the Foundation withheld

information which could have saved his life. Countless other parents – it must run into thousands – lost their children while the Foundation – the very organization which *should* have served our interests on this subject – dithered over life-saving advice. When they were most needed, when they could have been most effective, the Foundation failed to act. We decided to meet them – and this time we called in our boss, the editor of Thames Television's *This Week*, under whose banner our documentary was to be broadcast.

I'd first met Paul Woolwich when I was a new reporter on the BBC evening programme, *Nationwide* – and he was a deputy editor. I hadn't really known him. Now, over this lunchtime meeting with Joyce Epstein and Dr Shireen Chantler, I was to see him show the mettle which had made him a serious force in the world of news and current affairs.

'He was brutal,' Linda said to me afterwards. I had thought he was brilliant. He had calmly but ruthlessly, over a three-course meal and coffee, put it to the two women that they had failed Britain's mothers once, and were about to do so again.

'You have been effectively withholding vital, life-saving information,' he told them, fixing them with a steely stare. 'Now you seek to disarm Anne as she prepares to pass on the medical advice which you ignored. Everything has been carefully planned to achieve maximum impact,' he explained to them. 'This isn't just any old documentary, this is co-ordinated with special editions of *Woman* magazine and the *Sun* so that we can reach as many mothers as possible, and create the biggest impact we can with the press. If you try to cover yourselves now, you will simply neutralize the impact, and water down the message.'

He didn't say it, but I could see in the faces of the two women a distinct recognition that they were being threatened with exposure. 'Is that what you really want?' hissed Paul. 'Or are you, perhaps, more interested in saving face than saving lives?'

And here I experienced what others in the political world

probably go through every day – the reaching of a compromise in order to safeguard the overall objective. We offered the Foundation the chance to sit alongside us when we previewed the documentary to the press. There, they could unveil their risk-reduction posters and leaflets, and we would seem to be united. In return, Linda and I agreed that we would not go too hard on them in the programme. Though I would have to ask them one question – the only one that really mattered...Why didn't they tell us about the life-saving discoveries that had been made in New Zealand?

Once again I sat in the Foundation's main office, opposite Joyce Epstein and Dr Shireen Chantler. But this time I was with a full TV crew. And this time, I knew an awful lot more about cot death than when I had last been there. The two women looked uncomfortable. They pointed out that they had discussed the risk-reduction formula, and specifically the sleep position data, in their newsletters. But, I retorted, people only receive their newsletter if they're on the mailing list. *In other words, you have to have had a cot death already.* Couldn't they see that that was hardly adequate? Why hadn't they told the rest of Britain?

The two women shuffled in their chairs and shot each other uncertain glances. 'Well, some of our doctors still don't agree about it...' started Dr Chantler.

So they wanted to wait for political unanimity within their organization before telling ordinary parents how to save the lives of their children?

'It's very difficult to know when to go public with new medical information,' said Joyce, emphatically.

And we left it there. In some respects, of course, she was right. It *is* difficult. But it wasn't too hard for the New Zealanders to know when they should tell the public. And, in the county of Avon, it wasn't too hard for Dr Peter Fleming to know when to change his advice for the mothers under his care.

In both cases, the experts had chosen to act when their moral responsibility became clear. To the Foundation, it had never become clear. They wanted to be certain that it was completely safe to tell mothers to lie their babies on their backs. They wanted to be absolutely sure before they passed on the advice. Maybe, as had been strongly suggested to me by some scientists and doctors, the Foundation would rather have found the cause of cot death before finding an unexplained way of reducing the risk.

I do not doubt the sincerity of their intentions. In many ways, the Foundation has provided much-needed solace and a focal point for the grief of thousands of bereaved parents. But by playing it safe in scientific terms, they forgot their human obligation. If they felt it safe to discuss the sleeping position theory in their newsletters, then why not in a campaign for all mothers? By the end of 1989, the doctor whose work they were funding, Peter Fleming, was totally convinced that changing sleeping position would save lives. By March 1990 he knew from experience that it also did no harm, that it was safe advice. If the Foundation wanted safety, they had it then. They could have safely hung on to the coat-tails of the New Zealanders, who had themselves starting campaigning in July 1990. But no. They hesitated and we parents lost.

There was no doubt about it for me. The Foundation was at fault. But they were a charity, set up and run on voluntary contributions. What about the people who were paid to do the job of looking after the nation's well-being – the Department of Health? We'd asked for an interview with the Secretary of State for Health, William Waldegrave, or with his Health Minister, Virginia Bottomley. *Why had they both said no?*

Chapter 21

'Being a Health Minister is like being a fireman,' Jeffrey Archer said to me, with a lavish gesture. His hand settled on the cushion of his vast sofa, in the centre of his enormous living-room, in his immense apartment overlooking the Thames. He beckoned me to sit down.

'You just have a series of fires to put out – and you turn your attention on the biggest and most dangerous first...What you've got to understand is that, after you, she's got a deputation from the AIDS charity, then the breast cancer people, then the leukaemia people, then the bone marrow people – and they all want the same thing, action and money. What you've got to do is get yourself first in the queue by making the most fuss. Then she'll do something simply to make you go away.'

I had gone to the millionaire author, desperately looking for political advice. I could not get any response from either William Waldegrave or Virginia Bottomley – and I wasn't just after an interview for the programme. That was essentially Linda's problem. What I wanted was an audience with one of them – so that I could convince them that we in Britain should start a cot death campaign – like the New Zealanders.

I had gone to Jeffrey because I knew he was friends with the Prime Minister, John Major. And, in my experience, if you couldn't get anywhere with the minions, you went straight to the top. I told Jeffrey about the New Zealand and Avon evidence. 'We could save over half the lives which are now lost, if only we set up a campaign,' I said. And, to appeal to him on another tack, I tried: 'And wouldn't it look good for your government to be the ones who'd done it? Just before a general election?'

Jeffrey leaned back and shouted over his shoulder to his secretary, who was sorting out books and paperwork on the massive glass table at the other end of the room. 'When am I having dinner with Virginia?'

'Next Thursday,' came the reply.

He turned back to me. 'Look. I'm meeting Virginia soon, so I'll collar her then. In the meantime, let me give you a few lessons on how to put pressure on a minister.'

I was all ears.

'First, you draw up a list of about ten friendly MPs – ones who will ask a question in the House for you...'

'Easy,' I said. I knew of at least a dozen who would help.

'Something along the lines of 'What is the minister doing about the cot death rate' would do. OK?'

'Yes.'

'Then you get someone rather more important, say a former minister – even better, a former Health Minister – someone like maybe David Owen – to table an early day motion along the same lines...'

'Yes, I think I can manage that...' I knew David Owen would at least be sympathetic. I had spoken to him about possibly chairing the Diamond Cot Death Appeal fund. He had been brimming with research ideas about cot death.

'And by then, the minister will be seriously worried about what is going on. Right? Then we go in for the...'

'Kill?' I ventured.

'Final stage...' he went on. 'And if Virginia won't see you then, I will try to get you the PM. But let's give this a go first...' Jeffrey kissed me on both cheeks and briskly walked me to the door. I knew he was a sincere friend, but I suspected that he, too, was something of a fireman. And I had been this morning's little blaze.

While the documentary rolled on towards the editing stage, Mike and I knew we could not wait to convince a government which might never budge. We knew we must do what the New

Zealanders had done – and if we had to do it by ourselves, then so be it. We must make a television ad – to tell British parents that their babies should be sleeping on their backs.

Shirley Tonkin had given me a video cassette copy of her own ad. She had pressed it firmly into my hands. 'If your government won't do it, then do it yourself,' she had said to me sternly. 'It's your profession, isn't it? It's what you're good at. If you can't do it, then who can?'

She was right. But how do you make an advert? Where do you start? Mike and I played the VHS over and over again – until we knew it word perfect. It starts with happy music, a softly lit sitting-room, and the TV presenter, Judy Bailey cradling a baby in her arms. 'New Zealand has the highest cot death rate in the world but there are things you can do to lower the risks for your baby.'

She bends, and puts the baby on his side in a large cot. 'Make sure you place your baby on his back or side to sleep – not his tummy. If he's on his side, have the underneath arm well forward so that if he rolls, he'll roll on to his back where he's quite safe.'

And then, smiling... 'It's very simple and it's one of the most important safety measures for your baby.' And that was it. Just thirty seconds, followed by a sponsorship logo of Phillips, the electronics giant.

'That's what we'll do,' said Mike, as he ran and re-ran the tape. 'We'll have to get sponsorship to pay for the airtime. Surely all the babywear and baby products manufacturers will help...' First though, we had to make the ad. Neither Mike nor I had ever made an advert before, and the discipline of shooting such stuff is quite different from the live, studio-type television we were used to. We both came from the world of news, where one reporter shoots an entire story with just one cameraman and a sound engineer. Adverts needed a cast from a different galaxy. People like 'dolly grips', 'gaffers', 'clapper loaders' and 'focus pullers'.

However, my agent, Jon Roseman, had once owned a company which made everything from pop videos to TV ads. We rang him, and within minutes he was assembling a team. I faxed the New Zealand script to his home, and his wife, Pearl, started work on a storyboard. Everyone concerned agreed to work either for free, expenses only, or for a reduced fee. But the hire of equipment, studios and editing suites would be costly. Mike and I thought that the advert could justifiably be made with money from the Diamond Cot Death Appeal, still running in the *Sun*. We rang Kelvin MacKenzie, the editor, and told him the plan. 'Great!' he said. 'We'll support you all the way.' And he promised he would arrange for the money to be extracted from the charitable trust. Apparently, though the Charity Commissioners had been informed, the change of directors and change of use from the old charity name had still not been formalized.

'What?' yelled Mike at Kelvin. 'How come that has taken so long?'

Kelvin sighed down the phone. 'Come on, Mike, you know what lawyers are like...'

We were advised that it would take months if we waited for the paperwork to catch up with us – so the *Sun*'s lawyers set to work contacting the old directors, to get their permission for the money to be used. It was days before we heard anything. We kept ringing Kelvin. He returned our calls, only to sound more exasperated every time. 'Look. I feel as frustrated as you two...' Backwards and forwards went faxes, confirming the filming arrangements for the ad, its costs, its content, its aims and purposes. Still no cheque.

We wrote the script, copying exactly the New Zealand words, but with changes pertinent to Britain. Peter Fleming, in Bristol, approved the final draft. 'By the way,' he said, as we went through the script for the last time, 'I've heard again from the Department of Health. The expert working party meets next week, just about when your documentary goes out.'

Clearly this new Chief Medical Officer was not going to waste time. Maybe, he, too, was a fireman, angry that he had inherited such an explosive situation.

Now we had to get our ad passed by the ITC, the watchdog committee set up to safeguard standards. They quibbled over our figures. Was it 'nearly five' children dying every day of cot death in Britain, or 'over four'? Figures differed between the Foundation's numbers and the government's. Finally, we settled for 'at least four'.

We faxed the ITC approval to the *Sun*'s lawyers. Still no cheque.

I was adamant that our advert should feel optimistic rather than scarey, so we needed something upbeat to counterbalance the sad statistics. I knew just what I wanted. I tried it out on Mike...

'Do you think we could play a snatch of Elton John at the end of the ad? The bit from "Your Song", where he sings, "how wonderful life is while you're in the world..." Don't you think it would be nice?'

'Let's give John Reid a ring,' said Mike. John Reid was Elton's manager, and a friend of ours. Within a couple of hours, we had the message that Elton would be delighted to let us play the extract, free of charge, as long as the record company agreed. Very soon we had the confirmation we needed. It was all go. We faxed everything to the *Sun*'s lawyers.

Still no cheque. We were in danger of having to cancel the shoot, so in desperation, I rang the lawyers myself. The man I wanted was, of course, unavailable, so I screeched at his poor partner. 'Have you got children? Don't you realize that if we have to delay this advert you and your partner will have babies' lives on your conscience? Because every day we delay now, babies will be needlessly dying...'

It got me nowhere. We rang Kelvin. 'Don't start at me,' he sighed. 'I'm only the editor. You may think that's powerful, but it's nothing compared to lawyers...'

Just two days later, we found out what may have so preoccupied those lawyers. They were also the Queen's lawyers. And the very next day, the Duke and Duchess of York announced their separation. We went ahead and made the ad – and the money was released just in time.

It was beautifully lit – you couldn't see a trace of my anxiety or tiredness. And the baby – from a modelling agency – looked absolutely gorgeous. 'Every day in Britain,' I said to the camera, 'at least four babies die from cot death. New research shows you can reduce the risks for your baby. Sleep him on his back or side, not on his tummy. If he's on his side, have the underneath arm well forward so that if he rolls – he'll be on his back, where he's safe. This is not a cure but it really can help save your family from the tragedy of losing a precious young life...' And then Elton John took up the theme: 'How wonderful life is while you're in the world.'

But who were we to give out new medical advice? Since when did Anne Diamond and Mike Hollingsworth get their medical degrees? We knew we couldn't broadcast the ad without an endorsement from a reputable medical body. We couldn't even get to see the Health Minister. So it had to be the Foundation.

We rang Joyce Epstein. Would the Foundation accept the ad as a gift? In return, would they endorse it? We told them our plan. We would somehow (we didn't yet know how) find a sponsor. And then we would air the ad at a time when it would be seen by the most people, and create the most publicity – the *Coronation Street* advertisement break. In TV, if you want to achieve maximum sales, then you advertise around *Coronation Street* or *News at Ten*.

We knew that the airtime was expensive. But if things worked according to plan, we shouldn't have to pay for the ad after that. Because we would use the publicity to embarrass the government into adopting the ad themselves. There was just the sticky problem of finding a sponsor with enough money...

The girl from Mothercare gulped when I told her. 'How much?' she asked again, incredulous.

'£58,000,' I said, meekly.

'That's more than we've got left in the whole advertising budget,' she answered. 'There's no way...'

I interrupted quickly. 'We're going to try and get the TV companies to reduce their fees,' I told her.

'Yes, surely, for a charity they'll come right down...'

We knew we'd got Mothercare interested. But they hadn't been expecting to cough up quite so much dough. Not for just thirty seconds.

Luckily, an advertising expert from the *Sun*'s ad agency had offered to help. He was called Paul Booth, and he guided Mike and myself through what was to us virgin territory. Firstly – how were the TV tariffs set? It seemed by market forces only. In other words, the TV companies all charged individually to advertise in their own regions, and it seemed they could charge whatever they liked. Peak airtime was very popular, and the highest bidder won the time. So how could we get them to reduce their fees just for us? 'We're just going to have to ring round every company and beg,' said Paul. And the three of us sat down at the phones.

If Supi's death had made front-page headlines at the time, then cot death was even bigger news now, in the warm-up to the release of our documentary. So the advertising managers in most of the ITV areas knew immediately why our ad was so important, and were sympathetic. We were doing well. Every company had agreed a sizeable reduction – some had halved their normal rate. Every company, that is, except Thames and Central. 'I know the managing directors of both those companies!' I said eagerly. 'Let me see if I can try a bit of personal charm!'

I rang straight through to the managing director of Thames TV, Richard Dunn. He knew why I was ringing. I pointed out to him that our documentary was being broadcast under his company name. That he *had* to be able to do something.

He wasted no time on words.

'Leave it to me, Anne. I can't promise anything. Advertising people are a law unto themselves. But I'll try.'

Within the hour, we had a message that Thames would reduce their rate. But we had no such luck with Central.

Despite my appealing directly to the director of news and current affairs, Bob Southgate (who promised to take it higher), Central refused to budge. This was the company which had just bought its entire franchise for £2,000, while others had had to pay millions. This was the company for which I had once worked. If Lew Grade had still been in charge, they would have responded, I thought. But now it seemed that it was just run by money men, with no soul.

Mothercare, through their public relations lady, Jane Cookham, had indicated that they would pay, if we could get the cost down to £25,000. We were in trouble. We had booked the spot for Monday, 4 November on Thames, Granada, Yorkshire, Tyne-Tees, STV, Grampian, TVS/Channel, HTV and Anglia at a total cost of £27,327.50. There were no other sponsors around. For Mothercare, we were already over budget. And we simply couldn't afford the extra £17,000 wanted by Central.

Jane at Mothercare was unhappy. So was I. 'I don't think it would be right for us to broadcast a life-saving message to everyone except mothers in the Midlands,' she said. 'I don't know what more we can do...'

'I do,' said Mike. 'We'll run the ad everywhere else in Britain, and then you and I can go on *Central Weekend*, the Friday night show. They've been asking us if we'll do it. Let's tell them we will, so long as they show our ad in their programme.'

It seemed like the perfect solution.

Chapter 22

I knew the documentary was going to be successful when I saw tears in the eyes of a Fleet Street girl reporter. It was preview day, and every newspaper had sent someone to see it. This particular girl reporter – long, leggy, blonde and about thirty years old – came up to me afterwards. 'I've got to rush to file my copy,' she said, and then, in an embarrassed gush: *'I just want you to know that if I ever have a baby of my own, I will make sure that it sleeps on its back!'*

With that, the tears came – to both of us – and she clenched my hand quickly, and then left. And that reaction was exactly why we had made the documentary – to tell everyone that at last there was something you could do about cot death. Not just mothers – but *future* mothers. And fathers.

We had called it 'Every Mother's Nightmare' because that was what Nanny Sandra had said when she first arrived on that fateful day – and it's how everyone sought to describe it. I received lots of complaints, though, from fathers who pointed out that cot death was every *father's* nightmare, too. And, of course, it is. It's just that 'Every Parent's Nightmare' didn't have the same ring to it.

The next day was transmission day. It was also Hallowe'en, and the children had invited friends around for a spook party (liquorice spiders and green cake and the like). It was also *TV Weekly* day – and I had a hectic schedule. I left home at 6.30am to drive to Southampton. I'd be at the TVS studios by 9am, and straight into a production meeting. After a couple of coffees, I'd go into the studio, where we would rehearse as much as possible – and then into make-up. Then came the highlight of the day – a long working lunch, when we'd meet the guest, and go over the interview. Today it was Desmond Morris and Sarah Kennedy. Then we'd go back to the studio for a live transmission. *TV Weekly* was a lovely, fun programme – and the production team very close. They were bubbling with excitement, of course, about the news that TVS was to lose its franchise. What would they do? Become an independent company? Would the new franchise holder want to commission any more *TV Weekly*s?

After the programme was transmitted, we all met back in the Green Room for a glass of wine before going our separate ways. Everyone was talking about their future. I was preparing to dash, in order to make it home in time for the Hallowe'en tea, when the phone rang. Chris Riley, the editor, answered it, and spoke briefly. He looked over to me, and cupped his hand over the mouthpiece.

'It's for you. Someone from the Press Association. Says they want to speak to you – about cot death.'

I took the phone. A female voice greeted me. 'Hello, Anne, I just wanted your reaction to the news...'

'What news?' I asked, nervously. I sensed the room go silent around me.

'Well, we've just had a statement from the Department of Health. Basically, it says that the expert working party has met and decided that *from now on, all babies in Britain should be laid to sleep on their backs...*'

Chris saw my face – and he walked over and sat in the chair next to me. 'Are you all right?'

'Yes,' I said quietly, and looked up at him. 'The Department of Health has just said that all babies should sleep on their backs. From today onwards!'

The room erupted. Everyone, TV producers, directors, researchers – people who'd never changed a nappy in their lives – they all knew how important it was.

'Hello? Hello?' said the voice at the other end of the phone.

'Are you there? Can I ask you how you feel about this?'

I turned my attention back to the lady from the Press Association 'It's wonderful news, simply wonderful!' I said, and burst into tears.

The mobile phone was pretty busy in my car that evening, as I made my way home. Linda was ecstatic – and was hastily editing the Department of Health's statement onto the end of our programme. I rang Peter Fleming in Bristol. 'It was easy,' he said. 'The Chief Medical Officer gave us about six weeks to review all the latest research but it took us just one afternoon... It's wonderful, Anne. And it wouldn't have happened without this sort of pressure.'

But we both knew that the fight couldn't end there. It wasn't enough for the Chief Medical Officer to change the rules. What we needed now was a massive campaign to tell parents all about it.

The Hallowe'en party was almost a late birthday party for Oliver. It had not been intended as such, but the guest list inevitably included many little friends who had been invited in July, and who had been cancelled. They realized this, and brought presents – so Oliver had an unexpected boost to the proceedings. Smartie Arty came to entertain – though his eyes rolled skywards when he saw a room full of witches, wizards, ghosts and creepy crawlies. 'Aaaah!' he moaned. 'They're always more difficult to control when they're dressed up!' When the last cup of blood and the final worm sandwich had been consumed, and the children yawned their way off home, Mike and I slipped on our jackets to go down to Thames Television.

The documentary was to go out at 8.30. Before transmission, there was to be a small reception for everyone concerned. We both felt that we should be there, to thank the cast and crew. But we both wanted to be at home when the programme went to air. For the team, no matter how committed they had been, it was another programme. For us, it was Supi's life –

and our attempt to make some meaning of his death. We knew we would find it too emotional to witness in front of colleagues.

Paul Woolwich, *This Week*'s editor, offered me a glass of wine. His family, too, had suffered a near-miss cot death – and he had witnessed the family anguish it had caused. 'I just want to say well done. I know how hard it must have been. And just look at what has happened today. Things have already changed...'

Paul and I had had long discussions, over a couple of lunches, about life and the cosmos. Since our *Nationwide* days, we had gone very separate ways. He had pursued more serious current affairs television. I, meanwhile, had gone into 'tabloid television', and become what the papers called a 'star'. He knew my concerns about that. 'But if you ever wondered why you became "famous", now you know...' he added. 'This was it, wasn't it? You couldn't have achieved any of this if you hadn't been famous.'

We went home quietly, and watched the programme downstairs in the playroom with Mike's parents sitting, sobbing, on the red sofa. As the end titles started rolling, a voice-over announced that, from this day onwards, the advice given to every new parent was to be changed. British babies should now sleep on their backs or sides.

The phone rang – the first of many times that evening.

It was my mum. 'That was good,' she said simply. And it was. I played a part in it, but it was a monumental team effort – and the leader of that team was Linda. It had been her idea in the first place, and her sheer energy had built it into a powerful piece of television. Linda saved a great many lives that night, and I never thought to tell her so. I was hardly objective at the time – but later I came to realize that I was more proud of making that programme than practically anything else I have ever done in my career.

That documentary should have won an award.

Unfortunately, because of stupid TV politics, it was never entered for one. We could not, however, stop to think about that. We were in campaigning mode.

We had been invited on to the debate programme, *The Time The Place*, the following morning – but I was adamant we should refuse to take part. Its style was altogether too confrontational. It prided itself on being a British version of the *Phil Donaghue Show* or the *Oprah Winfrey Show*, but it was a poor copy. It merely opened up subjects for debate – and invited people to contradict each other. I knew I couldn't face that.

However, the ITV network mid-morning magazine, *This Morning*, had also invited us to appear. They occupied the next slot in the ITV morning schedule. We agreed, providing that they promised to show our ad, which was now edited and ready. So armed with a copy, we flew to Liverpool to be interviewed by husband and wife team Richard Madeley and Judy Finnigan. We knew that *This Morning*'s audience was largely mothers with small children. The sort who would be interested in our message. And the sort who would pass it onto others.

Richard and Judy were kind, and concerned. It shocked me that they hadn't seen our documentary the night before. But I quickly checked myself. When I had been on TV-am, no way could I always watch the programme or read the book which my guest had come on to 'plug'. It simply isn't possible – not when you're interviewing four or five people every day. Not when you have a family of your own at home, kids to bath and homework to help with, as Richard and Judy had. I realized that though Supi's death and our cot death crusade was *everything* to us, it was just another story to the rest of the media. We would have to work hard, and quickly, before the media got fed up with us, as they inevitably would.

So – cot death had been debated on *The Time The Place*, on *This Morning* and now we were off to Central TV to appear on their evening programme, *Central Weekend*. This was also a highly confrontational debate programme, and my instincts warned me against it. But we had agreed to appear for two reasons. First, because they had agreed to show our advert. And it was the only way we would be able to ensure that mothers in the Central area would have the chance to view it. Second, because the programme's producers had agreed to fly Shirley Tonkin over from New Zealand. I knew she would be a powerful ally in our fight to get a full-scale cot death campaign out of the government. But it was a horrid programme. Its logo was the silhouette of two people yelling at each other.

We travelled by car from *This Morning*'s Liverpool studios to Birmingham, where the Central studios were squashed in between several large Brummie roundabouts, a couple of flyovers and a six-lane highway. En route, both Mike and I were busy on our separate mobile phones. Mothercare were still fainting at the price of showing the ad. We had tried everything we could think of to reduce the price still further, but to no avail. Now we were trying other ideas for sponsors. Paul Booth, our advertising friend at Arc, was going through his book of likely sponsors. We thought that, since the publicity was now at an all time high, we might be lucky.

We were just nearing the outskirts of Birmingham when Jane Cookham phoned from Mothercare. 'Sorry I've been so long getting back to you, but it's because they've held a special board meeting because they were worried about broadcasting the ad to mothers everywhere except the Central region.'

We understood their problem – but hadn't we got around that, by having the ad played out on *Central Weekend*?

'Well, I'm afraid the board thought that that wasn't good enough. Either it would have to be broadcast to everyone, or morally, Mothercare shouldn't sponsor it.'

My heart sank. Were they going to pull out?

'So the board has just met. And they've agreed to pay for the full country, including Central. Though will you try and get the price down a bit further if you can?'

We whooped with delight. We rang Paul Booth at Arc straight away, and told him to confirm everything for the play-out at three minutes to eight, just after the Monday edition of *Coronation Street*.

We arrived at the Central studios, but only just in time. A producer met us at reception, and whisked us along the corridor towards make-up. 'There's just one problem,' he said as he flung us in the doors, where two make-up artists were waiting. 'I'm afraid we cannot show your ad for various technical reasons. So we've got a live baby for you instead.'

It was the dirtiest of TV tricks. Technical problems, my foot. They had just decided a live demonstration would be more fun. And it might even make Anne Diamond cry. They had blatantly contravened our basic agreement – to show the ad. What felt even worse was that the baby to be used as a prop was the tiny daughter of the show's presenter, Anna Soubry. There was no time to argue about it, because within minutes we were on air.

'Are you OK?' asked Mike, worried that I might be unnerved by having to handle a baby in public so soon after Supi's death. I was angry – but I could cope. And I was damned if they were going to make me cry.

They had set up a cot in one area of the studio, and asked me to demonstrate the new advice. I walked over to the cot, furiously thinking how I could turn this situation, cunningly designed to turn me into a victim, to my satisfaction. Anna Soubry handed me her little baby daughter. She was about four months old. I was careful not to flinch, though I could feel all eyes on me. Then I turned to Shirley Tonkin, who was sitting in the audience, and I invited her to come on to the studio floor with me.

'Now, Shirley, you explain what the new advice is...' And Shirley, ever the professional, talked me through it. At the end, I announced that our ad would be transmitted the following Monday, sponsored by Mothercare.

There was loud applause. I returned to my seat on the studio plinth, and Shirley returned to hers in the audience. Mike gripped my hand tightly. 'Well done,' he said. And the debate went on. I didn't hear another word. I was shaking with anger. But at least I had got the message across.

On the way out of the studio, I crossed paths with a woman I instantly recognized as Edwina Currie, the outspoken MP and former Junior Health Minister. Edwina was as famous for 'putting her foot in it' as for her political career. In fact, one had led nearly to the end of the other. She had lost her job in the ministry when she'd declared that most of Britain's eggs contained salmonella. It was a fact which most people perceived to be absolutely true, but she had to resign anyway.

Now Edwina put her foot in it again. She was waiting in the wings to go on air and debate the next subject in the show. But she saw me, walked over and patted me sweetly on the tummy. 'Congratulations, Anne! I didn't know you were expecting another!' I was dumbstruck, smiled stupidly and walked on. I heard a floor manager take her aside and point out to her that I'd only just had a baby, three months ago, and that had been the one which had died.

Maybe that's why, after the programme ended, Edwina made a beeline for me in the Green Room. It wasn't like her to apologize – but instead she offered to do something much more useful. 'I can get you in to see the Health Minister,' she said. 'I'll fix it up, and give you a call.'

Meanwhile, Mike was enjoying a large glass of wine with Shirley Tonkin. She had spent the day with Dr Kenneth Calman, the Chief Medical Officer. 'He wants to see you,' she said. 'They're still not convinced they need to do a campaign. They think they can just tell mothers through doctor's surgeries and maternity wards... You've got to convince them, Anne. This sort of message needs television. Just like we did it, only bigger and better.'

She gave me that look again. That platinum steel glare

which must have withered a thousand medical students and beat hundreds of problem children into meek submission.

'If you don't do it, who else is going to?'

Chapter 23

There are hidden costs in making a TV ad. No-one tells you that it takes time and money simply editing a Mothercare logo on to the end. No-one tells you that you have to book studio time simply to play the cassette on a machine, and send it up the telecommunications lines to every major ITV station. And no-one tells you that you have to pay for the cassette tape which records it at the other end. We were physically exhausted and at the end of our mental tethers by the time we'd had it confirmed that every ITV station was ready to play it out.

We watched every frame of *Coronation Street* that night. After the middle commercial break, our phone rang. Half of our family and friends had got it wrong, and had been watching the wrong commercial break. 'Where was it?' they cried.

So we all waited with bated breath for 7.57pm. Suddenly, there it was – between a baked beans commercial and another one for washing powder. And suddenly there it was – gone. The most expensive thirty seconds I'd ever been responsible for. Nearly £45,000 (including VAT) gone – just like that. I hoped someone had noticed it. Because we all felt a huge anticlimax. The only time I'd ever spent so much, so quickly, was when I had bought a house. But at least then I had had something to show for it. Now, we just felt empty. 'God,' exclaimed Mike. 'I hope that has the effect we planned.'

We went to bed that night, comforting each other that all advertisers must feel that way. But it must work, or the washing powder people wouldn't do it so much. And if that ad break was to result in increased sales of Ariel, then it should also cause increased awareness of our life-saving campaign.

The next morning, the newspapers responded – particularly interested in the angle that Elton John had given us a few bars of 'Our Song'. And by breakfast time we were inundated with requests for interviews. We went on TV and radio, to put the same point, over and over again. *Why should we British parents accept such shoddy treatment from our Department of Health? If New Zealand babies were worth saving, then why were British babies being so short-changed? We need a campaign and we need one now.* It was deliberately emotive stuff – real 'soundbite' material, but we could sense it was working.

We appeared on the BBC mid morning TV show *UK Today*, hosted by Miriam Stoppard, a TV doctor. She shook us heartily by the hand. 'You know we doctors have known about this sleeping position thing for years. It's absolutely disgusting that we've never done anything about it. I think the medical profession has a lot to be ashamed about. It shouldn't have had to take a celebrity's child to die...'

While we were driving back from the TV studio, near Westminster, the car-phone rang. It was the Chief Medical Officer, Dr Kenneth Calman's secretary. Could we make a meeting with him soon? A few days later, we arrived at his office in Whitehall. Mike had a VHS copy of our ad carefully tucked under his arm. Dr Calman, a genial Scot who was quick to tell us that he, too, was a father, met us with a warm handshake.

'I've been following what you've done, and I admire your courage,' he said.

That was a good start, I thought. At least the man is not hostile.

'Now tell me what you think we should be doing?'

Over a civilized cup of coffee and biscuits, we explained what had inspired us most about the approach being taken in New Zealand, and about Peter Fleming's local campaign in Avon.

'You medical men have done your work now,' Mike said. 'You've concluded that back is best. Now you must leave it to the communicators to get the message across...'

We explained, in as simple language as we could without sounding patronizing, that we were pretty experienced in broadcasting to the very audience that he needed to reach. We'd spent our whole careers in that very field. We showed him our tape.

'Can I keep this copy?' he asked.

We were only too delighted. Were we getting somewhere? Or was he another fireman intent on extinguishing a spark before it blew up into a damned great fire? In other words, was that the last we'd ever hear from him? I put it to Mike as we left Richmond House, the Department of Health building in Whitehall, and hailed a taxi to go home.

'No, I don't think so,' said Mike. 'He must recognize that this is no longer a little fire. It's already a bloody great inferno. And if I were him, just weeks into a new job, I wouldn't want to start my period of office in a burned-out wreck...'

The next day, Edwina Currie called. 'Can you make next Tuesday, 5.30pm?' she asked. She had got us in to see Virginia Bottomley.

Mike and I arrived at Richmond House reception with another VHS tape under our arms, and our brains well-tuned for an argument. Peter Fleming arrived with his assistant, Alison Stewart, and a brief-case full of research documents. They had spanking new research material (just completed), which showed that they had reduced the cot death rate in Avon by an overall seventy-five per cent since they had first started the new advice. We all had an expectant glow. Edwina came rushing up to meet us, looking brisk and puffed-up, like a headmistress in charge of a speech day. She almost dusted us off and straightened our ties, as we waited to be shown into the Inner Sanctum. It was a waiting-room, off a waiting-room, off another waiting-room. This was more nerve-wracking than going to see the Queen.

Eventually, we passed through an enormous oak door, and there, at the other end of a gigantic polished table, sat Virginia Bottomley with her famous smile. She was flanked one one side by her Chief Press Officer, Philip Aylett, and on the other by Romela Christopherson, her public relations officer. Edwina started to grovel. I hadn't expected such obsequiousness from the Member for Derbyshire South.

'Minister,' she grovelled. 'Thank you so much for sparing us a few minutes in your hectic schedule. Can I introduce...' Well, I hadn't exactly expected 'Hi, Ginny!' But this took me quite aback.

It was then I realized that we were indeed now meeting the Fire Chief. This was an exercise designed to smother our militant flames in a blanket of drool. We were clearly meant to shake the all-powerful hand, and then go home with a nice, rosy feeling that we had done our best. That we had gone to the top. Mike, Peter and I shot each other knowing looks. It was now or never. We brushed aside the small talk. If we were only being allotted a few minutes in the Health Minister's busy timetable, then we would waste no time.

'All the research from New Zealand and Avon shows that the cot death rate drops at least by fifty per cent in the first six months following a campaign,' I started. 'And it gets better. The figures then go on to show that the rate can drop still further in the next six-month period.'

Mrs Bottomley looked impressed for a second. 'How do those statistics translate into British figures?' she asked.

It's now or never, I thought. And I could hear Shirley Tonkin nagging in my ear... 'We are losing two thousand babies a year in the UK,' I said firmly. 'That's about four a day. So, with a properly targeted campaign, we could...' and then I corrected myself... '*you*...could save...three of them.'

I knew it sounded too simple. She leaned back in her chair,

and that smile returned. She turned away from me. Maybe she suspected I was talking journalistic hype. She looked at Peter.

'Surely not?'

Peter nodded. 'It's absolutely right. That's what the evidence says. It's been done in New Zealand, and I have done it myself in Avon.'

She raised her eyebrows for a moment's thought. 'I see...suppose we did do a campaign. How and where would we do it?'

Peter told her how he had mounted his campaign in Avon. And then Mike and I launched into our case for television. Peter agreed. It was the only way to successfully reach the whole nation. We were asking a whole generation of people to unlearn what had previously been taught. We were also asking a generation of doctors, midwives and health visitors to accept that what they had taught in the past was wrong. There would be pockets of opposition, of complacency and doubt. The only way to counter that was by creating a demand for the information from the mothers themselves.

'And the only way to get that sort of saturation marketing is television,' said Mike.

Mrs Bottomley turned white. 'Oh, no!' she butted in, with a dismissive hand. 'We couldn't possibly afford to use television...'

At this, Edwina chipped in. 'Oh, that's a pity, minister... Not even in the spring or summer, when the advertising rates are cheap?'

We were prepared for this one. Mike got the VHS tape out, and we outlined a plan for using the ad we had already made, and harnessing commercial sponsors. We had even had one famous children's cartoon character offered to us to help promote posters and leaflets.

'It's not just a financial consideration,' replied the minister. 'I don't believe that TV is necessary. Newspapers and baby magazines are the way to reach young mothers. Young mums don't watch television.'

This was unbelievable. I turned around to see if Mike was still beside me, half expecting to see that he'd fainted to the floor in sheer disbelief.

'No?' I said to the Minister... 'Then who watches *Neighbours*, *Home and Away*, *This Morning* and *TV-am*? Who watches *EastEnders* and *Coronation Street*, *The Price Is Right* and *Blind Date*?'

She looked blank. Maybe she thought I had lapsed into a foreign language. I was just about to launch into my theory about washing powder advertisers, when I was stopped. Edwina was up, and dusting us off again. I was actually still saying something when she pulled the chair out from underneath my bottom, and prepared to whisk me off.

'Right, well, we're so very grateful, minister, for your time. I know you're very busy so we won't keep you a moment longer. But thank you so much...' she said.

I was horrified. I could say that it was like being back at primary school, except that I don't ever remember being herded in such a way even then. I turned my back on Edwina, and faced Mrs Bottomley head on. 'So what is going to happen now?' I asked point blank.

She rose to her full height, and her lieutenants closed in. 'I think we all agree that we need to disseminate this new information to the public in as effective a form as possible. And I agree, that should probably be in the form of some sort of campaign in the printed media.'

'And what about TV coverage?' I asked. 'We all seem to agree that TV and radio is vital to its success, don't we?'

'Well, no, frankly I am not convinced... And anyway,' she added, smiling benevolently. *'You already seem to be achieving that very well for us...'*

I saw red, and brought my fist down on the table. 'No!' I said. 'No! That simply is not good enough!'

Mike brought his hand down next to mine. 'No!' he echoed. 'We will not go on exposing our private grief in public just in order to save you money. If you want our professional help, then we will gladly give it. But we will not continue to prostitute our grief.'

Edwina shuffled awkwardly, and made noises again to leave. Mrs Bottomley smiled again. 'We'll mull over everything you said,' she promised. 'And we will get back to you. I promise...we will get back to you...'

Chapter 24

She kept her word. Two days later, her letter arrived in the morning post. In it, she explained that the Department of Health would produce a printed leaflet: 'This message must be communicated professionally and in some detail. We will be using national newspaper advertising and ensuring that the concerned medical, nursing and voluntary organizations collaborate in the initiative...'

'In other words,' explained Peter Fleming, when I rang him, 'they're going to do no more than the absolute minimum.'

I just could not understand it. We couldn't have made it any plainer. We had outlined a simple formula which was almost guaranteed to save hundreds of lives, and yet they didn't really want to know. Couldn't they see, even at the basest level, the incredible public relations value of such a campaign? Especially before a general election? Their attitude seemed so cheapskate. I was depressed. I had put my all into that deputation to the minister. Maybe, I thought now, maybe I was wrong to have lost my temper.

But Mike was angry. He stormed to the phone, and got through to Philip Aylett, the man who had been at Mrs Bottomley's left hand. They started talking. I could tell that Mike was becoming agitated. At one point, he threatened to come to blows. Finally, he slammed the phone down.

'I don't believe it!' he spouted. 'That man is trying to rewrite history. He's airbrushed out everything we achieved at that last meeting. He denies nearly everything that happened. He says there was never any talk of using TV in the campaign... Honestly, it's just like that sit-com *Yes, Minister*. These civil servants think they can turn black into white. They think they can manipulate everyone. Well, he's not getting away with it.'

We both sat down at the word processor, and constructed a furious letter to Mrs Bottomley. By now we'd been invited on to more TV and radio shows. We had declined them for fear of offending Mrs Bottomley, as she planned her cot death initiative. Now we felt we had something more to say.

In the newspapers, on radio and again on TV, in Miriam Stoppard's show, we were asked the same question: 'Isn't it great that the Department of Health has finally announced a cot death information campaign?'

'No, it is not great,' we replied. 'The government is doing only the moral minimum. In New Zealand they had a TV campaign. British babies deserve the same.'

Three cheers for the British media. Mrs Bottomley's office was on the phone the next morning. Could we come down to Whitehall straight away? As we caught another cab – it was impossible to park anywhere near Whitehall so we couldn't drive our own car – I wondered if Mrs Bottomley had even thought of how we could afford to drop everything and come at her command. It cost a fortune in cab fares.

When we got to her office, she was sitting again at the big table. This time, she had an array of press cuttings in front of her, and she was tapping them, in an irritated manner, with her fingernail. 'This will not do,' she said. 'This will not do...'

I could see they were cuttings about our most recent TV and radio utterances.

'This sort of discord will not do. We must be seen to show a united front.'

We sat down. What was she going to say? Was she simply going to tell us off?

She continued tapping, obviously annoyed. 'I told you the last time we met that I do not consider TV coverage necessary to this campaign. Frankly, I have to say, that is still my opinion...'

I sat on the edge of my chair.

'But I have been persuaded, against my better judgement, that we *should* make a television advert. And we would very much like it if you would agree to present it for us.'

I looked her hard in the eyes. They were icy blue. It was impossible to tell if she was happy or angry. But across the table, Romela Christopherson beamed. I looked at Mike. I could tell that he was trying as hard as me to stop a cry of delight. Dammit, I thought, I'm not going to give her that satisfaction.

'Why not use the ad we've already made?' I asked.

'Well, we've looked at it, and taken all the due advice. And we believe it doesn't go far enough. We think we can now go one better than the New Zealanders. We can tell British mothers that back is best.'

It was true. All the research from New Zealand and Avon now showed that the advice should be to lay babies down on their backs. The half-way advice of lying on the side was now outdated. We in Britain could confidently go the whole hog.

Mrs Bottomley turned to Romela. 'Shall we show them the logo?'

Romela uncovered a large piece of artwork which had been lying on the table in front of her. It was a huge white square, with a grey cartoon of a baby asleep, on its back. The baby made the shape of a capital 'B', and it was lying on a bed of three letters, A, C and K.

'The campaign will be called 'Back to Sleep'. I rather like it. What do you think?' Mrs Bottomley asked.

Mike looked distinctly unimpressed. He said later that he couldn't understand why anyone would call a campaign 'Ack to Sleep', and I couldn't help but agree. The graphics were a bit confusing. Still, it had been rushed out.

'Now, will you agree to front the TV ad for us?' asked Mrs B. again.

I wanted to jump up and shout *Yes, of course I will! Isn't that what I've been on about for days?* Instead I heard myself saying: 'Can I think about it?'

'What did you say that for?' asked Mike as we walked back to reception.

'I don't really know,' I answered. 'But I'm damned if I'm going to lick her hand.'

When the government wants to spend money, it can spend money. They didn't hire just any old TV crew to make this ad. They hired the best. The director was the internationally famous photographer, Terence Donovan. It was a huge studio, positively awash with production talent. And they'd hired six professional babies, from a modelling agency. All bonny three- or four-month-olds. Old enough to smile, which is all they were required to do, on the very last frame. I was the only one there working for free. (I had momentarily dallied with the thought of charging a fee to the Department of Health, and then donating it to the Diamond Cot Death Appeal. But Mike said I shouldn't push my luck.)

We did about forty-eight takes. The twenty-fourth, and the last one, were the best. Ironically, by the time I'd got to take forty-eight, we'd come around to using the first baby again. It was a hard day. Terence Donovan wanted the whole message done in one single shot, with me walking into frame, approaching a cot, and lying the baby down on his back. It sounds simple enough, but it's murder when you've got to speak lines at the same time, walk in exactly the right spots, put the baby down at precisely the right moment, and get it to smile perfectly on cue.

Like the colour scheme for the Back to Sleep logo, everything was grey and white. My skin tones and the baby's were the only hint of colour. It's not how I would have done it – I'd have used warmth and colour. But then, I'm not Terence Donovan. He's the millionaire.

I wore a simple cream silk Marks & Spencers blouse, but I

was still rather chubby after my pregnancy. With all that had happened, I hadn't given my health or fitness a moment's thought. So the dress designer got a pair of scissors, and slit the blouse right up the back, so that it fell loosely and easily around the front. No-one would see.

At the end of the shoot, I wandered back to the make-up and wardrobe area. I glanced back at the mêlée of activity. Cameraman and producers, sound recordists and engineers, babies and their mothers, scriptwriters from the Health Education Authority. *'Oh, Supi, if only you were here to see all this,'* I whispered. *'This is probably the most important thing I'll ever do in my whole life and it's all because of you...'*

The Health Minister and I became, in her words 'a marvellous double act' on the morning that we launched the Back to Sleep campaign. I think, however, that she used the term sarcastically rather than out of any genuine pride. It seemed that wherever she turned up to be interviewed that morning, I was in her wake. By the look of astonishment on her face, I could tell that she had not been warned she would be sharing the spotlight.

We first met at TV-am at seven o'clock, where we sat on the breakfast couch together to be interviewed by Mike Morris and Lorraine Kelly. We presented the all-important united front, and I sat and smiled as the Health Minister proudly announced her life-saving initiative. To have bickered at this point about whose idea it had actually been, or to have reminded her that she had needed more than a little persuasion, would have diluted the message.

This was the moment that I, too, played politician.

The journalists weren't fooled – and many of them tried to get me to criticize the government. But today, I said, was not the day for such argument. Today we had news that every parent at home would want to hear. Political rowing would simply turn them off.

We continued on our cot death roadshow, in separate cars –

Mrs B. with her minder and me with my bacon sandwich – to Sky News and BBC Radio. Finally, we were interviewed in separate locations by *BBC Breakfast Time*. And then we stood together for photographs at the press conference, where the ad was played to reporters, and the campaign leaflets were on show.

I looked around the room. Everyone who was anyone in the cot death world was there. They had pulled together the Royal College of Midwives, the Foundation for the Study of Infant Deaths, Peter Fleming – even the Chief Executive of Mothercare, Derek Lovelock, who was promising to distribute the government leaflets in his stores. It was magnificent, even if Mike was still muttering about the clumsiness of the 'Ack to Sleep' message. We both giggled when one reporter came up to us and asked us what it meant. He couldn't see it either!

I read the words at the bottom of the poster. It said:

Cot death is comparatively rare.

Recent research, however, has shown that if babies are laid down to sleep on their back or side, the risk of cot death can be greatly reduced.

Don't be worried that they might be sick and choke when on their back. There is no evidence that this happens.

However, there are some babies with special medical problems who need to sleep on their front.

And some babies are used to sleeping on their tummy. Try the new position but if the baby finds it too distressing, it is probably wiser not to persist.

If you have any doubts at all, don't hesitate to contact your doctor, midwife or health visitor.

And remember, once babies are strong enough to roll over by themselves, they can sleep in any position they like.

The Department of Health's new leaflet explains in more detail how anyone who looks after a baby can help reduce the risk of cot death.

It's indispensable advice. And if you ask for your copy today, it won't just keep your baby safer, it'll help you sleep more easily, too.

The Freepost address was, quite by coincidence, in Bristol. I thought that was apt.

It was everything I'd wanted the campaign to be. Getting it out of the government had been, as they say, like pulling teeth. I congratulated the Health Minister, and she smiled sweetly. I had hoped, at this final moment, to see a hint of humanity, even compassion, in her eyes. She was a mother, too. Couldn't she see how important all of this was to me?

To give her her due, she was probably thinking of the next fire. She probably had another three or four deputations of desperate people waiting outside her office in Richmond House. She whisked off to her meetings, and her busy, busy schedule. I went back home – to try and figure out what we'd all do now the campaigning was over.

Chapter 25

They were right, of course, those cot death experts. They had all warned me that I should be at home grieving the death of my son, instead of blazing a campaign trail. I remember Shirley Tonkin's words: 'You may think you can avoid it, but grief must be lived through – or you won't properly recover. When you get home, it will hit you like a sledge-hammer...'

And it did. Maybe it was because the fire and fury of our crusade had now dissipated. The children were back at school – in fact, Oliver had started full time Big School, and the house seemed very empty. Or maybe it was just delayed reaction, but I sank into a deep hole of sadness, particularly at night. I just could not sleep. All night I would re-enact the trials of the previous weeks. I would sit in empty offices in Richmond House, thumping the table at various faceless politicians. Over and over again, I would replay the video tape in my head of the morning I found Supi dead. As Mike Morris had said in his letter, nothing would erase the vision. But I didn't want it erased, I just wanted a different ending.

Why hadn't I done what so many other women had told me in their letters? Why hadn't I followed my own mother's example, and put my baby down to sleep on his back, or side? Why hadn't we gone for our usual Christmas holiday in Australia? The Australian cot death campaign would have been in full swing that Christmas before Supi's birth, following the example of the New Zealanders. I would have seen it. I would have followed their advice. Supi would be alive.

And when I did fall asleep, I would have that dream, again

and again. I would run down that long corridor to the man behind the mahogany desk, screaming: 'Now, can I have my baby back?'

In the morning, Mike would look at me over the breakfast cereal. 'You look terrible!'

'Yes,' I would sigh. 'I've been campaigning all night...'

We decided to escape. We wanted to go as far away as possible. Now that I'd made the cot death advert, the last thing I wanted was to see it every time I turned on the TV. We rented a house in Palm Beach, just up the coast from Sydney in Australia, and took the whole family, including Mike's parents.

I'd long ago learned the best way to amuse little boys on a long, twenty-four-hour flight. Wads of paper, boxes of washable fluorescent felt tip pens and rolls of Sellotape. For what seemed like days on end, Mike's mum and I sat cutting out, drawing and sticking with Oliver and Jamie, putting our imaginations and creativity to their utmost challenge. We made glove puppets, Ninja Turtle masks, Christmas bunting and story books – and special carrier bags to stick on the back of the seat in front. It kept us going until Bangkok, when sleep overcame everyone – and we stayed comatose until the little plane on the computer graphic displayed above our heads entered Australasian airspace.

Sydney was where Jamie was born. We had come back to give him a birthday party on the beach. But you cannot escape grief. It follows you across the world. And even though we thought that a Christmas under a searing sun might not seem so emotionally charged as in Britain, it was.

We were shopping one afternoon, at Darling Harbour, where the Sydney-siders had developed their old harbour frontage into a spanking new shops and leisure complex. A procession was passing by, along the pedestrianized cobblestone street. There were children, dressed in biblical clothes, leading baby lambs, goats and piglets. The children were mesmerized. It was a pageant – and when three camels appeared, with some very regal-looking kings astride them – it became obvious that a nativity scene was about to be re-enacted.

We joined in the procession, which led to a vast grassy auditorium in the shadow of Sydney's famous Harbour Bridge. Programmes, songbooks, and candles were for sale. We sat on the grass, Mike, his parents, Toni and Bertie, Oliver, Jamie and I, and watched a magical, musical extravaganza of the nativity story, as the sun set in the sky beyond, and a huge moon rose above the Sydney Tower.

Australian children sing 'Silent Night', too. You can't get away from it. Not even if you run 12,000 miles from home. We sang along, holding our candles up to the dark sky, and wept for the little boy who should have been with us.

Back home, I went to see one of the doctors at our local GP surgery, Roy McGregor, another TV doctor whose practice happened to be near us. I knew Roy, mostly from having interviewed him on TV-am. Now I took one look at him, and started to blub.

'Please give me something to help me go to sleep,' I appealed to him. I was desperate for valium – anything that would knock me out.

To his eternal credit, he refused. He sat me down, and made me talk about the problem. 'What you want is a bit of counselling,' he said. 'It will make you feel a lot better than sleeping pills.'

I couldn't see how. Nothing was going to make me feel better, since the pain was being caused by Supi's death. And I realized now that nothing was going to bring him back.

'Give it a try, just give it a try,' he pleaded. 'If it doesn't help, then give it up and come back to see me. But promise me you'll see a counsellor first.'

He gave me the name of a bereavement counsellor he knew and trusted. She was called Vivienne and she lived five minutes from my front door. I rang her, and found that she was expecting my call. When I walked into the little room which she had set aside in her house for her work, I noticed straight away the box of tissues on the table. The tools of her trade? I wasn't the sort of person who ever cried in public. I always managed somehow, even on the most tense of occasions, to hold back until I was alone. But two minutes into our conversation, and I was pulling tissue after tissue out of the box, and blowing my nose like an emotional wreck. I was embarrassed to be so raw in front of a total stranger, but I just couldn't help it.

I don't know what we talked about, except that I loved Supi and wanted him back. But that night, I slept. So I went back to see Vivienne again, and my nights of sleep grew longer and more frequent. We talked about big things – like religious belief, and whether I believed that Supi had gone to Heaven. We talked about tiny things – minuscule worries that might have seemed insignificant to anyone else, but were beginning to haunt me. Like what should we do with his bedroom? Where should I put his clothes? Should I keep his mattress? Was it healthy for me still to sleep with his baby sleepsuit under my pillow? She taught me that nearly any feeling was OK, providing it didn't become obsessive.

At one point, when Mike and I were considering moving house, I told her that I was worried I might be leaving him behind in some way. Years before, I had seen a TV play called *The Stone Tapes*. It had explored the theory that spiritual energy could be absorbed by the very walls around us. I was still wrestling with the mystery of what had happened to Supi's spirit, the spark of life that had so clearly left his body that dreadful morning. I wasn't particularly religious, but I kept asking myself 'What if?' I didn't want to leave that room behind, his wallpaper, his walls.

'Well, if you are that worried, then take them with you...' Vivienne said.

'How?' I asked.

'Nothing is impossible,' she said. 'If you want to take that wallpaper with you, then steam it off the walls. Take the plaster, too, if you really want to.'

I laughed, nervously.

'I mean it,' she said. 'If you really want to do it, then you can. Think about it.'

And, of course, from that moment onwards, there was really no need. I stopped worrying about it. And when the day came to leave our London house behind, I had passed beyond my *Stone Tapes* theory, and on to something else. The point is, Vivienne had given me *permission* to feel the strangest and weirdest of feelings. She hadn't laughed, nor dismissed them – she had actually validated them. And while she couldn't bring Supi back, I was somehow feeling a little better.

On one of our last afternoons in that London garden, I was pottering in the flower beds while Oliver and Jamie played on the grass. I had become a keen gardener since Supi died, though very much a beginner. It somehow helped me to plant things, nurture them and watch them grow. Maybe I still needed visual confirmation that I could raise something living and keep it alive. They were chuckling loudly, and I turned around quickly to see what had amused them so much. I could swear I saw a little boy playing with them. I knew it was Supi. And I smiled. It was the first time, since we had lost him, that I had thought of Supi without the first sensation being one of pain. Now I knew I could remember him with feelings of joy as well. It felt like a release.

Chapter 26

'Do you think you'll ever have another baby?' It was a disarmingly direct question, but coming as it did from another bereaved parent, it didn't seem like a heartless intrusion. We were in Dublin, in the Green Room of RTE, the Irish television station – and we'd just appeared on the *Kenny Live* show, one of the highest rated chat shows in Ireland.

Mike and I were the guests of ISIDA, the Irish Sudden Infant Death Association. They were trying to pressurize the Irish government to launch a similar campaign to ours, but were having no success. When they'd rung us, they'd been so sincere, so committed, and so desperate, that we had wanted to rush to help them. When we got there, we found out why we were so drawn. They were all bereaved parents – none of them were professional charity workers. It seemed to make a difference. To us, at least.

Hardly were we on Irish soil, than out of the small delegation which met us, one couple stepped forward and hugged us eagerly. 'Anne, Mike, welcome! We're Una and Brian O'Brien.' I knew them straight away. They had sat down and written to us on the day Supi died, as soon as they heard the news. They were the couple from Ireland who had lost their baby daughter Sorcha, on July the twelfth exactly one year before. It's difficult to describe the immediate closeness you feel at a moment like that. When those two people had written, telling us their sad story and sympathizing with ours, they had formed a special bond. Every 12 July, while we are wrestling with the now twin emotions of happiness at Oliver's birthday, and sadness at Supi's anniversary, we think of Una and Brian too.

Now we were in Ireland, campaigning for Irish babies. We had spoken to their press, appeared on their chat show, and spoken to a meeting of experts and parents. They'd invited Peter Fleming, too. And for the first time, we saw him deliver a lecture. It was the lecture about the discovery in Avon of the breakthrough concerning sleeping position.

'If this doesn't convince our government, I don't know what will!' said Paddy Craven, ISIDA's chairman. And then he asked it again, softly. 'Do you think you'll ever have another baby, then?'

If anyone else had asked, I think I would have been offended. I would have taken it as an insult to Supi. But this man, and all the other people around us, knew what it was like to lose a child. They had written their own code of 'What To Do and Say' in a leaflet for the family and friends of newly bereaved parents. And number one on that list was *Don't tell them they've got a little angel in Heaven, because they don't want to hear it.* That made me warm to them straightaway. It had been said to us so often. They were right – you really don't want to hear about little angels in Heaven. You want your baby here on earth.

These people had been through it. And they also understood the mixed emotions you felt when considering having more children. They had felt the guilt, the worry and the feelings of betrayal. They *knew.* They had been there. I could talk to them. We were in the same boat.

Everyone watched for my response, including Mike. 'Oh! I don't know!' I laughed. 'Sometimes I think it would be nice, and the rest of the time I'm not so sure...'

'Ah, well, then,' smiled Paddy, a twinkle in his eye. 'Tis an accident you'll be wanting...'

But the accident was a long time coming. By the end of our second year without Supi, I was longing for another baby. By now, I knew that it wouldn't be Supi. And I was also sure that it wouldn't be a replacement. I just needed a live, kicking baby in my arms. It's like that friend of mine had said: 'You're still the mother of a four-month-old baby, even though the baby has gone.' It's not that Oliver and Jamie did not fulfil my maternal instincts. I loved them as much as I'd ever done. Maybe only another mother understands. I needed a baby. And that baby was Jake.

When I discovered I was pregnant, I was so excited I could barely contain the news. Mike was at work, and I had to wait several hours before I could sit him down and tell him. We had recently started working at the BBC in Birmingham, making a coffee-time programme called *Good Morning with Anne and Nick*. The BBC had come to Mike, and asked him to revamp their morning output. Eventually, it had come down to the creation of one programme – a magazine of topical features, fashion, chat and medical news.

It meant that Nick Owen and I could be reunited – something we'd wanted ever since he'd left TV-am – and we could present a show edited by Mike, in whom we both had utmost confidence. Where the BBC had a pretty shoddy reputation for its morning output, we knew Mike would be able to shield us from the notorious 'dead hand' of the BBC – and produce a show sufficiently bright and brilliant to beat *This Morning* on the other channel.

Ironically, the man from the BBC who came to our London house to persuade us to up sticks and go to Birmingham, was a cot death father, too. His name was David Waine. He and his wife Liz, had lost their baby daughter many years before.

Mike came home that evening in a flurry of paperwork, BBC memos, and videos, with his mobile phone forever ringing. I couldn't get a quiet moment with him until the children were in bed, and we were getting ready to sleep ourselves.

'Mike, I think I'm pregnant...' In fact, I *knew* I was. But I was going to break this news gently, in case he had a shock.

Instead, his eyes brimmed with tears. 'Do you think we can go through this again?' I asked him.

He looked at me and smiled. 'Of course we can,' he whispered, and then cried.

Nine months later Jake was born, the spitting image of his brothers. Maggie Thom delivered him, and the team of midwives who looked after him in his first few days were the same team which had cared for Supi. I sat up in my bed, cuddling my new little baby with the tuft of dark hair which had led his Dad to call him 'Spike', and counted my blessings.

Four. And as I was rocking my fourth, I heard Julia Somerville, the newsreader, on *News at Ten*. 'And finally... we've just heard that television presenter and cot death campaigner Anne Diamond has given birth to a baby boy. It is two years since the cot death of her third son, Sebastian. Mother and baby are said to be doing well.' And then Julia added her own congratulations, and said goodnight. I looked down at the little bundle and noticed that, for the first time in ages, my arms were not aching. They were full...of wriggling baby.

On the day Jake and I were due to leave hospital, Mike came in with Nanny Alex and the two big boys.

'We stopped off at the church and lit a candle for Supi,' said Alex. 'The boys told God that they loved their new baby. And do you know what they said then?'

'No, what?' I asked Oliver and Jamie.

Oliver took up the story. 'I asked God if we could keep this one,' he said. 'We can, can't we Mummy?'

Dr Rom came in to give Jake his final check-up. Just as he had done before with Supi, he gently undressed him, and went through his various bits and pieces. Hips OK, upper palette, lower palette, ten fingers (including two thumbs), ten toes. Everything complete and in full working order.

'This is a wonderful day,' he said quietly, but to the whole room. 'Little Jake is a new life – and we welcome him into the world. But we will never forget Sebastian. I never will. Whenever I give the sleeping position advice to my new mums, I am proud to tell them that Sebastian was one of my babies. Now you go off and take this little chap home. And, of course, when he goes to sleep, he will sleep on his...' At this, he turned to the boys, quizzically.

'Back!' they chorused.

Epilogue

I cannot say Jake's first few months were easy, because they were not. He caught a cold, and for many nights I lay awake just listening to him breathe.

We were enrolled, before he was born, on the CONI (Care of the Next Infant) scheme, a programme set up initially by the Foundation for the Study of Infant Death. This meant that we were put under the care of a local paediatrician specially trained in the care of families who go on to have another baby after a cot death. On the scheme, you can, if you want, borrow a breathing monitor. At first I had rejected one, having experienced monitors before. But I couldn't stay awake all night every night watching Jake's chest go up and down, so finally I succumbed.

I was lent a Densa monitor, the sort you fix around the baby's chest with elastic, just like the one I had seen in New Zealand. It was easy to use, and gave me great peace of mind. We hardly ever had a false alarm. We were also lent special baby scales, and kept a graph of his weight gain, so that the health visitor, nanny and I could easily spot any sign of trouble in his health.

I did something too, that I had never done with my first three children. I had Jake in bed with me all through the night. I don't know why I had never considered it before. Probably because I had been so proud to decorate and equip a brand new nursery for each of them. Maybe because I had always had a nanny to help. But it had never actually occurred to me, after the first few days, to keep them in my bed, nor even in my bedroom unless they were ill. It was a wonderful experience. Every night I would go to sleep happily, hearing him breathe almost in my ear. And in the mornings, he would turn to see me, and beam.

Mike, though, was not so thrilled. Naturally he had the same worries as me about our new baby surviving the night – but he's the sort of sleeper who cannot bear to be disturbed. Once he has woken up, he cannot get back to sleep. Many was the night I found him sitting up in bed watching satellite TV, watching over a sleeping Jake. I, meanwhile, had fed and changed the baby, trudged along the corridor to check the big boys, and happily dozed off again.

When Jake got so big that he kicked us in the ribs for space, we bought a marvellous invention called a Bedside Bed. It's basically a cot with three sides, designed to butt up against your own bed, and with adjustable height so that the baby's cot effectively becomes an extension to your own bed. I was still worried about the dangers of possibly rolling over on to Jake, or of him overheating underneath our duvet. This Bedside Bed, I thought, was the perfect solution. He was next to me, always within my arm's reach, and yet he was lying safely in his own environment, with his own bedclothes.

One morning I was contacted by Joyce Epstein, from the Foundation. She said they were arranging a press conference to announce new guidelines for mothers about co-sleeping. Would I come along and help? They had decided to actively campaign against the practice of mothers sleeping with their babies in the same bed. I squirmed with embarrassment. How could I advise mothers to do something which I was doing myself and enjoying? Was it really wrong to sleep with your child? I made some feeble excuse, and declined the invitation.

One night, when Jake was about eleven months old, I awoke in terror. The alarm on his breathing monitor was beeping loudly, and the red light flashing. I leaned over to him. His face looked shocked, and then he started to cry. I switched the light on, and looked him over. Once he had calmed down, he seemed fine. My heart was still leaping out of my chest. But nothing seemed to be wrong. Maybe he had simply held his breath a little too long. The monitor was programmed to go off if there was no breath for twenty seconds. I fixed it around his chest again, and we both settled down to sleep.

An hour later, the same thing happened. And an hour after that. And again. That night, Jake set the alarm off five times. I was shattered, and very worried. Was Jake, even at this mature age, showing a breathing problem? Could he have died those five times, if the alarm hadn't warned me? Or was the alarm going bananas?

I phoned our CONI paediatrician, Eve Fleming (no relation to Peter). I went into work as usual, to present my programme, leaving Nanny Alex with strict instructions to watch Jake like a hawk, and attach the monitor to him for his morning nap. Then, after the programme had ended, I rushed home, meeting Alex with Jake, and the monitor, at the paediatrician's surgery.

She checked him over. There was nothing wrong. In fact, he was the picture of health. Quite a bruiser.

'If you want, we could admit him to hospital for observation...but he seems to be quite well. It might be the monitor itself. We'll send it away to get it checked. Meanwhile, use a brand new one...'

So we tried again. But that night, the very same thing happened. In fact, the alarm sounded six or seven times. On the third night, I stayed awake all night, and watched what happened. Sure enough, the alarm sounded. But Jake had been breathing normally, or so it seemed.

I rang Peter Fleming, in Bristol. He could hear my tension down the phone. 'Do you want him to come in for observation?' he asked.

'I don't think so. Not yet, anyway. But I wish I knew why he's setting the alarm off so much...' Cot death was still possible. Even at eleven months.

'Well, if you can come here, I'll lend you a piece of hospital equipment called an oximeter. That will at least tell you if his oxygen levels are safe.'

So I drove that afternoon to Bristol, and received a crash instruction course on attaching such a monitor to a stroppy eleven-month-old baby. Basically, I waited until Jake was asleep, and then I taped a special device around his big toe. A red light shone through his flesh, and measured the oxygen levels in his blood. I had seen one before, on Supi when he had been in special care.

Meanwhile, Jake was also attached to his usual monitor. There were so many machines blipping and beeping that our bedroom looked like a hospital's intensive care unit. I stayed up all night again, staring at Jake, who slept on knowing nothing of the anxiety he was causing. At about two in the morning, the alarm sounded. My eyes shot to Jake. He was breathing normally. I looked at the oximeter. It was reading healthy levels of oxygen. *I* breathed again. It happened four more times that night. I left for work the next morning, troubled but happier at least that Jake seemed to be breathing well, despite the alarms.

'It sounds to me as though he's just too old to be using the monitor,' suggested Mark Porter, our TV doctor. 'Maybe it's time to think of giving it up. I know it's hard, but you're going to have to, at some point!'

And that's exactly what Peter Fleming reckoned, too. 'What we say at times like this,' he said, and I could hear the smile, 'is that the interface between baby and monitor is no longer working efficiently...'

So Mike and I summed up all our courage, and took Jake off his monitor. I think he was happy to see it go. We never looked back. There were often moments, particularly at night when Jake and I would cuddle before he dropped off to sleep, that I would tell him about the brother he'd never know. But he'd look at me with such mischievous eyes that I'd wonder. Did he know Supi? Had they, perhaps, bumped into each other in that place called Heaven, when they were souls all busy working out their karma? Or am I still kidding myself with fanciful notions, in the endless quest for peace of mind?

One thing's for sure – Jake has been an absolute miracle. He was never for one moment another child's replacement. From his first cry, he established his own strong personality. He filled my arms, and our lives with his boisterous demands. He has helped us overcome whatever emotional hurdles still stood in our path to recovery, and I'll always be grateful to him for that. Had Supi lived, we would probably not have gone on to have yet another child, our little Jacob. So we look upon him as a gift – not just from God, but also from Sebastian.

Now we have another gift, too, or more a surprise bonus – our little Conor, born on St Patrick's Day, 1995. Another little miracle, who looks at the moment exactly like his missing brother. But no doubt he'll develop in his own way – and will one day be his own man. We are blessed.

A while ago Oliver came up to me and patted my stomach. 'Exactly how many babies have you got in there?' he asked, as if he felt overloaded with the responsibility of being Big Brother to such a large team. I think that's it, Ollie. I'll tell you all about it when you're older.

Six months after the Back to Sleep campaign was launched, the cot death rate in Britain had halved. That means, in simplistic layman's terms, that about 500 babies *didn't* die who otherwise would have. Just in the first six months. A year later, the cot death rate had fallen by an overall sixty-nine per cent. And it continues to fall. More and more babies live to see the morning.

Once the message was relayed throughout Britain, it must have saved lives literally *overnight.* And when the Department of Health conducted a survey to find out how people had gleaned the new advice, they found that eighty-seven per cent of people had got it from the television ad. That made me feel better about thumping Mrs B.'s table.

I watched her, a year later, on the TV, talking about the need for a campaign to promote the measles vaccination. She said it would have to be as good as the cot death campaign. 'The Back to Sleep campaign is the most successful public health campaign we've ever had,' she said proudly.

Of course, that makes me feel good. But what of those wasted lives? My Sebastian isn't the only baby who need not have died. Four other babies died on the same day as Supi. Another four the next day, and the next , and the next – 2,000 that very year. And all that time, we could have been actively campaigning to save nearly two thirds of them. We were culpably slow to act.

Throughout this country there are mothers and fathers whose hearts are breaking for their lost children. I know. I've got letters from most of them. One of them's a lawyer, in Mortlake, London. She tells me we should sue the Government for negligence. Another is a GP, who feels so disillusioned with her own profession that she can hardly bear to go back to work. At times I am strong enough to be philosophical, and shrug my shoulders and tell myself not to look back with revenge or bitterness. At other times I miss Sebastian so much I want to throttle any sign of the complacency which allowed him to die. I'd love to sue somebody, if I thought it would do any good.

It's generally thought that the trend for lying babies on their stomachs came from the United States of America. That's where doctors first started to save tiny neo-nates, babies born well before their due dates, and where Special Care Baby Units were developed. They discovered that premature babies fared much better on their stomachs, and so the prone sleeping position quickly became a vital part of neo-natal care. Indeed, the popular image of the happy, well-tended baby became that of a baby lying on its tummy, sucking its thumb. I'm sure you've seen it.

Somehow, somewhere, *someone* then thought that the same principle should apply to ordinary, term, healthy babies, too. And that, it appears, is where they went wrong. Of course, the prone position is safe for the *vast majority* of babies. Oliver and Jamie slept on their tummies and lived. But for some babies, it is terribly dangerous, it makes them susceptible to cot death. The trouble is, no-one can tell you *which ones*.

Now, the world is turning upside down. Throughout Europe, in Canada, and even in America, governments are launching cot death campaigns. We nearly lost Dr Peter Fleming to the Canadians, in their enthusiasm to save lives. He had been helping them prepare their campaign, inspiringly called 'Sweet Dreams', when they sneakily offered him the chair of paediatric medicine at Toronto University. Only a grant of £100,000 from the Diamond Cot Death Appeal kept him in Britain, still working in Bristol, and continuing his vital research into cot deaths and how more lives might be saved.

Speak to any mum or dad in any hospital in any part of the world, and they'll tell you that they idolize the doctor who saved their baby's life. Well, Peter Fleming didn't save mine, but I think he *would have*, had we known him. One thing's for certain, he has saved countless hundreds – no, thousands – of lives. But he has never received so much as a thank you letter. Because those mums and dads who've been spared the tragedy of cot death don't even know it. I would like to say thanks, on their behalf, Peter. And to Shirley Tonkin, and Ed Mitchell, and all the other brave, stubborn and talented people in this country and elsewhere who cared enough to find out why our babies died – and, more importantly, what could be done about it.

There's a tiny little room in St Michael's Hospital in Bristol, with a large double bed and lots of wires linked up to monitors and an infra-red camera. Inside the bed, tucked up warmly under the duvet, is a young mother with her new baby. They're both fast asleep, subconsciously revelling in the almost primitive closeness of those first special days – and nights – together. But they're being watched, on a close circuit TV screen. Their heart rates, oxygen saturation, body temperatures, brain waves – and all sorts of bodily functions – are being carefully monitored, recorded and analysed. They are the latest recruits to the 'Sebastian Diamond Mother and Baby Sleep Laboratory'. A grand name for such a little room, designed to study the interactions between mothers and babies when they're sleeping together. It's part of the ongoing search for the answer to cot death.

When I first saw the sign on the door, I had to grab Peter's arm to steady myself. I had never seen Supi's name on anything before, even though he's old enough now for me to be sewing nametapes into his school uniform. I'm very proud of you, Supi, I thought. And then I looked at the next door, to the neighbouring laboratory. It said FSID – paid for and sponsored by the Foundation.

I thought of all the other little babies represented by those four initials. Babies every bit as wonderful and important to their parents as Sebastian is to us. Babies whose names did not make headlines, even though – added together – their deaths would have constituted one of the worst human disasters the world has known. Babies whose parents have been where we've been, and would do almost anything to prevent it happening to anyone else. Thousands of babies.

I asked my big boys the other day if they really could remember Supi.

'Oh yes,' replied Oliver. 'We used to play eyebrows with him...'

It was something I'd forgotten. Oh, God. It was something about him that I had forgotten. How could I possibly forget anything about him? And yet I had. He had used to sit in his bouncy chair, in the middle of the playroom, and beckon his brothers over – or so they thought – by raising his eyebrows and looking quizzical. Then they would wiggle their eyebrows at him, and it would always make him gurgle and chuckle.

'Mummy,' asked Jamie, 'is Supi still a baby, or is he getting older all the time, like us?'

I told Jamie the absolute truth. 'I don't know, I'm afraid. No-one knows.' And I turned the question around: 'What do you think?'

'I think he's a baby, because then he can play with baby Jesus.'

'Well, that's rubbish,' snorted Oliver. 'Because baby Jesus isn't a baby. He's a man, because the Romans crucified him...'

Nowadays we often have such deep, philosophical discussions. Like why Supi didn't leave a fossilized skeleton, as the dinosaurs did. That one required a very lengthy and difficult but always truthful – explanation!

We returned to Cyprus for another holiday – but everything had changed. John and Roswitha had moved away, after having a terrible car accident, and Oliver and Jamie were bored without instant access to a theme park. I unpacked my holiday clothes – the sort that only ever get worn abroad. And there, in the pocket of my sundress, was a baby's sock. It was Supi's.

I held it to my face, and breathed it in. It smelt of him. I buried my face in it, and breathed through it and cried, and wrung it in my hands. Until the sweet smell of little baby had gone for ever.

Conclusion

To answer Oliver's question (did we find the answer to cot death?), I think I can safely say yes, we did. A great deal of the answer anyway.

Cot death is, as the experts have long said, 'multi-factorial', by which they mean that it probably has many causes, some of which are now known, and some of which are not. I think that it is a matter of balance. While our babies may look robust, their lives are being affected every day and every night by many different factors, working both for and against them. Most babies, most of the time, have the weights happily stacked in their favour. But for babies like Sebastian, unseen dangers of which we are only just becoming aware, are massing against them. One too many and the balance tips.

Sebastian was a baby boy, the weaker sex physiologically. He was also premature with breathing problems. He had tiny little health difficulties, like the hydrocele and the oral thrush – unimportant in isolation – yet did they betray a slight fragility? He was four months old, known to be an age when all sorts of physiological changes are going on. It was a hot night, he was in a room on his own, he was lying on a sheepskin and he was in the prone sleeping position. I know now that we had chicken-pox in the house. Could that infection have caused, as it did in my older children, a sudden rise in body temperature? Cancel out just one of those factors, and he may well have survived the night.

If cot death is, as is becoming evident, something to do with a baby's inability to regulate his own temperature, causing or coupled with respiratory failure, then you can see how sleeping position is so important. If a baby is face down, he covers a huge part of the surface area he would normally use to dissipate body heat. Whatever was working against Supi that night, I strongly believe that turning him over would have given him that extra chance. It would probably have tipped the scales back in his favour.

Knowing that, and seeing what I've seen at the Sebastian Diamond Sleep Laboratory in Bristol, I would never leave a baby of that age on his own all night either. Despite all the problems that sleeping with your baby can bring – like your husband moving out of the room, your other children being jealous or your baby being difficult to wean out of your bedroom – I think you'd be stunned if you'd witnessed what I did.

In the Sleep Laboratory, Dr Fleming and his team watch the interaction between a mother and her baby as they sleep. On the first night, the mums and babies sleep as they normally do at home, either with the baby in the bed, or a in a cot next to the bed. For the second night, they do the opposite. On their third visit, they go back to their normal practice.

It was a first visit for this particular mum and baby – and they slept as they did at home, with the mother lying on her side, almost on her tummy, and her child nestling under the crook of her arm. Their faces were only a matter of three or four inches apart. At first when I saw their sleeping images, I worried that they were almost too close. One false move I thought, and the mother will be leaning on her baby. But that just didn't happen. What happened instead was a revelation to me, and a confirmation that nature really does know best.

There were many, many times in the night when mother and baby stirred – sometimes apparently in isolation from each other, at other times cutely in syncopation. It was rather like a dance. At one point, in the midst of a period of deep sleep for both of them, the baby started to fidget slightly, and in a sound almost below normal hearing levels, squeaked like a little mouse, though still fast asleep. The mother subconsciously caressed her child's head, rearranged the bedclothes around them both, patted and stroked the baby, and then settled back into stillness. She had never even half-woken. It was a fleeting moment of sweet tenderness, but it was also much more. Because when we looked at the monitor displays which we could superimpose on to the video, we could see that those few actions had all meant something.

When the baby squeaked and fidgeted, the read-out showed that his surface temperature was becoming warmer than his core temperature. Effectively that meant that the baby was becoming too hot. When the mother heard his noise, she acted. And even though she was asleep, she immediately sensed what her baby needed, adjusted the bedding and the baby's temperature instantly returned to a steady normal level. When asked about it the next morning, the mother was not aware that the incident, or any other periods of interaction, had happened at all. It was totally instinctive.

So what! I can hear the cry of co-sleepers up and down the land. Do I really need a sleep laboratory to tell me that it's natural for mothers and babies to sleep together? Well, no. I suppose I don't. But we now live in a society where it isn't always possible, or indeed desirable, to sleep with our babies. And we need to understand what it is we are *missing out on*, if we decide not to. It may be more than an aesthetic pleasure, it may be vitally important.

One thing we do know, is that you shouldn't sleep with your baby in the same bed as you if you or your partner have been smoking or drinking alcohol. An intoxicated mother can lose the instinct which stops us rolling over on to our babies. A parent who has smoked can go on breathing out toxic fumes in his or her breath for up to four hours after the last cigarette. And passive smoking is highly dangerous for babies. After sleeping position, smoking is the biggest single cause of cot death. All studies throughout the world agree that if experts could stop parents smoking, the cot death rate would plummet.

As for breastfeeding, the New Zealanders were adamant that their study showed it helped to prevent cot death, and so they included it in their risk reduction campaign. The British are equally adamant that although breastfeeding is best for babies in lots of other ways, it makes no difference when it comes to cot death. You can imagine my relief when I heard that one!

There's no doubt for me though, that babies who sleep on their backs sleep much more lightly and for shorter periods than babies who sleep on their tummies. Both Jake and Conor as tiny babies spent most of the night stirring, squeaking and squirming, and regularly kicking the bedclothes off. Many times during the night I would muse upon the natural way they were regulating their temperature, as I replaced the sheet over their legs, only to repeat the process an hour or two later.

Mattresses? Years ago, when it was alleged that babies may have inhaled toxic fumes from the fire-retardant chemicals on some cot mattresses, the government should have investigated the theory. In fact, they had failed to clear the matter up completely. Now, after yet more pressure from TV documentaries like *The Cook Report* on ITV, they have agreed on a full enquiry. Initial reports indicate that there is unlikely to be a link between cot mattresses and cot death. I have covered my mattress with a 'protective cot sheet', designed to protect a mattress from bedwetting, just in case. The scientists tell us that these sheets contain no harmful chemicals themselves, and would be an effective barrier against any chemicals in the mattress.

I am inundated with letters from worried mothers asking about various gadgets and wedges, designed to stop your baby from rolling over on to his tummy. Dr Fleming says that anything which falsely inhibits your baby's natural movements – and might therefore distress him – cannot be doing him any good. And anyway, they could contribute to overheating.

As for monitors, the popular line from the experts is that

'breathing monitors have never been known to save lives'. I think that's a medical cop-out. They simply don't know, and they are scared that every parent in the land will demand a highly expensive monitor. I use one because my baby died, but I also know what hell they are if you don't have full back-up from your GP, Health Visitor and paediatrician (all with cot death training) and thorough instruction in how to use and understand them. I'm tempted to say that with the risk reduction rules we already know, we do not need monitors, but I haven't the courage to give mine back. I do believe, however, that every parent in the land should be given full instruction on how to give a baby the kiss of life. When you think of it, it's criminal that we aren't all taught it at school.

We are still losing babies to cot death. Every week, ten families go through the hell we still endure. I get letters from women who scream at me from the page: 'Anne, we did everything you said, and we still lost our baby!' It's a curious fact that even before the Back to Sleep campaign, whenever there was a scare about cot death, the death toll went down fractionally. Indeed, some sceptics said at first that the Back to Sleep campaign was nothing more than the same reaction on a larger scale. That would suggest that parents suddenly take better care of their children after a scare, which in turn implies that parents are not usually taking *enough* care. That insults most of us.

What is clearly true, is that when there is heightened awareness of cot death and we are more conscious of the vulnerability of our little ones, we feel justified in feeling protective, even paranoid about our children's health and well-being. GPs always report a sudden influx of worried mothers with snuffly, grizzly babies. That may be a good thing. That's why 'going to your GP if you are worried' was included in the Golden Rules of the Back to Sleep campaign. That campaign should be repeated annually – it's absolutely guaranteed that it would result in a further drop in cot death.

Just in case anyone needed further proof, then they should look again at Avon. At the height of the national campaign, and after much campaigning on a local level too, they enjoyed a fifteen-month period where they had *no cot deaths at all. Not a single one. Since then, they have never lost a child to a non-smoking family. These are the facts – they are not opinions.*

Of course, cot deaths in non-smoking households are still happening, but it is rare nowadays for the death to be totally unexplained by known risk factors. Usually, it is possible to see now what elements may have heaped up against the baby and how that vital balance might have been tipped. Sometimes, it is clear that the child had breathing problems, had been premature, had rolled over on to its front, had caught a sudden infection or had suffered a number of problems together. We now know that heightened awareness improves the chances of vulnerable children – simply by giving the parents the right to worry.

I get very fed up with people who say that by talking about cot death, I could ruin a parent's enjoyment of their babies and make them frightened. Mums and Dads are frightened of cot death anyway. They are thirsty for information about it. Now, for the first time ever in the painful history of Sudden Infant Death Syndrome, there is something we ordinary parents can do about it. We can defeat the killer, and enjoy our babies all the more.

Useful Addresses

Cot Death Society (and Support for Bereaved Parents)
117 High Street
Worle
Weston-super-Mare
Avon
BS22 0HB
Helpline: 01836 219010

Diamond Cot Death Appeal
Registered Charity No: 801394
Midland Bank Account No: 01122940
Sortcode: 40-07-25
(You can give money at any branch with these details)

Foundation for the Study of Infant Deaths (FSID)
14 Halkin Street
London
SW1X 7DP
Cot death 24-hour manned helpline: 0171 235 1721
Tel: 0171 235 0965
Fax: 0171 823 1986

Irish Sudden Infant Death Association (ISIDA)
Carmichael House
4 North Brunswick Street
Dublin 7
Freephone helpline, open 9am-5pm: (01) 874 7007
Tel: (01) 873 2711/872 6199
Fax: (01) 872 6056

'Protective Cot Sheet'
Available from branches of Boots and Mothercare

Scottish Cot Death Trust
Royal Hospital for Sick Children
Yorkhill
Glasgow
G3 8SJ
Tel: 0141 357 3946 (9am-5pm)
Fax: 0141 334 1376

Sebastian Diamond Sleep Laboratory
Department of Child Health
St Michael's Hospital
Bristol

Stillbirth and Neonatal
Death Society (SANDS)
28 Portland Place
London
W1N 4DE
Helpline: 0171 436 5881
General enquiries:
0171 436 7940

The Bedside Bed Co.
398 Woodlands Avenue
London
E11 3QY
Tel: 0181 989 8683

The Child Bereavement
Trust
1 Millside
Riversdale
Bourne End
Bucks
OL9 5EB
Tel: 01494 765001
(Mainly for professional carers)

The Compassionate Friends
53 North Street
Bristol
BS3 1EN
Helpline: 0117 953 9639
Tel: 0117 966 5202
(A nationwide organization of bereaved parents offering friendship and understanding to other bereaved parents. I am a patron.)

The Twins and Multiple
Births Association
(TAMBA)
PO Box 30
Little Sutton
South Wirral
L65 1TH
**Twinline (helpline) eves and weekends:
01732 868000**
General enquiries:
0151 348 0020

Useful Publications

Coping With Cot Death Sarah Murphy (Sheldon Press, £5.99)

'Reducing The Risk of Cot Death' (leaflet)
Health Publications Unit
No 2 Site
Heywood Stores
Manchester Road
Heywood
Lancs
OL19 2PZ
Tel: 0800 555777
Report of the Chief Medical Officer's Expert Group on 'The Sleeping Position of Infants and Cot Death' (HMSO).
Available through HMSO bookshops and other booksellers.
Tel orders: 0171 873 9090
(This contains all the background information to the Back To Sleep campaign and some of the results and surveys)